I tapped on Clarita's door and when she didn't answer, I opened it and looked in. Her black-clad form lay stretched upon the bed, and I thought for a moment that she was weeping. But when I spoke her name, she sat up and stared at me with dry, ravaged eyes.

"Why did you lie?" I asked her softly. "Who was it who went along the hillside that day?"

For an instant I thought she was going to strike me. Her thin hand with its flashing rings came up, but I stood my ground and it fell back to her side just short of my face.

"You are like your mother," she whispered. "You ask for killing."

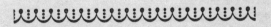

By Phyllis A. Whitney
Published by Ballantine Books:

*Published by Fawcett Books

Phyllis A. Whitney

The Turquoise Mask

FAWCETT CREST • NEW YORK

A Fawcett Crest Book
Published by The Ballantine Publishing Group
Copyright © 1973, 1974 by The Phyllis A. Whitney Trust

http://www.randomhouse.com

ISBN 0-449-00511-9

Selection of the Doubleday Bargain Book Club.

This edition published by arrangement with Doubleday, a division of Bantam Doubleday Dell Publishing Group, Inc.

Manufactured in the United States of America

First Fawcett Crest Edition: February 1975
First Ballantine Books Edition: December 1982

10 9 8 7 6 5 4 3 2 1

The
Turquoise
Mask

I

I had set my "arguments" out carefully on my drawing table. Every item was significant and to be considered soberly if I was to make a right decision. To act meant stepping into something completely unknown and facing what I had been warned against, while not to act meant continued loneliness and the frustration of never knowing the truth.

Across the street from my third-story window, New York brownstone fronts shone with a bronze gleam in the spring sunlight, and East Side cross traffic was heavy. I wouldn't miss New York. There was too much that was painful here. But New Mexico was foreign to me and it held a possible threat.

A little way off in the room my telephone waited mutely on an end table, and I knew that it could either reproach me forever or hurl me into action and doubtful adventure. As always, my instinct prompted me to the bold stroke, but I was trying to use the caution my father had always urged upon me. Too much spirit was as bad as no spirit at all, he used to say, and I was too ready to be headstrong. Now I would try to think before leaping.

But I had to decide.

There they lay, side by side—the objects that would

help me in my dilemma. There was the small, carved wooden road runner. The silver-framed miniature painting of a woman's face. The advertising brochure that carried illustrations by me—Amanda Austin. The snapshot taken twenty years ago, showing my father and mother and me when I was not quite five. A glossy page torn from a fashion magazine. My father's pipe with the crust of its last smoking still black in the bowl. The bracelet Johnny had given me—gold, set with sapphires, my birthstone. A slave bracelet, he had called it once, teasing me as he admired it on my wrist. That was why I'd placed it here—as a reminder of something I must never again forget.

Last of all were the two letters from Santa Fe, where I was born and which I had left shortly after that snapshot was taken—after my mother's death, when my father had brought me East to grow up in his sister Beatrice's house in a small New Hampshire town. I could return to her any time I wished. Aunt Beatrice would welcome me with stern kindness and no sentimental nonsense. She had never approved of my mother or her family. She had never accepted that one quarter of me that was Spanish-American, and she might very well wash her hands of me if I went to New Mexico. It wouldn't matter a great deal. She had never been what I thought of as "family." I suppose I had some romantic notion, gleaned from childhood reading, of boisterous, all-for-one, and one-for-all *families*. That was the experience I had never had.

I picked up the pipe with the blackened bowl and held it in my fingers as though I held my father's hand. I had not wanted for loving there. But he was gone—recently, suddenly. We had been happy together in this apartment. His work as an engineer often took him away for weeks at a time, but we were always glad to be together when he returned—companionable and content with each other, as far as we were able, and in spite of our different temperaments. He had lost my mother long ago, and I had lost Johnny because Johnny had walked away no more than a year ago. Now my father was gone too and the apartment was empty. My life was frighteningly empty. There were friends, of course, but now, suddenly, friends weren't enough.

I had to fill my life with something new, with something that would belong to me, in spite of all the warnings that had been given me.

My father, William Austin, had been a kindly, gentle man, though he had a good deal of New England stubbornness in him. Only once had I seen him furiously angry. One summer when I was ten years old I had gone rummaging in an old trunk and I'd found the very miniature which now lay on my drawing table. The bright, smiling face of the girl in the painting fascinated me. I could not miss the resemblance to my own face, and I took it at once to my father to ask who she was.

Never had I seen him so angry as when he'd snatched the small picture from me.

"That was a woman I once knew," he told me. "She was worthless—wicked! She is nothing to you and you are not to go snooping among my things!"

His unfamiliar anger frightened me, but it also raised a response of indignation and I stood up to him.

"She's my mother, isn't she?" I cried. "Oh, why won't you tell me about her? I want to know!"

He set the picture aside and held me so tightly by the shoulders that his hands hurt me. "You look like her, Amanda, and that's something I can do nothing about. But you're not going to be like her if I can help it. Not ever!"

His hurting hands raised my own anger and I sobbed with rage. "I *will* be like her! I *will* be like her if I want to!"

He shook me then until the angry sobs choked in my throat and I looked at him with terrified eyes. When he saw how he had frightened me, he turned away, and I will never forget the strange words he muttered: "That dwarf! That damnable dwarf!"

The words had no meaning for me then, but I'd known better than to ask questions.

Anger had spent itself in both of us. We drew apart

and for a few days we watched one another uncomfortably, until the soreness and the astonishment faded and we could once more turn to each other lovingly.

The miniature vanished and I never saw it again until I had come upon it recently among my father's things. He had called her wicked, but once he must have loved her, and he had never brought himself to destroy the portrait.

Always after that outburst of temper between us he had watched me warily, as if waiting for something to surface. But we'd never raged at each other again, and he went out of his way to be gentle with me. Now I reached across the table to pick up the round, framed miniature. She had been very young, hardly more than a girl, when this was painted. Doroteo, her name had been. I had only to hold the miniature up beside my own face in a mirror to see the resemblance. Not that I was any duplicate of the girl in the painting, for she was a beauty, with dark eyes, a great deal of thick black hair, and a smiling, sensitive mouth. I had the same black hair, and I wore it long in a heavy coil at the back of my head—in secret imitation of the portrait. I had the same eyes, the same sun-tinted skin, but my mouth was wide and my chin less rounded. I was no beauty.

Her face did not seem to me a wicked one. Spirited, yes, with a laughing mischief in the eyes—but not dangerous. I couldn't see her that way. I was spirited too, with a temper that was sometimes hard to control, and a determination that wanted its own way. But these things didn't make me wicked, though I suspected that they came from her.

I had never been able to get my father to talk about her or her family out in Santa Fe. When I wanted to know how she had died, he told me shortly that it was in a fall, and would say nothing more. His very silence told me there was more. From the time when I was very young I had sensed some horror about my mother's death— some devastating truth that he did not want me to know. Now perhaps there would be a way to find out. Though the question was, how wise would it be for me to know?

I wondered if my grandfather had painted the miniature, for I knew at least that he had been something of an artist, and that he had done some carving in wood. I set my mother's picture down and picked up the small, humorous carving of a road runner.

The bird stood upon a diamond-shaped block of wood, perhaps three inches long from its bill to its feathered tail. It was executed with a minimum of detail—merely shaped, with a forked tail and arrowed lines here and there which gave the effect of feathers. Tiny indentations marked its small round eyes and nostrils, a slashed line indicated the opening of the beak. Yet so skillful were these touches that the humorous whole was magically suggested. The figure had been carved of some clean white wood, but I had played with it as a child until it was smudged with gray, rubbed in with grime. I'd loved it dearly. It was a toy I used to take to bed with me at night—not soft and cuddly, but still somehow comforting.

I turned it over, knowing what I would find etched into the base of the under side. *Juan Cordova,* the scratched-in letters read. Once when I was eight, I had asked my father who the Juan Cordova was who had carved the road runner. I think he hadn't wanted to answer me, but we were honest with one another in most ways, and he finally told me. Juan Cordova was my grandfather in Santa Fe. He had given me the little carving when I was very small.

After that, my father had sometimes spoken of Juan Cordova, and his disliking had been intense. He was a tyrannical man who had ruined every human relationship he had touched, my father told me, and I was never to go near him for any reason. This of course made me more curious than ever.

The carving led me to the next in my collection of "arguments"—that dog-eared page torn from a magazine. I'd come across it when I was cutting out paper dolls one day when I was ten. The name at the top of the ad that ran down the entire page had arrested my attention.

CORDOVA, it announced in great block letters, and I had read every word of the ad eagerly.

CORDOVA was a shop in Santa Fe. It was one of the fine shops of the world, and it was owned and run by Juan Cordova. The ad spoke of his being an artist and craftsman himself, and a collector of fine articles, not only of Indian work, but of treasures from Spain and Mexico and the South American countries. There was a photograph of a portion of the shop's windows and I had looked at it many times and tried to examine in detail the carvings and ceramics and silver displayed in that window. To me, the ad said, "Come to Santa Fe." All through my childhood I had made up fantasies based on that ad and the fact that Juan Cordova was my grandfather. There was nothing frightening about it, as there was about the picture of my mother.

What else was left?

The snapshot—not very clear—of three people, with a low adobe house in the background. A man, a woman, and a child. The man was my father when he was young. The woman, my mother, wore her black hair wild at shoulder length and her face smiled gaily from the picture. With one hand she touched the shoulder of the child I had been. Whenever I looked at the small picture, it was as if something pulled at me—as if I could somehow step backward in time and recapture what it had been like to be nearly five and have both a father and a mother, a grandfather, and perhaps other relatives. But I could remember nothing of that time at all.

The letters were left, the bracelet, the brochure, and one other thing that was not tangible. I chose my grandfather's letter first and read it through once more, although I already knew it by heart.

Dear Amanda:

It has recently been brought to my attention that William Austin is dead. Come to see me. I want to meet Doroteo's daughter. They tell me that I have not long to live, so it must be soon. You can

*take a plane to Albuquerque, where your cousin,
Eleanor Brand, will meet you and drive you to
Santa Fe. Wire me your flight number and the time.
I await your response.*

Juan Cordova

There was something imperious about the letter. It
issued commands, rather than made a request. Still, a
dying man might feel he had no time for pleading, and it
meant something to me that he wanted to see his granddaughter. I would have to act soon, or be too late. My
father had not liked or approved of him, and he had
felt that Juan Cordova had damaged my mother. He
had never wanted me to see any of that side of my family.
Was I to heed him?

The second letter was from a grandmother whose name
I had never known until I'd found her letter hidden
away in my father's desk in a sealed envelope. It was
dated three years ago, but he had never told me of its
coming. My eyes followed the strong script down the page.

Dear William:

*I am very ill and I want to see my granddaughter
before I die. Besides, there is much we should talk
about. You have misjudged Doroteo cruelly, and
that is something which should be mended. Please
come to see me.*

Katy Cordova

But William Austin, for all his kindness, his gentleness,
had a stiff New England spine. He had not gone to see
her, and I'd lost that chance to meet my grandmother.
I had no idea whether she was still alive, but I thought not,
since my grandfather had not mentioned her in his letter.
Even more than I wanted a family of my own, I wanted
to know the truth about my mother and why my father
had "misjudged" her. Now, like his wife, Katy, Juan
Cordova had written me near the end of his life, and I

felt that this time the request could not be ignored. Still I held back, doubting myself.

What must I do? How must I choose?

I picked up the brochure I'd illustrated and flipped through its pages, considering. This was the way I earned my living. As a free lance I was moderately successful and I illustrated ad copy of all sorts, but what I wanted to be was a serious painter. My father had always encouraged me, given me something special in the way of independence, of reliance on myself. He had encouraged me to develop my talent and had sent me to art school. Painting was as much a part of me as my very hands. I had a certain talent, but I wanted to do something more with it, and that was the quality in me which Johnny Hall had never understood.

This brought me to the bracelet. I slipped it over my wrist and let the sapphires shine in the reflection from the nearest window. When he had gone away, I'd tried to give the bracelet back to him, but he had dismissed the idea lightly.

"Keep it," he'd insisted. "Keep it to remind you of what you're doing to your life."

Johnny had seemed such a safe love in the beginning. He was gay, lightheartedly adventurous, breezily dominating. He was absorbed in Johnny Hall, and since I was absorbed in him too, everything was lovely. Yet falling in love had not happened suddenly in that dangerous way my father had warned me against.

"Never let your heart run away with your head," he'd told me in my growing-up years. From the things he said, I gathered that he and my mother must have fallen in love with each other instantly—with that attraction which must be magical when it happens, and at the same time dangerous, because it may not last. I was safe enough. Such attraction had never happened to me. The beginning with Johnny was slow, gradual. We had come to like each other, to enjoy being together, and then had warmed to a closer relationship that promised a happy marriage.

If it had not been for my work and my painting! They were always getting in Johnny's way. I had deadlines to meet that spoiled his plans. It grew so that he did not even want me to take a sketchbook along when he went on outings. He wanted all my attention for himself. It was all right to earn my living with my little drawings, but that wouldn't be necessary after we were married. Then I would never need to pick up a drawing pencil or a paint-brush again, except as a sort of minor amusement.

"But I want to paint!" I told him. "I want my work to be good enough to be recognized."

He laughed and kissed me. "You'll get over all that when you have me to look after. I'll make name enough for both of us, and you can be just as proud of me as you want to be. I'll eat it up!"

By that time I was thoroughly in love, and tried to think in terms of compromise. As a matter of fact, he gave me very little time to think at all. He swept me along on a gay, impulsive, overweening tide of his own de-sires and wishes. My father was doubtful and a little sad, but then, he would lose me when I married. I tried to be what Johnny wanted, not talking about my work, hiding it from him.

The breaking point came when a small gallery show-ing was arranged for some of my work. I'd done a col-lection of paintings in various neighborhoods of New York, including a Chinatown scene, children playing on a Harlem street, a boy and girl standing in the stern of a Staten Island ferry, watching its wake, with the Man-hattan skyline in the background. There were a number of other scenes as well, for I'd enjoyed sketching and painting all around New York, even though Johnny thought it silly.

When the show was actually put on, it shocked me that he should resent it and be jealous of my work. He sneered at a modest review in the *Times,* which was remarkable to receive at all, and pointed out that Amanda Austin was pretty nearly as unheard of as before.

That was when I began to assert myself and produce

my sketchbook as I hadn't done before, even though I could see Johnny cooling before my eyes. He didn't want a career girl in his life, or even a wife who worked. He was old-fashioned and Victorian, and I began to cool a little too in the face of that realization. So when he walked out, I let him go. And when he was gone, I had for a little while a feeling of marvelous release and escape. I would never let myself in for a dominating male again. But I missed him just the same. I hadn't cooled as much as I'd thought, and there were times when I nearly phoned to tell him he could have everything his own way, if only he would come back. Something fiercely self-preserving kept me from calling.

Now a year had gone by and I was trying to ignore the ache of emptiness in me. I had my work, and I didn't want to fall in love again. I had a few men friends, but they were only that and I could take them or leave them, but it was all growing terribly flat—meaning nothing.

What I needed was a change of scene—a whole new way of life. I took off the bracelet and tossed it on the table. I wouldn't go on being lacerated because of an old love that hadn't worked out.

There was still one more thing to be considered. The intangible thing that was perhaps the strangest of all. That was my fearful nighttime dream. A frightening, recurring dream that verged on the edge of nightmare, and sometimes haunted me into the daylight.

It was always the same. There was a hard, bright light from the sky, and smudged charcoal-dark against that blue stood a tree. A very old tree, with black, twisted branches that seemed to reach toward me—as if the leafy ends were hands that would grasp and injure me. Always there was horror in my vision of the tree. A sense that if I stared at it long enough the ultimate terror would seize and engulf me. But I always woke up before whatever threatened me could happen. As a child, I'd sometimes wakened screaming, and my father had come to soothe and comfort me. As I grew older, the nightmare came less often, but it still troubled me, and I wanted to know its source. Was there such a tree out in Santa Fe? If I found the reality, would I understand the terror and be free of it?

Still—the dream was not the deciding factor. It was my grandfather's letter, the words my grandmother had written, and the miniature of my mother that made up my mind. I wanted to know the truth about Doroteo Cordova Austin—what she was like and how she had died. If there was some hidden tragedy there, I wanted it to be hidden no longer. As it was, I had roots on only one side of my family. On the other side there was empty soil that gave me an uneasy feeling. If there was darkness, it was a part of me, and I wanted to know about it. How could I understand myself when I knew nothing at all about half of my forebears? They had formed me too, and there had been times in my life when I felt an affinity to something other than my Aunt Beatrice's rock-bound New England, or my father's usually gentle ways. Sometimes there were storms let loose in me. Sometimes I too had an instinct toward that same highhanded imperiousness that showed itself in my grandfather's letter. There seemed to be a suppressed passion in me, something that needed an outlet now lacking.

So what was I? Until I knew, how could I offer myself in any sound human relationship? I had often surprised both Johnny and myself, and didn't know why. Now I must find out.

I reached for the telephone and dialed the number of an airline which flew into Albuquerque.

II

Outside the airport building there was a glare of afternoon sunlight where cars and taxis stopped to let out passengers or pick them up. I stood beside my bags, not far from the end doors and the baggage area, as the wire from my cousin Eleanor Brand had instructed me. No one had been there to meet me, and no one had come since I'd arrived, though others from my plane had already collected their baggage and gone.

I waited a little impatiently, with a traveler's anxiety. I had no idea what Eleanor would look like, and since I was standing in the appointed place, she would have to find me. I paid little attention to a woman, probably in her forties, who came rushing through a door, stopped abruptly, and stood looking toward the baggage section.

That is, I paid no attention to her at first, except for a quick glance which told me she couldn't be Eleanor. Somehow I expected Eleanor to be young. But when she continued to study me fixedly, I grew uneasy. This was more than the casual interest of a stranger, and I looked at her again, meeting her gaze with my own.

She had short, rather deliberately brown hair and hazel eyes with the beginnings of crinkle lines about them. She was not very tall, but she wore her smartly tailored tan slacks well. Her citron-yellow blouse set off the strand of turquoise and silver she wore about her neck. One sensed a woman who tried a little desperately for a semblance of youth.

When she realized that I too was staring, she seemed to recover herself and gave me a half-apologetic smile as she came toward me.

"You're Amanda, of course. You couldn't be anyone but Doro's daughter. I'm sorry I stared, but you stopped me cold and I had to take you in. The resemblance is startling. I couldn't help wondering how much you're like her."

Such frankness left me at a loss and I felt a bit prickly over being so openly examined.

"Are you Eleanor—?" I began.

"No, I'm not. Though I suppose I'm a second cousin or something." She led the way toward an exit door. "I'm Sylvia Stewart, and my husband and I live next door to your grandfather. Have you been waiting long? I got off to a late start because they didn't call me until the last minute and it's an hour's drive from Santa Fe. There's trouble at the Cordova house. Eleanor has disappeared. Completely gone. God knows where. Her bed wasn't slept in last night, and Gavin, her husband, was away until this morning, so he didn't know. Here's my car. Wait till I open up and put your bags in back."

I watched her store my sketchbook along with my two bags. I'd had no time to ask questions and I contained myself until Sylvia Stewart was behind the wheel and I beside her. At least she was a relative of sorts, and I could begin to learn about my family from her.

"Have they any idea what has happened to Eleanor?" I asked as we pulled away from the curb.

She gave me another studying look that seemed to weigh and consider, as though my appearance troubled her and she was searching for some conclusion about me. The insistence of her scrutiny made me uncomfortable because something I could not understand seemed to lie behind it.

Her shrug was expressive and probably critical. "Who's to tell what would happen to Eleanor? Maybe she's been kidnaped, murdered—who knows? Though I expect that's too much to hope for. She's probably gone off somewhere on her own just to drive Gavin mad. She's rather like your mother for doing the unexpected. That's the wild Cordova streak that Juan is so proud of."

I hardly knew how to meet this torrent of haphazard information, and I gave my attention to the city outskirts we traveled through. Everything was bathed in a glare of bleached light, and I remembered involuntarily the light in my recurrent dream—blazing sunlight reflected back at the sky from the earth colors—dun and ocher—all around.

No. Sand. The color of sand—of pale mud. The earth, the buildings, everything but a hazy cobalt sky was the color of sand. The landscape was a shock to eastern eyes accustomed to granite and concrete, or suburban greenery. Yet I liked the high intensity of light on every hand. It seemed familiar, and not just because of my dream.

"I never knew my mother when I was old enough to remember her," I said. "Apparently you did?"

"I knew her." The tone was dry, enigmatic. "I grew up with her. I grew up with all of them—the Cordovas, that is."

"It's strange to be coming here to a family I know nothing about."

Again she turned her head with that openly searching glance. "You shouldn't have come here at all."

"But why not—when my grandfather wanted me to come?"

"Oh, I don't suppose it could have been avoided, really. If you hadn't come, Paul would have gone to see you in New York."

I was completely at sea. "Paul?"

"Paul Stewart is my husband. You may know his books. He's writing one now that you may be a part of. That is, you could be if you remember anything about the time when you lived here."

The name of Paul Stewart was vaguely familiar, but I didn't know his books, and I didn't see what I could possibly have to do with whatever he was writing now.

"I don't remember anything," I said. "Nothing at all. Why should it matter when I was only a small child then?"

There seemed to be a visible relief in her response to my words that puzzled me all the more.

"Probably it doesn't. Anyway, Paul will tell you about it himself. I'm afraid I can't prevent that. Though I'll admit I'm against what he intends."

This seemed a blind alley. "How ill is my grandfather?"

"His heart is bad. Mostly he stays close to the house these days. To add to his troubles, there's a clouding of his vision, so that he can't see as sharply as he used to, and glasses won't help. Of course he's been threatening to die for years—to get people to do as he wants. But this time it's for real. The doctors don't know how long he may last and he's not a very good patient."

"Then I'm glad I've come in time. I haven't any other family. I don't even know whether my grandmother is alive. I know nothing about her."

"Katy died nearly three years ago." There was a softening in Sylvia Stewart's slightly brittle tones. "Katy was wonderful. I'll love her always. You know, of course, that she was an Anglo?"

"I don't know anything," I said.

"It's like your father to do that—isolate you, I mean." The softness was gone. "He told your grandfather off pretty thoroughly before he left. Though it was thanks to the Cordovas—to Juan—that the scandal about your mother was at least minimized and never erupted into the full-scale horror it might have become. Her death devastated Juan, and Katy's heart was broken. Everyone adored your mother."

There was a hint of bitterness in her last words, and I shrank from asking this tart, gossipy woman about my

mother's death. I didn't like the words "scandal" and
"horror." Whatever had happened, I wanted to learn about
it from a more sympathetic source. It came through rather
clearly that Sylvia Stewart had not liked my mother.

"What was your relationship to Katy?" I asked.

"Her sister was my mother. My parents died when
I was fairly young, and Katy took us into her family
and into her heart—my stepbrother, Kirk, and me. It
never mattered to her that Kirk wasn't related by blood.
She was just as good to him as to the rest of us. Just the
same, there wasn't any nonsense about her. Katy came
from Iowa farmlands and she hated adobe walls. But she
loved Juan and she put up with them without complaining.
After your father took you away, Katy used to send
you presents and write you letters. But they were all
returned and she had to give you up."

Until just before her death, when she'd written again,
I thought, and I mourned her sadly. How could my father
have done this to her and to me? No matter how
much he had disliked Juan Cordova, he shouldn't have
kept me from my grandmother.

"Katy could love without spoiling," Sylvia went on.
"In that way she was different from Juan. He has always
spoiled everything human he's touched with what he calls
affection. He loved my stepbrother, Kirk, more than his
own son, Rafael. I suppose they were two of a kind. But
I'd rather be loved by a man-eating tiger! That's what's
the matter with Eleanor. You can hope he'll spare *you*
his affection, Amanda."

This was something I'd have to find out for myself,
and I didn't mean to let this woman, second cousin or
not, prejudice me against my grandfather. I drew her
attention casually away from Juan Cordova.

"I suppose there are other relatives living?"

She was willing to talk. "Eleanor and Gavin Brand
live in the house. When Gavin married Eleanor some
years ago, he wanted them to have a house of their
own. But old Juan wouldn't have it."

As quickly as that, we were back on the topic of

my grandfather. I let her go on.

"Eleanor didn't want to move out anyway. She wanted to stay close to Juan so she could influence him. Gavin had to listen when it came to the house, since he's employed by Juan—though I'd say Juan is about the only one Gavin would listen to. Of course he should never have married Eleanor, but he was mad about her, the way men so easily are—just as they were about Doro. Are you like that, Amanda?"

The bitter note was in her voice again and I glanced at her. She was looking straight ahead at the road, and she seemed not to care whether her words distressed me.

"I've never thought of myself as a *femme fatale*," I said coolly. "Tell me who else lives in the house."

She waved a hand toward the window on my side of the car. "Don't miss the scenery, Amanda. That's Sandia Peak out there. The Sandia Mountains guard Albuquerque the way the Sangre de Cristo range guards Santa Fe."

I looked out at the massive bulk that made a close backdrop to the city, but it was not scenery which interested me most just now.

"I don't even know how many children my grandfather had—only that my mother was one of them."

"She was the youngest. Clarita was the oldest. Clarita —never married."

There seemed a slight hesitation in Sylvia's words, and again that bitterness I didn't understand. But she went on quickly.

"Clarita's still there in the house and it's a good thing your grandfather has her. Most things depend on Clarita these days. Then there was Eleanor's father, Rafael, who married an Anglo, as your mother did. You'll notice Katy had nothing to say about their names. They were all Spanish, thanks to Juan.

"When Rafael grew up, however, he would have nothing to do with being Spanish-American. He rebelled from all that Spanish heritage your grandfather dotes on. He wanted to be all Anglo and he wanted to raise his daughter that way. But when Rafael and his wife were killed in the crash of a small plane, Juan took over as always. So Eleanor moved into Juan's house and she's been very close to him. Closer than she ever was to Katy, in spite of the efforts Katy made with her. Eleanor always had her own self-interest at heart. You might say her first attachment was to her grandfather when she was small, and then to Gavin Brand, who was always in and out of the place. Now, who knows?"

Sylvia threw me one of her sidelong looks, and I suspected that she was testing the effect of all this upon me. I said nothing, and she went on without restraint, as if she were somehow eager to warn me away from my family.

"From the time she was in her teens, Eleanor was bound she was going to have Gavin for a husband, and she succeeded in snaring him." Tartness had turned corrosive in her dislike for Eleanor.

"What does Gavin do for my grandfather?" I asked.

"Everything! Mark Brand, Gavin's father, was Juan's partner when CORDOVA was first opened, and Gavin grew up in the business. Now that his father is gone, he's manager and chief buyer, since Juan can no longer get around very much. Gavin tries to hold Juan to a little sanity. It's really he who's held the store together."

I told Sylvia about the page I'd torn from a glossy magazine—that ad about CORDOVA—and of how I'd made up stories about it to amuse myself.

Sylvia shook her head. "Watch out for CORDOVA, Amanda. A long time ago it became the beast that rules the Cordovas. When we were young, we all knew the store came before any of us. Oh, not with Katy, but always with Juan. It's the monument on which his life is built. Gavin's rebelling though. There's a war going on between them over more than Eleanor. Gavin may not be pleased to see you here. You may be a threat."

I couldn't see how that was possible, but I let it go.

"You don't seem to like anyone connected with the Cordovas," I said.

I heard the soft gasp of the breath she drew in. "I wonder if that's true. Maybe I haven't much reason to like them—though they're my family as well as yours, and I grew up with Clarita and Rafael—and Doro. I suppose I hate to see Doro's daughter walk into the lair. Are you sure I can't persuade you to turn around and fly back to New York?"

I wondered why it should matter to her so much whether I stayed or left, but I didn't hesitate. "Of course not. You've made me all the more eager to know them—and make up my mind for myself."

She sighed and raised one hand from the wheel in a helpless gesture. "I've done what I can. It's up to you. I'd like to get away from Santa Fe myself and never see another Cordova. But Paul likes it here. It's good for his writing, and he's the only one I really care about. He's lived in the house next door since before your mother died. When I married him he wanted to stay there."

She was silent after that, and I gave my attention to the straight, wide highway we were traveling at seventy miles an hour, the city left behind. Mesa country stretched on either hand—the color of pale sand, dotted with juniper bushes. A tree was a rarity, except where there was a stream bed with its sprouting greenery. Uneven hill formations sprang from the dusty ground, and always in the distance there were mountains. Sometimes the near hills bore slashes of dun red and rust and burnt orange, and the always-present juniper grew like green polka dots up their sides.

I felt again that stab of familiarity. The brilliance of the light, the sand color, the wide sky above, the sense of space all around, as though the land ran on forever—all these were known to me. I had seen them before. A sense of excitement stirred in me, a feeling that I was coming home. This would be a wonderful landscape to paint. It was as if I had been born with an affinity for it. It invited me, belonged to me.

"I think I remember this," I said softly.

Sylvia Stewart threw me a quick look and I sensed again some anxiety in her. The speed of the car lessened briefly as she gave me her attention.

"Don't try to remember, Amanda. Don't try!"

"But whyever not?"

She would not answer that and gave her attention again to her driving.

The air was clear and intoxicating to breathe as we climbed toward high Santa Fe. There was little traffic at this hour and the straight road arrowed north into the distance, with now and then a crumbling adobe hut by the wayside, but no real habitation anywhere.

Recently, there had been a welcome rainstorm, and when the Sangre de Cristos came into view—the very foot of the Rockies—there was snow along the peaks. Below them the roofs of Santa Fe were visible. Anticipation began to quicken.

Once we were within the city limits, the approach turned into the usual honky-tonk that mars the outskirts of most American cities. There were the cheap hamburger stands, the gas stations, and motels.

"Pay no attention," Sylvia said. "This is an incrustation, not the real Santa Fe. We live up near Canyon Road where the artists hang out. It's an old part of town. But I'll drive you through the center first, so you can have a taste of the old city. As we'll tell you frequently, this town was founded ten years before the Pilgrims landed and it's the oldest capital in the country."

I knew that. I had always loved to read about Santa Fe. Now, however, I had a curious sense of a city set apart from the world. Where I had lived, you could hardly tell where one town ended and the next began, while all around Santa Fe stretched the wide mesa country, and behind it crouched the mountains, shutting it in, isolating it. I had a feeling that once within its environs, I was leaving all the life I knew behind, and this was a feeling I didn't altogether like. Foolish, of course. Santa Fe was an old and civilized city. This was where the conquistadores had come after marching through all those empty miles of desert. This was where the Santa Fe Trail had ended.

So it was that I came into city streets with a mingling

of homecoming, anticipation—and a curious apprehension. I supposed I could thank Sylvia Stewart for the latter, and I must get over it as quickly as I could.

We left the wide road as the streets narrowed and twisted. The buildings were the color of adobe, whether real or simulated, so there was again that glow of dull earth color drowsing in the sun. In the plaza that was the heart of the town the green of trees relieved the eye, and as we circled the central square, Sylvia pointed out the side street down which CORDOVA was located. Then she drove out of the plaza and past the Cathedral of St. Francis —that sandstone building with the twin towers that has the look of France about it. I knew of Archbishop Lamy who had erected it, and about whom Willa Cather had written in *Death Comes for the Archbishop*.

"My bookshop is down that way." Sylvia pointed. "My assistant is taking over today. You must drop in and see me soon. Now I'll take you home."

Home! Suddenly the word carried a ring of new meaning, in spite of my trepidation. For me it meant the end of a quest. I too was a Cordova, and no matter what Sylvia had said about them, I was eager to know my family.

We turned up the Alameda near where the Santa Fe Trail had once ended and followed a strip of green park above the dry bed of the Santa Fe River. We drove up the narrow spine of the hill that was Canyon Road, past studios and art galleries. Here the old adobe houses that had once been Spanish residences crowded close together, separated only by rounded adobe walls that enclosed houses and hidden patios. On Camino del Monte Sol we turned off and then took another turn down a narrow lane of old houses.

"There ahead—the one with the turquoise window trim and gate," Sylvia said. "That's your grandfather's house. Ours is beyond, where the next wall starts. Juan's is older than Paul's and mine—more than a hundred years."

I wanted to stop and search for recognition, but we

were past. Sylvia's next words brought disappointment.

"I won't take you there first. You'll come to our place and meet my husband. Then I'll phone Clarita and see if she's ready for you. Everything was in an upheaval when I left because of Eleanor."

Just past the Cordova house a garage faced on the narrow road, and Sylvia drove into it. From the back a door opened upon a bricked patio and we walked through. Adobe walls, shoulder high, shut out the street, and Sylvia led me across the patio and through a heavy wooden door into a long, comfortable living room with Indian rugs scattered over the floor, and a collection of Kachina dolls on two rows of shelves.

"You'll probably find Paul out in the *portal.*" Sylvia gestured. "Do go out and introduce yourself. I'll be along in a moment. Tell Paul I'm calling Clarita to let her know you're here and find out if Gavin has finally done away with Eleanor, as she deserves."

I went through the door she indicated and out upon a long, porchlike open space that was level with the patio it edged. In a rattan chair at the far end sat a man who was probably in his late thirties—certainly younger than Sylvia. His thick hair, sun-bleached, rose in a crest from his forehead and grew long at the back of his neck. He wore a beige sweater against the cool May afternoon and his legs were encased in brown slacks. He heard me and turned, rising from his chair.

He was tall and lean, with a thin, rather bony face, intent gray eyes, a long chin, and a straight mouth that moved into a slight smile at the sight of me. It was a face of considerable character and I liked what I saw. But there was more than that. Something unforeseen happened in that arrested moment of time. It was as if we looked at each other with a heightened awareness. An awareness that came from nowhere and was electric in its recognition. It was as if he had said, *I am aware of you and I'm going to know you better.*

I remembered that he was Sylvia's husband, and I had to break that arrested moment with its unexpected un-

dertones of attraction. It made me self-conscious and
suddenly wary. I tried to erase it by being flippant.

"Hello," I said lightly. "I'm Amanda Austin, Juan
Cordova's long-lost granddaughter. Sylvia told me to
come out here and wait until she's phoned to find out
whether Gavin Brand has finally done away with his
wife."

I expected him to laugh over the foolish words, but
instead the faint smile vanished and he bowed his head
gravely.

"How do you do, Miss Austin. I'm afraid you've made
a mistake. I'm not Paul Stewart. I'm Gavin Brand."

I could feel the awful sensation of bright, burning
blood rushing into my cheeks. My tongue felt numb and
my body stiffened. There was nothing I could say, no
amends I could make.

After a moment of hideous embarrassment for me, he
went on coolly. "As it happens, I'm rather concerned
about Eleanor. I came over here to talk to Sylvia and
Paul, to see if she might have dropped any sort of clue
that would lead us to her."

I could only stammer a hapless apology. "I—I'm sorry."

His nod was as grave as before and he seemed to remove himself to some remote plane that I could not
reach. I would have no welcome to the Cordova house
from Gavin Brand and it was my own fault.

The appearance of Sylvia and the man who must
certainly be her husband, Paul, rescued me from trying to
say anything more. Sylvia seemed surprised to find Gavin
here, and I caught the uncertain look she gave Paul.

"Hello, Gavin," she said. "I didn't know you were
out here. I see you and Amanda have already met.
Amanda, this is Paul."

Her husband came toward me, his hand outstretched.
Though he moved as lightly as a cat, he was a big man.
His hair, a sandy gray, was thinning at the temples, and
his eyes were a color I couldn't define. There was something oddly like a challenge in the look he gave me,
and I sensed an inner tension in him so that he made

me as immediately uneasy as Sylvia had done.

"I've been looking forward to meeting you," he said, and there seemed some special intent in his words. His look questioned me as it searched my face, and I felt at a loss to meet it. He went on at once, fortunately expecting no response. "You'll be welcome at the Cordovas'. Old Juan's been looking forward to your coming. Indeed, we all have. May I say you look very much like your mother. I remember her quite well."

Sylvia broke in hastily, as though she did not want him to talk about my mother. "Gavin, I've just spoken to Clarita. Word came in after you left the house. Eleanor's car has been found at White Rock on the road to Los Alamos."

"White Rock?" Gavin seemed baffled. "Why would she leave it there? Do either of you have any idea?"

Sylvia shrugged. "As well there as anywhere else when Eleanor takes a notion into her head."

Paul seemed to be thinking, but before he had anything to say, I caught the look he exchanged with Gavin Brand, and I could almost hear the antagonism that crackled between the two men. It was clear that they did not like each other.

When Paul Stewart spoke, it was almost grudgingly. "That White Rock branch of the road is also the way to Bandelier. I've heard her talk about the caves there with enthusiasm—as a hideaway. Once she suggested I use them for background in one of my books, and she's talked about what fun it might be to spend a night in one of those caves. It's possible she may have gone there."

"It's wild enough for Eleanor," Sylvia said, "and she's always gone for the outdoor life. Sleeping bags and all that."

"As a matter of fact, her sleeping bag is gone." Gavin seemed to be thinking. "At least it's a lead. I'd better get out to Bandelier and have a look."

"Then may I go now to see my grandfather?" I asked Sylvia.

She shook her head. "Not right away. Though Paul will

take your luggage over soon. There's more to come. Gavin, you know that small pre-Columbian stone head that Juan had in his private collection? I understand it's been missing for a week. Now it's turned up—on a bureau in your room."

Gavin stared at her and I saw how chill his gray eyes could become. "It wasn't there a little while ago."

"Clarita found it," Sylvia said, sounding waspish, as though she might be enjoying this. "She went straight to Juan to tell him, and the old man is furious. Now there's a new uproar going on. I think you'd better wait awhile before going to the house, Amanda."

Paul said smoothly, "They'll find out how it came there, of course."

"It can wait." Gavin did not look at him. "I want to find Eleanor before I deal with anything else. I'm going to drive out to Bandelier at once. It's a long shot, perhaps, but it's the only one I have at the moment. Sylvia, if there's any further word, will you phone the park rangers out there and have them give me a message?"

She nodded a bit grimly, and I stood helplessly by while Gavin strode across the *portal*. As he passed me, he paused and turned around with a speculative look.

"You can come with me," he said with calm assurance. "You shouldn't see Juan now. Eleanor's your cousin and I may need a woman along when we find her."

I didn't believe his reasons. He wanted to get me away from Sylvia and Paul. What he'd given me was more command than request, and clearly he expected no refusal. This was the last thing I wanted to do. I had no wish to be in the company of this cool, remote man to whom I'd been so instantly attracted, and whom I'd insulted so cruelly. It seemed, however, that I had no choice. He expected me to come and his will dominated my own, whether I liked it or not. At least going with him would be better than an idle marking of time.

"I'll come," I said, as though he had been waiting for my assent.

We went out of the Stewarts' house together and he

seemed very tall at my side. The crest of his sun-bleached hair shone in the clear light as we crossed the patio, and I thrust away the memory of that first attraction. He couldn't have been more distant if he'd existed on another planet.

III

Gavin took the road to Taos north out of Santa Fe. He drove at the maximum speed with an assurance that commanded the car as he had commanded me. I reminded myself that this was exactly the sort of man I did not like.

I had not expected to be traveling again so soon, and I regretted the further postponement of my meeting with the Cordovas. But thanks to my foolish words to Gavin, which had put me at a disadvantage, and his own rather highhanded commandeering of my company, here I was on the way to a national monument called Bandelier, of which I'd never heard before.

Most of the time we were silent, and once or twice I stole a sidelong look at my imperturbable companion. It gave me pleasure to dislike him, but at the same time the shape of his head, the planes of his face intrigued me as a painter. My fingers itched for a pencil so that I could catch an impression of that forceful head on paper. I wondered if I could paint him. I wasn't at my best in portraiture, but an interesting face always challenged me.

His voice broke into my thoughts. "I suppose you wonder why I took you away from the Stewarts so abruptly?"

33

"I did wonder—yes."

"I didn't want to leave you there for Paul to prey on."

"Prey on? What do you mean?"

"You might as well know—he's writing a book, and he wants to pick your memory, if he can."

"Sylvia said something of the same thing. But how can anyone pick a five-year-old child's memory? What sort of book is it?"

He stared grimly at the road ahead. "A chapter will deal with the Cordovas—specifically with your mother's death. How much do you know about that?"

I could feel myself tense. "I don't know anything, really. You see, my father would never talk about her or tell me what happened to her. All I know is that she died in a fall. That's one reason I've come here. Somehow, it's terribly important for me to—well, to know all about her. All about the Cordova side of my family."

He glanced at me and I met his look, to find unexpected sympathy there, though he went on without commenting on my words.

"Your grandfather is very much against Paul's writing about the Cordovas. And I agree with him. It will do no one any good to dig up an old scandal at this late date. You least of all."

I didn't like the sound of this. "Sylvia talked about a scandal too. But what scandal? If there is anything to do with my mother—scandal or not—I want to know it. Why shouldn't I?"

"Better let it rest," he said. "You'll only bruise yourself."

"I don't care about that—I want to know! This is maddening!"

He threw me a quick look in which there was a certain grim amusement. "The Cordova stubbornness! It sticks out all over you."

"Perhaps it's only my New England side," I told him.

Neither of us spoke for a while. When we turned off the Taos road toward the Jemez Mountains which rose beyond Los Alamos, we had the snow-crested Sangre de Cristos at our back, and I studied the landscape with the same interest I'd felt on the trip from Albuquerque. This was a different world from the one I was used to.

I was glad I had done some map studying before I'd left New York and knew something about the locality. Well over on our right appeared a massive, curiously black mountain, standing alone, with its sides rising straight up to the flat mesa of its top. I watched it intently as we drove parallel with it. Memory seemed to stir and a name came to me from nowhere.

"Black Mesa," I said, surprising myself. The name was not one I had noted on a map.

"So there are things you remember?" Gavin said.

"I keep having flashes of familiarity, so that I feel I've seen this country before. As of course I have. I must have made this trip with my parents when I was small."

We were driving through mesa country and the hills ahead were like sandy ships riding a juniper-green sea. Sometimes their tops were crowned by spiked pinnacles of rock and there were often caves in the sandstone. Perhaps all of this was known to me, though I had no further flash of recognition as I'd had with Black Mesa. But I could not relax and give myself to an enjoyment of the scene. Always there were questions to be asked.

"Did you know my mother?" I spoke the words into the silence that was broken only by the rush of the car.

"Yes, I knew her," he said, but offered nothing more, frustrating me further.

"My father would never talk about her," I repeated doggedly. "It's strange to have grown up without any memories or knowledge of Doroteo Cordova Austin."

"At fifteen, I found it hard to understand what Doro saw in your father," Gavin said. "He was her opposite in every way."

I wondered if he were prodding me to indignation, but he seemed too uninvolved for that, too indifferent.

"Can you remember me?" I asked.

"Very well." His straight mouth softened briefly. "You were an engaging little girl and very like your mother."

For just an instant I relaxed toward him. No matter what denials I'd made to myself, something in me wanted to like this man. His next words dampened my own softening, and I knew he would not for long make concessions to the past.

"It's too bad engaging little girls have to grow up," he said.

The words seemed simply an opinion calmly expressed. He was not taunting me, but he cared nothing about how I might feel. The earlier flash of sympathy I'd seen was gone, and I moved away from him in the seat, disliking the twinge of hurt I felt, and wanting to show my resistance to anything he might say. He didn't seem to notice, and we said nothing more until we reached White Rock.

"This is where Eleanor left her car," he told me. "I won't stop now to check with the police. If she went to Bandelier, it's possible she thumbed a ride from here."

It was a sand-colored New Mexico town, quickly lost in the landscape, and we were away on the winding road to the park.

"Do you know why she's gone off?" I asked, still prickling from his remark about growing up.

"She'll probably have a good many reasons," he said. "What the real one is I'd better not try to guess."

"Sylvia spoke about a wild Cordova streak in Eleanor that my mother had too. That sounds like nonsense to me—a wildness in the blood and all that."

"Juan will tell you it's anything but nonsense. But can't you speak for yourself? You're a Cordova."

"I like to think that I'm fairly well balanced," I told him.

"My congratulations." His tone was dry, and I was silent after that, my anger beginning to boil. I could not like Gavin Brand, and my sympathy for my cousin was increasing. I wouldn't even accept Sylvia's estimation of her until I had a chance to judge for myself.

After several miles, during which I simmered down a little, we reached the admission booth to the park, where Gavin stopped to pay an entry fee. He asked the man in the booth if he had noticed a tall woman with long fair hair who might have checked through with someone else yesterday.

The attendant shook his head. "Too many people come through for me to remember. There's probably been a lot of girls with long blond hair. I don't keep track."

"Doesn't the park have a closing time?" I asked as we drove through the entrance. "Don't people have to get out then?"

"The place is enormous, with miles of trails," Gavin said. "And there are always campers staying overnight. I don't think they make a head count when day visitors leave."

The road wound downward toward the bottom of the canyon and high cliffs rose on either hand, tree-covered on one side, steep volcanic ash on the other.

"Why is it a national monument?" I asked.

"The Indians were here until around 1500. You'll see the ruins of their dwellings and kivas. It's all being carefully preserved."

And he was being carefully polite—the courteous guide.

"But if there are miles of trails, how will you find her?"

"Paul thinks the caves interested her most, and they'd offer shelter. We can have a look at some of them. It depends on how far she'd be willing to wander off the main path, whether we'll find her or not. If she's here, I suspect it won't be far."

"But if she really wants to hide—"

"*If* she really does," Gavin said quietly, "then she can elude us. But I suspect that by this time, if she's here, she'll want to be found. Paul was pretty ready with information about where she might be. It could have been planted."

I did not understand in the least why Eleanor Brand

had suddenly run away from home to spend the night
in so unlikely a place. Or why any information about her
would be "planted."

However, I knew he would explain none of this. There
had been an edge to his voice when he spoke Paul's
name, and I decided to be bold, asking my question
swiftly.

"Why don't you like Paul Stewart?"

He gave me a look that said this was none of my
business, but he answered. "Dislike can be a complex
matter. For one thing, he has an avidity for stirring up
trouble. Stay clear of him."

Perhaps I would, or perhaps I wouldn't. In any case,
I meant to go my own way.

The sun was out now, but the air was chilly and I was
glad I wore a sweater.

"Doesn't it get pretty cold here at night?" I asked.

"Decidedly. But Eleanor could manage if she chose."

I wanted to ask why—why? But his manner held me off.

Near the small building of the Visitor Center, Gavin
parked his car and we got out. He glanced at the low-
heeled shoes I'd worn for travel and nodded.

"You'll be all right. It's not a difficult path or very
long."

The narrow road had been paved for comfortable
walking, and it wound into the open along the floor of
the canyon. Again I had the sense of a world wholly
new to me. The canyon ran straight, with steep cliffs
going up on either hand, wooded on one side, bare rock
on the other, so that it was as if one walked into a
wide slash in the earth, shut in on both sides, protected.
On our right the sheer cliffs rose toward the sky and
at their base in the pockmarked volcanic rock were
caves that Indians had used. There were dozens of these
and one could climb to them only over rough ground.

Gavin saw the direction of my gaze and shook his
head. "If she's here, she'll probably choose the easier
way. We'll follow the trail." He seemed assured in his
knowledge of her and not particularly worried.

There were the ruins of kivas along the path—those buildings which had once been used as meeting places for religious and ceremonial rites. There were stone ruins in the ground where the ancient pueblo of Tyuonyi had encircled a central plaza. It had once been three stories high, accommodating a hundred people or more, Gavin told me. At another time I'd have been more interested.

The trail turned toward the base of the cliffs and began to climb until we were edging along just below the caves and reconstructed cliff dwellings. For the first time I grew a little breathless at this slight exertion, responding to the unaccustomed altitude. Gavin noticed and slowed his pace, not without a certain consideration.

Now he stopped before each cave and looked inside. Where a wooden ladder was propped against the cliff, he climbed up to peer through the opening. We had mounted fairly high above the canyon floor, and there were occasional steps cut into the narrow, rock path. The cliff face was uneven, with indentations or sections that thrust outward, so that the trail turned like a string twisted across its surface. Only once did other visitors pass us, coming from the opposite direction, and the floor of the canyon, far below, with its winding stream and groves of trees, seemed empty. The vast reaches of Bandelier could swallow hundreds. We began to alternate now. I took one cave, and Gavin the next, so we could increase the speed of our search.

It was I who found her. At first, when I climbed the short ladder to look into shadowed cavern depths, I saw nothing. Then something at the back moved and I glimpsed a face peering from a sleeping bag on the rocky floor.

"Eleanor?" I said.

There were sounds at the back of the cave as she came out of her bag. But she did not approach me. She merely sat crosslegged upon the bag, staring at the patch of dark I must have made against the brightness outside. I could not see her clearly in the dim light.

"Who are you?" she asked, and I heard for the first

time the light, rather musical voice that belonged to
Eleanor Brand. It was a voice which lent itself to mockery.

I told her I was her cousin Amanda Austin, but she cut
me short with a wave of her hand that seemed imperious.

"Is Gavin there?"

"Of course," I said. "I've been helping him look for
you. He's been concerned."

"Has he really?" Here was more mockery, and she
still made no move to come out of the cave.

I waited helplessly on the ladder as Gavin crawled out
of the next cave and came toward me. When I gestured
and descended the ladder, he went up it at once, calling
to her through the opening.

"Come out, Eleanor. The game's over for the moment.
So roll up your bag and come out."

Her soft laughter, issuing from the cave, had a faintly
vindictive sound, but I could hear her preparations as she
rolled up her bag. Gavin backed down the ladder, and
she came to the rocky lip of the cave and tipped her
sleeping bag over, letting it drop to the path. Then she
backed out, her short alpine hikers finding the rungs of
the ladder, blue jeans, thick blue pullover sweater and
long blond hair coming into view, until she stood on the
path beside us, and I had my first view of my cousin
Eleanor.

She was older than I by five years or more, I judged,
and for all her unconventional position at the moment,
she was a poised and confident woman. And a very
beautiful one, with her violet eyes and thick lashes, her
full, slightly pouting lips, and that fine hair cut in bangs
across a smooth forehead, falling in a sheen over her
shoulders. It seemed untangled, as though she might have
been calmly combing it recently. She paid no attention
to Gavin, but looked straight at me, still mocking, hardly
friendly.

"So you're Doro's daughter? How much like her are
you?"

It was not a question I could answer, and I made no
attempt to reply. She was not really interested in me any-

way, in spite of her attempt to ignore Gavin.

He spoke to her curtly. "You were supposed to meet Amanda at the airport at Albuquerque. Sylvia had to go in your stead."

"I supposed she would. Juan should never have asked me to go in the first place. Why should I be happy about Amanda's coming, considering the plotting he's likely to do? So I went off by myself for a while. To state my independence and let you all worry a little. I had a lovely night. There were a million stars, and all those Indian ghosts were stirring down there in the canyon. I'm sure I heard their drums."

Gavin ignored this flight of fancy. "There is such a thing as consideration," he said.

She laughed softly again, maliciously. "Have I ever bothered about that?"

Gavin remained unmoved by what seemed a deliberate effort to irritate him.

"Are you hungry?" he asked her.

"Of course not. I had sandwiches and cans of orange juice. I've finished everything up."

"You planned well," he said dryly. "My arrival is properly timed."

"You can never let me go, can you? You always come after me!" Tall as she was, she was not as tall as Gavin, and she tilted her head back to look up at him with a look that challenged and provoked.

"Your grandfather was worried. He wanted me to find you."

"I thought he would be. That was a bang-up fight the three of us had yesterday, wasn't it? Maybe you'll both begin to think about what *I* want now."

Gavin turned away from her. "Let's get back to White Rock. We can pick up your car there and phone Santa Fe."

I had the feeling that this woman had the power to hurt him, and I felt an unexpected pang of sympathy for Gavin. I'd known what it was like to be hurt by someone you loved.

He went ahead of us along the cliff's face, carrying Eleanor's sleeping bag, and she gave me a small smile filled with malice and triumph as she went after him.

I followed uneasily behind. Something stubborn stirred in me, stiffening my resistance. It looked as if I would have to stand against them all. Well, Juan Cordova had asked me to come, and only he mattered.

When we were in the car heading for White Rock, no one spoke. We sat in the front seat, with me in the middle, and the miles of curving road wound away in heavy silence. What was unspoken throbbed beneath our quiet.

At White Rock we picked up Eleanor's abandoned car, and a change was made. She and I were to return in her car, while Gavin followed us in his own. I would have liked to protest this arrangement because I felt an instinctive reluctance to be alone with my cousin Eleanor. Even more than the others, she seemed to oppose my coming, and her uninhibited frankness about this left me thoroughly annoyed. Gavin, however, was ordering us both, and this was not the time to argue. At his biding, I got reluctantly into the passenger's seat of Eleanor's car, and he went around to the driver's side to speak to her.

"You'd better go straight back to Santa Fe," he said. "Amanda has been traveling most of the day, and I'm sure she'd like a rest." His manner toward her was withdrawn, remote, but I sensed that it covered some deep emotion—whether of anger or frustrated love, I couldn't tell. His guard of indifference hid a deeper seething, I was sure. What would he be like if he exploded? More likable, perhaps—more human?

Eleanor smiled at him brightly and he walked away to his own car. Without waiting for him to get in, she switched on the motor, and by the time we turned onto the highway we were going fast, and Gavin was nowhere in sight behind us. Eleanor seemed to relax a little, her hands assured on the wheel. I noticed the diamond-set platinum band on her left hand, and the large turquoise and silver ring on her right. They were beautiful hands, with long slender fingers, the sinews hidden by smoothly rounded flesh. I hid my own utilitarian hands in my lap. Mine were working hands, square, with spatulate fingertips. It didn't comfort me to know they were an artist's hands.

My cousin threw me a sudden questioning glance, bright with reckless promise. "We don't have to go back to Santa Fe, you know. There's a choice of roads. Gavin will be wild if we're not back at Juan's by the time he gets there. Shall we provoke him?"

The prospect of driving aimlessly about the countryside with this woman who didn't like me had no appeal, nor did it seem anything but pointless for her to defy Gavin and our grandfather any further.

"I think we'd better go back," I said. "I want a room of my own and a bed I can stretch out on."

Her lips curled in a smile that dismissed me. "I didn't think you'd pick up a challenge. And I suppose we do have to go back. I don't mind making Juan angry—but not too angry. Why did you come with Gavin to look for me?"

"He asked me to."

"Of course," she said. "Women usually do what he asks. But why did you come to Santa Fe? Whatever possessed you to say 'yes' to Juan's letter?"

"I suppose because I wanted to know the other half of my family."

This seemed to strike her as amusing. "You'll regret that soon enough. Juan will want to know what I think of you. What shall I tell him?"

"How can you tell him anything?" I was beginning to feel tired, and her behavior was increasingly outrageous. Any sympathy I might have felt was now on Gavin's side. No wonder he tried to remain distant and untouched. "You don't know me yet," I pointed out, a bit sharply. "There's nothing to tell."

She smiled secretly to herself, and I let the matter go,

though I could not help wondering what she might find
to tell Juan Cordova.

By the time we reached the main highway, dark clouds
were boiling up over the Jemez Mountains behind us, but
Eleanor only shook her head when I commented that it
looked like rain.

"Clouds often come up like that, but we seldom get
much rain. We need it badly."

Far ahead across the countryside a whirlpool of dust
rose in a spiral like a miniature cyclone, spinning along
above the junipers. A dust dance, I thought, and knew that
the phrase had again come, unbidden, out of memory. I
had seen those spirals before and been fascinated by
them. I glanced at the woman beside me.

"I don't remember you at all," I said. "Can you remember me?"

"I can remember your sitting on Grandfather Juan's
knee. I can remember being jealous. But that was when
we were babies, of course. I don't need to be now."

Yet she was, I thought. She deeply resented his sending
for me.

"I wonder what's happened since I've been gone,"
she went on. "What have you heard?"

"I haven't been to the house yet," I told her. "Sylvia
Stewart took me next door, where I met Gavin and her
husband, Paul."

"Gavin at Paul's house? That's quite mad. They don't
like each other."

"Gavin was concerned for you. And it was Paul who
suggested Bandelier's caves to him."

"Good for Paul. I really didn't want to stay another
night. But I had to let him find me dramatically."

"Why did you go off in the first place?" I asked her
bluntly. "Why stay there at all?"

She seemed not to resent my questioning. "That's complicated." Again there was the sidelong look. "Mostly
I had to give Gavin and Juan a chance to cool off and
start worrying about me. They're both a little afraid of
me, you know. They don't dare push me too far."

I wondered if the quarrel she referred to had in any way concerned me, but I didn't ask. Eleanor had wanted news and I volunteered the only bit I had in order to see her reaction.

"It seems that Aunt Clarita found some sort of pre-Columbian stone head in Gavin's room. Sylvia said it had been missing for a week."

The light laughter came again. "That's lovely! Though I'm glad I wasn't there or they might have said I'd planted it. Juan will be furious. What did Gavin say?"

"Merely that he'd have to look for you before he gave his attention to anything else. I'm afraid I don't understand what all this is about."

"You don't need to," Eleanor said. "You won't be staying in Santa Fe long enough for it to matter."

I was silent, not knowing how long I would be there, and not liking the way she had put it. There seemed something that was almost a threat underlying her words —and I wouldn't be threatened.

"He's very hard to please—Grandfather Juan," she went on. "You'll irritate him like everyone else, and he'll soon send you away. I'm the only one he can tolerate these days. I'm the only one he listens to. Except perhaps Gavin. But he'll stop listening to him soon. Gavin's grown too highhanded, too overconfident. This stone head, for instance."

"But of course he didn't take it," I said.

"Of course he took it. He's been slipping things out of the store for the last year or so. I suppose he has a market where he can sell them. Juan's got to wake up about him sometime."

I didn't believe any of this, and my sympathy for Gavin increased. His wife was completely vindictive toward him, and I wondered how much he was hurt by this.

Eleanor was silent for a time, and I made no further effort at conversation. When she spoke again, her question startled me.

"I supposed you've learned by this time why Juan has brought you here?"

I hesitated. "I thought he wanted to see Doroteo's daughter."

"Oh, that's the angle he'll undoubtedly play up. The daughter of his favorite child and all that. He's been rubbing it in with the rest of us. But there's a better reason than that. If you don't know, you soon will."

"Is it something to do with Paul Stewart's book?"

"So you've heard about that? I'm the one who put Paul up to it, really, and now he's determined to carry through and write it, no matter how Juan Cordova feels. Grandfather's furious."

"Then why do you want to see this book written?"

The mocking little smile was on her lips again. "Family scandals don't bother me. And this annoys Juan. After all the hushing up he's done over the years, he doesn't want it all dug up again now. But I don't mind. It may give me a lever over him."

"Hushing up of what?"

"You mean you don't know?"

"I don't remember anything, and I'm getting tired of all this hinting and secrecy. What on earth is it all about?"

"I could tell you, but I won't. Not after the orders Juan has laid down. No one is to talk to you about it until he does."

By this time I was thoroughly discomfited and angry. It was clear that my mother had been involved in something quite dreadful, and I could only cling for reassurance to the thought of Katy's letter and what she had written my father. But I didn't want to tell Eleanor about that, and open myself to more derision.

"Anyway, I haven't any memories about Santa Fe to tell anyone," I said.

"If that's true, Paul will be disappointed. But it's hard to believe you don't remember anything. Perhaps it will begin to come back, once you're in a familiar place."

I thought of the tugs of unexpected recognition I'd

already felt, and wondered if this was true.

By this time the outskirts of the city were coming into view and from the northern approach there was less honky-tonk than from the Albuquerque direction. I was relieved to find our journey ending, as I felt an increasing distrust of Eleanor, and a growing conviction that if she could injure me with Juan Cordova, she would.

In a short time we were driving through Santa Fe streets at a more decorous speed, and I tried to rouse myself in preparation for the encounters that were to come. After all that had happened since my arrival, I felt emotionally drained, and it was difficult to recover any sense of anticipation. If anything, a feeling of dread had replaced all eagerness.

We took a wide avenue that led uphill to the Canyon Road area and found our narrow lane with its adobe houses. The Cordova garage, with room for several cars, was tucked into a corner of the property where it abutted on an adobe wall. I got out of the car and looked around, wishing I could recapture my first feeling of excitement at sight of the house.

The afternoon had grown late, but turquoise-trimmed windows and painted gate still shone in bright sunlight, and rounded adobe walls encircled the house in smooth, pale ivory. Deliberately, I put everything else from my mind and thought of painting, of color. Ivory wasn't right. Flesh? No, that was too pinky. Pale apricot, perhaps? If I painted any of this I would try earth colors— red and yellow ochers and Venetian red. Perhaps a touch of viridian green for the shadows. Eleanor's voice brought me back from the thought of painting, made me stiffen for the next test.

"Has our adobe put you into a trance? Come along and I'll take you to Aunt Clarita."

We went in at the front, by way of the turquoise gate. The house seemed low and not particularly impressive— small to house a family—but that was its deception. I was to learn later that it had grown by addition to addition over the years, so that it ambled into many rooms and passageways, gaining its own individuality and character, as well as a sense of secrecy—of concealment behind closed doors and outer walls.

Eleanor led me across a narrow yard, through a carved wooden door and into the Cordova living room. I had come home to my beginnings, and I had no feeling now that there would be welcome for me here. Instead, adobe walls seemed to close me in tightly, shutting out sunlight, enveloping me in a cool gloom, holding me prisoner.

I tried to shake off such fantasy as I stood looking about the room. Nothing imprisoned me. I was quite free to walk away any time I wished. It was foolish to feel a faint prickling up my spine—as though there were something in this house for me to fear. Something hidden deep in old memory.

IV

The room was long and cool, with white painted walls and the contrast of dark wood. Overhead, the bare pine beams that supported the flat roof, and which I would learn to call "vigas," were dark brown stripes against the white ceiling, each ending in a wooden corbel where it met the wall. Navajo rugs, black, crimson, and gray in their striking patterns, were scattered across a polished red brick floor. The corner fireplace was adobe, rounded and smooth like the outdoor walls, with a crude, narrow mantel. Beside it along one wall stretched a built-in *banco,* a typical fireplace bench, piled with cushions of henna and pine green. Beside the chimney hung a long strand of red chili pods, drying and decorative, and within the fire-bricks of the hearth white piñon logs were piled, waiting to be lighted. Two dark leather chairs had been drawn up before the fireplace, with Indian rugs tossed over their seats and backs. All the furniture had a dark, Spanish look, with considerable use of leather and deep carving. From the center of the ceiling hung an ancient wrought-iron chandelier on a chain, casting a soft light in the cool, dim room.

All around on shelves and small tables were skillful wood carvings of desert animals. Probably they had

been created by Juan Cordova, but they were not like
my amusing little road runner. Each seemed to be per-
forming some cruelty, however natural to the species. A
horned toad had a half-eaten winged creature in its mouth.
The tarantula looked fearfully alive. I turned my attention quickly to a painting of the Sangre de Cristos
that hung upon one wall, the high snow peaks shining in
the sun, and a girdle of evergreens climbing the slopes
below. Here there was no threat of death by a predator.

My impression was of a room wholly southwestern
in character, yet I recognized nothing about it except for
some vague haunting of disquiet which existed in me.
I tried to tell myself that I had come home. Very soon
I would meet my mother's sister, my mother's father.
Eleanor and Gavin did not matter. I waited not only for
some greeting, but for a recognition within me that did
not come. There was no easing of that barely perceptible
pulse of anxiety that seemed to beat at the back of my
mind, carrying in it something close to fear. There was
some memory here, after all, but I did not know with
my mind what it was my senses remembered.

Eleanor said, "She'll have heard us. She'll be here
soon."

Doorways with carved wooden arches led off from
this central room, and in one corner were steps that
mounted to a little balcony at half-level, with a closed,
recessed door beyond it. As I glanced toward the door it
opened. A woman came out on the balcony and I saw
Clarita Cordova for the first time.

She was tall and very thin, not having turned to plumpness with the years, as many Spanish women do. She was
dressed almost wholly in black, even to her stockings
and black buckled shoes. Only at her throat fine ivory lace
in a modern ruff offered relief and threw reflected light
into her narrow face. Her hair was as black as mine, and
she wore it pulled severely down from a center part and
wound low at the base of her neck. From her ears hung
an unexpected touch of color in dangling turquoise and
silver that danced whenever she moved. She looked

wholly Spanish. If my grandmother Katy's blood had
come down to her, it did not show outwardly.

It was not her appearance, however, which made the
most impression on me, but the manner in which she
stood on her small balcony and stared at me with narrowed eyes, as though she weighed and judged me—
for whatever reason I could not tell. I was reminded of
the manner in which Sylvia Stewart had stared at the
airport, measuring me. All of them questioned me silently,
resented my presence, and held secret their thoughts
about me. I tipped my chin, staring back, resisting the
strange sense of some mental pressure this woman put
upon me. I would not be downed by these Cordovas. It
was my grandfather who wanted me here. And I wasn't
Spanish—I was from New England. Perhaps that was
one of the things I would discover about myself.

Almost gleefully, Eleanor let the moment grow long
before she spoke. "Aunt Clarita, this is Amanda. This
is your sister Doro's daughter." There was something
overly dramatic in her tone, as though she meant to
torment the older woman in some way with my presence.

Clarita gave me a slight nod of recognition and then
looked at Eleanor. It was a strange look—both affectionate and despairing, as she spoke to her in Spanish. Eleanor
shrugged her indifference and answered in English.

"I chose to go away. I'd had enough of all of you.
That's all there is to it."

Clarita came down the steps into the room. "We
will talk later," she said to Eleanor, and her attention
turned again upon me. Once more I felt that sense of
pressure, a sense that something I did not understand
was required of me. "So you are Doroteo's daughter?"
She held out her hand to me, though the gesture did not
seem wholly welcoming.

"And you are my mother's sister," I said, taking her
hand. It was thin, with jewels on the fingers, and it released mine at once.

A pretty young Spanish-American girl came into the
room and Clarita spoke to her.

"Rosa, you will take Miss Austin to her room, please. Your luggage is there waiting for you, Amanda."

The girl smiled at me with a flash of white teeth and stood waiting.

"You are tired, Amanda?" Clarita said. "You would like coffee—something to eat?"

"No, thank you. Just to wash and rest for a little while. My grandfather—how is he?"

Clarita's dark eyes were large and placed deeply beneath the bony structure of her brows. When her heavy lids closed over them, the sense of pressure upon me seemed to lighten.

"He is not well today. Eleanor has disturbed him. It is best if you do not see him at once."

I was no longer impatient to see him, but all too willing to postpone the meeting until I felt rested and stronger. The experience of meeting Clarita had further dampened any eagerness I might have felt. My father had been right. Nothing about this house or family reassured me. There was something ominous in the very air—some warning that was part of the walls and dark vigas, of those omnivorous carved creatures my grandfather had made.

"Go with Rosa then," Clarita said, gesturing toward the maid. "There is time to rest before dinner. We have given you our one upstairs room. It belonged to Doroteo when she was young. Eleanor, I wish to speak with you."

I went with Rosa through an arched doorway into another room that seemed an extension of the living room, except that a passageway toward the rear of the house branched off from it, evidently leading to bedrooms, and at one corner a flight of narrow stairs rose toward an open doorway above. Rosa climbed the stairs, and I followed.

Here was welcome contrast to the dark room downstairs. This was a high place of windows—windows on three sides, set deep into thick adobe walls. A bright room with white walls, overhead vigas, and a splash of color where a Navajo blanket hung against the white.

Over the small, rather narrow bed was a framed painting of mesa country—rather good. I liked the shadows across the sunny land, the chiaroscuro of light and dark. Had that picture been here when my mother was a girl? I thought not—its execution was too modern. The very brush strokes belonged to today.

Yet this was my mother's room. It had known her as I did not. The views from the windows were those she had seen. I moved from one window to the next, looking out, and a whisper of familiarity went through me again. Perhaps long ago someone had held me up to those windows and I had delighted even then in the beauty they framed. The Sangre de Cristos with snow on their crests were visible from one side, the more distant Jemez Mountains which I'd approached with Gavin that afternoon were on the other. A third window looked out upon the surprise of a large patio behind the house, and gave onto a vista down the hillside into an arroyo. Something quivered in me, like the kindling of old fear. What was it everyone expected me to remember?

Rosa motioned to where my bags and painting gear stood near a wall. "All is ready for you. This is best room. It is better than downstairs." Her smile wavered and she gave an odd little shiver.

"I'm sure it is," I said. "Thank you."

Perhaps I understood what she meant. Up here I was above those outer walls that sealed in the Cordovas. Up here I was free—except when I looked out toward the arroyo. That was when something stirred that led to horror. I didn't want to recapture that feeling, whatever it was, and I turned quickly away.

Rosa went out of the room, leaving uneasiness behind her. I tried to shake it off. I mustn't give in to some absurd and unhealthy haunting.

The bathroom was in a passageway near the foot of the stairs, and when I had taken a few things from a bag, I went down to freshen up. From the door to the living room I could hear the murmur of voices, speaking in Spanish again, and I suspected that Eleanor was being reproached for her escapade. I could imagine how casually she would dismiss any lecturing from Clarita. Yet her aunt, in spite of her severity, had seemed to show an affection for my cousin.

The bathroom had been remodeled and it sparkled with decorative Mexican tiles. There was a wide mirror over the wash basin and I looked into it as I brushed my hair and recoiled the knot at the back of my head. Cool water freshened and rested me a little, and I felt better with a touch of lipstick to make me look courageous. Now I would lie down on the bed that had been my mother's, and see if I could renew myself before the ordeal of dinner. But I was not to do that right away.

When I climbed back up the flight of stairs to my room and went through the door I had left open, it was to find Eleanor standing in the center of the room, obviously waiting for me. She had changed from wrinkled jeans and pullover to violet linen that matched the color of her eyes. Her windblown bangs had been fluffed, and her hair had been brushed to a smooth sheen and hung down her back nearly to her waist, longer than mine. I had no wish to see her, but here she was, and I was aware that she appraised me, just as I did her.

"You're all Anglo, aren't you?" she said. "In spite of all that black hair. Juan won't like it."

"What difference does it make? My mother was his daughter."

"Just as my father was his son. But I'm the one who is all Spanish in temperament, in spite of the fact that I'm fair. Juan knows that Spain is in my blood and he's proud of that."

I found it hard to carry on any sort of conversation with her. "Does he permit you to call him by his first name?"

"Permit? What is that? Sometimes I do and sometimes I don't. Oh, don't think I call him that to his face. Not the hidalgo. We all have to play to his delusion."

I wished she would go away. I had no desire to discuss our grandfather with Eleanor Brand. But I might as well find out all I could if she wanted to talk.

"What delusion is that?"

She shrugged lightly. "That he comes down straight from the conquistadores—a son of old Spain. He forgets the children of Montezuma with whom the conquistadores mated. Don't expect to find this a typical Spanish-American family, Amanda. Chicano is not a word that is used in this house."

"And does Clarita share this—delusion, as you call it?"

"She's Spanish to her fingertips. You'd never guess that Katy was her mother. But it doesn't get her anywhere with Juan. He thinks she's a poor thing for a Cordova."

I hadn't thought her a poor thing. I'd sensed a good deal of Spanish pride in the woman, as well as some dark force that I didn't understand.

"Why did you come to my room?" I asked Eleanor.

She moved about gracefully in her violet frock, glancing at the picture over the bed, looking out the window toward the arroyo. When she turned back to me, I thought for a moment she meant to say something pertinent, but she only shrugged again.

"Go away, Amanda. Don't stay here. No one wants you. Not even Juan. He'll only use you if you stay. He'll play with you—the way those carved monsters downstairs play with their victims. He's carnivorous, really."

"Aren't you being melodramatic?" I said.

Her eyes narrowed a little as she looked at me and her mouth had a tight, drawn set that had a hint of cruelty. I wondered if that was a trait of Juan's too, revealed in those carvings.

"We're a melodramatic family," she told me. "We are always at stage center. Go away before we hurt you."

"Whether I stay for a while or not is between Juan Cordova and me," I told her. "It's being made perfectly clear by everyone else that I'm not wanted here. But it's my grandfather who asked me to come. And he's the one I want to see."

"You may harm yourself by staying."

"Harm myself? How?"

"You'd better remember all that wild Spanish blood that flows in the veins of the Cordovas. It's better if you don't find it being used against you. It will do you no good."

"But I have some of that Spanish blood. It surfaces at times."

She looked at me as though I had said something significant. "Then you do have it too? The blood of our legendary dwarf?"

"What are you talking about?" I demanded.

But she had finished with her purpose in coming here. With a flick of her fingers she turned away and went out of the room, moving as gracefully as a dancer.

Until she had gone lightly down the stairs, I stood quite still, looking after her. Then I went to close the door. There was no bolt or key, or I would have locked it. When it was shut, I flung myself upon the bed, longing for rest and quiet and a stilling of the throb that had begun in my head.

Dwarf—there was that frightening word again. But I didn't know what it meant, and I must not think of it now. I closed my eyes and tried to drift into nothingness. I didn't want to think about the lack of welcome for me in this house. And I didn't think of it. With my eyes closed I saw—unexpectedly—Gavin Brand's face, with its marked cheekbones and straight mouth, his fine head crowned with thick, fair hair that grew to a point at the back of his neck. And then I remembered that same face a moment later when he had turned cold and remote and ready to dismiss me as someone he did not care to know.

But I didn't want to think about Gavin either. I didn't want to think of anything. I could only wait and see how events developed. I could only wait for the meeting with my grandfather. It was he who had sent for me, he who wanted me here. I must have faith in that fact. None of the others mattered. I had already given up my fantasy of a close, warm relationship with

my family. I couldn't imagine any genuine warmth between me and Clarita. Nor with Eleanor. Of them all,
I really liked Sylvia Stewart best. But she too had warned
me away, and apparently her husband was engaged in a
writing enterprise that was stirring up the Cordovas,
and which concerned me because it concerned my mother.
I was being plunged into some strange maelstrom that
seemed to have surfaced at my coming. My mother was
involved, and something hung over this house which
had not died with her death. Juan Cordova must tell
me what it was.

My thoughts stopped surging at last, and I fell wearily
asleep. When I awakened, Rosa was tapping at my door
to tell me that dinner would be served shortly. Daylight
had faded and the lights of what must be Los Alamos
twinkled against distant mountains. The breeze that
came in the windows was cool.

I rolled off my bed, found a light switch and went to
look in the dressing table mirror. It was an old mirror,
its silvering marred, and I knew my mother must once
have looked at herself in this glass. Strange that a mirror
and the spaces of a room which had known a human
body intimately could bear no trace of what was gone.
There was a yearning in me to reach out to the woman
who had borne me and find her again in this house where
she had grown up. *She* would not have set herself against
me or tried to send me away. But I could only find her
through those who remembered her. That was my mission now. To discover her, to penetrate the mysteries, the
shadows, and find my mother, whatever she had been.
Only then would the odd feeling of terror subside, and
I'd be free to go home when I pleased.

I unpacked a few things hurriedly and hung them up.
The wrinkles weren't too bad. I put on a cowrie shell
print with a coral belt and was ready to go downstairs.

The big dining room was at the far end of the house
from the living room, on a horizontal plane with the
street, and kitchen and pantries opened off it. I followed
the sound of voices into a room that had the usual dark

vigas overhead. A long, linen-covered refectory table
was set with heavy silver and fine crystal, and the Spanish
chairs had dark leather seats and tall backs, ornate with
carving. Against the white walls hung several good paintings. I recognized one of John Marin's floating land-
scapes, and two others belonged certainly to the private
world of Georgia O'Keeffe—sand and bones which suited
this country where she had made her home, not far from
Santa Fe.

The family stood about waiting for me, with glasses
in their hands, and I paused in the doorway for a moment,
studying them. Clarita with her dark eyes and her black
dress and turquoise earrings. Eleanor with that brightly
malicious look upon her, and Gavin, standing a little
apart from the two women, his manner as detached as
though he hardly knew them. I was relieved to find in
myself nothing of the sense of attraction that had flashed
through me when I'd seen him earlier today. He was
only my cousin Eleanor's unfortunate husband and he
meant nothing to me.

Clarita saw me first. "We thought it best to let you
sleep," she said, and moved to the head of the table,
motioning me to a chair at her right. Gavin went to the
far end, opposite Clarita, while Eleanor sat across from
me. There were great stretches of empty table between
us.

When we were seated, I spoke to Clarita. "Grandfather
doesn't join you for meals?"

"He prefers to eat alone in his room," she said. "Rosa
takes him a tray. Tonight he is particularly upset because
of Eleanor." She threw her niece a despairing look and
busied herself with serving the food.

Eleanor, still in her violet linen, with the inevitable
New Mexico silver and turquoise about her neck, looked
subdued for the moment and rather watchful. Once or
twice I caught her gaze upon me in speculation, and at
other times she watched Gavin as if she were not altogether sure of his reactions.

Clarita, clearly trying to do what was proper, made

conversation by asking if I knew about Santa Fe's Fiesta, which was held in September.

"That's when we burn Zozobra," she explained. "He's the monster figure that represents gloom. There will be music and fancy dress on the floats and much excitement. Visitors come from everywhere."

"That's something for you to see, if you're an artist, Amanda," Eleanor put in. "I noticed your painting gear. But of course you probably won't be here by that time."

No one at the table wanted me to stay that long, and I said nothing.

Gavin paid no attention to this idle interchange. He was intent upon his own thoughts, as was clear when he spoke abruptly into the new silence.

"This is the first time we've all been together since Eleanor got home. I want Amanda to hear this too. Who put that stone head in my bedroom today?"

A moment of further silence met his words, and I could feel tension in the air. Then Clarita spoke.

"It was I who found it. I think we know how it came to be there."

I had a feeling that Clarita and Eleanor were closing forces against Gavin, accusing him.

He returned Clarita's look coldly. "There's no doubt about who is behind these tricks, but I hadn't expected you to back Eleanor up."

Clarita's manner was as distant as his. "We have a guest," she pointed out. "This is not the time for such discussion."

"Our guest is one of the family," Gavin said flatly.

Eleanor's soft laughter mocked him, and I wished myself well away from such family feuding. I wanted no family like this one.

Unexpectedly, it was Eleanor who drew the conversation onto safer ground by asking me about my painting.

A little stiffly I told them about my work and my wish someday to be a real painter. Surprisingly, Clarita showed an interest.

"My father was something of a painter at one time,"

she said. "And Doroteo liked to sketch."

I snatched at that. "I want to know about my mother. Do you have any of her sketches?"

Again silence fell upon the table and I was aware of Gavin's eyes upon me, faintly pitying. Why pity? I wondered. Rosa came to serve the plates as Clarita filled them, and for a little while we were busy with our meal. My unanswered question hung in the air until Eleanor leaned toward me across the table.

"This is a house filled with secrets, Cousin Amanda. You'd better not go dragging them out of the shadows. Of course you could hardly know that Aunt Doro's name isn't often mentioned here. Least of all to our grand-father."

This was something I didn't mean to accept, and I looked around at them all defiantly. "But I mean to mention it. That's one of the reasons why I've come here —to learn about my mother. My father would never talk about her either. Yet I have a right to know. All I've been told was that she died in a fall, but I don't even know how or where."

Clarita choked and put her napkin to her lips.

With a too innocent air of concealing nothing, Eleanor spoke to me openly across the table. "There was a picnic outdoors. Several of us were there that day. I can't remember very much, but I've been told that, at least. Katy was there, and Sylvia—though she wasn't married to Paul Stewart at that time. Gavin was there too, though he was only fifteen. The trouble is most of us didn't see what happened. It was all out of our sight." She fluffed her fair bangs with a childish gesture that did not match the wisdom of her eyes.

Clarita stared at her niece with an air of stunned horror, until Gavin reached out and placed a hand on his wife's arm. "That's enough, Eleanor. You're upsetting Clarita, and you know Juan's wishes."

"But why?" Eleanor asked quickly. "Why shouldn't Amanda be told what happened? Aunt Clarita needn't be upset. She didn't even go to the picnic that day. She was ill and couldn't come, and Juan wasn't there either."

"It might have been better if I had gone," Clarita said hoarsely. "Perhaps it would never have happened if I had been there."

"But how did she fall? How?" I persisted.

Clarita recovered herself. "We will have no more of this subject. Do you understand—all of you? And I will not have my father disturbed with questions, Amanda. What happened nearly killed him, and I will not have him made ill over it now. You are here because he wanted you to come. Only for that. But there must be rules about your meeting him. You are not to ask him anything about the death of your mother. If he chooses to speak of it himself, that is something else."

I felt again that force she possessed. It put a pressure upon me and I found it hard to resist, as her will bore down upon me, defeating me. Juan Cordova was apparently Clarita's charge and she would protect him at all costs. I was ready to give in until she pushed me too far.

"You will promise me this," she insisted.

I recovered my own will and shook my head. "I can't promise," I told her, and Eleanor laughed as if she approved.

"You can see Amanda is a Cordova," she said.

Clarita ignored her. "It will not make you happy to learn about your mother," she assured me.

Gavin made an effort to draw the lightning away, and I was briefly grateful to him as he began to talk about the firm of CORDOVA. Until I found that this too was a dangerous subject.

"Paul is going to put in the Penitente display you asked him to loan the store, Eleanor," Gavin said. "I'm not sure it's a good idea."

Eleanor nodded with no great enthusiasm. "He wants to advertise the book he's written on the subject. And Grandfather was pleased. He'd like to turn the store into a museum anyway."

"Which he can't be allowed to do," Gavin said, and

I heard the grim note in his voice.

"*You're* not likely to stop him," Eleanor taunted. "He'll do as he pleases. But it's interesting to see you standing against him after all these years. Amanda, how much do you know about our albatross?"

"CORDOVA is scarcely an albatross," Clarita broke in. "We live and eat well because of it."

"And who comes first in any crisis—the store or us?" Eleanor sounded angry. "You know very well that the store has been held over us all our lives. We can't do this, and we can't do that, because the store might suffer. My parents ran away from it, but after they died Juan brought me back here. And I was foolish enough to marry a man who is owned by CORDOVA."

"Eleanor!" Clarita said warningly.

She paid no attention. "Oh, you'll feel it too, Amanda, if you're here long enough. It's Juan Cordova's life and blood, and he cares about none of us as he does about all those treasures he's collected for the store. It ruined your life, Aunt Clarita, because he could never spare you from the work you did for him. He made you a slave to it, and it kept you from having any happiness of your own. But it's not going to ruin my life!"

"No one but you can ruin yours," Gavin said grimly.

Eleanor turned her interest back to me. "Don't ever accept any part of it, Amanda. If you do, it will destroy you, just the way it destroyed your mother."

"That is ridiculous," Clarita said, but she looked a little pale, as though Eleanor's words had got home to her.

"Why?" Eleanor persisted. "Amanda's father wanted to take Doro and the baby away from Santa Fe. You told me that, Aunt Clarita. But Juan said if she went away he'd leave her no share of the store and his fortune. So she stayed. And look what happened to her! Wait till he tries to buy you, Amanda. The way he's bought Gavin and me!"

"Be careful," Gavin said evenly. "You go too far, Eleanor."

By this time we had reached dessert, but I could eat

nothing more. The meal had been disastrous, and Eleanor's efforts to mock everyone and stir up emotional storms left us all upset and antagonistic.

I don't know whether she would have subsided or not, for at that moment Rosa came into the room looking excited. She spoke in Spanish to Clarita, and I saw my aunt close her eyes, as if against the inevitable. Then she opened them and looked at me.

"Your grandfather is asking for you," she said. "I will take you upstairs to see him, but you are not to stay more than ten minutes."

Again Rosa broke in with words in swift Spanish.

Clarita sighed. "He wishes to see you alone. There's nothing else to be done. You will have to go to him now."

This was what I had been waiting for—yet with the moment upon me I felt frightened and unready. I cast a quick glance around the table, seeking for help, for reassurance. Eleanor was eating a piece of fruit with an air of concentrated unconcern. Clarita, clearly disapproving, restrained herself with difficulty. Only Gavin looked at me with some consideration—where I had expected none.

"Don't be afraid of him, Amanda. Don't let him intimidate you."

While this hardly sounded promising, at least it helped me to brace myself against the coming interview. This was what I had come here for, and I must make up my own mind about my grandfather. All the others had disappointed me. Clarita, Eleanor, even Sylvia, would never seem close to me as relatives. But Juan Cordova remained.

I pushed back my chair from the table and the others rose with me.

"Rosa will take you to him," Clarita said. "Remember that he is ill. Don't upset him or stay very long."

The little maid threw me a quick look and hurried off through connecting rooms toward the other end of the house.

"Wait a moment," I called after her. "I want to get something from my room."

While she waited, I ran up my private flight of stairs and took the little road runner from one of my bags. Then I rejoined her.

"I'm ready now."

She took me to the foot of the steps which led to the small balcony off the living room.

"Better you go up alone," she told me.

I hesitated for a moment, looking about that southwestern room with its dark Spanish furniture and bright Navajo rugs. But all I saw was the carved tarantula on the table near a lamp. It looked ready to move, to pounce. Yet the same man had carved my amusing road runner, and it was reassuring to feel its outlines hard in my hand.

I reached for the railing and mounted the balcony steps.

V

The door of Juan Cordova's room stood open and I stepped through the gloom. At the window, draperies were drawn and no lights burned. Only a glow from the balcony behind me picked out general shapes. The room was a study, not a bedroom, and across it I discovered a man's straight figure seated behind a desk. He did not droop as a sick man might, but sat facing me with a manner of pride and assurance.

"I am here," I said hesitantly. Now that the moment was upon me, I found myself both fearful and hopeful.

He reached out a hand and touched a switch. The gooseneck lamp on the desk beside him was bent to turn full upon me and it was as though I were lighted suddenly by a spotlight. Shocked and startled, I stood blinking in the glare, unable to see the man behind the lamp, and disturbed that he should do such a thing. With an effort, I recovered myself, and I walked out of the circle of light and around the desk. Any possible moment of sentiment between us in this first encounter had been lost, and clearly that loss was deliberate. There would be no affectionate welcome for me from my mother's father. Indignation erased my shock.

"Is this the way you always greet visitors?" I asked.

His chuckle was low, amused. "I like to see how people react. Come and sit down, Amanda, and we will look at each other in a kinder light."

He stood up and touched another switch that lighted an amber glow overhead. Then he turned off the glaring lamp and waited for me to seat myself in a leather chair near his desk. As I sat down, I hid the road runner carving beneath my hands in my lap. Bringing it here had been a sentimental gesture, and this was clearly no time for sentiment.

In the softer light I studied him boldly, still prickling with resentment from his cruel greeting. Juan Cordova was tall, I noted, as he sat down, retying the sash of the maroon silk robe which hung loosely upon his spare frame. His gray hair was brushed close to a finely shaped head, and his face was lined and drawn by illness, though the proud beak of the nose denied all weakness and somehow reminded me of a falcon. It was an infinitely proud face, its expression not a little arrogant— with a falcon's arrogance—even to the posture of his head and the way he held his leanly carved chin. But it was the eyes, most of all, that arrested my own gaze, almost absorbing me into the fierceness of his look. They were eyes as dark as Clarita's, as dark as my own, but they glowed with an intensity of spirit that gave no quarter to age or illness or weakness of vision, and made an almost palpable effect upon me.

My own eyes dropped first because I had, instinctively, to protect myself from some strange emotional demand he seemed to make upon me. I had felt this before— from Clarita and Paul—some inner questioning. It was a demand that had nothing to do with affection. If I had expected to find an old man, beaten by illness, someone whom I might pity, I was quickly disillusioned. No matter what his body had done to him, his spirit was invincible and I could see why those around him must fear him a little. I had hoped that I would be wanted by him, and his look told me that I was—not because he had love to give, but because he had a purpose in bringing me here. In these few moments I stiffened against him, aware that this was a man I might need to battle.

"You look like her," he said. It sounded more accusation than praise.

"I know," I agreed. "I have a miniature you painted of my mother when she was young. But she must have been beautiful and I am not."

"It is true you are not like Doroteo in that respect. *No importa*—the resemblance is there. You have the family hair, thick and lustrous, and I like the way you wear it. I wonder how much you are like her in spirit?"

I could only shake my head. "How can I know?"

"You are right. *Quién sabe?* You do not remember her, of course?"

"No—I wish I could. I don't even know a great deal about her because my father never wanted to speak of her. I've even been told not to talk about her to you."

Something in those fierce eyes seemed to flinch for just a moment, and then the very flinching was dismissed.

"It is still painful to think of her, speak of her. But now that you have come, I must face my own pain."

He used a certain formality in his speech, as though he had grown up accustomed to another language, seeming thoroughly Spanish. Clarita's speech was rather like her father's, I realized, perhaps copied from him.

I waited, having nothing to offer. His pain was none of my affair, since he had not chosen to greet me warmly as belonging to his family.

"If your father would not speak of her, Amanda, perhaps he was more willing to speak of me?"

"To some extent, yes."

"He had no love for me."

Again I was silent, agreeing, and again Juan Cordova chuckled. There was bitterness in the sound and no mirth.

"I remember our parting. I will never forgive William for taking you away, but I can still understand how he felt. Now I suppose I am to prove myself to you—prove that I am not so evil, so wicked as he portrayed me?"

"I expect you will do as you please, Grandfather."

Oddly, he seemed to like my resistance. "You interpret me well already. And you will have to take me as you find me. I will pretend nothing. I am quite likely all the things he has told you I was. But we must get to know each other on a basis of our own. Why did you accept my invitation to come here?"

I made a small, helpless gesture. "I've already been asked that several times. It seems to be part of the Cordova arrogance to invite me here, and then demand why I've come."

"I do not deny that we can be arrogant. But you could have refused to come. Especially with your father's warnings."

"I had to see for myself. One half of my family I know very well. The other half is a blank page. Naturally, I want to fill it in."

"Perhaps you will not like what you find."

"That seems quite possible. I've hardly received a warm welcome here, but I'm beginning to learn about the Cordovas, and what being a Cordova means."

That seemed to rouse his indignation. "You don't know the least beginning of what it means to be a Cordova!"

"What I've learned, I don't want to be."

He smiled at me thinly, his face lighting briefly. "You have a certain arrogance yourself, Amanda. You are instinctively more Cordova than you know."

Impatient, and moving in angry denial, I sprang up from my chair. On the wall behind him hung a narrow mirror in which I glimpsed myself—and was astonished. The stranger in the glass looked proudly Spanish with her black hair and flashing dark eyes, and there was nothing of humility in her. I hadn't known I could look like that, and I turned away from my reflection, rejecting it.

"If there is evil in me, then it lives on in you," Juan said slyly.

I knew he meant to torment me and I stood up to him. "All right—I'll accept that. But I think there was no evil in my mother. The miniature you painted tells me that she was gay, perhaps a little reckless, but not wicked."

"Sit down," the old man commanded. "Tell me what you know about her death."

I took my chair again, shaking my head. "Nothing. My father told me only that she died in a fall."

"And no one here will tell you the truth. As I've told them not to. I wanted you to come to me."

"I've come. And now I'll put it to you directly. Is it true that she died in a fall?"

His thin hands were clenched together on the desk before him, and he stared at them for a moment before he looked back at me, his face expressionless and deeply lined.

"Yes, she died in a fall. But first she killed a man. The law calls her a murderess, and then a suicide."

It was as if I had been suddenly frozen in my chair. My muscles tightened in rejection of his words, my hands were clenched about the carving of the road runner as tightly as his own were clasped on his desk. My breath seemed locked in my chest. Only by a terrible effort was I able at last to move, to cry out.

"I don't believe that! I will never believe it!"

There was pain in his voice. "That is what I said in the beginning—that I would not believe. But of course there was a police investigation and the result left us no choice. Clarita saw what happened. She stood in the window of the room you now occupy and she saw it all. Even I had to accept the truth in the end."

"Katy didn't accept it," I said.

His look sharpened. "What do you mean by that?"

"My grandmother wrote my father a letter before she died. She said he had misjudged my mother, and she wanted him to bring me to visit her. He never told me about the letter. I found it among his papers after he died, but I didn't know what it meant."

"Katy did that?" He seemed both astonished and outraged. "She should not have acted without consulting me."

"Would you have told her not to write?"

"But of course. I would have known it would be no use. Your father would not change. Katy wanted to deceive herself up to the end. She wanted to believe what was not so."

"Could she have had some reason for believing it wasn't so?"

The fierce, dark eyes examined me, probing as though his clouded vision sought for clarity. "I wish I could think that. She had only a mother's heart. She had the love she felt for a daughter."

"Perhaps there's wisdom in love."

He answered me in a tone more gentle than I had heard from him. "I loved Doroteo too. As she loved me. We were very close, your mother and I. That is why I have sent for you to come here."

I believed him. And yet I didn't quite believe him. That air of gentleness was uncharacteristic. Surely if he had brought me here because he loved Doroteo, and thought with any warmth of her daughter, he would have greeted me differently. My uncertainty strengthened me and hardened me against him as I spoke my thought.

"I can't believe you sent for me because of any love for my mother."

Again he spoke in sudden anger. "You know nothing of me!"

It no longer mattered whether he kept me here or sent me away. It didn't matter at all, I told myself. I had been terribly shocked, and there was still a trembling within me. Tears burned in my eyes and I hated my own weakness.

"I already know that you're arrogant, and perhaps a little cruel," I told him, blinking weakness away furiously.

His own anger seemed to die. "You are more like Katy than like Doroteo. They both had spirit, but Katy would fight for more. Perhaps you have possibilities. I can offer you nothing but hurt when it comes to the past, though perhaps there were extenuating circumstances. I have tried to believe that."

Possibilities? I didn't like the sound of the word. What

use he had for me, I didn't know, but I would be on guard against anything that might violate my own feelings. Now, however, was the moment to learn as much as I could.

"Who was the man my mother is supposed to have killed?"

"His name was Kirk Landers. He was the stepbrother of a second cousin of yours—the woman who brought you to Santa Fe today. Sylvia Stewart. They both grew up in this house because Katy took them in when their parents died."

I tried to digest this, remembering Sylvia's uneasiness with me. She must have felt a reluctance to meet the daughter of the woman who was supposed to have killed her stepbrother.

"What were the extenuating circumstances?" I asked.

Juan Cordova sighed deeply. "That is a long story. Shall we save it for another time?"

He looked suddenly tired and old, and I remembered Clarita's warning not to stay with him for long. The effect of that shocking revelation he had made still seethed in me violently, but I must not push him now in his illness.

"I'd better go," I said. "I've tired you."

One long-fingered, aristocratic hand reached out to rest on my arm. I could feel the strength of his fingers. If there was weakness in this man, it was not something he chose to accept.

"You will stay with me until I say you may go."

My private resistance to such male authority stirred in me, but he was old and ill, as well as domineering, and I let the command pass with only a small effort to deny it.

"Aunt Clarita warned me that—"

"Clarita is sometimes a fool! She will do as I say."

Even though he knew her so much better than I, I had the sudden feeling that he underestimated his older daughter. Clarita had more to her than surfaced in her obedience to her father.

"Tell me," he said more gently, "do you remember

anything at all about the day your mother died?"

"I don't remember anything of that time. Since I've come here, I've had a few flashes of recognition. But these seem to do with places, not people. I suppose the people I might remember have all changed in twenty years."

"It's probably just as well," Grandfather said. "Paul Stewart is planning to write a book about famous murders of the Southwest."

So that was the answer—a book about murder! This was what they had been hinting at, and why no one had wanted to come right out and tell me what his book was about.

"You mean he is going to—to include—" I faltered to a stop.

"Yes. He means to write about Doroteo and Kirk."

"But that's dreadful. He should be stopped. Can't you—"

"I have tried. Without success. Naturally, I don't want these happenings resurrected at this late date. It can only hurt those who are living. The affair has been mostly forgotten, except by us. Now he will renew interest in it, and we will have to live through it all over again."

Sorrow seemed to crush him, and for the first time I felt a sympathy for him. In spite of his arrogance, he had suffered too, and my coming here must be a goad to old pain.

"Sylvia told me that Paul would have gone to New York to see me, if you hadn't happened to bring me here."

"Yes. He is questioning anyone who was present at the time of the tragedy. I suppose even a five-year-old might have memories that he could find useful. But now you can tell him that you remember nothing, and he'll have to leave you alone. Perhaps it will help if you can be as discouraging as possible."

"I'll certainly try, if he questions me," I promised.

"Now tell me something about yourself," he said. "What do you do? What do you want to do?"

"All I want to do is paint."

He laughed softly, delightedly, the bitterness gone, the mood change instant, and in its suddenness unnerving. My own emotional transitions were made less quickly.

"So there is such a thing as heritage! The strain has come down through the family. Along with other things less pleasant. I am an artist manqué. So I give myself to the collecting of the art of others. As an appreciator and critic, I have few peers. Doroteo had the talent too, but she would not work at it. She did not care enough."

"I care. I work very hard. It's the way I earn my living, though mostly in small ways. I've had a showing of my paintings at a gallery in New York, and I've even sold a few. I'm already eager to paint in Santa Fe."

"Good—this is a fine country for painters, and a town that is kind to them. What is that you've been fondling in your hands ever since you came in? It looks like a carving."

I remembered the figure of the road runner and handed it to him across a corner of the desk.

"You made this for me when I was very small. I've kept it ever since. It was the toy I took to bed with me at night when I was young and sometimes frightened."

He took the carving and turned it about in his hands. I knew he was sensing the smoothness of the wood with his fingers, noting the indentations of the carving. His love for wood as a medium was evident in the sensitivity of his touch, and perhaps too his sorrow because he could no longer create, as once he had done. I felt a bond of understanding with him, because I too wanted to create.

"Yes, I remember this," he said. "I remember the high hopes I had for you as Doroteo's daughter. You loved me quite innocently then. Without wanting anything from me." Sudden suspicion came into his voice, and my brief sense of a bond was broken. "What do you want from me now?"

These changes of mood ruffled me, but on this I could answer him readily. "Nothing except what you want to give, Grandfather."

The look he returned was arrogant, proud—it gave

me no relief. "There is little I can give you. But there may be something I want of you."

"I'll give it, if I can," I said.

"You are like Doroteo. Generous. I am surrounded by those I can no longer trust. Those who are my enemies. I suffer over this. But then—the essence of your true Spaniard is his ability to suffer. To suffer and to laugh. But laughter turns to mockery after a time."

He seemed to go into a brooding silence, and I tried to draw him from it.

"I would like to know something about my grandmother," I said gently. "What was Katy like?"

His expression softened and he opened a drawer of his desk and took out a picture in an oval frame—another miniature. "This I painted too, before any of the children were born."

He handed me the picture and I saw again the gift he must have had for portraiture. The young face that looked out at me had strength and character. She was a woman who might have hated adobe walls, as Sylvia Stewart had said, but she'd have loved her husband with a loyalty that would permit no weakness. Her hair was fair, like Eleanor's, and she wore it short in the picture and fluffed youthfully about her ears, yet there was maturity in the blue eyes and a forcefulness about the chin. Here was a woman who had been able to cope.

My grandmother, I thought, and felt a stirring of recognition in me. She was not a stranger to me. I could recognize kinship, even though I resembled her outwardly not at all.

He took the picture back from me and put it away. "She did not look like that as I remember her. I wanted her to have long hair, and she grew it for me. Her hair was thick and heavy as the gold it resembled. She wore it high on her head, and it gave her a look of poise and assurance. She could have been a great Spanish lady— my Katy."

Katy, from the farmlands of Iowa! Had she ever expected to play the role of a Spanish lady?

"I wish I could have known her," I said.

Juan Cordova made a sound of distress that carried anger in its depth. "She had the right to know you. Your father took you away."

"I suppose he did what he thought was best. He wanted me to grow up in a different environment."

"And away from me."

The words were flat, certain, and I did not contradict them.

"Enough of all this," he went on. "I have no time for sentiment. No time for the past. The present is short and there is much to be done. We must make plans."

I suppose it was sentiment I had come for, but I was beginning to see that I would not have it from Juan Cordova. I could only wait to hear about his plans.

He was silent for a few moments, thinking, and as I waited uneasily, not trusting any plans he might make for me, I looked about the room. There were the inevitable white walls, the brown vigas that graced every ceiling. Burgundy draperies were drawn across the windows, but since the room was only a little higher than the floor of the living room, it could not have looked out upon any distant view, as my room did. There was a door which led into the darkness of a bedroom beyond. And all about, set on bookcase shelves and small tables, were the treasures of a lifetime. My eye was caught by the handsomely carved and painted figure of a bullfighter swirling his cape. On a lower shelf stood a buff-colored pottery bowl with brown buffalo pounding their hoofs as they ran endlessly from hunters around its circumference. It looked as if it might be old and valuable. Here, however, were none of those frightening desert creatures I had seen downstairs. Perhaps Juan Cordova himself played their role, and I wondered if I was the victim upon whom he would next pounce. I put the uneasy thought aside and let my gaze move on about the room.

On the walls were hung paintings of Santa Fe scenes —the Cathedral of St. Francis casting the shadows of its twin towers across a stone walk; a row of adobe houses that might belong to this very neighborhood; a scene on the Alameda and another in the sun-speckled plaza. Undoubtedly these had been painted by local artists, and they made me want to find my own scenes, try my own conception in color of what I saw.

"I have decided," my grandfather said abruptly, and his voice was strong, assured, banishing all weakness. "There are things you will do for me at once."

A warning of resistance stiffened in me, but I answered quietly. "I'm waiting, Grandfather."

"First you will speak to Clarita." His tone was harsh, commanding. "She guards me like a dragon because the doctor has said I must conserve my strength. There is to be no more of that. You are to come here to me whenever you wish, and without waiting for her permission. Tell her so. Then you will tell Eleanor that she is no longer needed to accompany me when I walk in the patio. From now on, you will come with me on my walks. As for Gavin—you will tell him that he is to take you through the store and show you all that is important for you to know. You will now become one of the family, and you are to learn the store, Amanda. He will teach you. If all this is clear, you are to go at once and begin."

My gasp must have been audible. It shocked me that I should be brought in from outside and set above everyone in the house. Such an act was anything but just, and I didn't mean to be so commanded. Setting out to anger members of my new family with these highhanded orders was not for me. What he planned, I didn't know, but I suspected that it wouldn't be something I'd want. What I had wanted from the Cordovas had another value.

"No," I said. "I won't do any of these things."

There was a small silence as though he listened to the echo of my words without fully understanding them.

"You said?" he murmured.

"I said I wouldn't go about giving orders to the people in your household. If I'm to visit here, I want to be friends with them. I'm certainly not going to set myself above them and tell them what to do."

Perhaps it had been a long time since anyone had spoken so to Juan Cordova. I saw the angry flush mount in his face, saw the tightening of his hands into fists where they lay before him on the desk. He lost his temper.

"You will do as I say, or you may pack up and go away at once! I will not endure such foolishness. Your mother betrayed us all. Your father was a fool—stupid and mindless in his behavior. I have not forgotten or forgiven the words he spoke to me before he left, and I will not tolerate disobedience from his daughter. You will not go the way of Doroteo. Or—if that is the pattern—you can leave at once."

I pushed my chair back and stood up. I was trembling and my muscles were tense as my own rage spilled out.

"Then I will pack up and go! The only reason I came here is because I love my mother. Even without knowing her, I love her. If some injustice had been done her, I wanted to set it right. And I won't listen to words against my father. How could someone like you possibly know his worth and his goodness? He was so far above any of the Cordovas that—that—" I choked on my anger and there were tears of rage in my eyes. As I started for the door, I shoved my chair aside so furiously that it fell over on the floor with a bang. I didn't care. I was through with this dreadful man.

His sudden ringing laughter brought me to a halt before I reached the door. Juan Cordova was laughing. I turned about in further outrage and stared at him.

"Wait," he said. "Come back here, Amanda. I am pleased with you. You will do, as none of the others will. The Cordova strain comes through. You are a young, wild thing with a temper. You are a part of me and of your mother. Come—sit down, and we will talk more quietly."

The unexpected gentleness of his voice warned me. He could not be entirely trusted. Yet the tone of it hypnotized me. With hands that still shook, I righted the chair and sat down in it. I had no intention of forgiving him easily, no intention of trusting him, but something in me did not want to run away.

"I'm waiting," I said, and hated the way my voice trembled.

He rose from the desk and bent toward me. His long fingers touched the weight of my hair at the back, moved lightly down my face, as though the artist in him sought for deeper knowledge than the eyes could give, reached my chin and tipped it upward. I sat frozen, resenting his touch, finding it more possessive than loving.

"I remember the small Amanda," he said. "I remember holding her in my arms. I remember reading to her of Don Quixote while she sat on my knee."

He was trying to beguile me. "Don Quixote when I was less than five?" I said.

"But of course. The meaning of the words is not important to a child. It is the interest of the adult and the music of the sound." I did not move, and he sensed the resistance in me, drew away, sat down. Not hurt, but still amused, and obviously pleased because he had so upset me. He was a dreadful old man—wicked and quite dangerous.

"Now we will talk again," he said. "All the things I've stated to you must be done, but you are right. It would not be good to antagonize the household yourself. I will take care of my orders. The others are used to the outrageous from me, as you are not, and they cannot run away—as you can. So I have them where I want them. At least, you are good for me. I feel more alive at this moment than I have in months. You may go now. And tomorrow we will begin."

"I'm not sure I want this," I said. "What is it you wish of me?"

"That depends on what you have to give. It will be best, however, if you do not go stirring up old fires, old wounds. All that could be done about your mother's death was done at the time. Let it rest, Amanda, and do not bother yourself talking with Paul Stewart. Now, good night."

"Good night," I said. But I did not promise that I would let the matter of my mother's death go. I had not been told everything yet, by any means.

I went through the door and out upon the landing. Only Eleanor sat in the living room below. She had a book in her hands, but I didn't think she was reading. She looked up at me wih a searching glance.

"You were shouting," she said. "You must have made Juan very angry."

"He made me angry," I said sharply. "I think I'll go to bed now. I'm very tired—after all the graciousness that's been extended to me by the Cordovas."

"Of course," she agreed, unruffled, and rose smoothly from her chair. "I'll come with you and see if everything is right in your room."

I had no wish for her company, but there was no way to discourage her. She followed me up the flight of stairs to my room and waited while I opened the door.

Someone had lighted a lamp on the bed table, and the shaggy white rug on the floor nearby glowed yellow. Something rested in its center that did not belong there. I bent to pick it up.

The little object lay heavy in my hand, and I saw that it was made of some black stone formed roughly in the shape of a mole, with a pointed snout and rudimentary legs. Bound to its back with sinew thongs were an arrowpoint and several colored beads, including a piece of turquoise that had been threaded onto a thong. These things looked old and were stained with some brownish color. Strangely, I felt a revulsion toward whatever they represented. There seemed no reason for so strong a flash of repugnance, but the feeling was there. Atavistic. This was some sort of Indian relic, I was sure, and it had not been left in my room for any but an evil purpose.

I looked at Eleanor and saw that her gaze was fixed with bright interest on the black stone I held.

"What is it?" I asked.

She raised her shoulders in a slight shiver. "It's an Indian fetish. That's probably dried blood on the back. There's a ritual where the fetish is fed blood."

In my hand, the black stone felt cold and heavy as a threat. But I refused to let the matter of its presence go.

"Why is it here?"

"How would I know? Someone must have put it there. Let me see."

She took the thong-wrapped stone from me and examined it closely. "I think it's a Zuni fetish, and I know where it came from. It's been missing ever since Gavin brought home several fetishes to exhibit in the store. Genuine fetishes are hard to come by these days because no self-respecting Indian will sell anything so personal. I think this is a hunter's fetish. It's supposed to bring good luck in the hunt. Gavin told me it was a rare one because it's in the form of a mole. Moles belong to the nether regions and they aren't highly thought of as fetishes, so there aren't many of them. Still—a mole has its virtues. It can burrow in the dark and lay traps for larger animals."

She was all too well informed, and there was mocking intent in her words.

"But why would someone leave it here?"

"Perhaps it's a warning, Cousin. Perhaps you are the prey." There was an odd light in her violet eyes that did not reassure me.

"And who is hunting me?" I challenged.

Her hands moved gracefully and I was reminded again of a dancer. "Who knows the hunter until he strikes? It could be any of us, couldn't it?"

I stared at the black stone mole in her hands. "Why should I be anyone's prey?"

Eleanor laughed softly, and I heard the ruthless echo of Juan Cordova in the sound. "Isn't it obvious? I heard some of what our grandfather said to you. He means to use you against us. He means to try to frighten us."

From the living room below, a voice called up the stairs. "Is anyone at home? I've been wandering around without finding a soul."

"That's Paul." Eleanor's eyes lighted with a pleasure I did not like. "I'll give the mole back to Gavin, Amanda. Don't worry about it. Or"—she paused—"perhaps you *had* better worry about it." Then she moved toward the door. "I expect Paul wants to talk to you."

I shook my head. "Not now. I don't want to see anyone tonight." I'd had enough of the Cordovas, and in particular of Eleanor. "Good night," I said in firm dismissal.

For a moment she regarded me intently, but I didn't waver and she shrugged as she went toward the stairs. At the last minute she turned back with that bright look in her eyes.

"You really aren't afraid, are you, Amanda?"

I met her look, asserting my own courage and dignity. The small victory was mine, and she ran lightly down the stairs. From below, as I closed the door softly, I could hear the sound of voices—low, conspiratorial.

Was I afraid?

I hadn't come here with any wish to be used as a weapon for some veiled warfare that might be going on in this house, a weapon with which those who might oppose Juan Cordova could be subjugated. But neither did I mean to be threatened by those who opposed him. I would not let either side use me, and there was nothing to keep me from going home at once, if I chose. There was nothing to hold me here—except my own will. Was the wish to stay stronger than the desire to run?

Once more I had the feeling of adobe walls closing in on me, holding me a prisoner. Had Katy ever felt like that? And how had my mother felt, here in this room? Nothing I had learned about her seemed like the behavior of a prisoner—she who had grown up happily in these walls. Yet she had died, and a man had died too—they said because of her.

Feeling a little sick, I went to a window and spread the

curtains that had been drawn across it. A cool night wind touched my face and under starlight the snow on pointed peaks glistened against the deep, dark blue of the sky. At least this room was above the walls. Here, at least, I was not closed in. Except by my own thoughts.

A past that had always seemed distant and something to be gently unraveled—a story to give me pleasure and a new knowledge of myself—now seemed imminent and threatening. I had been in this house at the time when they must have brought them back to it—Kirk Landers and my mother, Doroteo, both dead. Yet I had no memory of loss, of suffering. Whatever existed deep in my consciousness was smothered in a mist through which no light penetrated. I did not want to remember that time in order to help Paul Stewart with his book, but now that I knew there must be something hidden in me, something lodged in the recesses of my own mind which had experienced a time of tragedy, I wanted to seek it out for myself, bring it into the open, know it for whatever it was. Katy had known—something. Or discovered something later. If I stayed here, could I perhaps find out what it was? Could I free my mother's memory of that dreadful stamp of murder and suicide? How futile was such a wish?

I couldn't know until I had stayed for a few days, at least, and had learned everything I could about the past. There were so many gaps that were still not filled in, and I still knew nothing at all about what dreadful thing had risen to cause violence between my mother and Sylvia Stewart's stepbrother.

No, I could not leave right away. Not even if some threat to me existed in this house. What had happened long ago was all going on still. It had not ended with my mother's death, and perhaps my coming had stirred sleeping terrors. I must stay and find out. For myself I must allay them.

VI

Weariness enveloped me the moment I was in bed. I fell soundly asleep and heard nothing of the whisperings of a strange house. It must have been well into the early, dark hours that the dream began to take shape in my sleeping mind. I knew with a sense of dread that it was coming, yet I was chained by sleep, unable to waken and protect myself from the vision that grew in my mind.

The tree was there. That dreadful, haunting tree—so enormous that it hid the sky, reaching upward with twisted black branches. I cowered close to the ground, staring up into that sickly green canopy that held all horror, that enclosed me in frozen terror. The thing was alive with movement, trembling, writhing, reaching toward me. In a few moments it would grasp and smother me with that awful green. Already, I could hardly breathe. A heavy limb lowered itself slowly, moving with a strange life of its own, to rest upon my chest and I struggled to fight it away, to cry out, to scream for aid that I knew would never come in time.

I sat up in bed struggling with the bedclothes, fighting for my breath. My nightgown was soaked with cold perspiration and the sharp breeze from the window chilled me into consciousness. I did not immediately know where I was because the familiar horror lingered. I could see the tree as though it grew within the walls of my room, and I fought to free myself of the clinging vapors. As always, there was a sense of loss in me, of abandonment.

I had been on feared and well-known territory. As a child I had dreamed of the tree and when I awakened screaming, my father had held me in his arms to soothe and quiet me. Yet his arms never obliterated that terrible sense of loss. I could never tell him how bad the dream was—how frightful. Sometimes it was hours before I knew I was safe with him in a real world, and there was no tree, no black limbs to twine about me and stop my breath with the smothering green of their leaves.

Even now that I was grown and awake, the sense of terror returned to me in waves, and it was a long while before the haunting faded and I was able to sleep again.

When I awakened the next time, the sun was up, but I felt drained and weary, as I always did when the nightmare had returned. Somehow I knew that I had come close to the source of the dream. I had come to the place where the tree waited, and I must find it in reality this time. Only when I knew why it haunted me would I be free of it.

When I came downstairs, the cook was still in the kitchen, though no one was left at the table. She served me cheerfully enough, and my appetite returned as I drank hot coffee and revived a little.

In bright daylight, I could put the dream away and face a present that, while not wholly attractive, was at least real and could be dealt with, as the dream could not. I would see Juan Cordova as soon as possible and try to clear the air between us. I would let him know that I would not be used for some purpose which might be unfair to others in his family, and I would also persuade him to tell me the full story of my mother's death.

The still disturbing puzzle of the mole fetish which had been left in my room remained, but I supposed this too would be made clear eventually. There were those who did not want me here, but I would not be frightened off like a child. The word "evil" which had come to me last night was only something to make me smile by daylight. I was not without courage, and I would stand up to whatever must be faced. I'd come here to learn who I was, and I wouldn't go away until I knew.

When I'd finished breakfast, I went into the living room and approached the short flight of steps to my grandfather's room. Clarita stood on the balcony.

"I'd like to see my grandfather," I told her.

She loomed above me, a black figure, with her thin arms folded across her body, and her aging face looked down at me in disapproval.

"That isn't possible this morning. Your visit yesterday excited him too much. He isn't well and he can see no one."

Her concern for her father seemed genuine, but she was still the guardian dragon, as he'd called her. Though he had given me instructions as to what I must say to her, I would not give her his orders. She had a right to tell me what I might do in this house, and I couldn't oppose her. I would see him eventually because he would ask for me. I would wait till then.

I went up to my room, feeling restless and at loose ends, and got out my sketchbook and a pencil. These always served me when I needed release from tension. I let myself out through a rear door to the patio, finding the air marvelously clear and bracing, the morning sky pure turquoise. Behind the house, the garden was surprisingly spacious, stretching down an incline toward the back. It was not, however, a garden in my sense of the word. There were areas of bluestone, where nothing grew, and there was little grass. Since such a small amount of rain fell that constant watering would have been necessary to keep anything growing, no great effort had been made to provide flower beds. There were clumps of cholla and other cactus, and the native gray-green chamiso bushes one saw everywhere. Fluff from a cotton-wood tree floated to the ground, whitening an area around its base, and a path wound downhill toward a small building on the lower level of the property. Beyond it was a rear gate which must open on the hillside. Around all of this ran the adobe wall, shutting in the Cordovas, sealing them away from the world. They had, indeed, had secrets they wanted to conceal behind their walls.

The small building at the bottom of the property offered a contrast to the rest of the neighborhood. Though the walls were adobe, redwood had been used for the roof and it slanted to a high peak, like the roof of a church, so that I wondered if it might be a chapel of some sort. Its construction was modern and graceful, appealing to the eye, and it drew me, so that I walked down to view it more closely.

The typical carved wooden door was closed, and thick curtains covered its windows, unlike the windows of a chapel. A nearby rock, flat enough to sit upon, gave me a perch, and I sat down and opened my sketchbook.

In a few quick lines I caught the outline of the building, blocking in a cottonwood tree nearby and a clump of cholla by the front door. I made notes about the colors I might use and took the liberty of sketching in the rise of a mountain above the adobe wall, though none was visible from this angle. For me, the interest of painting, the satisfaction, was never in copying a scene exactly, but in creating my own impression of what I saw, finding a dimension caught only by me, selecting and rejecting, searching for an expanded vision, until the result pleased me, existed as mine.

I did not notice the nearby gate in the side wall, or hear it open until Sylvia Stewart called to me.

"Good morning, Amanda."

Apparently this gate led into the Stewarts' patio and the two families moved back and forth to visit each other as they pleased.

She wore fawn slacks and an amber sweater, and her hair with its deliberate shade of brown was brushed straight back from her forehead. I found myself looking at her through my new knowledge, wondering whether, because of her stepbrother, she resented me as Doroteo's daughter. All the time we had been together yesterday she had known what was said about my mother, and I had not. But there seemed no particular uneasiness in her this morning.

"May I see what you're drawing?" she asked, and came to look over my shoulder.

I had turned another page, to make a careful study of a cottonwood tree, but now I flipped back to my drawing of the chapel-like building.

"Juan will like that," she said. "Though you ought to put in his pride—those climbing Castilian roses against the wall. They're the only flowers the Cordovas give much attention to. Do you know what it is you've drawn?"

"It looks like a chapel."

"In a way, it is. To Juan it's quite sacred. He keeps his private collection of art treasures there. Most of them are paintings from old Spain. Rumor has it that one of them is a Velázquez. But there are other things too. Sometimes I suspect that not everything has been legitimately come by."

She laughed wryly and I did not comment. It was one of her typically barbed remarks.

"I suppose you've seen the collection?" I asked.

"Of course—since I'm counted as one of the family. But he shows it to very few people, and it's his own private passion that he's not given to sharing. Don't try to walk in. There are burglar alarms everywhere. You have to know the right combination or you set them off."

"Did the pre-Columbian head disappear from here?"

"Not exactly. It belongs here, but I understand that Juan had given permission for it to be put on display in the store with a special exhibit. It's from that exhibit that it was taken. If it's true Gavin is to blame, he could easily have picked it up from the store."

"But why would he do a thing like that?"

"I don't think he did. I suppose you've met all of our family by now? How do you like them?"

"I've hardly had time to get acquainted," I said.

Closing my sketchbook, I stood up from the rock, and at once she gestured toward the gate in the adobe wall. "Do come over and visit Paul. He's been waiting to talk to you, and you might as well get it over with."

I looked at her questioningly.

"By this time you've been told more about the book he's working on, haven't you? Its subject, that is?"

I answered her evenly. "If you mean has my grandfather told me about my mother's death—he's given me the bare facts. I know what's supposed to have happened, and that your stepbrother died. I don't think I can accept his account."

"Not accept it?" Sylvia was clearly startled.

I tried to explain. "I can't accept it—emotionally. My grandmother Katy wrote a rather strange letter to my father before she died, and said that he'd misjudged my mother. What do you suppose she meant by that?"

Sylvia walked off a few steps, her back to me. My words had somehow disturbed her.

"Before she died, Aunt Katy left me something for you," she said. "She told me if you ever came here I was to give it to you."

Eagerness alerted me, but I felt impatient with Sylvia.

"Then why didn't you tell me? Why didn't you give it to me yesterday? Perhaps she's left me some message that will clear up her letter."

Sylvia came slowly back to me, her expression faintly pitying. It was the same look I had seen in Gavin's eyes at the dinner table last night, and I resisted it, waiting for an answer to my questions.

"I had the package with me when I met you," Sylvia said. "But you knew nothing about your mother's death, and I didn't want to throw everything at you at once. It was better to wait a little. Now you're going down a blind alley, Amanda. Don't deceive yourself with fantasies. What happened, happened. I never liked your mother, but all that has nothing to do with you. I'm trying to be fair about that and not let old emotions mix in because it was my stepbrother who died. I suppose they've told you that Clarita saw the whole thing?"

I nodded, waiting.

"There's no getting around that. Once Clarita fancied herself in love with Kirk, you know. That was when we were all around twelve and thirteen, and used to go out to the *rancho* for holidays and weekends."

"The *rancho*?"

"Yes—the *Rancho de Cordova*. It belonged to Juan's father—your great-grandfather. He raised horses and we used to love to go there. It's a ghost place now. Juan doesn't keep it up, though he employs a married couple who stay at the hacienda. Of course Clarita got over that childhood infatuation. By the time Kirk died she was in love with—someone else. She didn't even like him by that time."

I thought with a feeling of shock of Clarita, who had seemed to me eternally middle-aged. It was hard to imagine her a love-sick girl. Now, because of my mother, Clarita too might hold old prejudices against me.

"Of course Doro was in love with Kirk too in those *rancho* days," Sylvia went on. "I grew up with them. I saw the whole thing from the beginning."

I didn't want to think of my mother in connection with any man but my father.

"I don't believe I'm making up fantasies," I said. "But perhaps all the truth hasn't come out. That's what I want to know."

"Then come and see Paul. He knew her too, though he was outside the family then. I'll have to be running along soon. My bookshop usually opens at nine o'clock, but I'm late today."

Juan Cordova had told me not to trouble myself by talking to Paul, but of course I would pay no attention. I hadn't felt strong enough to face Sylvia's husband last night, but I could manage it now. There was nothing in the way of memories I could give him, though there might be something he could tell me. Besides, I wanted whatever it was Katy had left for me with Sylvia.

She moved to the gate in the wall as I packed up my painting gear.

"You might as well know that I hate what Paul is doing," she said over her shoulder. "I agree with Juan that all of this should be left alone. But my husband is a strongly determined man, and he seems to have a bit between his teeth about this. I blame Eleanor. She likes to stir up trouble and annoy Juan, and she's convinced Paul that he'll be doing history a favor with this book. I've heard her tell him that he mustn't pay any attention to Clarita or Juan's feelings. Or mine, for that matter. Of course it's not really to anyone's interest for him to write it. Not even Paul's. But he likes to play with fire."

She had grown oddly excited as she spoke, and only quieted herself when she saw I was staring at her.

I left my painting things beside the stone I'd perched upon and joined Sylvia at the gate. Before we went through, she put a hand on my arm, halting me.

"Be careful, Amanda. I have a feeling that all those heated emotions Doro stirred around her like a whirl-wind have never quite died down. The repercussions can still damage those who are living. You among them."

It was a strange warning, though I'd felt something of the same thing myself. I didn't try to answer her as I went through the gate between the two gardens. How could I be careful when I didn't know what it was that I must guard against?

We crossed a patio that was smaller than that of the Cordovas' and stepped into the Stewarts' living room, with its brilliant Indian rugs and rows of Kachina dolls. At the far end a door stood open on Paul's study. He was pacing about his desk restlessly and he looked around when he saw me, his face, with its wide cheek-bones and cleft chin, brightening as though I were a gift Sylvia had brought him. For the first time I noticed that his eyes were the pale yellow-green of chrysolite, with an intensity in them, a probing quality in their gaze, as though he sought to draw out some inner signif-

icance that might be hidden from him. My instinct to
resist such probing was strong now. I wasn't sure what I
must defend, but I was on guard against him.

"Hello, Amanda," he said, and came toward me with
a step that was buoyant for so big a man. "How are you
settling in with the Cordovas?"

"I've met them all," I said carefully, avoiding the
demand upon my will that seemed to light his strange
eyes.

"As I've told you, Amanda doesn't remember anything," Sylvia said quickly. "It's as though everything is
being told her for the first time."

"Come and sit down," he said, drawing me toward
a living-room chair with a blue-and-brown rug flung across
it.

Sylvia made a futile gesture toward delay. "Do look
at that chair covering before you sit down, Amanda.
Juan gave it to us one Christmas years ago. The things
he finds for the store are superb. That indigo color is
hard to come by, and the brown isn't dyed. It's the
natural color of the sheep."

I duly examined this treasure before I sat down.
Sylvia's slight flutter seemed uncharacteristic, but I hadn't
seen her in the presence of her husband for long before.
In any case, my main attention was given to Paul.

"They've told me about your book," I said bluntly.
"I don't like what you plan to do. In any case, I can't
be of help to you. There's nothing at all I can remember
of that time."

"I didn't expect it to be so easy," Paul said. "Such
memories are apt to be deeply buried. You'd instinctively
try to protect them from view, forget them—wouldn't
you? But perhaps they can be coaxed to emerge."

My sense of wariness increased. There had already
been small flashes, an edge of memory, though I wouldn't
tell him that. And my dream had come again last night,
brought on, undoubtedly, by the impact of these once
known surroundings. Nevertheless, if I were to remember
something terrible, I wanted to share it with no one,

least of all with this man who seemed avid for such knowledge.

"I don't want to remember, that's true," I told him. "Nothing has come back. I have no recollections of my grandfather's house, of the patio garden—nothing. And no one I've seen has brought back any feeling of recognition. My cousin Eleanor, Aunt Clarita, my grandfather are all strangers to me."

"You see, Paul?" Sylvia said, almost pleading with him.

He turned his head with its sandy-gray hair to look at his wife, and thus presented me with his profile. Strangely, it did not seem to match the rather engaging look he displayed full face. Seen from the side, he wore the profile of a faun—sharp-featured, playful, hinting of dangerous delights. I could well see that he might hold a fascination for women.

The look reproached Sylvia now, though he went on calmly, losing nothing of that deeper intensity I'd glimpsed in him.

"The surfacing of memory is a fascinating phenomenon. I've seen the forgotten emerge from hiding bit by bit until a picture became clear that was not clear in the first place. I'd like to try this with you, Amanda."

Underlying the calm assurance of his manner, I sensed excitement—some quality that courted danger. As Sylvia had suggested, this was a man who would play with fire for the fun of it. I sensed in him a tendency to enjoy the macabre, and I knew that whatever happened, he must not be allowed to write about my mother. Why Sylvia should be so concerned about Paul's project, I didn't know, but I could understand why my grandfather did not trust this man.

Sylvia broke in again, and I heard strain in her voice. "No, Paul—no. Let her alone. Don't do this. It could be dangerous."

He glanced at her with those pale eyes and she seemed to shrink back from his look. "Dangerous to whom, my dear?"

"To—to all of us. I mean emotionally, of course.

Please let her be, Paul. You have enough material for your book without the Cordova affair. And I don't want to upset Juan and Clarita. Or Gavin, for that matter."

He came to sit in a chair opposite me, leaning toward me with all his intensity turned in my direction. "Someone is always upset in these efforts. Obscure relatives threaten to sue. Indignant letters are written. I've been through it before with other books. Since I deal mostly with facts, it all comes to nothing. Besides, the Cordova case is what set me off on the idea of doing this book in the first place. This is one murder I was close to. I knew all the actors personally. I was there at the time. Most of the people involved are still at hand, even though the two main actors are gone."

"You weren't close to it—you weren't!" Sylvia cried.

"If you mean that I wasn't actually there when it happened, that's true. But I must have arrived ten minutes later—which is close enough. And I remember everything."

"Then I don't think you need to bother about the nonexistent or hazy memories of a five-year-old," I said.

He looked at me with a certain amusement, as though I had said something funny. "You don't know, do you? You really don't know?"

"I don't know what you're talking about."

"Then perhaps we ought to tell her. Don't you think so, Sylvia?"

"No—no, I don't!" Sylvia cried. "It's up to them to tell her the whole story."

"And color it as they please?"

"That's Juan Cordova's right."

He shrugged and leaned back in his chair. "I'm willing to wait. There's plenty of time."

His quiet certainty that I would talk to him eventually disturbed and angered me. "It doesn't matter whether you wait or not. Even if I should remember anything, I wouldn't talk about it. I've already told you that."

"Not even if what you might remember should change

the story about your mother? What if it should exonerate her in some way?"

I stared at him. "What do you mean?"

"Nothing at all. It's just a possibility that we can't overlook." He made a bland gesture with his hands which was belied by that tantalizing light in his eyes. "As Sylvia has suggested, we'll wait for the time being. I'm always here if you should want to talk to me. Does that satisfy you, Sylvia?"

Almost imperceptibly she relaxed, though she didn't answer him, but looked at me instead. Her interest now lay in changing the subject.

"Did you find out yesterday why Eleanor ran away?" she asked.

Since Paul had seen Eleanor last night, it seemed strange that Sylvia had not been told her story. However, there was no reason why I shouldn't talk about this, and I gave an account of our finding Eleanor in the cave and bringing her home. "She seems to have wanted to get away from her family—"

"And worry them to death," Sylvia put in.

"Gavin's a brute," Paul said.

What had Eleanor told him? I wondered, and felt unexpectedly indignant.

Sylvia contradicted this at once. "He's not a brute at all. You know him better than that. Eleanor wants a divorce, so I wouldn't put it past her to try to goad Gavin. There's a whole nest of hornets being stirred up. Juan is bound that she's not going to leave Gavin and he's using every card he can play to keep them together."

Was I one of the cards? It seemed likely.

"What does Gavin want?" I asked.

"Eleanor, of course," Paul said. "She means money and the control of the store to him. He'll never let her go unless she forces his hand. She's finding herself helpless in a difficult situation, so she takes imprudent courses."

"She's about as helpless as a tarantula," Sylvia snapped, sounding like herself again. "But let's stop talking about the Cordovas. It's not pleasant for Amanda. I've some coffee perking in the kitchen. I'll go and get it. Show her a copy of *Emanuella*, Paul. I've always thought it was your best book."

Paul smiled, and I was not sure I liked the smile. It seemed to take too much for granted—as though he assumed that I would side with him in any controversy, and that if he waited long enough I would come over to his way of thinking.

"Sylvia is prejudiced," he said when she'd gone. "Against Eleanor, I mean." He leaned toward me, and I felt again the submerged intensity in this man that filled me with foreboding. "You're a lot like your mother. You take me back to another time. Before all the trouble. Would you be surprised to hear that I once thought myself in love with Doro? Foolish, of course. She was already married, and Sylvia was the right woman for me."

Perhaps she heard him as she came back into the room with a tray of coffee cups and set it down on his desk. Perhaps he had intended for her to hear. I did not like or trust Paul Stewart, and I hoped that my mother had ignored him.

"He hasn't shown you the book," Sylvia said, and when she had poured our coffee she went to a bookcase and took down a volume in a mustard dust jacket. "Take this along and read it sometime, Amanda. It's semi-nonfiction. Paul based the story on old Spanish history. We went over to Spain when he was doing the research and stayed awhile in Madrid. As a matter of fact, it's Cordova history. At least of that branch of the family which stayed in Spain."

I took the book from her, interested in the family connection. When I flipped open to the copyright page, I saw it had been published a few years after my mother's death.

I had taken only a few sips of coffee when Eleanor came brightly through the door. Her hair was brushed to a sunny shine this morning, and her tall person looked beautifully trim in a dove-gray trouser suit.

"I've been looking for you, Amanda," she told me. "Grandfather wants to see you at once. So you'd better hurry."

I took another sip of coffee and stood up. "Thank you, Sylvia. I suppose I'd better go. Did you say you had a package for me?"

Sylvia remembered and jumped up. She ran out of the room and was back in a moment with a lumpy brown envelope.

"Here you are. I almost forgot. Katy was very weak when she gave me this, but she managed to whisper a few words. She said, 'Tell her to go to the *rancho.*' "

I took the envelope and moved toward the door. Both Eleanor and Paul had watched this interchange, but neither Sylvia nor I explained.

"Come back soon," Paul said, and his look seemed to challenge me with that amused assurance, as though he knew I would be back.

Eleanor gestured with a careless hand. "You know the way. I needn't go with you. I'll have some of that coffee, Sylvia, if you don't mind."

Sylvia turned away to pour the coffee, and in that instant I saw the quick exchange of looks between Paul and Eleanor. What I saw I did not like. Some pact, some understanding existed between them, and I had a feeling that it had to do with me.

The gate stood open in the adobe wall and I went through to pick up my painting gear and go into the house. Clarita was in the living room, talking to Rosa. When she saw me her eyes went carefully blank, and she made no effort to stop me as I set down my gear and the small package on a table. The book *Emanuella* I took with me. Perhaps I'd ask Juan about it. Evidently she had received her own orders by now and liked me none the better for them. I wished I could reassure her, but there was no way to do it at the moment.

As I mounted the steps to the balcony, I heard voices and I approached the doorway hesitantly. Gavin was there with my grandfather. Juan Cordova sat behind his desk, white-faced, his eyes closed, his lips thin with tension. Gavin stood above him, and I heard his words as I reached the door.

"This isn't something you can order as you please," he said grimly. "We've been over this ground before, and I won't be changed."

"Grandfather?" I spoke quickly, not wanting to hear what was not intended for my ears.

Gavin turned his cool look upon me and I found myself wishing that he might have been an ally, instead of one more antagonist. There were matters I might have consulted him about, if I were able. But he turned his back, dismissing me, and walked to a window, where the burgundy draperies had been drawn aside to let in New Mexico sunlight.

"Come in, come in, Amanda," Juan Cordova said testily. "Where have you been that it took so long to find you?"

I went to stand before his desk. "I was next door with Sylvia and Paul."

He stared me down with his fierce, falcon's look. "I told you not to talk to Paul Stewart."

"I know. But I didn't promise you not to. However, you needn't worry that I might help him with his book. There isn't anything I can tell him. He said something strange, though. He wondered if anything I could remember might help to exonerate my mother."

"Exonerate? I hardly think that is his purpose. But we will speak of this again. Now sit down for a moment. I've been talking to Gavin about you. I want him to show you the store this morning. It is necessary for you to learn as much as you can about what it means to the Cordova family."

I didn't like the implication. "Why?" I asked as I sat in the chair beside his desk.

The heavy lids closed over his eyes as though he found it difficult to deal with me. He looked anything but kind.

"The store is part of your heritage. You must learn about it."

"I've heard it called an albatross," I said, and drummed my fingers lightly on the book Sylvia had loaned me.

Gavin turned from the window. "It's all of that, if you let it be. But you're forewarned. All right, Juan—I'll do as you ask. If Amanda is to go through the store, we'd better start now."

"One moment, Gavin," Juan said. "Have you learned anything more about the pre-Columbian head someone put in your room?"

"I didn't expect to," Gavin said. "All these happenings are meant to look bad for me, and no one is going to admit anything. I can only count on your trust in me."

"To a certain extent you may count on it," Juan said. "To a certain extent. I'm not sure who can be trusted any more. But shortly after I've spoken to her, you will take Amanda to the store and introduce her to the best of it. She and CORDOVA may be important to each other."

I stood up, speaking hastily out of embarrassment. "Of course I'd like to see the store—as a visitor. I've known about it since I was a little girl and it has always fascinated me. Isn't it possible for you to come with us?" I said to my grandfather.

I could hear the weariness of ill health in his voice as he replied. "Not today. Leave us alone for a moment, Gavin. I want to speak with Amanda."

Gavin went out, but there was an angry glint in his eyes that did not promise well for our tour of the store. He had never been an ally, but this talk of showing me CORDOVA might make him an enemy.

My grandfather beckoned me closer. "I want you to do something for me in the store. I go out very seldom these days, and I have an errand for you. You are to notice one display case in particular while you are in the store. You will find it on the second floor—a tall glass case containing articles of Toledo steel. Locate the cabinet. Look at it so that you can find it again. Do you understand?"

"I don't understand at all," I told him. "But I'll do as you wish."

"Good. I will explain another time. Now go and join Gavin. But report to me when you return. I want to know what you think of CORDOVA. And—listen to me carefully, Amanda—you are to say nothing to Gavin about the cabinet. Do you hear me?"

"I hear you," I said. "I'll do as you wish."

Some strange relief seemed to wash over him. He smiled at me with a certain air of triumph, as though he had not been sure he could bend me to his will, and was pleased that he had. I suspected that I had been bested in some way I did not understand, that I was being made sly use of. But the matter didn't seem important, and in this case I would do as he wished.

I went down to the living room where Rosa was busy working and Clarita had disappeared. Gavin waited for me.

"I'll put this book of Paul Stewart's and my other things in my room, and get my handbag," I said, holding up the volume.

Gavin looked at it with distaste. "It's a good thing your grandfather didn't notice what you've got there. He long ago ordered every copy in the house of that book to be given away or thrown out. He won't be pleased about your reading it. He doesn't feel that Stewart did well by Emanuella."

"Then I shan't tell him," I said, and hurried up the stairs to my room.

Now the book interested me all the more, but I had no time for it at the moment. I tossed it down on the bed, glancing quickly at the white rug where the fetish had lain, relieved to find nothing there. I liked that episode less every time I thought of it. But now what mattered was Katy's package. That could not wait. I ripped open the sealed flap and looked inside. All the envelope contained was a small blue jeweler's box of the sort that might hold a ring. There was no paper, no message. I pressed the catch and the lid of the box opened. Inside, tucked into the satin slit where a ring might have rested, was a tiny brass key. Nothing else. I had been left a puzzle to which I had no answer, except that I had been told to go to the *Rancho de Cordova*. There was no time to ponder over this now, since Gavin was waiting, and I was eager to see the store for myself.

Juan was right—it was a part of my heritage, whether I liked it or not, and it would tell me more about the Cordovas. Gavin was clearly reluctant to be my guide, and I found myself regretting that. He mustn't become my enemy. If he didn't so obviously disapprove of me, he might have helped me when it came to the things I wanted to know. I might even have told him of Paul Stewart's effort to put some pressure on me to remember what had happened at the time of my mother's death. But I couldn't do that unless I broke through the barrier Gavin held against me.

For the first time, I wondered if that was possible. In spite of the way Juan's words had antagonized him, perhaps, as he showed me about the store, I could find a way to allay the suspicions he held against me, whatever they were. I needed a friend badly, and I went downstairs to join him with a new intent in me, a new purpose.

VII

CORDOVA fronted spaciously on a street that branched off from the plaza. I saw that only a portion of its glass windows had been photographed in that ad I had long ago torn from a magazine. The wide store front was impressive, and there was an elegance, a luxury about the windows with their exotic treasures discreetly displayed.

Gavin opened a glass door and let me precede him into the shop. It was an old building, and I had an immediate sense of great space, high ceilings that lost themselves in upper gloom, of polished counters and wall shelves that followed long aisles to the rear of the store, all handsomely arranged to attract the eye and tempt those who might appreciate the beautiful and unusual.

Daylight penetrated only a little way past the front windows, and the vast interior was illuminated by artificial lighting. Inside, visitors moved about decorously, and women behind the counters waited on customers with grave courtesy. A hush that shut off traffic sounds from outdoors gave the shop an aura of restrained and almost awesome dignity. It was not a place in which boisterous behavior would be tolerated, any more than such behavior would be endured in a museum. Juan

101

had apparently made an elaborate effort to turn CORDOVA
into a shrine for the rare objects he worshiped. I
found the effect a little oppressive and somehow it made
me feel irreverent, contrary.

"Does anyone ever laugh in here?" I asked Gavin.

Apparently he had been waiting for my first reaction,
and I had surprised him. His smile came slowly.

"So you aren't going to be intimidated, after all?"

I stood before an ancient Spanish chest with heavily
carved drawers and wrought-iron pulls. On top of it
stood a bowl of beaten brass from Guyana, and several
carved trays and boxes made of rare Paraguayan woods,
all labeled with discreet small signs.

"It's not that I don't appreciate all these beautiful
things," I said, "but I can't help thinking of what Eleanor
said about CORDOVA—that it was always put above the
human beings connected with it. So that now, when I'm
here, I have a feeling of resistance to its—well to its
smothering perfection."

Gavin reached past me to touch the surface of an
exquisitely carved bowl. "The man who made this knew
how to laugh. He was close to the earth, perhaps ignorant,
by our standards, but he could create beauty with his
hands. Juan knows nothing about him. He has always
been interested in the product, not the man, except as the
artist can be used. For the purist, that may be the way
to look at it."

"But you're interested in the artist apart from his art?"

"Yes—perhaps because I've traveled a lot and come
to know some of the people who sell us their work.
It's not disembodied for me, since I care about the
craftsman who is alive and working today. A good many
of the things we carry here have men and women behind
them who live in Spain and Mexico, or in the South and
Central American countries. I've come to know some
of their families and a good deal about their personal
skills and talents. When my father used to go abroad
for Juan, he always looked for sources, instead of deal-

ing with some middleman. I've done the same thing. Craftwork *is* a living thing."

His head with its thick crest of fair hair was held high, so he could look all about him, and his gray eyes saw more than mere objects, wherever he looked. I liked him better for his explanation, and my brief sense of irreverence faded.

We moved on past a rug with a Kachina design in brown and white and black, displayed against a near-by wall, and I paused before a Mexican sunburst mirror next to it, looking at Gavin behind me in the round of glass. For the first time since I had met him, he seemed alive and concerned, instead of being far away and always on guard. It was interesting to see his eyes take on warmth and excitement when he was involved in the things he cared about. Perhaps this was the man I had sensed in that moment when I had first seen him and felt that breath-stopping attraction I couldn't quite shake off.

"Are you and my grandfather at odds about the store?" I asked.

At once his guard was up again. "I work for him," he said curtly, and moved on to a table graced by an intricate wrought-iron candelabrum, with fine Indian pottery arranged around it. Against the wall beyond leaned a stack of great, carved doors of Spanish colonial design, such as I had already seen at the Cordovas' and the Stewarts'.

"Those doors are made in the city," Gavin said. "They're known everywhere as Santa Fe doors."

He was again the guide Juan had instructed him to be, and I had lost my tenuous contact. I could only follow as he turned down the next aisle and paused before a cabinet with a glass front. A sign indicated that these objects belonged to pre-Columbian times and were being loaned to the store for exhibit. There were bits of stone, shards of pottery, and ornamentation from ancient buildings. One piece was a stone head with bulging, exaggerated features, broken off at the neck, but otherwise intact.

"Is that the head that disappeared?" I asked.

"Yes—the one I'm supposed to have stolen."

"Why would anyone play such a trick on you?"

He gave me a distant glance. "It's hardly your concern."

Prickling indignation swept me and I would not be intimidated by Gavin Brand either. "Grandfather seemed to think that everything about CORDOVA was my concern."

"Why?"

"I suppose because I'm one of the family and should know about such things. What else? Surely Grandfather doesn't believe in any robbery when it comes to that stone head, does he?"

"There was a robbery. Someone took the head out of this locked case. Someone who had access to the key that's kept in the store."

He moved away, indifferent to what I might believe, continuing our tour of the first floor. Now and then he paused to explain something casually, or stopped to point out some article with an admiration that shone through his indifference toward me. I felt increasingly resentful of his attitude. All his barriers were up, and my wish to break through them was obviously futile. Yet I didn't want to accept this as final defeat.

We reached the back of the store and a corner where articles of woven grass were displayed. The scent of the grasses was fragrant and all pervading. There was no one about back here, and when Gavin would have moved on, I stopped him.

"Please let me apologize for that ridiculous remark I made when we first met. It was stupid, but I wish you wouldn't go on holding it against me."

At least his look focused on me, though he seemed surprised. "I'd forgotten all about it. It was never important."

"Then why must you—" I began, but he broke in on my words, suddenly willing to be frank.

"Juan brought you out here to use you, and you're stepping right into his trap. I suppose it will serve you to step into it, but you might as well know that I'll oppose you all the way. There are prior rights."

I stared at him in outrage, so furious I couldn't speak. I didn't understand his talk about traps or about my willingness to be used. Too angry to answer him, I moved on to the next display, unable to examine it calmly.

"The better things are upstairs." He was my impersonal guide again, grimly doing his duty. "A good deal of what we show down here is for the tourist trade. Or else it consists of imported objects that Santa Feans buy."

There was a strong smell of leather as we walked through a section given over to Spanish leather goods—belts and pocketbooks, and even boots and saddles. Near the front of the store, a wide flight of stairs rose toward the floor above, and I mounted them beside Gavin, still seething. But at least I remembered Juan's words—that it was up here I would find the cabinet of Toledo steel, the case he had instructed me to notice for some reason he hadn't explained. I would take care of my mission as soon as I could, and then I would turn my back on Gavin and the store.

At the head of the stairs a glass-enclosed ceramic flamenco dancer waited to greet us, and beyond her the floor turned into a museum of fine arts and crafts. Here much of what was displayed was fabulously expensive, exquisitely wrought. This was CORDOVA, restrained in its presentation of superb workmanship, less crowded than the floor below, yet stamped somehow with the same arrogant confidence that characterized Juan Cordova. There was no entreaty to buy, for here that function seemed a privilege. For the first time, I began to sense the element of proud family that ruled both the store and the Cordovas.

"I could never belong to all this," I said impulsively. "It would try to dominate and rule, wouldn't it? It would have to be possessive. You'd have to give your life for it."

Gavin glanced at me with mild curiosity. "I didn't expect you to understand that."

I thought with resentment that what he expected of me had little concern with reality. But in spite of the effect the store might exert upon me, I was quickly lost to the rich fare it presented on every hand. The artist in me was beguiled in spite of myself.

Hand-embroidered shawls from Spain were glorious and I stopped to finger silken fringe and study the design of great, embroidered blossoms. This was like painting on silk. Brilliant blankets and rebozos and ponchos from Bolivia caught my eyes as I moved on, only to be drawn along to the next display of a stunning suede jacket from Argentina.

"There's nothing machine-made here," Gavin informed me. "Behind everything you see there's a craftsman or a woman talented at design and needlework." His tone had warmed again, though not toward me. "Juan has let me have my hand up here, and none of these things are confined in a museum. Because we can sell them, we help to keep these crafts alive and their creators productive."

The anger he could so quickly arouse in me was dying. I could understand the importance of finding the artist a market, and I touched with respect an inlaid box of exquisite woods from French Guiana.

"Even though it's possessive, CORDOVA is more than I thought," I said. "Sylvia Stewart called it the beast that ruled the family. And I can see the enormous amount of effort and expense that must go into keeping it alive. But perhaps it's worth it."

"It's worth it if we keep our feet on the ground and don't get lost in clouds of antiquity, which is what Juan, more and more, seems to want. He buys museum pieces he would never sell. He gets carried away by the idea of collecting and displaying, instead of selling. But this isn't a musty museum—it is something to keep men and women earning and productive, to preserve skills that might be lost. It must be kept *alive*—not allowed to die in the dust of a mere collection."

There was a passion in this man—a love for hand-wrought beauty, but also a belief in the worker behind it that I found myself relishing.

"What will happen to the store when Juan dies?" I asked.

He answered me curtly. "Eleanor will inherit it. That's the way his will reads."

"What about Clarita?"

"She's taken care of in other ways. Though I don't think Juan has ever been fair to Clarita, considering all the work she's put into the store. She used to manage this entire floor and she knows CORDOVA as Eleanor never will."

"Another one who's given her life to it? Perhaps CORDOVA is omnivorous like Juan. What will Eleanor do with it, if she inherits?"

"That remains to be seen. She'll hardly be possessed by it." His tone was dry.

"But of course you'll continue to manage it, buy for it?"

"There's no guarantee of that."

"If Eleanor has any sense—"

His look told me that once more this was none of my business, and I broke off. I could see how there might well be some sort of war going on under the surface in Juan Cordova's house.

We walked on past other displays, but I was beginning to feel sated, as one does sometimes in a museum. There was too much to see, too much to absorb. If it was possible, I would come back here again. I wanted more, but not now, and I wondered with a certain self-distrust if I too was beginning to be possessed by the store's power to absorb the Cordovas.

As I passed a shelf, my eye was caught by a carving done in some reddish-brown wood and I stopped to look at it more closely. It was about eight inches high— the head of an Indian woman with wide cheekbones, a nose with flared nostrils, and a generous mouth. The lines were swift and modern, suggesting, rather than expressing, detail. I took it in my hands and felt the smooth grain of the wood like satin under my fingers.

"How beautiful!" I said. "Where did this come from?"

Gavin thawed a little. "A woodcarver in Taxco did that. He's part Indian and supremely gifted. The only trouble, from our viewpoint, is that he carves very few pieces. He doesn't care about money, and he'll work only when the vision comes to him and he can produce something superb."

I set the carving regretfully back on the shelf. I would have liked to own it for myself, but I didn't trouble to look at the price label glued discreetly to the base. I knew what it must cost.

"How lucky he is to do only the work he really cares about," I said, thinking of my brochures, my drawing for advertising projects I often didn't care about. "Sometimes I've wished——" but I stopped, remembering that Gavin Brand would not care what I wished.

"You want to be a painter, don't you?" he said.

I was surprised that he would comment. "More than anything. But no matter what I might wish, I have to work at jobs that are often less than creative."

"And probably good for you. My Taxco friend is an exception. Ivory towers don't work for most artists. Or for the rest of us, for that matter. Men need to be engaged in life. Otherwise our viewpoints become desiccated and narrow."

As Juan Cordova's had? I wondered. Gavin was involved with more than the mere perfection of all this rich merchandise which the store presented. How much was he involved with Eleanor, and how much was Eleanor concerned with what lay outside herself?

But again, this was none of my business.

"Don't let anything stop you. Be a painter," he said, and moved on to the next display.

I heard him in surprise. He had cut through to an understanding I hadn't expected of him. He had not softened toward me particularly, but he respected what I must do.

"You haven't seen my work," I said. "How do you know that I shouldn't be discouraged from going ahead, that I shouldn't be stopped?"

"No one should be stopped. You can create for your own satisfaction, if for nothing else."

"That's not good enough. That's the ivory tower bit. I suppose I want to say something in my work that someone else can see and enjoy. If there's no one to appreciate, you're only looking in a mirror."

He smiled at me—for once without suspicion or disliking, so that his face lighted and lost its somber quality.

"You're right, of course. This is the thing Juan is forgetting. He has created CORDOVA, yet he's becoming a miser about it. He wants it all for himself and his family—like that art collection of his. He's forgotten what is fundamental—the sharing and appreciation of art by many. Will you show me some of your work sometime?"

"I—I don't know," I said. I was suddenly both hopeful and oddly shy. Gavin had taste and perception. He would be honest, and if he didn't like what I showed him, it would hurt me. It would matter.

He didn't press me, but allowed me the right of uncertainty, and I was unexpectedly grateful.

"Here is something you must see," he said, and we stopped before a glass counter in which fine silver and turquoise jewelry was displayed against a background of black velvet.

"These are things from the Southwest," he told me. "From some of our best Indian craftsmen. Your grandfather said you were to choose whatever piece you like. He wants you to have something in turquoise from CORDOVA."

I was touched and pleased, and I bent over the glass, searching. The girl behind the counter drew out a tray and set it before me so that I could finger the lovely gleaming rings and brooches and pendants. I did not want a ring or necklace; so I finally picked out a brooch, inlaid with turquoise, jet and coral, and outlined with the points of a silver sunburst.

"This one, I think," I said. I pinned it to the shoulder of my blue linen and the girl brought a mirror on a stand, so that I could see how it looked.

"A good choice," Gavin approved. "That's Zuni work and of the finest."

I was turning away from the counter when a tall cabinet in the center of the floor caught my eye. I walked over to it at once to look at the swords and knives it displayed. *Toledo Steel,* the card in the case read. I could not imagine why my grandfather had wanted me to locate and remember this case, but I looked around to check it against other displays, so that I could find it again.

Gavin seemed uninterested in such cutlery. "You've just about seen the store," he said, turning distant again. "Have you had enough? Do you know all about CORDOVA now?"

"As you very well know, I couldn't learn all about it in months of study," I assured him. "But I'm glad to make a beginning."

Apparently my choice of words was unfortunate. His face was expressionless, all feeling suppressed. "Yes— you're expected to go on from here, I gather."

We were walking down an aisle and there was no one nearby to overhear. I spoke to him quickly, bluntly.

"What is it my grandfather expects of me? What does he want?"

He answered me with careful indifference, as though the words he spoke did not matter. "Perhaps an heiress. Perhaps only a weapon to threaten us with." He might have been speaking of the weather.

"But I don't want to be either of those things!" I cried. "I don't want anything from him, except perhaps an affection I'm not likely to find in his house."

He didn't believe me. His silence was skeptical and I went on heatedly, even though I knew it was no use.

"Certainly I don't want to threaten anyone. Though

someone seems to be threatening me." I told him abruptly about the mole fetish which had been left in my room yesterday.

He seemed unsurprised. "What can you expect? If you're determined to stay here, you're sure to stir up antagonisms. Juan will use you, as he tries to use everything he touches."

"Perhaps I won't let him use me."

"Then there's no point in staying, is there? Why do you want to stay?"

"Why do you want me to go away?" I countered. "What are you afraid of? I don't really know my grandfather yet. I want to know him for myself, not just through the eyes and prejudices of others." There was still more to it. There was the matter of my mother, but I didn't want to tell him how I felt about that, and have him laugh at me. "If my staying here is Cordova stubbornness, then let it be that way."

"The stubbornness of Spain or New England?" he said. "There's not much to choose between, is there?"

To my surprise he was not wholly mocking. He might dislike and disapprove of me, but I had the feeling that he had, strangely, begun to respect me. Nevertheless, I resented his calm assurance as he strode toward the stairs ahead of me, obviously relieved that his guide duty was over, taking it for granted I would follow. All that was contrary in me resisted, and I turned down an aisle I had not seen and came to a halt before an open display case.

The key was in the lock of the door which stood ajar, as though someone must be working on the display, and the contents of the case took my startled attention.

In the center was a crude, two-wheeled wooden cart with spikes protruding all around the upper edge. It was filled with large rocks upon which sat the figure which had startled me. It was made of carved wood—the skeleton of a woman with a wig of scrawny black locks, and a bow and arrow fixed in her bony hands. Her eyes were hollows and her teeth grinned eerily in her skull's face.

"Attractive, isn't she?" said a voice behind me.

I turned in surprise, to find Paul Stewart at my shoulder, holding up a vicious-looking three-pronged whip in one hand. When I stared at the whip, he gave the thongs a little flick with the fingers of his other hand.

"This is a *disciplina*. Just part of my Penitente collection," he said. "Of course you've heard of the Penitentes of the Southwest? I offered to loan my collection to Juan for the store, and he was pleased. So I've brought these things over and I've been arranging them. How do you like the lady in the cart?"

His pale, chrysolite eyes turned from me for a moment to look down the aisle, and I saw that Gavin was standing a little way off, clearly waiting for me with some impatience. I stayed where I was.

"What is she?" I asked Paul.

He bent his big frame and carefully arranged the whip to best effect among the other articles in the case.

"She's *La Muerte*. Or Doña Sebastiana, if you wish. That's what they call her. You'd better pray to her for a long life. That arrow poised in the bow is intended for some nonbelieving bystander. She's sitting in one of the death carts they pull in their processions. The stones that fill the cart make it heavy, so that those who pull it punish themselves."

"You've written about all this, haven't you?"

"Yes. I found it fascinating. I've been into Penitente country a good many times and managed to get myself trusted enough so they'd talk to me. That whip is one they use for self-flagellation. The wooden clackers are *matracas* and they can make a hideous noise. The flints down in the corner there—the *pedernales*—are used to inflict surface wounds, and you'll see there's a candle lantern and a crucifix. The sect is dying out to some extent, but *Los Hermanos,* The Brothers, still exist back in the hills. They're Hispanic in descent and Catholic, of a sort, though the Church has denounced their practices."

Near the center of the case Paul Stewart had taken care to display several copies of the book he had written and I read its title, *Trail of the Whip*. Doña Sebastiana herself graced the jacket, and Paul's name was in black letters across the bottom.

"I'll loan you a copy, if you like," he said.

I shivered slightly. "I still have *Emanuella* to read, and I think she'll be more to my taste."

"I'm not so sure," Paul said. "You may find out too much about the Cordovas in those pages."

"The Cordovas are what I want to know about," I said lightly, and turned to walk toward Gavin.

Gavin stood near the stairs, and he made no comment as I joined him. I sensed that Paul Stewart's presence in the store was not something he liked, and if the choice had been his, he might have dispensed with the Peni-tente display. I sensed, too, disapproval of me because I had stopped to talk to Paul. But Gavin was not my keeper and I would do as I pleased.

We went down to the lower floor and out to the side street, where he had left his car. On the way to the house I tried to unbend my resentment enough to thank him.

"I'm sure no one else could have told me as much about the store as you have," I said. "I appreciate your taking the time."

He gave me a casual nod without speaking, and his very silence dismissed me. He had simply been doing what Juan Cordova had ordered him to do. I had ar-rived nowhere with my foolish hope that we might be-come better friends during my tour of the store. In fact, part of the time I wasn't sure I wanted him for a friend anyway.

He let me out at the turquoise gate and said he was returning to work. When I crossed the narrow yard to the unlocked front door, there was no one about, and inside the house I climbed the steps to my grandfather's rooms, knocking on the door. He called to me to come in. I entered, to find him lying stretched out on a long leather couch, a cushion propped beneath his head, and his eyes closed.

"I've seen the store," I told him. "You asked me to come back afterwards."

He gestured toward the chair beside his couch, his eyes still closed. "Come then and sit down. Tell me about it."

I tried haltingly to obey, but my impressions were too recent, too many, and I hadn't begun to digest them. I found myself quoting Gavin, speaking about the store's use in helping so many skilled craftsmen to keep working.

He shrugged this aside. "We are not a charitable institution. Fine work is well paid for. Tell me what you liked best."

I told him about the wood carving from Taxco and he opened his eyes to look at me approvingly. "Ah, yes— the Tarascan woman. Beautiful. I wanted to bring her home and keep her in my study, but Gavin would not permit me."

"Permit you?" I echoed in surprise.

He smiled at me slyly. "These days Gavin must be my eyes, my hands, my will. It doesn't do to oppose him too much. Did you find something in turquoise for yourself?"

I touched the pin on my blouse. "Yes. Thank you, Grandfather."

"Come closer," he said, and reached out to touch the pin, sensing the inlay with his fingers. "Zuni. A good choice. Did Gavin help you?"

"I chose it myself," I told him, and couldn't help the slight tartness that crept into my tone. I was not leaning upon Gavin.

"And did you see the case of Toledo steel?"

"Yes. I know where it is. Why did you want me to see it?"

"Later, later," he said testily. "Tell me what you think of Gavin?"

This was not a question I wanted to answer and it took me by surprise. I formed my words cautiously.

"He seems to know everything about the store. He made a very good guide."

"I know all that. What do you think of *him?*"

Since he would allow no evasion, I tried to answer honestly.

"He seems to understand the man behind the craft. He believes that art should be a living thing—something with meaning for the living. And in the case of craftwork, a living for the creator."

"He has been lecturing you, I see. But you're still talking about the field in which he's an expert. What do you think of him—of Gavin himself?"

Again, I tried to be honest, though this was not a subject I wanted to discuss. "I think I would like him if he permitted me to. But he doesn't like me. He believes that I mean the Cordovas some harm."

There was a wicked glee in the old man's laughter. "They are all sure of that. I have poured poison in the ant heap and they are scurrying to save themselves."

"I don't like to be regarded as a household poison."

His glee included me. "They don't know what I am going to do about you, and I've frightened them badly."

"I didn't come here to frighten anyone. I don't like this role you've thrust upon me."

"Why did you come then?"

It was the old question, and he had not understood my reasons. The attraction of a family for someone who had no family was beyond his comprehension.

"I came because of my mother," I said. "I know now that there's something I need to remember. Grandmother Katy left me a small ring box containing a key. She gave it to Sylvia to keep in case I ever came here, and she left me a message too. She said I was to go to the *rancho.*"

He flung back the light covering and sat up on the couch to stare at me in astonishment. "What does this mean? Sylvia has been like a daughter, yet she has never told me of this. Why?"

"I'm afraid you'll have to ask her."

He sat there pondering. "Before she died, Katy tried to tell me some wild thing of which I could make nothing."

"Then she knew something!" I cried. "She really did know something. What if Paul Stewart is right and some memory of mine might be used to exonerate my mother?"

"It is all so long ago." He shook his head in unhappy memory. "It is not an experience I want to go through again."

"But you loved Doroteo."

"That too was long ago. Now I am an old man, beyond loving or being loved."

"Then I'm sorry for you," I said.

He rose from the couch, and his height gave him dominance over me. His height and his arrogance.

"I want pity from no one. Mine is an enviable state. I have all that I want, and there is no one who can inflict pain upon me."

"And no one who can bring you joy?" I said.

"You speak your mind like a Cordova. What do you intend to do with this key and ring box?"

"I'll get someone to take me out to the *rancho*. Perhaps something there will help me to remember."

He moved to the chair behind his desk, pulling the maroon silk of his robe more tightly across his chest.

"If there is a real need for you to remember, perhaps I can help you. But not if you mean to talk about these things to Paul Stewart."

"How can you help me?"

"I will think about this and we will speak of it again. If there should be a way to change our beliefs about what happened with Doroteo and Kirk Landers, that is something I would like to explore. Doroteo was my beloved daughter, and Kirk was more like a son than Rafael. Perhaps he loved me more than my own son did, and he loved Spain. He should have been born to me."

This was a new view of Kirk, and I listened in mild surprise.

"Never mind," he went on. "I have little faith that the past can be changed. And now there are more urgent matters pressing upon me. You have made a beginning with the store, Amanda. We will go on from there."

I didn't care for the sound of that, but he reached for papers on his desk and nodded a cool dismissal. He wanted nothing more of me now. On my way down to the living room, I realized that he still hadn't told me why he'd sent me to look at the cabinet that held swords from Toledo.

No one was about, and I stood upon a Navajo rug and looked around thoughtfully. Nothing spoke to me with a clear voice. The room with its cool gloom seemed strange to my eyes—all white walls and brown vigas and Indian ornaments. Yet something hovered just beyond the edge of vision—something that waited to pounce. I remembered the mole fetish and Eleanor's hinting that I was the hunter's prey. But I wouldn't accept that. I would not play mouse for Juan Cordova or prey for a hunter. I would stay here only long enough to find out what I wanted to know about my mother, and then I would turn my back upon adobe walls and encroaching mesa, get away from here forever.

As I walked toward the stairs to my room, I wondered why this decision filled me with no relief. Was there, after all, a spell exerted by mountains and desert, and adobe-colored towns? Something seemed to draw me, hold me here, yet whatever it was pulsed faintly with a sense of danger at the same time. What if Doroteo had not, after all, pulled the trigger of that gun which had killed Kirk Landers? What if she had not killed herself? Was there someone still living—someone who knew the truth and would be on guard against me if I meddled with matters that were thought settled and long buried?

The house was very still, yet I never had the sense of being alone in it. There were too many windows and passages, too many rooms opening one out of another. Was I being watched, as was so easily possible? I turned about quickly and caught a faint movement at a door that led to the patio. For an instant I was prompted to run to the door and see who was there—but I did not. An odd prickle of panic went through me and I fled up the stairs to my room, wanting only to close my own door between me and the rest of this silent, watching house.

But when I reached my room, I saw that it would do no good to close the door. Once more, Eleanor waited for me. She wore dove-gray trousers and a sleeveless turquoise blouse, and she sat cross-legged in the middle of my bed, with the book *Emanuella* open on her knees.

"I've been waiting for you," she said. "I see that someone has loaned you *Emanuella*."

"Sylvia said I should read it."

"She's right—you should. Though it may frighten you badly. It did me. Do you know who Emanuella was?"

I shook my head, wondering why Eleanor had come to my room.

"Legend has it that she was an ancestress of ours. Rather a notorious one, because of all her affairs at the court of Philip IV of Spain. Paul learned about her after he married Sylvia, and he went to Madrid to do some research on her before he wrote the book. Grandfather is proud of what he claims is the line of descent and he makes a lot of it. Emanuella was supposed to have a passionate disposition and a temper that we're all expected to inherit. But when Paul wrote the book, Grandfather was furious because he claimed she was a little mad. Her cousin Doña Inés wound up in a madhouse. Do you suppose the strain really comes down to us, Amanda?" Her eyes were bright and wide, with that appealing air of innocence that I didn't trust. I knew there was nothing innocent about her intent.

"I shouldn't think so," I said carelessly. "It would be a pretty diluted strain if it did."

"Velázquez painted the mad one—Doña Inés," Eleanor went on, tossing the book aside on the bed. "Velázquez himself is a character in Paul's story. Has Grandfather told you any of this, Amanda?"

"No," I said. "And I'm afraid it all sounds too remote as a scandal to get very excited about."

Eleanor uncurled herself and stretched out her legs in their gray trousers. "Not so remote, perhaps. Grandmother Katy took it seriously. I think she used to watch all of us for signs of the wild strain that Grandfather is so proud of. Only he won't call it madness."

"From what I've heard of Katy, she sounds too sensible for that."

"I remember her very well," Eleanor said. "She wasn't always calm and sensible. When I was small I can remember her walking in the patio and wringing her hands together as though there was something she couldn't bear. Once when she didn't know I was near I heard her talking to herself about being trapped in silence. I've always wondered what she meant."

I wondered too, and thought of the little key I'd put away in my handbag. Was that trap of silence about to be sprung open? Was I to be the instrument? I walked to one of the room's three windows and stood looking through the deep recess, down into the patio. I could imagine Katy walking its paths with a warm sun beating upon adobe walls. Eleanor came quietly to stand beside me.

"From here you can see the place where the family used to picnic," she said softly, slyly. "Do you see where the hillside dips into the arroyo beyond our back wall?" She pointed. "There's a very old cottonwood tree down there that gives a lovely shade. And there's a place where the hillside levels out beneath it. Do you see where the path winds down to the clearing?"

My gaze followed her pointing finger and I remembered my earlier uneasiness when I'd looked out toward the arroyo. I could see the path she indicated, and the clearing itself in the midst of that green growth that sprang up wherever there was a trace of water in New Mexico.

"Yes, I can see it," I said.

I would have turned from the window, but she put her hand on my arm to hold me there, and I felt malice in her grip.

"Your mother died on the ledge below the clearing." Her voice was light—and deadly. She meant to wound, to torment. "Because of the juniper bushes it's hidden from those who were there above at the picnic. But you can see the ledge from here. There are rocks along the hillside, forming the ledge. Do you see them?"

I could only nod, my throat constricted. The pressure of her fingers hurt my arm.

"That's where they struggled—your mother and Kirk Landers. Though he was away in Taos when it happened, Mark Brand, Gavin's father, was visiting here at the time and he had a gun. Doro must have gone into his room to get it, and everyone thinks she went down there to kill Kirk Landers."

"I don't believe that," I said tightly.

Eleanor shrugged graceful shoulders and took her hand away from my arm. "What difference does it make whether you believe it or not, when it really happened? I've heard Paul say that Doro was like Emanuella. She was in love with men. Many men. But she had a passionate nature and she couldn't bear to be—what's the old-fashioned term?—spurned. She was in love with Kirk when she was young, but he went away and changed. So she killed him."

My breath was coming quickly and I could feel the perspiration breaking out on my cheeks and neck.

"What if none of this is true? You said they couldn't be seen from the picnic ground above."

"That's the angle that interests Paul. But you forget there was a witness—Aunt Clarita. She'd stayed home, since she had a headache. But she got up for fresh air and she stood at this very window and saw the whole thing. She saw Doro fire the gun, while Kirk struggled with her. There was blasting going on in a nearby lot that day, so no one heard the shot. But Aunt Clarita knew when it was fired because she saw Kirk fall and your mother fling herself over the ledge into the arroyo. She could swear to all this later and there weren't any who would doubt Aunt Clarita's word."

The light, breathless voice at my side was still for a moment, but I was aware of the air of triumph with which she awaited my reaction. I felt a little sick and somehow angry as well. Stubbornly, I refused to accept.

"You wanted to know, didn't you?" she went on. "No one else would tell you the truth, but I think it's only fair that you should know the details of what happened. Of course, it's too bad the other witness couldn't be coherent about what she saw."

"There was a second witness?"

"Yes. Hasn't anyone told you? *You* were there on that ledge with your mother. You saw everything that happened and you were a lot closer than Clarita. But you were too terrified to talk. Gavin says you were speechless for quite a while after what happened. Your father was away that day, and it was Gavin who found you crying your heart out, and he brought you back to the house. Everyone else was too busy with the tragedy to think about you until you could be taken to Grandfather. All that part I saw, because Gavin brought me along too. Oh, he could be kind enough in those days. Not the way he is now."

Because I was shivering and the breeze felt cold, I moved back from the window.

"You came to my room for some reason?" I asked, knowing how stiff I sounded.

"Yes, of course. And I've told you what I came to tell you. Now you know everything that happened, so you can go back to New York and not worry Grandfather any more."

She turned from me with a light flick of her fingers that dismissed me, and went out of the room. Whatever malice she'd intended had been accomplished. I didn't want to look out that window again. I closed my door against further unwelcome guests and threw myself upon the bed. Eleanor wanted me gone, and that was why she had told me. But I couldn't accept her story. I still rebelled against the published version of what had happened, yet I had only my own instinct about my mother to guide me. Even my father had believed the worst of her. Only I, who knew her so little, believed in her. I flung an arm across my eyes to shut out the bright Santa Fe light.

I had seen what happened. I had seen it all—and I knew and remembered nothing. Or perhaps some instinct in me still remembered the truth and this was why my belief seemed unshakable, so that I had to stay and uncover the past.

VIII

I must have fallen asleep, for when I awakened it was nearly time for lunch. Something hard lay on the bed beneath my hand and I saw it was the book by Paul Stewart. I sat up and stared at the back jacket, where a photograph of the author had been used.

The picture must have been taken years ago, for he looked youthfully handsome and more like a faun than ever. His sharp-featured face with those pale eyes gazed out at the world with an expression that seemed to invite danger. He was hardly the ivory tower writer, but looked like a man who enjoyed living, and who might court danger for the sheer satisfaction of defeating it. Only a few years before this picture was taken, he had—as he'd told me himself—been in love with Doroteo Austin. Yet he had married Sylvia. And now he chose to bring to life the circumstances under which Sylvia's stepbrother had died, and which his wife opposed having resurrected. Besides all this, some relationship seemed to exist between Sylvia's husband and Gavin's wife. Eleanor too seemed to be stirring something up, and I had again a feeling that the past hung over the present, dangerously imminent and involving all of us. Perhaps involving me especially, because of whatever lay buried in the memory of the child I had been.

I was sharply aware of the window that looked down upon the arroyo and drew me toward it with invisible threads. There was something down there which compelled me, and inevitably I would have to obey the summons. But not now. Not yet. Nevertheless, I went to the window and looked out.

At once my attention was fixed on the patio below. Near the gate which joined the Cordova and Stewart properties, Paul and Eleanor stood talking. They were in open view and there was no reason why they should not be there, yet there was something that suggested the clandestine in their interest in each other, in their whispered conversation. If I'd had to title the picture they made, I'd have called it *The Plotters,* and I wondered why that impression was so strong.

A memory flashed into my mind of Paul as I had seen him today in the store with the *disciplina*—that three-pronged whip of the Penitentes—in his hand. He had startled me unpleasantly then, and it wasn't hard to imagine his using the whip. Though not, I thought, on himself.

As I watched, Paul turned from Eleanor and disappeared through the gate to his own house. She, with a small, secret smile on her lips, ran across the patio to the garage, out of my view. As I stood there, I heard a car start, heard it move out of the garage and down the road.

Beyond patio and wall the path Eleanor had pointed out led along the hillside above the arroyo. Abruptly I faced my room. I was not yet ready to deal with what awaited me down there. Before I answered that summons, I wanted to talk to Clarita. Both Juan and Eleanor had told me she'd seen what happened, but I wanted to hear it from her own lips. I wanted to watch her face and listen to the tone of her voice when she told me.

When I was ready for lunch I went downstairs apprehensively. I wasn't anxious to face Eleanor again so soon, or for that matter, any of the rest of the family.

However, neither Eleanor nor Gavin was there, and only Clarita sat at the head of the table. As I took my place, she regarded me with her curiously intent look, though her words were casual enough.

"We are having only an omelet. I hope that will suit you. Often I lunch alone, and I prefer something light."

"That will be fine," I said. This was my opportunity, and I began to wonder how I might bring up my question. I knew I must move with care, since this was a subject she abhorred. Her guard must be down first, and that might be difficult to achieve.

The omelets arrived, and were made with tomatoes, green pepper and onion, lightly browned, with the edges firm. I found I was hungry and I ate with relish and relief, since the others weren't there and there need be no crosscurrents of hostility. However, nothing in my aunt's manner gave the opening I wanted, and I said nothing of what was uppermost in my mind.

Again Clarita wore her favorite black, with little concession to fashion. Only her dangling turquoise earrings gave her a touch of elegance and did not look foolish against her thin cheeks. She had the same manner of pride that characterized Juan Cordova, and which she had probably learned from him.

"You visited CORDOVA this morning?" she asked, when the omelets had been served.

"Yes. Gavin took me all around the store. There's more on those shelves than I could see in a lifetime."

Her look grew distant, remembering. "I used to know all of it. I trained the women who work on the second floor. As my father trained me. If I had been a man, Gavin would never have been put in charge over me. But my father doesn't believe in the business ability of women."

Her words carried a hint of hostility toward Juan, which I hadn't expected. For the first time I was aware that underlying her concern and care for her father, lay something else—an antagonism—that seldom surfaced.

"Surely you'd proved your worth to him in the store," I said.

"Gavin knew my worth. He always consulted me, as his father used to do before him. I had a certain influence when I worked for CORDOVA."

"Why did you stop?"

The rings on her fingers flashed blue and amber light as her hands moved about the table. "I am no longer interested in such things."

Her answer allowed of no questioning, but it seemed to hide more than it revealed. I ate in silence. We had little to talk about. But at the end of the meal she surprised me.

"I have something to show you in my room. Will you come with me?"

She rose from the table and I followed her into the long, bedroom wing and through the first door. No sun fell through the windows into Clarita's room, and it had a muted, austere look. The blanket on the narrow bed was an Indian weave in brown and white, and on the floor nearby lay a shaggy brown rug. The rest of the floor was of dark, wide boards, richly polished and bare of any covering. On the wall above the bed, Clarita had hung a row of very old *santos,* those pictures of saints that were commonly seen in the Southwest, and on a shelf were two *bultos*—saints carved in the round and also clearly old. On a table near a window, various small objects had been collected, and she waved me toward them.

"These belonged to your mother," Clarita said. "I came upon them in the storeroom and I thought they might mean something to you."

I approached the table hesitantly because of unexpectedly quickening emotion. Emotion so sudden and shattering that I didn't know how to cope with it. These were feelings long buried, yet able to rise and devastate me. For an instant the old dream-vision of a tree was sharp in my mind, and I swayed as if I were dizzy.

Clarita was watching. "Is something wrong?"

The child which had risen with such sudden passionate grief, subsided, sank below the surface, and I managed to recover my adult self.

"I'm all right," I said. But the child had frightened me.

On the table lay a pair of silver and turquoise earrings of exquisite design. Zuni work again, with the typical inlays of coral, turquoise, and jet in the form of small winged birds that must once have graced Doroteo's lovely ears. There was a long-toothed Spanish comb with a high curved back that might have held up a mantilla, and I could almost see her wearing it—gay in Spanish dress. The small prayer book fell open when I picked it up, to reveal pressed rose leaves between the pages, and I set it down with hands that were quick to tremble. Last of all was a single satin baby shoe, embroidered in pink. I picked up the shoe and my eyes filled with tears that were a release and a relief.

"Are these the only things of hers that are left?" I managed the words.

Clarita nodded. "They are a few things my mother packed away in a box when everything else of Doro's went out of the house."

"Why? Why were her things sent away?"

"Your father wanted to keep nothing of hers. And my father ordered everything to be given to charity. He wanted no reminders of her around. But Mother stole out a few things and set them aside. She said they were for you. But I had forgotten about them until now."

I couldn't stop my tears. The impact of emotion had been too great, too unexpected. Grandmother Katy had thought of me again with these small treasures that had been my mother's. Clarita stood silently by and let me weep. She offered me no sympathy, no kindly understanding, and her eyes were bleak.

When I'd dried my tears, she spoke to me without emotion. "They are for you to keep. I would not want my mother's wish to be forgotten. Here is the box she packed them in." She brought a small sandalwood case from under the table and gave it to me.

I picked up earrings, comb, prayer book, and shoe, one by one, and placed them on the nest of cotton in the box. Having wept, I felt a little steadier, less vulnerable to the frightening child that haunted me. Touching them seemed to bring Doroteo a little closer to me as an adult, and in coming closer, her demand upon me was all the greater—the demand I had put upon myself. Somehow I must talk to Clarita.

"The shoe is badly embroidered," she pointed out critically. "Doro had no skill when it came to sewing, and she would not apply herself. Our mother could teach her nothing."

All the more reason I would treasure the small shoe which she had tried awkwardly to embroider because it was for me. I closed the box. This was the moment for the next step.

"Thank you for thinking of these things, Aunt Clarita," I said. "Now I wonder if you will do something more for me?"

Though her expression did not change by a flicker, I sensed that she was immediately on guard—and I wondered all the more what secret it was that she guarded. I went on resolutely.

"Will you tell me what it was you saw that day when you stood at the window in Doroteo's room? When you saw what happened between her and Kirk?"

Clarita turned toward the door, offering me her stiff back and the heavy black coil of hair on the nape of her neck, the twinkling earrings.

"I have already told you that these things we do not discuss."

"But they are being discussed," I said gently. "My grandfather has told me that you saw what happened. And so has Eleanor. What I want—what I have a right to as Doroteo's daughter—is to hear this from you. Please tell me."

I half expected her to walk out the door and leave me standing there, rebuked, but instead she whirled toward me with a violence that left me startled. I had not thought her an emotional person.

"You might as well know that I was not fond of Doroteo. Sylvia was more a dear younger sister to me than your mother ever was. I owe nothing to you as Doro's daughter. If you have heard what happened from both my father and Eleanor, then you know all there is to know. I did not grieve when Doro died."

"But you grieved for Kirk," I said, and stood my ground.

She came close enough to put an angry hand on my arm. "I did not grieve for him! Once, long ago, Doro and I loved him when he was a young boy. And I hated your mother then because he liked her best. Later it was different. But I do not wish to talk about these things. I have suffered enough. Remember that you are the daughter of a woman who committed murder, and you have no rights in this house."

The violent emotion that shook her frightened me, but I would not step back from her touch.

"You forget something," I said. "You forget that I too saw what happened. I was there. Closer than you. Close enough to see and hear as well."

The shock of my words made her drop her hand from my arm, and step back from me. For just an instant I saw open fright in her eyes. Then her guard was up again, all emotion erased, her face as expressionless as usual, her eyes bleak, but unrevealing.

"So what did you see? What have you to reveal that would be any different from that which I saw very clearly with good eyesight?"

"Nothing," I said. "Nothing yet. But perhaps there will be a way of remembering. My grandfather has said he'd try to help me remember, if that's what I wish. Aunt Clarita, were you really in Doroteo's bedroom that day when it happened? Did you really stand at her window?"

Nothing moved in her eyes, her face. She simply walked to the door and stood aside, gesturing me through. There was nothing to do but walk past her and back to the living room. She did not follow me, and I stood in the cool, dim room, feeling shaken by a confrontation more extreme than I had expected or intended. Clarita would tell me nothing more now, but she'd already told me one thing. She had told me of her youthful disliking for my mother and her consequent lack of any liking for me.

Adobe walls were tight about me. Beyond them mountain and mesa seemed to close me in. For a little while I had to escape. I wanted to tell someone what had happened to me. Gavin, I thought. I would go downtown to the store again and see if it was possible to talk to Gavin. Yet I knew in the same breath that I would not. We hadn't ended our morning as friends. He wouldn't welcome the sight of me, and he was too closely involved with the Cordovas to listen to me with any sympathy. But I had another cousin—Sylvia Stewart. Tart of tongue though she might be, she had more honesty in her than the others, and she might be willing to listen to me as no one else would. Sylvia would be in her bookstore downtown.

I took the sandalwood box to my room, and stopped there long enough to clip on my mother's earrings. The small winged birds seemed to flutter at my earlobes, and the Zuni work matched my grandfather's gift of the brooch. When I'd picked up my handbag, I ran downstairs and went out through the front door. The little key was with me again, though when I'd have the chance to use it, I didn't know.

Perhaps I could have had the use of a car, if I'd asked, but I didn't want to speak to anyone in that house in my present mood. The central plaza downtown was no great distance and I could find my way along Canyon Road and down the Alameda.

Walking calmed me to some degree. When I reached the plaza, dreaming in cool May sunshine, with its white wrought-iron benches and its memorials—a center of quiet, while traffic moved all around—I paused before the monument trying to focus on everyday things. There was a plaque and I read the words.

TO THE HEROES WHO HAVE FALLEN IN THE BATTLE WITH
SAVAGE INDIANS IN THE TERRITORY OF NEW MEXICO

I wondered what New Mexico Indians thought of this plaque. But of course these words belonged to another century and different thinking.

I left the plaza, crossing to the long adobe building that was the Governor's Palace which now housed a museum. On the sidewalk, beneath protruding brown vigas, Indians sat against the wall, displaying turquoise and silver jewelry spread before them on squares of cloth. Passers-by stopped to examine their wares, while the Indians, both men and women, regarded them impassively, urging nothing upon them. Hunched beneath shoulder blankets, they waited for whatever might come. Both "heroes" and "savages" were gone and these Pueblo Indians regarded the rush and avarice of the Anglos with a quiet, superior wisdom. It was a scene I would like to paint.

Walking about the square, I found the street Sylvia had indicated when she drove me through town on my arrival, and I moved slowly past the windows of small shops until I came to one which displayed books. When I stepped inside, I found Sylvia busy with a customer.

Her short brown hair was slightly rumpled and she looked at me through dark-rimmed glasses, gave me a nod and a signal to wait. The shop was small, with a single window at the back, and it was crowded with bright-jacketed books. They stood in neat rows on wall shelves and were piled in orderly fashion on a central table. In an alcove there was a desk and typewriter, where her assistant was working.

I found the books by Paul Stewart easily, since his wife had given them prominent display. I found *Emanuella, The Trail of the Whip,* and several others. I was browsing through a volume on the Pueblo Indians, when the customer left, and Sylvia came over to me.

"How are things going?" she asked.

I put the book back on the shelf. "I'm not sure. I've just had rather a row with Aunt Clarita. She gave me some things that had belonged to my mother and I asked her to tell me exactly what she saw that day when my mother died."

"Did she tell you?"

"No. She seemed terribly upset and she wouldn't talk about it. I did something rather foolish. I reminded her that I'd been there too that day, and that I had seen everything that happened."

Sylvia gasped. "Do you mean you've begun to remember?"

"No—not at all. But Clarita looked positively frightened for a moment, and then she turned into stone again. I think she's hiding something."

Sylvia picked up a book and blew imaginary dust from its top a little too casually. "That's unlikely, I should think."

"I even asked her if she was really there at the window where she could see what happened."

"You *have* stirred her up! Clarita is the most underestimated member of the Cordova family. There's a lot more to her than she ever shows the world. Juan always discounted her and let her know it, yet she's held that household together and been a loving mother to Eleanor. When we were young, she was very good to me, and I'm fond of her."

"She said you were like a sister to her."

"Katy appreciated her quality of loyalty and her sense of duty, but I think she guessed too that Clarita, when she was young, had a passionate nature. There was a time when she was blindly in love with Kirk—but that changed with the years, and a good thing. Only Juan, I think, kept his affection for Kirk—perhaps because Kirk tried to pattern himself after Juan Cordova. Sometimes I found it hard to take that Kirk was more Spanish than Spain. We fought a bit because he didn't want me to marry Paul."

But it was not Kirk who interested me most at the moment. I wanted to talk about Doroteo first, and I dared a question in the face of this outpouring. "Was Paul really in love with my mother at one time, as he says?"

Sylvia shrugged a little too elaborately, and I suspected that there might be certain matters on which she too would not be altogether honest. Perhaps in self-deception?

"I think that was a little fantasy he developed while he was writing *Emanuella*—that he had once been in love with Doro. All the way through writing that book he admittedly saw Doro in Emanuella. But it hadn't any reality in fact, as far as I know."

Her voice had turned a little hard, and when a customer came into the shop, she hurried from me, as though relieved to end our conversation. She hadn't, after all, been a satisfactory person to talk to. The interplay of all those emotions which had dogged the Cordovas and those involved with them was a complex thing.

While she was busy, I stepped to a rear window and looked through glass upon an unexpectedly pleasant vista. The building which housed Sylvia's shop ran around the hollow square of a large patio. There were trees and shrubbery growing there, and brick walks crossed one another. On a stone bench near the center, Paul Stewart sat writing in a notebook.

He was not a man whose company I enjoyed, and I hadn't liked the way he wanted to study me, extract from me those buried memories. I'd wondered besides about his relationship with Eleanor. But now there were things he could tell me, and I might do a little extracting myself.

Back in the shop's alcove was a door to the courtyard. "May I go outside?" I asked Sylvia.

She nodded and I went through the door. There was the pungent scent of juniper warming in the sun, and snowball bushes displaying their white puffs. Iris grew along a walk and birds sang in this quiet place where traffic sounds were muffled and distant, and a blue sky arched overhead. Running part way about the hollow of the patio was a sheltered walk, with a wooden gallery overhead, and offices and shops opening off it. Again I had a sense of enclosure, of a place that tried to shut out the world. A Spanish family had once lived here, treasuring privacy, turning its back on all that lay outside. But increasingly, I didn't like being shut in.

I walked toward Paul, my footsteps echoing on brick, and he looked up at me, smiling, though his eyes appraised and questioned.

"Am I interrupting?" I asked, glancing at the notebook.

He flipped it closed. "Not at all. I needed to get away from my typewriter and do some thinking. Have you been visiting Sylvia's shop?"

"Yes. I've even been looking at some of your books. Is there one you can especially recommend?"

"I only know what the critics tell me. I'm a masterful writer to some, too fanciful in my nonfiction for others. Of course, I'm half fiction writer deliberately. I let my imagination go with *Emanuella*. It's really a novel."

"Your wife says you had my mother in mind when you were writing that book. What was Doro like?"

He answered with a slight edge to his voice. "She was unforgettable. Beautiful, and a little wild. Perverse, tantalizing. Mercurial. All the things Emanuella must have been. Are you any of these things, Amanda Austin?"

I shook my head, smiling back at him, though it was as if we dueled, and I thought once more of a faun with all its whimsicality and mischief-making ability.

"What you're describing sounds like my cousin Eleanor."

"Possibly. But Eleanor is her own woman."

"And I think my mother was not very much like her."

"Have they told you yet?"

I knew what he meant. "That I was there when it happened? Yes, Eleanor took care of that."

"I made her see that she must. You couldn't really

begin to remember until you knew that. Now it will surface. Will you tell me what you discover?"

I didn't think I would, but I evaded a direct reply, because I wanted him to answer me.

"You've told me a little about my mother. What was Kirk Landers like?"

He seemed to answer carefully. "Women thought him pretty dashing, and he enjoyed that. He wanted to masquerade as a Spanish *caballero,* a young Spanish don. I can't say I cared for him."

"Sylvia says he didn't want her to marry you."

"He had a prejudice against me. I'm not sure why. I think Juan sent him off with a bribe to get him away from Doroteo until they both grew up, and then Doro married your father—which didn't please Juan very much. Of course when Kirk came home, his nose was pretty much out of joint, with Doro married, and Clarita no longer looking at him in adoration."

Paul fingered the hinges of his notebook and his smile had a secret look, as though he glimpsed a joke he didn't mean to tell me. When he looked up, there was speculation in his eyes.

"In any case, Amanda, there's a way to help you remember, if you'll let me try."

I didn't trust him at all, but I was curious to know what he meant. When I merely waited, he flipped open his notebook again.

"I've been sitting here jotting down bits and pieces out of my memory, trying to reconstruct what happened, and recall where everyone was at the time. But I'm not getting anything significant. I've thought of going back to the actual place where the picnic was held, to see what might return to my mind. Will you come with me?"

Even though he took me by surprise, I didn't hesitate. There were things this might tell me, and I already knew I had a rendezvous with that particular spot.

"When?" I said.

"What better time than now? My car's outside, and we can drive there directly. Unless someone looks out

of that high window, no one at the Cordovas' needs to
know we're there."

"All right," I said. "Let's go back through Sylvia's
shop. I'd like to tell her what we plan to do."

He seemed to hesitate, as though he'd rather have
gone directly through the archway to the street. Then he
came with me as I started across the patio.

The shop was empty of customers, and Sylvia was un-
packing a carton of brightly jacketed books. Her eyes
went to Paul's face, and in that look I knew how much
he meant to her.

"We're going to see what we can resurrect from the
past," he told her. "We're going back to the picnic
place to see what we can learn."

That odd, dancing light was in his eyes again, and
Sylvia looked her alarm, as though this was something
she feared. However, she offered no objection. Perhaps
she knew objecting would do no good. She went quickly
to a small artificial tree set on a counter and hung with
tiny squares. From it she selected one and brought it
to me.

"You must have an *Ojo de Dios*. To protect you
against evil."

Her tone was light, but I sensed meaning beneath the
surface, as though she was warning me. The piece I
took from her was hardly an inch square, made of two
crossed sticks, wound about with strands of colored yarn
to form a pattern in red and green and white. In the
center was a spot of black.

"What is it?" I asked.

She seemed anxious to hold me there talking, and she
explained in detail, while Paul moved restlessly about the
shop, examining book titles.

"The Zapotec Indians make one of these for every
child at his birth. They cross two twigs and wind yarn
about them, beginning at the center—for the years of
a child's life. There are bright colors and dark, for the
gay and the sad. The years go very quickly there at
the beginning, but they grow longer and slower at the

outer edge. They used to hang one on the wall to re-
present all the years of a life. Nowadays they're regarded
as good luck charms against evil spirits. That black
spot in the center is the Eye of God—the *Ojo de Dios*.
Put it in your bag and keep it with you."

I saw now that above a bank of bookshelves hung
a row of larger squares of the same sort, made of various
colored yarns. I thanked her and dropped the little token
into my bag, but somehow I felt uneasy. Why should
she warn me against Paul? She stood close to me, watching, and she said something odd for a woman who
seemed as practical-minded as Sylvia.

"That's an evil place he's taking you to. I wish you
wouldn't go."

Paul heard her and laughed. "There's no such thing
as an evil place. There are only evil people."

"Not my mother," I said.

He smiled at me and that strange gleam was back in
his eyes. "No, not your mother. Perhaps she was reckless and wild, but not truly evil."

"Kirk was reckless too," Sylvia said quickly, "but he
wasn't evil either. In spite of everything."

"Then that leaves no one who was evil." Paul seemed
to challenge her.

For an instant there was fright in Sylvia. I could
sense it in her tightened lips, in the look she gave him.
Then she reached out to touch my arm.

"Don't let him torment you with all this. Let what's
gone be forgotten."

"Come along, Amanda," Paul said curtly, and the
look he threw his wife was not one of affection.

But I had ceased to pay attention. I'd known all
along that the arroyo would summon me, and the moment was here. This was what I must do.

😈😈😈😈😈😈😈😈😈😈😈😈😈😈😈😈😈😈😈😈😈

IX

We drove back to the Stewarts' garage, and on the way Paul had little to say. I was aware of the occasional glance he turned in my direction, aware again of something in him that probed and searched. For what? What compulsion drove him that he *had* to know about the past?

From the house we went on foot, and he led the way out to the rear where the hillside curve followed above the arroyo. He pointed out that there were other ways to reach the picnic place from above, but this diagonal path which ran behind the Cordova wall was quicker.

"It's the path you and your mother took that day when she was hurrying to meet Kirk," he said.

His will was pressing upon me, exerting a force that I had to resist. If I wasn't careful, he would make me "remember" something that had never been.

"How do you know that Doroteo went out to meet Kirk?" I asked.

"They think she'd taken Mark Brand's gun from his room. She must have had it with her. She must have known she would meet him."

I shivered in warm sunlight, and let him lead the

way. The path we followed meant nothing to me. There seemed no memory here. Cottonwoods and poplars grew thickly above the dry arroyo, where water would sometimes rush furiously, coming down in a spill from the mountains. There were the usual clumps of chamiso and juniper. We came quickly upon the open space beneath a cottonwood tree, and stood in its shadow, looking around.

Paul's hand was on my arm, its pressure light, but somehow compelling. "This is where they used to picnic. Can you remember it? Can you remember anything?"

I could only shake my head. The place was strange to me. It was not familiar as the mesa country seemed beyond Santa Fe. Perhaps something in me, always on guard, had buried the memory of this hillside so deep in my consciousness that it was forever blocked from rising.

A steep, rocky path led from the clearing to the ledge below—a ledge that was out of sight of the picnic place because of the brush. Paul led the way again, and I followed him, my sandals slipping on the rough earth as we went down. The ledge below gave way in turn to a steep bank sloping to the bottom of the arroyo, and as I reached it something in me quivered—and was still. For an instant, memory had fluttered, only to be rejected by whatever it was that stood so relentlessly on guard.

How quiet everything seemed. There was no noise of blasting now, but only a faint whispering as breezes touched the treetops and wild shrubbery. I was aware —as though I stood on some dangerous verge—but I was still untouched.

"This is where it happened," Paul said softly.

Stepping to the edge of the steep bank, I looked down, and now I was shivering and a little sick. This was not because I remembered, but only because of all I'd been told of what had happened here. I turned about slowly, my eyes searching the nearer ground, and then seeking what lay farther off.

Up the hillside I could see adobe walls that surrounded

the Cordova house, and I could see that one high room which had been my mother's, standing up above the lower roofs. I could see the window from which Clarita had looked that day—the window of what was now my room. Hillside and house and window were all as they had been long ago. Only I was not the same. I had been a small child then. I was a woman now. A woman who could remember—nothing.

As I stared at the window, something moved beyond the glass, and I knew someone was watching us. But the light was wrong and I couldn't see who it was. It didn't matter. Let them worry that I had come here, if they chose.

Paul no longer touched my arm, and he had stepped back a little to let me be alone. I turned toward him and saw that pale yellow-green of his eyes, felt the pressure his will once more exerted upon me.

"Tell me what you're thinking," he said. "Tell me what you see."

"I don't see anything except what's here. It all seems strange to me."

He was watching me closely. "Let me remind you. Your grandmother Katy and Gavin were in the clearing above when it happened. Eleanor was with them. She was about ten at that time. Two or three neighbors had joined them. Juan was at home because he never liked picnics and he wasn't well that day. Clarita wasn't feeling well either, and she was lying down in Doro's room, which was more airy than her room downstairs. At least that's the story she tells. Sylvia and I were just leaving the house. We came along the lower path, and Kirk must have been waiting for Doro right here when she arrived. Doesn't any of this come back to you?"

Nothing did. There had been only that quiver of memory when I'd looked down into the arroyo, but it was nothing clear that I could recognize and account for. Paul Stewart's presence disturbed and distracted me. How could I remember anything with that intense demand he put upon me?

"Why does it matter so much to you for me to remember?" I asked. "A child's recollections can't mean anything. Not in so young a child."

"I'd like something fresh for this section of my book, of course," he told me. "But if you can't remember, you can't."

"Perhaps it would help if I could stay here alone for a little while," I said.

"If you like. I'll go back to my typewriter. You know the way home." He was almost curt now—as though he had satisfied himself about something and had no further use for me.

I nodded and he went back along the hillside by the way we had come. Immediately, I was closed in by a pocket of silence. City sounds were far away, and few cars came along the quiet lane above.

What had it been like to be five years old on that long ago day and stand here on this hillside with my mother? What had I seen and heard? Surely I must have been terrified, shattered, hysterical. Yet there was no emotion in me except for that which conscious knowledge provided. This was the place where my mother had died. She had fallen down this steep bank into the arroyo, and the fall had killed her. But first she had deliberately raised the gun she'd brought with her and had shot Kirk Landers.

No! There was something wrong. Something I could not believe in what I'd been told. Since this ledge where they had stood revealed nothing to me, I climbed back to the clearing, and this time I faced the cottonwood tree that I had only walked beneath before. At once a piercing, terrifying sense of recognition flashed through me. This was the tree of my nightmare. It was tall and spreading and thickly leaved, its branches gnarled with age. It commanded the hillside and it must have seemed a giant to the little girl I had been.

Nearby stood a weathered wooden bench, probably left by those former picnickers, and I sat down on it abruptly because my knees were trembling. This was where I must have sat as a child, facing the tree. I had stared at it in my desperate state until I saw it above all else, and it had marked me with a haunting—the symbol of something terrible that a young mind had washed away.

This was the beginning of memory and I was frightened. The tree of my dream was centered in some mirage of horror and I could feel the misty visions sweeping back upon me in waves of vertigo. I put my head down upon my knees and let the dizziness wash over me. My handbag was under my cheek, and I could feel in it the shape of the sketchbook I took with me everywhere. Let me exorcise the tree by drawing it, I thought. Let me register its reality so that I would not dream of it in terror ever again.

As I reached into my bag the little "Eye of God" Sylvia had given me came to my fingers. I held it for a moment, half smiling. Let its spell against evil work now, if ever it did.

Then, with my pencil in hand, and the sketchbook open on my knees, I began to draw, shaping the gnarled form of the tree—the trunk and the branches, the foliage that had seemed to reach out to smother me in my dream. The drawing that took shape on paper was more like my nightmare than was the real tree. Its limbs seemed to writhe as if with eerie motion, its leaves appeared to flutter in a raging wind.

I closed my eyes to shut out the horror that seemed embodied in what I had drawn, and at once there was new motion before my eyes. Shadowy figures struggled and fought each other for their lives, and horror had a color—the color of scarlet, of blood. But nothing was clear. There was no real remembering.

Sounds reached me from the path above. Someone was coming down from the direction of the road. Someone real in a real world. I could not bear it if Paul had come back. He must not see me like this—on the verge of dreadful discovery, my hands wet with perspiration, so that the pencil was slippery in my fingers,

and my mouth was dry. I opened my eyes reluctantly
and looked at the man who stood before my bench. It
was Gavin Brand.

He must have seen terror in my face. Quietly he sat
beside me on the bench and looked at my open sketchbook.

"You've caught more than the image of a tree," he
said. "You've caught the spirit of it. When I was a small
boy, I used to think that some trees were alive, as men
were alive. I used to think there were trees that could
menace me."

I began to breathe in deeply, steadying myself. "I
remember this tree," I said. "Sometimes I've dreamed
about it in a nightmare. It's a dream I've had all my
life."

"I can understand its haunting you. I was here, you
know. I brought you up from the ledge below and got
you to sit on this bench for a while. I had to leave you
because there was need for help. I climbed down into
the arroyo with Paul Stewart and helped to bring your
mother up. Nothing could be done for Kirk. When I
came back, the way you looked frightened me. You'd
stopped crying, and you were sitting there staring at that
tree with a fixed look that was hard to break."

"I must have imprinted it on my memory, while I
wiped out everything else."

"It's likely. Katy was concerned about you, but she
was trying to see to what must be done, and carry on in
spite of her own shock. She asked me to take you and
Eleanor back to the house."

I could say nothing. He was telling me the whole
terrible story, and it left me shaken—though I could
not feel that I'd been there. Gently he reached out and
took one of my damp hands into his.

"This is the way I held your hand that day. You
clung to me and didn't want to let me go. When you
went to sleep that night, you wanted me to sit beside
your bed for a while. You were so young and frightened,
and I suppose I was frightened too. I'd never come up

against violent death before. Something pretty ghastly
had happened to people I knew. I'd always liked Doro.
She was gay and a bit frivolous, I suppose, but she was
kind, too. She never hurt anyone."

He broke off with an exclamation, staring at me.

"Those earrings you're wearing! Your grandfather gave
them to her. She had them on the day she died. I remember those little birds at her earlobes when we brought
her up from the arroyo."

His hand about my own steadied me, comforted me.
I reached up with my free hand and touched coral and
turquoise. But I did not pull the clips from my ears.
They made me feel as though I were coming closer
to Doroteo.

"Thank you for telling me all this," I said. "I don't
remember, really. Perhaps I don't want to remember.
But sometimes the curtain lifts a little and when it does
I feel dizzy and terrified. Yet I've got to face it. I must remember. I know that I saw someone struggling, but I
don't know for certain that it was my mother and Kirk."

"It must have been," he said. "There was no one else
there."

I tried to steady myself, tried to thrust terror away and
return to a real and present world.

"How did you happen to find me here just now?"

"I was looking for you. I went up to your room, and
when you weren't there, I looked out your window and
saw you here with Paul. I didn't like that. You should
stay away from him. He means nothing but mischief.
So I came along by the upper road."

I drew my hand from his and wiped it with my handkerchief. It was good to be looked after for a while, but
I couldn't let him dictate to me whether or not I would
see Paul Stewart. If Paul was on my road to discovery,
then I would of course see him.

"Why were you looking for me?" I asked.

A slight smile touched his somber face. "A guilty
conscience, perhaps. I've been thinking over some of
the things I said to you this morning. I was too harsh and

I felt it might be in order to tell you I was sorry. Since I had to come back to the house from work to see Juan, I looked for you."

"You were fair enough," I said. "If you thought Juan was going to use me in some way against Eleanor, you'd have to protect her."

He said nothing, and there was silence between us. I was feeling calmer, and somehow safer. Once, when I had been a child, Gavin had protected me, and now I had again a feeling of security in being with him. Since he wasn't being harsh and critical, I could relax and let down my guard. Perhaps he was the one who could help me.

"Will you take me to the *rancho?*" I said.

"The *Rancho de Cordova?*" He was surprised.

I told him then about the message from Katy and the small package she had left for me with Sylvia. I had no idea what I must search for at the *rancho,* but sooner or later I must go there, and perhaps it would be best if Gavin could take me, rather than one of the others.

He didn't hesitate. "I'll stop at the house and phone the store. Then we'll go out there. I don't know what you can hope to find, but I'll take you, if you wish. Katy must have had some intent in mind. She was a wonderfully sane and sensible person."

I closed my sketchbook upon the nightmarish drawing of the cottonwood tree, and stood up, turning my back on the real tree.

"Thank you. I feel better now. I'm ready to go."

He nodded his approval, and I thought how kind he could be when he was not condemning me.

We took the short-cut path along the hillside to the back gate of the Cordova house, and there were no more twinges of memory to trouble me. Inside, Clarita was not about. I waited in the living room while Gavin made his call, and then we went out to his car and drove away from Canyon Road.

The highway led south out of the city, in the direction of Albuquerque, but in a little while we turned off on

a road that led toward Los Cerrillos, The Little Hills.
Again there was empty country and straight roads. I
settled back in the seat and let the wind from the open
window blow in my face. After my experience in the
clearing, I wanted only to be quiet for a little while
and renew my forces. Gavin seemed to understand and
there was no idle conversation between us on the half-
hour drive away from Santa Fe.

I was almost drowsing when Gavin spoke to me.
"There's the hacienda ahead—the *Rancho de Cordova*.
Most of the land has been sold and it's not what it was
in the old days when Juan's father was alive."

Juan's father—my great-grandfather, I thought.

He pulled the car up to a curb before a long, low
adobe building. Francisco and Maria, the couple Juan
had placed in charge of the hacienda, came to the door
to welcome us. They knew Gavin, of course, but had
come here since Doroteo's day, so they did not remember
my mother. They greeted me warmly, however, as a
granddaughter of Juan Cordova.

We stepped into the dim, cool *sala,* where strings of
chili and Indian corn hung from the vigas, and the
furniture was dark and shabby and old. Gavin explained
that I wanted to see the place and asked permission
to show me around.

"Está bien," Maria said, with a wave of her hand,
offering me the house.

As we stood at a window, looking out into an empty
courtyard, he told me a little about what the *rancho* had
once meant to the countryside.

"There was always fighting in the early days. And when
the Pueblo Indians attacked Santa Fe, most of the
Spaniards in the area were killed. Settlers out here came
to the *rancho* for protection. Later, when the Spaniards
were gone, Union troops sheltered here when they were
fighting Rebel forces."

I looked out at the empty courtyard of bare earth,
baking dry and cracked beneath the sun. A long *portal*

with wooden pillars stretched along one side of the open space, and at the back was a building of adobe bricks.

"Once that was an army barracks," Gavin said.

I could look out and see phantom horses and men stirring the dust, see my great-grandfather moving among them with that pride of bearing that Juan Cordova, his son, would also carry. New England's chill rocks seemed very far away, and I knew that I belonged to this place of sun and dust as well.

"It sleeps now," Gavin said. "Few of us come here to visit. But when Clarita and Rafael and Doroteo and Sylvia were young, it was never quiet."

"And Kirk?" I said.

"Yes, of course. I only remember him after the time when he came back—just a little while before his death. I suppose I knew him when I was a child, but I have only a vague memory of him as rather wild and dashing— dramatic. I was younger than the others, and I was only a small boy when they all used to come out here. I've been told that Doro was a great rider, though a little reckless. She and Kirk used to ride together. Eleanor and I rode too, when we came out here as children. But all that's gone. Juan keeps no horses here now."

We turned from the sunlight of the empty courtyard and Gavin led the way into the long, shadowy house and down a corridor, off which many rooms opened.

"I don't know what to look for that might be unlocked by so small a key," Gavin said. "Will you let me see it?"

I took the ring box from my bag and sprang the catch. The little key was tucked into its satin nest.

"Perhaps a jewel case," I said.

He nodded. "We might as well begin here—with what used to be your mother's room."

I stepped across the sill and looked about. The room was empty of belongings, impersonal. Dust covers had been thrown over the bed and there were no rugs on the floor, or pictures on the wall. All traces of Doroteo Austin had long been removed.

Moving about the room, I opened empty drawers and examined the graceful rosewood desk. In only one drawer did I find something that brought a flicker of recognition. It was a glass paperweight and when I picked it up snowflakes flew over mountains that resembled the Sangre de Cristos, and over the twin church towers of St. Francis.

"I believe I used to play with this when I was little," I said. "Do you suppose anyone would mind if I keep it?"

"I'm sure not." Gavin's tone was kind.

He seemed a different man from the one I'd toured the store with this morning. For some reason I didn't wholly understand, he appeared to have accepted me without the rancor and suspicion he had harbored toward me earlier. In the same way my own resentment toward him had faded because he had indeed become the friend I'd needed. With a new, quiet assurance I felt I could talk to him when the time came—and he would listen. Such knowledge brought with it a warmth that was comforting.

Since there was nothing here in my mother's room that could be unlocked by a tiny key, we went on to the next door, which Gavin opened for me.

"This was your grandmother Katy's room whenever she came to the *rancho*."

I stepped past him eagerly and came to a shocked halt. Someone had been here ahead of us. As though one of those whirlwinds had struck it, everything in the room had been stirred about in great haste and without any effort to replace the things which had been moved. The room was still furnished, and little effort had been made to dispose of the possessions of the woman who had once occupied it. What was here had been thoroughly disturbed.

Drawers were turned out, their contents left on table or floor. Boxes in a closet had been unpacked, and even the bed had been stripped. While I stood looking about in astonishment, Gavin summoned Maria. She came quickly to look past us into the room, exclaiming aloud.

"But only yesterday I cleaned in here, Señor Brand. Everything was in order, nothing like this!"

"Have you had any visitors at the *rancho* since then?" Gavin asked.

The woman shook her head vehemently, then paused, looking around for her husband. When he came down the hall she spoke to him in voluble Spanish. He nodded, seemed to agree about something and then shrugged eloquently.

Gavin explained for my benefit. "Earlier this afternoon, a little while before we arrived, Francisco heard a sound in this part of the house. When he came into the hall to investigate, he saw nothing. The doors were closed, and all was quiet, so he didn't look into any of the rooms, believing he must have been mistaken. Now he remembers that a little later he heard a car moving away from the hacienda. But when he went to look out a window it was already well in the distance and he couldn't recognize it."

Maria started into the room, greatly distressed and anxious to tidy everything up. I stopped her quickly.

"Please," I said. "Can you let it be for now? I would like to look at some of these things myself before you put them away."

She glanced at Gavin for his consent and then gave me a troubled nod before she went out of the room.

My efforts were desultory. In such confusion, I didn't know where to begin. I found myself picking up a sewing box that had been my grandmother's, poking in among scissors and spools, before I set it down and turned to something else. Nothing I touched required a small brass key to open it. In neither room had I found a jewel case. Nevertheless, I kept on halfheartedly, knowing that someone had been here ahead of me, and that probably whatever could be unlocked by such a key was already gone. My hands moved almost absently among Katy's things, but my mind was busy.

"As far as I know," I told Gavin, "only three people knew about this. Sylvia gave me the envelope sealed, but perhaps she could have opened it in the past and sealed it up again. And I told Clarita and Juan. No one else, until I told you."

"If Sylvia knew, Paul could have known too."

"Yes, and Eleanor, I suppose. But then why wouldn't one or the other of them have investigated here at the *rancho* sooner?"

"Perhaps nothing became crucial until the key was put in your hands."

Most likely, it was Clarita who had come here, I thought. But I let the matter go and went on with my fruitless search.

A large cardboard box had been half emptied, and when I poked through the contents which had been dumped on the floor, I came upon a Mexican costume that a man might have worn. I held up the tight trousers of dark blue suede, trimmed with silver buttons down the sides, and started to pick up the embroidered, braid-trimmed jacket, when Gavin took the things from me without ceremony.

"You don't want these," he said, and thrust them away on the high shelf of a huge armoire.

I wondered at the abrupt removal, but I was emptying out the rest of the box and my attention was distracted. Something made of wood, like a hollowed bowl, fell out and skittered across the floor. I reached to pick it up, turned it over in my hands—and without warning was caught by a wave of cold terror that washed through my fingertips.

What I held in my hands was a carved wooden mask, and I could only stare at it in a frozen state of shock. The entire face had been painted a smoky shade of blue, with the features outlined with great skill in silver and turquoise inlays. The eyebrows were curves of tiny turquoise stones above the eyes outlined with turquoise and silver. The nostrils were silver slits, but it was the mouth that was most arresting. It was in the shape of an oval—the open shape of a scream—and again the outline was done in silver and turquoise. Staring at the blue face, I could feel my own mouth round to that screaming shape and it was all I could do to suppress the sound that surged in my throat.

From across the room Gavin saw and came to me at once.

"What's the matter, Amanda? What's happened?"

When I couldn't answer at once, he took me by the shoulders and held me gently, and I saw warmth in his eyes and sympathy. "Something's frightened you again."

"Yes!" I held up the mask with hands that shook. "It's—like the tree. I've seen this before and it's part of the nightmare— it's connected with that time."

Gavin took the blue mask from me and examined it. "I've seen this before too—when I was small. Long before your mother died. It seems to me—yes, it used to hang on a wall here at the hacienda. I can remember the very place out in the *sala*."

"But how can *I* remember it?"

"Don't try," he said, and I had the feeling that he knew more about the mask than he was telling me.

I paid no attention to his warning. I *had* to remember, and I took the mask back from him, studying it, forcing myself to meet its evil, slitted gaze.

The mouth seemed to shout at me from the blue face, crying out in some silent agony that matched my own. Whoever had created this mask had meant it to agonize, and I could agonize with it.

"I can't remember," I said. "It's just that I have a terrible sense of horror and danger. But I know it has something to tell me."

A smaller cardboard box lay on the bed, with a leather book in it. He dumped out the book and put the mask in the box, closed the lid over that dreadful blue face.

"There—it's out of your sight for now."

I reached for the box. "I'll take it back to the house with me. There's something about it I've got to remember."

"All right," he said. "If you must. And now—here's the brass lock for your key."

He picked up the leather book that had fallen on the bed and held it out to me. I saw at once that it had a brass hasp with a small lock in it. Without ever taking the key from my bag, I knew it would fit. But there was no need. One end of the hasp had been ripped from the leather, and the book was no longer locked.

"It must be a diary," I said as I took it from him.

When I raised the leather cover and looked at the flyleaf, I found Katy Cordova's name written there in the same strong script I had seen in the letter she'd sent my father. The year of the diary was the year of my mother's death.

As I flipped through them I found the pages thick with that same writing. Here was the answer Katy had left for me. Here was the answer to everything.

A little feverishly, I turned the pages, reading dates, looking for the month of my mother's death—which was this very month of May, though I didn't know the date. When I came to the passage about the picnic, I began to read eagerly, forgetting Gavin, forgetting the room about me. Yes, she had written of her plans for the day—she had set down the names of those who would come. My eyes skimmed as I turned the pages and came abruptly, shockingly, to the end of the diary. Only a core of torn edges remained at the central binding. Whatever else Katy had written for that time and the rest of the year had been ripped from the book.

I held out the leather volume to Gavin. "She was writing about the picnic. She must have written about what happened—but it's all gone, torn out. Someone came here—probably today—and tore out these pages. Someone who is frightened."

Gavin took the book from me and stared at the rough edges where only a word or two of script remained. "It looks as if you're right. But don't count too much on what was written here, Amanda."

"I'm counting on it—I am! Those pages have to be found."

"If there's anything revealing in them, they've been destroyed by now."

Limp with disappointment, I sat down on the bed. Now what was I to do? Where was I to turn?

"Perhaps we'd better go back to town," Gavin said. "I've put off an appointment until late afternoon, but I do need to be back for it. And I think this is all we can do here."

I agreed, my thoughts rushing ahead. "Yes—I'll go back now. I'll talk to Grandfather. I'll show him the mask and the diary. If I can only get him to believe what I believe, perhaps he can help me."

"What do you believe?" Gavin asked gently.

"That my mother didn't kill anyone. And perhaps she didn't fall by intent down the bank. Perhaps someone pushed her because she witnessed what happened."

Gavin shook his head at me regretfully. "I'm afraid you're fantasizing. You're hoping for too much."

I snatched the diary indignantly back from him. "This is the evidence! Katy wanted me to know. She felt I had a right to know."

"To know what? Don't you think that if your grandmother had known that Doro was innocent she would have cried it from the hilltops? I remember Katy. I remember her courage. And I remember how much she loved your mother."

"She might not if the truth would injure someone else she loved. She might figure that it was better to save the living than to exonerate the dead. But she still wanted *me* to know."

"Come along," Gavin said. "We'll turn this mess over to Maria and get back to town."

We told Maria and Francisco *Hasta la vista* and I went with him. I knew he was growing impatient with me, but I didn't care. I was on my own headlong course, and I didn't mean to let anything stop me.

X

When Gavin left me at the house and drove back to the store, I went at once to Juan Cordova's study, taking with me the box that contained the mask and the diary. Clarita was not about to interfere, and his door was open.

"Come in," he called when I appeared.

I placed the box on his desk. "Here's something I want you to see."

He did not look at the box because as I came close he was staring at me. "Where did you get those earrings?"

"Clarita gave them to me. They belonged to my mother. Gavin says you gave them to her."

"Take them off!" he said harshly. "Take them off!"

I understood his pain and I slipped off the Zuni birds, dropped them into my handbag. Then without preliminary I reached into the box and drew out the mask, to place it before him. This time I knew what to expect, and I felt less of a tendency to panic with terror at the sight of it.

"Do you know anything about this?" I asked.

For an instant, the sight of the mask seemed to bring him some unwanted memory, and a grimace of pain crossed his face. But he thrust it aside and picked up the mask, examining its detail with his fingers.

"I've wondered what happened to this. An Indian friend made it for me long ago when the children were young. They were always fascinated by it, and we used to keep it on a wall out at the *rancho*. This is particularly fine work, though of course not traditional. It was made for no ceremony, but because my friend was an artist and wanted to create something original. Where did you find it?"

"In Katy's room at the *rancho*," I said. "Gavin drove me out there because of the message she left me. When I found this, I recognized it."

There was no change of expression in that face that reminded me of a falcon. He merely repeated my words. "Recognized it?"

"I don't know why I know it, but I do. And it frightens me. I thought perhaps you could tell me why."

"Why should it frighten you? You must have seen it on the wall at the hacienda when you were small, but as far as I know, you never had any fear of it. Our own children used to play with it sometimes when they they were little—even though it was forbidden. I didn't want a work of art damaged, but you'll find a few nicks in the wood and in the blue paint, as well as a stone or two missing. I can remember one day when I caught Kirk Landers leaping around with it on his face. In those days he had a gift for pantomime, and he could be very amusing." Juan sighed deeply.

None of this meant anything to me.

"I went down to the arroyo," I told him. "Paul Stewart took me there. He thought I might remember something if I saw the place where—where it happened."

"And did you?"

"Only the cottonwood tree. I can remember that. Everything else seems wiped away. Why did Grandmother Katy choose that place for a picnic anyway? Why not eat outdoors more comfortably in your own patio?"

"The walls—she wanted to escape the walls out on the open hillside."

"I've felt that way too—a little," I admitted. "But now I want to remember about that place. You told me you'd try to help me. When will you begin?"

His smile was meant to be kind, but it seemed a little fierce. "Why not now? Sit down, Amanda, and relax. You're wound up with tension."

I put the mask back in the box. Later I would show him the diary. "If you don't mind, I'd like to keep the mask for a while. Perhaps it will encourage something to come back to me."

"You may keep it for now," he said.

I sat in the chair opposite him and waited. For a moment or two he seemed lost in his own faraway thoughts and there was a sadness in the downward droop of his mouth. He closed his eyes, and when he began to speak he did not open them.

"As you may know, I didn't go to the picnic that day. When Gavin brought you back to the house, Katy had already come to tell me what had happened. I had been ill and she wouldn't let me go out to that place afterwards, though she had to go back. I sat here in this room and grieved because I had lost my daughter under terrible circumstances and lost a foster son as well. Gavin brought you to me here. You were white-faced and no longer crying, though your cheeks were streaked with tearstains. You sat on my knee and leaned your head above my heart and we tried to comfort each other. Do you remember any of this?"

I closed my eyes, like Juan, and tried to seek out memory. Could I recall strong arms about me, a strong, adult heart beating under my cheek? The vision seemed very real, but I didn't know if this was memory.

"After a while you began to babble a little. You said your mother had fallen and someone was covered with blood. I held you and tried to talk to you. I told you your mother would never have willingly hurt anyone, but she must have been maddened by anger with Kirk."

I opened my eyes. "Were these the extenuating circumstances you mentioned?"

"Yes, perhaps. I couldn't explain it all to a child, but I had sent Kirk away when he got the idea that he wanted to marry your mother. She was too young for marriage, and he was too young for responsibility. I told him he must go away and prove himself. When they were both older, we would see. When he came back, nearly ten years had passed and Doroteo had married William Austin. He was not the man I would have chosen, but she was happy with him. I had to recognize that. Then Kirk came home and he would not believe that he had to give her up. He'd undoubtedly had affairs in the meantime, but something brought him back to Doroteo. She wanted none of him and she had our hot Cordova temper."

This was not the story Eleanor had told me—of Doroteo using that gun because she had been "spurned." But this story seemed closer to the possible truth.

"Don't you remember?" my grandfather said.

"Remember what?"

"Something happened between them one day, when she was angry with him. He had said he would go to your father and tell him of their love for each other when they were young. By then, I think, it would not have mattered to William. But your mother was furious and she struck Kirk in the face. You were there, Amanda. You were in the living room, which is not so very different now from the way it used to be."

The sound of a slap seemed to echo out of the past. As if through a mist I could see a beautiful and angry woman flinging out her hand. I had been frightened, but she hadn't been angry with me. When the man had gone from the house, she had caught me up and held me close to her. Almost I could remember some flower scent she had worn.

"You are remembering, aren't you?" Juan Cordova said.

I brushed my hands before my eyes. "A little, perhaps. Something."

"Good. Then we have made a beginning. You mustn't

try too much at once. We'll attempt it again another
time."

"But remembering a slap doesn't bring back anything of that time on the hillside."

"It's a beginning, and it gives you something to tell
Paul. I gather that you're talking to him in spite of
my wishes?"

"Why should I tell him that?"

"He must understand that Kirk was tormenting your
mother. That he drove her to what she finally did. If
he must write this book, then I would like him to be
gentle with Doroteo. You must remember that Paul
knew her in those days. He knew about her wild temper—
the blood of the dwarf that has come down to us."

I stopped him with an outflung hand. "There's that
phrase again—'blood of the dwarf'! Eleanor used it to
me, and my father once mentioned a dwarf. What does
it mean? You must tell me."

"Yes," he said. "It's time you knew." He opened
an upper drawer in his desk and took out a ring of
two keys, examining them with his fingers, as though
he could distinguish them better that way than with his
eyes. When he came to some conclusion, he dropped the
ring back in the drawer and closed it.

"Not now," he said. "We will go after dark, when no
one will be watching. After dinner tonight you will come
to me here and I will show you something. You have
the right to know all our family secrets. Perhaps they
will be your responsibility someday. But I am tired now.
Come to me later. *Por favor.*"

I couldn't let him off as easily as that. "I'll come, but
there's something else I must show you now."

From the bottom of the box I took Katy's diary
and set it before him. I didn't need to ask if he knew
what it was—he recognized it at once and drew it toward
him, opened the flyleaf to look at the date of the year.

"This has been missing," he said. "She kept diaries
for many years—before Doroteo died, and up to the
time when she became ill. After Katy was gone, I read

them all. But the book for this year was not among them. You found it at the *rancho?*"

I nodded. "It was in a box with the mask and other things."

"I asked Clarita to search for this book, but she never found it. Or at least she told me she had not."

I opened the book to the last pages, where the leaves had been torn out, leaving only jagged scraps at the center.

"We think this was done today. Has Clarita been away from the house?"

He fixed me with that fierce gaze. "She has been here all afternoon. She looked in on me several times. Clarita would not do a thing like this."

"What would I not do?" Clarita asked from behind me.

I turned my head as she came into the room. For once she did not look like a middle-aged Spanish lady. She had put on cinnamon brown slacks and a dark red blouse, and she wore no jewelry. The effect was different, younger, and somehow less subservient to Juan Cordova.

He answered her words coldly. "You would not, I think, go out to the *rancho* and disturb your mother's possessions. You would not tear pages from her diary."

"Naturally not. This has been done?" In spite of her denial, I sensed tension in her.

"Tell her, Amanda."

I obeyed. "Since Katy had left me a message to go to the *rancho,* and left me a key, Gavin took me out there today. We found this book with the hasp of the lock torn loose and the last pages ripped out. The pages which must have told about the picnic and my mother's death."

"Such pages would not matter," Clarita said. "She knew only what was known to all of us from the beginning."

"I have told Amanda that you were in the house all this afternoon, and that you looked in on me several times."

"That is true." Clarita spoke with dignity and assurance, but I did not know at all whether she was telling the truth or whether Juan might be shielding her. Something had made her tense.

"I found one other thing out there," I said, and took the turquoise mask from its box, holding it toward her.

Her gasp was one of repugnance, and she took an involuntary step backward.

"The mask disturbs you?" Juan asked, quickly alert.

"You know very well why it does," she said. "It was found there that day. The day when Kirk and Doro died. The child was holding it. My mother took it from her. Later she packed it in a box with other things and removed them to the hacienda. I have not seen this again until now. It is a thing of ill omen, Amanda."

"I know," I said. "I had an immediate feeling of fright when I saw it."

"No one has told me of this." Juan sounded irritable. "The mask was always hung on a wall at the *rancho,* but the last time I went there it was gone, and I did not ask about it. How could it have come to the picnic place?"

If Clarita had any notion, she didn't betray it. She simply reached past me to pick up the diary from the desk, and she would have carried it away if I hadn't stopped her.

"Please, Aunt Clarita. I'd like to read the pages that are left, if I may. I know so little about my grandmother. And this book would cover part of the year when I was five."

She gave it up to me reluctantly, and I put it and the mask into the box I'd brought from the *rancho.*

"I'll go to my room now," I said. "Is there anything else you wanted of me, Grandfather?"

There was nothing, and Clarita stood away from the door to let me by. Juan spoke as I went out.

"You will remember our plans, Amanda?"

I told him I would remember, and I would come to his study after dinner.

The afternoon was already growing late and shadows lay long across my room when I returned to it. On the bed Paul Stewart's *Emanuella* still awaited my attention, but I was not ready to dip into its pages. My grandmother's diary interested me more because it had to do with the past which pressed with a growing threat upon the present.

I sat down in the chair by a window and began to skim through the pages. Katy had expressed herself vividly, and there were passages I would read with more care at another time, but now I was filled with a strange uneasiness that made me read as though I awaited some revelation. It was as if I stood before a curtained doorway, knowing that it was within my power to fling the curtain aside in time to witness something terrible that was happening beyond. Yet my hand could not move to push aside the curtain. Somehow my will and my vision were blocked. Perhaps this book would give me the power to open that curtain.

Katy had loved life and loved her family, yet she had worn no rose-colored glasses with which to deceive herself. She had lived in a real world in which she made allowances for those she loved, permitting them to be themselves—not always approving, but always loving. Her love for Juan, her husband, came through her words, yet she could be exasperated with him at times. Clarita she worried about and prayed for secretly.

Once she wrote, "Clarita is doomed to unhappiness. I have no use for the man she loves and I do not think he will marry her." She couldn't have meant Kirk at the date of the writing, and I wondered who the man had been whom Clarita had loved in her adult years.

Doroteo was Katy's joy, and she delighted as well in her two small granddaughters, Eleanor and Amanda.

Where she wrote about us, I read more carefully, taking sustenance from the words. Her affection for me—for Doroteo's daughter—came through warmly in the strong script, and tears burned my eyes as I read. Here

was the family I had sought. If only this darling grandmother had lived long enough for me to know her after
I was grown.

When she wrote about Eleanor, however, there was
something a little strange, something pained and off-key,
as though she forced herself. The affection was there, but
there was something else beneath it—a sadness, a fear,
a regret?—that made me wonder if Eleanor had shown
disturbing traits even as a small child.

She wrote of Kirk Landers' return to town and there
was distress and uncertainty in her words, giving way to
relief as she seemed to realize that whatever Doroteo had
once felt for Kirk was over, and that Doro would never
be turned from her husband. But she fretted about Kirk
in these pages. She and Juan had loved and raised him
as a son, as his stepsister, Sylvia, had been their daughter.
But now Kirk was disturbing the climate of a happy family
because he was so unhappy himself. Juan was trying
to guide and advise him wisely, and he was the only
one Kirk seemed to listen to.

I turned the page and Paul Stewart's name leaped
at me from the script. Kirk didn't want Paul to marry
his stepsister, and one day there had been a violent
quarrel between them, in which Kirk had given Paul a
dreadful beating. It had been Katy who'd found them
fighting down in the lower patio of the Cordova house.
She had managed with difficulty to break up the fight—
and not before both men had gained a few battle
scars, though Paul's hurts were far worse than Kirk's.
Katy's writing became a bit erratic as she told of what
had happened, and she closed the episode with these
words, "Such angry wounds won't easily heal. Juan
mustn't know. He has been ill, and he is still weak. He
loves Kirk deeply, and I won't have him upset by Paul."

There was a space of a few days after that in which
she didn't write. Then came the time of the picnic, and
the preparation for it. A dull passage that was more a
listing than anything else—of food to be prepared, of
guests to be invited. But there was something wrong in

the very writing, because Katy was one to make the prosaic come to life, one to lace her own sense of humor into words with keen perception. There was none of that now—only the wooden setting down of words that might have been a cover for seething emotions she did not want to express.

Then the time of the picnic arrived, and the words suddenly ended, leaving me once more frustrated and questioning, because there were no more pages to be read. Fingering the bits of torn paper at the center of the diary, I found here and there a meaningless word that remained. And one not so meaningless—a word standing by itself near the bottom of what had once been a page. The word "mask."

I sat with the book open in my lap, trying to force that curtain back. But only mists swirled before my eyes and something in me resisted all memory. I had seen something too terrible to be endured by so small a child, and all my forces of self-protection had worked through the years to keep it buried. Now the curtain would not stir. Only through a crack now and then had I glimpsed whatever lay behind the present. Juan himself had helped me more than anyone else, and I must go to him again at another time, but my probing had left him exhausted and I must move gently there.

What was it about the mask?

I went to the box, which I'd left on my bed, and took out the blue carving. I was getting used to it now, and the immediate reaction of terror had faded. But I knew it meant something to me—something agonizing, like its silent scream.

On a sudden whim, I carried it to the dressing table that must once have been my mother's, and sat down to face myself in the glass. With hands that were not quite steady, I raised the mask and placed it before my face. Through the slitted eyes of turquoise and silver I could just make out the mask in the glass, with my own hair sweeping back darkly above the line of blue. The quiver of terror returned. The mask was evil. It intended evil.

The rounded mouth shouted silent obscenities at me. I was I no longer. I was the victim, toward whom evil was intended. I was the hunted.

From across the room Sylvia's voice startled me.

"Since your door's open, may I come in? Clarita said you were up here."

I stared at her in the glass, my vision narrowed by blue slits, and there was an instant in which I seemed unable to stir. Then I removed the mask, laid it upon the rosewood surface before me, and turned around to face Sylvia. I still couldn't speak.

She took my silence for invitation and came toward me across the room. "You're white as a sheet. Have you been frightening yourself with bogeymen?" She reached past me and picked up the mask. "Blind Man's Buff," she said softly.

"Clarita said they found me holding it the day my mother died," I told her.

She nodded, her own expression guarded. "Yes. I remember. Oh, not that you had it—I don't remember that. I was too concerned about Kirk and Doro to think of anything else. But I know Kirk had taken it with him when he went to that place."

"Why? Why did he take it?"

"He didn't explain anything to me. I only know that he was wildly upset, and he went rushing off along the hillside by way of the lower short cut. Doro must have followed him, taking you with her. I didn't want to go that way. I was frightened about what might happen, and I hurried along the upper road to find Katy, who'd gone ahead with one of the picnic baskets. I didn't know where Paul was and I went alone."

A vague questioning stirred in my mind, though I didn't know what it was I questioned—only that something she had said didn't match something I already knew.

"Why did you mention Blind Man's Buff?" I asked.

She set the mask down as though she didn't like the feel of it and turned toward the window chair. "Mind if I sit down? It's a long story. Do you really want to hear it?"

"Yes. I want to hear everything I can."

Light from the window fell upon her insistently brown hair and showed the small lines about her eyes that had begun to make themselves evident. She lowered darkened lashes, shutting out the room, as though she were making a voyage backward in time.

"When we were small, we used to play Blind Man's Buff out at the *rancho,* and whenever we could sneak that mask off the wall without being caught, the one who was 'It' put it on. It made the game all the more scary, and you couldn't really see very well with it on, so it was as good as a blindfold. Of course playing with it was forbidden, because it's a valuable piece. But it fascinated us and added to our fright in being chased by whoever wore it. By the time we were twelve and older, we didn't play such games any more—except out at the *rancho,* where they'd become a sort of ritual. Kirk used to put on the mask and chase Doro. I thought myself too old for such nonsense, and so did Clarita. Paul wasn't around then, of course. He bought the house next door after we were all grown up."

"Who else was there?"

"Sometimes Gavin, though we thought him too young in those days. Rafael was there, of course."

"Eleanor's father?"

Sylvia took her hands from her face and looked at me. "Yes. Eleanor's father. He was always there. He made trouble even then."

"Rafael? No one has said much about him before. Except that he wanted to be an Anglo and he got away from the Cordovas as soon as he could. I hadn't heard that he was a troublemaker. Perhaps Eleanor takes after him."

Sylvia seemed to shake herself, as though some confusion had risen in her mind, and she wanted to be free of old memories. "I don't want to talk about all this. It's gone. Buried. It needs to be forgotten."

But I didn't think anyone was forgetting it. That was
the trouble. It was a long while before her hesitation to
speak about Eleanor's father returned to me and brought
an answer.

In any case, I didn't urge her further. Here and there
the bits and pieces were being given me that would
eventually add up to the whole—the truth that I was
seeking.

I motioned toward the diary, where it lay on my bed.
"I went out to the *rancho* today. With Gavin. That's
where I found the mask—and an old diary of Katy's
as well. It covers the months up to the time of the
picnic. The rest has been torn out."

In Sylvia's quiet I sensed an alertness, as though she
waited.

"There was a fight, wasn't there?" I went on. "Between
your stepbrother and Paul Stewart? Katy wrote about
it."

"I—I think there was something of the sort. I was
away on a visit at that time."

She didn't want to acknowledge the fight, for some
reason. I had the feeling that she was evading her own
knowledge of it as something she could not face—or
wanted to forget.

"It doesn't matter," I said. "None of this helps me.
I've only a crumb or two more to tell Paul."

She made an effort to recover herself. "That's what
I came over to hear. Paul sent me to find out whether
anything more was stirring yet."

I wasn't going to tell Sylvia the thing Juan wanted
Paul to know. Since Kirk was Sylvia's stepbrother, she
might try to block those "extenuating circumstances."
If I talked to Paul at all, I would tell him myself.

"What happened after—they died?" I asked. "Did you
stay on with the Cordovas?"

"Of course. It was my home. I couldn't blame the
others for what Doro had done. And Paul was living
next door. By that time we were interested in each
other. Well, I'd better be getting home—since you

haven't anything more to contribute to the book right now."

I wondered at her concern with something she disapproved, but let it go. When she had disappeared down the stairs, I stood for a few moments in the center of the white rug where the Indian mole fetish had lain, looking after her. The question she had aroused was stirring in my mind. Now I knew what it was.

Sylvia had said that she'd hurried along the upper road to look for Katy at the picnic place. Alone. She'd been upset because Kirk had left the house carrying the turquoise mask. But earlier Paul had told me that he and Sylvia had come late to the picnic together. The two stories didn't match, and I wondered which one of them was lying. If he hadn't been with Sylvia, where had Paul been that day, and when had he arrived at the picnic?

I went back to the dressing table and picked up the mask. Its silent cry of anguish was an enigma in itself. There were too many questions. Why had Kirk Landers gone along the hillside carrying it? And what had it meant to Doroteo Austin?

XI

Soon after I left the dinner table that evening, I went to my grandfather's study and found him waiting for me. There was a change in him—a quickening that made him seem more alive and fiercer than ever. At once I was wary. Whatever he intended, I was not sure I would want to accommodate him.

"*Buenas tardes,*" he said eagerly. "Now you will tell me where each one is."

"I don't know. They all went off in different directions. But they aren't sitting around downstairs, if that's what you mean."

"No matter," he said. "Come with me, Amanda."

He rose from his desk and stepped into the darkened room behind him—the bedroom I hadn't seen until now. A lamp near the big, four-poster bed came on at his touch and I went into the room for the first time.

It was all dark brown against the white of the walls, from the high, carved posts of the bed, to the bed covering and a dark Spanish rug on the floor. Beside a carved table stood a monk's chair, square-wrought, with dark leather across the back, and a crimson velvet cushion over the stretched leather seat. The arms were square-cut and broad, and I could imagine Juan sitting in it as though it were a throne, ruling his domain.

There was nothing Indian in this room. The only relief which offered rich color was a great painting that occupied most of the wall opposite the bed, where he could lie in comfort and look at it. Though why anyone should want such a picture for a bedroom where rest was essential, I couldn't guess.

Fire flared at the painting's center, climbing toward a storm-angry sky and beginning to envelop the man at the stake. Hooded figures with crosses upheld marched about the fire, and a little way off an old woman stood wringing her hands—perhaps suffering for her son who was being burned by the Holy Inquisition.

My grandfather saw the fixed direction of my gaze. "A fine painting and very old. The artist is not known, but I found it long ago in a shop in Seville."

"It seems a strange choice for a bedroom."

He stared me down with proud arrogance. "That scene is part of Spain, part of the Spanish character. We cannot shrug our heritage away in gentler times."

"I'm not sure I like that Spanish heritage," I said. "I haven't any taste for torture in the name of religion."

"I accept what is in my blood, Amanda. And so must you. There are times when one must rule by the brand and the scourge. Come with me."

The falcon's untamed ferocity was upon him again, and I shivered inwardly. I would hate to bring my grandfather's anger down upon me.

I'd wondered why he'd brought me to this room, and now I saw. He went to a door that I had thought was a closet, and opened it upon stone steps running down into darkness, at the end of which was a faint radiance.

"A secret passageway?" I asked lightly.

His tone reproved frivolity. "I do not like a room in which there is only one exit. Nor did the men who built this house. Step carefully now. The light is dim."

He went ahead of me with confidence, since poor vision did not matter here. He knew his way, his hands touching narrow walls on either side as he went down the steps. I followed with less confidence, letting one foot feel for each step as I went down. There were not many steps before the passageway leveled and moved toward the dim bulb which hung from the ceiling at the far end. There Juan Cordova stopped before another door. Before he opened it, he put his ear against the wood panel, listening to whatever lay beyond.

"I think there is no one there," he said.

Under his hand, the door opened quietly, and I followed him into the softly lighted patio. The passageway had not taken us outside Cordova walls, but only by a direct means to the patio.

I offered him my arm, but he had brought his stick and he moved down the flagstone walk without faltering, and I walked at his side. Ahead of us, at the lower end of the patio, rose the small adobe building with the peaked redwood roof that held the Cordova art collection. I knew where we were going now, though I didn't know why our going there should be secret—something concealed from the rest of the house.

A dim lamp burned in the upper part of the patio, its rays barely lighting our way to this lower end. The small building was a dark shadow among other shadows, and thick curtains had been pulled across its windows. I felt a tensing in me as we neared the door—as though I approached some revelation that was to be dreaded. Perhaps this was a feeling I'd caught from my grandfather's manner, since it was as if he approached some blood rite that was half mystical in nature.

At the door he took out the ring of keys he had brought with him, and as his hands moved over a square metal box near the door, he seemed to stiffen.

"The alarm is already off," he said.

At the low sound of his voice, a portion of shadow detached itself from a patch of chamiso and came toward us.

"What are you doing here, Clarita?" Juan's tone was irritable.

She emerged into dim light, wearing black again, as

she had at dinner, her face pale under starlight. "I
have been watching. Watching *him*." She gestured toward
the adobe building. "You need no key. He is in there
now."

Juan uttered an exclamation of annoyance and pushed
the door wide. Whatever his intent toward secrecy, it
had been defeated.

"Who is there?" he called sharply.

From around a bend that led into a wing at the far
end of the central room, Gavin Brand came into view.

"What are you doing here?" Juan asked in quick
suspicion.

"You know I have keys," Gavin said. "There was
someone around outside a little while ago. I wasn't
quick enough to catch him. He got away from me."

"Got away?" Juan challenged skeptically. "In this enclosed space?"

"He managed." Gavin was curt. "Perhaps through the
back gate, though there was no one in sight on the hillside when I looked out."

Or through the side gate into the Stewarts' yard? I
thought, though I said nothing. There was no reason
for such a suspicion, and I wondered why it came to
mind.

Clarita drifted into the room behind us. "Perhaps
it was I you heard? I have been here for a little while,
watching you."

"I came in to check whether everything was all right,"
Gavin said, paying no attention to her. "As far as I can
tell, nothing has been touched. No one has broken in
or taken anything from the collection."

I'd stood back a little during this interchange, looking
about the interior of the building. It was strangely like
a church, with its high cathedral ceiling raftered to a
peak overhead, and a chapel-like hush in the room when
the voices stopped. One felt a sense of that awe which
was reserved for the mystical—as if this were a place of
worship. As perhaps it was—Juan Cordova's worship of
the art men had created. I remembered that Sylvia had

said he collected these things for his own passion and pleasure, and did not readily share them with others.

On shelves along a portion of wall were sculptured pieces and fine carvings from Mexico and Central and South America, as well as ancient Indian pottery from all the Americas. But mostly there were Spanish paintings—not all of them from earlier centuries.

I recognized a Picasso from the blue period—a man and woman standing on a beach at the water's edge, with gray-blue ocean and sky all around, and blue reflected in the sand under their feet, in their very clothes. There was a gypsy study by Isidore Nonell, who had influenced the young Picasso—a swarthy-complexioned girl against a green wash background. The impressionist Sorolla had lent his sunlight effects to a woman in a head scarf walking among the flowers of a sunny park.

In spite of his clouded vision, which kept him from seeing sharply, Juan Cordova knew every item in the room, knew its place and its history, and he paused to tell me about this art he had acquired over so many years. He was clearly not pleased that Clarita should be here or Gavin, since for some reason this was a tour he had wanted to conduct alone with me, without the knowledge of the household. But he bore up under the circumstances and gave his attention to the paintings and to me.

I had exchanged a single glance with Gavin, and found him oddly guarded and not like the sympathetic man I'd met at the picnic place and who had driven me out to the *rancho*. He did not want me here, and I wondered why.

"I have been thinking," Juan said, his eyes on the wall of Spanish pictures, as though he strained to see them. "Perhaps the time has come when I should share some of my treasures with the world. In my own way."

Gavin was silent, waiting, and I sensed resistance in him. Clarita seemed to hang on her father's words.

Juan went on. "I have decided to select five or six Spanish scenes and display them at the store. Gavin, you will have a space cleared for them, so they can be hung well apart."

"The insurance problems will be enormous," Gavin said flatly, "and there is no space."

"Then you will put away wall hangings, rugs, weaving, so you can make space."

"We are not a museum." Gavin was angry but controlled. "The craftsmen you would displace depend on our sales for their living. If you want these things shown, loan them to a museum."

"They must appear under the Cordova name," Juan said harshly.

"Articles have been taken from the store lately," Clarita put in. "Perhaps it is wiser not to risk what is valuable."

Juan ignored her, starting down the aisle. "We will speak of this later, Gavin. Come, Amanda, there is more for you to see."

There was nothing to do but go with him, though my sympathy lay with Gavin's intention for the store.

Before a portrait hung halfway down the room, my grandfather paused and touched my arm lightly. "It is there before you. Look at it well. That is Doña Emanuella. Unfortunately, she was not painted by a great artist, but the portrait is good, adequate. It conveys her personality, her likeness."

I looked up at a painting which had been done rather in the manner of Velázquez, though the artist had far from his mastery. He had portrayed a dark girl in a black lace mantilla, with a cluster of pink flowers pinned to the round neck of her yellow court dress. The gown came snugly in at a waist that seemed all the more slim because of skirts which flared widely over an underframe at each side, in the seventeenth-century style of Philip IV's court of Spain.

She stood half turned, and with one hand she seemed to beckon with a full-blown yellow rose. Her mouth had a sulky look, though gaiety danced in her eyes. I could imagine that I looked again at a portrait of Doroteo

Cordova—and perhaps to a lesser extent and with a little more imagination, at my own face.

"You see the resemblance?" Juan asked.

"I suppose I want to see it."

"And a resemblance to yourself?"

I was silent, and unexpectedly, Gavin spoke for me. "Yes, for herself too. There's a chance likeness there. I saw it the first time we met."

Had that been part of the reason for the current of recognition that had leaped between us on that first meeting? Was it because he had seen Emanuella and Doroteo in me, rather than recognizing me for myself? I felt somehow disappointed.

"There was passion in Emanuella," Juan said. "Spirit. Fire."

"I am none of those things," I said hastily, wanting to stand on my own ground.

"Are you so sure?" Gavin said. "Perhaps you're all of them more than you recognize. Not that I believe these characteristics have come down to you from a legend."

I glanced at him in surprise and saw the guarded look was gone, and in his eyes was that same warmth that had existed briefly at the *rancho* this afternoon. Because the look disturbed me, I turned away, knowing I might be too ready to respond. That way lay danger.

Juan did not see this interchange, all his attention given to the portrait, as he peered to see its detail, but I heard Clarita's faint sniff of disapproval. She was staring at me with a high flare of color on her cheekbones and a challenge in her dark eyes. I gave her look for look, while Juan went on speaking of Emanuella, and Clarita's eyes turned away first, though with an air of proud disdain.

"Emanuella was a great beauty and she married young and was mother to several children," Juan went on. "I've always thought her reputed immorality overrated. She was a little wild but not wicked."

"Paul Stewart seemed to think otherwise," Gavin said.

"Stewart!" There was distaste in Juan's voice. "He fell in love with her picture in his writer's way and he wrote about her to suit himself. Just as he was half in love with Doroteo."

"He has never had a woman worthy of him," Clarita put in irrelevantly, and I glanced at her in surprise. Clarita—Paul? Was he the man Sylvia had hinted about?

"He's supposed to have done a good deal of research on Emanuella in Spain," Gavin said.

"Research!" Juan was emphatic. "He colored his facts. He made her what she never was. Amanda, you can be proud of the bloodline that comes down to you from that glorious woman."

He really believed in that bloodline, I thought, and I looked up at the sulky, beautiful face with its crimson mouth, lightly tinted cheeks and smoothly combed black hair, glimpsed beneath the fine lace of the mantilla. For just a moment I felt close to my mother. Then the sense of nearness fell away and I was looking into the face of an enchanting stranger. It was romantic to think that some bit of this glamorous woman had come down to me, but I didn't really believe it. She belonged to another world and another time.

"When you speak of the bloodline, you can't forget the other portrait," Clarita said tartly. "The Cordovas must claim her too as a relative. Inés as well as Emanuella."

"I am not likely to forget." Juan gestured and we moved on to look at more pictures.

There was a portrait of Cervantes, in which a strange yellow-green light glowed from the landscape behind him, touching his long thin face and the ruff about his neck. Next came a bullfight scene, with a fallen matador and blood streaking the sand of the ring, and then one of Spagnoletto's scenes of torture and martyrdom that would have made a good companion piece for the Inquisition painting in Juan's bedroom. I preferred the following painting of a Spanish street on a misty, rainy night, with a glowing nimbus shrouding the street lamps.

Before this I stood for a long while, studying the effect the artist had achieved so well with his pigments.

There were others, but Juan Cordova grew impatient. "Enough of all this! You can come back another time, Amanda, and look to your heart's content. Now we will see the masterpiece."

Strangely, Gavin hesitated. "Must she see it?"

"But of course she must. Perhaps it will be her heritage someday."

Clarita made her odd little sound of distaste, and Gavin glanced at me with sympathy. "Don't let it give you bad dreams at night."

I was curious now, and when Juan moved on toward the hidden wing, I walked at his side.

The portrait dominated a small alcove. If the building was given over to the mystical worship of beauty created by gifted painters, this was the central image before which one did homage.

The painting hung against one white wall, framed in gilt and nearly life size. Unmistakably the incomparable artist, whose work I had seen in museums and in reproductions, had painted this and it was dramatic in its impact. The subject was a woman gowned in dark bottle green which had been banded with strips of creamy white. Like the dress of the other portrait, her skirts were extended widely at each side over a hidden frame, but this time the waist was thick, the woman stunted. The size of the dog which lay at her feet with its ears cocked told her true proportions. She was a dwarf, with flowing dark hair and a flat, pushed-in face. There was a strange serenity about the face, yet the dark eyes that looked straight out of the picture had something frightening about them.

"The dwarf," I murmured, and felt a sense of shock. But surely the relationship to Juan was only, as Eleanor and Gavin said, a legend.

"Yes," my grandfather said. "Doña Inés. She was cousin to Emanuella and a maid of honor to Maria Teresa, the Infanta."

"Velázquez," I said. "No one else could have done this."

Juan Cordova looked pleased. "I'm glad you recognize a masterpiece. Yes. Velázquez painted it. It is the famous lost painting of one of the dwarfs he liked to portray in Philip's court."

"But how did you ever—?"

"Come to possess it?" Juan Cordova chuckled, and the sound was sly, wicked. "That is nothing we need to go into now. It has had many travels before coming into my hands. Eventually it will be sent back to Spain. But for now, it is the portrait of an ancestress and I treasure it for many reasons."

"Not all of them pleasant," Gavin said. "Perhaps you'd better tell her the story, since you've gone this far."

If there had been friction between them a short while ago, Juan seemed to have put it aside, but I did not think he would have forgotten.

"Inés was a fiercely passionate woman," Grandfather said. "And apparently she adored the cousin she could not resemble. She murdered one of her cousin's lovers—or at least a nobleman she thought was Emanuella's lover. She stabbed him to death in his bed one night. An attendant apprehended her and she was sent to prison. She was never executed because she went completely mad. So now you have the story of our famous dwarf. That, too, is the blood that comes down to us."

I stared at that strangely serene face, with the eyes that suggested madness, and I could not help shivering. I remembered my father's voice speaking of that "damnable dwarf."

"Any such strain—if it ever existed—has obviously long since been diluted," Gavin said. "Don't worry about it, Amanda."

"It is there," Juan Cordova contradicted coldly. "The passion, the fury, the lack of restraint. It crops out in all of us again and again. In myself. In Doroteo. In Eleanor. Even in you, Clarita. About Amanda, I do not know."

I looked up at the portrait with a growing sense of dismay. What Gavin said was surely true, yet I remembered the way my father had watched me, the way he had fought any signs of temper in me. But there was no reason to be afraid. No real reason.

"I'm not like that," I said.

Gavin reached out a hand and turned off the light that gave the painting its individual illumination. "I'll admit it's haunting. But you'll throw it off as soon as you turn your back on it, Amanda. Your grandfather has too much of an obsession with these supposed female ancestors."

"I am proud of them," Juan Cordova said, and I knew that, strangely, this was true. He actually took pride in fancying this wild strain in himself and in others of his blood.

I was aware of Clarita there beside him, her dark gaze on the portrait with a certain avidity, as though she had, in this too, patterned herself after her father, worshiping at the shrine of the dwarf.

"Perhaps you encourage the strain to exist," I said to Juan. "If your children grow up haunted by that picture and its story, every small loss of temper might be frightening. Or—it might become something to indulge."

Gavin agreed. "Exactly. That's what has happened to Eleanor. Juan has encouraged her to indulge herself in wildness because he's proud of this supposed strain."

"The strain is there." Clarita echoed her father. "We cannot escape it." In the bright lighting that illumined the rest of the paintings, her face seemed stark, colorless—a Spanish portrait in black and white, with the eyes shining darkly in her pale face.

The old man did not look at her. "This is not so," he said in response to Gavin. "It isn't possible to encourage what isn't there. The strain is visible in all the Cordovas. But in Eleanor it is only a youthful unruliness."

"Then it's time for her to grow up," Gavin said. He sounded hard again and unrelenting. This was the side

of him I did not like. He would approve and encourage—
up to a point where a woman wanted to go her way.
Then he could be as domineering as my grandfather. My
feelings toward him were ambivalent, and in either phase
I could feel the other side near. He would never be for
long the kind and sympathetic man I had known this
afternoon.

I turned away from the now unlighted picture of the
dwarf Inés, leaving it to its own demented gaze, and
moved out of the wing. My steps echoed on the tile
floor and Juan Cordova must have heard me, though he
stayed where he was, speaking earnestly to Gavin. Clarita
stayed with them. I didn't want to hear any further
arguments between them, and I returned to the painting
of Doña Emanuella and looked up into those dancing,
provocative eyes. There was no madness there.

At the other end of the room the voices rose a little,
but I paid no attention.

How had Emanuella felt about her cousin, the dwarf?
Had she loved her, been kind to her? Or had she suffered because of her? How much had Paul Stewart un-
covered in the research he had done in Spain? I wanted
to dip into his book and read his account of these two
women who had existed so far back on my family tree.

Now the voices intruded, rising in heat, and I became
aware that Eleanor was the subject of their contention.
When I glanced in their direction, I saw that the two
men had come around the corner of the wing and stood
in full view. They had forgotten me, but Clarita had not.
She remained a little apart, staring down the room in
my direction as though she willed me to turn away,
commanded me not to listen. I began to listen with full
intent.

"We can't stay together any longer!" Gavin cried.
"It's impossible. Eleanor doesn't wish it and neither do
I!"

"Eleanor doesn't know what she wants," Juan protested.

"Do you think that's true of me?"

"I think you have a responsibility."

"Not any longer. Eleanor wants to be free of all restraint. She doesn't want the trust fund you've set up for her. She wants the money itself in her own hands. But if you give it to her—"

"I will not give it to her," the old man said. "You know in your heart you cannot leave her. But if your marriage breaks up I will change my will and leave everything to my other granddaughter, Amanda."

His voice was strong, assured, and it carried with no effort at concealment. It carried to the open doorway where Eleanor had suddenly appeared, her face white, her eyes blazing. She had heard it all, and I thought in sudden alarm—or did I imagine it?—that there was a look of the dwarf about her, for all her golden perfection as contrasted with that dark, stunted figure.

If she saw me, she gave no sign, but rushed past me down the long room, to stand defiantly before Juan Cordova, a tall, slender figure, with her hair falling over her shoulders.

I was suddenly aware of Gavin, his attention not upon Eleanor, but upon me—challenging me in some way, any warmth toward me gone from his face, so there was only a waiting coldness there. But this was no time for me to probe whatever he expected. Eleanor held stage center.

"You can't do this, Grandfather!" she cried. "I won't stay with Gavin. I hate him! I'm the one you should think of now—not Amanda. I'm the one you must take care of."

Juan moved toward her, his expression proud and unrelenting. "You will always be taken care of—modestly. But if you leave Gavin, everything will go to Amanda."

She flung herself upon him, pounding clenched fists against his chest so that for an instant he staggered under the impact. Then he righted himself and held her to him, stilled her beating hands, soothing her until she quieted. I was stunned by this outpouring of emotion. In the face of it any words from me would have been feeble indeed. I stayed where I was in silence.

"Perhaps you've only a little while to live!" Eleanor
wailed, clinging to him with a childlike appeal I could
not believe was real. "And when you're gone there will
be no one to look after me. There will be only what
you leave to take care of me."

He spoke to her in soft Spanish and there was the
sound of endearment in his tone, yet I felt sure that he
promised her nothing. Gavin walked past them stony-
faced, and came in my direction. There was no kindness in him.

"Why haven't you said something to stop this?" he
demanded. "I thought you were the one who wanted
nothing from him. But of course if you stand by and do
nothing, everything will fall into your hands, won't it?
The store, the money—everything CORDOVA stands for."

I felt outrage rising in me and a deep wounding as
well, though this I thrust aside and would not accept.
In no way had I meant to be used like this by my grandfather. Gavin was wildly unfair, and I wouldn't be driven
away or stopped in my real purpose because of his
words or because of Juan Cordova's machinations.

"Go away, Amanda," Gavin said in the same cold
fury. "Leave Santa Fe!"

I remembered wryly the time when I had wondered
if he might not seem more human if he ever exploded.
Now the explosion had come and it was deadly chill—
inhuman.

Nevertheless, I stood up to him. "I wouldn't have
come here in the first place if I'd known I'd be used
like this. But now I won't be driven away."

My words seemed to echo into a sudden silence. For
a moment the chapel-like hush lay upon the room and
Doña Emanuella looked mockingly down from her place
on the wall. Then Gavin gave me a last look and went
out the door. When he had gone, Juan put Eleanor from
him and came quickly toward me down the room, his
stick tapping on the tiles, but used very little for support.
Excitement had given him strength.

"Of course you will not go away, Amanda. You are the one I can trust. There is just a little time left for me, and you must stay with me."

I couldn't answer him warmly. What he had done was unforgivable. "I've told you why I mean to stay," I said. "I won't leave until I've found out the truth about what happened to my mother. I think it's beginning to come back to me, a little at a time, and for me nothing else matters."

He gave me a long, searching look and nodded gravely. Then he went past me out the door. There was much to be said, but this was not the time to say it.

Eleanor came running from the back of the gallery, but she didn't follow him immediately. She paused instead to stare up at the painting behind me.

"That one doesn't belong to me," she said of Emanuella. "She is all yours—and your mother's. It's the other one I belong to. The wild, mad one. Perhaps you'd better remember that."

She went past me out of the room and left an echoing silence behind her. The lighted gallery was quiet, yet the atmosphere of awe and worship which Juan Cordova so carefully cultivated was gone, and the air seemed to pulse with the unrestrained emotion that had flowed through it with Eleanor's passing. Here, tonight, something had been unleashed that would not quickly be restrained again. Something of it had touched all of us. I felt shaken by its surging—and more than a little alarmed.

I had forgotten Clarita, until she moved at the back of the gallery, and came toward me with her air of calm arrogance.

"It has begun again," she said as she came opposite me. "I have been waiting, and it has begun."

"What has begun?" I demanded.

Dark eyes were strangely expressionless in her pale face. "It is the death march. If you are very still you can hear the footsteps. They are the footsteps of Inés, coming down to us over the centuries. I have heard

them before." She came close to me. "I have heard them
along the hillside, when your mother died. You had
better save yourself, Amanda."

She was a little mad too—like all of them—and I
stepped abruptly away from her.

"Go back to the house," she directed. "Go quickly
through the dark. I will lock up here."

I had no desire to linger in her company, and I went
out the door into the cool Santa Fe night. Stars seemed
very bright, and the dim patio lamp could not rival them.
Ahead of me the house glowed with lights, and I
walked toward them, hurrying. It was a night in which
to slip swiftly past clumps of shadow and regain as
quickly as possible the safety of walls and rooms, of
warm color and lighted lamps.

No one was in sight when I stepped indoors, though I
could hear Eleanor's voice sounding from our grandfather's study. What they had to say to each other, I
did not care. None of his plans concerned me, because
they were not acceptable to me, no matter what Gavin
believed. But as I went up to my room, the sense of
wounding returned, and once more I thrust it away.
I wouldn't be caught by such a trap again. He was
easy to hate, but he would also be more than easy to
like. To love? The thought made me angry with myself, and I dismissed it at once. I was a stronger woman
than that.

When I was in my room, I turned on a lamp beside
the shabby armchair, picked up the book by Paul
Stewart, and settled down to read. Now I wanted to
know about Emanuella. And about Doña Inés.

XII

The story of *Emanuella* was a fictionized version—"as based upon . . ." so there was no telling which parts were fact, and which fiction. Nevertheless, I read eagerly, and some of the time I could not fling off the feeling that I was reading about my mother.

Paul Stewart had been skillful in bringing his characters out of the past and his scene to life. Emanuella was all fire, completely alive, yet with a certain sweetness about her. Everyone seemed to adore her and she lived on adoration. How much of this was research, I wondered, and how much of it was Paul's memory of Doroteo?

But as the narrative continued, a note of brilliant wickedness was introduced into the depiction of the heroine. "Brilliant" in the sense of being vivid, glittering, dramatic—revealing all too clearly that the author himself, if he had been in love with Emanuella-Doroteo, saw her as provocative in her very iniquity. Had this been my mother? I couldn't believe it, and I could see why the book had angered Juan, and why he did not want Paul to touch the subject of Doroteo again.

I read on, trying to put the thought of my mother from my mind. The story re-created a lively picture of Philip's court, with mystery and a sense of horror

185

emerging as Inés stepped onto the scene.

It had been King Philip's whim to bring to Madrid from abroad whatever dwarfs he could find to amuse him. Often they were jugglers, tumblers, jesters—a motley, entertaining crew. And the young Velázquez, new to the court under the patronage of King Philip, found them interesting subjects for his early work. There was one dwarf, however, who was no jester, but cousin to a lady of the court, daughter of a nobleman. She was Doña Inés, feared a little, perhaps, but respected, and assigned as lady in waiting to the Infanta. Maria Teresa loved her and made her a playmate and confidante. Perhaps she was more nurse than anything else. For all her stunted size and abnormal appearance she was a woman of dignity and power. Yet Paul drew her in his story as evil, and my flesh crept as he described her fatal devotion to the cousin who was all that she was not.

It was growing late, but I read on. The house about me was very still and from my high room I could glimpse the distant lights of Los Alamos, and on the other side I could see by starlight the Sangre de Cristos. Santa Fe was asleep, but I was not. Once I put my book aside and went to look down into the dark patio in the direction of the Stewarts' house. There lights burned, and there was a distant sound of voices. Paul Stewart, who had written these pages, and his wife, Sylvia, who had gone with him to Spain when he was doing his research, must still be up. In the stillness the woman's voice held a note of disquiet, as though she might be agitated, disputing something.

I turned back to my reading. Emanuella had married well—a gentleman of Madrid, and her children were healthy and beautiful. But there was always a restlessness upon her. Her husband's adoration no longer seemed enough. When a younger man, newly come to Philip's court, began showing more than a little interest in her, she responded. He was handsome, rich, with a wandering eye for women. Emanuella was caught, and Inés, ever watchful, saw what the outcome would be. Her beloved cousin might well risk her marriage, injure the children, whom Inés adored, and the husband who was devoted to her. She counseled Emanuella against this young Don Juan, but of course she was not listened to.

All through the narrative Paul pointed up the taint of wild blood in the family of the cousins. A trait inherited and perhaps exploited when it was convenient. There were storms of temper on Emanuella's part and much excitability. Strangely enough, Inés carried this trait of character with more control and dignity than her cousin showed. Only now and then did she explode in wild anger, and then everyone was far more afraid of her than of Emanuella.

In the face of threat, Doña Inés knew what she must do. While one of the palace guards was sleeping she stole out and took the dagger from his belt. Her hands were small, but powerful, and there was strength in her handling of the weapon. She crept into the room where the young man lay sleeping and stabbed him to death. Only then did her control shatter and she began to scream.

When a guard rushed into the room, he found her there, screaming, bloodstained—and quite mad. It was when she was imprisoned that Velázquez painted her. Serenity had been restored because she no longer knew or cared who she was, had no knowledge of what she had done. So that calm, misshapen dwarf's face looked out of the picture, but the eyes were entirely mad.

I sat with the book open upon my lap, haunted by this tale of horror Paul had written so vividly. It all came too close to home. I had wanted to know what made me, what I had descended from, but I didn't want to believe my mother was like Emanuella, or that the blood of Inés still flowed in the veins of the Cordovas—as my grandfather was determined to believe. On any family tree there were all possible combinations of traits if you went back far enough. There was madness and sanity, and good and evil. But the affairs Paul Stewart had written about had nothing to do with me.

Yet, coming unwanted, there was a vivid picture in my mind of Doroteo with a gun in her hand as she went to that place where she would find Kirk Landers. If she had lived, would she have gone mad afterwards, as Inés had done?

I closed the book sharply, and the slap of sound was startling in my quiet room. The story had put an unwelcome spell upon me—as though I must, after all, believe that murder had been done in the recent past. But I would not accept the murderer, as others had labeled her.

Then in that silent room, as if it were a living presence, a gift from the past, a new thought occurred to me, and it pointed clearly to Doroteo's innocence. A woman who went out with a gun in her hand to commit a murder did not take a loved child with her to witness violence. All the doubting fell away from me. How simple, and how clear an answer. Now my course was plainer than ever.

Someone knew the truth. How was I to find that person and make him talk to me? Whether retribution was done at this late date or not, I didn't care a great deal. But I wanted to know the truth as Doroteo's daughter, and I wanted her immediate family to know.

Paul's book could tell me nothing more, and I put it aside, picked up my sketchbook and pencil and began to sketch idly. I was drawing the tree again, shaping it as I remembered it from recent reality—not from my dream. The branches no longer seemed grotesque, but merely ancient, and the leaves were dry and dusty from the long drought, but not like bony fingers that reached for me. I began to feel a certain reassurance as my pencil moved on the page and what came to life on paper was only a very old tree—not the embodiment of evil. It soothed me to draw the real tree instead of the one that belonged to nightmare, and I even began to feel a little sleepy. In a moment I would go back to bed, but first I would compare my new sketch with the one I'd made in the clearing.

I flipped over the pages to the earlier drawing and knew at once that this was a mistake. I should never have looked at my drawing again tonight. In a rush that enveloped me the sense of horror was back. My eyelids felt heavy, the drawing began to swim before my eyes, and the lights in the room began to pulse. Now I was seeking some hazy, dream-laden answer, trying to see with a child's eyes, trying to return to the terrible past the tree represented, all sense of ease vanishing. Behind my lids weaving pictures moved and there were figures to be seen as if through mist.

Some sort of struggle was going on and I sensed again the terrifying stain of scarlet spilling across my vision. Before young, frightened eyes, forms struggled together in the mists. Not two people—but *three*. I could not recognize who they were. But there were shapes that seemed to writhe in some dreadful death dance. There seemed a tremendous noise inside my head —the sounds of nearby blasting, perhaps. Then another explosion. Afterwards, the hillside was quiet and the three were gone. There was only that frightful mask left on the ground beside the small child who watched, weeping, and who reached down to pick it up.

The fog seemed to swirl like a blown veil before my eyes. Then light flashed through bright zigzags through the mist—and I was fully awake and in the present. The room about me was bright and quiet. The drawing of the tree lay upon my knees, and now it was only a sketch I had made, a thing without life of its own.

Yet I remembered something. Three. There had been three. Or was any of this rational? I did not know, but I was seized by the conviction that I was on the right trail. My mother and Kirk had been there—but there had been another one as well. And perhaps it was the third who had fired the gun. The third who had come secretly along the hillside, and escaped as secretly, so that none of those at the picnic above had any realization of his presence. Clarita had lied.

I couldn't bear to think of this any longer. I must

empty my mind, think of something else—let anything that chose come to me. Absently, I added shading to the foliage of the sketch, then flipped over to another page and let my pencil move as it wished upon the paper. I hardly realized what I was drawing until the shape and look of Gavin's face began to emerge on the paper. When I saw what I was doing, I stopped at once, but now I couldn't stop my treacherous thoughts. The face I had drawn would have been the one he'd shown me that afternoon, when I sat beside him on the bench and he had held my hand as kindly as he'd done when I'd been a child. That, I reminded myself, was not his true face. He would fight for Eleanor with her grandfather, and he would shut me out, condemn me for being something I was not. Roughly I scratched over the lines I had drawn, and closed the book, put it aside.

As I undressed and made ready for bed, I felt emotionally drained. I could no longer think clearly, and I didn't know what my next move must be. There was no one to whom I could turn for counsel. If I told anyone the thing that had come to me, all of them would be against me. Perhaps even Sylvia. Only Paul would welcome eagerly anything I had to tell. He would use every crumb and give me no counsel worth having. He might even lead me in some wrong direction. What was I to do?

I turned out the lights and slipped between the sheets, drew up a blanket. The high mountain air was cool and Santa Fe nights were wonderful for sleeping. But I lay awake and listened to the house. It did not creak and groan in quite the same way that old wooden houses do, but there seemed a whispering of movement abroad. The lower bedrooms of the others were in an addition which had long ago been built onto the house. Only my grandfather's room and my own were isolated from the others.

Once I thought I heard footsteps on the narrow flight of stairs that mounted to my upper room. I tensed myself on one elbow, listening to the darkness with all my being. But there was no further sound. Either the stairs themselves had creaked in the changing temperature, or someone sat on the steps, patiently waiting for me to relax and go to sleep. Or to rise out of curiosity and go to some dangerous rendezvous?

I couldn't bear the suspense of not knowing, and after a while I left my bed and went softly to the door. It opened quietly upon the stairs that led down to the room that was an extension of the living room. Moonlight found its way through deep windows, touched the light patches of Indian rugs on the floor, flung the furniture into jet shadow. It also silhouetted the stairs. No one crouched upon them. But nevertheless, there was movement.

In the room below one of the shadows moved. It did not dart, but moved slowly, with great stealth. Moonlight did not reach to my place at the head of the stairs and the moving shadow seemed not to sense my presence. I had no impulse to cry out, to ask who it was. I was filled with a dread curiosity. I had to know what was meant by this action. At least the shadow was not creeping toward Juan Cordova's room, though I had the feeling that if there was danger, it was not to me.

Maddeningly, the moon went behind a cloud and the chiaroscuro of the room was wiped out. Now there was no light and dark, but all was shadow. I could no longer distinguish movement, though there seemed a faint whisper of sound as if something drifted across the room below. Then I heard the soft creaking of a door and knew that the night visitor sought the patio.

I turned quickly back to my room and ran to a window in the thick adobe wall. I climbed into the embrasure so that I could see directly down into the patio. The moon was still hidden, but there was starlight, and in the patio a single lamp burned on a standard. I could just make out the slow movement of that stealthy figure as it followed the path downward toward the little house at the far end of the garden. Lights were out now at the Stewarts' and there was no one down there to hear or see. But if there was a tampering with the lock, the alarm would go off. This I knew. Unless the person who stole toward Grandfather's precious collection had a key. He had come from inside the house, so he might well have one.

I had to rouse someone. This might be another trick to be played upon Gavin, like the one with the stone head. No matter who it might be, our thief must be exposed. He would be trapped if he let himself into the little house and we could catch him there. I must call someone so that the culprit could be discovered.

I put on my robe and for the sake of quiet crept barefoot down the stairs. The door that led into the bedroom wing stood open, and a dim lamp burned on a small table, lighting the long hall with its closed doors on either hand.

Time was slipping by and I couldn't wait. Clarita's room was nearest and I turned the knob slowly, gently, so there was no sound. I didn't want to rouse the house so our thief—if that's what he was—would be alerted to escape. Softly I pressed the door and a wedge of darkness opened before me. The dim light from the hall gave me little help. I could barely make out Clarita's bed across the room, but there was no sound of breathing, and I could make out no mound of sleeping body beneath the covers.

Gathering my courage, I ran across the room in my bare feet. Clarita was gone from her bed. So it was she I must follow, and I needed no help for that.

I left the hall with its other sleepers, and ran through the living room to a patio door, where I let myself outside. The area still lay in shadow, with the moon hidden, but now the patio light had been turned off. Nothing stirred. No shadow moved along the walk, and all seemed to be quiet down near the building which held the collection. Nevertheless, someone had come out here. Alarm stirred in me. The very quiet seemed menacing.

Bricks were cold to my feet as I stepped outside and started down the walk. The faint rush of sound behind me came without warning—only another whisper in the night. There was no time for me to turn, to protect myself. Searing pain struck me across the shoulders and then came again and again, slashing furiously, so that I stumbled and fell to my knees, half stunned, trying vainly to escape the flailing whip. My own screaming split the night.

The blows stopped as suddenly as they'd begun, and there was an outcry from farther along the walk, the sound of a fall. I crouched dazed on my hands and knees, aware only of stinging pain. In the house lights flared on, but it seemed an age before Gavin came running down the walk. He paused beside me but I waved him on.

"Down there! Someone fell!"

He went past me and I heard Juan's choked voice. "The whip!" he moaned. "It was the *disciplina!*"

I managed to stand, to move toward the place where Gavin knelt beside my grandfather. But before I had taken three steps, I saw the thing that lay in my path, its three leather prongs outflung on the tile.

From the house Eleanor came running. She flung herself upon the old man, uttering cries of alarm. Where was Clarita? my stunned mind questioned, and I looked around to see her tall figure in the lighted doorway that led from the patio. She neither moved nor cried out, but waited while Gavin and Eleanor helped her father back to the house. Then her words reached me clearly.

"Go and phone for the doctor, Eleanor." There was no emotion in her tone.

The three moved past me, with Juan faltering between them, and I saw that he was fully dressed and wearing a heavy leather jacket. Perhaps that had spared him what I had suffered. Clarita let them by and then moved toward me, but before she could ask questions I spoke to her.

"I went to your room," I said. "You weren't in bed."

She ignored that. "Are you hurt?"

"A little," I said.

"Then come inside," she ordered, and turned back to the house.

Awkwardly, I reached back to touch my throbbing shoulders, but when I would have followed her, a voice spoke to me out of the lower shadows. Paul's voice.

"Can I be of any help, Amanda? What seems to have happened?"

I didn't trust him. The *disciplina* still lay at my feet and I picked it up with repugnance. The cruel thongs that would have lacerated bare flesh hung limp in my hand as I held it out.

"This belongs to you," I challenged.

He came toward me and took the whip questioningly. "So it does. There was another theft from the store today. My Penitente display has been rifled. This whip was taken, and so was the figure of Doña Sebastiana from her cart. But what's the whip doing here?"

"That's what I'd like to know," I said. "Someone struck me with it and then struck my grandfather, knocking him down on the walk. How could anyone be so cruel?"

Sylvia came running through the gate from the other house, a coat flung over her night clothes.

"Paul—what is it? I heard voices—someone screamed."

He said, "Go back to bed, Sylvia. I'll be along in a moment."

He was stroking the thongs of the whip gently across one palm, but as the moon came out from behind its cloud, his eyes were fixed on me with bright curiosity. By moonlight all he needed were the pipes and a cloven hoof.

"Who did this, Amanda? Who do you think did it?"

"I don't know," I said dully. I wasn't going to tell him about Clarita being out of her bed, or of my hearing sounds from the living room. I didn't want to talk to him at all. As I turned toward the house, he let me go, and I didn't look back until I reached a glass door. Then I looked around to see that both Paul and Sylvia were gone, and the whip with them.

Inside, Juan Cordova lay weakly on a leather couch in the living room, and Clarita was holding a wine glass to his lips. Eleanor stood by, her eyes alive with excitement rather than concern, and when they met mine across the room she gave me a smile filled with malice.

"What happened, Amanda? Were you whipped too? You see what can happen to you if you don't go away from Santa Fe!"

Gavin was kneeling beside Juan, talking to him quietly, and he looked up sharply at Eleanor. "What do you know about this?"

"I?" Her reproach was exaggerated. "Do you think I would ever injure my grandfather?"

The old man roused himself and pushed Clarita's glass away. "It was not Eleanor. She had nothing to do with this. Amanda, you were struck down first—did you see who it was? I had just come from the passage that leads to my bedroom when I heard you scream, and then he was upon me. In the darkness I couldn't see the attacker."

"Nor could I." I went closer to his couch. "I heard something but I couldn't turn in time to know who struck me. When the whip first lashed me I stumbled and fell, and I didn't see what happened clearly. I think someone rushed past me, but I was dazed."

He sighed and closed his eyes. "Whoever used the whip was strong. I have enemies, enemies."

"Are you going to call the police?" I asked.

Except for Gavin, they all looked at me as though I'd uttered some obscenity.

"There will be no police," Juan Cordova said harshly, and Clarita nodded dark agreement.

Eleanor laughed. "We never call the police, dear Amanda. There is too much guilt among us. Who knows what a policeman might turn up?"

"That is not the reason," Juan said coldly. "The papers are too much interested in Cordova scandal. It is not good for the store. There is nothing to be done anyway, since the culprit has escaped. We will handle this ourselves."

My eyes met Clarita's and she stared me down boldly, disdainfully, not caring what I thought. Where she had been, and why Juan Cordova had gone outside, I didn't dare ask, but Gavin had no compunction about asking direct questions.

"Why were you in the patio at this hour?" he demanded of Juan.

The old man answered readily. "I couldn't sleep. When I looked out the window I saw someone down there. Since there have been thefts, I feared for the collection. By the time I came outside, someone had turned off the outdoor light. I was starting down the path when I heard Amanda scream." He paused and seemed to draw a certain dignity about him, as though he would not allow himself to appear old and ill and half blind. "I would have gone to her aid. *Naturalmente.* But there was no time before I too was struck down."

Eleanor's voice had a little rasp in it when she spoke and she surprised us all. "You know very well who used that whip, don't you, Grandfather?"

The old man gasped softly, and at once Clarita was at his side. "Let him alone, Eleanor. This is no time for your teasing."

The doorbell rang, and Gavin went to let the doctor in. Clarita rose from her knees with quiet dignity and went past me to greet him. And in passing she spoke one word to me in a deadly whisper.

"Cuidado," she said, and went to take the doctor's coat and invite him in. Dr. Morrisby was a small man, gray-haired and in his mid-fifties. He came in shaking his head and scolding Juan gently.

"In trouble again!" he said. "Can't you keep my patient quiet, Clarita?"

No one answered him. Gavin explained in as few words as possible that we had an intruder on the grounds. When the doctor had assured himself that Juan had not

been seriously injured, spared by his heavy jacket, Gavin
asked him to have a look at me.

He came upstairs to my room. "A bad business," he
said as I lowered my robe. "The Cordovas have an attraction for violence. I attended your mother at the time
of her death."

There were tender welts across my upper back and
shoulders from which my light robe had hardly shielded
me, but at his words I had no further interest in my own
hurt.

"Do *you* think she committed suicide?" I asked him
flatly.

He drew up my robe gently over the sore places and
turned away to write a prescription for ointment. There
was the matter of putting his glasses on and taking them
off—all delaying tactics, I suspected—before he answered
me. When he did his voice was kind, thoughtful.

"Doro was my patient from the time she was quite
young. She had a gift for happiness. When she loved, she
loved with all her heart, and sometimes she claimed
that her heart was broken. But I doubt that she ever
hated, and she always recovered. I believe that she loved
your father in a more adult way than she'd ever loved
that boy who died, and she was happy with him. It
was hard for me to understand why she would take
the action she did, or to believe that she would kill herself."

I thanked him warmly, and his eyes were pitying as he
said good night.

"I will give this prescription to Clarita, so she can
have it filled for you," he said, and went downstairs.

Alone in my room, I sat on the bed for a few moments,
thinking about the doctor's words. And of that warning
Clarita had whispered to me: *Cuidado!* In spite of Juan's
belief that the real attack had been aimed against him, I
didn't believe it. I was the one whom the attacker had
meant to frighten. Juan had been lightly struck, so that he
supposedly would not be able to identify my assailant.
But Eleanor, who read her grandfather with a cool and

calculating eye, believed that Juan had known who it was.

There *had* been someone on my stairs. The sounds had been intended for me to hear. Perhaps they had been bait to make me curious and entice me into the patio. It would not have been Juan down there in the living room, since he had his own passageway to the patio, if he chose to be secretly abroad.

Someone was growing afraid. Someone who wanted to warn me away from Santa Fe before I remembered too much. Was it that shadowy third one who struggled in the mists of my memory, and would not make himself known? What had Clarita said earlier about a death march? That it had begun again, and that she'd heard the footsteps before, when my mother had died? But Clarita was given to the ominously mystical.

Anyway, nothing further was to be gained by puzzling over all this now. I slipped off my robe and went to bed somewhat gingerly, trying to favor my shoulders. My thoughts would not stop their churning, however.

Downstairs Gavin had been kind to me again. He had been concerned for my hurt. But of course his kindness had been impersonal—simply the sort of thing he would extend to anyone who had been injured. It did not mean that he thought differently about me, or was ready to retract the harsh words he'd flung at me earlier in the evening.

Tears that I resented were wet against my pillow and I found that my teeth had begun to chatter with a reaction of nerves. I could feel the lash of the whip—intending to hurt, intending to warn. Warn of what might come next if I didn't go away?

I was so alone. There was no one to whom I could turn with confidence. The fetish had been the first hint of warning. Now it was growing worse. And I must keep my own counsel, lest he who was afraid be forced into more dangerous action. Or she? Clarita? Eleanor? But Eleanor wouldn't care about the past. She had been only ten when my mother died.

I tried to think of Gavin's hand holding mine, comforting me. I could remember the feeling of his fingers about my own, and that was all I wanted. If he loved Eleanor, it didn't matter—if only he would befriend me for a little while.

Sleep came while I was clinging to that memory—and at once I began to dream about the tree. But this time I was strong enough to sit up in bed and fling off the nightmare. When next I fell asleep, sore and exhausted, my dreams were harmless, and I couldn't recall them when I awakened to morning sunlight.

There was a stiffness to my back and shoulders when I got out of bed, but I could tell by the bathroom mirror that the red welts were less marked. If I stayed, I would live to face the next attack, I thought wryly. *If* I stayed. Was it worth it to risk what was now becoming a more determined warning to me to go away? I didn't know. Doroteo Cordova Austin seemed a faraway stranger to me this morning, and I was simply the daughter who did not know her—and who was afraid and terribly uncertain.

No one was at the table when I went to breakfast, and I ate very little. Coffee was warming and savory, and I began to make a plan for my morning. I needn't decide at once whether to stay or to go. I must give my mind time to quiet so that I could choose wisely. Whatever happened, I didn't want to run away in a panic—and have to live with an act of cowardice for the rest of my life. So this morning I would paint. I would go out into the street and find a vista that appealed to me, and I would give myself to catching it on canvas.

Decision helped. When I left the table and started toward my room, I felt momentarily eased. From the foot of my stairs, I could look through into the living room, and I saw that a bustle was going on. Clarita was there, directing Rosa, and plumping up the small henna cushions strewn across the couch. She looked up and saw me, nodding indifferently.

"How is my grandfather?" I asked.

"Overly stimulated." She shook her head in disapproval. "He wants to come downstairs to sit for a while. And he wishes to see you."

I stayed where I was, waiting. After a moment, she sent Rosa away and came toward me.

"And you? Did you sleep? How are you feeling this morning?"

"Sore and stiff," I said. "Does anyone know what really happened?"

"My father feels that he has enemies. Someone got into the patio last night while he was there. You were in the way."

"I certainly was. But what were you doing up?"

Her head went back at such blunt questioning, and she made an effort to stare me down. When it didn't work, she went back to her cushion plumping, and surprised me by answering.

"I knew my father was up and about. I was concerned for him."

Whether this was the truth or not, I didn't know. She had not come outside quickly, as had Gavin and Eleanor.

"I'm going out to paint," I told her. "Do you suppose my grandfather still has an old easel he could let me use? I brought none with me."

"There is one in the storeroom. I will get it for you."

"Thank you. I'll collect my gear and then come down and talk to him."

She nodded stiffly. "I have the prescription Dr. Morrisby ordered for you. You cannot apply it yourself."

She insisted on coming with me to my room, and while I lay on my bed, she smoothed the ointment matter-of-factly over my shoulders. She had neither sympathy for me nor compassion, but she would do her duty to a guest in her house.

When she'd gone, I changed to slacks and a sweater, and picked up my sketchbook. By the time I went downstairs, Juan Cordova was stretched out like a recumbent emperor upon the leather couch, and Clarita was no-where in sight. She had kept her word about the easel, however, and it stood propped near the door.

XIII

Rosa knelt before the hearth tending a fire of white piñon logs. Their pungence filled the room and I knew this was a scent out of my childhood—the scent of Santa Fe, of New Mexico, of the Southwest.

Juan Cordova seemed in a strangely benign mood, considering what had happened to us last night.

"How are you feeling?" I asked, sitting beside him in a chair near his couch.

He waved my query aside with a careless hand, perhaps because of Rosa's presence. "The thing I come downstairs for, Amanda, is this fire. Not only the warmth, but the fragrance. I remember it from my boyhood—out at the *rancho*."

"I remember it too," I said. "It's unforgettable."

"Odors breed memory. You are beginning to remember this room?"

But I wasn't. There were no flashes to remind me that the very young Amanda had ever been here.

He went on conversationally. "You know it was the women who built the adobe fireplaces in every house in the early days. And it was the women who polished the inside walls to a gloss, rubbing them with sheepskin on their hands."

Rosa stood up and regarded the narrow mantel over the fireplace. With a quick movement she stroked the ledge and brought her finger away gritty, shaking her head. There was always dust in Santa Fe.

"There's nothing more," Juan told her, and she gave us a quick smile and ran off to another part of the house.

"I am too rough for them," Juan Cordova muttered. "I am not defeated yet. They wait for me to die. Perhaps they try to hurry my dying. But I am still alive. And you, Amanda? It is you I am concerned about. Through no fault of your own, you have been drawn into our troubles."

"I'm all right," I assured him. "But I don't understand what happened. Or why it happened."

Even when he was lying down, his look could be fierce, intimidating. "It is not necessary for you to understand, but I think you must go away, Amanda."

"That's not what you said yesterday. I haven't forgotten the way you tried to use me against Eleanor and Gavin. They're both angry with me now, and for no fault of mine."

His soft laughter recalled how he had disconcerted us all, and he was not above enjoying the memory. Then he saw my face and sobered like a naughty child. But he was not a child in any sense, and I didn't like the pretense. I listened to his words in distrust.

"You must go away, Amanda, because it is no longer safe for you here. You are becoming involved in what you do not understand."

"Because I'm beginning to remember too much?"

He dismissed my words. "We have been over all that. There is nothing to remember that will serve your mother now. I have faced that fact long ago. I have tried to go along with this pretext that there is something you might remember that would exonerate your mother. I would like to believe that too, but I have had to face reality long ago. Now you must face it. So you must leave, because there may be danger for you here."

"But if there's nothing of importance for me to remember, how can there be danger? You contradict yourself."

"No—danger, if there is any, lies in the present. Because of what I may do with my will. Danger because of—Doña Inés."

"That's nonsense. Danger from whom—Eleanor, Gavin, Clarita?"

He flushed at what he must have regarded as my impertinence in contradicting him, but he let it pass.

"You do not understand these matters. I feared I might force some risk upon you, but I did not think it would come so quickly, or be so vicious. Now you must go away."

"Then you do think last night's attack was meant for me, not you?"

He repeated obstinately, "You must go away."

And, as obstinately, I resisted. "Not yet. You can put me out of your house, of course, but unless you do, I'll stay awhile longer. You brought me here, and now you must put up with me. I think I'm coming close to something."

"I did not know what a true Cordova I was bringing here," he said with surprising mildness, and I had to relent and smile at him. At once he held out his hand. "That is better. A dark brow does not become you. You give me pleasure when you smile. I am reminded of the portrait of Emanuella."

He was beguiling me, but his falcon's look did not match his tone. I began to gather up my painting gear, preparing to leave him.

"Wait," he said. "If you will not go away at once, then there is something you can do for me tonight."

"If I can." I was immediately cautious.

"Last night, while I lay trying to sleep, someone came and stood beside my bed, watching me. When I reached for the light, this person went away."

"Clarita, perhaps?" I said. "She was concerned for you last night."

"Clarita knows she must announce herself when she comes near me. She knows I will not be secretly watched.

But then there was the attack later in the patio, when I got up, being unable to rest because of concern for my collection. There are those who plot against me, Amanda. But I cannot see the face of my enemy."

This all seemed a little fanciful. There was no one who could get to him except the members of his household, and I could not see one of them threatening him seriously. He was quite capable of weaving fantasies in order to prevail upon my sympathy.

"What is it you want me to do?"

"I am no longer able to drive a car. I can go nowhere without being taken, so I cannot do this for myself. You will go to the store for me this evening."

"Go to the store?" I echoed. "To CORDOVA—at night?"

He went on calmly. "In the daytime you would be seen, your action noted. Surprise is on my side. Slip out of the house quietly, so no one will know you have gone. I will order a taxi for nine o'clock. It will wait for you where our road turns into Camino del Monte Sol. I will give you a key. Two keys."

He fumbled in the pocket of his robe and as he held out the ring I took it from him reluctantly.

"One is to the back door of the store. It will also deactivate the alarm. Let yourself in and go upstairs to the cabinet of Toledo swords. The second key will open it. There is a carved wooden box on the floor of the cabinet. Bring it to me. And tell no one."

The keys were cold in my fingers and I did not like the feel of them. Nor did I in the least like the prospect of going into that place at night when no one was there. It was eerie enough in the daytime, and too much had happened to me.

"You are not afraid of an empty store?" he challenged me.

"Of course I am. After last night, I don't want to go anywhere that's empty and dark. Why don't you send Gavin?"

"How far can I trust Gavin? How far can I trust any of those who work against me? You I can trust because you want nothing of me. You must do this for me, Amanda. And of course it will not be dark in the store. Certain lights are left burning all night. And no one will know you are going there."

His strong will compelled my own, bent me to his way, as he had done before. There was no affection between us, but perhaps there was a certain respect.

"All right," I said. "I'll do as you wish."

His thin lips twisted in the semblance of a smile, and once more I sensed triumph in his dominance over me.

"Gracias, querida, gracias."

"What's in the box you want me to bring you?" I asked.

"When you bring it here to me, perhaps I will show you. But it is a Pandora's box and you are not to open it yourself. Promise me that."

"I promise," I told him, though I wondered what possible difference it would make if I knew the contents.

"Good. Then you may go about whatever you want to do with your day. I will sit here for a time where the fire can warm my bones."

"I'm going out to the street to do some painting," I said. "Clarita has found your old easel for me. I'll take a sandwich and not bother anyone for lunch."

He nodded as though his thoughts were already far away and I knew he was again deep in his own concerns and fear. But what he was afraid of I didn't know.

The morning was bright when I let myself out through the turquoise gate and walked along the dusty edge of the road, looking at adobe walls with their hand-rounded tops, and at the low houses behind them. Hills rose close by, while farther away were the snow-peaked Sangre de Cristos, and I wondered what it was like up there in the snow, far above the pines

There was little traffic on this blind road, and I found a sheltered place in the shadow of a poplar tree where the sun would not shine upon my canvas. There I put up my easel. I had brought several small canvas boards in my sketchbox and when I'd set one of them in place,

I made a finder of my hands to separate the picture I might want from its surroundings.

A portion of winding road with an adobe wall following it, an open gateway with a low house and a poplar at its door—these seemed right for composition and reflected this part of Santa Fe. I might put a small hill into the background as well. With that feeling of anticipation mingled with uncertainty about my own ability that often came to me when I began to paint, I squeezed coils of pigment onto my rectangular palette. This would be a picture of sunlight on adobe, and that was tricky to catch. You achieved sunlight by suggesting it to the eye, not by trying to color it in as an entity in itself. This could be accomplished by the exaggeration of contrast—by using both the highest and lowest values, and touching in highlights with a judicious use of white. I liked oils for sunlight because natural light penetrated and was refracted, so that the surface had a luminous effect—as though one mixed sunlight into the oil paints themselves.

When I had sketched quickly with charcoal, I went to work, and everything but the scene before me faded away. I could forget about Gavin, and even about that moment last night when a whip had slashed across my shoulders. None of that had reality in this sunny scene, and the hours slipped past as I worked.

There was the familiar smell of turpentine and the paints themselves, all mixing with the warming scent of the sun upon adobe—like sun-baked pine needles. Yet the air was cool and comfortable. I concentrated intensely, lost in a quiet joy because I was doing what I liked best to do, and nothing else existed. The picture was coming to life on canvas, and I thought it would not be too bad. I wasn't sure I'd caught exactly the right hues for adobe, but the effect was close. I'd been right about a touch of veridian green for the shadows of the houses. Burnt sienna seemed right for a patch of dried grass, and cadmium red, light, to touch in the poplar's shadow at the bole of the tree.

I was so far away from everything but my canvas that I jumped when a soft voice spoke behind me.

Jarred back to reality, annoyed at being interrupted, and aware of a crick in my neck and the weight of the palette on my thumb, I looked around at Eleanor. When I'd seen her in the gallery last evening, she had been furiously angry. Yet here she stood, a slim figure in jeans and white blouse, with the medallions of a silver concho belt slung low on her hips, smiling as though there had been no flaring anger between us. I didn't trust her, but I decided to go along with this suspiciously amiable mood and see if I could find out what lay behind it.

"How are you feeling, Amanda?" she asked.

I moved my shoulders gingerly, not wanting to remember.

"I'm all right."

She regarded me intently. "Who do you think used that whip last night?"

"I'm not trying to guess," I said. "Do you know?"

"Perhaps *I* can guess."

"Then you'd better tell your grandfather."

She changed the subject abruptly, studying my canvas. "I wish I could do something like that."

"Anybody can paint," I said, offering her the usual cliché.

"I don't think that's true." Eleanor stood back to look at my picture. "Not to do it as well as you can. Or as those artists did who painted the pictures in Juan's collection."

I laughed as I stroked in a bit of cadmium yellow. "Don't mention me in the same breath. I'm hardly in that class."

"Don't be so modest! I can't paint, but I've looked at paintings all my life, thanks to Juan. I didn't expect you to be so good."

With my brush poised in the air, I turned to look at her in surprise. Her fair hair was caught back at the nape of her neck with a torn blue ribbon, her pale bangs were ruffled, and her face was devoid of all make-up, so that it looked guileless and surprisingly young. I had never seen her like this before, and I was instinctively on guard. When the Cordovas chose to disarm, they could be all too convincing.

"Do you care if I stay to watch?" she asked, and dropped onto a patch of dry grass by the roadside, not waiting for my assent. I turned back to my work, hoping that she'd soon grow bored and go away. But she seemed in a mood to talk, and though I didn't encourage her, she wandered amiably into words as though we were the best of friends.

"I understand you went out to the *rancho* yesterday. Did Gavin tell you anything about the place?"

"A little," I said.

"It used to belong to Juan's father—Antonio Cordova, our great-grandfather. He should have been a Spanish don. He always claimed that Spain was the mother country, and that Seville, not Madrid, was the historical capital of the Americas. It was Seville which sent out the explorers and the missionary priests."

For me, this was a new family name I hadn't heard before.

"Did you know Antonio Cordova?"

"He died before I was born. But I've heard about him all my life. Clarita used to tell me stories of her grandfather. He was furious when his son married an Anglo woman—our grandmother Katy—and moved into Santa Fe to start a store. Clarita says Juan had to be enormously successful to prove to his father what he could do. It's too bad that Antonio died before CORDOVA became as famous as it is today. You went through the store too yesterday, didn't you?"

"Yes—it's impressive." I tried to concentrate on my painting. The scene was coming rather well, in spite of Eleanor's interruption.

"Someday CORDOVA will belong to me," she said and there was a hint of defiance in her words, as though she dared me to disagree.

I didn't pick up the bait. "It will be a big responsibility. It's a good thing you have Gavin to manage it and buy for it."

She jumped up and moved off a little way, then came back to me, kicking at the dirt with one stub-toed shoe.

"Let's not talk about Gavin."

I shrugged and went on with my painting.

After a moment or two she tried a different tack. "Clarita says you found that old turquoise mask out at the *rancho* and brought it home. Why?"

"Because I remember it. It made some connection in my mind with—with what happened."

Excitement kindled. "That's lovely! Paul will want to hear about this. What did it make you remember?"

"Nothing. Except that I was afraid. Sylvia says when they were all children, they used to play Blind Man's Buff with the mask at the *rancho*."

"Yes. Clarita's told me about that. One day when Kirk was wearing the mask, he caught Doro and took it off and kissed her. Clarita saw, and she was still angry when she told me the story. In those days she wanted Kirk herself, and she resented the fact that he liked Doro best. Of course she got over him later. He wasn't the love of her life."

"Who was?"

"Don't you know?" she asked slyly.

I wasn't going to play games. "Anyway, my mother ended by being in love with William Austin," I reminded her.

"That's not how Clarita's story goes. She thinks that Doro was still in love with Kirk when he came back after being away for all those years."

I said nothing more. I had no wish to argue such points with Eleanor, and I didn't know why she was talking about any of this.

"When Gavin drove you out to the *rancho* did you go through Madrid?" she asked. In the local manner she put the accent on the first syllable of the town's name.

"I don't know. Why?"

"He may have taken you by the other road. You'd know if you went through Madrid. It's a ghost town now, though it was once a thriving mining town. There are Cordova roots out there, and it would be a perfect place for you to paint. If you like, I'll drive you out there sometime."

"Thanks," I said, and gave her a direct look. "Why are you feeling better about me today? You were pretty angry with me yesterday."

"How suspicious you are, Amanda!" Eleanor's violet eyes gave me a wide look of innocence that did not convince me. "We're cousins, aren't we? So isn't it time we got acquainted?"

"Who do you think used that whip last night in the patio?" I returned her own question with a suddenness that made her blink.

For a moment she only stared at me. I went on. "Paul says several things were taken from the Penitente display."

"I know. He told me. Doña Sebastiana still hasn't turned up. But I don't know why anyone should want to attack Grandfather."

"I don't believe anyone did. I think I was the one they were after. He was struck down so whoever it was could get away."

She regarded me coolly, appraisingly, her earlier pretense of amiability gone. "Then I should be very much afraid, if I were you, Amanda."

"Why? Because I'm coming close to something revealing?"

"Aren't you?"

I told her then—told her I'd remembered that there had been three figures struggling together the day when my mother had gone to meet Kirk, and not two as Clarita claimed and everyone believed.

She listened with a bright avidity that I found chilling. Yet I'd felt I had to tell her. She would spread this around, of course. She would tell Paul and perhaps Clarita. She might even tell our grandfather. And now I might be in greater danger than ever. But this was the only way I knew in which to bring that hazy third figure into the open where he could be recognized.

She gave my painting another glance of pretended interest, and then said a casual *Hasta la vista,* and went off toward the house. Though it was past noon, the sun seemed a little less bright, and the air a trifle more chilly.

I moved about, stretching and flexing my fingers. Then I sat down on a low adobe wall and ate my sandwich, drank from a thermos. To go back to the house would break my mood even more than Eleanor had broken it, and as soon as I could I returned to my work and let it absorb me.

Only once after that did I surface, returning to the thought of the Cordovas with a jolt. In spite of my preoccupation with my work, and the successful distraction it offered, the thought of tonight and what I'd promised to do for my grandfather was not as far away as I would like. His plan still repelled me and I wished I hadn't agreed to something I didn't want to do. I had let his will overpower me again. When I returned to the house, I would simply tell him I'd changed my mind. I no longer felt safe and protected by adobe walls, and I had no intention of frightening myself further with the errand he had set me.

Coming to this decision gave me a sense of relief, and now I could paint the afternoon away, nearly finishing what I'd started. Sometimes it took days to complete a picture, but today I'd worked long and steadily and accomplished a lot.

I scraped my palette, dipped my brushes in turpentine and wiped them and my hands on the paper towels I'd brought along instead of paint rags. My sketchbox would hold a wet canvas without smearing it, and I packed everything away and returned to the house.

Clarita met me in the living room, and she seemed in something of a fluster. "Father is coming down to dinner tonight, Amanda. And we are having company. Sylvia and Paul. Sylvia was over just now and my father invited them. So put on a good dress and come down on time."

She looked as though some ordeal were facing her, and I think she might have rebelled if she could. I wondered what had given rise to this sudden party, and the unusual factor of Juan Cordova coming down for dinner. But Clarita rushed off toward the kitchen to supervise preparations, and there was no time to ask.

When I reached my room, I took out my painting and set it in the embrasure of a window where it could dry in the air. I liked the look of my adobe walls and winding road, yet it was not a sentimental picture. There was a certain starkness about the hot sky and baking earth. It was not really a Santa Fe picture, but one that suggested the oasis of a village in desert country in midsummer—a timeless scene. A brown-clad brother who was new from Seville might come riding up that road on a burro at any moment. Perhaps I would even paint him in. A glow of satisfaction was my reward. This was the first of my New Mexico paintings, and I knew there would be more. I had a special feeling for this land that lent emotion to my brush.

Painting had brought relaxation from tension for a time, but it had tired me too, and now I might lie down and rest before dinner. My room was cool and dim with late afternoon light, and I turned toward the bed, about to throw back the coverlet—only to stop in surprise. Slightly mounded, something lay beneath the covers—something with a vaguely human form.

A tremor of warning went through me, and with it came that awareness of something menacing and secret that I'd first felt about this house. With my deepest senses I knew what the house knew—and there was terror all about me. Yet still my conscious mind told me nothing.

With an effort, I managed to fling back the covers and stood staring at the thing that grinned back at me from the pillow. All of last night's horror re-engaged me, and I could almost feel the sting of that three-pronged whip across my shoulders. Doña Sebastiana stared at me with hollow eyes, and bared, grinning teeth in her skull's head. Her bow and arrow seemed pointed at my heart and it was her bony figure which made the slight mound beneath the covers.

I ran to my door and called shrilly for Clarita. She heard me and came running up the stairs, to stand beside me, staring at the thing on the bed.

"*La Muerte,*" she said softly. "The carts are rolling. The footsteps are coming nearer. The death march."

If I listened to her I might go a little mad too. I grasped her by the arm and shook her roughly.

"Stop that! I won't be frightened by such tricks. I won't be threatened. This is Eleanor again, isn't it? Just as the fetish was Eleanor!"

"And do you think it was Eleanor who whipped you last night?" Clarita whispered. "Do you think it was Eleanor who whipped her grandfather?"

"Juan must be told about this," I said, and moved toward the door.

At once she blocked my way. "No. He has borne enough."

I pushed past her and ran down the stairs. Juan was no longer in the living room and I went up to his balcony and looked into his empty study. Then I stepped to a window and looked down into the patio. Only a little way off he lay in a lounge chair with a pillow under his head and the late afternoon sun warming him. But even as I found him, Clarita came outdoors, and I saw agitation in the way she bent above her father. She had reached him first, and I couldn't know what she might be telling him. Nevertheless, I must see him for myself.

When I went out to the patio she was still there, but though she faced me with a bitter anger in her dark eyes, Juan saw me, and there was nothing she could do when I dropped to my knees beside his chair. There was no way in which Clarita could stop me from telling him what I had found in my bed. He closed his eyes at my outpouring, but he heard me through before he spoke. Then he opened his eyes and looked at Clarita.

"Leave us, please," he said.

She was reluctant to obey, and for a moment I thought she might take a strong enough stand to oppose him. But old habit ruled, and she bowed her head so that the blue earrings swayed at her jawline. When she'd gone into the house, Juan spoke to me.

"You will go away soon, Amanda," he said weakly. "Tomorrow we will arrange for your plane back to New York. The risk is becoming too great. I should never have brought you here, but I had thought this was one way to stop Paul Stewart from trying to use you for his book. Here we could protect you from him. Or so we thought."

It was time to tell him. There was no longer any secret about what I knew, since I'd told Eleanor.

"There were three on the hillside when my mother died," I said. "I don't know who the other was, but there were three figures struggling together."

Weakness seemed to leave him, and he sat up in his chair and reached for my wrist with strong, thin fingers. "This is what Katy tried to tell me before she died. This is what I would not believe."

"Do you know who it could have been?" I asked.

He stared at me, not answering, and his fingers hurt my wrist. "It's too late to do anything now," he said. "I will not have all that old tragedy resurrected again. What is done is done."

"To protect the living?" I said.

He flung my hand away from him as though the touch of it had become suddenly distasteful. "To protect you. Doro's daughter. You must leave here at once."

"I won't go," I said. "Not now when I am coming so close to the truth. Don't you *want* to know, Grandfather?"

The weakness was upon him again. "I am old. I cannot bear any more. Tonight there will be a little party I have planned for you in farewell. And after dinner you will slip away and do for me what I asked. I am in danger too, Amanda, and only you can help me now. Then we will talk again about your returning to New York."

I rose from my place beside him without answering. His dark, fierce eyes watched my face, and I think he saw my opposition, my disbelief in *his* danger.

"I have told Clarita to take that—object from your bed and give it to Paul Stewart when he comes tonight. It must be returned to the display in the store. We will meet again at dinner, Amanda."

I walked slowly back to my room. I didn't know whether I would go away or not, but I knew now that I would have to do as he wished and carry out the mission he had set for me later tonight. Perhaps it was the last thing I could do for him.

Doña Sebastiana was gone from my room, but Rosa was there changing the sheets and pillowcase. I was grateful to Clarita, for I'd have felt a repugnance to touch the sheets where that figure had lain. Rosa's eyes looked big and a little frightened, and I knew she must have seen what had been hidden in the bed. She made no attempt to talk to me, but hurried with her work, and escaped as quickly as she could—almost as though an evil spell had been laid upon me and she didn't want to come too close.

I lay down on top of the covers and tried to rest. I wanted nothing more of terror, of threat. Perhaps it would be better to do as Juan Cordova wished, and go away. But I knew that my life could never be the same again, and always there would be the unanswered questions and the memories of Santa Fe and this old house. There would be memories of Gavin, too, but I couldn't help that. I was never able to put him completely from my mind. Where was the borderline between being whole of heart and foolishly in love? I might rage against him when he angered me, yet a part of me yearned toward him, and that made me angry with myself. There must be a way out of this tunnel.

When it was time to dress, I did so with care, since this might be my last night in the Cordova house. Perhaps whatever occurred at tonight's dinner party might help me make up my mind. I must watch for some answer.

I had brought one dinner frock with me. It was an eggshell white, with long sleeves that fell in points over my wrist, a long slim skirt with a slit to one knee, and a rounded neckline. The lines were simple and it was without decoration, so I pinned my Zuni brooch near the neckline and clipped on my mother's earrings. No matter whom they might upset I wanted to wear her little birds tonight. My lipstick was a light mandarin—not too pale, and I left my eyes alone. Men weren't fond of heavy eye shadow—that was a female choice of make-up— and tonight I dressed for Gavin. Never mind whether I had any good sense or not. Very soon now I might never see him again.

When I went downstairs a little late, I found them having drinks in the living room—all except Gavin, who was missing. Eleanor wore black in contrast to my white, with a diagonal of fringe across the front, like a Spanish shawl, and she had piled her hair high upon her head, graced with a Spanish comb and a flower, and plastered down her bangs in spit curls. There were pearls about her neck, and at her ears, and she looked stunningly beautiful. Apparently recovered from his earlier weakness, Juan sat near the fire, and could hardly take his eyes off Eleanor for pride. She need not, I thought, worry about losing her fortune to me. His look approved my own appearance when I entered the room, but it was Eleanor who held his real affection.

Clarita, surprisingly, wore a long robe of claret velvet, trimmed with an edging of old gold, and her earrings were great golden hoops. I found myself staring at her, seeing for the first time that she could be a remarkably handsome woman when she chose not to efface herself. Sylvia Stewart was thoroughly modern in a powder blue tunic and trousers, and Paul had pleased himself and worn a comfortable plaid jacket with a southwestern bolo tie.

I wondered where Gavin was, but no one mentioned him.

Though Paul's attention often wandered to Eleanor, he shortly attached himself to me, and I knew he'd probably had her latest report about my elusive memories. He drew me aside and tried to probe a little, and when I had nothing more to tell him, he grew insistent.

"I've always been sure that something was kept off the record that day," he told me. "And you're the one who knew what it was, Amanda. Are you sure you haven't found the answer?"

Intent, his yellow-green eyes seemed to demand the truth from me, and I found myself resenting him more than ever.

"Perhaps it would help if we could know exactly where you were that day," I said, deliberately baiting him. "You told me that you and Sylvia were coming along the upper road together on the way to the picnic, but Sylvia says that she was alone that day."

He stared at me fixedly for a moment, and then laughed aloud, so that heads turned to look at him.

"So you'd like to tie me into it," he said. "Do you think I'd really want to write about a murder I'd committed?"

"I don't know," I said.

"Sylvia must have forgotten." His words were casual.

I let the matter go. "Anyway, I'm not sure of anything—except that they all want me gone."

"I can see why. They want you gone before you turn their comfortable lives upside down to any greater extent. I've heard about the will. Eleanor was pretty furious for a time, but she seems to have calmed down. I advised her to."

"It won't matter," I told him lightly. "I'll probably be gone by tomorrow."

"So they're sending you away?"

"I haven't decided yet," I said, and moved off toward Juan Cordova, where he sat on the leather couch near the fire.

He nodded to me and I saw his gaze flick to my earrings, but he did not tell me to take them off, as he had done before. Nor did he attempt to engage me in conversation. I suspected that he was more tired tonight than he wanted us to know and was concentrating on his inner forces so that he could get through the evening.

Paul had returned his fascinated attention to Eleanor, who was thoroughly alight in her black gown, moving once more like a dancer, her long fringes swaying as though she played a role, and as though her dance might be mounting to a climax. Not only Juan Cordova watched her, and Paul, but Clarita too, and I saw the pride of maternal possession in those dark eyes. To Clarita, Eleanor would always be her child. But Clarita watched Paul too, with a certain fondness born, I wondered, of long ago love?

Oddly, Sylvia, who usually fitted in anywhere, was on the outside tonight. She stood a little apart from the others and watched them all as though she held a seat at a play in which she wanted no active part. When I was able, I moved quietly to her side.

She looked at me with a start that told me I hadn't been one of those she studied. "Why tonight?" she said. "Why a party *tonight?*"

"I suppose because I'm expected to leave tomorrow. But you were looking at them so strangely. Tell me what you see."

"Calamity." She grimaced. "That's what Eleanor is— calamity. She's like Doro in that. She won't be happy until she blows everything sky high."

"Did my mother really want to have that effect?"

"Perhaps not consciously. But she never saw what was coming."

"Is that why Gavin isn't here tonight? Because of what Eleanor might do?"

"But he is here," she said.

I looked past her and saw him in the doorway. Without defense, our eyes met across the room, and for an instant I saw his light. Whether my own betrayed me in return, I didn't know, and he looked away at once, his guard immediately raised. Clearly he was surprised by the party.

Clarita went quickly to welcome him and explain, and I suspected that they'd deliberately not warned him ahead of time, lest he stay away. So one more factor of disruption had been introduced into the room.

Strangely, it was Clarita who pulled everything together as we went into the dining room and took our places at the table. She dominated the room quite magnificently in her claret red gown, and I saw Eleanor watching her in astonishment. Something had enlivened Clarita and given her a strength I had not seen before. By way of contrast, Juan seemed to shrink to a lesser size, and the usual hubris he radiated was gone. If it hadn't seemed impossible, I might have thought that my arrogant grandfather was afraid of his elder daughter.

It was Eleanor, however, who dropped the first pebble into the pool and started the ripples widening across already muddied water.

"I happened on an interesting fact today," she announced. "Have any of you remembered that this is Kirk Landers' birthday?"

Sylvia gasped softly and Clarita flashed a look at her.

"No, it is not," Clarita said.

With an effort, Juan Cordova reached for his wine glass, ignoring his daughter. "There was a time when Kirk was very dear to us, as you are, Sylvia. Why should we not remember a lost son with a toast?"

I had the feeling that he was defying Clarita in some way, and perhaps tormenting Sylvia.

Eleanor caught up her glass at once. "You give the toast, Sylvia."

Juan nodded benignly at his foster daughter, appearing more like himself. "We are waiting, Sylvia," he said.

Looking about to dissolve in tears, Sylvia did not touch her glass, but only sat there, shaking her head miserably. "I—I can't. Eleanor is being cruel."

"Let me then," said Paul, and that bright green gleam was in his eyes as he raised his glass. "To one we all miss. To one who died too soon and too young. To Kirk Landers!"

I remembered that those two had quarreled, and knew this for mockery. Juan and Eleanor raised their glasses. Gavin looked angry and did not touch his. Nor did I touch mine, since I'd never known Kirk Landers except as a small child, and I had too many questions in my mind. Clarita reached for her glass last, as though she forced herself—and knocked it over. In the ensuing distraction, with cries for Rosa and the process of mopping, Sylvia jumped up from her place and ran from the room.

Gravely Juan and Eleanor clinked each other's glasses and sipped wine, their eyes meeting in affection. Then Juan glanced at Clarita.

"You had better go to Sylvia," he said.

Clarita faced him down the length of the table. "No! I have no comfort to offer anyone. This was a cruel thing to do. A mockery, as you know very well."

"I'll go to her," I said, and slipped from the table.

She had run into the living room and flung herself full length on the leather couch. The scent of piñon wood was pungent on the air. I went to sit beside her, touching her shoulder gently. "Don't be upset. Eleanor is heedless."

"She's utterly cruel." Sylvia took several deep breaths to quiet her emotion, and looked up at me tearfully. "This isn't Kirk's birthday, as she knows very well. This is the anniversary of the day he died."

I stared at her in dismay. I hadn't known. I'd never known the exact date. Then this was also the anniversary of my mother's death.

"Why would Juan"—I faltered—"why would he gather us for a dinner on such an anniversary?"

"I don't know, I don't know!" Sylvia cried. "Perhaps to torment someone. Perhaps to remind. Perhaps really only because he's sending you away tomorrow."

"Then let's go back to the table. I want to go back, so I can watch."

"No!" Sylvia cried. "Don't wake up the sleeping. Don't call back the ghosts!"

I stared at her. "You always surprise me. When I first met you, I thought you were worried about something, but I also thought you were contained and controlled. I thought you were the unruffled type."

She sat up beside me, suddenly defiant. "I am. I must be. God knows I've practiced long enough!"

I pounced on the word. "Practiced—what do you mean?"

"Nothing, nothing. Let me alone, Amanda. If you'll wait for a moment till I run to the bathroom and wash my face, I'll go back to the table with you."

"I'll wait," I told her.

She hurried off, brushing against the end table as she went. The ugly tarantula fell off into my lap and I picked it up and replaced it on the table with repugnance. I remembered my thought that Juan Cordova was omnivorous. Tonight he had joined with Eleanor to prove that fact. If Sylvia was right, he had meant to disturb someone, and he knew very well who that someone was. But whom would he protect, if he knew the truth? Clarita, perhaps. Sylvia, possibly. Paul—surely not.

I heard Gavin's steps as he came into the room, regarding me gravely. "Is Sylvia all right?"

"She's pulling herself together. She'll be back in a moment."

"Juan says you're going away tomorrow."

"Juan doesn't know. I haven't decided."

"It's best if you do go," he said. "What happened last night was meant for you, no matter what Juan believes."

"Yes, I think so too."

"And it may happen again—and be worse."

"Do you know who it was?"

He was silent, and I knew the answer. Gavin believed

that his wife was behind the attack upon me, but he would not say so.

"Please believe me," I said. "I don't want anything from Juan in his will. He hasn't changed it yet, and I don't think he will. Eleanor is his darling."

"Eleanor is the daughter of Rafael—a son he thoroughly disliked. You are Doro's daughter."

"I'm not the one he cares about," I said. "I've been watching the way his eyes follow her. There's no danger to anything she wants. He'll take nothing away from her. And I need to stay. Gavin, I'm close to the truth of what happened. There are cracks in the surface. They're widening."

Sylvia came back in time to hear my words. "You mustn't stay now. I urged you to go in the beginning, but now everything is much worse. What can it matter to you, Amanda, whether some buried 'truth' comes out? What good will it do your mother if it only harms someone still living?"

"I don't know the answer to that. I only know that I must stay."

She gave me a long, despairing look and started for the dining room. Gavin waited for me, as relentless as Sylvia, and I went with him.

Salt had been sprinkled on the wine stain and a padded cloth mounded beneath it. Clarita looked strained, nervous, and no longer able to carry off the wearing of her handsome gown. Juan, on the contrary, was himself again. If anything, he looked renewed by what had happened, and he and Eleanor were talking to each other animatedly. Eleanor glanced around as we took our places at the table.

"I'm sorry," she said, mockingly contrite. "Grandfather tells me that I'm wrong about my dates. So I apologize. Anyway, he's feeling much better these days, and I've coaxed him into taking a little outing with all of us. Tell them, Grandfather."

While Clarita served the meal with hands that shook a little, Juan spoke to us cheerfully. "It has been too

many years since I have been out to the *rancho*. So we
are all going there one day soon. We will drive out in the
morning, have lunch, and come back in the late afternoon."

"I don't think—" Sylvia began, but he shook his head
at her gently.

"You too, of course. And Paul. It will be like the
old days. It is unfortunate that Amanda will not be
here, but otherwise it will be a family party."

I put my hand lightly on his arm. "But of course
I will be here. I'm not going away yet, Grandfather."

Around the table heads turned toward me, eyes were
fixed upon my face, and I had the feeling that one of
those who stared was angry and perhaps dangerously
frightened. But I looked only at Gavin. His face was
cold, shutting me out, condemning me.

Eleanor laughed softly. "Then we'll all be together.
What fun, Amanda! If only Kirk and Doro and Grandmother Katy could be there too, our party would be
complete."

She was once more stepping upon dangerous ground,
but no one said anything, no one reproached her frivolity.
After that the meal turned into an ordinary dinner, even
though I sensed awareness, watchfulness below the surface. Once more I had time to think ahead to the errand
Juan had planned for me. And to be again afraid of
what I must do. I had no taste at all for an excursion
into the dark reaches of the store at night. Now even
less than ever.

XIV

Though it was Saturday night, the plaza was quiet by nine o'clock, and few people were about on the streets. Most of these were wandering *turistas*.

I paid off my taxi near the plaza, since, when I was through with Juan's errand, I could go to the Fonda del Sol and phone for another. As I walked quickly toward the store, I could hear sounds of gaiety from the direction of the Fonda Hotel, but there was no one in sight when I walked down the side street and around to the back of CORDOVA.

The key Juan had given me slipped easily into the lock, but I hesitated for a moment before I pushed open the door. If I'd had any choice, I would have preferred to turn around and go home right then, but the thought of Juan Cordova's displeasure forced me to open the door. He had told me that lights were left on in the store overnight, and I found them dim but welcome as I stepped inside and closed the door softly behind me.

At once I was in an alien world, cut off from all I knew. It was a shadowy world of faint light and no sound. The daytime bustle was gone with the flow of customers on the main floor. The quiet was so intense

225

that it was as if my coming had caused the great open space of the store to hush and hold its breath, waiting for me to make some move. At night this place had a life and being of its own—the entity that was CORDOVA seemed alive.

I stood very still in the center of an aisle near the back door and listened. The smothering silence seemed without boundary. Scents of leather and sweet grasses came to me, mingling with other exotic odors that were closed into the store at night. But I mustn't stand here, I thought, listening for some whisper of sound, waiting for an imaginary footfall. Last night's attack upon me had undermined my courage, and I was sharply aware that while someone could come to my aid quickly in the patio, here no scream of mine would ever be heard and no one would come if there was danger.

But this was nonsense. Who but Juan knew that I was here? I wasn't a child to be afraid of the dark and a strange place, and I must get this over with quickly.

The nearest aisle led to the front of the store, and I followed it, walking with light steps so as not to disturb the sleeping hush. Near a lighted window I stood for a moment looking out into the street where nothing moved.

When I turned toward the stairs that led to the floor above, I had again the strange feeling that, for all the quiet about me, the store had a living spirit of its own. This was the beating heart of the thing which ruled the Cordovas, and would rule me if I let it. All about me rich stacks of merchandise were piled—offerings on a temple's altar. And the gods of the temple lurked just out of my line of vision, waiting for sacrifices.

I shook myself impatiently and started up the stairs. If there was anything here to fear, it would be living, not imaginary, and I did not feel that anyone was here. Juan had not wanted my mission to be known, so no one could be lying in wait for me, ready to strike.

The great cavern of the first floor continued to lie breathlessly still below me as I mounted the stairs. Only the creaking of wooden steps broke the blanketing silence and seemed startlingly loud. At the head of the stairs, behind glass, the figure of the flamenco dancer glimmered at me in dim light. She looked as though she might burst into movement at any moment and I could almost hear the beat of wild music. I was reminded of Eleanor tonight in her high comb and swinging fringe.

As I left the stairs, the upper floor seemed suddenly a maze, a labyrinth in which I no longer knew my direction. When a cold hand touched mine, I stifled a cry, before I realized it was only the mailed glove of a set of Spanish armor, standing lifesize beside me. I hadn't seen the armor before. I hadn't come this way. Where had Gavin led me so that I had found the cabinet of Toledo steel? I no longer knew the course I had taken and I could recognize no landmarks.

Confused by the dim aisles, with the lighting up here even fainter than it was downstairs, I moved haltingly. The clinging silk of a Spanish shawl brushed my arm, and I tried to remember where I had seen those splendid shawls.

This wouldn't do at all. I stood still, trying to regain my sense of direction, and listening in spite of myself to the utter silence. Or was it silence? Had a faraway door creaked open? Had I heard a whisper of voices? Were those feet upon the stairs? I was not imagining this time.

Laughter that sounded like Eleanor's crashed suddenly through the upper reaches of the store, echoing to the high ceiling. Because my knees weakened, I grasped a nearby counter to steady myself and shake off the alarm that swept through me. Now I could hear someone running on the stairs, hear another pair of feet coming after her, another voice speaking.

Paul Stewart's voice!

"The display is over here. Have you brought the whip?"

"Of course," Eleanor's voice replied. "And you've brought the Lady. Let's fix up the display and then explore. I wonder if all these things have a life of their own when no one is watching? I've never been here before at night."

"Nor have I," Paul said, sounding less enthusiastic.

It was all right, I told myself. They didn't know I was here. For some odd reason—probably Eleanor's whim—they had brought the Penitente things here tonight to return them to the display. I had only to be quiet and wait, and they would go away, never dreaming I was present in the empty store. Why I felt it vital to keep my presence secret, I wasn't sure, but I knew I wanted neither of them to discover me.

They made no attempt to be quiet themselves. I heard the showcase opened and the sounds of rearrangement as Doña Sebastiana was restored to her place in the stone-filled cart. In fact, they were making enough noise in the quiet store so that I could move again myself, under the cover of sound. When I reached the place where my aisle met a cross aisle, I looked carefully around.

Now I could see it. The case of Toledo swords was a tall cabinet, rising above others in its vicinity, and I made my way toward it, stepping softly. I had slipped my second key into its lock, when Eleanor's voice halted me to listen intently.

"How did you like the way I managed to plan a trip to the *rancho*?" she asked.

Paul's laughter held approval. "You handled it perfectly. The old man fell right in with what you wanted."

"I thought I could coax him. Do you know what he told me before tonight's dinner? He said we could use the fact of the date to make someone worried and uncomfortable. But the only one who went to pieces was Sylvia. I wonder why? Do you suppose she's worried about you?"

"Worried about me?" Paul repeated her words evenly.

The taunting little laugh came again. "Why not? You and Kirk hated each other, didn't you? Isn't it possible—" Perhaps something in Paul's expression stopped her, for she broke off.

Now she seemed to back down. "Oh, don't think I care about what happened that day. I'm interested in *now*. Amanda's getting around Juan, and I don't like it. But when they all go out to the *rancho*—perhaps tomorrow if I can work it—they'll be out there for most of the day. Then it won't matter what Juan does about his will. I don't like that trust he's set up for me anyway. I want money in my hands—so I can be free of Gavin, free of them all."

"Come here," Paul said.

There were faint sounds that were not of struggle, and I suspected that he was embracing her, kissing her. Silencing her? Poor Sylvia, I thought, and disliked Paul even more intensely than before. I no longer wanted to wait for them to go. All I wanted now was to get the box I had come for, and escape from the store before those two discovered me.

I turned the key and the cabinet door creaked faintly as it opened.

"What was that?" Eleanor said.

She and Paul were quiet, listening, and I kept very still. After a few moments their attention returned to the display, and when there were sounds again I reached quickly into the bottom of the cabinet to find the flat case Juan had told me to bring him. My fingers touched the carving on the lid as I drew the box out. When I closed the cabinet door, it creaked again, betraying me.

"I'm sure I heard something," Eleanor said. "Let's look around."

They were moving in my direction, and I dropped below the level of the nearest counter and crept in the direction of what I hoped was the stairs, carrying the box with me. Since they made no attempt at secrecy in their approach, I could tell where they were, and it was easy enough to keep out of their way.

The flamenco dancer loomed above me and I found the stairs. But try as I would for quiet, the ancient wood groaned under my feet, and I heard Eleanor cry out again.

"There *is* someone here! The stairs are creaking!"

I ran down without trying for stealth, and found my way toward the back door. Eleanor and Paul had left it open, but there was a light outside, and I knew I would be silhouetted against the outdoors if I stepped into the doorway. The stack of great wooden Santa Fe doors offered me a hiding place, and I stepped behind their shelter, clutching Juan's carved box to me.

Across the store, the two ran down the stairs, and I heard Eleanor whisper, "Whoever it is must be down here. Hush, Paul. Don't make any noise."

Now they were both as silent as I, and I lost track of their location. At any moment they could creep upon me, and I quivered at the thought. Eleanor would not share her secrets readily, and neither would Paul. I had heard too much. Perhaps I'd better chance the door and escape into the narrow side streets of Santa Fe. There would be less chance of their catching up with me then. Moving as softly as I could, I stole toward the escape of the open door. The stuffiness lessened, and a hint of breeze came through the doorway, welcoming me. I crept toward the opening.

There was a single instant of awareness before it happened—an instinctive premonition of danger, so that I ducked my head just as the blow fell, and I was spared its full, deadly impact. Crashing lights on a wave of pain went through my brain as I sank into oblivion.

For a long time the darkness behind my eyelids seemed to pulse with a beating of pain. Faraway voices seemed to be discussing my plight. Someone was calling my name, calling me back to pain that I wanted to escape.

"Amanda, Amanda, Amanda," the voice urged, insisting on my return.

The mists cleared slowly and I seemed to be floating in some dim void where my only contact with reality was the sound of my own name being repeated over and over. I opened my eyes to dim light and a face bending over me.

"That's better," a voice said. "You're coming round now."

Gradually the misty weaving of my surroundings steadied and I could see Paul Stewart kneeling beside me, with Eleanor standing just behind him, her face shadowed in the dim light of the store.

"Can you sit up?" Paul asked me. "We'd like to get you home, Amanda."

As he drew me to a sitting position, memory drifted back. I recalled being in the store, remembered the Penitente case and Paul and Eleanor—and my errand for Juan. Feebly I moved my hands about, concentrating only on the latter, seeking the carved box I must take to Juan—as if it were more important at the moment than anything else. The case lay under me. My hands found it and drew it from beneath my body, while Eleanor and Paul watched.

"What were you doing here, Amanda?" Eleanor demanded. "Who struck you down?"

Didn't you? I wanted to ask, but the throbbing increased and silenced me as I got to my knees, and clutched at Paul, steadying myself.

"Someone tried to kill me," I said. "Didn't you see who struck me?"

Eleanor shook her head, all her mockery gone. Paul leaned over and picked something up from the floor.

"Quetzalcoatl," he said, and held up the brass figure for me to see. "The Plumed Serpent—one of the Aztec gods. He's made a good bludgeon."

How much of this was acting? I wondered. Eleanor moved her head and light caught the glitter of excitement in her eyes.

"But who would hide in the store and strike you down? We heard you fall, but there was no one here when we reached you. What did you come here for, Amanda?"

I found that my legs would hold me, and my head

was clearing. The throbbing lessened as I righted myself. Gingerly I felt the back of my head and discovered a
rising lump. But there seemed to be little blood, if any,
and I knew I had spared myself the full force of the
blow by moving at the moment it fell. All I wanted now
was to get away from these two. I could trust neither
one. Either might have struck me down. But my arms
were weak and the box I clasped dropped to the floor
with a clatter.

At once Eleanor leaned to pick it up. "What's this?
What are you taking away from the store?"

With an effort, I reached for the box, but she drew
it away and set it on a counter. There was no way to
stop her as she pressed the clasp and raised the lid. The
interior of the box was lined with midnight blue velvet,
its contents wrapped in a chamois skin which Eleanor
unwound, revealing a slender dagger with an ornate
handle.

There was a roughness in Paul's voice when he spoke.
"What do you want with that, Amanda?"

For just an instant I thought of saying that I needed
it to protect myself against someone who'd strike me
on the head with Quetzalcoatl, but that would do no
good. Secrecy was no longer possible.

"Juan Cordova asked me to bring him the box," I
told them. "I didn't know what was in it."

Eleanor whistled softly, looked at Paul. Then she
replaced the weapon in its wrapping and closed the
box, gave it back to me.

"I suppose you'll have to take it to him," she said.
"But I don't like this at all."

Paul held my arm as we went out the door, and
Eleanor ran ahead to open her car. I was helped into
the back seat, where I slumped into a corner. We drove
home without incident, and no more questions were asked.
It was good to breathe deeply of the night air, and my
headache faded to a dull throb. I didn't try to think
of anything.

When we reached the house there was a hasty,

whispered consultation between Paul and Eleanor in the front seat. Paul helped me out and waited long enough to see whether I was able to walk. Then he told us a quick good night and cut through the patio to his own side gate, while Eleanor took my arm and steadied me through the living-room door.

"Shall I help you up to your room?" she asked.

I shook my head. "Not now. I'm going to see Juan first. He asked me to come to him when I got back."

For a moment Eleanor looked as though she might say something more—perhaps ask for my silence, perhaps ask how much I'd heard of her conversation with Paul—but she must have known it would do no good, for she shrugged and made a slight grimace.

"I'll go get Clarita. She'll want to have a look at that lump on your head."

I tried to tell her not to bother, but she went off, and I moved reluctantly toward my grandfather's study. I had no wish for long explanations. All I wanted was to sit in my room and try to recover myself. But there was no help for it—I had to face Juan Cordova.

He was lying on his couch, waiting for me.

"I've brought the box," I said, and put it into his hands.

He sat up, almost fondling the case, his fingers moving in appreciation over the carved lid.

"I know what's in it," I said. "Why did you want the dagger?"

He made a sound of annoyance and opened the box. With careful fingers he unwrapped what lay within and held it up by the handle, forgetting me for the moment as light caught the blade in a bright flash.

"There is no better steel than that of Toledo," he murmured. "And this handle is of fine Toledo Damascene. I purchased it myself in a shop there many years ago."

"Why did you want me to bring it to you?" I persisted.

With a suddenness that startled me, he thrust the dagger beneath his pillow on the couch. "I do not mean to lie here helpless, defenseless. But I told you not to open the box, Amanda."

"I didn't open it," I said. "Eleanor did." And I told him that she and Paul had been in the store, apparently to return the Penitente things to their display case, and that I had been trying to escape without their discovering me when I was struck.

He was silent for a long time after my account, his gaze fixed on the wall beyond my head. When he spoke his face seemed to collapse into the fallen lines of despair.

"What am I to do? Where can I place my trust? Which one of them did this to you, Amanda?"

"I don't know whether either of them did," I said.

"But who else would go to the store? Amanda, this is no longer a choice you can make. You are not safe in this house."

"Because the one who killed my mother is afraid of me?"

He made a choked sound. "No one killed Doro. She died by her own will. It was Kirk Landers who was shot."

"You believe what you want to believe!" I cried. "You won't be shaken from your own stubbornness."

He looked at me with pain in his eyes, but as I started to say more Clarita burst into the room in an agitated state. She was dressed in black again, with only one of the gold hoops she'd worn at dinner still gracing an ear.

"What is this, Amanda? My father has told me of this foolishness in sending you on an errand to the store at this hour. Now you have been hurt. And I suppose you have come crying back to him?"

"That's enough!" Juan said sharply. "I wish to know all that happens. There are to be no secrets held from me."

"Isn't it time you went to the police?" I asked.

Both Clarita and Juan made sounds of repudiation.

"I will not advertise our troubles in the newspapers," Juan insisted. "We have been through all this before."

Clarita bowed her head in agreement. "Come with me,

Amanda, and I will look at your bruise in a good light. It must be bathed and perhaps bandaged."

"Go with her," Juan said. "We will talk more tomorrow, before you start for home."

"Right now this is my home," I said, "inhospitable as it seems to be," and I followed Clarita out of the room.

She led me to a bathroom where she opened a medicine cabinet, so thoroughly annoyed that she spat angry little cries as she took out what she needed and examined the back of my head.

"Why must you be where you should not be? Why must you provoke trouble? You will be killed if you continue like this. You must heed my father and leave Santa Fe tomorrow."

"Who is it that wants to kill me, Aunt Clarita?" I asked softly.

She dabbed roughly at the lump on my head with cotton dipped in disinfectant, and the skin must have been broken because it stung.

"Ask no more questions. Close your eyes. Close your ears. Be quiet until you can get away."

"What did you do with the diary pages, Aunt Clarita?"

Again her hand on my head was rough. "I don't know what you are talking about. Stand still. I must fix a patch over this spot."

I stepped away from her, declining to have my hair stuck up with a taped patch. "The lump isn't important."

She gave up in further annoyance, but she was not through with her questions. "He told me he'd sent you to the store, but what did he want you to bring him?"

"You'll have to ask him yourself," I said. "Or ask Eleanor. She knows."

Clarita flicked her hands at me in dismissal. "Eleanor is being wronged. But go to bed now. Here—I will give you something to help you sleep."

"Perhaps I'd better stay awake," I said, though I accepted the pills from her.

"As you please," she said.

I started toward the door, leaving her to put away

her bottles and bandages—but then I turned back.

"Where did you lose your gold earring, Aunt Clarita?"

Her hands flew to her ears and I knew that she was unaware that one was missing. "I'd started to undress," she said. "I haven't been away from the house, so it's undoubtedly on my dressing table."

"Undoubtedly," I said, and went out of the room, leaving her with a look on her face that I didn't like.

I took the capsules she'd given me to my room, but I didn't swallow them, nor did I go immediately to bed. Instinct told me that my senses must not be dulled artificially. I needed to be alert, lest there be some further move against me. Though probably I was safe enough now. No one was likely to attack me in my room.

I went to turn down the covers of my bed and stopped with my hand on the spread. The Zuni fetish lay against the pillow. It was the same one I had found before, and which Eleanor had taken away to return to the exhibit in the store. The small, heavy stone with its rudimentary carvings of the legs and head of a mole, its bloodstains and its thong binding of arrowhead and turquoise beads, all were the same. Now I knew I would not sleep.

This was too much. Somehow it seemed the last, shattering straw, as frightening as the whip and the blow on my head. It meant that whoever threatened me would not let up for an instant. The hunter was close on my trail, and he wanted me terrified.

I paced about my room with the ugly little stone in my hand, and found there was no order to my thoughts. There were only desperate questions in every direction in which I might turn. And now there was constant terror as well.

When the knock came on my door, I dissolved into trembling despair. My room was remote from the others. There was no escape from it except down the narrow stairs where this visitor, whoever it was, must stand. The knock came again, and a voice. Gavin's.

"Amanda, are you there?"

Relief swept through me and I ran to open the door.

It didn't matter that he was displeased with me, that he distrusted me, I simply clung to him, shaking so that my teeth chattered.

He held me quietly, impersonally, and it was enough that his arms were about me and that I loved him, however hopelessly. He, at least, would let nothing harm me. He was not involved in any of this plot.

His warmth and closeness soothed me, and my shivering stopped, my chattering teeth stilled. I became all too aware that his arms merely supported me, and that it was I who continued this embrace. I stepped back from him, still feeling shattered but in better control of myself.

"I—I'm sorry," I faltered. "I just—let go for a moment."

"I know." His voice was kind. "Clarita has told me what happened to you in the store. I came to see if you were all right."

"She—she gave me some sleeping pills, but I don't want to take them. I'm afraid to go to sleep. Look!"

I held out the fetish to him and his eyes seemed to cloud as he looked at it.

"It was there on my bed," I ran on. "Where someone also put the death-cart figure."

His composure seemed to crack a little as he took the fetish from my hand.

"Eleanor," he said. "She likes to play such games. I'm afraid there's a cruel streak in her—as there is in Juan. But she's unlikely to take any serious action."

I wasn't sure about that, and I walked away from him to a window and looked down into the patio. Nothing moved in bright moonlight. A single light burned at the Stewarts' house. Someone was taking serious action. I just didn't know who it was.

"I don't know what to do," I said.

He didn't answer me directly. "It's not terribly late. Put on your coat and come with me. I'll take you for a drive and make you sleepy without pills."

I turned from the window with a feeling of unreasonable joy. All my emotions were exaggerated tonight—out of bounds. Of course I would go with him—anywhere, and gladly.

While I wound a scarf around my neck and took out my coat, Gavin stepped to the window embrasure where I'd propped my small painting to dry.

"May I?" he said, and drew it out.

I froze with my coat still on its hanger. Here was more emotion. I couldn't bear it if he thought poorly of what I'd done.

He held up the canvas in both hands and studied my brilliant scene of village road and stark hot sky.

"It's good," he said, and I breathed again. "It's very good. You've painted your own feeling into your pigments, as a true painter should. You must show this to Juan."

He put it aside and came to help me with my coat, and I was awkward about finding the sleeves because I was too happy to concentrate on mundane matters like putting on a coat. Gavin liked what I had done, and my feelings were off on a new and joyful path. I had to make an effort to contain myself and not bubble with foolish happiness like a child. For me, just then, only the moment existed, and I would not look ahead or use my wits. I would not look behind. It was enough to be with him, and I asked for nothing more.

No one saw us as we went downstairs and out to the garage. I got into the front seat beside Gavin, and he eased the car onto the narrow road, where I'd done my painting in a time that seemed utterly remote from now.

"There's a full moon tonight," he said. "I know where I can take you."

We followed the quiet streets of Santa Fe and then turned onto a side road that led off toward the mountains. Before long the highway began to rise, winding and climbing into the Sangre de Cristos. Our headlights cut the darkness and the moon shone down on forests of ponderosa pine, with stands of aspen still above us.

Gavin knew the road well and he drove with confident skill. I let myself relax beside him, breathing the night scent of pine trees which had warmed all day in the sun. The world was all the more intensely beautiful because of my unreasoning happiness. If only this drive could go on forever, I would be content and ask for nothing more.

Once or twice Gavin glanced at me as though my mood puzzled him and he might be wondering what had become of all my fears. It was colder now, but the air was bracing and nothing could chill me. When we came to a lookout place, Gavin pulled off the road and let me gaze over the lights of Santa Fe, sparkling at our feet, and off to the faraway lights of The Hill— Los Alamos. I let beauty hold me. I would have liked to paint a night picture of this—something I'd never attempted. Again Gavin was watching me, rather than the scene he knew so well.

But he said nothing, and in a few moments we started up the mountain again. There were patches of snow in the crevices now—white and shining, with shadows of indigo. We were climbing in low gear, and suddenly the tall trees gave way to scrubby growth, and we were in the open below the snow peaks. Santa Fe was no longer in view. A dark building rose on our right and we could see the framework of the ski lifts climbing to the fields above us. Nothing moved. Deep silence lay over the peaks. Again Gavin stopped the car and we got out into invigorating cold. Our breath frosted on the air and I wrapped my scarf about my head to keep my ears warm.

Gavin held out his hand to me and I took it easily as we walked about the open area where cars would park for the winter skiing. His hand was as warm as mine was cold, and once he stopped to chafe my fingers. The moon had an icy radiance and this was a world far removed from threats of violence, from the darkness of murder. There was no evil in this clear air. Happiness was a mountaintop at night and the companionship of Gavin Brand.

As we turned back to the car we ran, our hands still clasped together, though when he reached the car he did not open my door at once, but just stood looking at me for a moment. Then he drew me into his arms in hungry despair.

"I knew from the first that you spelled trouble," he said ruefully. "I meant to make you dislike me, distrust me."

"I don't do either," I said with my cheek against the rough cloth of his jacket.

He turned my face up to him and kissed me with a tenderness I'd never known before. "What am I to do about you?"

It had happened to me—just as it had once happened to my father and his Doroteo—and I had no wish to struggle against it. This was a natural force which would go its own way, and there was no stopping it. My quiet joy had heightened.

"Let's never go back," I said with my cheek against his jacket. "Let's just go away and make a life of our own."

His arms tightened about me, though he didn't answer my foolish words. Down in Santa Fe the Cordovas waited for us, and there nothing had been settled.

"*You* must go away," he said at last. "Your safety means everything now. Juan is going to be angry, and so is Eleanor."

I could think of nothing but my new love. "You aren't going to do what Juan wishes, anyway," I pointed out. "Can't we stay together?"

He released me and opened the car door, waited until I was in my seat, and then walked around to the driver's side. When he was behind the wheel he turned the engine key, switched on the heater, and we sat for a little while in silence, not touching each other. I knew there was nothing more I could say or do. I had declared myself without reservation, and whatever happened now would be up to Gavin.

"I don't know whether I can make you understand,"

he said. "It's true that I've told Juan I want to get out
of this marriage, just as Eleanor does. But it isn't a
simple matter and I can't cut off the past with a sharp
knife."

"Do you still love her a little?"

He slipped an arm behind me on the back of the seat.
"I love you, even though I wish it hadn't happened. But
once I loved her a great deal, and I haven't entirely got
over my feeling of responsibility for her. She can be
heedless. Juan knows that. He knows that I've kept her
on a steadier path than she might otherwise have followed."

"If you leave her now, will he put you out of the
store?"

"It's likely. But that isn't what matters most. I want
to see her land on her feet and not destroy herself."

"With Paul Stewart?"

"Paul will never leave Sylvia. He's roamed a bit before this. Eleanor is too sure of herself, too sure that
the world revolves around her. She can't help that. It's
what Juan has taught her. But she may be in for a shock
with Paul. There are matters which must be settled before
I can be free. You came here in the middle of turmoil.
Will you go away and wait for me?"

"I'll wait as long as you like. But I won't go away.
I can't go away now."

He put the car in gear, backed around and started
down the mountain. We drove in low gear most of the
way, and this time we didn't stop to look at the view.
Once Gavin tried helplessly to say something, but only
broke off. Not until we reached the Cordova garage did
he pull me to him again, and I clung a little tearfully as he
kissed my mouth and my wet eyelids. But there were
no more words to be spoken and I understood that a
wall not of our own making rose between us, and until
it was leveled, he could not be wholly free to come to
me. I could only wait until all the problems were solved,
even though they were problems I didn't wholly understand. Of course they would be solved—I must believe

in that. It was all I had to hold onto.

The Cordova house was asleep when we left the car in the garage and went inside. Gavin did not touch me again, and his look was bleak when we said good night. I went to my high room and took the capsules Clarita had given me. I'd plunged from my high peak of joy, and I wanted to go quickly to sleep and for a little while to think about nothing.

XV

The next morning was Sunday, and when I went down to breakfast they were all gathered at the table, except Juan. Clarita had been up and out to early Mass, and she greeted me guardedly, inquiring about my head. The lump was there, and it was tender, but not unduly painful. I found myself speaking in a subdued manner, as though a heavy restraint lay upon me.

There were polite murmurs from Eleanor and Clarita when I said I was feeling better. Only Gavin was silent, and after a single searching look, he didn't glance at me again, so that I had the feeling that during the night his burden had increased. Clearly depression rode him this morning, and it did not bode well for our happiness.

No one discussed last night's occurrences—as though in that direction quicksand lay which none of them wanted to test. I had brought the Zuni fetish to the table with me, and when I'd taken my place I pushed it across to Eleanor.

"I think you must have left this in my room," I said. "I thought you might want it back."

Gavin raised his head and stared at her, but Eleanor only laughed.

"Since it keeps turning up, I'll keep it for a lucky

243

piece," she said, and set it beside her place, neither acknowledging nor denying any part she might have had in placing it in my room.

Clarita spoke to me. "Juan has phoned to make a reservation for your flight to New York. Sylvia will drive you to Albuquerque this morning. There is a local plane, but the trip is apt to be bumpy, and this will get you there more comfortably in plenty of time. You must pack right after breakfast."

They were all looking at me, including Gavin, and I raised my chin obstinately. "I'm not ready to go."

Clarita began to fuss, but Eleanor cut in, silencing her. "In that case, Amanda, you can come with us on our visit to the *rancho*. Juan is feeling fine today, and he wants to go. You'll come too, won't you, Gavin? Since it's Sunday?"

She had put on a pretty, pleading look, and though he responded with no warmth, he agreed to make the trip. I suspect that, like me, he wondered what she was up to.

"We'll bring Sylvia and Paul along as well," Eleanor rushed on. "It will be like old times out at the *rancho*. We'll wake the place up."

Her excitement seemed real enough, but its cause was faked. Something she had no intention of revealing motivated Eleanor, and as I buttered crisp toast, I wondered what this exodus meant. Last night at the store she had been plotting about it with Paul, but I had heard nothing worth reporting to Gavin or Juan.

Only Clarita seemed against making the trip. "I do not wish to go," she said, looking the picture of black gloom.

Eleanor was after her in a flash. "Why not, Aunt Clarita?"

"I do not care for that place."

"Because of its memories?" Eleanor persisted.

"Perhaps I will stay home today."

"No!" Eleanor cried. "I won't let you stay home. You never have any fun, and this will be good for you. Please come with us, Aunt Clarita."

She left her place and ran to Clarita's side, coaxing and cajoling until the older woman gave in, sighing.

"Very well, *querida*. But I have a feeling that no good will come of this. Old ghosts should be allowed their quiet."

Eleanor threw a sharp glance at me. "Amanda doesn't think so—do you, Amanda?"

"Perhaps the old ghosts have no quiet," I said. "But if you think they're stirring out at the *rancho*, I'd like to be there to meet them."

Eleanor's eyes were bright with some secret malice. "Then it's settled!" she cried. "We're practically on our way."

After breakfast there was a flurry of preparation. Clarita reluctantly canceled my plane reservation. Sylvia was called and asked to change her plans and come with us. It developed that Paul wanted to work on his book today and would not give in to any coaxing. This latter fact alerted me, yet there was still nothing to give me a clue as to Eleanor's intent. I would simply have to wait and keep my own watch for anything untoward that might happen. I felt as though I were marking time, waiting for some unseen explosive to go off and perhaps damage all of us. Perhaps even Eleanor, who held a torch to the fuse.

This morning I was no longer as sure of myself as I had been last night. What had happened on the mountain seemed distant and unreal, especially in the face of Gavin's remote air and his lack of effort to speak to me. It all seemed part of a dream, rising to false heights of joy that inevitably meant a later plunge to despair. For the last year or so I had managed to move on a fairly even plane emotionally, without extremes of happiness or sorrow. It was safer that way. Since last night, however, my feelings had taken on a quicksilver quality and were all too ready to dart about, changing their character from one moment to the next, running the scale from high to low. Now a sense of foreboding haunted me, and the barrier was there that I could not see beyond. The barrier between Gavin and me.

Back in my room I tried to cheer myself by putting on my favorite beige slacks and a buttercup-yellow blouse, but the sunny combination seemed to mock me in the mirror. That was when I had another bad moment. The plan for going out to the *rancho* had made me think of the mask again, and I opened the drawer and rummaged under the clothes where I had hidden it. The mask was gone.

I looked in several other places, lest my memory had played a trick on me, but the mask was no longer in my room. In the end, I gave up my search and went downstairs, but the fact that it was missing seemed ominous. The mask had meant something to me, and someone, clearly, did not want me to have it.

There were six of us going on the trip, and it had been decided that we would take two cars. Juan and Clarita and Eleanor would go in one, with Eleanor driving, while Gavin would drive Sylvia and me. Except for Paul, who stayed behind with his book, we all assembled near the Cordova garage as the cars were backed out. Juan was brought downstairs last, and he leaned on Clarita only a little as she helped him into the back seat of Eleanor's car. Some quickening force seemed to possess him this morning, and he had come thoroughly to life.

I stood well back in the garage, watching them settle Juan in his place, not projecting myself to his attention. He gave me a single look of annoyance and I looked away at once. He was displeased with me because I wouldn't leave, and there was nothing I could do about it.

Something on the garage floor caught my eye as I stood there, and I bent to look more closely before I picked up the fine hoop of gold that was Clarita's matching earring. How it came to be in the garage when she had gone nowhere last night, I didn't know.

I went to her just as she was about to get into the back seat with Juan. "Your earring," I said. "I just found it there in the garage."

She snatched it from me impatiently and without a thank-you, dropped it into her handbag. All her attention was given to Juan, and she had no time or interest for me. Or perhaps it was just that she had nothing to say to me, and wanted to attempt no explanation.

In Gavin's car I managed to sit on the outside, with Sylvia in the middle. Last night's dream was far away and he was so much on guard against me this morning that I couldn't bear to sit next to him.

Sylvia had heard sketchily from Paul what had happened to me at the store, and she was full of questions, which I answered rather shortly. Strangely enough, she did no speculating as to who might have struck me. She seemed to have more concern about the fact that Eleanor had coaxed Paul into going to the store at that hour to restore the Penitente display, and I knew that she was worried about her husband.

Eleanor was already on her way ahead of us and she was driving as fast as usual, so that we did not even catch a glimpse of her car during the trip. Gavin drove more moderately, but he kept to the top of the speed limit and I sensed the nervous energy that spurred him.

In a way, I was glad to be going out to the *rancho* with all of them this morning. I would have a chance to observe the Cordovas in a familiar atmosphere that might recall old actions, might lead to revelations. I had no knowledge then of what Eleanor might be planning.

When we reached the hacienda and went inside, we found Juan and Clarita in the long *sala,* Juan sitting before a lively fire of piñon logs, and Clarita hovering about, trying to make sure he was comfortable. The brief rebellion that she had instituted last night when she wore the dress of claret velvet, had vanished, and she seemed to be Juan's serving maid as always. Only when she looked at me did she stiffen with displeasure—perhaps because I had found her earring where she did not want it to be found.

Eleanor had disappeared, and no one knew where she had gone.

"The *rancho* is home to her," Juan said when Sylvia inquired for her. "She knows every corner."

"So do I," said Sylvia. "Let me show you about the place, Amanda."

Gavin had matters concerning the store to discuss with Juan, and he had no time for me this morning. I went with Sylvia, back into the dark reaches of the house, where narrow passageways with plastered walls led to series of rooms. The house had been built all on one floor, and it meandered into small, rather dark rooms packed with ancient and often shabby furniture. I had seen a little of it with Gavin.

"You should have been here in the days when they used to entertain out here," Sylvia said. "Juan and Katy loved to have house parties, and they would fill every room with guests. In those days there were enough horses for everyone to ride who wanted to, and Kirk was the best rider of them all. Juan used to say that Kirk should have been his natural son, instead of Rafael, who did nothing but disappoint him. Kirk took up the Spanish ways and made them his own. He had that wild streak that Juan admires and he might have been one of the Cordovas, instead of a foster son. When he and Doro died, Juan lost a son as well as a daughter."

I'd had only glimpses of Kirk before and I listened with interest.

Sylvia had opened the door to a small, rather cell-like room, which had been denuded of most of its furnishings. With one exception, there were no hangings on the walls, or rugs on the floor, and the single, narrow wooden bed was stripped to its springs, a table by the window was bare, and the bureau void of ornament. The single exception hung against the wall just over the head of the bed, and it was a large duplicate of the little *Ojo de Dios* I carried in my purse.

"I gave him that," Sylvia said, her eyes on the red and black and yellow strands of wool wound outward from the central Eye of God. "A lot of good it did him!"

She wandered idly to the tall dresser and pulled open an empty drawer. If this had been Kirk's room, I wanted to miss nothing, and I went to stand beside her. The drawer was empty, and she slammed it shut, opened another. This time there was an old newspaper inside, and Sylvia drew it out curiously and opened the pages, exclaiming as she spread them on the bare table.

"That was the year!" Sylvia said softly.

I knew what she meant. It was the year of the tragedy, but an earlier date. Sylvia turned to the second page and her hand was arrested on the paper. I saw why. Smiling at us from center page was a photograph of a young man in an elaborate costume of tight trousers, white shirt, short embroidered jacket and broad sombrero caught under his chin with a strap of leather thongs.

"Juan sent to Mexico for that *charro* outfit for Kirk," Sylvia said. "And he wore it as though he'd been born to silver and leather and embroidered braid. He was as good a horseman as Juan, and when there was a fiesta he rode his own palomino."

Her voice was low, lacking emotion, as though she thought aloud, without any awareness of me, standing beside her.

The photograph showed him full length, smiling arrogantly into the camera, and his narrow, full-lipped face was as handsome as the face of any man I'd seen. But there was something about it—something I couldn't quite put my finger on. . . .

"You can see why women were mad about him," Sylvia went on in that same even, rather dead voice. "Doro and Clarita were only two out of many. Though they were the two closest to him. I think Juan always wanted him for Doro, because that would make him doubly his son."

"But I thought Juan sent him away so he couldn't marry her?"

"That was mainly Katy's doing. She persuaded Juan

that Doro was too young. Katy loved Kirk, but she
didn't want Doro to marry him. So the arrangement,
supposedly, was that he would go away for a few
years. Juan got him a job in South America—Ecuador—
since he spoke Spanish well and would feel at home.
He was to come back to Santa Fe in a few years and
then marry Doro, if they both still wished it. When he
did return, of course, Doro had married your father,
and Kirk was furious. Doro was more beautiful and fascinating, and Kirk fell in love with her all over again.
He still thought Doro would run off with him, and I
don't think he was ever convinced that she could love
someone else. Anyway, he was on their hands again,
and since he knew horses so well, Juan put him in
charge out here, and he worked on the *rancho* until the
day he died."

I studied the faintly insolent young face in the picture.
It wore a confidence that was supreme—as though he
knew very well that women and horses would obey him.
There was no heartbreak in his eyes, but there seemed
a steely determination.

What was it that bothered me about his face? As
though I had seen it somewhere before—as though,
somehow, I knew Kirk Landers very well.

"He doesn't look like you," I said to Sylvia.

"Of course not. He wasn't related to me by blood. He
was my stepbrother. I'm glad we weren't alike."

A cool note had come into her voice and I threw her
a quick look. Until now I had taken it for granted that
she had been fond of her stepbrother, but the tone of her
voice seemed to repudiate him.

"What did you think of him?" I asked. "As a sister?"

"I detested him. He was cruel and thoughtless and
selfish. He hurt Doro more than once, and he played
with Clarita because it amused him to. Because I wanted
Paul, he was against Paul, and he nearly killed him in
that fight they had. If he'd lived, he might have come
between Paul and me."

She folded the newspaper roughly with hands that

showed mounting emotion, and almost ran out of the room. I stood for a moment longer, looking about me, trying to get the measure of the man my mother had loved when she was young and before she had met my father. But if there was a haunting presence here, it told me nothing.

There was one thing, however. I thought I recognized the *charro* costume Kirk wore in the picture. Those were the same garments which had been stuffed into that box with the mask and diary, and which Gavin had taken from me without explanation. I remembered wondering why at the time, and now I wondered again.

Since Sylvia had given up guiding me about the house, I found my way back to the *sala,* and found her kneeling before the adobe hearth, warming her hands at the blaze as though something had chilled her to the bone. Clarita sat a little apart in the room, where shadows hid her face, and I had a sense of her watching and listening presence, as though she wanted to be there without calling attention to herself.

Gavin stood up as I came into the room to make a place for me between him and Juan, and my grandfather smiled at me tightly, still not forgiving my obstinacy.

As I sat down, he pointed to a space at one side of the rounded adobe chimney. "That is where the turquoise mask always hung when the children were small, Amanda. We must bring it back and hang it there again."

"It's gone from my room," I told him. "I'd put it into a drawer, but someone has taken it away."

Gavin looked at me sharply. "More tricks?"

"I don't know," I said. "I'm just as glad to have it out of my room, because it haunts me. But I didn't take it away myself."

Maria came to tell us that our lunch would be served in the dining room.

Juan asked where Eleanor was, and Maria said she was looking through old cartons in Señora Cordova's former room. Maria would call her to lunch.

The dining room was long and narrow, and so was the dark wooden table with its woven straw place mats. High-back chairs with cracked leather seats awaited us, and dark paintings of somber Spanish scenes hung upon the walls, none lighted clearly enough to be appreciated. Arched windows set in deep walls looked out upon the courtyard of parched, dry earth.

"I used to hate this room when I was small," Sylvia said. "It never made me feel like eating. I used to expect one of those figures from Grandfather Juan's pictures of the Inquisition to come walking in, all hooded and threatening."

"This is foolish," Juan said. "There was always good conversation here, and laughter and fine wine. The hacienda is rich in Spanish tradition."

Maria lighted creamy white candles in candlesticks of pewter and the flames dispelled the gloom a little. We did not wait for Eleanor, but were served tacos with a delicious meat filling, though a little hot with chili for my taste. There was Spanish rice and *sopapillos*—those pillowlike puffs of thin bread, which I especially enjoyed.

We were halfway through the meal when Clarita, who sat at the end of the table facing the door, gave a sudden cry and put her napkin to her lips. Sylvia stared at the door, turning so white that I thought she was going to faint. From where I sat, Juan's chair blocked the door, but I saw the grim look on Gavin's face, saw him push back his chair.

Juan, made aware by behavior around the table that something was happening behind him, twisted about and stared toward the door. A lithe figure in dark blue moved into view, and I saw the tight suede trousers, trimmed down the sides with tarnished silver buttons, the short jacket ornamented in white braid and embroidery, a white sombrero topping the whole—and I saw something else. Where the face should have been beneath the rolled brim of the sombrero, was a blue mask, its features formed of silver and turquoise, the mouth rounded in an "O" that seemed a silent scream.

Clarita cried out—a single name, "Kirk!" and covered her face with her hands.

Sylvia said harshly, "Don't be silly—it's Eleanor!"

The figure in the *charro* costume pranced a little, sweeping the sombrero from her head in a bow, whirling about the table as she showed herself off.

I could hear the screaming when it began, and I covered my ears to shut out the terrible sound. I didn't know until Gavin came around the table and shook me gently by the shoulders, that it was I who screamed.

"Stop it, Amanda, stop it. You're all right," he said.

Juan spoke for the first time. "Take off that mask, Eleanor. You are upsetting Amanda. What is this prank you are playing? What are you trying to do?"

Eleanor flung aside the sombrero and unfastened the mask, laying it on the sideboard. Her own face was a mask in itself—a mask of heightened excitement and cruel curiosity.

"What do you remember, Amanda? What do you see?" she urged me tensely.

Before Gavin could move to stop her, she came around the table and knelt beside me in her tarnished silver and leather.

"Look, Amanda, look!" she whispered, and pointed to the breast of the jacket. There were dark stains across the heart, brownish where they touched white braid, and the material had been broken by something that had left a scorched hole.

I had stopped screaming, but I was trembling so desperately that I clung to Gavin to keep my hands from shaking, and I buried my face against his heart. He held and soothed me gently, and there was a silence all around the room. Clarita was the first to break it.

"Oh, wicked, wicked!" she cried to Eleanor. "Sometimes you are as wicked as he was." And I knew she meant Kirk. I had never before seen Clarita angry with Eleanor.

Sylvia pushed back her chair and walked out of the room, without a look for anyone, as though she had need to recover privately. Only Eleanor and Juan continued to stare at me, with Gavin there beside me, holding me to him, smoothing my hair, whispering softly to calm me. I clung to him and wept, not caring who saw me, or what they might think.

"You have outdone the Cordovas," Juan said at last to Eleanor. "I suggest that you go and get into your own clothes. Then have Maria wrap those things in a parcel and bring them to me. They must be disposed of. I did not know they had been saved."

"My mother saved them," Clarita said in a choked voice. Now she was watching me too, weighing what she saw with a look as dark as Juan's.

Eleanor paid no attention to Juan, still playing her cruel role. "I remember, if you don't, Amanda, though I didn't see what happened. Kirk was wearing this very *charro* outfit when he came to meet Doro on the hillside that day. I'd seen him in it before at fiestas, and I saw him that day, too, when they carried him up the hill afterwards. I saw the blood, just as you did, Amanda, but I didn't go to pieces over it the way you did."

Her eyes were bright with defiance of her grandfather, of Gavin, of all of us. She snatched up the sombrero and put it back on her head, taunting me, and when I closed my eyes against the sight, I could still see, vividly, that figure with the great sombrero on its head, and the turquoise mask covering its face. But I knew it was Kirk I was seeing, not Eleanor. Kirk ripping the mask from his face and dropping it to the ground, so that it fell beside me. I could almost hear him speaking to my mother, threatening her. Yes, I could remember the voice—rough and threatening. And I could almost see her frightened face. She was crying out, "No, no!" as she struggled with an adversary. There was a blast of sound and I saw the dreadful, staining blood, heard the crash of her body, falling endlessly. Afterwards everything went blank and I could remember only that

I was sitting on a bench with the blue mask in my hands, staring at that terrible cottonwood tree which seemed to my young eyes the spirit incarnate of evil.

Gavin was holding a water glass to my lips. I sipped weakly and the vision faded. Sylvia had made a supreme effort to recover herself and she returned to the dining room. Her hands drew me away from Gavin, her voice whispered to me softly.

"Let it go, Amanda. Don't try to bring everything back."

I wanted only to continue clinging to Gavin, but he had stepped back, to leave me to face Sylvia's ministering. When I put a hand to my face I found it wet with tears, and I felt exhausted.

Eleanor was still there, still prying and intent. "You've remembered, haven't you, Amanda? Tell us what you saw!"

Weakly, I moved my head from side to side. "No—it nearly came clear, but not completely. I can remember Kirk. I can remember my mother's fright. But nothing else—nothing."

Someone sighed as if in deep relief, and when I opened my eyes I saw it was Sylvia. But it was Eleanor I must look at now. Look at and recognize. Because now I knew. I knew why I'd sensed familiarity in the photograph of Kirk Landers. His picture had looked like Eleanor in this very mood.

Strength began to flow through me, and I pushed Sylvia away. Eleanor and Kirk—why? I stared at Juan and at Clarita, and I saw vestiges of resemblance to Eleanor there. But Kirk had not been related to the Cordovas at all. Or that was what Sylvia had told me. So why?

Juan had not moved from his place and now he spoke down the table. "Perhaps you will feel better, Amanda, if you finish your lunch."

I looked with distaste at the food on my plate, and Clarita rose from her place. "I will get her some soup from the kitchen." She spoke without liking for me, without sympathy, though she would minister to me.

Eleanor, still defying her grandfather, slipped into her chair at the table and began to eat hungrily, still dressed in Kirk's Mexican *charro* costume, with that dreadful powder burn and the brown stains on the front. But now Juan had recovered his own inner power and this time when he spoke to her his voice crackled.

"You will eat nothing more until you have changed your clothes," he told her. This time she did not dare to disobey. Her defiance melted and she slipped from her place like a scolded child and ran out of the room.

Clarita returned shortly with a cup of heated broth, and I drank it gratefully. Eleanor came back as I finished, changed into her own slacks and blouse.

Gavin said, "I'll take you home now, Amanda. You've had enough."

"Then I'll come with you!" Eleanor cried.

"No," Gavin said. "You will not."

Juan looked at Sylvia, and she said, "I'll drive back with you, if I may, Gavin."

He nodded to her shortly, and we went out to the car. At the table Juan, Clarita and Eleanor sat like images, watching us go.

This time Gavin placed me next to him in the car, and Sylvia sat on the outside.

"Juan is furious," Sylvia said nervously. "He wants you to stay with Eleanor, Gavin. He won't stand for— for you and Amanda. You've floored us all, I must say."

I knew they had seen plainly how I felt. It was my own fault, my own weakness. And I didn't seem to care.

"There's not much he can do about it," Gavin said grimly.

"He can fire you."

"If he wants to. But he still needs me."

I knew I should murmur something about being sorry, apologize for giving my feelings away so thoroughly, but I didn't want to. I leaned my head against Gavin's arm as he drove, and once he reached over to stroke my cheek, so that I knew he wasn't angry with me. I loved him so much that I couldn't bear it. Yet when we had driven a few miles in silence, I knew there were things I had to ask.

"I know now why that picture you showed me of Kirk seemed familiar," I said to Sylvia. "He looks like Eleanor."

"Kirk?" Gavin sounded surprised. "I've never thought that. But then, I can't much remember what Kirk looked like."

"You're imagining it," Sylvia said with a lightness I couldn't believe in. Whatever the truth was, Sylvia knew.

"Was Juan Kirk's father?" I asked bluntly.

Gavin exclaimed and Sylvia seemed to choke on the words she'd been about to speak. "Oh, no, no, of course not!" she cried.

"Then why did Kirk have the Cordova look?"

"He didn't have!" Sylvia insisted heatedly. "Not at all, Amanda!"

I paid no attention. "If he did inherit it, then Kirk and my mother might have been half brother and sister," I said.

Sylvia shook her head vehemently. "You're going down a completely wrong road. There was nothing like that. Kirk was my stepbrother."

"Then tell me the truth," I said.

She only shook her head again, denying knowledge of anything, denying my claim that Kirk had the Cordova look in his face.

I went on, thinking aloud. "If Doroteo had wanted to marry Kirk and he was really her brother, then Juan couldn't have allowed that, could he? What if it was Juan who came along that hillside? Juan who killed Kirk?"

"And pushed his favorite daughter down the bank?" Sylvia was derisive.

"What if Clarita lied about what she saw from the window?" I went on. "What if she has protected her father all these years?"

"Don't!" Sylvia cried. "Amanda, don't. Juan was ill that day. Katy had put him to bed. But if you want to know something, Clarita was never anywhere near that window from which she claimed to be looking. All her avowals to the police were false."

I turned my head to stare at her, and so did Gavin. Sylvia was looking straight ahead at the highway that rushed toward us, with the rooftops of Santa Fe in the distance, and the mountains rising beyond.

"Are you making this up?" I asked.

Once more she had turned as pale as she'd been when Eleanor came prancing into the dining room in Kirk's costume.

"I'm not making anything up. Paul saw her that day. He saw her outside the house where she couldn't have seen a thing on the hillside. And she's been lying ever since."

I remembered that Sylvia had earlier given away the fact that she and Paul had not come to the picnic together that day.

Gavin asked the next question. "Then why didn't Paul go to the police with what he knew?"

"He chose not to. He was sorry for Clarita. She'd gotten over her young crush on Kirk by that time, just as Doro had. It was Paul she was in love with, and she'd begun to see Kirk through Paul's eyes. She knew he was thoroughly bad."

I leaned my head back against the seat and closed my eyes. It was as if a picture I had been looking at for some time had suddenly shifted in character, and all the recognized brush strokes now meant something new and different.

I couldn't bear to think about it any more. Far ahead the snow crests glistened in the sun and I remembered what it had been like to be up there among the peaks last night, alone with Gavin. How clean and pure the snow had seemed under the moon. How clear and simple love had seemed then. Now it was neither. Yet somehow another corner had been turned and Eleanor had put herself outside of Gavin's consideration. I wondered what she would do now. She might be amusing herself with Paul, she might be eager for a divorce, yet I had the suspicion that she would not easily release to a rival something she had once owned. If Gavin loved me, she would hate me for that very fact.

I could cope with nothing more. I let myself go limp, forced my mind to empty. No one spoke in the car, though now and then Gavin threw me a concerned glance. There was no strength in me to reassure him. Eleanor's prank had wrung me out emotionally and all my ability to think and feel had been washed away. I was numb, and I didn't want painful sensation to return.

When we reached the empty house, Gavin held me close for a moment that might have been comforting if I could feel anything, and then turned me over to Sylvia. She came up to my room with me and offered to stay for a while.

"I'll be all right," I assured her. "I just need to be quiet and—and catch my breath."

In a way, Sylvia was more disturbed than I in this unfeeling state. She moved restlessly about the room, and I had the sense that she didn't want to go home to Paul right away. In fact, she admitted this after her third round of the room.

"Paul will want to know everything that happened, and I—I don't want to talk about it. What Eleanor did was dreadful. She believes it will drive you away and still help Paul with his book if she can stir things up, but I don't think they should be stirred up. Forget about today, Amanda. Let it be."

This was the old song that Sylvia was forever singing, and I wondered at her deep concern.

"I haven't any other choice," I said. "I'm very close —but I'm not there. And until the fog clears completely, there's nothing I can do."

She stopped her pacing and stood beside my bed. "If it does clear, what will you do?"

"I don't know," I said. "How can I even guess? I

suppose I'll go to Juan if what I remember clears my
mother."

"I'll tell Paul you can't remember," Sylvia said. "I'll
tell him not to pay any attention to Eleanor."

I closed my eyes, only wanting to be alone, and in a
little while she went away. When her steps had stopped
echoing on the stairs, I lay quiet on the bed, listening to
silence. After a time it was broken by the arrival of the
other three. I heard Clarita helping Juan to his room,
and when I got up and looked out the window, I saw
Eleanor running across the patio toward the Stewarts'
gate, and I knew she was losing no time in talking to
Paul.

When I lay down again, I managed to fall asleep,
and I didn't waken until Rosa came up my stairs bringing a tray Clarita had sent up to me. It was a simple
meal of soup and cheese and fruit, and I managed to
eat it, as I could not have done a full dinner. When Rosa
came to take the tray away, I lay down again, more
awake now, more alive, yet still unsure of what it was I
must do next.

The room darkened, and the light in the patio came
on, throwing a slight radiance against one window. I lay
in the dark and thought of Gavin and wished myself
into the future, when all problems might be solved and
I could be with him for good. If that time ever came.
The present returned to me sharply when I heard Juan
calling my name.

When I went to open my door, I found him at the
foot of the stairs, his back to the lighted room, so that
I could not see his face.

"Come down to me, Amanda," he said softly.

A deep breath gave me a semblance of courage, and
I went down the steps. Whatever I expected in the way
of chiding did not come.

"I want you to do something for me," he said, and
held out a ring with two keys.

I took them from him, my look questioning.

"There's no one else I can send," he told me. "I'm

too weary to walk down there tonight, and my eyesight can't be trusted. I want you to check the collection for me."

"Check the collection?" I echoed.

"Yes. We've been away most of the day. I always look at it immediately after being away. I want you to be my eyes this time. I want to know if everything is all right."

"But I won't know if anything is missing," I objected. "I should think Gavin—"

He gave me a dark look. "Not Gavin. It isn't necessary to check everything. There is just one thing that matters —the Velázquez. I want to make sure it is safe. I have worried about it all day."

"But someone nearby would have heard the alarm if it sounded, and you'd have been told."

"Not necessarily. Don't argue, Amanda. Just go out there now. And then come to me in my study."

I looked reluctantly at the keys in my hand. "All right, I'll go." At least it was something that he didn't mean to lecture me now.

"You remember? The burglar alarm key first. Then the other. And when you come to me, follow the passage from the patio, so no one will see you. The door is open."

I nodded, and he turned back toward his room, leaning heavily on his stick, as though all his strength had been used up in our day's excursion.

I let myself out to the patio through the living-room door. No one was about, and I turned down the flagged walk to the building with its peaked redwood roof. Using the keys in proper succession, I let myself in the door.

With curtains drawn as always, it was very dark inside. I found a switch at the right of the door and turned on the indirect lighting. Scenes of Spain sprang to life along the walls, but I paid no attention to them, walking rapidly toward the alcove at the back. There I touched the switch that lighted Velázquez's painting of Doña Inés.

It took only a moment to assure me that the picture was safe. I stared at that strange, indented face of the stunted woman with the dog at her feet, then turned off the light and returned to the main room. As far as I could see, nothing had been disturbed. There seemed to be no vacant places on the walls, or on any of the shelves which held carved figures and ceramics.

Once more the painting of Doña Emanuella caught my attention and I stood before it, trying to see in that bright face with the sulky mouth the image of my mother. If only she had lived. Not Emanuella, but Doroteo. She had cared about me as Grandmother Katy had cared about her daughters. As my father had cared about me. None of the other Cordovas would serve. I had been seeking a mirage to expect anything from them.

But now there was Gavin. The thought of him warmed and comforted me, and I tried to tell the Doroteo I saw in the picture that at last I had someone of my own, as she had had. Someone who loved me. But she only smiled her tantalizing smile, and I knew Doroteo had not been like the girl in the picture.

Dreamily I switched off the lights and went outside. Paul Stewart stood waiting for me in the patio. He was the last person I wanted to see, but there could be no escaping him now.

"I saw the light as you went in," he said. "I wondered who was there."

I locked the door and reactivated the alarm. "Juan gave me the keys. He was worried about the Velázquez."

"I'm sure no one has touched it," Paul said. "I haven't been far from my typewriter all day. I'd have heard any disturbance."

"That's what I assured Juan," I said, and started past him.

"Eleanor told me what happened today," he went on. His eyes had that pale green light I didn't like, and I knew he must have praised Eleanor for her wild prank.

"She didn't succeed," I said coolly. "I've remembered

nothing more. But she managed to upset everyone. It was a dreadful thing to do."

Paul paid no attention to my disapproval. "Will you promise me one thing—if it all comes suddenly back in your memory, will you tell me first?"

"Of course I won't. Why should I?"

"It might be better for everyone if you did," he said quietly, and turned away to disappear through the gate in the wall.

I watched him go and then walked slowly toward the entrance to the passageway to Juan's rooms.

The door was unlocked, as promised, and I let myself into the narrow tunnel. A pool of light thrown by the bulb at this end illuminated the beginning of the stone-paved way, but it grew darker near the steps at the far end, and for a moment I hesitated. Too much had happened to me lately. But as I paused, the door of my grandfather's room opened in the distance, and he called to me.

"Is that you, Amanda?"

I answered him, and moved along the passageway. He had stepped back from the doorway, and it was empty when I climbed the steps and entered the bedroom. It too was empty, but lighted, and I averted my eyes from the agony of the man in the painting who burned endlessly at the stake.

Juan awaited me in his study and he wore a long brown robe with a monk's cowl thrown down at the back. For a moment I stared at him in dismay because he looked all too much like one of the dark, hooded figures which circled the fire in the painting.

But he was waiting for me, and I went into the room and dropped the keys on the desk before him, and watched as he put them away in a drawer.

"I don't think anything has been touched," I told him.

He seemed to relax in visible relief and his hands unclenched where they rested on the desk before him. He was obsessed by the Velázquez painting and I wondered if that was good for his peace of mind.

"Why don't you send it back to Spain?" I asked.

"No! Not in my lifetime."

"But you say you can't see it clearly any more."

"I can see it with my inner eye. I can see it with my mind and my heart, and I can touch it with my fingers. It is my greatest pleasure."

"It would never have been Katy's greatest pleasure," I said. "I think Katy believed in what was human."

"If Katy had lived, much would be different in my life," he said. "Now a picture becomes important."

"It isn't even a very beautiful picture," I objected. "I'll agree that it's magnificently painted, but there's a sort of horror about it. I prefer the picture of Emanuella."

"Then that painting shall be yours. I give it to you now. Let me keep it upon that wall while I live. Afterwards, it is for you to own. I will put this in writing."

At once I was on guard. Juan Cordova was not a sentimental man, nor given to gestures of generosity. This was an attempt to win me.

"Thank you," I said quietly, and moved toward the door.

At once he stopped me. "Wait. Sit down for a moment, Amanda."

The lecture would come now, I thought. Because of the way I'd betrayed my feeling for Gavin. But he surprised me.

"What happened today? What came back to your memory?"

"Nothing. I remembered seeing Kirk in that *charro* costume wearing the mask. Why do you suppose he wore it?"

"Katy believed it was because Doroteo used to adore him when they were younger and he dressed like that. And they used to play some game of flirtation with the mask. So he wanted her to remember that time. He wanted her to run away with him. Which she would never have done."

"Yet someone came along the hillside and shot him.

Not my mother. I've remembered that much. I know it wasn't Doroteo."

I heard a choked sound behind me and turned in my chair to see Clarita standing there. She looked outraged, indignant.

"Of course it was Doro! I saw it with my own eyes—"

I stood up to face her. "No, you didn't see anything, Aunt Clarita. I learned that much on the drive home today. Paul saw you outside the house. You couldn't have been anywhere near that window when it happened."

Juan reached across his desk and caught me by the hand.

"What are you saying? What do you mean?"

Clarita uttered another choked cry, put her hands over her face and fled from the room. The pressure of Juan's fingers forced me back into the chair.

"You will explain yourself," he said.

I repeated what Sylvia had told us in the car and Juan listened to me with a stunned expression.

"All these years I have believed her," he said. "Why did she lie—if she was lying? Why?"

"To protect someone, I suppose," I said.

With difficulty he roused himself and released my hand. "Go and find her. Bring her here to me, Amanda. And then leave us alone."

He had forgotten all about Gavin, and I went away in relief. The living rooms of the house were empty, and I went into the bedroom wing. I tapped on Clarita's door and when she didn't answer, I opened it and looked in. Her black-clad form lay stretched upon the bed, and I thought for a moment that she was weeping. But when I spoke her name, she sat up and stared at me with dry, ravaged eyes.

"What do you want? Haven't you done enough damage for one day?"

"Your father wants you. He said I was to bring you to him at once."

She waved her hand at me in dismissal. "I will go to him. There is no need to bring me."

As I knew very well, when Juan gave an order, he meant it literally, and I stayed where I was. After a moment she got up from the bed and came toward me.

"Why did you lie?" I asked her softly. "Who was it who went along the hillside that day?"

For just an instant I thought she was going to strike me. Her thin hand with its flashing rings came up, but I stood my ground and it fell back to her side just short of my face.

"You are like your mother," she whispered. "You ask for killing."

Then she pushed me aside and went out of the room. I followed her to the foot of the balcony steps and watched until I saw her go into her father's study. When the door closed, I fled to my own room and got ready for bed.

I felt more than a little frightened. The corner into which I'd painted myself seemed to be narrowing. Before long there would be no way in which I could turn. All my motions were automatic as I undressed and got beneath the covers. Gavin seemed very far away.

XVI

That night a dream wakened me. It was not the dream of the tree, but it was so vivid, so horrible, that I sat up in bed and turned on my bed lamp. My small travel clock showed three-thirty. I tried to recall the details, but they were already fading. Something about a dog. Something quite dreadful about a dog. But there was no dog in this house, nothing to make me dream about one. I had not had a dog as a pet since I'd been a child in my aunt's house in New Hampshire.

I slipped out of bed and went to the window where I could look down into the patio. The usual night light burned, and I could see the pale glimmer of adobe and redwood at the far end, but nothing moved down there. All was blank and empty.

Suddenly I remembered.

Of course. *She* had been in the nightmare too. It was the picture of Doña Inés with her dog that had made me dream. She had been part of the nightmare. Looking at the painting again had disturbed me. But what was it about the dog? There had been something —something eerie, something monstrous. I couldn't remember.

I went to the other window and stood with a cool

wind blowing in upon me. Once more I could see moonlight shining on the snow peaks. Night hours were the worst. They would always be the lonely time—the time when courage fades and I am sure that nothing in my life will ever come right. Now something dark and threatening seemed to menace me, and Clarita's words echoed in my ears.

"You ask for killing," she had said.

But I didn't want killing, I wanted to live—as my mother had wanted to live. Because now there was Gavin. Yet there could be no turning back. I had gone too far. Eleanor had gone too far. There was no safety anywhere, and I had to live, somehow, until it was over.

Questions were sharp in my mind. Where had Paul really been at the time Kirk had died? Where had Clarita been? For that matter, where had Sylvia been at a time when she was angry with her stepbrother for quarreling with Paul?

I managed to sleep a little, and there were no more dreams that I could remember in the morning. I rose early and found only Clarita at the breakfast table. Her hair was not smoothed as usual, and for once she wore no earrings. It was as if something in her had begun to give up. I wondered what had passed between her and Juan, but I was not likely to know because she barely spoke to me. Indeed, I think she hardly saw me there at the table.

Eleanor didn't appear at all, but Gavin joined us, and Clarita did not speak to him either. A restraint lay upon all of us, and though Gavin looked at me with concern, he made no attempt at conversation.

Not until I was about to leave the table, did he make his suggestion.

"Amanda, will you come to the store with me this morning? I've already phoned Paul and he'll join us there. We can't let the matter of the attack on you pass without some investigation. Perhaps we can reconstruct a little and find an answer. I'll also ask the salesgirls to check on whether anything is missing from their stock."

"What if it was Paul who struck me?" I said. "Or even Eleanor?"

Gavin sighed. "Anything is possible. But that's all the more reason why we have to make this effort. We'll both keep our eyes open for leads."

Clarita rose gravely from the table and went away toward her room without comment. I thought of her earring on the floor of the garage.

"Perhaps we should take Clarita with us," I said.

Gavin dismissed that as idle humor and looked at me down the table. I wanted to be in his arms, and I knew he wanted me there, but we both held back. Quick, stolen embraces under the roof of this house were not what either of us wished. Ahead of us were the mountains which had to be climbed. Higher than the Sangre de Cristos.

Paul met us at the store, as planned, and we went through a mock-up of all our actions of that night. It came to nothing. Paul seemed more than eager to help, but I didn't trust him, and I sensed a secret mockery behind all he said and did. Gavin and he were carefully polite to each other, but the enmity between them showed, and if Paul Stewart had come to the store with something to conceal, it was still carefully hidden by the time we left.

Only one thing of any consequence happened during the hour we spent wandering the aisles of CORDOVA —and that occurred inside my own head. I began to worry again about my dream of the night before. What was it that disturbed me about Doña Inés and her dog? I began to wonder if the dog in the painting could have something special to tell me. The thought brought with it an impatience to get back to Juan's house, and to somehow have another look at the collection.

Luck played into my hands. When Gavin drove me home, and then went back to the store, Rosa met me at the front door and told me that Clarita had taken my grandfather for a drive. That left the field clear.

The moment Rosa went about her work at the far end of the house, I ran up the balcony steps and entered Juan's study. The drawer of his desk was locked, as I might have expected, and the keys to the collection were there, where I couldn't get them. While I was wondering what to do, I heard a sound that froze me. A sound that came from Juan's bedroom.

I could have escaped. I could have fled out his study door and gone to another part of the house without being seen. But I had to know who stirred in his empty room while Juan was away. It took only a moment to drop down behind his long sofa and crouch there perfectly still.

The sound that came from his bedroom was one I recognized. It was the closing of a door. Someone had come up the passageway from the patio and let himself into Juan's bedroom. A moment later there were steps into the study and the sound of a drawer being unlocked and opened. I peered around the end of the couch and saw Eleanor standing there. Her key was in the lock of the very drawer I had wanted to open, but she was not taking out the collection keys—she was putting them back.

From the living room, Rosa called to her, and Eleanor closed the drawer hastily and went out to the balcony to answer. I lost no time. In a moment I had the drawer open, the collection keys out, and had closed it again. When Eleanor came back to lock the desk and take away the key, I was once more hidden.

When she removed her key from the desk drawer, she didn't linger, but went quickly out of the room, leaving by way of the balcony. I sprang up and hurried after her. When I reached the bedroom wing, I was in time to see her go through her own door at the far end of the hall. I tapped on the wood, and after a moment's hesitation she called to me to come in.

I stepped into a room that was entirely Eleanor's, and I knew she didn't share it with Gavin. Curtains and spread and rug were of soft colors that complemented her gold and cream. But I gave the room no more than a glance. It was Eleanor who held my attention.

She stood upon a pale blue scatter rug in the center of the floor, and I could see that she was still nervous. Her fingers played with the silver medallions of the concho belt slung low on her hips, and her eyes studied me with a wary regard.

"Why did you have the keys to the collection?" I asked.

She brushed a hand over the dishevelment of her blond hair. "What are you talking about?"

"I saw you just now in Juan's study when you put them back. Perhaps you wanted to know about the Velázquez too? You needn't worry. It hasn't been touched. He sent me to check."

She laughed and seemed to relax a little. "Good for you. If you must know, I was a bit worried and I had a look myself. Perhaps he infects us all with his concern about his great treasure."

"Would you keep it as he does—if it were yours?"

"Of course not." She answered easily. "I'd sell it on some black market and be rich for the rest of my life."

"Surely it ought to go back to Spain," I said.

"And if he writes you into his will, you'll send it there?"

"He won't do anything of the kind. He'll never take away what is yours. And I don't want anything he can give me—except the truth about my mother."

"As if you'd have anything to say about it!" She sauntered off the island of the rug and dropped onto a low ottoman, clasping her hands about her knees. A frown drew her brows together as if in puzzlement, and her mouth pursed quizzically. "Are you really like that, Amanda? Do you really care so little about money?"

"I can always earn money. Not a lot, but enough for what I need."

"And I suppose you're counting on Gavin anyway?"

"There isn't anything in Santa Fe that I count on."

She ducked her head down to her clasped hands for

an instant, and when she brought it up again she was smiling at me in a manner more friendly than I'd seen until now.

"It doesn't matter, Amanda. I don't want him anyway. Once he thought I was marvelous—but somehow he got over that. As I got over how I felt about him. But let's not talk about Gavin."

She rose from her stool and came swiftly toward me across the room. I stiffened, and she saw and laughed ruefully.

"You don't trust me at all, do you, Amanda? Not that I can blame you. That was an awful thing I did yesterday. I didn't really understand how it might affect you. Juan has been scolding me."

She seemed surprisingly contrite, but I knew she still didn't understand the effect she'd had on me. Eleanor lacked the faculty of empathy, and she would never understand how other people felt. What she had done could not be erased by an apology, and I turned toward the door. Before I had taken two steps, she was after me, clinging to my arm.

"Amanda, let me make it up to you. I told you I'd drive you out to Madrid one of these days so you could paint. Let's go now. Besides, there's something I want to show you out there—something you ought to see."

"What?" I asked bluntly. I had no desire to go with her anywhere, least of all to an empty ghost town.

"Something about your mother, Amanda. There's something out there I've never shown anyone. But I'll show you now, and it will answer a lot of your questions."

"Do you mean you know the answers?"

"Some of them."

"Then tell me here and now. We don't need to go anywhere."

Her hands moved in a helpless gesture. "You'd never believe me. You have to be shown."

I hesitated for a moment longer, thinking of the keys to the collection, a lump against my thigh in the pocket of my slacks. But Juan was away and perhaps he would not look for them for a while. And I could do what I wanted to do when we came home from Madrid. Inés and her pet could wait.

Eleanor saw indecision in my eyes, and she smiled at me with that charm I had seen her exert before. "Get your painting things, Amanda. You can have all the time out there you like."

"I'll just take my sketchbook," I said, and hurried off toward my room.

"Meet you in the garage," Eleanor called after me.

I picked up a sweater and my handbag with the sketchbook in it, and hurried down to join her. I'd made up my mind and I didn't dare linger to weigh whether what I was doing was sensible or not. In any case, Eleanor was unlikely to try anything in broad daylight, while I was watching her.

When I was beside her in the front seat, she wheeled the car a bit wildly out of the garage, and turned around in the street with a squealing of tires. It was as though she wanted to get away as quickly as possible. Without our being seen? I wondered.

Just before we pulled away, Clarita drew up in her car, with Juan Cordova in the front seat beside her. They both stared at us in surprise, and I leaned in the window to shout to Juan.

"Eleanor's driving me out to Madrid. I'm going to do some sketching."

Our car pulled away so fast that I wasn't sure they'd heard me, and Eleanor looked sulky.

"Why did you do that? You shouldn't have told anyone we were going out there."

"Whyever not?"

"You'll see," she snapped at me.

The narrowness of Canyon Road and its traffic slowed her down, but once we were out on the highway, turning south, she let out the car, going faster and faster, well over the speed limit. I wondered how many tickets for speeding she collected in the course of a year, and how she had managed to keep her driver's license. Los

Cerrillos, with their individual humpy hills, seemed to move toward us rapidly, and I could see the Ortiz Mountains rising beyond.

"It's wonderful to get away!" Eleanor cried, her sulkiness gone. "Don't you feel sometimes that Grandfather's house smothers you, walls you in?"

"I've felt that," I agreed. "But I'm surprised you feel that way."

"Of course I feel that way. Juan, Gavin, Clarita—all of them want to hold me down, keep me in a prison. But I'm going to escape. I'm going to show them all!"

She was becoming increasingly keyed up as we left Santa Fe behind, and I was filled with a growing uneasiness. I couldn't imagine Eleanor settling down and waiting for me quietly while I did some sketching, and my puzzlement as to why she was really bringing me out here grew. Once or twice I protested her speed, and she would heed me for a mile or two, and then press her foot on the gas pedal again so that the wind would whistle by. I hoped that Madrid was not far away.

Some twenty miles or so out of Santa Fe we found ourselves on a canyon road, and I saw ahead the houses of a town dotting a slope of hillside. Eleanor slowed the car.

"Here we are. Take a good look at it, Amanda. This is our history too. Once a great-uncle of ours ran a coal mine here, and we still own some property. But it's a dead town. As dead as the Cordovas."

Slipping past the car windows, the gray houses on the slope were derelicts. There was no adobe here, and all the houses were built of splintery gray frame. They stood with broken windows and sagging doors, looking drearily out upon nothing. Eleanor drove on slowly, until more weathered, unpainted houses lined each side of the road, with others crowding behind in what had once been a fair-sized town. She was right—this would be something to sketch and paint.

"Thousands of people lived here once," Eleanor said, slowing the car to a crawl. "That was when the mines flourished. A million tons of coal came out of just one seam in this area, and thousands of people flocked in. I've heard Juan tell how at Christmas time the ridges, the houses, the canyon sides were covered with lights at night. But now it's all dark and dead. A true ghost town. Like ours has been turned into a ghost family, Amanda."

Pulling the car off to the side of the road, she set the brake, opened the door and jumped out. Then she came around and opened my door.

"Come along! We've arrived, and there's something I want to show you before you start sketching.

Suddenly I didn't want to go with her. Crowding all about on the hillside, the ghost houses seemed inimical. They didn't want their sleep disturbed. They didn't want to be reminded of the life they no longer led. But Eleanor had already run across the scrabble of dry grass at the side of the road and was wandering in among the houses as they ranged above us.

"There's a sign that tells us to keep out," I called after her.

She turned and waved an arm at me, beckoning. "Who's to see? Besides, we belong here. We're ghosts too, aren't we? The ghosts of the great Cordova family!"

I got out of the car and followed her uneasily as she wound among the irregularly set houses, running ahead, pausing now and then to make sure I was coming.

The place set its spell upon me, and I almost forgot my cousin. I climbed broken steps and looked past a sagging door into a bare room, where floorboards had buckled and something brown scurried down a hole in the corner of a room. I backed away hastily, and after that limited myself to staring through broken panes of glass into long-abandoned interiors. Only the sound of my own steps disturbed the sleeping hush.

Ahead of me, Eleanor waited, the canyon wind blowing her bangs and lifting the tendrils of her long fair hair. I could feel the gusts on my face, and it was a chill gray wind that had nothing to do with the blue sky overhead, and bright New Mexico sunlight. It was a wind that belonged to the sleeping Madrid.

"These are the houses where the miners lived," Eleanor said. "The Cordova house was much grander, but it's long gone. It burned down one night, and no one ever knew how the fire started. Everything we touch turns to ashes."

With an effort I tried to resist her, tried to resist the very mood of the town around me.

"CORDOVA is hardly a pile of ashes," I said. "I suspect that it will always keep you nicely."

"Hush!" she whispered. "Don't laugh at them, Amanda. Don't make any sounds to wake them. They're all asleep and it's best to let them stay that way."

Unwilling to accept her fantasies, I tried to shut away the eerie sound of her voice. If I came here to paint, I might be willing to enter into such a mood, but I had no desire now to stop and sketch, and my growing feeling was that I'd like to turn my back on this place and go quickly away.

Ahead of me Eleanor moved on again, and I called after her.

"Let's go back. I've seen enough. I can sketch a bit in the car, and perhaps come here another time to paint."

Eleanor stepped from shadow into bright sunlight and flung out her arms. "Can you imagine what it's like at night, Amanda? I wonder if all the old ghosts come out and dance by moonlight? I'd like to be one of them. Maybe I am one of them."

I wasn't a child to be frightened by ghosts, but the uncanny mood which ruled her touched me. I'd had enough of Madrid, and I turned about and started down the hill, picking my path between the derelict houses, staying away from broken windows and empty doorways. At once Eleanor shouted to me, forgetting her own edict of silence.

"Wait! Don't go back yet, Amanda. We're almost there. You haven't seen what I can show you. You want to know about Doro, don't you?"

Her shouting roused a clacking of echoes among the bare, stark houses, as if they too shouted in protest at my departure, rattling their skeleton bones. I had begun to think that all her earlier talk about my mother had been pretense to get me out here for some reason that might put me at her mercy in this dead place. But she had come to a halt beside one of the gray houses where there were still panes of glass, where dark green shades had been drawn before all the windows, and the steps had been repaired, though unpainted.

She beckoned to me. "Come," she said, and I surrendered, turning about to climb the hillside and stand beside her. "Go in," she directed. "I've unlocked the door. Go in."

She spoke with the authority of Juan Cordova, and I found myself obeying. I climbed the three gray steps and put my hand on a cracked china doorknob.

"Open it," said Eleanor behind me.

I turned the knob and stepped into a strange world. At once she came up the steps and closed the door, so that we were shut together into a room that came out of the long ago.

In this place of abandoned dwellings and empty rooms, this room was completely furnished. There was wallpaper sprigged with blue cornflowers, instead of whitewashed walls, and at the three windows of this main room hung blue and white crisscross curtains. There was a wide brass bed, a small table with a marble top, a wooden rocking chair, and an easy chair upholstered in red plush. True, the wallpaper hung in strips in one corner, the curtains were limp and gray-hued, a nest had been built by some animal in the center of the blue bedspread, the brass bed knobs were tarnished, the red plush chair was worn shiny in the seat and raveled across the back, and there were cobwebs everywhere. Yet this room had been used and left furnished.

"Why?" I said. "Why?"

"Doro and Kirk fixed it up like this when they were

young—before Kirk went away, and Doro met your father. Clarita says they brought pieces of furniture from the hacienda, and bought other things. Doro made the curtains, which is why they're lopsided. It was their hideaway. When Juan and Katy thought they were at the *rancho*, well chaperoned, they would come here. What a romance they must have had!"

"But why has it been left like this? Does Juan know?"

"Probably. He knows everything. But he's shut it out of his consciousness. He won't accept what he doesn't want to accept. A love nest for Doro and Kirk was never in his picture. Katy knew, Clarita says, and she just locked it up after Doro and Kirk died. Clarita found the key to Katy's things one time, and when I was in my teens she brought me out here to tell me about her younger sister and the wicked young man she loved. Wicked in Clarita's lights."

Stirring up dust wherever I moved, I wandered about the room, aching a little for the broken romance my mother had suffered, even though I wouldn't be here if it had continued.

"Of course she never came here any more after Kirk went away and she met your father," Eleanor went on. "When they were both dead, Clarita brought your father here and showed this room to him. She said he had to understand about the woman he had married, so that he would take his daughter away from the Cordovas and never come back again."

The marble of the small table felt chill under my hand, and I whirled around angrily. "It's Clarita who was wicked. What a dreadful thing for her to have done!"

"She had to make him understand why Doro had killed Kirk. He wouldn't believe in their love until she showed him this."

"Clarita has no business calling anyone else wicked!"

Eleanor's smile was enigmatic and I didn't like the way she looked, or the fact that she'd brought me here.

Apparently the house had two rooms, for a second door opened at the back. It was ajar and to help regain my composure I left Eleanor, to walk through it. There was a rusty enamel sink under a window, and ancient pipes, a bare wooden table and two rickety chairs. No effort had been made to fix up the kitchen and if there had been a stove, it had been removed.

In one corner stood a small battered trunk, and I went over and raised the lid. Only emptiness and a lingering odor of mothballs greeted me. Except for one thing. I leaned over in surprise and picked up the tiny bonnet made of yellowed satin and lace—a baby bonnet which lay in the bottom of the trunk. The uneven stitches told me that Doroteo had made this too, but if she had made it for me, how had it come to this place on which she'd never looked back?

When I'd closed the trunk, I carried the bonnet into the other room to show Eleanor.

"What do you make of this?"

Eleanor had no interest in baby clothes. She was watching me with something electric about her that made me uneasy.

"Amanda," she said, "do you believe the old stories about the Cordova curse that came down from Doña Inés? Do you think there's a strain of madness in all of us?"

Her eyes were alight with some excitement I did not like, and there was no kindness, no friendliness in her smile. Perhaps there was a little madness in all of us. Even in me, who had thought herself outside the reach of the Cordovas.

She went on softly, while I moved about the room again, trying to shake off the spell she was weaving.

"I wonder what she was really like—Inés? I wonder how she felt when she stood beside that bed in the middle of the night with the blood of her victim staining her hands and her gown. Was Emanuella afraid of her then?"

There was something insidious about her words, about the very tone of her voice. I had to face up to her and I mustn't let her frighten me.

"It was you behind that fetish I found in my room both times, wasn't it?" I said. "And you who put Doña Sebastiana in my bed? Was it you, too, who used the whip in the patio and—"

"And struck my grandfather down?" Eleanor cried.

"He wasn't hurt. And perhaps you used the brass statue of Quetzalcoatl in the store?"

As she stared at me, her face looked utterly white beneath the frame of her long hair. "I haven't been as clever as all that. The fetish, yes. And those tricks on Gavin with the stone head and other things. Aunt Clarita helped me because we both wanted him in wrong with Juan. But they were silly attempts and they never worked. I didn't do any of the other things, and perhaps that was my mistake, Amanda."

Her eyes were fixed upon me so intently that I felt myself held by her gaze. Yet I knew I must get away from her. Something was building. If there was madness, it was activated now, and I could believe nothing she said except that she meant me harm. I dared not turn my back to her, and I began to move stealthily backward toward the door, a step at a time. She didn't seem to notice because she was looking around the room. Her attention fixed itself upon a narrow, splintery board that had fallen from the molding of a window, and with a quick, darting movement she sprang toward it, picked it up with both hands. I could see the rusty nails protruding from one end as she fixed me again with the bright excitement of her look.

"So you thought you would take my inheritance, Amanda? And now you want to take Gavin. But you aren't going to, you know. There's no place to run to. This will be worse than a *disciplina,* Amanda. If I choose, you may never leave this little house where your mother used to come. It might take them years to find you. And when they did, you'd look like Doña Sebastiana in her death cart."

I couldn't stand there and wait for her to come toward me, to strike me. I had to be quicker than she was—I had to get away. Whirling toward the door, I made a dash for it, tearing it open, flinging myself down the steps—and straight into the arms of Gavin Brand.

XVII

Gavin held me, steadied me, and for a moment I clung to him in helpless relief. There was no movement in the room behind me, and when I had control of my legs, I turned and stared at Eleanor.

She held the splintered board in one hand, and she was laughing. "Oh, Amanda! I really frightened you, didn't I? You were such a sitting duck, I couldn't resist. Gavin, where on earth did you spring from?"

He answered her coldly. "Juan saw you and Amanda taking off in your car with all that wheel squealing, and he was worried. When Amanda called out that you were going to Madrid, he had Clarita phone me to come after you."

Eleanor flung down the board with a violent gesture. I could imagine her with the whip that she'd denied.

"Please—I'd like to go," I said to Gavin.

He put an arm around me and walked away from that small, haunted house, leaving Eleanor to its ghosts. More than ever, she was my enemy now, and there was nothing I could do about it. In Gavin's car I put my head against the seat back and closed my eyes. I could sense his anger with Eleanor as his hands grasped the wheel and he turned about on the highway. But he was angry with me too.

"Why did you go with her? Why did you trust her?"

"She said she would show me something about my mother," I told him. "And she did. Did you know that room existed? Did you know my mother used to come there with Kirk?"

"I didn't know. Clarita told me where to look. But what good does it do for you to know?"

I was still holding the yellowed lace bonnet in my hands and I help it up for him to see. "Perhaps this is *my* Cordova madness. That I want to put together all the pieces about my mother."

I folded the bonnet and put it away in my bag. Whatever I learned seemed to add more questions, never to answer them. I couldn't even be sure whether Eleanor had meant me real harm, or only wanted to vent her spite by frightening me.

"The way never opens," I said miserably.

Gavin didn't answer, and I knew it was closed for him too as the wedge between us grew wider. He would be happy with me only if I went away, as would my grandfather.

As we neared Santa Fe, I thought again of the keys in my pocket. I must visit the collection before Clarita or Juan knew I was home, and now Gavin must come with me.

We entered the city with silence growing between us, and there was nothing we could find to say. When we reached Canyon Road, I asked him to come with me out to the collection, and told him something was troubling me about the picture. He parked the car and we entered the patio through the garage. If anyone saw us, at least no one called out.

When we reached the building with the peaked roof, I gave the keys to Gavin and he opened the door. We stepped into inner darkness and stood for a moment listening. There was no sound anywhere, not indoors or out. He led the way through dimness to the alcove at the back and turned on the switch for the lamp above the Velázquez. In an instant the painting was flooded with light.

Doña Inés looked down at us with her strange, demented eyes that now seemed a little like Eleanor's eyes as I had seen them in a ghost town that morning.

It was not the dwarf who interested me, however, but her dog. The animal lay at her feet—silver gray, with its forepaws outstretched, its hound's ears cocked and pointed.

"Look at the dog!" I cried to Gavin. "Velázquez never painted a dog so clumsily."

Now that I was paying careful attention and not taking something for granted, other details sprang to view. The tiny hand of the dwarf, curled against her breast, the face itself, all were subtly wrong. The very texture of the master—never to be matched—was missing.

"This was never painted by Velázquez," Gavin agreed.

"We've got to tell Juan!" I reached for the switch and turned off the light. When we'd locked the door, we hurried toward the house together.

We found my grandfather in his study and he fixed me with a cold look as we burst in. "Was it you who took my keys, Amanda?"

I placed them on the desk before him, but when Gavin would have spoken, I put a hand on his arm.

"When you used to paint," I said to Juan, "did you ever learn by copying old masters?"

"Yes, of course. I visited museums in various countries, and I made many copies. It's a good way to learn. When the Velázquez came into my hands, I made a copy of that. Probably it is still around somewhere, if you'd like to see it. Though I did the dog badly—I was never good at painting animals."

Gavin and I looked at each other. Clarita had heard us talking and she came upstairs to the study.

"The Velázquez is missing from the collection," Gavin

said. "The picture that's been hung in its place must be the one you painted long ago."

The old man did not move or speak. He sat frozen at his desk, his eyes fixed upon Gavin. Clarita made a soft, moaning sound and sank into a chair, though it seemed to me that she was watching her father warily.

"Surely this is the time to bring in the police," I said to Gavin.

He shook his head. "There'd be a tremendous uproar and publicity. The painting might be taken away, if it was recovered."

"Exactly," Juan said coldly. "Which I will not have. As long as I live it is mine. What happens later does not matter."

"Then how can you recover it?" I asked.

"I will recover it. Where is Eleanor?"

"We left her in Madrid," Gavin said. "I got there in time to prevent her from tormenting Amanda."

Juan looked at me. "This is why I sent Gavin after you. I didn't want her to do some reckless thing that might injure her."

"She might have injured me," I said dryly.

"Why did you go with her, then?"

Clarita began to utter little sounds of distress, as though she wanted to prevent me from speaking, but I answered him without heeding her.

"Eleanor wanted to show me something out there. Do you know that the house where my mother and Kirk used to meet is still there, and that a room in it is furnished?"

"What are you talking about?" Juan's fierce, dark gaze pinned me, demanded the truth from me, but before I could go on, Clarita broke in.

"Please, please—it is nothing. I can explain everything."

Juan turned that dark look upon his eldest daughter. "You have had to do too much explaining today. Do you remember what I told Katy? Do you remember that

my order was to have that house torn down, and everything in it destroyed?"

For just an instant before Clarita bowed her head,
I saw the look of malice she turned upon him, and I
knew that if Juan had an enemy to fear, it was Clarita.
But she answered meekly enough.

"Yes, I remember. But my mother would not do it.
Everything else of Doro's had been destroyed or disposed of. Only this was left, and my mother wanted
to keep it. Though Doro never went there after Kirk
left Santa Fe."

"Then it is to be destroyed now," Juan said. "I will
not have that place left standing."

I broke in. "But, Aunt Clarita, she must have gone
there at some time after he left. Because of this."

I opened my handbag and took out the bonnet of
yellowed lace and dropped it on the table before Juan.
As he stared at it blankly, Clarita gasped, and a strange
thing happened. She left her chair, and it was as if she
left her body, her former spirit. As I watched in astonishment and some dismay, she became the woman I had
seen briefly at the dinner table—the woman who had
worn claret velvet and comported herself with the arrogant confidence of a Cordova. Even in her habitual
black, she seemed now to grow in stature—and in
subtle menace.

"No," she said. "Doro never returned to Madrid." She
reached past me and picked up the bonnet, stood looking at it in her hands as though it fascinated her. Then
she held it out to Juan. "Do you remember this, my
father?"

He stared at the small scrap of lace and satin with
an air of dread, and he did not answer her. After a
moment she went proudly out of the room, carrying
the bonnet with her.

Juan made no effort to stop her, and as she had grown,
inexplicably, he seemed to shrink in his chair. The lines
in his face grew more deeply etched. Paying no attention to either Gavin or me, he stood up and crossed

the room to his long couch. I expected him to lie down upon it, but he did not. Feeling beneath the pillow, he reassured himself that something was there, and returned to his desk. I knew he had searched for the dagger.

"My enemies gather," he said dully. "Go now and leave me. I must think. When Eleanor returns, send her to me."

Though Gavin might have stayed to argue, he accepted the edict when I did, and we went down to the living room together.

"What is happening?" I cried, and Gavin shook his head unhappily.

"I don't know, Amanda. Except perhaps about the painting."

"You know what's happened to that?" I asked in surprise.

"I can guess. But I'm not going to make any wild accusations. We'll wait until Eleanor comes back from Madrid."

However, she did not return to the house for the rest of the day. Gavin went to the store, and my grandfather remained alone. As did Clarita in her room, without going near him. I wondered what had transpired when he had accused her of lying about being at that window.

By midafternoon, I decided that I must talk to someone, and the logical person was once more Sylvia Stewart. Without telling anyone where I was going, I ran down through the patio and let myself into the next-door yard. Across the Stewart *portal* the living-room door stood open. I called out Sylvia's name, but had no answer. Yet I could hear a light, clicking sound coming from Paul's workroom.

No matter what I was interrupting, I had to find Sylvia, and I stepped to the door and looked in. Paul was nowhere in sight, but his wife sat at the desk. The sound I'd heard was the idle tapping of a pencil as she drummed it on the desk, but she didn't know I was there, so absorbed was she in the yellow second sheets be-

fore her. Her brown head was bowed over the manuscript,
her lips slightly parted as she read with excitement.

It was necessary to interrupt, and I spoke softly so
as not to startle her. "Sylvia?"

Nevertheless, the startling was extreme. She dropped
her pencil and jerked around to face me, a bright flush
rising in her cheeks as she stared at me.

"I'm sorry," I said. "I did call out when I came in
the door from the *portal*, but you didn't hear me."

Her dazed look told me she was still far away, though
the flush in her cheeks indicated that guilt of some sort
was surfacing.

"I thought you were Paul!" she cried. "He'd have a
fit if he knew I was reading his manuscript. But he got
a phone call a little while ago and went out, so I took
this chance."

"Is that his book about Southwest murders?" I asked.

"Yes. And the chapter about the Cordovas is going to
be all right." For some reason she seemed tremendously
relieved. "I was afraid he would stick too closely to the
facts, but he's fictionizing again. It will be all right."

When she turned back to the pages, I stepped close to
her chair to look over her shoulder, but at once she
flipped the sheets face down.

"No, Amanda. I can't let you read this unless Paul
says so. It's one thing to pry when I'm his wife, but
something else when it comes to letting other people
see."

She pushed away from the desk and turned off the
typewriter lamp. "Let's go where we can be comfortable.
What's been happening? You look thoroughly keyed up."

I couldn't let the matter of Paul's book go so easily.
"If he fictionizes—when he's dealing with facts—won't
he chance trouble from Juan Cordova?"

"Perhaps not. He's glamorizing Doro and making out
Kirk a villain. I don't think Juan will object to that."

While I trailed her back to the other room, she waved
me into a chair and flung herself down on a couch
with bright canary pillows tossed among the brown.

"Can I get you something to drink, Amanda?"

"Thanks, no. Why are you so relieved about Paul's book? What did you think he'd write?"

With an elaborate effort, she busied herself finding a pack of cigarettes, offering it to me, tapping one out for herself when I refused—all the while plainly marshaling what she would say to me.

"After all, that whole affair is pretty thin ice, isn't it?" she said. "If Paul were clumsy, he might crash us all through into freezing water."

"What do you mean?"

"Oh, nothing much. If it's what you're curious about, he isn't making anything of that brainstorm you had about a third person appearing on the hillside. Though he is doing quite a thing about the frightened child and her loss of memory."

"I don't like that," I told her. "And perhaps that third person will come clear."

With a shrug, Sylvia blew smoke into the air. "I'm afraid he's given up asking you. What's wrong, Amanda? Has something happened to bring you here?"

"I just wanted to talk. Sylvia, what do you know about a house the Cordovas own out in Madrid?"

Her eyes widened as she stared at me. "Don't tell me that place is back in the picture?"

"Eleanor took me there today. She said my mother and your stepbrother used to meet there."

"That's true enough. Fixing up the house and trying to keep it secret was one of Doro's wilder fantasies. And Kirk had as wild a streak as she had, so he went right along with it. I warned him that there'd be an explosion if Juan Cordova ever found out. And of course there was. Doro was his darling and he loved Kirk like a son. But they were both too young, and he was a proper Spanish father. So he packed Kirk off to South America and put Doro into Katy's care as though she were a nun. Which she certainly wasn't."

"And then he ordered the house destroyed?"

"Yes, he wanted all evidence of their affair wiped out."

Her nervous smoking made me even more edgy and I wished she would put down her cigarette. Ever since I'd first met Sylvia, I'd known that some deep worry was eating away inside her, and I still wanted to know what it was.

"What do *you* believe?" I asked her. "Do you think it could have been Juan on that hillside, angry with Kirk because he'd come back to bother Doroteo?"

"Maybe it was!" Sylvia pounced on my words so eagerly that I knew she didn't believe in them. Why should she want me to go down a side road, unless there was something she wanted to hide?

"You don't believe that," I contradicted. "Because Juan wouldn't have minded their marrying if Doro hadn't been so young. He was fond of Kirk, but wanted to give them both time to grow up and know their own minds. Katy urged that too. And they were right. Because she forgot about your stepbrother and fell in love with my father. But there's more I wanted to talk about."

I hesitated, wondering whether to tell her about the whole dreadful episode with Eleanor. When I'd decided not to, I went on.

"While I was poking around out in that house, I found an old baby bonnet my mother must have made for me. But when I brought it home and asked Clarita about it, she behaved strangely. She said Doro had never gone back to that place after Kirk left. So who took a bonnet of mine out there and left it?"

Sylvia ground out her cigarette with another of her nervous gestures. "Clarita was lying. Doro did go back. She went back for one last time. Clarita was with her. But I won't talk about that, so you needn't ask me. Let it alone, Amanda."

How often she had said that to me—"Let it alone." But I would never let it alone now, though I didn't press her at the moment. There was another question I wanted to ask.

"Sylvia, who was it that found Kirk's body, and then my mother's? Why has no one ever told me that?"

She stared at me without answering, and I went on.

"It was Paul, wasn't it? He wasn't with you on the road, as he let me think earlier. After he saw Clarita away from the house, he came along that path by himself—and found them both. It was he who raised the alarm, wasn't it?"

"Why do you think that?"

"You're stalling," I said. "I remember his being there."

The words seemed to echo through the room and dash themselves against the white painted walls, astonishing me as well as Sylvia.

"You—*remember?*" Sylvia repeated softly.

In strange confusion I tried to examine the thing that had just come to me. I seemed to see a man rushing about, calling people, trying to be helpful. He was a younger version of Paul.

"I think I remember. Something is coming back to me."

"The third one in the struggle?" The words were almost a whisper.

"I don't know."

Suddenly I didn't like the way she was looking at me— no longer in her half-jesting, easy manner, but with something inimical in her eyes. I stood up and moved toward the door.

"Thanks for letting me talk, Sylvia. I'll run along now."

She was not like Eleanor. In spite of the way she looked, she might have let me go without a word to stop me, but I stopped myself, pausing in the doorway.

"Did you know," I said, "that Juan's Velázquez has been stolen? The painting of Doña Inés is gone from the collection. An old student painting of Juan's has been put in its place."

The pallor that had replaced her earlier flush was alarming. She looked so sick and faint that I stepped back into the room.

"Are you all right? Can I get you a drink of something?"

But as I had always suspected, Sylvia was a woman of strength when she had to be strong. She sat erectly on the couch and stared at me without blinking.

"I'm perfectly all right," she said. "Why shouldn't I be?"

I put her to no further strain, but went out the door onto the *portal*. When I turned and looked back, she was sitting exactly as I had left her, staring after me, and I knew she would do so until I was out of sight.

The gate in the wall stood ajar, and I went through it and back to the house. I'd been given no answers to anything except the one fact that Paul Stewart had found Kirk's body the day he had been shot.

Eleanor had still not returned, and she did not appear during dinner or later in the evening. With Paul gone too, I wondered if they had met somewhere and were plotting together. Perhaps they were already busy trying to sell the Velázquez on some black market. If Eleanor had given him the keys, Paul could have spirited it out of its frame and made the substitution the day we were all out at the *rancho*. It seemed clear now that this must have been why Eleanor had wanted us away from the house, and why Paul had stayed home. But how was anything to be proved? Eleanor wanted money in her hands, and this could be a way to get it, as well as a daring escapade of the sort that would be to her liking. In a way, she was only taking what belonged to her, since she would inherit the painting anyway. But the injury to Juan Cordova was great—perhaps because he too suspected what had happened, as undoubtedly Gavin had. And Clarita? She knew Eleanor best of all, and I remembered her little performance of shock, during which she had watched her father warily while she was moaning in distress.

In any case, since that moment when she had picked up the bonnet she had become the woman who had worn claret red the night of Juan's party. She had finally come out of her room, and she moved about the house with her head high—clearly in command. I heard her telling Juan that he'd had a difficult day and he had better go to bed early. A role of authority she would never have dared assume toward him earlier. I saw him again that evening, though only to tell him good night, and he seemed a weary and beaten man. For the first time I had a feeling of sympathy for him, but I would not insult him by showing it. As Clarita's strength increased, his own faded.

Gavin did not appear at all, and I had no idea where he was, or exactly how things stood between us. The climate of the house was uneasy, and all my early dread of it seemed to have returned, so that I moved quickly and kept an eye upon the shadows. Something must be done, and I must do it. But what? And what, if anything, did the sudden flash of memory I had had about Paul mean?

I took some books up to bed and read for a while before I fell asleep around eleven o'clock. I'd placed a chair under the knob of my door, since I had no lock and key, and I knew that anyone who tried to enter would have to waken the house as well as me. So I could fall asleep without fearing an intruder.

It was after one in the morning when a sound woke me. It had been distant—not at the door of my room. I left my bed and ran to remove the chair from beneath the doorknob. Was Juan abroad again? There was a sound from the living room, as though someone hurried through it. Going toward Juan's room?

I put on a robe and slippers and went softly down the stairs. Everything was quiet, and there was no sound from Juan's room. Perhaps I had been wrong, but it might be better to rouse Clarita or Gavin, so we could investigate together.

When the scream came from the direction of the

balcony outside my grandfather's room, it shattered all silence. That was Eleanor's voice. After the first cry of fright, I could hear her screaming, "No, no!" hysterically.

Clarita and Gavin came in moments, but I was the first one up the balcony steps. Juan's study was dark and as I fumbled for the switch, the scene sprang to life to show Eleanor, fully dressed, standing beside Juan's desk. Evidently he had been sleeping on the couch, for it was covered with rumpled bedclothes, but now he stood grasping Eleanor by one arm, and he held the Toledo dagger in his other hand.

"He was going to stab me!" Eleanor wailed. "I felt the knife!"

The old man tossed the dagger onto the couch and reached for Eleanor with both hands.

"Hush, *querida,* hush. I would never hurt you. But when I heard someone come close to my couch, I grasped the dagger and sprang up. I thought you meant me injury. I didn't know until I touched you who it was."

She pressed her head against his shoulder, still sobbing, clinging to him, letting him smooth her hair, comfort her. She was no longer the woman I had seen in Madrid. Since those moments when she had threatened me, all the venom had gone out of her, and the adventurous spirit with it.

Clarita stood proudly back, somehow giving the impression that she could take charge if she chose, but did not wish to.

Gavin waited for only a little of Eleanor's sobbing. "What were you doing here in the dark?" he asked her. "At this hour?"

She hid her face against the old man's shoulder and would not answer. One hand flicked behind her, and I heard a tinkle that was familiar. When I picked it up from the carpet and held it out, the ring of keys was still warm from her hand.

Gavin took it from me gingerly. "What did you want with these, Eleanor?"

Again she would not answer, and Juan Cordova

looked at us over her head, recovering some of his authority.

"Let her be. I have frightened her badly. I left my bed to sleep here, so my enemy would not find me where expected. I did not know it was Eleanor—but thought it was someone who meant me harm."

"Was it you who came that other time and stood by Grandfather's bed?" I asked Eleanor.

She recovered herself slightly so there was a hint of defiance in her voice. "I came once before. I didn't think he knew."

Again Gavin tried to question her. "Where have you been? We've been looking for you since early afternoon."

This time she chose to reply. "I stayed in Paul's study. He let me stay there while he worked. Not even Sylvia knew I was there. I didn't want to see any of you."

This, I knew, was a lie. Paul had not been in his study. But Sylvia and I had. So why this stealthy visit to Juan's study, and why the filching of his keys?

"Come, Eleanor." Clarita spoke with decision. "You have caused enough trouble today."

"Go with her," Juan said, and Eleanor walked away from him and let Clarita put an arm about her shoulders. Her eyes looked a little glassy, whether from tears or because she was staring so fixedly at nothing, I couldn't be sure.

Juan returned to his couch and picked up the dagger, thrust it once more beneath his pillow. "No one will get to me," he said. "You can see that I am able to protect myself."

"Against what?" Gavin asked. "Against whom?"

The old man did not answer. "Tell Clarita to stay away," he said, and settled himself beneath the covers. Gavin helped to pull up the blanket, but at Juan's request we did not turn off the lights when we went away.

Gavin put his arm about me as we descended to the living room. "Are you all right, Amanda?"

"I don't know," I said. "I feel as if I were walking a ridge with a precipice on either side. Walking it blindfolded. Perhaps I'm the one playing Blind Man's Buff behind the turquoise mask. If I could take it off, I'd see everything clearly. But I can't remove it. If I look into a mirror I'll see it on my face."

"No, you won't," he said, and turned me about gently to face the fireplace.

I saw it then—where someone had hung it against the rounded chimney. The mask looked out over the room, and I shivered, turning away from it, clinging to Gavin.

He held me close, kissed me. "I've wanted to tell you," he said. "I'm leaving this house late tomorrow. I'm taking the first steps."

Cold waters seemed to close over my head. His presence was my security. No matter which way I had turned, he had been there to guard me. The steps he was taking had to be—yet now I would be vulnerable, open to any one of them who wanted to attack.

"I want you out of this house too," Gavin went on. "And you will be soon. But for the moment you'll be all right. I've talked to Clarita."

I looked up at him. "Clarita?"

"Yes. I've made her understand. She doesn't approve of divorce, but she knows that neither Eleanor nor I can be held any longer in this marriage. Juan can't have his way, and I think in a sense she's glad to oppose him. But now she'll watch out for you. I doubt that there'll be any danger from Eleanor again. In fact, now that you've faced them all down, I don't think anyone will try to threaten you."

I didn't know this for sure. I didn't know it at all, but he had never believed in what I was trying to prove. That someone else had killed Kirk, and not my mother.

He raised my chin and kissed me again, not tenderly this time, but roughly, so that I felt a sense of rising storm in him—and liked it. Here was a man who would respect me as a person—some of the time. And he would dominate me some of the time, so that I might have to fight him for my own existence. If I chose to fight. Perhaps I wouldn't always, and yet I knew that he would never hurt me when my defenses were down. And he would always want me to paint—so the rest didn't matter.

He turned me about and faced me in the direction of my room. "Go back to bed. You've stood enough for today."

Without looking back, I fled up the stairs to my room. Once more, I propped the chair beneath my doorknob before I got into bed, and then I went quickly, deeply, sweetly to sleep.

In the morning it was Clarita who awakened me, rapping sharply on the door and demanding that it be opened to her. I slipped out of bed and removed the chair, so that she could come into the room prow first like a battleship in full array.

"Gavin has talked with my father, and he has gone to the store for the last time today," she told me. "From now until the time you leave, you are to go nowhere without me. Gavin wishes it to be so."

I remembered a gold earring on the floor of the garage, and was silent, making no promises. Perhaps Gavin trusted her, but I did not. Yesterday I had seen Juan afraid of her and I knew it was against her he would defend himself with that dagger.

"What plans have you made for today?" she demanded.

"None. Perhaps I'll paint for a while here in my room. I have a picture to be finished. Perhaps I'll spend some time with my grandfather if he wants to see me."

"He will not want to see you. He is ill today. Dr. Morrisby has already come and he wants him to be very quiet. The last few days have been too much for him."

"I understand," I said meekly, not trusting her.

"Our doctor has had two visits to make here," she went on. "Sylvia is ill as well, and staying home from her shop. I have already been over to see her."

I could guess what might be wrong with Sylvia. She hadn't taken lightly my word that the Velázquez had been stolen. I suspected that she knew very well that her husband and Eleanor were involved, and today she had gone to pieces. But I said none of this to Clarita, merely murmuring my sympathy.

With a regal nod, Clarita went away, and I marveled at the change in her. Always she had been kept under the thumb of Juan Cordova. But now somehow their roles had been reversed, and I had the feeling that while he was afraid of his older daughter, she was no longer afraid of him. The change, I suspected, was more psychological than real, and it had something to do with that baby bonnet.

When I had breakfasted alone and returned to my room, I set up Juan's easel. My room that had once been Doroteo's was high and light, and would serve me well. When my painting of an imaginary desert village was in place, I set out the colors on my palette. I knew exactly what I was going to do to finish the picture. Coming up from the end of that narrow, winding road I would paint a burro, and on his back would be riding a Franciscan brother in a brown robe, with a knotted white belt about his waist. I could see him vividly in my mind, and he would add exactly the right touch to my ageless New Mexican painting.

But when I went to work, that rare and mysterious magic which sometimes occurs took over. One never counted on it. One worked with or without it. But sometimes when it came the work prospered beyond the means of an artist's talent, and he surpassed himself. Sometimes he even painted what he had not at first intended. It was like that now, and I knew the colors on my palette were wrong. I scraped them off and started fresh because accumulations of wrong colors could be a distraction and a discouragement.

The burro was not a burro. It was a palomino. And the man who rode it was not a Franciscan brother, but a Mexican *charro* in dark blue suede, with silver buttons and white braid and a broad white sombrero. He rode jauntily up into the foreground of my picture, his left hand light on the reins, and his face—tiny though it was—was Eleanor's.

I worked intently for an hour or more. The figure was small, not dominating the scene, but done in greater detail than its surroundings. And all the while I was telling myself something—something I knew with my feelings, but not with my conscious mind.

When the figure in dark blue riding his spirited horse was completed, I picked up the painting and carried it carefully downstairs. There were three people I wanted to show it to—Sylvia, Clarita and Juan. Strangely, Eleanor didn't matter. That inner thing that had caused me to paint was still ruling me, and it must be obeyed. First Sylvia—whether she was ill or not.

Clarita was not about, and I was glad to postpone that confrontation.

This time I found Sylvia Stewart lying in a deck chair where the sun slanted across the *portal*, a light Indian blanket tossed over her. She greeted me without pleasure and I told her I was sorry she wasn't feeling well, and asked if Paul was home.

"I've done a picture," I said. "I'd like you to see it."

She nodded languidly, and I turned the small canvas about. Sylvia stared at it with no great interest, and I brought it close so that she could focus on the rider of the palomino. At once she closed her eyes and turned her head away from me.

"You've caught the way he used to look," she said helplessly. "How did you know? That jaunty air of Kirk's, the expression on his face."

"I painted Eleanor," I said. "You weren't telling me the truth out at the *rancho*—none of you was telling the truth. Juan was Kirk's father, wasn't he? Kirk was Eleanor's uncle. The Cordova likeness is there in all of them."

Sylvia opened her eyes and stared at me. "You don't know, do you?" she said. "You truly don't know."

I remembered Paul saying those very words to me before, when they had concerned my mother.

"Hadn't you better tell me?" I asked.

"No. Never. It's not up to me."

She would be adamant, I knew. There was granite in Sylvia when she made up her mind.

"There's something else," I said. Carefully I set up my painting against a table, where nothing would smudge the wet portions. "There's the Velázquez."

She made no attempt at evasion. "What about it?"

"Do you think Paul and Eleanor have taken it away to sell?"

With a deep breath that seemed to strengthen her, she sat up and threw off the blanket. "I don't think so. Let's go and see."

"Did they tell you about taking it?" I asked, following her into the house.

"No. I guessed after you were here. And I checked to make sure. They didn't worry about how well they hid it."

Crossing the living room, she opened the door of a closet and rummaged about inside. When she didn't find what she was looking for, she dropped to her knees and padded about into the corners and over the floor with her hands. There was alarm in her eyes when she looked up at me.

"This is where Paul must have put it when he rolled it up. It was here yesterday."

Neither of us had noticed that the typing in the room beyond had stopped, and neither was aware of Paul until he stood behind us at the closet door.

"Put what?" he asked.

Sylvia didn't trouble to look up at him. "The Velázquez," she said from her creeping position.

I saw his face change. The green in his eyes had an angry glitter as he leaned over to grasp his wife's arm and pull her to her feet. Sylvia cried out and began to rub her arm when he released her.

"What are you talking about?" he demanded.

She continued to rub, but she answered him with spirit. "Oh, Paul, you're better at this sort of thing when it's done on paper. I'm sure everyone has guessed by now about your plotting with Eleanor. I suppose it was safe enough, because Juan would never punish her. But what have you done with the painting? You couldn't simply take it away and sell it. Not as quickly as this!"

Pushing past us both, he searched the closet himself. When he couldn't find the rolled-up canvas on the floor, or standing in a corner, he pushed things off the shelves, turned everything upside down and emerged at last in a rage.

"What's she trying now?" he demanded, and walked to a table where a telephone stood. In a moment he had dialed the Cordovas' number and was talking into the receiver. "She must be there, Clarita. Do look for her."

The phone at the other end was put down and for a time there was silence. Sylvia and I sat on the couch, waiting, not looking at each other. Paul's face was dark with anger and I would not have liked to be Eleanor at that moment.

"Everyone's guessed by now," Sylvia told him. "There's nothing you can do but return the painting. Why did you do this wild thing anyway?"

He turned his angry look upon her, and she winced away. Then Clarita was back on the line, and Paul listened.

"Thank you," he said in a dull voice, and hung up. "Eleanor can't be found. Her car's in the garage, but she's nowhere about. And apparently the Velázquez has disappeared with her. I suppose she could have taken a taxi. I suppose she could be halfway to Albuquerque by now."

"Then it's not your responsibility," Sylvia said. "There's nothing Juan can do about it, if Eleanor has the painting. You're lucky if you can get off so easily."

He rushed out of the room and onto the *portal*, his eyes searching the patio, the area about the house, as though he might still discover her. By chance his look fell upon my painting—and was arrested. He picked it up to hold it at arm's length, studying the small adobe village, the cottonwood trees, and winding road with that small meticulously painted figure riding up it.

"Why Eleanor?" he asked me.

"It's not supposed to be Eleanor," I said. "It's Kirk."

He stared as if the picture hypnotized him, but when he spoke, it was not of my work.

"No, she hasn't skipped out and taken the painting with her. I think I know what she'd do. Yesterday we were together awhile, and she was vacillating, uncertain —not like herself. She mentioned once that she'd like to go out to Bandelier again, to think things through. She has some sort of affinity for the place. This time she must have taken a taxi all the way—to throw us off by leaving her car behind."

"Then I hope you all let her go," Sylvia said fretfully. "She only does it so someone will chase after her and plead with her to come home."

"That's not what she wants," Paul said grimly. "But this time *I* am going after her. I'm going to bring her back."

Sylvia was up from the couch in a flash, flinging herself upon him, "No, Paul, no! Don't go now while you're angry. Wait awhile—wait!"

I stared at her in surprise, but Paul paid no attention. He was already heading for the garage. When I had picked up my painting, I left without either of them noticing me. It didn't matter. What Eleanor did now, or what happened to the Velázquez, no longer interested me. My own direction was clear. I could mark Sylvia off the top of my list. Clarita was next.

All was dim and quiet in the bedroom wing, and the first door—Clarita's—stood open. I paused on the threshold to call her name, but there was no answer. Just as I was about to leave, something I saw stopped me. A yellowed streamer of satin ribbon hung from beneath the lowered lid of a camphorwood chest.

In a moment I was across the room, lifting the lid of the chest. The baby bonnet lay on top of the piled contents, and something else lay there too. Eagerly

I reached in to pick up the top sheet of a sheaf of papers. Fading script seemed to spring at me from the page, and I saw the ragged inner edge, where the sheet had been torn from a book. All the pages beneath bore similar tears. So it had been Clarita out at the *rancho* that day, speeding away in a car, Clarita who had tumbled Katy's room in her search, and torn out the diary pages. Here beneath my hand lay Katy's words, and the answer to everything.

I began to read, standing where I was, following down the page the strong handwriting now so familiar to me. The words dealt, not as I had expected, with the day of Doro's death, but with reminiscence. She had been writing of the past.

> *It rained all that day. When I remember it, I always think of rain beating on the roof of that little house in Madrid. It was all we could do to climb the slope of hill and get her to the cabin because her time was already upon her. Clarita came with me, and old Consuelo, who knew about such matters. We boiled water for sterilizing, and listened to her moaning. All the while Clarita muttered angrily. I tried to hush her, but that day she was made only of anger against both of them. I did my best. My darling was frightened and needed affection, and I could give her that at least. She was my youngest and I had no blame for her, no anger in me. But we all knew Juan must be dealt with after it was over.*

I'd reached the bottom of the sheet, and I set it aside in the chest and picked up the next page. I knew what the baby bonnet meant now. It had never been intended for me. I wasn't born until five years later.

"What are you doing with my things?" The low, deadly voice spoke behind me and I whirled around.

Clarita's lips were pale, her eyes blazing, but I had to face her without wavering.

"I'm beginning to see," I told her. "My mother went back to that cabin to have her baby, didn't she? The baby who was born five years before me."

With a violent gesture, Clarita snatched the paper from my hands and tossed it back in the chest. She slammed down the lid, nearly catching my fingers beneath its edge. She wouldn't have cared if she had broken my hand, and I felt far more afraid of her than I had of Eleanor in Madrid. But there was no Gavin now to rescue me, no one about in this empty wing.

"You meddle," Clarita said, and her voice held its deadly level. "You've been meddling ever since you came here."

Carefully I moved away from the chest, edging toward the door. All this had happened before, in another place and another time, but this time the intent was more dangerous. Nevertheless, I had to face her, I had to know.

"It was you in the patio with the whip, wasn't it? Even to whipping your father, whom you hate. It was you in the store, wielding that brass statue of Quetzalcoatl. You'd kill me if you could because of all the hatred in you. For me and for my mother. Why? Because she was the favored one always?"

Her eyes never left mine, her expression never changed, but she stood utterly still, and there was a difference— as though all life and hope were seeping from her. Now a great deal was coming clear to me. By the time I'd reached the doorway, she still had not moved, had not tried to stop me. In a moment I would be free to escape her. But there was even more to be said.

"Now I understand about you and my grandfather. You had to bend to whatever Juan wanted because Eleanor has been like a daughter to you, and you knew he could disinherit her to spite you, if he chose. But after she took the Velázquez, you knew she would have money enough for the rest of her life, and you wouldn't bow to him any longer. The turning point must have come when you held that bonnet in your hands and you thought of what all of you had been through. So you weren't afraid any more. He had too much pride of family to betray what had happened. But I know now who came along that hillside with a gun in hand. You hated Kirk by then, didn't you? Not only because he wouldn't look at you when you were younger, but also because of what he'd done to your sister, and thus to Juan and your family."

With an effort, Clarita managed to break her frozen posture, and she made a lunge toward me. But I was already gone from the doorway, running down the hall and into the main house. I left my painting behind. It didn't matter now. I understood about the thing some hidden consciousness had told me, and there would be no need to show my work to Juan. What Katy had written changed all that.

I ran across the living room and up the balcony steps to Juan Cordova's room. I didn't know how much he had discovered over the years, or how much he knew now, but he had to be told all the truth, and at once.

With both his hands flat upon its surface, he sat behind his desk. His skin looked gray and his eyes sunken. An inch away from his fingers lay the dagger with the Damascene handle, and he was staring at it. Because I knew Clarita would follow me, I burst into words that were not altogether coherent.

"I've seen what Katy wrote in her diary!" I cried. "Clarita had the missing pages hidden away in her room. So I know about the baby that was born in Madrid. I know everything."

He did not move or look at me. He was a very old man and life was nearly over for him. It would not be possible for him to bear very much more. I was suddenly sorry that I'd burst in on him so explosively, but I had had to before Clarita could do something drastic. She was already there behind me in the doorway, though she didn't cross the threshold but merely stood there in silence.

Juan must have sensed her presence, for he raised his

eyes slowly from the dagger. When he spoke his voice was low and hoarse.

"What have you done, Clarita?"

His elder daughter extended her hands in a gesture of despair. "It is not what I have done. It's this one—this viper you have brought into your household!"

"Where is Eleanor?" Juan asked, ignoring her spite. Clarita was silent again.

"Bring her to me," Juan said. "I must speak with her at once. I will tell her everything myself."

"No—no!" Clarita took a step toward him. "She will never forgive me. Or you. She will never forgive the deception."

"I will tell her," he said dully.

"I'm afraid you can't tell her anything for a while," I put in. "Paul Stewart thinks she's gone to Bandelier again. He's gone after her. Because of the Velázquez. They took it, you know. They plotted its theft between them."

When he chose, Juan's eyes could still blaze as fiercely as Clarita's and he turned that searing look upon me, so that I winced beneath it, and drew back. But he only waved me aside.

"Paul has gone to Bandelier—after Eleanor?" Life seemed to return to him. With no evidence of weakness, he stood up from his desk and walked toward his daughter. "Then you will take me there. We must follow them at once. The Velázquez must be recovered, and Paul must not be alone in that wilderness with Eleanor."

"But, Father—" Clarita began, only to have him hush her fiercely. "At once. You will drive me."

He went out of the room and she hurried to help him on the steps. It was clear that his will was once more ascendant, and he would have his own way. I didn't wait to hear them leave the house, to hear the starting of the car, but picked up Juan's phone and dialed CORDOVA's number.

When Gavin's voice came on, I told him quickly that Eleanor had gone out to Bandelier and Paul had gone after her. That now Juan was forcing Clarita to drive him there. I attempted to tell him nothing more, since there was no time, and he responded with blessed speed.

"I'll get out there," he told me. "I'll be leaving at once. Juan shouldn't be making that drive."

When I heard the click of the phone, I hung up and went slowly out of the room. There was nothing I could do now. The wheels were turning without me, and they couldn't be stopped or swerved from the course they would follow. I didn't know what would happen to Clarita now, or how what she had done all those years ago would affect all our lives in the present. The coming hours would be anxious ones, but at least Gavin would be there, and he would search for Juan and the others. Once more Eleanor had turned us all toward Bandelier.

XVIII

As I moved through quiet rooms, I remembered that this was Rosa's afternoon off, and the house was empty. No one was nearby except Sylvia, in the next house. Now if I chose, I could return to Clarita's room and read the rest of those diary pages. But I had no desire to. I felt a little limp. The full story would come out now, and it could wait. It was enough for me to know that Doroteo Austin had never been guilty of murder. Why and how she had died, I still didn't know, but perhaps her spirit could rest, now that all the truth would be known.

Only Doroteo's own quiet room could offer me solace, I thought, as I climbed the stairs. I wanted to be quiet and understand, not only what had happened on that hillside, but all the ramifications of that secret birth in the little ghost town of Madrid.

My door stood open as I had last left it, and I walked unsteadily into the room. In reaction to wildly spent emotions, my legs felt rubbery, and I wanted only to lie for a while on my bed and let the earth spin around me. But someone had been there, for a long roll of canvas lay upon the bed.

It took me only a moment to partially unroll it from

the bottom of the painting until Doña Inés' small feet, and the feet of the dog which crouched beside her came into view. With hands that shook, I unrolled farther until the full figure of the dwarf was displayed. This was the real Velázquez—fragile, precious—though how it had come to be left on my bed, I didn't know. Eleanor must have put it there.

Behind me I heard the faint swish of sound, and turned just in time to catch the movement of the bedroom door as it swung shut. I whirled about—and faced my cousin Eleanor. No—my sister Eleanor.

She wore her jeans and concho belt, and she stood with one foot crossed jauntily over the other, and her arms akimbo.

"Hello, Amanda," she said, her head tilted in cocky defiance. "How do you like my turning honest woman and giving back the painting?"

I glanced toward the bed and then at her. "I thought it must be you. But why—why?"

"I'd have preferred to return it to its frame," she said. "I went out yesterday to see if I could do it by myself—when you caught me putting back the keys. Then last night I tried to get the keys from Grandfather's desk, but he caught me. And he hasn't been out of his study all day. So I thought I'd leave it here before I went away."

"Away where?"

"I don't know. I've been packing. Perhaps I'll go out to California as a start. Gavin can get his divorce. And afterwards if Juan wants me back, perhaps I'll come. After everything has simmered down and he's forgiven me for what I've done."

I couldn't wait any longer. It was necessary to tell her what I knew.

"You started something in Madrid yesterday."

"Yes, I know. I couldn't live with myself very well afterwards. I've done other things, but I've never seen myself as vicious before. But now I know what I can be like. The Cordova heritage—from Doña Inés."

"That's foolish. Anyway, the Madrid episode is over. What matters is that bonnet I found out there. It wasn't one Doro made for me, Eleanor. It was one she made for you."

Her look was more curious than shocked. "Well, go on," she said. "Tell me the rest."

I explained then about my growing awareness of the way she and Kirk resembled each other, though I'd gone down a wrong road at first in seeking a relationship. I told her about my painting and what I'd found in Clarita's room when I went to show it to her. As well as I could remember it, I quoted the page I'd read from Katy's diary.

She heard me out thoughtfully, surprisingly calm. "So Doro and Kirk were my parents. And that makes me your half sister, doesn't it? How strange, Amanda. You don't know how strange. Sometimes I've felt so remote from my parents. I didn't seem to be anything like them. When they died, I was secretly a little shocked because I didn't care enough. When Juan knew I'd been born to Doro—and I'm sure Katy would have told him at once—he must have found a way to get Rafael and his wife to take me as their own. And then, when they died, he and Katy took me themselves, and raised me in the same house with Doro. I always felt close to her, and I was sad when she died. It's funny though— I don't remember Kirk at all. When you came here I was jealous of you because you were Doro's daughter. Remember what I said about the portrait of Emanuella out in the collection? That none of her belongs to me? I was lying. I wanted to belong to her and to Doroteo. And now I do. But I must be like Kirk too. It isn't all Cordova wildness."

I heard her out, not entirely trusting, not able to accept this new mood. She had meant me so much harm, and I didn't believe in lightning changes.

Softly she began to laugh. "Wait until Paul hears all this! What wonderful material for his book. What a story it will make!"

This was the normal Eleanor. "You mustn't tell him!" I cried. "Think of Juan!"

"Of course I'll tell him. Juan can't stop me. I'll go and tell him now."

I remembered then. "You can't. When Clarita couldn't find you in the house—because you were probably up here where she wouldn't look—he decided that you'd gone out to Bandelier again. You might as well know he's furious with you, and he's gone out there to find you. To get the painting back."

Her laughter increased. "Oh, lovely, lovely! I'll go after him and confront him with a few things."

I sighed. "Thanks to this idea of Paul's, Clarita and Juan have gone out there too—because Juan doesn't want you there with Paul. And I've called Gavin, so he's followed them. Though I think it's Juan he's worried about. Grandfather seemed beaten and old this morning."

Eleanor, who had hardly been able to contain her laughter, suddenly stopped. "I'll go right away and call off the search."

There was certainly nothing amusing about this wild goose chase. I remembered the rage in Paul's eyes, and I didn't like to think of Eleanor out in that wild place, confronting him, as she very well might.

"Don't go," I begged her. "There's no point now."

"Oh, yes there is." The laughter was gone, but she was still lightly amused. "Think of them all searching that place for me, and not finding me. We can't have that. If I'm the treasure they're hunting for, I'd better be there."

She was on the stairs now, running down. I doubted this new, sweet concern, but I went after her.

"I'll go with you. Just give me time to change shoes."

For a moment she hesitated, looking back at me, then she nodded. "I'll wait."

I ran up to my room and changed into slacks and walking shoes.

When we were in the car on the way to Bandelier, I

became aware of a further change in Eleanor. She was no longer amused, no longer pleased with the idea of confronting them all and making them look foolish. Something had happened in her thinking to sober her and give her a strange edge of anxiety between the time when I'd left her to change my clothes, and when I'd joined her in the garage.

All desire to talk had left her, and she drove at her usual high speed, but with a new urgency, so that it was not merely as though she tried to escape something, but as if she was thrusting herself toward something that frightened her badly.

Only once did I try to question her on the way, and then she behaved as though she didn't hear, or at least had no intention of answering.

A memory returned to my mind while we were traveling—of Sylvia the time I'd spoken to her of Eleanor's father. She had given a strange answer that I couldn't fit with what I knew of Rafael. Of course! Sylvia had been speaking of Kirk. So Sylvia knew.

When we reached the open space in front of the Visitor Center at the park, Eleanor at once checked the other cars. All were here, and we had gone only a little way on foot along the trail before we ran into Gavin.

He hadn't found the others yet, and he was clearly surprised to see Eleanor and me together. I explained about the mistake and apologized for sending him out here. He brushed my words aside. "It's Juan I'm worried about. He looked pretty bad this morning and he shouldn't be wandering around out here, even though Clarita is with him."

I wondered how much protection Clarita would be in any case, but there was no time for explanations now. It was best to find those two right away. Paul I didn't care about.

It was decided that Gavin would take the lower trail that followed the stream through groves of trees along the floor of the canyon, while Eleanor and I would take the path that led upward past the caves along bare, unwooded rock. At least we had no need to look into the caves today. There would be no one hiding in them.

Eleanor started off by rushing ahead of me, and I was hard put to keep up with her. Once I called out and asked her to wait for me, begging her not to go so fast. She astonished me by turning to show me a look of anxiety that was not far from tears and thoroughly unlike Eleanor.

"We've got to hurry!" she cried. "They should never have come out here—never. I don't know what will happen. If only we could find Paul."

Paul was the one I cared least about, but after that I didn't try to control Eleanor's hurry. We stumbled along the cliff path, sometimes slipping on rocky surfaces in our haste, running when we found a level space, holding onto rough walls as we helped ourselves through tight passages cut from rock. We met no one, nor did we see anyone in the glimpses we had of the lower trail far below us.

Across the canyon, on the steep, wooded cliffs opposite, no trails were visible, though there must be those that climbed among the trees. But it was unlikely that Juan or Clarita, or Paul, for that matter, would be up there. They would expect to find Eleanor at an easier level.

On a space of trail where there were steps up and down, and a narrow walk hugged the cliff, Eleanor rushed ahead of me again. New York city canyons hadn't prepared me for clambering over New Mexico rock at this altitude, and I stopped for a moment to catch my breath, watching her slim figure silhouetted against the cliff ahead of me, where she stood at the top of steps carved into the rock. She seemed frozen in a position that was unnaturally still. I hurried to join her in that high place. The moment I brushed her arm, she whirled and ducked back down the trail.

"I don't think they've seen us. Quick, Amanda, get out of sight. Let's climb into one of the caves."

I stayed where I was, protesting. I wasn't afraid of Clarita out here in the open, with Juan behind her. "But why—why?"

"Clarita's down there, and she'll have seen you by now. Juan must be with her."

I glanced up the trail from where I stood, and saw Clarita looking up at me. We both turned away at the same moment, and I rejoined Eleanor, out of sight.

"Clarita saw me," I said. "But she turned back. Why don't we go and meet them?"

"No, no!" She grasped my arm and fairly dragged me toward a ladder that led to the lip of a deep cave. She pushed me up the ladder and scrambled after me as I crept into cool darkness.

"Keep your head down and lie flat," she directed.

There was no denying her urgency and I stilled my questions and obeyed. *I* knew what Clarita had done, but surely Eleanor didn't.

We lay close together on the stone floor and there was a smell of rock dust in our noses, the hardness of rock fighting our flesh. Beside me, Eleanor lay with all her senses alert, listening, every muscle in her body strained to hear some betraying sound.

"What is it?" I whispered. "Clarita won't hurt us out here. All we have to do is stand up to her. There isn't any gun this time."

"I know, but now I'm afraid," she said. "I'm terribly afraid. Amanda, while you were changing your clothes, I went into Clarita's room and read the pages of Katy's diary. I had to read about that baby in her own words. But then I read farther. I read about the day of the picnic."

"I didn't get to that," I admitted. "But it doesn't matter. I know because I confronted Clarita there in her room. But she's beaten now. She can't hurt us. Let's go out and—"

Eleanor pulled me back roughly. "Wait—I'll look. Stay here. Stay down."

She crept to the lip of the cave, where she could

look out and down the trail. Then she scrambled hastily
back to me.

"Now we know the enemy," she said. "It's not *we* who
are in danger, Amanda. It's *you.* Only you. Keep quiet.
Don't make a sound."

For a moment or two I lay beside her as still as
she wished. But I couldn't believe what she said, and
if I was careful I could see out for myself nearer the
lip of the cave. I could hear someone moving about on
the trail below, hear a murmur of voices. Then footsteps
went past, and I crept closer to the edge in order to look
over. Behind me Eleanor caught hold of my foot, tried
to pull me back. But I was close to the ladder now and
I wrenched away. The small struggle dislodged a chip
of rock and sent it skittering over the edge to the
stone path below.

That alarmed me, and I too lay still, listening. There
was no sound at all. Behind me Eleanor, perhaps
shocked by the clatter of the falling stone, was equally
still and her hand was no longer on my foot. After a
moment I crept to the top of the ladder and looked
down. Looked down upon Kirk's white sombrero that
was rising toward me up the ladder. Before I could
move back, the rolled brim tilted to reveal the face
beneath, and I stared directly into the turquoise slits of
a blue mask.

In the flood of terror that followed, I tried to slide
backward into the depth of the cave. But the blue mask,
thrust toward me, was coming up the ladder, evilly intent beneath the brim of the white sombrero.

In an instant everything flashed back from that other
time, and I cried out, knowing the truth, remembering
that day on the hillside, remembering the loved face, and
the gun that had spat death for Kirk Landers. Remembering Doroteo struggling, trying to save Kirk as she
fought her father, then losing her own balance, falling
down the bank to lie dead in the arroyo.

All this in a moment of memory.

Behind me Eleanor cried out. "No, Grandfather, no!"

The man on the ladder snatched off sombrero and mask and I looked down upon that fierce falcon's head —and the face of death. One thin hand thrust out to clasp my arm and hold me there.

"So you have remembered everything—and you have destroyed everything for me. You have injured me with my daughter's daughter. Because of you she must know what should never have been known. It is the end."

I saw the upward flash, saw the dagger in his right hand, and tried to roll away from him. But his grasp held me with a madman's strength. There was no way to escape that upheld blade. Then Eleanor was upon me, pushing me, rolling me aside in the instant that the knife rose to its height and came swiftly down, tearing into human flesh. There was blood again, and I was sharply aware of the figure on the ladder—Juan Cordova's terrible face looking up at us for an instant before he teetered and fell backward on the rock below. In the same instant I saw Clarita coming back from one end of the trail, and Gavin running toward us from the other.

But only Eleanor concerned me now—her soft moaning, and that bloody wound in her shoulder. My sister, who had saved me. Clarita came past Juan and up the ladder to kneel beside us. At once she ripped off Eleanor's cotton blouse and used the unstained part of it to stanch the blood. Gavin was bending over Juan Cordova on the path.

"Eleanor will be all right," Clarita told him. "You must go and phone for an ambulance."

Gavin stood up. "Juan is dead. I'll go to the Center and phone at once."

When he'd gone, I spoke to Clarita. "Eleanor saved me. But now I remember it all. It was Juan who shot Kirk. But I still don't understand why."

Clarita answered me evenly, without emotion. "It is time for the truth. Now you must know. There must be an end to hating. It is not your fault, though I too have hated you. When Kirk came back to Santa Fe and learned that Doro had borne his child, he threatened to go to William Austin with the whole story unless Doro ran away with him. She came to meet him on the hillside that day to tell him she would not, even if he ruined her marriage. But she told her father first of Kirk's threat. Juan was in a rage, and he took a gun from Mark Brand's room and came along the hillside to threaten Kirk. His anger was so great, and when Kirk laughed at him, he shot and killed him. Doro fell while she was struggling with him to get the gun away."

"I know," I said and heard my own choked voice as though it were someone else's. "Did you see it from that window after all?"

"No. I was away from the house, where Paul saw me. But afterwards Juan called me to his room and told me what I must say. He told me that not even Katy was to know the truth. But mother was too wise for that. He did not tell her, but she forced the truth from me. She had to go along with my story to save her husband, and she never let him know she knew until she was dying. However, she had written it all down in her diary, so as to keep a record. After you came I went out to the *rancho* to get those pages and hide them from you."

"Why didn't you destroy them?"

She gazed at me coldly. "Because it was necessary to hold something over my father's head. He ruled me, and I bowed to him because he threatened to disinherit Eleanor—who was like my own child—if I did not do as he wished."

"And the whip?" I said. "That time in the patio? And the brass figure in the store?"

"He wanted to drive you away. You were becoming too dangerous, and to him you were not Doro's first-born—Eleanor was. He feared to have her learn the truth of her birth and discover that he had killed her real father and caused her mother's death. Eleanor was the only one he loved left alive. It was he who made sounds that would lure you into the patio that night where he could use the whip, and then pretended the attack upon himself. I drove him to the store that other night, and he went inside alone, looking for you. And found you. But it was I—because he ordered it —who brought him the whip and the Pentitente figure. I who placed Doña Sebastiana in your bed. I too wanted you to go away. It would have been better for you as well as for my father. Yet the real guilt lay in the past, and not with you."

I looked down at my grandfather where he lay with that fierce visage turned upward toward the sky. Beside him lay the sombrero and the turquoise mask. I went down the ladder and picked up the hat to lay it gently over that unguarded face.

"Why did he bring the hat and the mask here?" I asked Clarita. "And the dagger?"

"He wanted to frighten Paul so that he would stay away from Eleanor. My father was always given to the dramatic. He knew Paul would remember those things from that other time on the hillside. And the dagger would threaten him. But when I saw you above us in the trail, he was not far behind and he saw you too. So he used his masquerade in another way."

I pressed my hands over my face and began to weep softly into them. I wept for us all, and because of my lost, foolish dream of finding a family. Surprisingly, Clarita put a hand on my shoulder.

"*Pobrecita,*" she said. "Do not cry. It is over now."

I took my hands away from my wet face. "But you —you seemed to grow stronger, even today."

"As he grew weaker, he began to fear me more. When he saw that bonnet you brought from Madrid, I thought I could control him. It reminded him of all I could tell if I chose. I was wrong. Much of this is my fault— because I did not speak out and stop him."

Eleanor had lain weak and silent, listening to us, making no sound, and now she reached for Clarita's hand. "It doesn't matter that Doro and Kirk were my parents. *You* are my true mother."

Clarita bent to caress her as though she had been a child, and there were tears in her eyes.

The park men came with two stretchers, and Juan and Eleanor were carried back to the Center to await an ambulance. Clarita followed them. Gavin and I waited until they were gone. Then Gavin bent to pick up the blue mask.

"What shall we do with this?" he asked.

I took it from him. Stepping to the edge of the trail, I flung it out into a growth of cactus and chamiso far below. When it had fallen out of sight, I put my arm through his and we walked back to the Center together. I never wanted to see that mask again.

Paul was waiting for us, and his eyes were alive with excitement. He had his story now—the full, lush story that would make his book. Or so he thought. Later that evening Sylvia ended his dream. She told him quietly that she would leave him for good if he used one word of the Cordova story in his writing, ever. And Paul did not want to lose Sylvia. She had known about Doro's baby, known who Eleanor was, but Sylvia had always feared that Paul might have shot Kirk, and she was terrified lest this come out. She could see Paul playing with fire in writing his book, though perhaps disguising his role even further. She thought that if Clarita had guessed, she might have protected Paul out of old affection.

When the ambulance had gone ahead, and Clarita, Eleanor, and Paul were gone on their separate ways, Gavin and I followed in his car. I lay weakly back in the seat with my eyes closed until I felt the car stop. When I opened them I saw we were at a lookout point and that the bare opposite wall of the canyon stood up with all its stark striations markedly visible in the intense New Mexico light.

There was no need for words. Gavin's arm held me with my head against his shoulder. The sun had shone on all my terror for the last time. But it would be a long while before I would forget that moment when I had looked down into the eyes of the turquoise mask.

**Praise for the novels of *New York Times* and
USA TODAY bestselling author**

GENA SHOWALTER

The Darkest Night
"A fascinating premise, a sexy hero and nonstop action,
The Darkest Night is Showalter at her finest, and a
fabulous start to an imaginative new series."
—*New York Times* bestselling author
Karen Marie Moning

"Dark and tormented doesn't begin to describe these
cursed warriors called the Lords of the Underworld.
Showalter has created characters desperately fighting
to retain a semblance of humanity, which means
the heroines are in for a rough ride. This is darkly
satisfying and passionately thrilling stuff."
—*Romantic Times BOOKreviews*, 4 stars

"Amazing! Stupendous! Extraordinary! Gena Showalter
has done it again. *The Darkest Night* is the fabulous
start of an edgy, thrilling series....An exceptional
novel from an extraordinary author, *The Darkest Night*
is one of 2008's must reads for any paranormal fan."
—*Fallen Angels* reviews

"Not to be missed...the hottest new
paranormal series of 2008."
—*Night Owl Romance*

The Darkest Kiss
"In this new chapter the Lords of the Underworld
engage in a deadly dance. Anya is a fascinating blend
of spunk, arrogance and vulnerability—a perfect
match for the tormented Lucien."
—*Romantic Times BOOKreviews*, 4½ stars

"Talk about one dark read.... If there is one book
you must read this year, pick up *The Darkest Kiss*...
a Gena Showalter book is the best of the best."
—*Romance Junkies*

GENA SHOWALTER

HEART OF THE DRAGON

HQN™

Recycling programs
for this product may
not exist in your area.

ISBN 13: 978-0-373-77350-3
ISBN-10:   0-373-77350-1

HEART OF THE DRAGON

www.HQNBooks.com

Printed in U.S.A.

Dear Reader,

Since the first title in my Atlantis series, *Heart of the Dragon,* was published in 2005, I've been asked how I thought to combine the lost city of Atlantis with the creatures of lore. The answer is simple: what if. What if the gods hid their greatest mistakes inside Atlantis and that's why it's buried under the sea?

That single question branched into a thousand others, each more intriguing than the last. What if a dragon shape-shifter is forced to guard the portal that leads to his home, tasked with killing anyone who enters—even the woman of his dreams (*Heart of the Dragon*)? What if a modern man is sent inside the forbidden city to steal its greatest treasure... who just happens to be a beautiful female he can't resist *(Jewel of Atlantis*)? What if the king of the nymphs can seduce everyone he encounters—except the woman he loves (*The Nymph King*)? I hope you'll join me on these journeys through Atlantis, where the creatures of myth and legend walk, peril lurks around every corner and forbidden passions ignite. Even readers familiar with the books might find a few new surprises in these slightly revised versions!

And in March 2009 don't miss *The Vampire's Bride,* my brand-new tale of Atlantis, where I answer the question readers have been asking for years: what if the villain in all those earlier stories, the vampire king who has tortured and hated and warred, got a story of his own?

Wishing you all the best,

Gena Showalter

You survived a childhood of mind-numbing pain and abject humiliation. You survived a childhood of utter terror and unimaginable horror. Somehow, some way, you survived a childhood with me as your babysitter. Thankfully I've found a better outlet for my...creative spirit.

To Auston and Casey Dowling. I love you both. To Debbie Splawn-Bunch, who wouldn't let me title this book *Extra Crispy Love.*

PROLOGUE

Atlantis

"DO YOU FEEL IT, BOY? Do you feel the mist preparing?"

Darius en Kragin squeezed his eyes tightly closed, his tutor's words echoing in his mind. Did he feel it? Gods, yes. Even though he was only eight seasons, he felt it. Felt his skin prickle with cold, felt the sickening wave of acid in his throat as the mist enveloped him. He even felt his veins quicken with a deceptively sweet, swirling essence that was not his own.

Fighting the urge to bolt up the cavern steps and into the palace above, he tensed his muscles and fisted his hands at his sides.

I must stay. I must do this.

Slowly Darius forced his eyelids to open. He released a pent-up breath as his gaze locked with Javar's. His tutor stood shrouded by the thickening, ghostlike haze, the bleak walls of the cave at his back.

"This is what you will feel each time the mist summons you, for this means a traveler is nearby,"

Javar said. "Never stray far from this place. You may live above with the others, but you must always return here when called."

"I do not like it here." His voice shook. "The cold weakens me."

"Other dragons are weakened by cold, but not you. Not any longer. The mist will become a part of you, the coldness your most beloved companion. Now listen," he commanded softly. "Listen closely."

At first Darius heard nothing. Then he began to register the sound of a low, tapering whistle—a sound that reverberated in his ears like the moans of the dying. *Wind*, he assured himself. *Merely wind.* The turbulent breeze rounded every corner of the doomed enclosure, drawing closer. Closer still. His nostrils filled with the scent of desperation, destruction and loneliness as he braced himself for impact.

When it finally came upon him, it was not the battering force he expected, but a mockingly gentle caress against his body. The jeweled medallion at his neck hummed to life, burning the dragon tattoo etched into his flesh only that morning.

He crushed his lips together to silence a deep groan of uncertainty.

His tutor sucked in a reverent breath and splayed his arms wide. "This is what you will live for, boy. This will be your purpose. You will kill for this."

"I do not want my purpose to stem from the deaths of others," Darius said, the words tumbling from his mouth unbidden.

Javar stilled, a fiery anger kindling in the depths

of his ice-blue eyes, eyes so unlike Darius's own—unlike every dragon's. All dragons but Javar possessed golden eyes. "You are to be a Guardian of the Mist, a king to the warriors here," Javar said. "You should be grateful I chose you among all the others for this task."

Darius swallowed. Grateful? Yes, he should have been grateful. Instead he felt oddly...lost. Alone. So alone and unsure. Was this what he truly wanted? Was this the life he craved for himself? His gaze skimmed his surroundings. A few broken chairs were scattered across the dirt and twig-laden ground. The walls were black and bare. There was no warmth, only cold, biting reality and the lingering shadow of hopelessness. To become Guardian meant pledging his existence, his very soul to this cave.

Gaze narrowed, Javar closed the distance between them, his boots harmonizing with the drip, drip of water. His lips pulled in a tight scowl, and he gripped Darius's shoulders painfully. "Your mother and father were slaughtered. Your sisters were raped and their throats slit. Had the last Guardian done his duty, your family would still be with you."

Pain cut through Darius so intensely he nearly clawed out his eyes to blacken the hated images hovering before them. His graceful mother twisted and bent, lying in a crimson river of her own blood. The bone-deep gashes in his father's back. His three sisters... His chin trembled, and he blinked away the stinging tears in his eyes. He would not cry. Not now. Not ever.

Mere days ago, he had returned from hunting and found his family dead. He had not cried then. Nor had he shed a tear when the invaders who plundered his family were slaughtered in retribution. To cry was to show weakness. He squared his shoulders and raised his chin.

"That's right," Javar said, watching him with a glint of pride. "Deny your tears and keep the hurt inside you. Use it against those who hope to enter our land. Kill them with it, for they only mean us harm."

"I want to do as you say. I do." He glanced away. "But—"

"Killing travelers is your obligation," Javar interrupted. "Killing them is your privilege."

"What of innocent women and children who mistakenly stumble through?" The thought of destroying such purity, like that of his sisters, made him loathe the monster Javar was asking him to become—though not enough to halt this course he had set for himself. To protect his friends, he would do whatever was asked of him. They were all he had left. "May I set them free on the surface?"

"You may not."

"What harm can children do our people?"

"They will carry the knowledge of the mist with them, ever able to lead an army through." Javar shook him once, twice. "Do you understand now? Do you understand what you must do and why you must do it?"

"Yes," he replied softly. He stared down at a thin, cerulean rivulet that trickled past his boots, his gaze following the gentleness and serenity of the water. Oh, that he possessed the same serenity inside himself. "I understand."

"You are too tender, boy." With a sigh, Javar released him. "If you do not erect stronger defenses inside yourself, your emotions will be the death of you and all those you still hold dear."

Darius gulped back the hard lump in his throat. "Then help me, Javar. Help me rid myself of my emotions so that I might do these deeds."

"As I told you before, you have only to bury your pain deep inside you, somewhere no one can ever hope to reach it—not even yourself."

That sounded so easy. Yet, how did one bury such tormenting grief? Such devastating memories? How did one battle the horrendous agony? He would do anything, anything at all, to find peace.

"How?" he asked his tutor.

"You will discover that answer on your own. Much sooner than you think."

Magic and power began swirling more intently around them, undulating, begging for some type of release. The air expanded, coagulated, leaving a heady fragrance of darkness and danger. A surge of energy ricocheted across the walls like a bolt of lightning, then erupted in a colorful array of liquid sparks.

Darius stilled as horror, dread and yes, anticipation sliced a path through him.

"A traveler will enter soon," Javar said, already tense and eager.

With shaky fingers, Darius gripped the hilt of his sword.

"They always experience disorientation at first emergence. You must use that to your advantage and destroy them the moment they exit."

Could he? "I'm not ready. I cannot—"

"You are and you will," Javar said, a steely edge to his tone. "There are two portals, the one you are to guard here and the one I guard on the other side of the city. I am not asking you to do anything I would not—and have not done—myself."

In the next instant, a tall man stepped from the mists. His eyes were squeezed shut, his face pale, and his clothing disheveled. His hair was thick and silvered, and his tanned skin was lined with deep wrinkles. He had the look of a scholar, not of war or evil.

Still trembling, Darius unsheathed his weapon. He almost doubled over from the sheer force of his conflicting emotions. A part of him continued to scream to run away, to refuse this task, but he forced himself to remain. He would do this because Javar was right. Travelers were the enemy, no matter who they were, no matter what their purpose.

No matter their appearance.

"Do it, Darius," Javar growled. "Do it now."

The traveler's eyelids jolted open. Their gazes suddenly clashed together, dragon gold against human green. Resolve against fear. Life against death.

Darius raised his blade, paused only a moment—

stop, run, do not—then struck. Blood splattered his bare chest and forearms like poisoned rain. A gargled gasp parted the man's lips, then slowly, so slowly, his lifeless body sank to the ground.

For several long, agonizing moments, Darius stood frozen by the fruit of his actions. *What have I done? What have I done!* He dropped the sword, distantly hearing a clang as the metal thudded into the dirt.

He hunched over and vomited.

Surprisingly, as he emptied his stomach, he lost the agony inside him. He lost his regret and sadness. Frigid ice enclosed his chest and what was left of his soul. He welcomed and embraced the numbness until he felt only a strange void. All of his heartache—gone. All of his suffering—gone.

I have done my duty.

"I am proud of you, boy." Javar slapped his shoulder in a rare show of affection. "You are ready to take your vows as Guardian."

As Darius's shaking ceased, he straightened and wiped his mouth with the back of his wrist. "Yes," he said starkly, determinedly, craving more of this detachment. "I am ready."

"Do it, then."

Without pausing for thought, he sank to his knees. "In this place I will dwell, destroying the surface dwellers who pass through the mist. This I vow upon my life. This I vow upon my death." As he spoke the words, they mystically appeared on his chest and back, black and red symbols that stretched from one shoulder to the other and glowed with inner fire. "I exist for no other purpose. I am Guardian of the Mist."

Javar held his stare for a long while, then nodded with satisfaction. "Your eyes have changed color to mirror the mist. The two of you are one. This is good, boy. This is good."

CHAPTER ONE

Three hundred years later

"HE DOESN'T LAUGH."

"He never yells."

"When Grayley accidentally stabbed Darius's thigh with a six-pronged razor, our leader didn't even blink."

"I'd say all he needs is a few good hours of bed sport, but I'm not even sure he knows what his cock is for."

The latter was met with a round of rumbling male chuckles.

Darius en Kragin stepped inside the spacious dining hall, his gaze methodically cataloging his surroundings. The ebony floors gleamed clean and black, the perfect contrast for the dragon-carved ivory walls. Along the windows, gauzy drapes whispered delicately. Crystal ceilings towered above, reflecting the tranquillity of seawater that enclosed their great city.

He moved toward the long, rectangular dining table. The tantalizing aroma of sweetmeats and fruit should have wafted to his nostrils, but over the years his sense of smell, taste and color had deteriorated.

He smelled only ash, tasted nothing more than air, and saw only black-and-white. He'd willed those senses away. Better, easier to exist in a void. Only sometimes did he wish otherwise.

One warrior caught sight of him and quickly alerted the others. Silence clamped tight fingers around the chamber. Every male present whipped his focus to his food, as if roasted fowl had suddenly become the most fascinating thing the gods had ever created. The jovial air visibly darkened.

True to his men's words, Darius claimed his seat at the head of the table without a smile or a scowl. Only after he'd consumed his third goblet of wine did his men resume their conversation, though they wisely chose a different subject. This time they spoke of the women they had pleasured and the wars they had won. Exaggerated tales, all. One warrior even went so far as to claim he'd gratified four women at the same time while successfully storming his enemy's gate. For a nymph, that was possible. A dragon? No.

Darius had heard the same stories a thousand times before. He swallowed a mouthful of tasteless meat and asked the warrior beside him, "Any news?"

Brand, his first in command, leveled him a grim smile and shrugged. "Perhaps. Perhaps not." His light hair hung around his face in thick war braids, and he hooked several behind his ears. "The vampires are acting strangely. They're leaving the Outer City and assembling here in the Inner City."

"They rarely come here. Have they given no indication of why?"

"It cannot be good for us, whatever the reason," Madox said, jumping into the conversation. "I say we kill those that venture too close to our home." He was the tallest dragon in residence and always ready for combat. He perched at the end of the table, his elbows flat on the surface, both hands filled with meat. "We are ten times stronger and more skilled than they are."

"We need to obliterate the entire race," the warrior on his left supplied. Renard was the kind of man others wanted to guard their backs in battle. He fought with a determination matched by few, was fiercely loyal and had studied the anatomy of every species in Atlantis so he knew exactly where to strike each to create the most damage. And the most pain.

Years ago, Renard and his wife had been captured by a group of vampires. He'd been chained to a wall, forced to watch as his wife was raped and drained. When he escaped, he brutally destroyed every creature responsible, but that had not lessened his heartache. He was a different man than he'd been, no longer full of laughter and forgiveness. What Darius hated most was that a rogue group of dragons had mimicked the tale, doing the same thing to the vampire king, who had not been responsible for Renard's tragedy, but who now blamed Darius for it. Thus, a war erupted between their races.

"Perhaps we can petition Zeus for their extinction," Brand replied.

"The gods have long since forgotten us," Renard said with a shrug. "Besides, Zeus is like Cronus in so many ways. He might agree, but do we really want him to? We are all creations of the Titans, even those we loathe. If Zeus annihilates one race, what is to stop him from wiping out others?"

Brand gulped back the last of his wine, his eyes fierce. "Then we will not ask him. We will simply strike."

"The time has come for us to declare war," Madox growled in agreement.

The word "war" elicited smiles across the expanse of the room.

"I agree that the vampires need to be eliminated. They create chaos and for that alone they deserve to die." Darius met each warrior's stare, one at a time, holding it until the other man looked away. "But there is a time for war and a time for strategy. Now is the time for strategy. I will send a patrol into the Inner City and learn the vampires' purpose. Soon we will know the best course of action."

"But—" one warrior began.

He cut him off with a wave of his hand. "Our ancestors waged the last war with the vampires, and while we might have won, our losses were too great. Families were torn asunder and blood bathed the land. We will have patience in this situation. My men will not jump hastily into any skirmish."

A disappointed silence slithered from every man present, wrapping around the table, then climbing up the walls. He wasn't sure if they were considering his words, or revolt.

"What do you care, Darius, if families are destroyed? I'd think a heartless bastard like you would welcome the violence." The dry statement came from across the table, where Tagart reclined in his seat. "Aren't you eager to spill more blood? No matter that the blood is vampire rather than human?"

A sea of angry growls grew in volume, and several warriors whipped to face Darius, staring at him with expectation, as if they waited for him to coldly slay the warrior who had voiced what they had all been thinking. Tagart merely laughed, daring anyone to act against him.

Do they truly consider me heartless? Darius wondered. Heartless enough to execute his own kind for something so trivial as a verbal insult? He was a killer, yes, but not heartless.

A heartless man felt nothing, and he felt *some* emotions. Mild though they were. He simply knew how to control what he felt, knew how to bury it deep inside himself. That was the way he preferred his life. Intense emotions birthed turmoil, and turmoil birthed soul-wrenching pain. Soul-wrenching pain birthed memories… His fingers tightened around his fork, and he forced himself to relax.

He would rather feel nothing than relive the agony of his past—the same agony that could very well become his present if he allowed a single memory to take root and sprout its poisonous branches.

"My family is Atlantis," he finally said, his voice disturbingly calm. "I will do what I must to protect her. If that means waiting before declaring war and angering every one of my men, then so be it."

Realizing Darius could not be provoked, Tagart shrugged and returned his attention to his meal.

"You are right, my friend." Grinning broadly, Brand slapped his shoulder. "War is only fun if we emerge the victor. We heed your advice to wait most readily."

"Kiss his ass any harder," Tagart muttered, "and your lips will chap."

Brand quickly lost his grin, and the medallion hanging from his neck began to glow. "What did you say?" he demanded quietly.

"Are your ears as feeble as the rest of you?" Tagart pushed to his feet, leaving his palms planted firmly on the glossy tabletop. The two men glared at each other from across the distance, a charged stillness sparking between them. "I said, kiss his ass any harder, and your lips will chap."

With a growl, Brand launched himself over the table, knocking dishes and food to the ground in his haste to attack Tagart. In midspring, reptilian scales grew upon his skin and narrow, incandescent wings sprouted from his back, ripping his shirt and pants in half, transforming him from man to beast. Fire spewed from his mouth, charring the surface of everything in its path.

The same transformation overtook Tagart, and the two beasts grappled to the ebony floor in a danger-ous tangle of claws, teeth and fury.

Dragon warriors were able to change into true dragons whenever they desired, though the transfor-mation happened of its own volition whenever raging emotions gripped them. Darius himself had not experienced a change, impromptu or otherwise, since he discovered his family slaughtered over three hundred years ago. To be honest, Darius suspected his dragon form was somehow lost.

Tagart snarled when Brand threw him into the nearest wall, cracking the priceless ivory. He quickly recovered by whipping Brand's face with his serrated tail, leaving a jagged and bleeding wound. Their infuriated snarls echoed as deep and sharp as any blade. A torrent of flame erupted, followed quickly by an infuriated hiss. Over and over they bit and lashed out at each other, separated, circled, then clashed together again.

Every warrior save Darius leapt to his feet in a frenzy of excitement, hurriedly taking bets on who would win. "Eight gold drachmas on Brand," Grayley proclaimed.

"Ten on Tagart," Brittan shouted.

"Twenty if they both kill each other," Zaeven called excitedly.

"Enough," Darius said, his tone even, controlled.

The two combatants jumped apart as if he'd screamed the command, both panting and facing each other like penned animals, ready to attack again at any moment.

"Sit," Darius said in that same easy tone.

Rather than obey this time, they growled gutturally at each other. Not so the rest. They sat. While they might wish to continue cheering and taking bets, Darius was their leader, their king, and they knew better than to defy him.

"I did not exclude you from the command," he

said to Tagart and Brand, adding only slightly to his volume. "You will calm yourselves and sit."

Both men leveled narrowed gazes on him. He arched a harsh brow and motioned with his fingers a gesture that clearly said, "Come and get me. Just don't expect to live afterward."

Minutes passed in suspended silence until finally, the panting warriors assumed human form. Their wings recoiled, tucking tightly into the slits on their backs; their scales faded, leaving naked skin. Because Darius kept spare clothing in each room of the palace, they were able to grab a pair of pants from the wall hooks. Partially dressed now, they righted their chairs and eased down.

"I will not have discord in my palace," Darius told them.

Brand wiped the blood from his cheek and flicked Tagart a narrowed glare. In return, Tagart bared his sharp teeth and released a cutting growl.

They were already on the verge of morphing again, Darius realized.

He worked a finger over his stubbled chin. Never had he been more thankful that he was a man of great patience, yet never had he been more displeased with the system he had fashioned. His dragons were divided into four units. One unit patrolled the Outer City, while another patrolled the Inner. The third was allowed to roam free, pleasuring women, losing themselves in wine or whatever other vice they desired. The last had to stay here, training. Every four weeks, the units rotated.

These men had been here two days—a mere two days—and already they were restless. If he did not think of something to distract them, they might very well kill each other before their required time elapsed.

"What think you of a tournament of sword skill?" he asked determinedly.

Indifferent, some men shrugged. A few moaned, "Not again."

"No," Renard said with a shake of his dark head, "you always win. And besides that, there is no prize."

"What would you like to do, then?"

"Women," one of the men shouted. "Bring us some women."

Darius frowned. "You know I do not allow females inside the palace. They pose too much of a distraction, causing too many hostilities between you. And not the easy hostilities of a few moments ago."

Regretful groans greeted his words.

"I have an idea." Brand faced him, a slow smile curling his lips, eclipsing all other emotions. "Allow me to propose a new contest. Not of physical strength, but one of cunning and wits."

Instantly every head perked up. Even Tagart lost his wrathful glare as interest lit his eyes.

A contest of wits sounded innocent enough. Darius nodded and waved his hand for Brand to continue.

Brand's smile grew wider. "The contest is simple. The first man to make Darius lose his temper, wins."

"I do not—" Darius began, but Madox spoke over him, his rough voice laden with excitement.

"And just what does the winner gain?"

"The satisfaction of besting us all," Brand replied. "And a beating from Darius, I'm sure." He offered them a languid shrug and leaned back in the velvet cushions of his chair. He propped his ankles on the tabletop. "But I swear by the gods every bruise will be worth it."

Eight sets of eyes swung in Darius's direction and locked on him with unnerving interest. Weighing options. Speculating. "I do not—" he began again, but just like before he was silenced.

"I like the sound of this," Tagart interjected. "Count me in."

"Me, too."

"And me, as well."

Before another man could so easily ignore him, Darius uttered one word. Simple, but effective. "No." He swallowed a tasteless bite of fowl, then continued with the rest of his meal. "Now, tell me more of the vampires' doings."

"What about making him smile?" Facing Brand, Madox shoved eagerly to his feet and leaned over the table. "Does that count? It's a show of emotion and as rare as his temper."

"Absolutely." Brand nodded. "But there must be a witness to the deed, or no winner can be declared."

One by one, each man uttered, "Agreed."

"I will hear no more talk of this." When had he lost control of this conversation? Of his men? "I—"

Darius snapped his mouth closed. His blood was quickening with darkness and danger, and the hairs at the base of his neck were rising.

The mist prepared for a traveler.

Resignation rushed through him and on the heels of that was cold determination. He eased up, his chair skidding slightly behind him.

Every voice tapered to silence. Every expression became curious.

"I must go," he said, the words flat, hollow. "We will discuss a tournament of sword skill when I return."

He attempted to stride from the room, but Tagart leapt up and over the table and swiveled in front of him. "Does the mist call you?" the warrior asked, casually leaning one arm against the door frame and blocking the only exit.

Darius gave him no outward reaction. But then, when did he ever? "Step out of my way."

Tagart arched an insolent brow. "Make me."

Someone snickered behind him.

With or without his approval, it seemed the game had already begun. This wasn't like his men. They must be more bored than he'd thought.

Darius easily lifted Tagart by his shoulders and tossed the stunned man aside, slamming him into the far wall. He thudded to the floor in a gasping heap. Without facing the others, Darius asked, "Anyone else?"

"Me," came an unhesitant and unrepentant reply. A blur of black leather and silver knives, Madox rushed to stand at his side, watching him intently, gauging his reaction. "I want to stop you. Does that make you angry? Make you want to scream and rail at me?"

An unholy light entered Tagart's eyes as he scrambled to his feet. He curled his fingers around the hilt of a nearby sword and stalked to Darius, his motions slow and deliberate. Never once pausing to consider the stupidity of his actions, he pointed the razor-sharp tip of the blade at Darius's neck.

"Would you show fear if I vowed to kill you?" the infuriated man spat.

"That's taking things too far," Brand growled, joining the growing group around him.

A drop of blood slithered down Darius's throat. The nick should have stung, but he felt nothing, not a single sensation. Only that ever-present detachment.

No one realized his intentions. One moment Darius stood still, seemingly accepting of Tagart's assault, but the next he had his own sword unsheathed and directed at Tagart's neck. The man's eyes widened.

"Put your weapon away," Darius told him, "or I will kill you where you stand. I care not whether I live or die, but you, I think, care greatly for your own life."

One second dragged into two before a narrow-eyed Tagart lowered his sword.

Darius lowered his own weapon; his features remained stony. "Finish your meal, all of you, then retire to the practice arena. You will exercise until you have not the strength to stand. That's an order."

He strode from the chamber quite aware he had not given his men the reaction they craved.

DARIUS DESCENDED the cave steps four at a time. Ready to finish the deed and resume his meal in private, he removed his shirt and tossed the black fabric into a far corner. The medallion he wore, as well as the tattoos on his chest, glowed like tiny pinpricks of flame, waiting for him to fulfill his vow.

Expression blank, mind clear, he tightened his clasp on his sword, positioned himself to the left of the mist…and he waited.

CHAPTER TWO

GRACE CARLYLE ALWAYS hoped she'd die from intense pleasure while having sex with her husband. Well, she wasn't married, and she'd never had sex, but she was still going to die.

And not from intense pleasure.

From heat exhaustion? Maybe.

From hunger? Possibly.

From her own stupidity? Absolutely.

She was lost and alone in the freaking Amazon jungle.

As she strode past tangled green vines and towering trees, beads of sweat trickled down her chest and back. Small shards of light seeped from the leafy canopy above, providing hazy visibility. Barely adequate, but appreciated. The smells of rotting vegetation, old rain and flowers mingled together, forming a conflicting fragrance of sweet and sour. She wrinkled her nose.

"All I wanted was a little excitement," she muttered. "Instead I end up broke, lost, and trapped in this bug-infested sauna."

To complete her descent into hell, she expected the

sky to open and pour out a deluge of rain at any moment.

The only good thing about her current circumstances was that all this hiking and sweating might actually help her lose a few pounds from her too-curvy figure. Not that losing weight did her any good here. Except, perhaps, in the newspapers.

New Yorker found dead in Amazon
A shame. She was hot!

Scowling, she swatted a mosquito trying to drink her arm dry—even though she'd applied several layers of ucuru oil to prevent such bites. Where the hell was Alex? She should have run into her brother by now. Or, at the very least, stumbled upon a tour group. Or even blundered upon an indigenous tribe.

If only she hadn't taken an extended leave of absence from AirTravel, she'd be soaring through the air, relaxed and listening to the hypnotic hum of a jet engine.

"I'd be in an air-conditioned G-IV," she said, slashing her hand like a machete through the thick, green foliage. "I'd be sipping vanilla Coke." Another slash. "I'd be listening to my coworkers discuss stiletto heels, expensive dates and mind-shattering orgasms."

And I'd still be miserable, she thought, *wishing I were anywhere else.*

She stopped abruptly and closed her eyes. *I just want to be happy. Is that too much to ask?*

Obviously.

So often lately she battled a sense of discontent, a desire to experience so much more. Her mother had tried to warn her what such discontent would bring her. "You're going to get yourself in trouble," she'd admonished. But had Grace listened? *Noooo.* Instead she'd followed her aunt Sophie's lovely bit of wisdom. Aunt Sophie, for God's sake! The woman who wore leopard print spandex and cavorted with mailmen and strippers. "I know you've done some exciting things, Gracie honey," Sophie had said, "but that's not really living. Something's missing from your life and if you don't find it, you'll end up a shriveled old prune like your mom."

Something *was* missing from Grace's life. She knew that, and in an effort to find that mysterious "something," she'd tried speed dating, Internet dating and singles bars. When those failed, she decided to give night school a try. Not to meet men, but to learn. Not that the cosmetology classes had done her any good. The best stylists in the world couldn't tame her wild red curls. After that, she'd tried race-car driving and step class. She'd even gotten her belly button pierced. Nothing helped.

What would it take to make her feel whole, complete?

"Not this jungle, that's for sure," she grumbled, jolting back into motion. "Someone please tell me," she said to the heavens, "why satisfaction always dances so quickly out of my reach. I'm dying to know."

Traveling the world had always been her dream, and becoming a flight attendant for a private charter had seemed like the perfect job for her. She hadn't realized she would become an airborne waitress, jaunting from hotel to hotel, never actually enjoying the state/country/hellhole she found herself in. Sure, she'd scaled mountains, surfed the ocean waves and jumped from a plane, but the joy of those adventures never remained and like everything else she'd tried, they always left her feeling more unsatisfied than before.

That's why she had come here, to try something new. Something with a bit more danger. Her brother was an employee of Argonauts, a mythoarchaeological company that had recently discovered the crude glider constructed by Daedalus of Athens—a discovery that rocked the scientific and mythological communities. Alex spent his days and nights delving deep into the world's myths, proving or disproving them.

With such a fulfilling job, he didn't have to worry about becoming a shriveled old prune. *Not like me,* she lamented.

Wiping the sweat from her brow, Grace increased her pace. About a week ago, Alex had shipped her a package containing his journal and a gorgeous necklace with two dangling, intertwined dragon heads. No note of explanation accompanied the gifts. Knowing he was in Brazil and looking for a portal that led into the lost city of Atlantis she'd decided to join him, leaving a message on his cell phone with details of her flight.

With a sigh, she fingered the dragon chain hanging at her neck. When Alex failed to pick her up at the airport, she should have returned home. "But nooo," she said with deep self-loathing, suddenly more aware of her dry, cotton mouth. "I hired a local guide and tried to find him. '*Sí, senhorina,*'" she mimicked the guide. "'Of course, *senhorina.* Anything at all, *senhorina.*'"

"Bastard," she muttered.

Today, two miserable days into her trek, her kind, considerate, I-only-want-to-help-you guide had stolen her backpack and abandoned her here. Now she had no food, no water, no tent. She did, however, have a weapon. A weapon she had used to shoot that bastard in the ass as he ran away. The memory caused her lips to curl in a slow smile, and she lovingly patted the revolver resting in the waist of her dirty canvas pants.

Her smile didn't last long, however, as the midday heat continued to pound against her. In all her wildest dreams, her need for fulfillment had never ended like this. She'd envisioned laughter and—

Something hard slammed into her head and jostled her forward. She yelped, her heart pounding in her chest as she rubbed her now throbbing temple and skimmed her gaze over the ground, searching for the source of her pain.

Oh, thank you, thank you, she mentally cried when she spied the rosy-colored fruit. Mouth watering, she studied the delicious-looking juice seeping from the smashed remains. Was it poison-

ous? And did she care if it was? She licked her lips.
No, she didn't care. Death by poison was preferable
to walking away from this unexpected treasure.

Just as she reached down to scoop up what she
could, another missile crashed into her back.

She gasped and jerked upright.

Spinning, she sent her narrowed gaze through the
trees. About ten yards away and fifteen feet up she
discovered a small, hairy monkey holding a piece of
fruit in each hand. Her jaw dropped open in disbelief. Was he...smiling?

He swung back both of his arms and launched
each piece at her. She was too stunned to move and
simply watched as they splattered against her pants,
stinging her thighs with their impact. Laughing,
proud of himself, the monkey jumped up and down
and waved his limbs wildly through the air.

She knew what he was thinking: *ha, ha, there's
nothing you can do about it.* This was too much.
Robbed, abandoned, then assaulted by a primate who
should pitch for the Yankees. Scowling, at her wit's
end, she picked up the fruit, claimed two mouthwatering bites, paused, claimed two more bites, then
launched what was left. She nailed her target in the
ear. He lost his smile.

"Nothing I can do about it, huh? Well, take that,
you rotten fuzz ball."

Her victory was short-lived. In the next instant,
fruit sailed at her from every direction. Monkeys
littered the trees! Realizing she was outnumbered
and outgunned, Grace grabbed what fruit she could,

ducked behind a tree, jumped over a swarm of fire
ants and ran. Ran without knowing what direction
she traveled. Ran until she was certain her lungs
would collapse from exertion.

When she finally slowed her pace, she sucked in
a breath, then bit into her bounty. Sucked in another
breath, then bit into the fruit again, continually
alternating between the two. As the sweet juices ran
down her throat, she moaned in surrender.

Life is good, she thought.

Until another hour passed. By then her body
forgot that she'd had any nourishment, and lethargy
beat rough fists inside her, causing her feet to drag.
Her bones were liquefying, and her mouth felt dryer
than sand. But she kept walking, each step creating
a mantra in her brain. Find. Alex. Find. Alex. Find.
Alex. He was out here somewhere, looking for that
silly portal, perhaps blithely unaware of her
presence. Why couldn't he have been at the coordi-
nates his journal had claimed he'd be? Where the hell
was he?

Unfortunately the deeper she roamed through the
jungle the more lost and alone she became. The trees
and liana thickened, as did the darkness. At least the
scent of rot evaporated, leaving only a luscious trace
of wild heliconias and dewy orchids. If she didn't
find shelter soon, she would collapse wherever she
found herself, helpless against nature. Though her
vaccinations were up-to-date, she hated snakes and
insects more than hunger and fatigue.

Several yards, a tapir and two capybaras later, she

had made no progress that she could see. Her arms and legs were so heavy they felt like steel clubs. Not knowing what else to do, she sank to the ground. As she lay there, she heard the gentle song of the insects and the— Her eardrums perked. The peaceful trickle of water? She blinked, listening more intently. Yes, she realized with excitement. She was actually hearing the glorious swoosh of water.

Get up, she commanded herself. *Get up, get up, get up!*

Using every bit of strength she possessed, she pushed to her hands and knees and crawled into a thick tangle of vegetation. Forest life pulsed vibrantly around her, mocking her weakness. Brilliant, damp green leaves parted and the ground became wetter and wetter until becoming completely submerged by an underground spring. The clear, turquoise water smelled clean and refreshing.

Shaking with the force of her need, she cupped her hands together, scooped up the cool, heavenly liquid and drank deeply. Her parched lips welcomed every wet, delicious drop…until her chest began to burn, hotter and hotter, like she was swallowing molten lava. Except, the sensation came from the outside of her body, not the inside.

The heat became unbearable, and she shrieked. Jolting up, her gaze locked on to the twin dragon heads dangling from the silver chain around her neck. Both sets of ruby eyes were glowing a bright, eerie red.

She tried to jerk the thing over her head but was

suddenly propelled forward by an invisible force. Arms flailing, she broke past an amazingly thick wall of flora. Light gave way to muted dark as she was dragged, grunting and fighting, several yards. Finally, she stilled, and the medallion cooled against her chest.

Her eyes grew impossibly round as she studied her new surroundings. She had entered some sort of cave. *Drip. Drip.* Droplets of water beat against the rocky floor. A cool, welcoming breeze kissed her face as relief nearly buckled her knees. The tranquil ambiance flowed into her, helping to calm her racing heart and labored breathing.

"All I need now is the powdered eggs, canned beans and coffee that were in my pack and I'll die happy."

Too exhausted to care what might be inside, waiting for a tasty human to appear, she scrambled deeper inside the passage and down a steep incline. The ceiling constricted and lowered, until she had to crouch and kneel. How long she crawled, she didn't know. Minutes? Hours? She only knew she needed to find a smooth, dry surface so that she could sleep. Gradually a ribbon of light appeared. The welcome beam snaked around the corner like a summoning finger. She followed.

And found Paradise.

Light crowned a small, iridescent pool of...water? The dappled ice-blue liquid seemed thicker than water, almost like a clear, transparent gel. Instead of lying on the ground, however, the pool hung upright at a slight angle, much like a portrait on a wall. Yet there was no wall to support it.

Why wasn't it spilling over? she wondered dazedly. Her foggy brain couldn't quite sort through the bizarre information. Balmy tendrils of mist enveloped the entire haven. A few ethereal strands reached the cavern top, swirling, circling, then gently dipping back down.

She uttered a nervous laugh, and the sound echoed all around her.

Grace reached out carefully, meaning only to touch and examine the strange substance. At the moment of contact, a violent jolt exploded within her, and she felt as if her entire being was sucked into a vacuum, pulling her, tugging her in every direction.

The world crumbled, breaking around her piece by fragile, needed piece, until finally ceasing to exist. Terror unfurled and consumed her. She was falling slowly, falling down. Her arms reached out, desperate for a solid anchor, yet no tangible object greeted her palms.

That's when the screams began. High-pitched, disharmonized, like a thousand screeching children running all around her. She covered her ears to block the sound. She needed the noise to stop, had to make it stop. But the screams only grew louder. More intense.

"Help me!" she cried.

Stars burst like fireworks at her side, spinning her round and round. Spinning her up and down. Waves of nausea churned inside her stomach, and she tried valiantly to regain any sense of time or place.

Suddenly everything quieted.

Her feet touched a hard surface; she swayed but didn't fall. The nausea slowly receded. Cautiously she shifted her feet, ascertaining that she truly stood on a stable foundation.

In. Out. Relieved, she drew in a breath and slowly let it out. In. Out. When her head cleared, she cracked open her eyelids. A haze of dew still rose from the small pool like strands of pale, glistening ivy composed entirely of fairy dust. The beautiful sight was spoiled only by the stark contours of the gloomy cavern—a cavern that was different from the one she'd first entered.

Her brows furrowed. Here, the rocky walls were covered with strange, colorful markings, like liquid gold upon forgotten ash. And…was that splattered blood? Shuddering, she tore her gaze away. The floor was damp, burdened with odd-shaped twigs, rocks and straw. Several crudely carved chairs pushed against the far corner.

Instead of miserable humidity, she inhaled air as cold as winter ice. Air that possessed a sickeningly metallic bite. The walls were taller, wider. And when she'd first entered, the dappled pool had been on the right side, not on the left.

How had her surroundings changed so drastically and quickly without her moving a step? She shivered. What was going on? This couldn't be a dream or a hallucination. The sights and smells were too real, too frightening. Had she died? No, no. This certainly wasn't heaven, and it was too cold to be hell.

So what had happened?

Before her mind could form an answer, a twig snapped.

Grace's chin whipped to the side, and she found herself staring up into cold, ice-blue eyes that swirled in startling precision with the mist. She sucked in an awed breath. The owner of those extraordinary eyes was the most ferociously masculine man she'd ever seen. A scar slashed from his left eyebrow all the way to his chin. His cheekbones were sharp, his jaw square. The only softness to his face was his gloriously lush mouth that somehow gave him the hypnotic beauty of a fallen angel.

He stood in front of her, at least six foot five and pure, raw muscle. He was shirtless, his stomach cut into several perfect rows of strength. A six-pack, she mused, the first she'd ever seen in real life. Shards of mist fell around him like glittery drops of rain, leaving glistening beads of moisture on his bronzed, tattooed chest.

Those tattoos were glowing, but more than that, they appeared alive. A fierce dragon spread crimson wings and seemed to be flying straight out of his skin, like a 3-D image come to dazzling life. The dragon's tail dipped low, past the waist of the black leather pants. Around its body were black symbols that boasted curling slashes and jagged points. These stretched the length of his collarbone and around the biceps.

The man himself proved more barbarous than his tattoos. He held a long, menacing sword.

A wave of fear swept through her, but that didn't stop her from staring. He was utterly savage. Fascinatingly sensual. He reminded her of a caged, wild animal. Ready to strike. Ready to consume. Danger radiated from his every pore, from the dark rim of his crystalline, predator eyes, to the blades strapped to his boots.

With a flick of his wrist, he twirled the sword around his head.

She inched backward. Surely he didn't mean to use that thing. My God, he was lifting it higher as if he really did mean to… "Whoa, there." She managed a shaky laugh. "Put that away before you hurt someone." *Namely me.*

He gave the lethal weapon another twirl, brandishing the sharp silver with strong, sure hands. His washboard abs rippled as he moved closer to her. Not a trace of emotion touched his expression. Not anger, fear, or mischievousness, offering her no clue as to why he felt the need to practice sword-slicing techniques in front of her.

He stared at her. She stared back, and told herself it was because she was too afraid to look away.

"I mean you no harm," she managed to croak out. Time dragged when he didn't respond.

Before her horror-filled eyes, his sword began to slice downward, aimed straight for her throat. He was going to kill her! On instinct, she swiped her gun from the waist of her pants. Her breath snagged in her throat, burning like acid as she squeezed the trigger. *Click, click, click.*

Nothing happened.

Shit. *Shit!* The cylinder was empty. She must have used all of her bullets on her bastard of a guide. The gun shook in her hand, and terror wrapped around her with the chill of a wintry storm. Her gaze scanned the cave, searching for a way out. The mist was the only exit, but the savage warrior's big, strong body now blocked it.

"Please," she whispered, not knowing what else to do or say.

Either the man didn't hear her, or he didn't care what she said. His sharp, deadly sword continued to inch closer and closer to her neck.

She squeezed her eyelids tightly shut.

CHAPTER THREE

DARIUS UTTERED a fierce curse and allowed his sword to pass just in front of the woman, never actually touching her. The action danced a delicate breeze through the red tendrils of her hair. The fact that he could see the actual color, a tempest of carmine that tumbled around her shoulders, startled him enough that he hesitated to destroy the possessor of such brilliance.

He fought past his shock and gripped his weapon at his side, trying to prepare his limbs to wreak destruction. Trying to force icy determination through his veins and push away any thoughts of mercy or sorrow. He knew what he had to do. Strike. Destroy.

That was his oath.

But her hair… His eyes basked in their first intake of color in over three hundred years. His fingers itched to touch. His senses longed to explore. He should have hated it. He'd *wanted* his senses barren. Hadn't he? But he'd looked at her, thought of the family he'd once loved, and his determination had cracked. That crack had been all his senses needed to activate.

Kill, his mind demanded. *Act!*

His teeth gnashed together, and his shoulders tightened. His tutor's voice echoed through him. *"Killing travelers is your obligation. Killing them is your privilege."*

There were times, like now, he loathed the tasks he performed, but never once had he hesitated to do what was needed. He'd simply continued on, assassination after assassination, knowing there was no other alternative for him. His dragon life force had long since overpowered his mortal side. There was a conscience living inside him, yes, but it was shriveled and decayed from lack of use.

So why was he hesitating now, with *this* traveler?

He studied her. Freckles dotted every inch of her skin, and streaks of dirt marred her jaw. Her nose was small and elfin, her lashes thick, sooty, and so long they cast spiky shadows on her cheeks. Slowly she opened her eyes, and he sucked in a heated breath. Her eyes were green and flecked with ribbons of blue, each color dusted with determination and fear. These new colors mesmerized him, enchanted him. Made his every protective instinct surface. Worse...

It shouldn't have—gods, it shouldn't have—but desire coiled inside him, powerful coils that refused to loosen their grip.

When the woman realized his sword tip pointed to the ground, she crouched down ever so slightly, clutching an oddly shaped metal object. He could only assume she was in attack position. She was frightened, true, but to survive she would fight him with all of her strength.

Could he really destroy such bravery?

Yes. He must.

He would.

Mayhap he truly was the heartless beast Tagart had called him. No, surely not, he thought in the next instant. The very actions that made him evil made him a keeper of the peace and provided safety for all residing in Atlantis.

There could be no other way.

Yet looking at this newest intruder, really looking at her, he *felt* like a beast. Her features were so guile-less, so angelic, sparks of some unfamiliar emotion crackled within him. Concern? Regret? Shame?

A combination of all three?

The sensation was so new, he had trouble identify-ing exactly what it was. What made this traveler so different from the others that he hesitated—and, gods forbid, felt desire? The fact that she resembled a delicate fairy queen? Or the fact that she was every-thing he'd always secretly wanted—beauty, gentle-ness and joy—but knew he could never have?

Unbidden, his gaze drank in the rest of her. She was not tall, but had a regal bearing that gave her an air of height. Her skin was smudged with grime and sweat that did nothing to detract. Her clothing fit her rounded curves to perfection and paid her beauty proper homage.

More unwelcome sensations pulsed through him, unnamable sensations. Hated sensations. He should feel nothing; he should remain detached. But he felt; and he wasn't. He yearned to trace his fingertips all over her, to immerse himself in her softness, to bask in her colorful brilliance. He yearned to taste, yes, actually taste her entire body and drive away the flavor of nothingness.

"No," he said, more for his benefit than her own. "No."

He *must* destroy her.

She had broken the law of the mist.

All those years ago a Guardian had failed to accomplish his duty, had failed to protect Atlantis, and in turn brought about the deaths of many people—people Darius had loved. He could not, *would* not allow even this fairy queen to survive.

Knowing this, Darius still remained in place, unmoving. His cold, hard logic warred against his primitive, male appetite. If only the woman would glance away…but seconds turned to minutes, and her gaze remained fixed on him, studying. Perhaps even appreciating.

Desperate to escape the mental hold she had on him, he demanded, "Turn your gaze, woman."

Slowly, so slowly, she shook her head, whisking red tendrils around her temples. "I'm sorry. I don't understand what you're saying."

Even her voice was innocent, soft and lyrical, a caress of his senses. Yet he had no idea what she had said.

"Damn this," he muttered. "And damn me."

The corners of his lips twitched in a scowl. He

commanded himself to remain indifferent to her even while he sheathed his sword and closed the distance between them. There was no reason to do what he was about to do, but he could not stop himself. His actions were no longer controlled by his mind, but by some force he didn't understand or want to acknowledge.

She gasped at his approach. "What are you doing?"

He pressed her back, crowding her until she met the rock-lined wall; she kept the metal object directed at him, the silly thing clicking over and over again. Did she truly expect to protect herself from a dragon warrior with such a useless object? He easily pried it from her fingers and tossed it behind his shoulder. Unbeaten, she lashed out, kicking and hitting and scratching like a wild demon.

He secured her by the wrists, pinning them above her head. "Cease," he said. When she continued to squirm, he sighed and waited for her to tire. Only a few minutes passed before her movements slowed, then halted altogether.

"You'll go to prison for this," she said, dragging in breath after breath.

Her warm exhalations caressed his chest, their intoxicating sweetness a tangible entity that prodded his memory, another gentle reminder of the family he couldn't quite banish from his mind. He almost jerked away from her, but the scent of fear and orchids enveloped him, a sensual declaration of her appeal. He'd smelled nothing but ash for so long; he couldn't help but luxuriate in this new fragrance. Inhaling deeply, he pressed against her, brushing her body with his, closing all hint of separation. The need to touch her, any part of her, refused to leave him.

She shivered. From the cold? he wondered. Or from a turbulent desire similar to his own? Her nipples were pebbled against his ribs, erotically abrading, and as he watched her nibble her soft bottom lip, the arousal he felt for her became a storm. A desperate, wild storm. A storm so intense it was like a supernatural entity. His dragon's blood flowed to his cock like a freshly sprung river, hot and consuming.

His lips curled into a self-disparaging smile. The moment he realized he was actually smiling, he frowned. How his men would have laughed to crown this dainty creature the winner of their wager. Yet he couldn't seem to make himself care. By the gods, he'd never felt anything so perfect, so right.

His captive blinked up, and their gazes collided. Had white-hot sparks of awareness visibly enveloped them at that moment he would not have been surprised.

This woman is your enemy, he reminded himself, gritting his teeth and shifting his hips so that his erection remained a safe distance away.

"The mind is open, the ears will hear," he bit out. "Understand we do, apart or near. My words are yours—your words are mine. This I speak. This I bind. From this moment, through all of time."

Still watching her, he said, "Do you understand my words now?"

"Yes. I—I do." Her eyes widened, darkening with renewed flecks of alarm. Her mouth opened and closed several times as she struggled to form a coherent rejoinder. "How?" was all she could manage. Her voice was strained. Then, she added more strongly, "How?"

"I cast a spell of comprehension over your mind."

"Spell? No, no. That's not possible." She shook her head. "I speak three languages, and I had to work hard to learn every one of them. What did you do to me? What did you do to my brain?"

"I have already explained that to you."

"Don't tell me the truth, then." She laughed, the sound emerging desperate rather than humorous. "None of this matters, anyway. Tomorrow morning I'll wake up and discover this was all a horrible nightmare."

No, she wouldn't, he thought, hating himself more at that moment than ever before. Tomorrow's dawning she would not wake at all. "You should not have come here, woman," he said. "Do you care nothing for your life?"

"Is that a threat?" She fought against his hold. "Let me go."

"Cease your struggles. Your actions merely press your body deeper into mine."

She immediately stilled.

"Who are you?" he demanded.

"I'm an American citizen, and I know my rights. You can't keep me here against my will."

"I can do anything I like."

All color drained from her face because there was no denying the truth of his words.

To prolong her demise like this is cruel, his mind shouted. *Close your eyes and strike.*

Once again his mind and body acted as separate entities. He found himself releasing her and stepping backward. She leapt away from him as if he were a bloodsucking vampire or a hideously misshapen Formorian.

He focused all of his might on her destruction, looking anywhere except her enigmatic, sea-colored eyes, thinking of anything except her fierce, admirable spirit. Her shirt was torn and gaped down the middle, revealing the hint of two perfect breasts encased in pale pink lace. Another spark of desire flared inside him. Until his gaze locked on the two sets of rubied eyes that hung in the valley of her breasts.

His breath snagged as he studied the ornament more intently. Surely that was not...could not be...

But it was.

A frown cemented his features, and his fingers fisted so tightly his bones almost snapped. How had this woman come to possess such a sacred talisman? The gods awarded every dragon warrior a Ra-Dracus, a Dragon's Fire, upon reaching manhood, and a warrior never removed his gift, not for any reason save death. The markings etched at the base of this one were familiar to him, but he could not recall exactly to whom it belonged.

Not this woman, that much he knew. She was not a dragon, nor was she a child of Atlantis.

His frown deepened. Ironically the very oath that commanded him to harm her also compelled him to keep her alive until she explained how and why she had the medallion. Reaching out, he attempted to remove it from her neck. She slapped his palm and scampered backward.

"Wh-what are you doing?" she demanded.

"Give me the medallion."

She didn't cower at his hard tone as most would have done. Nor did she jump to obey. No, she returned his gaze with unflinching courage. Or stupidity. She remained firmly in place now, hands at her side.

"Don't come any closer," she told him.

"You wear the mark of a dragon," he continued. "And you, woman, are no dragon. Give me the medallion."

"The only thing I'll give you is an ass-kicking, you rotten thief. Stay back."

He leveled her with a resolute gaze. She was defensive and fearful. Not a good combination when trying to obtain answers. He almost sighed. "I am called Darius," he said. "Does that ease your fears?"

"No, no it doesn't." Contrary to her words, her muscles relaxed slightly. "My brother gave me this necklace. It's my only link to him these days, and I'm not giving it up."

Darius worried a hand down his face. "What is your name?"

"Why do you want to know?"

"What is your name?" he repeated. "Do not forget who holds the sword."

"Grace Carlyle," she reluctantly supplied.

"Where is your brother now, Grace Carlyle?" Her name floated easily from his tongue. Too easily. "I wish to speak with him."

"I don't know where he is."

And she did not like that she did not know, he realized, studying the worry in her eyes. "No matter," he said. "The medallion does not belong to him, either. It belongs to a dragon, and I *will* have it back."

She studied him for a long, silent moment, then offered him a sunny if brittle smile. "You're right. You can have it. I just need a moment to take it off." She raised her arms as if she meant to do as she'd claimed—take it off. But in the next instant, she darted forward until she stood poised at the mist's entrance. His arm snaked out and jerked her back into the hard circle of his body. She gasped on impact.

Had his reflexes not been so quick, he would have lost her.

"You dare defy me?" he said, perplexed. As leader of this palace, he was used to having his every command obeyed. Well, before today and his army's game. That this woman opposed him was shocking, yet somehow added to her appeal. She was not a warrior and had no defense against him.

"Let me go!"

He held steady. "Struggling is pointless and merely delays what must be done."

"What must be done?" Instead of calming, she beat her pointy little elbows into his stomach. "What the hell must be done?"

He whirled her around and used one of his hands as a shackle, locking her against him, chest to chest, hardness to softness.

"Be still!" he shouted. Then blinked. Shouted? Yes, he'd actually raised his voice.

Amazingly enough, she stilled. Her breath came shallow and fast. Amid the growing quiet, he began to hear the beat of her heart, a staccato rhythm that reverberated in his ears. Their gazes narrowed on each other and looking away proved impossible. Minutes ticked by unnoticed.

"Please," she at last whispered, and he wasn't sure if she was asking him to release her or hold her more tightly.

He used his free hand to smooth up the velvety soft expanse of her neck, then gently flick her hair out of the way. The heat of her beckoned him to linger, and he fought the urge to glide his hands across her every feminine peak and hollow, from the plumpness of her breasts, to the slight roundness of her stomach. From the exotic slope of her legs, to the hot wetness of her center.

Was she the kind of woman who could accept and return his animal passion? Or would she find him more than she could handle?

The thought jarred him, and he gave a brutal

shake of his head to dislodge it. Whether she could handle him or not didn't matter. He wasn't going to bed this woman.

And yet...

He easily imagined Grace naked and in his bed, her body splayed for his view. Her arms open and waiting for him. She would smile slowly, seductively, and he would inch his way atop her, graze his tongue over every curve and hollow, enjoy her as he'd never enjoyed another—or let her enjoy him—until they both collapsed.

The fantasy caused his desire to intermingle with tenderness, each sensation sparking off the other as they raced through him.

Desire he could tolerate. Tenderness he could not.

For years he'd tried to suppress his physical needs, but he'd learned that was impossible. So he'd begun to allow himself the occasional woman, taking them hard and fast, then leaving them quickly afterward. He didn't kiss, didn't savor. Just took them with utter detachment, an easily forgettable coupling.

He needed that same detachment now, which meant he needed to ignore Grace's appeal. With that firmly rooted in his mind, he hurriedly unhooked the chain's clasp from around her neck, though he was careful not to bruise her.

"Give that back," she demanded, pulling against his hold. "It's mine."

"No. It is *mine*."

Her expression turned venomous.

Without removing his gaze from her, Darius secured the medallion around his own neck, causing it to clang against the other Ra-Dracus. "I have many questions for you, and I expect you to answer every one," he told her. "If you utter a single untruth, you will regret it. Is that clear?"

A strangled breath slipped past her lips.

"Do you understand?" he reiterated.

Wide-eyed, she nodded slowly.

"Then we will begin. You told me you want to give the medallion back to your brother. Why? What does he plan to do with it?"

"I—I don't know."

Did she lie? The angelic cast of her features suggested no untruth had ever passed from her lips. Thinking of her lips brought his gaze to them. They were plump lips. Lips made for a man's pleasure. He ran his hand down his face, unsure what to believe, but knowing he should not imagine those lips slipping up and down his shaft, her red hair spilling over his thighs.

"Where did he acquire it?" Darius ground out.

"I don't know," she said hollowly.

"From who did he acquire it?"

"His boss."

His boss…Darius's jaw ticked. That meant there were more surface dwellers involved. "How long has the chain been in your possession?"

She closed her eyes for a moment, silently counting the days. "A little over a week."

"Do you know what it is? Or what it does?"

"It does nothing," she said, her brow furrowed. "It's just a necklace. A piece of jewelry."

He regarded her intently, studying, gauging. "How, then, did you find the mist?"

She pushed out a breath. "I don't know, okay. I was walking around that damn jungle. I was hot and tired and hungry. I discovered an underground spring, stumbled upon the cave and crawled inside."

"Did anyone enter the cave with you?"

"No."

"Are you certain?"

She glared up at him, daring him to do what he would. "Yes, damn it. I'm certain. I was alone out there."

"If you have lied…" He allowed his threat to hang in the air unsaid.

"I told you the truth," she snapped.

Had she? He honestly didn't know. He only knew that he wanted to believe every word she uttered. He was too captivated by her beauty. Too entranced by her scent. He should kill her here and now, finally, but still he couldn't bring himself to hurt her. Not yet. Not until he'd had time and distance to put her in proper perspective.

I'm a fool, he thought. Darius grabbed her by the waist and hoisted her over his shoulder. She began kicking immediately, and her nails raked down his back.

"Put me down, you Neanderthalic bastard!" Her shrieks echoed in his ears. "I answered your questions. You have to let me go."

"Perhaps a little time in my chamber will make those answers of yours improve. Surely you can do better than 'I don't know.'"

"Improve? Improve! If I'd given you different answers, I would have been lying."

"We shall see."

He strode up the cave stairs and into the palace above. She continued to squirm and kick, and he continued to hold her firmly with his arms. He was careful to avoid his men as he carried her to his chamber. Once there, he tossed her atop the velvet covered mattress and tied her flailing arms and legs to the posts. Seeing her splayed on his bed made him sweat and ache. Made him rock-hard. Gods, he couldn't deal with her now, not when she looked so…eatable. Without another glance in her direction, he turned and strode into the hall. The door closed behind him of its own accord.

Sooner or later, the woman would have to die…by his own hand.

CHAPTER FOUR

ALONE IN THE ROOM, Grace tugged and squirmed until she freed her wrists. She untied the knots at her ankles and jerked upright. Alex had tied her up many times when they'd been children, so escaping seemed like child's play. Besides that, her captor had not tied the knots that tight. As if he'd been afraid to hurt her. She dragged in a shaky breath as her gaze darted throughout the spacious interior, taking in every detail. Other than the gloriously soft bed she sprawled upon, a tiered ivory chest was the only other furnishing. Colors…so many colors glistened from the jagged walls like rainbow shards trapped in onyx. There was a cream and marble hearth, unlit and pristine. The only exit was a door with no handle.

Where the hell am I? she wondered, panic rising.

Fear and adrenaline pounded furiously through her blood. A man who could afford this type of luxury could afford an impregnable security system. She fisted her hands on the sapphire velvet coverlet as another thought invaded her mind. A man who could afford this type of luxury could afford to kidnap and torture an innocent woman with no consequences.

Shooting to her feet, she tried to fight past her fear. *I'll be okay. I'll be okay.* She just needed to find a way out of here. Before *he* returned. She raced to the door, clawing at the tiny seam. When that didn't work, she pushed, trying to force the doors to split down the middle. The thick ivory remained firmly in place, refusing to budge even a little. She expelled a frustrated screech. She should have expected no different. Like he'd make escape that easy.

What was she going to do?

There were no windows to crawl through. And the ceiling…she glanced upward and gasped. The ceiling was comprised of layered crystal prisms, the source of the room's light. A thin crack stretched across the middle from one end to the other, giving way to a spectacular view of swirling, turquoise liquid. Yet the liquid didn't drip through. Fish and other sea creatures—those were *not* mermaids, she assured herself—swam playfully through the water.

I'm underwater. Underwater! She banged her fists against the door. "Let me out of here, damn you!"

No response was forthcoming.

"This is illegal. If you don't let me out, you'll be arrested. I swear you will. You'll go to prison and be forced to have intimate relations with a man named Butch. Let. Me. Out."

Again, no response. Her punches slowed, then stopped altogether. She rested her cheek against the coolness of the door. *Where the hell am I?* she wondered once more.

Something tugged at her memory…something

she had read. A book or a magazine, or...Alex's journal! she realized. The bottom dropped from her stomach, and she squeezed her eyes shut as the full implication hit her. Her brother had written about a doorway from earth to Atlantis, a portal surrounded by mist. Her mouth formed an O as a section of his text invaded her mind, clicking in place like the piece of a puzzle. Atlantis was not the home of an extraordinary race of people, but of horrible creatures found only in nightmares, a place the gods had hidden their greatest mistakes.

Her knees weakened and her stomach clenched. Turning, placing her back to the door, she sank to the cold, hard ground. It was true. She had traveled through the mist. She was in Atlantis. With horrible creatures even the gods feared.

Let this be a dream, a dream I'll awaken from any moment. I promise I won't complain about anything ever again. I'll be content.

If the gods heard her, they ignored her.

Wait, she thought, shaking her head. She didn't believe in ancient Greek gods.

I have to get out of here. She'd wanted danger and fulfillment, yes, but not this. Never this. En route to Brazil, she'd imagined how intrepid she would feel helping Alex, how accomplished she would feel proving or disproving such a well-loved myth.

Well, she'd just proved it—and she felt anything but accomplished.

"Atlantis," she whispered brokenly, staring over at the bed. The comforter appeared quilted from glass, yet she knew exactly how soft it was. She was in Atlantis, home of minotaurs, Formorians, werewolves and vampires. And so many more creatures her brother hadn't been able to name them all. Her stomach gave another painful clench.

Just what type of creature was her captor?

She searched her memory. Minotaurs were half bull and half human. While *he* may have acted like a bull, he had not possessed the physical characteristics of one. Formorians were one-armed and one-legged creatures. Again, he didn't qualify. Could he be a werewolf or a vampire? Yet neither of those seemed right, either.

With his dragon tattoos, he seemed more like, well, a dragon. Could that be right? Didn't dragons have scales, a tail and wings? Perhaps he was the only human here. Or perhaps he was a male nymph, a creature so sexual, so potent and virile, he could not be released into human society. That certainly explained her hopelessly powerful reaction to him.

"Darius," she said, rolling his name across her tongue.

She shivered twice, once in fear and once in something she didn't want to name, as his image filled her mind. He was a man of contradictions. With his swirling, ice-blue eyes, harsh, demanding tone and rock-solid muscles, he personified everything cold and callous, everything incapable of offering warmth. And yet, when he touched her, she'd felt molten lava run through her veins.

The man reeked of danger, resembling a warrior

who lived with no laws but his own. Like the deliciously tantalizing warriors she read about in romance novels. This was no novel, however. This man was real. Raw and primal. Purely masculine. When he spoke, his voice resonated a dark, barely leashed power reminiscent of midnight tempests and exotic, foreign lands. Despite everything, she had been drawn to him in the cave.

Despite everything, she was *still* drawn to him.

Never, in all of her twenty-four years, had a man stirred such sensuous awareness inside her. That this man did, a man who had threatened her—several times—blew her mind. He'd even tried to slice her in half with that monstrous sword of his. *But he didn't hurt you,* her mind whispered. *Not once.* His touch had been so gentle…almost reverent. At times, she'd thought his gaze was pleading with her to touch him in return.

"You need your head examined, young lady, if you actually find that man attractive." Her mother's stern voice reverberated in her mind. *"Tattoos, swords. Not to mention the beastly way he carried you over his shoulder. Why, I was horrified."*

Then her aunt Sophie piped in, *"Now, Gracie baby, don't listen to your mother. She hasn't had a man in years. You should offer him a little somesome. Does Darius have a single, older brother?"*

"I truly do need my head examined," she muttered. Her relatives were taking residence inside her mind, dispensing bits of advice whenever they wanted.

A wave of homesickness hit her in a way she hadn't experienced since her first week of summer camp all those years ago. Her mother might be reserved and exacting from years of caring for Grace's sickly father, but she loved and missed her. Her aunt loved her, too, and would have hugged her tight.

She drew her arms around her stomach, trying to mask the hollowness. Where had Darius gone? How long before he returned?

What did he plan to do with her?

Nothing good, that much she suspected.

The air here was warmer than in the cave, but the cold refused to leave her, and she trembled. Her gaze flicked up the jagged walls, to the ceiling. Climbing up might earn her scratched and bloody palms, injuries she'd willingly endure if the crystal ceiling opened wide enough for her to slip through and swim to safety.

She eased to her feet, her legs shaky. First she needed sustenance or she'd collapse—and then she'd never escape.

On top of the dresser was what looked to be a bowl of fruit and a flagon of wine. Drawing in a deep breath of sea-kissed air, she approached. Her mouth watered as she reached out and palmed an apple. Without giving herself time to contemplate the likelihood of poison, she quickly ate—more like inhaled, she thought—the delicious fruit. Then another. And another. Between bites, she sipped the sweet red wine straight from the flagon.

By the time she stepped to the edge of the wall, she felt stronger, more in control. She gripped two small ledges and hoisted herself up, balancing her feet on the sharp ebony. Up, up she scaled. She'd once climbed the Devil's Thumb in Alaska—not her favorite memory since she'd frozen her butt off—but at least she knew how to climb properly. She dared a peek down, gulped, and thought lovingly of the harness she had used on Devil's Thumb.

She reached the top, and her palms were indeed bruised and raw, throbbing. Using all of her might, she pushed and clawed at the crystal. "Come on," she said. "Open for me. Please open for me." Hope curdled in her stomach as the damn thing remained firmly closed. Near tears, she maneuvered her way down to the lowest outcropping and hopped to the floor.

She shoved her hair out of her face and took stock of her options. There weren't many since she was stuck in this room. She could passively accept whatever Darius had planned for her, or she could fight him.

No deliberation was required. "I'll fight," she said, resolved.

By whatever means necessary, she had to get home, had to find and warn her brother about the dangers of the mist—if it wasn't too late already. An image of Alex popped into her mind. His dark red hair artfully arranged around his pale face; his body lying motionless in a coffin.

She pressed her lips together, refusing to consider

the possibility a moment longer. Alex was alive and well. He was. How else would he have sent her his journal and the medallion? Stamps were not sold in the afterlife.

Her gaze scanned the room again, this time looking for a weapon. There were no knickknacks. No logs in the hearth. The only item that might work was the bowl holding the fruit, but Grace wasn't sure how much damage she could do to Darius's fat (okay, sexy) head with a surprisingly flexible bowl.

Disappointment swam through her. What the hell could she do to escape? Make a trip cord of the sheets? She blinked. Hey, that wasn't a bad idea. She raced over to the bed. When she lifted the silky linen, her palms ached sharply.

Despite the pain, she tied each end on either side of the sliding doors. Darius might look indomitable, but he was as vulnerable to mishap as everyone else. Even the myths of old spoke of every creature, be they human or god, as being fallible. Or in this case, fallable.

Though she lived in New York now, Grace had grown up in a little town in South Carolina, a place known for its friendliness and politeness to strangers. She'd been taught to never purposely hurt another human being. Yet she couldn't stop a slow smile of anticipation as she studied the sheet.

Darius was about to take a tumble.

Literally.

DARIUS STALKED into the dining hall. He paused only a moment when he realized he no longer saw colors, but once again saw merely black-and-white. He inhaled a disappointed breath. When he realized he smelled nothing, he stilled. Even his newly developed sense of smell had deserted him.

Until now, he hadn't realized just how much he missed those things.

This was Grace's doing, of course. In her presence, his defenses had crumbled and his senses had come alive. Now that there was distance between them, he had reverted to his old ways. What kind of power did she wield that she could so control his perceptions? A muscle ticked in his jaw.

Thankfully his men had not waited for his return. They had already adjourned to the training arena as he'd ordered. Though they were several rooms over the sounds of their grunts and groans filled the air.

Lips drawn tight, Darius moved to the immense wall of windows at the back of the room. He gripped the ledge above his head and leaned forward. As high upon the cliffs as this palace sat, he was granted a spectacular view of the city below. The Inner City. Where creatures were able to relax and intermingle. Even vampires, though he did not spy the masses his men had encountered.

Crowds of Sirens, centaurs, cyclops, griffins, and female dragons ventured from shops and strolled the streets as merchants peddled their wares. Several female nymphs frolicked in a nearby waterfall. How happy they appeared, how carefree.

He craved that same peace for himself.

With a growl, he pushed himself from the ledge and paced to the edge of the table, where he gripped the end with so much force the fire resistant wood-stone snapped. He had to get himself under control before he approached the woman—Grace—again. There were too many emotions churning inside him: desire, tenderness, fury.

He stabbed and pounded at the tenderness; he kicked and shoved at the desire. They proved most resilient, hanging on to him with a viselike grip. The lushness of her beauty could charm the strongest of warriors from his vows.

By the gods, if he experienced these sensations simply from holding her wrists, from gazing into her vibrant eyes, what would he feel if he actually palmed her full, lush breasts? What would he feel if he actually parted her luscious thighs and sank the thickness of his erection inside her? His tormented moan became a roar and echoed from the crystal above. Were he ever to have that woman naked and under him—he might perish from an overload of sensation.

He almost laughed. He, a bloodthirsty warrior who was thought to possess no heart and had felt nothing more than detached acceptance for three hundred years, was agonizing over one small woman. If only he hadn't smelled her sweetness, a subtle fragrance of flowers and sunshine. If only he hadn't caressed the silkiness of her skin.

If only he didn't want more.

What was it about her that defeated centuries of

safeguards? he wondered. If he figured out the answer to that, he could easily resist her.

Fight, man. Fight against her enchantment. Where is your legendary discipline?

With an almost brutal slash, he jerked a shirt from one of the wall hooks. He pulled the black material over his head, covering both of the medallions he wore. The etchings at the bottom of the one Grace had worn flashed before his mind, and in a sudden burst of clarity he placed the stolen medallion with its owner. Javar, his former tutor.

Darius frowned. How had Javar lost such a precious treasure? Did Grace's brother wield some strange power that allowed him to slip through the mist, fight Javar and win the sacred chain? Surely not, for Javar would have come to Darius for aid—if he still lived, his mind added.

Darius had spoken to his former tutor by messenger only a month ago. All had seemed well. But he knew better than anyone that a life could change in the space of a single heartbeat.

"You have to do something, Darius," Brand growled, flying into the room. The long length of his opalescent wings stretched to fill the doorway. Without a pause in their glide, his clawed feet smoothly touched the ground. He began striding closer. His sharp, lethal fangs were bared in an ominous scowl, a beacon of white against his scales.

Darius gave his friend a hard stare, careful to withdraw all emotion from his features. By word or deed, he refused to let any of his men know just how precariously he clung to his control. They would ask questions, questions he did not want to answer. Questions he honestly had no answers for.

"I will not speak with you until you calm down," he said. He crossed his arms over the width of his chest and waited.

Brand drew in a deep breath, then another, and very slowly his dragon form receded, revealing a bronzed chest and human features. His fangs retracted. The cut on his cheek had already healed, a courtesy of his regenerative blood. Darius fingered the scar on his own cheek. He'd acquired the injury from the nymph king years ago during battle and he'd never understood why he'd been left with such a mark.

"You have to do something," Brand repeated more calmly. He claimed the only clothes left on the hooks and tugged them on. "We're ready to kill each other."

Darius had met Brand not long after he'd moved into the palace. They'd both been young, barely more than hatchlings, and both their families had been slain during the human raid. From the beginning, he and Brand had shared a bond. Brand had always laughed and talked with him, made sure he was invited to participate in every dragon activity. While Darius had declined—even then he had kept himself a strict mental distance from others—he'd found companionship with Brand, found someone to listen to and trust.

"Blame your silly game," Darius said with a slight growl, reminded of the previous antics, "not me."

The corners of Brand's lips suddenly stretched to full capacity. "Emotions from you already? I'll take that to mean you want my head on a platter."

"Your head will do…to start." Forcing himself to appear relaxed, he clasped a chair and eased down backward. He rested his forearms against the velvet-trimmed back. "What caused you to transform this time?"

"Boredom and monotony," came his friend's dry tone. "We tried to begin the first round of a tournament, but couldn't stop fighting long enough. We're on the verge of complete madness."

"You deserve to be driven mad after the chaos you caused earlier."

Brand's smile renewed. "*Tsk, tsk, tsk,* Darius. You should be thanking me, not threatening me."

He scowled.

Brows arched, Brand said, "Don't tell me I'm about to win the wager. Not when there is no one here to witness my victory."

His scowl intensified. "Other than the game, what can I do to help ease this boredom?"

"Will you reconsider bringing us women?"

"No," he quickly answered. Grace's lovely face glimmered in his mind, and his lower abdomen contracted tightly. There would be no more women in his palace. Not when such a tiny one as Grace caused this type of reaction in him.

Brand did not seem to notice his disconcertment. "Then let us play our game. Let us try to make you laugh."

"Or rage?"

"Yes, even that. It is long past time someone broke through your barriers."

He shook his head. Someone already had, and he *hated* it. "I'm sorry, but my answer remains the same."

"Every year I watch you grow a little more distant. A little more cold. The game is more for your benefit than it is for ours."

With the fluidity inherent to all dragons, Darius shifted to his feet, causing the chair to glide forward. He did not need this now, not when he struggled so fiercely for control. One grin and he might crumble. One tear and he might fall. One scream and his deepest agonies might be unleashed. Oh, yes. He knew if ever the day came that he lost total control, he would be destroyed in a maelstrom of emotion.

"I am this way for a reason, Brand. Were I to open a door to my emotions, I would not be able to do my duty. Is that something you truly desire?"

Brand tangled a hand roughly through his braids. "You are my friend. While I understand the importance of what you do, I also wish you to find contentment. And to do so, something needs to change in your life."

"No," he said firmly. When Grace had stepped through that portal, his life had changed irrevocably—and not for the better. No, he needed no more change. "I happen to embrace monotony."

Realizing that argument held no sway, Brand changed his tactics. "The men are different from you, then. *I* am different. We need something to occupy our minds."

"My answer is still no."

"We need excitement and challenge," Brand persisted. "We yearn to discover what the vampires are up to, and yet we are forced to stay here and train."

"No."

"No, no, *no.* How I weary of the word."

"Yet you must make peace with it, for it is the only one I can offer you."

Brand stepped to the table, casually running his finger over the surface. "I hate to threaten you, and you know I would not do so if I felt there were any other way," he added quickly. "But if you do not allow us *something,* Darius, chaos will reign supreme in your home. We will continue to fight at the least provocation. We will continue to disrupt the meals. We will continue—"

"You have made your point." Darius saw the truth to his friend's words and sighed. If he did not relent in some way, he would know no peace. "Tell the men I will allow them to finish their wager, if they swear a blood oath to stay away from my chambers." His eyes narrowed and locked on to Brand. "But mark my words. If one—just one man—approaches my private rooms without my express permission, he will spend the next month chained to the bastion."

Brand's chin tilted to the side, and his golden gaze became piercing. Silence thickened around them as curiosity tightened his features. Darius had never barred anyone from his chambers before. His men had always been welcome to come to him with their troubles. That he withdrew that welcome now must seem odd.

He offered no explanation.

Wisely Brand asked no questions. He nodded. "Agreed," he said, giving Darius a friendly slap on the shoulder. "I believe you will see a remarkable change in everyone."

Yes, but would the change be for the better? "Before you reenter the training arena," Darius said, "send a messenger to Javar's holding. I desire a meeting."

"Consider it done." With a happy swagger to his step, Brand strode from the room as quickly as he had entered.

Alone once more, Darius allowed his gaze to focus on the staircase and climb upward toward his rooms. An insidious need to touch Grace's silky skin wove a tangled web through his body, just as potent as if she were sitting in his lap.

Brand had spoken of the men going mad, but it was Darius himself who was in danger of madness. He pushed a hand through his hair. Leaving Grace had not helped him in any way; the image of her atop his bed refused to leave his mind. He realized he was as calm as he would ever be where that woman was concerned. Which meant not calm at all. Best to deal with her now, before his craving for her increased.

Stroking the two medallions he wore, he followed the path his gaze had taken until he stood poised at the doorway. She would give him the answers he wanted, he thought determinedly, and he would act as a Guardian. Not a man, not a beast. But a Guardian.

Resolved, he released the medallions and the doors opened.

CHAPTER FIVE

NO HINGES SQUEAKED. In fact, not a single sound emerged. Yet one moment the bedroom doors were closed and the next, the two panels were sliding open.

Grace stood to the left, unseen and hidden by the shadows cast by the thick ivory. When Darius stepped past her, his feet tangled in the sheet—aka trip cord.

He propelled forward with a grunt.

The moment he hit the ground, Grace jumped onto his back, using it as a springboard, and raced into the hall. Her head whipped from side to side as she searched for the right direction. Neither appeared better than the other, so she ran. She didn't get far before strong male hands latched on to her forearms and jerked her to a halt. Suddenly she was heaved onto Darius's shoulder, too shocked to protest as she was carried back to his room. Once there, he slid her down his body. She stilled, feeling the buttery softness of his shirt and the heat of his skin past her clothes. Their bodies were so close she even felt the ripple of his muscles.

Without releasing her, he somehow caused the doors to slam together, blocking her only exit. She watched, her gaze widening. Breath froze in her lungs as failure loomed around her. No. *No!* In a mere two seconds, he'd snatched away her best chance for freedom.

"You will not be leaving this place," he said without a hint of anger, only determination. And regret? "Why are you not in my bed, woman?"

Overwhelmed by her failure, she whispered, "What do you plan to do with me?"

Silence.

"What do you plan to do with me?" she cried.

"I know what I *should* do," he said, his voice now a low growl that vibrated with anger, "but I do not yet know what I *will* do."

"I have friends," she said. "Family. They'll never rest until they find me. Hurting me will only earn you their wrath."

There was a concentrated hesitation, then, "And what if I do not hurt you?" he asked so softly she barely heard him. "What if I only offer you pleasure?"

Had the callused surface of his palms not brushed her forearms, she might have been frightened by his words. Now she was oddly enthralled. Every fantasy she'd ever created rushed through her mind. Naked, writhing bodies—on the floor, against a wall, inside an airplane. Her cheeks fused with heat. *What if I only offer you pleasure?* She didn't answer him. Couldn't.

He answered for her. "No matter what I offer you, there is nothing you or anyone else can do about it." His voice hardened, losing its sensual edge. "You are in my home, in my personal chambers, and I will do whatever I want. No matter what you say."

With such a dire warning ringing in her ears, she snapped from whatever spell he'd woven and called upon her terrorist training from flight school. SING, she inwardly chanted. Solar plexus, instep, nose, groin. Spinning, she elbowed him in the solar plexus, then slammed her foot into his instep. She swung back around and shoved her fist into his cold, unemotional face. Her knuckles collided with his cheek instead of his nose, and she cried out in pain.

He didn't flinch. He didn't even bother to grab her wrist to prevent her from doing it again.

So she did.

She drew back her other arm and let it fly. On impact, she experienced a repeat of the first punch. Throbbing pain for her, smug amusement for him. No, not amusement, she realized. The blue of his eyes was too cold and hollow to hold any type of emotion.

He arched a brow. "Fighting me will only cause *you* hurt."

Her gaze slitted, incredulous, clashing with his. After everything she'd endured these past two days, Grace's temper and frustration erupted full force. "What about you?" She jerked her knee up, hard and fast, gaining a direct hit between his legs. Groin: the last section of her training.

A slight breath whooshed from his lips as he hunched over and squeezed his eyes shut.

She raced to the door and began clawing at the seam. "Open, damn you," she railed at the exit. "Please. Just open."

"You do not look capable of such a deed," Darius said, his voice strained. "But I will not underestimate you again."

She never heard him move, but suddenly he was there, his arms braced next to her temples, his hot breath on her neck. She didn't try to fight him this time. What good would that do? He'd already proved he did not react (much) to physical pain.

"Please," she said. "Just let me go." Her heartbeat thundered in her ears. From fear, she assured herself, not from the sensual strength of his body so close to her own.

"I cannot."

"Yes, you can." She twisted, facing him, and shoved him backward. The impact, though slight, caused him to trip once more on the sheet. He took her down with him and when he hit, he rolled them over and pinned her.

Automatically she reached up to push him away from her. But her fingers caught in his shirt, causing the neckline to gape. Both of the medallions he wore sprang free and one of them plopped against her nose. She gasped. Which one belonged to Alex? The one with the glowing eyes?

What did it matter? she thought then. She'd come here with a medallion, and she was leaving with one.

Determination thudded like a drum inside her chest. To distract him, she screamed with all the power her lungs allowed. She flailed her legs and wrapped her sore hands around his neck, as if she meant to choke him. She hurriedly worked one of the clasps, and when she felt it unlatch, she jerked her hands down and shoved the chain into her pocket. She gave another ear-piercing scream to cover her satisfaction.

"Calm down," he said, his features pinched.

"Bite me." She screamed again.

When she quieted, he said, "I would be most upset if you damaged my ears."

Upset? He would be most upset. Not infuriated, not lost in a rage. Simply mildly upset. Somehow, with this man, that seemed all the more frightening than out-of-control fury. With a deep, shuddering breath, she relaxed into the floor. After all, she had what she wanted, and fighting him did nothing more than press their bodies together, as he was fond of reminding her.

His brows winged up, and he blinked, broadcasting his shock at her easy compliance.

"That easily?" he asked, suspicious.

"I know when I'm beaten."

Darius used her stillness to his advantage and allowed more of his muscled weight to settle atop her. He braced her wrists above her head—something he obviously liked to do, since it was the third time he'd done it to her—causing her back to arch and her breasts to lift for his view.

"You wish for me to bite you?" he asked, dead serious.

Briefly she experienced confusion. Then she realized what he meant. Oh, my God. She *had* told him to bite her. Something dark and hot twisted in her stomach, something she had no business feeling for this man. An image of his straight white teeth sinking into her body and taking a little nibble filled her line of vision. Erotic and sexual; except…

If he were a vampire, she'd just given him an open invitation to make her his next meal.

"I didn't mean it literally," she managed to squeak out. "It's just a figure of speech." With barely a pause, she added, "Please. Get off me." He smelled so good, so masculine, like the sun, the earth and the sea, and she was sucking in great gulps of that scent as if it were the key to her survival. He was beyond dangerous. "Please," she said again.

"Too much do I like where I am."

Those words echoed in her mind with such clarity her body offered a reply: *I like where you are, too.* She ran her teeth over her bottom lip. How did he do this? How did he make her feel strangely captivated and oddly entranced, yet fearful at the same time? He was quite possibly a bloodsucking vampire. He was also so sexy he made her mouth water. Made her ache in places she'd thought dead from disuse. Made her crave and fantasize and hunger.

Get a hold of yourself, Grace. Only an idiot would lust after a man of questionable origins and even more questionable motives.

What did he want from her? She studied his face, but found no hint of his intentions. His features were completely blank. Her gaze probed deeper, taking in the scar that slashed down his cheek, raised and puckered, interrupting the flow of his dark eyebrows. This close, she noticed the slant to his nose, as if it had been broken one too many times.

He was darkly seductive. Dangerous, her mind repeated.

That's it, she realized reproachfully. *That's why I'm so attracted to him. I'm a danger junkie.*

"What did you do to your hands, woman?" he suddenly demanded. His features were no longer blank, but projected a fierceness that was beyond intimidating.

"If I tell you," she said, faltering in the face of that severity, "will you let me go?"

His eyes narrowed, and he brought one of her palms to his mouth. Heated lips seared her flesh before the tip of his tongue flicked out, licking and laving the wounds. Electric currents raced through her arm, and she almost experienced an orgasm right then and there.

"Why are you doing that?" she asked on a breathless moan. Whatever the reason, his actions were utterly suggestive, endearingly sweet, and she gasped at the deliciousness of it. "Stop." But even as she spoke, she prayed he didn't heed her command. Her skin was growing increasingly warm, her nerve-endings increasingly sensitive. A drugging languor floated through her, and God help her, she wanted that tongue to delve further, to explore deeper territory.

"My saliva will heal you," he said, his voice still fierce. But it was a different kind of fierce. More strained, more heated, less angry. "What did you do to your hands?" he asked again.

"I climbed the walls."

He paused. "Why would you do such a thing?"

"I was trying to escape."

"Foolish," he muttered. One of his knees wedged between the juncture of her thighs. The ache in her belly intensified as their legs intertwined.

He exchanged one hand for the other, swirling his tongue along the peaks and hollows, making her aware of all sorts of erotic things. The way his eyes flickered from ice-blue to golden-brown. The way his soft, silky hair fell over his shoulders and tickled her skin.

If he planned to hurt or kill her, surely he wouldn't concern himself with her comfort like this. Surely he would not—

He sucked one of her fingers into his mouth. She moaned and gasped his name. He whorled his tongue around the base. This time, she moaned incoherently and arched up, meshing her nipples into his chest and creating a delicious friction.

"That is better," he said roughly.

Her eyelids fluttered open. His expression taut, he held her hands up for her view. Not a single blemish appeared on the healthy, pink skin.

"But—but—" Confusion overshadowed her pleasure. How was that possible? How was any of this possible? "I don't know what to say."

"Then say nothing."

He could have left her sore and bruised, a punishment for trying to escape, but he hadn't. She didn't understand this man. "Thank you," she said softly.

He nodded, the action stiff. "You are welcome."

"Will you let me up now?" she asked, dreading—anticipating?—his response.

"No." He placed her left palm at her side, but held firm to the right. His fingers continued to caress and trace every line, as if he couldn't stand to break contact. "What did your brother plan to do with the medallion?"

Briefly she considered lying, anything to stop the flood of conflicting desires running rampant. Then, just as briefly, she considered not answering him at all. She knew instinctively, however, that he would not tolerate either from her and that would merely prolong their contact. So she found herself saying, "We've been over this before, and I still don't know. Maybe he wanted to sell it on eBay. Maybe he wanted to keep it for himself, for his private collection."

Darius's brow furrowed. "I don't understand. Explain to me this eBay."

As she expounded on the concept of the online auction, he glowered furiously.

"Why would he do such a thing?" Darius asked, genuinely perplexed. "Selling such an item to a stranger is the epitome of foolishness."

"Where I'm from, people need money to survive. And one way to make money is to sell our possessions."

GENA SHOWALTER87

"We need money here, too, yet we would never barter our most prized possessions. Is your brother too lazy to work for his dinner?"

"I'll have you know he works very hard. And I didn't say he *was* going to sell it. Only that he might. He's an auction addict."

Darius expelled a sigh and finally released her hand, bracing his palms on either side of her head. "If you mean to confuse me, you are doing a fine job. Why would your brother give you the medallion if he had any desire to sell it?"

"I don't know," she said. "Why do you care?"

In stalwart silence, he watched her, looked past her, then watched her again, his dark thoughts churning behind his eyes. Instead of answering her, he said, "You claim to know nothing, Grace, yet you found the mist. You traveled through. You must know something more, something you haven't told me."

"I know I didn't mean to enter your domain." The faintness of her voice drifted between them. "I know I don't want to be hurt. And I know I want to go home. I just want to go home."

When his features hardened dangerously, she replayed her words through her mind. What could she have possibly said to have such an ominous effect on him?

"Why?" he demanded, the single word lashing from him.

She crinkled her forehead and gazed up at him. "Now *you* are confusing *me*."

"Is there a man waiting for you?"

"No." What did that have to do with anything? Unless...surely he wasn't jealous. The prospect amazed her. She was not the kind of woman to inspire any kind of strong emotion in a man. Not lightning-hot lust and certainly not jealousy. "I miss my mom and my aunt, Darius. I miss my brother and my apartment. My furniture. My dad made all of it before he died."

Darius relaxed. "You asked me why I care about the medallion. I do so for *my* home," he said. "I will do anything to protect it, just as you will do anything to return to yours."

"How can my owning the medallion hurt your home?" she asked. "I don't understand."

"Nor do you need to," he replied. "Where is your brother now?"

Her eyes narrowed, and her chin raised in another show of defiance. "I wouldn't tell you even if I knew."

"I respect your loyalty, and even admire it, but it is to your benefit to tell me whether he traveled through the mist or not."

"I told you this before. I don't know."

"This is getting us nowhere," he said. "What does he look like?"

Pure stubbornness melded the blue and green of her eyes together, creating a churning sea of turquoise. Her lips pursed. Darius could tell she had no plans to answer him.

"This way I can know if I have already killed him," he prompted, though he wasn't sure he would recognize any of his victims if he ever saw them again. Killing was second nature to him, and he barely glanced at them anymore.

"Already— Killed him?" She uttered a strangled gasp. "He's a little over six foot. Red hair. Green eyes."

Since Darius had not seen colors before Grace, the description she'd just given meant nothing. "Does he have any distinguishing marks?"

"I—I—" As she struggled to form her reply, a tremor raked her spine and vibrated into him. Her eyes filled with tears. A lone droplet trickled onto her cheek.

His arm muscles constricted as he fought the need to wipe the moisture away. He watched it glide slowly and fall onto her collarbone. Her skin was pale, he noticed, too pale.

The woman was deathly afraid.

The clamor of his conscience—something he'd thought long expired—filled his head. He'd threatened this woman, locked her inside a strange room, and fought her to the ground, yet she had retained her fierce spirit. The concept of her brother's death was breaking her as nothing else had been able.

There was a good chance, a very good chance, he *had* killed her brother. How would she react then? Would those sea-eyes of hers regard him with hatred? Would she vow to spill his blood in vengeance?

"Does he have any distinguishing marks?" Darius asked her again, almost fearing her reply.

"He wears glasses." Her lips and chin trembled. "They're wire-rimmed because he thinks they make him look dig-dignified."

"I know not what these glasses are. Explain."

"Cl-clear, round o-orbs for the eyes." Her trembling had increased so much she had trouble forming her words.

He pushed out a breath he hadn't known he'd been holding. "A man wearing glasses has not entered the mist." He knew this because he would have found the glasses after the head rolled to the ground—and he hadn't. "Your brother is safe." He didn't mention there was a chance Alex could have entered the other portal. Javar's portal.

Grace began to cry in great sobbing howls of relief. "I hadn't wanted to think of the possibility…and when you said…I was so afraid."

Perhaps he should have left her alone just then, but the relief radiating from her acted as an invisible shackle. He couldn't move, didn't want to move. He was jealous that she felt this strongly for another man, no matter that the man was her brother. More than the jealousy, however, he felt possessive. And more than the possessiveness, he felt the need to comfort. He wanted to wrap his arms around her and surround her with his strength, his scent. Wanted her branded by *him*.

How foolish, he thought darkly.

The love she possessed for her brother was the same he had felt for his sisters. He would have fought to the death to protect them. He would have… His lips curled in a snarl, and he banished that line of thought to a hidden corner of his mind.

Grace pressed her lips together but another sob burst free.

"Stop that, woman," he said more harshly than he'd intended. "I forbid you to cry."

She cried harder. Big fat tears rolled down her cheeks, stopping at her chin, then splashing onto her neck. Red splotches branched from the corners of her eyes and spread to her temples.

Hours passed—surely these long, torturous moments could not be mere minutes—until she at last heeded his order and quieted. Shuddering with each breath, she closed her eyes. Her long, dark lashes cast shadowed spikes over the too-red bloom of her cheeks. He held his silence, allowing her this time to gather her composure. If she began crying again, he didn't know what he'd do.

"Is there…anything I can do to help you?" he asked, the words stilted. How long since he'd offered comfort to anyone? He couldn't recall, and wasn't even sure why he'd offered now.

Her eyelids fluttered open. There was no accusation in the watery depths of her gaze. No fear. Only pitying curiosity. "Have you been forced to hurt many people?" she asked. "To save your home, I mean?"

At first, he didn't answer her. He liked that she wanted to believe the best in him, but his honor demanded he warn her, not lock her in delusions about a man he'd never been. Nor would ever be. "Save your pity, Grace. You fool yourself if you think I have ever been forced to do anything. I make my own choices and act of my own free will. Always."

"That doesn't answer my question," she persisted.

He shrugged.

"There are alternatives. You could talk to people, communicate."

She was trying to save him, he realized with no small amount of shock. She knew nothing about him, not his rationale, not his past, not even his beliefs, yet she was trying to save his soul. How...extraordinary.

Women either feared him or wanted him, daring to take a beast into their beds; they never offered him more than that. He'd never wanted more. With Grace, he found himself desirous of all she had to give. She called to the deepest needs inside him. Needs he hadn't even realized he possessed.

Admitting such profound desire, even to himself, was dangerous. Except, he suddenly didn't care. Everything but this moment, this woman, this need, seemed utterly insignificant. It didn't matter that she had passed through the mist. It didn't matter that he had an oath to fulfill.

It didn't matter.

He dropped his gaze to her lips. They were so exotic, so wonderfully inviting. His own ached for hers, a soft press or a tumultuous crush. He'd never kissed before, hadn't cared to try, but right now the need to consume—and to be consumed—by that heady meeting of lips proved stronger than any force he'd ever encountered.

He gave her one warning. Only one. "Stand up or I will kiss you," he told her roughly.

Her mouth dropped opened. "Get off me so I can stand!"

He rose, and she quickly followed. They stood there, two adversaries caught in a frozen moment. The withdrawal of her body from his hadn't lessened his need, however. "I'm going to kiss you," he said. He meant to prepare her, but the words emerged more of a warning.

"You said you wouldn't if I stood," she gasped.

"I changed my mind," he said.

"You can't. Absolutely not."

"Yes."

Her gaze darted from his mouth to his eyes, and she licked her lips just the way *he* wanted to lick them. When she dragged her gaze up again, he met her stare, holding her captive in the crackling embers of his own. Her pupils dilated, black nearly overshadowing the brilliant turquoise hue.

He recaptured her in his arms and dragged her back down to the floor. "Will you give me your mouth?" he asked.

A sizzling pause.

I want this, Grace realized dazedly. *I want him to kiss me.* Whether the fire of his desire had simply burned into her, or the desire was all her own, she wanted to taste him.

Their gazes locked and she sucked in a breath. Such desire. Blistering. Had there ever been a man who had looked at *her,* Grace Carlyle, like this? With such longing in his eyes, as if she was a great treasure to be savored?

The outside world receded, and she saw only this sexy man. Knew only the need to give him something of herself—and take something of him. He was living, breathing sexual gratification, she mused, and more dangerous than a loaded gun, yet as gentle and tender as a bed of clouds. *I truly am a danger junkie,* she thought, loving the contradictions of him. Was he a brute or a lamb—and which did she crave more?

"I shouldn't want to kiss you," she breathed.

"But you do."

"Yes."

"Yes," Darius repeated. Needing no more encouragement, he brushed his lips against hers once, twice. She immediately opened, and his tongue swept inside. She moaned. He moaned. Her arms glided up his chest and locked around his neck. He instinctively deepened the kiss, slipping and sliding and nipping at her mouth just the way he'd imagined. Just the way he wanted, uncaring if he were doing it right.

Their tongues thrust and withdrew, slowly at first, then growing in intensity, becoming as uncivilized as a midnight storm. Becoming wild. Becoming the kind of kiss he'd secretly dreamed of, the kind of kiss that caused the strongest of men to lose all sense of self—and be glad for the loss. Her legs relaxed around him, beckoning him closer, and he fitted himself into her every hollow, hard where she was soft.

"Darius," she said on a raspy pant.

Hearing his name on her lips was sheer bliss.

"Darius," she repeated. "Tastes good."

"Good," he whispered brokenly.

Caught in the same storm, she boldly rubbed herself against the hardness of his erection. Rubbed herself against all of him. Surprise mingled with arousal in her expression, as if she couldn't believe what she was doing but was helpless to stop. "This can't be real," she said. "I mean, you feel too good. *So* good."

"And you taste like—" Darius plunged his tongue deeper inside her mouth. Yes, he tasted her. Truly tasted her. She was sweet and tangy all at once, unfailingly warm. Flavored as delicately as aged wine. Had he ever sampled anything so delicious? "Ambrosia," he said. "You taste like ambrosia."

He buried one hand in her hair, luxuriating in the softness. His other hand traveled down her shoulder, down the slope of her breast, her ribs and over her thigh. She quivered, tightening her legs around his waist. He brought his hand back up and did it all over again. She purred low in her throat.

He wondered what she looked like just then, and wanted to see her eyes as he took his time with her, as he pleasured her in a way he'd never done with another woman. The concept of watching her, *seeing* her take her pleasure, was as foreign as his desire to taste her, but the need was there. He tore himself away from her mouth, breaking the kiss—surely the most difficult task he'd ever performed—and lifted slightly.

His exhalations came shallow and fast, and as he gazed down at her, his jaw clenched. Her eyes were closed, her swollen lips parted. The fiery red of her tresses was an erotically tousled mass around her face. Her cheeks glowed a rosy-pink, and the freckles on her nose seemed darker, more exotic.

She wanted him as desperately as he wanted her. His shaft hardened dangerously with the knowledge. She probably felt the same hopeless fascination and undeniable tug that he did. A tug he didn't understand. His soul was too black, hers too light. They should despise each other. They should have desired distance.

He should have desired her death.

He didn't.

She slowly opened her eyes. The delicate tip of her tongue darted out and traced her lips, leaving a glistening trail of moisture. How soft and fragile she was. How utterly beautiful.

"I'm not ready for you to stop," she said with a seductive smile.

He didn't respond. Couldn't. His vocal cords suddenly seized as something constricted in his chest, something arctic and scorching at the same time. Affection. *I should not have kissed her.* He jerked up and onto his knees, straddling her hips.

How could he have allowed something like this to happen, knowing he had to destroy her?

He was the one who deserved death.

"Darius?" she said questioningly.

Guilt perched heavily on his shoulders, but he fought past it. He always fought past it. He could not allow even guilt in his life if he hoped to survive.

As he continued to watch her, her expression turned to confusion and she gingerly lifted to her elbows. Those long, red curls cascaded down her shoulders in sensual disarray, touching her in all the places he yearned to touch. Her shirt gaped open over one creamy shoulder.

Silence thickened between them. Smiling bitterly, he wet the tips of two fingers and traced the lushness of her lips, letting the healing qualities of his saliva ease the puffiness and erase the evidence of his possession. She surprised him by sucking his fingers into her mouth just as he'd done to her earlier. Feeling the hot tip of her tongue caused his every muscle to bunch in expectation. He hissed in a breath and tugged his fingers away.

"Darius?" she said, her confusion growing.

He'd come here to question her, but the moment he'd seen her, touched her, *tasted* her, those questions had fled. Yes, he'd managed to ask her one or two, but the need to capture a glimmer of her innocent flavor had been so fierce he'd soon forgotten his purpose.

He'd forgotten Javar. He'd forgotten Atlantis.

He would not forget again.

If only he could prove her duplicitous, he could kill her now without a qualm, then rip her image from his mind. As it was, he wasn't sure he could force himself to even chip one of her pink oval-shaped nails. The thought unnerved him, battered against him, and filled him with the urge to howl at the gods. Failure to act against her would mean breaking his vow and surrendering his honor. But hurting her would mean obliterating the last shreds of his humanity.

Gods, what was he going to do?

He felt shredded as he lunged to his feet. A cold sweat popped on to his brow, and it required all of his strength to spin and stalk to the door. There, he paused. "Do not attempt to escape again," he said, not glancing back at her. If he faced her, he might lose the strength required to leave her. "You will not like what happens if you do."

"Where are you going? When will you be back?"

"Remember what I said." The thick ivory opened for him, and he stepped into his bathing room. Then the door sealed automatically, not emitting a single noise as it blocked her dangerous beauty from his view.

Grace sat where she was, shaking with…hurt? He'd wanted her, hadn't he? If so, why had he left her reeling from the intensity of his kiss?

Why had he left her at all?

He'd walked blithely away, almost callously, as if they'd done nothing more than discuss their least favorite disease. She laughed humorlessly.

Had he merely toyed with her? While she panted and ached for him, while she bathed in the decadence, the wildness and the exquisite need, had he merely sought to control her? To gain the answers he seemed to think she possessed?

Perhaps it was best that he'd left, she thought furiously. He was a confessed assassin, but if he'd stayed, she would have stripped herself naked, stripped him naked, then made love to him right here on the floor.

For that one moment in his arms, she'd finally felt whole and she hadn't wanted the feeling to end.

This hunger he awakened inside her...it was too intense to be real, but too real to be denied.

Beneath his cold, untouchable mask, she'd thought she had seen a fire blazing inside him, a tender fire that licked sweetly rather than devoured needlessly. When he'd gazed down at her so carnally and said, "I want to kiss you," she'd been so sure the fire was there, simmering under the surface of his skin.

Her long repressed hormones cried out whenever he was near, assuring her that any intimate contact with him would be wild and wicked. The kind she'd fantasized about for years now. The kind she read about in romance novels, then lay in bed, wishing a man was beside her.

Enough! You need to find a way out of here. Forget about Darius and his kisses.

Though her body protested something so sacrilegious, forgetting such an earth-shattering experience, Grace pushed the kiss to the back of her mind then dug the medallion from her pocket and anchored it around her neck, where it belonged. *Ha! Take that, Darius.*

She vaulted to her feet and spun in a circle, hoping that by searching the chamber this second time, she'd find a way out. A hidden latch, a sensor, *something*. When she saw only the same jagged walls, with no break in the pattern, she cursed under her breath. How did Darius enter and exit without so much as a word or touch?

Magic, most likely.

She blinked in surprise at the ease with which she entertained such a concept. Magic. Yesterday she would have committed anyone who claimed magic spells were real to a psych ward. Now, she knew better. She could speak a language she'd never learned.

Not possessing any magic of her own, she decided to ram into the door with her shoulder. She prayed she didn't break a bone as she girded herself for impact.

One breath, two. She rushed forward.

She never hit.

The door slid right open.

She nearly tripped over her own feet but managed to slow her momentum. When she stopped, she glared over at the door. If she didn't know better, she'd swear it was alive and purposefully tormenting her. There had been no reason for it to open this time. No reason except the medallion... Her eyes widened and she fingered the warm, ridged alloy at her neck. Of course. It had to be some sort of passkey, like a motion detector. That explained why Darius hadn't wanted her to have it.

I can escape, she thought excitedly. She surveyed her new surroundings. She wasn't in the hallway she'd expected. She was in some type of bathing room. There was a lavender chaise longue piled high with beaded, satin pillows; a large glistening pool rested inside a stone ledge. Towering, twisted columns. Multiple layers of sheer fabric hung from the ceiling. A decorator's dream.

In each of the three corners was an archway leading off somewhere. Grace debated which direction to take. Sucking in a deep breath, she raced through the center route. Her legs ate up the distance as she pumped her arms. The walls consisted of one jewel stacked upon another. From ruby to sapphire, topaz to emerald, the gems were interspersed with weblike gold filigree.

There were enough riches in this one little hallway to feed an entire country. Even the least avaricious of people would have trouble resisting such allure. That was exactly what Darius guarded against, she realized, the greed of modern day society. Exactly why he killed.

With all of this obvious wealth, she expected servants or guards, but she remained alone as she ran and ran and ran. A light at the end of the hallway caught her eye—and no, she didn't miss the irony of that. Huffing from exertion, she headed straight into the light. She may not have an exciting life to get back to, but at least she had a life. She had her mother, her aunt Sophie and Alex. Here she had only fear.

And Darius's kisses.

She scowled, not liking the heady thrill she received from the remembrance of his lips against hers, of his tongue invading her mouth oh, so sweetly. Of his body pressing into hers.

Lost yet again in the memory of such a soul-searing kiss, she didn't hear the frenzied male voices until it was too late. A table of weapons whizzed past before Grace spurted to a halt. Sand flicked around her ankles. Her mouth dropped open, as did the pit of her stomach.

Oh, my God.

She'd escaped Darius only to throw herself at six other warriors just like him.

CHAPTER SIX

GRACE STOOD at the edge of a huge arena of white stone and marble that resembled a restored Roman coliseum. Only the ceiling marred the illusion, boasting the same sea-covered crystal dome that comprised the rest of the...building? Castle?

Wide and long, the arena spanned the length of a football field. The air was scented with sweat and dirt, courtesy of the six men brandishing swords and basically trying to annihilate each other. Their grunts and groans blended with the cringe-worthy clang of metal. They had yet to notice her.

Her heart thudded in her chest, and she whipped around, intent on running back down the corridor. When she spied yet *another* warrior, this one just entering the far end, she scooted to the side, out of sight. Had he seen her? She didn't know; she only knew the nearest exit was blocked. *The nearest exit was blocked!*

"Calm down," she whispered. She'd wait two minutes. Surely the hallway would be clear by then; surely for such a short amount of time she could stay right here and remain unnoticed. Then she'd escape. Simple. Easy.

Please let it be simple and easy.

"Who taught you to fight, Kendrick?" one man snarled. He was the tallest man present, with broad shoulders and ropelike muscles. His pale hair was pulled back in a low ponytail, and the long length of it slapped his cheek as he shoved his opponent to the ground. "Your sister?"

The one called Kendrick jumped to his feet, sword raised in front of him. He wore the same black leather pants and black shirt as the others. He was obviously the youngest. "Perhaps it was *your* sister," he growled. "After I tumbled her, of course."

Grace's jaw dropped as green scales momentarily appeared on the first man's face. When she blinked, they were gone.

The tall blonde sheathed his sword and held out his hands. He motioned for Kendrick to approach him. "If I actually had a sister, I would kill you where you stand. Since I do not, I'm merely going to beat you senseless."

A man stepped between the two combatants. He had brown hair and surprisingly sad features. He was unarmed. "That's enough," he said. "We are friends here. Not enemies."

"Shut up, Renard." A boy only slightly older than Kendrick jumped into the argument. He pointed the tip of his sword at the sad one's chest. Wet strands of brown hair clung to his temples and framed the dragon tattoo that stretched up from his jawline. "It's time you and all the other *lucifaeres* learned you're not infallible."

Renard's golden eyes narrowed. "Remove the weapon, little hatchling, or I will gut you where you stand."

The "little hatchling's" face paled, and he did as commanded.

Grace inched backward a step. *Breathe,* she commanded herself. *Just keep breathing.* They were going to kill each other. Good news: If they were dead, they couldn't stop her from escaping.

"Smart move," another male said. This one had strawberry-blond hair and a breathtakingly beautiful face, which thoroughly contrasted with the fact that he was polishing a two-pronged hatchet. Dry amusement gleamed in his golden eyes. "Renard has killed men for less. I guess it helps that he knows exactly where to cut them, where to make them bleed and suffer for days at a time before finally, mercifully dying."

At his words, cold sweat beaded on Grace's forehead. She managed another inch backward.

"He's only trying to scare you," one of the younger boys gritted out. "Don't listen to him."

"I hope you kill each other." The heated phrase came from a black-haired warrior who slammed his weapon into the ground. "Gods know I'm tired of listening to all of your whining."

"Whining?" someone said. "That's rich coming from you, Tagart."

Kendrick chose that moment to launch himself at the large blonde. With a howl, the two men fell to the ground, fists flying. Every other man present paused only a moment before throwing himself into the fray. Oddly enough, every one of them seemed to be smiling.

Grace cast a quick glance to the hall. Empty. Relief threatened to topple her. She kept her eyes on the combatants and moved another inch backward…then another…then another.

And backed herself right into the table of weapons.

In a sudden symphony of disharmony, the different metals clanged together and tottered to the floor.

Then…silence.

All six men stopped, whirled and faced her. In the space of a few seconds, their bloody and bruised expressions registered shock, then happiness, then wicked hunger. Her breath snagged in her throat. She scrambled behind the table, specks of dirt flying about her shoes. A thin piece of wood would not stop these men, she knew, but she garnered a little courage with a barrier between them. She tried to lift a blade but it was too heavy.

A solid wall suddenly crowded her from behind. A very much alive, solid wall.

"Like to play with a man's sword, do you?"

Strong male arms wound around her waist—and they weren't Darius's. This man's skin was darker, his hands not quite as thick. But more than that, he didn't cause the same wave of arousal that Darius stirred in her. This man's embrace caused only fear.

"Remove your hands this instant," she said calmly, mentally applauding herself. "Otherwise you'll regret it."

"Regret it, or keep loving it?"

"Who do you have there, Brand?" one of the warriors asked.

"Give me a moment to find out," her captor answered. His rough voice drew closer to her ear, becoming a suggestive rumble. "What are you doing here, hmm?" he asked. "Women are not allowed in this palace, much less the training arena."

She gulped. "I—I—Darius is—"

He tensed against her. "Darius sent you?"

"Yes," she answered, praying such an admission would scare the man into freeing her. "Yes, he did."

A chuckle rumbled from him. "So he heeded my advice, after all. To keep us from teasing him, our leader sent us a whore. I never expected that. What's more, I never expected him to act so quickly."

Her mind only registered one portion of his speech. A whore? Whore! If they thought she was paid to have sex with them, they'd most likely see any resistance on her part as a game. She shuddered.

"Excited already, little whore?" He chuckled again. "Me, too."

Applying the same technique she'd used on Darius, she jabbed her foot atop her captor's instep, then rammed her elbow into his stomach. He *umphed* and loosened his hold. She twisted, jerked back her fist and let it fly. Her knuckles collided with his jaw. On impact, his chin snapped to the side, whipping his sandy-colored braids across his cheek. He howled and released her.

Free now, she attempted to run. The other warriors

had already encircled her, however, halting any progress. Her heart stopped beating. Their bloodlust seemed to have deserted them entirely—leaving only lust.

One of them pointed at Brand. "I guess she doesn't like you, Brand." He laughed.

"I'm willing to bet she'll like me."

"None of us like you, Madox. Why would she?"

"Why don't you send her over here to me? I know how to treat a woman."

"Yes, but do you know how to eat one?"

They erupted in laughter.

Eat her? Good God. They were cannibals. They wanted her to whore for them and then become their evening snack. Worse and worse. A tremor shook her, trekking down her spine, then spreading over the rest of her body. Death by human banquet. No, thank you.

Brand, the one who had grabbed her, rubbed his jaw and smiled at her with genuine amusement. "Did you bring any friends, little whore? I do not think I want to share you with the others."

As he spoke, "the others" began tightening the circle around her. She felt like a slab of beef at a barbecue for the starving. Literally. All they needed to make the meal complete was a knife, a fork and an extra large bottle of easy-squeeze ketchup.

"I want her first," the warrior with the thickest shoulders said.

"You can't have her first. You owe me a favor, and I'm collecting. She's mine. You can have her when I'm done."

"Both of you can shut up," the most beautiful of the group said—the one who'd polished his hatchet. "I have a feeling the little whore will want me first. Women like this face of mine."

"No, I don't and no, you can't have me first," Grace announced. "No one can have me. I am not a whore!"

The man with the tattoo on his jaw grinned at her suggestively. "If you don't want to be our bedmate, you can be our meal."

She gasped, moving in circles to avoid their outstretched hands. *Threaten them, scare them.* "I taste sour," she rushed out. "I've been known to cause major heartburn."

Their grins widened.

"Acid reflux is serious. It can cause cancer of the esophagus. It can erode your stomach lining!"

Closer, closer they came.

"I belong to Darius!" she rushed out next, grasping at any frenzied thought her mind produced.

Each of them ground to a halt.

"What did you say?" Brand asked, giving her a blistering frown.

She gulped. Perhaps claiming Darius as her lover hadn't been such a good idea. He could have a wife—why did she suddenly want to destroy something?—and these men could be said wife's brothers. "I, uh, said I belong to Darius?" The words flowed out as more of a question than a statement.

"That's impossible." Brand's frown became a vehement scowl, and his gaze bored into her, inspecting, taking her measure for a different scale than he'd previously used. "Our king would not claim a woman such as you for his own."

King? A woman such as her? Did they think she was good enough to eat for dinner, good enough to whore for them, but not good enough to belong to their precious leader, Darius? Well, that offended her on every level.

She couldn't be any more irrational, she knew, and blamed her overwrought emotions. They'd run the gamut today and were no longer hers to command. She'd always been emotional, but usually controlled her impulses.

"Is he married?" she demanded.

"No."

"Then yes," she said, not taking the time to analyze her relief, "he would welcome a woman such as me. In fact, he's expecting me back. I'd better be going. You know how upset he gets when someone's late." Nervous laugh.

Brand didn't let her pass. He continued to study her with unnerving intensity. What was he searching for? And what did he see?

Suddenly he grinned, a grin that spread and lit his entire face. He was extremely handsome, but he wasn't Darius. "I believe she speaks the truth, men," he said. "Look at the love mark on her neck."

Quick as a snap, Grace brought her hand up to her neck. Her cheeks warmed. Had Darius given her a hickey? She was struck first by shock, then by an unexpected, unwanted and ridiculous surge of pleasure. She'd never had a hickey before.

What's wrong with me? Jolting into motion, Grace shoved her way past Brand, past the others. They let her go without protest. She sprinted down the hallway, fully expecting them to follow. She heard no footsteps, and a quick glance behind her showed she was alone. When she reached the fork inside the bathing area, she trudged around the opening on the left. A salty breeze hit her in the face. She prayed she'd made the right decision this time.

She hadn't.

At the end, she found herself in a large dining hall. Darius was there, sitting at an enormous table, his eyes focused on the far wall of windows as if he were in deep thought. A heavy air of sadness enveloped him. He looked so lost and alone. Grace felt herself freezing, felt her muscles locking in place.

He must have sensed her, or smelled her, or *something,* because his gaze abruptly leveled on her, widening with puzzlement, then narrowing with ire. "Grace."

"Stay where you are," she said.

He growled low in his throat and sprang up, a panther ready to strike. And like a panther, he leapt over the table, coming straight toward her. She glanced around wildly. A side-table rested next to her, decorated with a multitude of breakable items. She swiped them to the ground, causing vases and bowls to shatter and sprinkle glass in every direction. Perhaps that would slow him, perhaps not. Either way, she pivoted on her heel and bolted.

Arms pumping frantically, shoes thumping into the

ebony, she snaked the corner and rushed through the final hallway. She didn't have to glance back to know Darius was closing in on her. His footsteps resonated in her ears. His fury bored intense, determined flames into her back.

At the end of the corridor, she spied a downward spiraling staircase. She quickened her speed. How close was she to victory? How close to failure?

"Get back here, Grace," he called.

Her only response was the shallowness of her breathing.

"I'll come after you. I'll not rest until I find you."

"I'm tired of your threats," she growled, throwing the words over her shoulder.

"No more threatening," he promised.

"Doesn't matter." Faster and faster, she pounded down the stairs.

"You don't understand."

At the bottom of the last step, she spied the opening to a cave. And there, just ahead, the mist swirled, calling to her, beckoning. *Home,* her mind shouted. *Almost home.*

"Grace!"

With one backward glance in his direction, she hurled herself into the fog.

Instantly her world spun out of control, and she lost the solid anchor beneath her feet. Dizziness assaulted her; nausea churned arduously in her stomach. Round and round she plunged and spun, so jerkily, so erratically the dragon medallion tore from her neck.

Screeching, she reached out and tried to scoop the chain into her hands.

"Nooo," she cried when it danced out of reach. But in the next instant, she forgot all about the necklace. Stars winked in every direction, so bright and blinding she squeezed her eyelids closed. Grace flailed her arms and legs; she was more scared this time than before. What if she landed in a place more terrifying than the last? What if she didn't land at all, but remained in this enigmatic pit of nonexistence?

Loud screams resounded, piercing her ears, but one stood out from the others: a deep male voice that continually bellowed her name.

CHAPTER SEVEN

ONCE SHE REGAINED her sense of stability, Grace crawled through the cave. Warm, humid air brushed her skin, thawing her inside and out. Following flashes of light, she soon emerged from the rocky exit. Familiar sounds of the Amazon welcomed her: the screech of howler monkeys, the incessant drone of insects, the hurried rush of a river. Utterly relieved, she jackknifed to her feet. Her knees almost gave out, but she forced herself to move forward, to put distance between this world and the other.

As she ran, the backdrop of sounds tapered to quiet. Sunlight faded, leaving a horrendous darkness. Then, rain burst from the sky, pelting and soaking her. Under the weight of the water and darkness, she was forced to seek shelter beneath a nearby bush. *Hurry up, hurry up, hurry up.*

Finally the rain ended and she popped up, once again dashing through the forest. Gnarled tree limbs reached out, clawing at her face, slapping at her arms and legs, splashing remaining raindrops into her eyes. She wiped them away and kept moving, never breaking stride.

Shards of sunlight gradually returned, winking in and out between clouds and foliage, illuminating a treacherous path of trees, dirt and rocks. Twigs snapped beneath her boots. Every few steps she tossed a fearful glance over her shoulder. Looking, always looking, fearing the worst.

I'll come after you, Darius had said. *I'll not rest until I find you.*

She shot another look over her shoulder...and slammed into a male chest. Grace flew backward, landing on her back with a thump. The man she hit was barely taller than she was and flew backward, as well, remaining supine, gasping for breath. She came up swinging. She'd escaped a horde of warriors, and she wasn't going to be captured or assaulted now.

"Whoa, there," another man said, stepping over his fallen comrade and holding up his dirt-smudged, empty palms. Droplets of water sprinkled from his baseball cap. "Calm down. We won't hurt you."

English. He was speaking English. Like the man lying on the jungle floor, this one was of average height with brown hair, brown eyes and tanned skin. He was thin, not corded with muscles and he wore a beige canvas shirt. The Argonaut logo was stitched over the left breast, an ancient ship with two spears erected on either side. The name Jason perched above the ship.

Jason of the Argonauts, she thought with a humorless, inward laugh.

Alex worked for Argonauts. She rolled the name

Jason through her mind, wondering if Alex had ever spoken of him, but she found no reference. It didn't matter. He worked with her brother and that was good enough.

The cavalry is here.

"Thank God," she breathed.

"Get up, Mitch," Jason said to the fallen man. "The woman isn't hurt, and it doesn't speak well of you if you are." To her he offered a canteen of water. "Take a drink. Slowly. You look like you need it."

She grabbed the canteen eagerly and gulped down all that her stomach could hold. The coolness. The sweetness. Nothing had ever tasted so good. Except for Darius, her mind whispered. Tasting him was an experience with no equal.

"Slow down," Jason said, reaching for the flask. "You'll make yourself sick."

She wanted to snarl and snap at him, but allowed him to reclaim his property. Water dribbled down her chin, and she wiped it away with the back of her hand. "Thank you," she panted. "Now let's get the hell out of here."

"Wait a minute," he said, closing the distance between them. He grasped her wrist and placed two fingers over her pulse. "First we need to know who you are and what you're doing here. Besides that, you're clearly nearing exhaustion. You need to rest."

"I'll rest later. Explain about myself later." She hadn't seen Darius exit the mist, hadn't heard him, but she wasn't taking any chances. He could kill both of these men with a mere snap of his fingers.

Jason must have caught her desperation, because she watched with widening eyes as he withdrew a 9mm Glock. Alex always carried a weapon when he went on expeditions, so the sight of it shouldn't have bothered her, but it did.

"Is there someone after you?" He didn't spare her a glance. He was too busy scanning the wooded area behind her.

"I don't know," she answered, gaze darting through the trees. What she wouldn't do for her own weapon right now. "I don't know."

"How can you not know?" he demanded. Then he softened his tone, and added, "Clearly you're spooked. If you *were* being followed, what would we be dealing with? A tribesman? An animal?"

"Tr-tribesman." Her voice barely rose above a whisper. "Is there anyone out there?"

"Not that I can see. Robert," he shouted, gaze boring into the trees.

"Yeah," came a distant, rough voice. She couldn't see the one who had uttered the response and figured he was hidden in the thick stumps and leaves.

"Robert is one of our guards," Jason explained to her. To Robert he called, "See any natives out there?"

"No, sir."

"You sure?"

"One hundred percent."

After Jason put on the gun's safety, he anchored the weapon in the waist of his jeans. "No one's after you," he told Grace. "You can relax."

"But—"

"Even if there were someone out there, we've got scouts all around us and they'd never make it anywhere near you."

So Darius *hadn't* followed her. Why hadn't Darius followed her? The question echoed through her mind, plaguing her, confusing her. "You're sure there's not a large, half-dressed man out there?" she asked. "With a sword?"

"A sword?" Dark intensity filled Jason's eyes, and he studied her. His body seemed to loom around her, bigger than she'd thought. "A man with a sword was chasing you?"

"Sword, spear, they're all the same, right?" she lied, not sure why she did so.

Jason relaxed. "No one's out there but my men," he said confidently. "The tribes out here won't bother us."

This didn't make sense. Darius had been so intent on catching her. Why hadn't he followed her? She was torn between fear and—surely not—disappointment.

Her thoughts scattered as a wave of dizziness swept through her. She swayed and scrubbed a hand across her forehead.

"How long have you been out here?" Jason asked. He wrapped a parka around her shoulders. "You might have been bitten by a diseased mosquito. You're shaky and flushed, and I'm willing to bet you've got a fever."

Malaria? He thought she had malaria? She laughed humorlessly, fighting the knot twisting her stomach. She was tired and weak, but she knew she didn't have malaria. Before flying into Brazil, she'd taken medication to prevent the illness.

"I'm not sick," she said.

"Then why— You're scared of us," he said. He grinned. "You don't have anything to fear from us. Like you, we're Americans. Hardly dangerous."

Another wave of dizziness overtook her. She clutched the parka closer to her chest, drawing on its warmth as she recovered her equilibrium. "You work for Argonauts, right?" she asked weakly.

"That's right," he said, losing his smile. "How did you know?"

"My brother works there, too. Alex Carlyle. Is he here with you?"

"Alex?" came another male voice. "Alex Carlyle?"

Grace turned her attention to…what was his name? Mitch, she recalled. "Yes."

"You're Alex's sister?" Mitch asked.

"That's right. Where is he?"

Mitch was older than Jason, with salt and pepper hair and slightly weathered features. Lines of tension branched from his eyes. "Why are you here?" he asked.

"Answer me first. Where's my brother?"

The two men exchanged a glance, and Mitch shifted uncomfortably on his feet. When she returned her attention to Jason, he arched one of his brows. He appeared calm and casual, but there was a speculative gleam in his eyes.

"Do you have any identification?" he asked.

She blinked at him and spread her arms wide. "Do I look like I have identification?"

His gaze roamed over her, lingering on her breasts and thighs, barely visible under the camouflage slicker. "No," he said. "You don't."

Unease stole through her. She was a lone woman, days away from civilization, in the company of men she didn't know. *They're Argonauts,* she reminded herself. *They work with Alex. You're fine.* Hands shaky, she pushed wet hair back from her face. "Where's my brother?"

Mitch sighed and wiped a trickle of rain from his brow. "To be honest, we don't know. That's why we're here. We want to find him."

"Have *you* seen him?" Jason asked.

Disappointed, worried, Grace rubbed her eyes. Clouds were beginning to fill her vision. "No. I haven't," she said. "I haven't heard from him in a while."

"Is that why you're here? Looking for him?"

She nodded, then pressed her fingertips to her temple. The simple action had caused a sharp, unabating ache. What was wrong with her? Even as she wondered, the pain in her temples knifed to her abdomen. She moaned. The next thing she knew, she was hunched over vomiting, every fiber of her being clenched in rebellion.

Jason and Mitch leapt away from her as if she were nuclear waste. When she at last finished, she wiped her mouth with her palm and closed her eyes.

Mitch skirted around and handed her another canteen of water. He remained a safe distance away.

"Are you all right?" he asked.

Stomach still churning, she sipped. "No. Yes," she answered. "I don't know." Where the hell was her brother? "Were you part of Alex's team?"

"No, but we do work with him. Unfortunately, like you, we haven't heard from him in a while. He simply stopped checking in." Jason paused. "What's your name?"

"Grace. Did you just arrive in Brazil?"

"A couple of days ago."

She hated her next question, but she *had* to ask. "Do you suspect foul play?"

"Not yet," Mitch answered. He cleared his throat. "We found one of Alex's men. He was dehydrated pretty badly, but said Alex had left him to follow another lead. The man's at our boat now, hooked to an IV."

"Where did this other lead take him?" she asked.

"We don't know." His gaze skidded away from her. "Do you know what Alex was looking for? His teammate babbled about, uh, Atlantis."

"Atlantis?" She feigned surprise. Yes, this man worked with Alex. Judging by his words, however, he hadn't known Alex's agenda. That meant her brother hadn't wanted him to know, and Grace wasn't going to be the one to tell him. Besides, how did she explain something so unbelievable? "I thought he was trying to prove the legend about the female warriors. You know, the Amazons."

He nodded, satisfied with that. "How long have you been out here?"

"Since Monday." Two miserable days that felt like an eternity.

"Last Monday?" Jason asked, rejoining the conversation. "You've survived out here—on your own—for seven days?"

"Seven days? No, I've only been here for two."

"Today is Monday, June 12."

Holding back her gasp, Grace counted the days. She'd entered the jungle on the fifth. She'd spent two days wandering through the interior of the rain forest before traveling through the mist. Today should be the seventh. "You said today is the twelfth?" she asked him.

"That's right."

My God, she'd lost five days. How was that possible? What if— No. She immediately cut off the thought.

The possibility continued to flood her, however.

She pushed out a breath. If it weren't for those missing days, she wouldn't entertain the idea at all. But...what if everything she'd just endured was merely a figment of her imagination? Like a mirage in a desert? What were the chances of there being a man who could teach her a new language with a magic spell? Or lick her wounds and heal her?

Or kiss her and make her want to weep from the beauty of it?

Unconsciously she reached for the medallion at her neck. Her fingers met only skin and cotton, and she frowned. She'd lost it in the mist. Hadn't she? She just didn't know, because in all actuality she could have lost it anywhere in this godforsaken jungle.

Her confusion grew, the truth dancing just beyond her grasp. Later, she decided. She'd worry about sorting truth from fiction later. After she'd had a shower and eaten a good meal.

There was no way to explain her suspicions to these men without sounding totally and completely insane, so she didn't even try. "Yes, last Monday," she said weakly.

"And you've been alone the entire time?" Jason asked skeptically.

"No, I had a guide. He abandoned me."

That seemed to pacify him, and he relaxed his stance. "Did you see Alex at all?" He patted her shoulder in a gesture meant to comfort her.

She pretended to stumble backward a step, dislodging his hand. She didn't want to be patronized or coddled. She just wanted to find Alex. When she'd first entered the Amazon, she hadn't worried about him, hadn't worried that he might be lost or hurt somewhere. Or worse. He was smart and resourceful, and had traversed jungles like this before, so she'd just assumed he was not in any real danger.

"I wish I had seen him," she said. "I'm concerned about him."

"Do you know anywhere he might have gone?" Mitch asked. "Anything about that lead?"

"No. Wouldn't his teammate know?"

"Not necessarily." Jason sighed, a pronounced sigh that revealed a hint of too-white teeth. "All right," he said. "I need to stay here and continue searching, but I'm going to have Patrick—that's another member of our crew—"

Patrick stepped from the shadows in a swath of camouflage, holding a semiautomatic. A startled jolt sped through her at the sight of the man and his gun. He ignored her upset and tipped his chin to her by way of introduction.

"He won't hurt you," Jason continued. "I'm going to have Patrick get you to our boat. It's loaded with medical supplies. I want you hooked to an IV ASAP."

"No," she said after a moment's thought. Alex might still be in the jungle, alone and hungry. He might need her; he'd always been there for her, through the years of their father's cancer, and she wanted to be there for him. "I'll stay with you and help you look for him."

"I'm afraid that's impossible."

"Why?"

"If you're hurt, or worse, it's my ass in a sling. Let Patrick take you to the boat," he cajoled. "It's docked on the river and not far from here, about an hour's hike."

He didn't want her help here, fine. It would be better to spread out the search, anyway. "I'll go into town and—"

"You're two days from civilization. You'd never make it alone. And I'm not sending any of my men into town right now. I need them here."

"Then I'll stay here. I can help," she said stubbornly. She would *not* be thwarted.

"To be honest, you'd be more of a hindrance. You're clearly near collapse, and we'd waste precious time having to carry you."

Though she didn't like it, she understood his logic. Without strength and energy, she would be a burden. Still, helplessness bombarded her because she desperately wanted to do something to aid her brother. Perhaps she'd question the man on the boat, the one who had spent time with him.

She gave Mitch and Jason a barely perceptible nod. "I'll go to the boat."

"Thank you," Jason said.

"We'll keep you apprised of our progress," Mitch added. "I promise."

"If you haven't found him in a day or two," she warned, "I'm coming back in here."

Jason lifted his shoulders in a casual shrug. "I'll give you a piece of advice, Grace. Go home when you've regained your strength. Alex may already be there, worried about *you.*"

Her back straightened, and she leveled him with a frown. "What do you mean?"

"If he's anything like me and his lead fell through, first place he'd go was home. To regroup, see his loved ones."

That made sense. "Anyone check to see if he bought a plane ticket?"

"We have people at the airport now, searching, but don't have any answers yet," Mitch said, shifting on his feet. "Because this is the last place he was seen, we're to stay here and search until the office hears from him."

Could Alex be home? The concept was so welcome after everything she'd been through that she latched on to it with a vengeance. She turned to Patrick. "I'm ready. Take me to the boat."

CHAPTER EIGHT

ONCE AGAIN seeing only black-and-white, Darius flattened his palms above his head, against the rocky cavern wall. He stared into the swirling mist. She'd escaped. Grace had actually escaped. Everything inside him urged him to vault into her world and hunt her down. *Now.* However, his reasons were not what they should have been. It was the beast inside him that craved her nearness—not the Guardian.

Teeth gnashing together, he remained in place. No matter his desires, entering the surface world was not an option. Not until he appointed a temporary Guardian. Darius uttered a brutal curse into the mist, hating that he must wait. Yet beneath his impatience was an undeniable pang of relief. Grace would live a while longer, and he *would* see her again, no matter where she went, no matter how many days passed.

He dropped one of his hands and clasped his medallion from beneath his shirt. When he felt only one, he stilled. Frowning, he reached inside his pocket, encountering only the buttery soft glide of leather. His breath became as chilled and frosted as the mist, and dark fury pounded through him. Not only had Grace escaped him, and quite easily, too, but she had also stolen the Ra-Dracus. His hands fisted so tightly his bones threatened to grind to powder.

The woman had to be found. Soon.

With one last glance at the mist, he stole out of the doomed cave and up into the palace. Seven of his warriors were waiting for him in the dining hall.

They stood united, each of their arms crossed, each of their legs braced apart. The stance for war. In the center was Brand. His lips were thinned in displeasure, and his brow was stern. There was a mischievous gleam in his eyes that didn't quite match the rest of his expression.

"Do you have something to tell us, Darius?" his first in command said.

Darius paused midstep, then he, too, assumed a prebattle position. His men had never waylaid him like this, and he cursed himself for allowing their game. "No," he said. "I have nothing to tell you."

"Well, *I* have something to tell *you*," Zaeven growled.

Madox placed a warning hand on the young dragon's shoulder. "That tone will get you nothing but a beating."

Zaeven mashed his lips together in silence.

"I do not have time to play your silly game right now."

"Game?" Renard said, exasperated. "You think we're playing a game?"

"What else would you be doing here if not trying

to win your wager? I told you to stay inside the practice arena for the rest of the day. That is where I expect you to be." Darius pivoted and strode toward the hallway.

"We know about the woman," Tagart called, stepping forward. A scowl marred the clean lines of his features.

Darius paused abruptly and spun to face them. He schooled his features to reveal only mild curiosity. "Which woman is that?" he asked with false casualness.

"You mean there is more than one?" Zaeven jumped in front of Tagart. His features lost their steely edge.

"Shut up," Brand told the boy. He refocused on Darius. His next words lashed out as sharply as a sword. "I'll ask you again. Do you have anything to tell us?"

"No." Darius's tone was absolute.

Tagart's scowl darkened with a flash of scales. "How is it fair that you are allowed to have a woman here and we are not?"

Brittan leaned against the far wall. He crossed his feet at the ankles and grinned with wry humor. The infuriating man found amusement in every situation. "I say we share the woman like the nice little fire lizards we are."

"There is no woman," Darius announced.

Their protests erupted immediately. "We saw her, Darius."

"Brand touched her."

"We even fought over who would have her first."

Silence. Thick, cold silence.

Very slowly, very evenly, Darius roamed his gaze over every man present. "What do you mean Brand touched her?"

The question elicited different reactions. Brittan chuckled. The younger dragons paled, and Madox and Renard shook their heads. Tagart stormed from the room, muttering, "I've had enough of this."

Brand—the gods curse him—rolled his eyes.

"You're missing the point," Brand said. "For years we have followed your orders and your rules without dispute. You said women were not allowed, and so we have always forgone pleasures of the flesh while residing in the palace. For us to discover that you have a whore hidden in your chambers for your own personal use makes a mockery of your rules."

"She is not a whore," he growled. Instead of offering an explanation, he repeated his previous question. "What did they mean you touched her?"

His friend pushed out an exasperated sigh and threw up his hands. "That's it? That's all you have to say?"

"Did you touch her?"

"She backed into a table, and I helped right her. Now will you concentrate?"

Darius relaxed…until Madox muttered, "Yes, but did you have to 'help' her for so long, Brand?"

With surprise his lips thinned.

With disbelief his jaw tightened.

With fury his nostrils heated with sparks of fire.

Darius recognized the emotions and did not even try to mute them. All three hammered through him, hot and hungry, nearly consuming him. He didn't want any man save himself touching Grace. Ever. He didn't stop to examine the absurdity of his possessiveness. He just knew it was there. He didn't like it, but it was there all the same.

"Did you hurt her?" he demanded.

"No," Brand said, recrossing his arms over his chest. "Of course not. I'm insulted that you even have to ask."

"You will not touch her again. Not any of you. Do you understand?" His piercing gaze circled the group.

Each man wore his own expression of shock during the ensuing silence. Then, as if a dam had broken, they hurdled rapid-fire questions at him.

"What is she to you? She wore your mark on her neck."

"Where is she?"

"What's her name?"

"How long has she been here?"

"When can we see her again?"

He ground his teeth together.

"You have to tell us something," Madox snapped. *Or there will be a revolt,* rang in the air unsaid.

Darius tilted his head to the left, felt the bones pop, then tilted his head to the right, felt the bones pop. Control. He needed control. "She only just arrived," he said, offering them a bit of information to pacify them. He liked and respected all of his men. They'd been together for hundreds of years, but right now they were nearly more than his precarious discipline could withstand. "She has already left."

Several moans of disappointment harmonized, from the deep baritones of the elders, to the crackling timbres of the young.

"Can you bring her back?" Zaeven asked eagerly. "I liked her. I've never seen hair that color before."

"She will not be returning, no." A sharp pang of disappointment caught him off guard. He wanted to see her again—and he would—but he wasn't supposed to desire her here, in his home, lighting the room with her very presence. He wasn't supposed to look forward to their encounter, to sparring with her or touching her. Neither was he supposed to mourn her loss.

It wasn't the woman herself he wanted, he assured himself. Merely her ability to regenerate his senses. Senses he'd once *fought* to destroy.

"There has to be a way we can bring her back," Zaeven said.

They didn't know that she was a traveler and must die, and he didn't tell them. They had never understood his oath, so how could he explain this most loathsome task of all?

"Brand," he barked. "I need to speak with you privately."

"We aren't finished with this conversation." A muscle ticked in Madox's temple. "You have not yet explained your actions."

"Nor will I. The woman was not my lover and was

not here to see to my personal pleasure. That is all you need to know." He pivoted on his heel. "This way, Brand."

Without another word or even a backward glance to ensure his friend followed, Darius strode to his chambers. He sank stiffly onto the outer lounge and jerked his hands behind his head.

How had his life become so chaotic in only a few short hours? His men were near revolt. A woman had bested him—not once but twice. And though he'd had sufficient time, he had failed to do his duty. His hands curled into fists.

Now he had to leave all that he knew and travel to the surface.

He despised chaos, despised change, yet the moment he'd encountered Grace he'd all but welcomed both with open arms.

Brand stepped inside and stopped when he reached the edge of the bathing pool. Darius knew that if he could see colors right now, Brand's eyes would be a deep, dark gold filled with bafflement. "What is going on?" his friend asked. "You are acting so unlike yourself."

"I need your help."

"Then it is yours."

"I must journey to the surface and—"

"What!" Brand's exclamation rang in his ears, followed quickly by a heavy pause. "Please repeat what you just said. I'm sure I misheard."

"Your hearing is excellent. I must journey to the surface."

Brand frowned. "Leaving Atlantis is forbidden. You know the gods bound us to this place. If we leave, we weaken and die."

"I will not be gone more than a single day."

"And if that is too long?"

"I would go still. There has been a...slight complication. The woman was my prisoner. She escaped." The confession tasted foul in his mouth. "I must find her."

Brand absorbed that information and shook his head. "Do you mean you let her go?"

"No."

"Surely she did not escape on her own."

"Yes, she did." His jaw clenched.

"So you did not let her go?" Brand persisted, obviously stymied by the concept of his leader's failure. "She managed to outwit you?"

"How many ways would you have me say it? I locked her up, but she found a way out." *Because she slipped the medallion from my neck when I was distracted by the feel of her body under mine,* he silently added.

Slowly Brand grinned. "That is amazing. I'm willing to bet that woman is like a wild demon in bed and—" His words ground to a halt when he noticed Darius's thunderous glower. He cleared his throat. "Why did you have her locked away?"

"She is a traveler."

His grin faded, and his eyes lost all sparks of merriment. "She must die. Even a woman can lead an army to us."

"I know." Darius sighed.

Brand's tone became stark. "What do you need me to do?"

"Guard the mist while I am gone."

"But I am not truly a Guardian. The coldness of the cave will weaken me."

"Only temporarily." Darius sent his gaze to the domed ceiling. The seawater that encompassed their great city churned as fiercely as his need to see Grace. The temptress, the tormentor. The innocent, the guilty. Just what was she? Waves crashed turbulently against the crystal, swishing and swirling, driving away all sea life. Just as quickly as one wave appeared, another took its place, leaving a splattering of foam on each individual prism. Was this an omen, perhaps, of his coming days? Days of storms and turmoil?

He heaved another sigh. "What say you, Brand? Will you remain in the cave and destroy any human who passes through the portal, be they man or woman, adult or child?"

With only a brief hesitation, Brand nodded. "I will guard the mist while you are gone. You have my word of honor."

"Thank you." He trusted Brand completely with this task. Only a man who had lost loved ones to a traveler truly understood the importance of the Guardian. Brand would let no one through.

Brand inclined his head in acknowledgment. "What am I to tell the others?"

"The truth. Or nothing at all. That is up to you."

"Very well. I will leave you now so that you may prepare for your journey."

Darius nodded and wondered if there was any way to actually prepare himself for another encounter with Grace.

THE MESSENGER he sent to Javar's holding returned as the sounds of the day began to fade. Darius was submerged from the waist down in his bathing pool, gazing out at the breathtaking view of ocean beyond the window he'd bared only an hour ago. Its viewing had become a nightly ritual, granting him some measure of tranquillity. He motioned for the young dragon to share his news.

Standing at the edge of the pool and shifting nervously from foot to foot, Grayley said, "I'm sorry, but I was unable to deliver your message. Does that," he gulped, "make you want to yell at me?"

Darius's eyes narrowed, and his hand stilled over the warmth of the water. "Did you purposely act against my orders merely to win your game?"

"No, no," the boy rushed out, game forgotten. "I swear. The guards refused my entrance."

"Guards? What guards?"

"The guards who told me to leave. The guards who said I was not wanted there."

"And Javar?"

"Refused to speak with me, as well."

"Did he tell you this himself?"

"No. The guards informed me of his refusal."

Darius frowned. This made no sense. Why would

Javar refuse a messenger entrance? That was their usual way of communication, and neither of them had ever refused the other. Besides, why would a dragon refuse another dragon?

"There is something else," the dragon said, hesitating. "The guards…they were wholly human and carried strange metal objects like weapons."

Human. Strange metal objects… He jolted to his feet, sloshing water over the rim of the pool, then stalked naked to his desk and withdrew a sheet of paper and writing ink. He gave both to Grayley. "Draw the weapon for me."

What the young warrior drew appeared larger than what Grace had carried, yet was roughly the same design. Darius absorbed that information, mulled it over, then came to a decision. "Gather my men in the dining hall. After that, I wish you to find the unit on patrol in the Outer City. Vorik is acting as leader. Tell him I want him and the others surrounding Javar's palace, unseen, detaining any who enter or leave."

"As you command." The young dragon bowed and rushed to do as he was bid.

Darius dried himself with the nearest robe before jerking on a pair of pants. What a mess this was becoming. He'd thought Javar alive, and had hoped his tutor had merely lost his medallion. Now that seemed implausible.

What were humans doing inside his tutor's palace? Humans. Plural. More than one. Perhaps an army. Frustrated, Darius shoved a hand through his hair. Grace's arrival was no coincidence. The answer lay with her and her brother. He was sure of it. Finding her, he realized, was no longer a luxury. Finding her was a necessity.

His warriors awaited him inside the dining hall. They sat at the table, silent, unsure of his intentions. He positioned himself at the head. Before they could think to begin their game, he said, "You wanted something to do, and now I am giving it to you. I want you to prepare for war."

"War?" they all gasped, though there was an undercurrent of excitement in every voice.

"You are letting us declare war upon the vampires?" Madox asked.

"No. Humans have overtaken Javar's palace, and they carry strange weapons. I do not yet know if they have killed the dragons inside, nor do I know what they are planning. But I have sent Grayley to the Outer City where he is to inform Vorik's unit to surround the palace. Tomorrow's eve, you will join them."

"Tomorrow?" Madox pounded a fist into the table. "We should act today. Now. This instant. If there is a chance the dragons are alive, we must do what we can to save them."

Darius arched a brow. "What good are you to them if you are dead? We do not know what kind of weapons these humans wield. We do not know how to protect ourselves from them."

"He's right," Renard said, leaning forward. "We must discover what these weapons do."

"I will be traveling to the surface," Darius said. "I will learn what I can."

"The surface?" Zaeven gasped.

"You cannot," Madox growled.

"Lucky bastard," Brittan said with a wry smile.

"Go now," Darius told them. "Sharpen your weapons and prepare your minds. Brand, your new duties will begin immediately."

His friend opened his mouth to question him, but changed his mind. He nodded in understanding.

Chairs skidded as they rushed to obey; then the shuffle of their footsteps sounded.

Darius shut himself in his personal chambers. With Brand now guarding the mist, he closed his eyes and pictured Javar's palace. Within seconds, he stood inside the very walls he imagined. Except, these walls were barren, devoid of any type of jewel or decoration. He frowned.

A billowing mist stretched to the prismed ceiling, and as he floated into the next room, he noticed what looked to be ice crystals scattered across the floor. Those crystals produced the mist. He bent down and smoothed his palm over a few shards, wishing he could hold them in his hand and feel their coolness. Why weren't they melting? His frown deepened, and he straightened. Unlike the emptiness of the first room, human men abounded in this one. No one saw him, for he was like the mist. There, but not there. Able to observe, but unable to touch.

Some of the occupants were striding in and out, holding weapons just as Grayley described. Attached to their backs were strange, round containers with a single tube that stretched from the top. The men who weren't holding weapons were holding spikes crafted by Hephaestus himself. They jammed those spikes into the wall and pried at the jewels. Where had these humans acquired tools of the gods?

Had he been a man who allowed emotions to rule him, Darius would have morphed into dragon form. Prongs of fury simmered to life just beneath his skin. He watched a female vampire glide casually inside the room and lick her lips as her gaze caressed the humans. A trickle of blood fell from her chin, testament of a recent feeding. She stopped to speak with a human.

"Tell your leader we've done all that was required of us," she said in the human language, trailing a finger over his now pale cheek. "We are ready for our reward."

The man shifted nervously, but nodded. "We're almost ready to venture further."

"Do not take too long. We might decide to turn our appetites to you." With one last lick of her lips, which sent the man rearing backward in fear, she left as casually as she'd entered. Her white gown flowed behind her in sensuous waves.

Darius watched in shock. Vampires and humans aiding one another? Inconceivable. Perplexed, he moved his gaze over the rest of the chamber. Sections of the walls and floor were blackened from fire. In a far corner lay the broken, dead body of a dragon. Veran, one of Javar's fiercest soldiers.

A white film covered him from head to toe. He bore several injuries, yet there was no blood around him.

What type of weapon could destroy such a strong creature? Vampires were strong, yes. Humans were resourceful, yes. But that wasn't enough to capture an entire dragon palace. His fury increased. Darius found himself reaching for one of the humans, intent on curling his fingers around the bastard's vulnerable neck, but his hands drifted through the man like mist.

Now more than before he knew he could not send his own army here until he learned just how to combat these men and their weapons.

Darius searched the rest of the palace. He did not find a sign of Javar or any more of his men. Had the rest met the same fate as Veran? Or had they merely abandoned this place? Left unsure, he whisked himself back inside his own chamber. Answers. He wanted answers. Answers he suspected lay with Grace. If he hoped to gain what he wanted from her, he needed to be focused, distant. Utterly unfeeling.

Heartless.

He only wished he did not feel so alive each time he thought of her. So vital.

Well, he *would* remove the sight of her from his mind. All of that glorious hair tumbling down her shoulders. Eyes more vibrant than the sea. He would even remove the sound of her voice from his ears. That sweet voice entreating him to continue their kiss.

Instead of forcing her from his thoughts, he only managed to strengthen her hold.

He easily saw himself carrying her to his bed, laying her down and stripping the clothes from her body. He imagined himself parting her sweet thighs, luxuriating in the softness of her skin, then sliding deeply inside her. He could see her head thrashing from side to side. Could almost hear her moans of rapture.

Desire became a heady essence in his veins, and his cock strained to an unbearable thickness. He growled from the pain of it. Jaw clenched, he removed the medallion from his neck and held it in his palm. "Show me Grace Carlyle," he commanded.

The twin dragons glowed incandescent with energy. Power whirled inside them, mighty, burgeoning, and when it became too much for them to bear, blood-red beams shot from their eyes, creating a circle of light. Inside the light, air crackled and thickened.

Grace's image formed in the center.

In that instant, his senses came to life. He still didn't understand how a simple glance at her could undo centuries of safeguards. She lay in a small bed, and he studied her. Her eyes were closed; her cheeks were pale, making the freckles scattered across her dirt-smudged nose and forehead appear darker. Her carmine curls were wound atop her head, all but a few loose tendrils framing her temples.

She wore the same dirty shirt, and some sort of small, clear tube protruded from her arm, partially covered by the thin white sheet draping her from the chest down. Two male humans approached her bed.

Darius scowled as his possessiveness resurfaced.

"Looks like the morphine is working," the man with dark hair said, his voice a smooth baritone.

"Not just morphine. I gave her three different sedatives. She'll be out for hours."

"What are we going to do with her?"

"Whatever she wants us to do." He chuckled. "We're to play the gracious host."

"We should just kill her and be done with it."

"We don't need the attention her disappearance would bring—not when her brother is already missing."

"She won't stop searching for Alex. That much is obvious."

"She can search all she wants. She'll never find him."

The dark-headed one reached out and trailed his fingers over Grace's cheek. She didn't awaken, but mumbled something unintelligible under her breath. "She's pretty," he said.

A low, menacing snarl rose in Darius's throat.

"She's too fat," the other said.

"Not fat, just not anorexic. She's soft in all the right places."

"Well, keep your hands to yourself. Women know when their bodies have been used, and we don't need her bitching about it. The boss wouldn't like it." With a disgusted shake of his head, he added, "Come on. We've got work to do."

The two humans walked away—which saved their lives. Grace's image began to fade. With much regret Darius hung the chain back around his neck.

Soon. Soon he would be with her again.

CHAPTER NINE

"HOME," Grace sighed as she tossed her keys and purse on the small table beside her front door. She padded to her bedroom, the sound of honking cars filling her ears. Sunlight burst directly into her line of vision from the open blinds, too bright, too cheery.

She was not in a good mood.

She'd spent the past week with the Argonauts. While they had been perfectly solicitous of her, they had failed to find any clue as to her brother's whereabouts. Neither had she. Every day she'd called his cell phone. Every day she'd called his apartment. He never answered. She'd had no luck tracking down what flight he'd taken out of Brazil. *If* he'd taken one. The federal police had been no help.

She finally caught the red-eye and here she was, though she didn't know what she was going to do. File a missing person's report here like she'd done there? Hire a P.I.? Uttering another sigh, she picked up the cordless phone perched on the edge of her desk. Three new voice mails, all of them from her mom. Grace dialed her brother's number. One ring, two. Three, four, five. The answering machine picked up.

She called his cell. Straight to voice mail.

She hung up and punched in her mother's number.

"Hello," her mom answered.

"Hey, Mom."

"Grace Elizabeth Carlyle. My caller ID says you're calling from home." Accusation layered her voice.

Grace pictured her sitting at the kitchen counter, one hand on her hip while she glared at the red checkered curtains hanging over the window.

"I flew home last night."

"I didn't realize Brazil had yet to embrace modern technology."

"What are you talking about?"

"Phones, Grace. I didn't realize there were no phones in Brazil."

She rolled her eyes. "I left you messages." She had purposely called when her mom wouldn't answer.

Ignoring her, her mom said, "Not once did I get to talk to my only daughter. Not once. You know how your aunt worries."

"Is that Gracie?" a second female said in the background. Her "worried" aunt Sophie was probably standing over her mom's shoulder, grinning from ear to ear.

The two sisters had lived together for the last five years. They were polar opposites, but managed to complement each other in a strange sort of way. Her mom was schedule-oriented and thrived on fixing other people's problems. Sophie was a free spirit who *caused* problems.

"Yes, it's Grace," her mom said. "She's calling to tell us she's alive and well and not being held hostage in the jungle like you feared."

"Like *I* feared?" Sophie laughed. "Ha!"

"How are you feeling, Mom?" Her mom's health had been dismal lately. Weight loss. Fatigue. They didn't know exactly what the cause was.

"Fine. Just fine."

"Let me talk to her," Sophie said. Slight pause, crackling static, then, "Did you get lucky?"

"I don't want to hear this," her mom groaned in the background.

Automatically Grace opened her mouth to say yes, she'd made out with a sexy, tattooed warrior and had nearly given him everything a woman could possibly give a man. Then she clamped her mouth closed. Dreams, or mirages, or whatever Darius had been, did not count in Sophie's estimation.

Over the past week, she'd mulled over her experience in Atlantis. She always came back to the same conclusion. None of it had been real. Couldn't possibly have been real.

"No," she said, careful to keep the disappointment from her voice. "I didn't."

"Did you wear the outfit I bought for you?"

The leopard-print spandex skirt with matching low-cut, too tight shirt? "I didn't have a chance."

"Men go crazy for that sort of thing, Gracie honey. They're like fish. You have to hook them with the proper bait, then reel them in."

Her mom reclaimed the phone with a muttered,

"I will not allow you to give my daughter lessons on seduction." Then to Grace she said, "How's Alex doing? Is he eating enough? He never eats enough when he goes on these expeditions of his."

With each word, dread uncurled inside of Grace. "So you haven't talked to him?" she asked, hoping her fear and uncertainty were masked. "He hasn't called you?"

"Well, no," her mother said. "Is he back? He's back, isn't he, and just didn't call?"

"No, I just—" Just what? Don't know if he's eating enough because no one's heard from him in several weeks?

"What's going on, Grace?" Worry tinged her mom's tone. "You took this trip specifically to see your brother. Why don't you know how he is?"

"Does this have anything to do with the man who called us?" Sophie asked, her voice clear enough that Grace knew she was still standing over her mom's shoulder.

"What man?" she demanded. "When?"

"Someone called for Alex about a week ago," her mom said. "Asked if we'd heard from him, if we knew where he was. Grace, what's going on? You're worrying me."

To tell the truth, or not tell the truth… She loved her mom and hated to cause her any worry. Yet, as Alex's mother, Gretchen had a right to know that her son was missing. The worry might make her sicker, though. She'd tell her, Grace decided then, but not now, and not over the phone. She'd wait a few days and see if she learned anything new. No reason to cause her mom anxiety until absolutely necessary.

"You know how Alex likes those doughnuts," she said, evading. And not lying. "I can say with one hundred percent surety that he's not eating right." He never did.

"So he's okay?" her mom asked, relieved.

"I'd tell you if anything was wrong, wouldn't I?" Again, evading and not lying, since she'd posed the words as a question.

"You've always told the truth," her mom said proudly, then *tsked* under her tongue. "I swear, your brother is a walking advertisement for heart disease. Maybe I'll send him some soy muffins. I can FedEx them. Does FedEx deliver to Brazil?"

"Not in the heart of the jungle."

"I'll send him a Cindy Crawford workout DVD," Sophie called.

"I doubt his tent has an electrical outlet."

"He has to go to his hotel room sometime," her mom said.

Grace rubbed her temple. "I hate to do this, but I've got to let you go."

"What! Why? You haven't told me about your trip. Did you do any shopping? Did you visit with the natives? I hear they walk around…" She paused and uttered a scandalized gasp, "Naked."

"Unfortunately I didn't see them. Which is too bad, since I'd promised to take pictures for Aunt Sophie."

"Speaking of Sophie, she's wondering if you brought her a souvenir."

"I was not," her aunt said.

"I'll come by in a few days and give you all the details. Promise."

"But—"

"Bye. Love you." Grace gently placed the receiver in its cradle and cringed. Oh, she was going to be punished for that one. A never-ending lecture, followed by a reminder every time her mother needed a favor. "Do you remember the time you hung up on me? I cried for days."

Rolling her eyes, Grace punched in one last number. Her friend Meg was head of reservations for a major airline, so she had Meg check all databases for Alex's name. He wasn't listed, but that didn't mean anything. He could have flown private.

Not about to give up, Grace stuffed her keys, wallet and a can of Mace into her favorite backpack. She caught a subway to the Upper East Side. She *needed* to find her brother, or at least find proof that he was okay. He'd always been there for her as a child. He was the one who bandaged her cuts and bruises. He was the one who held and comforted her when their dad died. They both traveled extensively, but they always managed to make time for each other.

Please, please let Alex be home, she inwardly recited, a mantra in rhythm to the rocking of the car against the rails. If he was home, they could spend the rest of the day together. Maybe have dinner at Joe Shanghai in Chinatown, a favorite restaurant of theirs.

Soon she was strolling past the security desk at

Alex's apartment building. He'd lived in the ritzy building only a short time. Despite her few visits, the doorman must have recognized her because he let her pass without a hitch. After a short elevator ride, she found herself knocking on Alex's door. When he didn't answer, she used her key and let herself inside. Only three steps in, she paused with a gasp. Papers were scattered across the thick, wool carpet.

Either someone had broken in, or her brother the neat freak had left in a hurry. "Alex," she called, remaining in the foyer.

No response.

"Alex," she called again, this time louder, more desperate.

Not even the shuffle of footsteps or the hum of a fan greeted her.

Though she knew she shouldn't, knew she should call for help first, Grace withdrew her Mace, holding the can out as she inspected every inch of the spacious apartment. Her need to know Alex's whereabouts completely obliterated any sense of caution.

There was no intruder lying in wait for her, but there was no sign of her brother, either. She walked to the living room and lifted a framed photograph of her and Alex, smiling and standing in Central Park, the sun glistening around them. Her aunt had taken the picture several months ago when they'd all decided to jog around the park. Two minutes into their run, Sophie had panted that she was too tired to continue. So they'd taken a break and snapped the picture. The memory made her ache.

Disheartened, Grace locked up and leaned her back against the door. She had no idea what to do next or— A man strolled past. "Excuse me," she called, an idea forming. She flashed him a quick, I'm-a-sweet-Southern-girl smile that proclaimed you-can-tell-me-anything. She only hoped it worked. "You live in this building, right?"

He nodded wearily. "Why?"

"Do you know Alex Carlyle?"

"Yes." Again, he asked, "Why?"

"He's my brother. I'm looking for him and was wondering if you'd seen him."

Her words relaxed him, and he gave her a half smile. He even held out his hand to shake. "You're Grace," he said. "The picture Alex has of you in his office is of a little girl. I thought you were younger."

"At the office?" Grace asked. "You work for Argonauts?"

"Nearly everyone here does. They own the building." He paused, his smile fading to a frown. "Unfortunately I haven't seen your brother in weeks. He hasn't been home, or even to work."

"Do you know anyone he might have contacted?"

"Well, Melva in 402 has been picking up his mail…I saw her this morning. She's rent controlled," he whispered, as if it were a shameful secret. "Argonauts can't get rid of her. Not legally at least."

Grace gave him her biggest, brightest smile. "Thank you," she said, taking off. Her first break. Another elevator ride and she was hammering on Melva's door.

"Coming. I'm coming," a craggy voice called. Moments later, the door swung open. Melva was thin, wrinkled and wrapped in a fluffy white bathrobe. She held herself up with a walker. The only difference between her and every other great-grandma across the country was that she wore a diamond choker and sapphire earrings.

"Can I help you?" she asked, her rough voice testament to years of smoking.

"I'm Grace Carlyle. I'm looking for my brother and wondered if he'd contacted you recently."

Melva's wrinkled gaze studied her. "Sister, eh? That slyboots never mentioned a sister. I'll have to see some ID."

Grace slid a photo ID from her wallet and allowed Melva to glance at the picture. The old woman nodded in satisfaction. "I haven't seen Alex for a while now. I have his mail, though. It's been piling up in his box. He asked me to collect it for him, but I was under the impression he would return last week."

"If it wouldn't be too much trouble, I'd like to take his mail with me."

"Give me a second. I'm still recovering from hip surgery and it takes me a bit longer to get around." She slowly turned, her diamonds twinkling in the light, and disappeared beyond the foyer. When she returned, she wore a fanny pack stuffed with different sized and colored envelopes. "Here you go." She braced one hand on the walker and handed Grace the letters with the other.

"Thank you so much." Grace quickly riffled through the contents. When nothing jumped out at her, she crammed them in her backpack. She'd go through them more thoroughly when she returned home. "Do you need help getting back inside?"

"Oh, no." Melva waved her off. "I'll be fine."

Spirits buoyed, Grace bounded outside. But her good mood didn't last. All too soon she felt an ominous gaze slicing into her back, observant, penetrating. The sensation unnerved her, and she glanced over her shoulder. Nothing appeared out of the ordinary. After everything that had happened with Alex, however, she didn't try to convince herself that her imagination was playing games. She increased her pace and slipped one hand inside her backpack, wrapping her fingers around her Mace.

Instead of going straight home, she stopped in a coffee shop, a souvenir shop and a bakery, trying to lose herself in the crowds. By the time she felt safe, the sun was beginning its descent. She reached her apartment building as darkness fell completely. She gathered her own mail, then bolted herself inside her little efficiency. *What have I gotten myself into?* she wondered, securing all of the window locks. A thirst for danger seemed so silly now.

Exhausted both mentally and physically, she tossed her backpack onto her nightstand and sank into the chair at her desk. She booted up her computer and checked her e-mail. When she saw one was from Alex's return address, dated yesterday morning, she broke into a huge smile and eagerly pressed Open.

Hey Grace,
I'm fine. I've got a lead elsewhere and had to
follow it. Sorry for the note, but there wasn't time
to call. I'll probably be out of touch for a while.
Love,
Alex

As she read, her smile faded. She should have been
relieved by the note. This was, after all, what she'd
wanted. Contact with Alex. But if there'd been no
time to call, how had there been time to type a note?

With that question floating in her mind, she stripped
to her tank and panties, poured herself a glass of wine
and sprawled across her bed. She meticulously sorted
through Alex's mail. Junk mostly, with a few cards and
bills thrown into the mix. She checked her own. Her
eyes widened then subsequently narrowed when she
came to a postcard from her dad. *Her dad!* A man who
had died many years ago after a long battle with lym-
phoma. Confused, she shook her head and read it again.

Gracie Lacie,
Can't come to see you as planned. I've been de-
tained. I'll contact you. Don't worry. I'll be fine.
Yours,
Dad

This was Alex's handwriting and had to be some
sort of code. But what did it mean, other than
someone had sent her a false e-mail? Perhaps the
same person who had "detained" Alex. Why had he
been detained? And for how long?

Where was he now?

She studied the postmark. Sent from Florida, one week ago. A lot could have happened in a week. Alex said not to worry about him, but she couldn't help herself. She *was* worried. None of this made sense. Why Florida? The lead? Should she travel there?

Well, she certainly couldn't go tonight. She wouldn't do anyone any good in this condition. Moonlight had settled comfortably inside her bedroom, and the scent of unlit apple cinnamon candles filled the air, exhausting her further. Grace drew in a shaky breath and set the mail aside. She closed her eyes and leaned against the mountain of pillows behind her, wondering what to do next. If only Darius were here...

He's not real, she reminded herself. Unbidden, his image floated to the forefront of her mind. With his harshly angled face, he radiated rawness and sheer male virility.

She should have known the moment she first saw him that he was a figment of her deepest fantasies. Real men were nothing like him. Real men lacked the savageness, the fierceness and didn't taste like fire, passion and excitement when they kissed her.

Real men didn't chase her down and threaten to hurt her, then tenderly caress her in the next heart-beat of time.

A shiver of remembrance swept through her, until she recalled one last fact about him. Real men didn't blithely admit to being an assassin.

His confession had startled her, made her feel unexpected sorrow for him because even though he'd claimed he made his own choices, that he was never *forced* to kill, she'd glimpsed flickers of agonizing despair in his eyes. She'd glimpsed endless torment. And at that moment, his eyes had been without any shred of hope.

No man should be without hope.

Grace rolled to her side, taking a pillow with her. *Forget about Darius and get some rest.* Nothing mattered but Alex. Perhaps the key to finding him would come to her after a good night's sleep.

But how could she have known that key would come in a six foot five, two-hundred-and-fifty-pound package?

CHAPTER TEN

DARIUS STOOD at the edge of the bed, staring down at Grace.

She was surrounded by a multitude of colors. A pink satin sheet beneath her, a waterfall of red curls around her shoulders and an emerald blanket draped over her. The sight was intoxicating. She looked more relaxed than she had in his vision. Sleeping peacefully, languidly, her expression was soft and innocent. The moment he'd first seen her, his only thoughts had been of joining her. How he longed to reach out and stroke the pale delicacy of her skin. How he longed to comb his fingers into the silky cloud of her hair.

Perhaps he should fulfill his oath here and now, he mused, simply to end this strange fascination he had with her. But he knew he wouldn't. He was too much a man of strategy. He liked all facts before him, and much still remained a mystery. He needed to know more about these surface dwellers and their weapons. Only then would his army be able to storm Javar's palace and conquer everyone inside.

Darius had spent several hours searching for

Grace, following magical wafts from the spell of understanding. Since no Atlantean could survive outside of Atlantis for long, he should have been filled with a sense of urgency now that he'd found her.

He wasn't.

He lingered.

His breath ragged, Darius continued to drink in the sight of his tormentor. She wore a thin white shirt, leaving her shoulders bare and glistening in the moonlight. Leaving her full breasts clearly outlined. Her nipples formed shadowed circles he longed to trace with his tongue. He watched the rise and fall of her chest, watched the life that radiated from her. The longer he studied her, the more starved and desperate he felt for her. What would her heartbeat feel like under his palms? Steady and gentle? Or hurried and erratic? His blood sang with vitality, rushing to his cock and hardening him painfully.

I do not want to hurt this woman, he thought. *I want to relish every moment in her presence.* He shook his head against such dishonorable thoughts.

He had lived so long by his oath of death and destruction that he knew not what to make of these newly acquired desires—desires that had not muted with the distance between them.

Desires such as these could drive a man from his chosen path, push him and beat him down until he collapsed from regret.

Grace muttered something under her breath, then gently, delightfully moaned. What did she dream of?

He would be lying if he denied that he wished her to dream of him. She fascinated him in so many ways. Her resourcefulness. Her bravery in challenging him as few men had ever dared. Her defiance.

What would she do if he lay down beside her on the bed? If he stripped the clothes from her body and tasted every inch of her honey-smooth skin—lingering, savoring, sinking deeply into the hot moistness between her thighs? Sliding, slipping, slowly pumping?

He tore his gaze from her. *Gird yourself against her. Distance yourself from the situation. Stay sane. Sure.* This woman posed a greater threat than any army. She had plunged through the mist and completely destroyed his sense of order. She had violated his innermost thoughts, ignored his commands and lured him to dishonor with her beauty.

And yet she still lived. Perhaps he should bed her, forget her like his other lovers.

Yes. Take her like you took the others: primitive, savage and quick. A fine plan. But... With *this* woman, Darius desired something slow and easy. Something gentle. Like their kiss.

If he didn't lure his mind away from her, he would do something foolish.

As he observed the rest of the room, he saw floral curtains hanging over both windows, each a symphony of colors. Pink, yellow, blue, purple... A rainbow. A mirror consumed one wall, while flowers and vines were painted on another. Green leaves and purple grapes bloomed in feigned sunlight. Grace was a woman who enjoyed the sensuality of life. Things he, too, enjoyed of late.

Grace, Grace, Grace. His mind chanted her name. If he could have one more taste of her, perhaps he could forget her without bedding her. A bedding would be too intimate, he decided. A kiss would be enough to satisfy him, but not enough to ruin him.

Liar. The last kiss left you raw. You can allow nothing. Still. He found himself approaching the side of the bed. Compelled by a force greater than himself, he leaned down and inhaled her exotic fragrance. His eyes closed as he relished the carnal sweetness of her. Lost in her dreams, she instinctively tried to mold herself against him.

He knew, though, that if she'd awoken just then she would have fought him. If she fought him, he would cave. Not knowing what else to do, he uttered a temporary peace spell that would keep her relaxed for the first few moments after she woke.

When he finished, he straightened. "Grace," he said softly. "Awaken." He would question her. Nothing more.

"Hmm," she muttered. Her eyes remained blissfully closed as she shifted, causing the pale pink and emerald linens enfolding her to wrinkle and bunch.

"Grace," he said again. "We must talk."

Slowly her eyelids fluttered open. She offered him a drowsy sweet smile. "Darius?" she asked breathlessly.

At the sound of his name on her lips, his mouth went dry, and he found himself unable to reply.

"You're here." Her smile widening, she stretched her arms over her head and purred low in her throat. "Am I dreaming?" She considered her words, and her brow wrinkled. "This doesn't feel like a dream."

"No dream," he said, the words ragged. The color of her eyes was far more beautiful than any other color he'd ever encountered.

"So you're real?" she asked, not the least afraid of him.

He nodded, knowing the peace spell was responsible for her languor. It was irrational, he knew, but he wished he himself had caused such a reception, not his powers.

"What are you doing here?"

"I have more questions for you."

"I'm glad you came," she said.

"I need the medallion, Grace. Where is it?"

She watched him for a long, slumberous moment, then eased up and wound her arms around his neck, crushing her breasts into his chest. She tugged him closer until they were nose to nose. "Questions later," she said. "Kiss now."

His nostrils flared at her demand—but not in anger. A traitorous fire licked through him. He'd meant to relax her, not arouse her. Gods, he'd cast the peace spell to *avoid* touching her, yet here she was demanding that he do so! "Release me," he said softly, knowing he could pull himself away if only he could find the will.

"I don't want to." Her fingers toyed with the hair at the base of his neck, and her eyes beseeched him.

"Every night I've dreamt of our kiss. It's the only thing I've ever done that made me feel complete, and I want more." She frowned slightly. "I don't know why I just told you that. I— Why am I not afraid of you?"

I deserve a beating, he berated himself, but he lowered his head anyway. Her admission lured him as surely as a chain around his neck. He was helpless against her allure. Any moment the aura of peace around her would wither, and she would jerk away from him. Until then… "Open," he told her. And he didn't care what type of man this made him. Dishonorable, so be it.

She immediately obeyed. His tongue swept inside, swirling and searching. His rough moan blended with her airy sigh. She was a mélange of flavors: warm, delicious, mesmerizing. It was a taste he'd experienced only once before, the first time they kissed. He wanted to experience that sweetness again and again.

She clutched at his shirt, then kneaded his neck, opening herself up, silently demanding he hold nothing back. He was humbled that she responded to him so openly, so uninhibitedly and so quickly. A deep-seated yearning to let her goodness seep into him blossomed and heightened. How desperately he wanted to press deeply inside her, over and over, and take her in every position imaginable until this hunger for her vanished.

He eased himself on top of her, allowing them both to lie in her bed as he'd imagined doing moments before. He gently rolled them to their sides.

Had she been coaxing him to his death, he gladly would have followed. The full lushness of her breasts cushioned his chest. Besides the thin shirt, she wore a small patch of lace between her thighs. She was the most erotic little creature, and he resented the minimal barriers preventing complete skin to skin contact.

She settled one leg over his waist, cradling him intimately, and he sank deeper into the apex of her legs. He hissed in a breath at the exquisite pleasure. He knew he should shove her away, knew he should begin the questioning. He did not have much time, for he already felt the weakening effects of leaving Atlantis.

But he could not stop. Was helpless. Desperate for her.

He had to have this woman.

His lust for her was dangerous, forbidden, but time slipped outside of reality, and Darius allowed himself to *feel* instead of think. As he did so, the very things he'd always despised became his greatest allies. Tenderness. Passion. Greed. Warm, female flesh tantalized him. Her sweet, feminine scent drugged him. Smooth and perfect. A sheen of sweat covered his brow.

As if she read his mind and discerned his needs, she sucked on his tongue, nibbled on his lips, and slanted her mouth for greater penetration. She taught him the way of it, consuming him bit by enticing bit. And he let her do it. He would have begged her to continue if necessary.

He trailed one hand over her body, tracing the velvety texture of her skin, first along the column of her spine, then over the roundness of her bottom. She moaned, and he slid his fingers between her legs, allowing them to travel up and over her panties, her moist heat, then under her shirt.

"I love the feel of your hands," she gasped when his fingertips grazed her nipple. He circled the hard bud with the tip of his finger. "So good."

She'd said as much to him before and still he relished the words. They made his every nerve dance and clamor to please her. He licked her neck and rubbed against her, nestling his erection in the pulsing heart of her desire. Their gasps blended, his strained, hers hoarse. Which only made it clear they both needed more.

"I want you naked," he said raggedly.

"Yes, yes."

Impatient to see her, he tore the folds of her shirt in two. She didn't flinch from his action; instead she arched her back, offering herself to him. Silently telling him to do with her what he would. Her breasts sprang free, revealing two rosy nipples, both pebbled and wanting. In the moonlight, her slightly rounded stomach glowed like fresh cream, and a small, silver jewel winked from her navel. He paused and fingered the stone.

"What is this?" he asked.

She wet her lips. "A belly-button ring."

He'd never heard of such a thing, but praise be the gods for its creation. The eroticism of seeing a jewel nestled in the hollow of her stomach nearly felled him. His muscles taut, he bent his head and flicked his tongue over the little bud. She gasped and shivered. His body jerked in response.

"I shouldn't have done it," she said, gripping his shoulders, urging him on with the sting of her nails. "I'm not skinny enough."

"You are the most beautiful sight I have ever beheld."

Her heavy-lidded gaze met his. She opened her mouth to protest, then cupped his jaw and compelled his lips to hers. He slanted his chin, taking more of her, sinking into her. As his fingertips continued to caress the jewel, he trailed kisses along her shoulder and neck, then moved to her breasts. Biting her lip, moaning, she bowed toward him, letting him suck her nipples deeply, hungrily. He wanted to taste all of her at the same time: her stomach, her nipples, the core of her.

"Darius?" she said, her tone thick and drugged with arousal.

"Hmm?" Though his body urged him to finish what they'd started, he continued to savor. Continued to feast on her.

"I want to possess you, body and soul."

He stilled, gazing down at her and thinking he must have misheard. No woman had ever said such a thing to him before. Perhaps he'd left them too quickly. Or perhaps they'd been as unconcerned with him as he was with them. "Tell me what you wish to do to me." His voice emerged hoarse, choked.

"I want to give you pleasure." Her eyes were like turquoise flames. "So much pleasure."

"How?"

"By kissing you like you're kissing me. By touching you like you're touching me."

"Where?" He couldn't stop the questions. He needed the words.

"Everywhere."

"Here?" He skimmed his hand inside her panties, felt the softness of her hair, and dove two fingers inside her silky wetness.

"God, yes!" she screamed. Her eyes closed, and she moved her hips with his fingers. She moaned, "That feels...that makes me... Ohmygod."

"Do you want to touch me like this, sweet Grace. Between my legs?"

"Yes. Oh, yes." Grace uttered a ragged exhalation and coasted her hands under his shirt and across the bold, black tattoos on his chest. The tips of his nipples speared into her palms as a deep thrum of pleasure rocked her entire body.

His fingers were stretching her, but oh, Lord, the pleasure. Darius's thumb found and circled her clitoris. Lost in the magic of sensation, she gripped his forearms and let herself be swept away. So close... almost there.

"Seeing you like this," he whispered, "touching you like this gives me more pleasure than I deserve."

He crushed his lips to hers in a deep, open-mouthed kiss that stole the breath from her lungs. He was kissing her the way a man kissed a woman right before sinking into her body. Kissing her the way she needed to be kissed. Her knees squeezed his waist, and she gripped his butt in her hands. His fingers never stopped working her.

"I want so badly to make you mine," he said through gritted teeth.

Something hot and wild exploded inside her just then, not allowing either of them to go slowly. He wanted to make her his woman, but she *needed* him to do it. She fisted her hands in his hair, holding him captive while she deepened the kiss. Other men had kissed her, but this was the first time she ever experienced a kiss with her entire body. This was the first time a man had ever made her feel as if she were his entire world.

His thick erection pulsed against her thigh and the need to have it inside her, a part of her, consumed her heart and soul. "You're so thick and hard. I want you, Darius," she told him, the words coming from a secret place within her. The most honest part of herself, a part she couldn't deny, though she knew she should. "I do. Make love to me."

"I—" A hint of reason swept into Darius's consciousness. He couldn't make love to this woman. To do so and then to destroy her would be more vile than anything he'd ever done in the past.

She ran the tip of her tongue over his neck, up his chin, and placed little nips along the column of his jaw. "I want to do this with you every night. Just…" Kiss. "Like…" Nibble. "This."

Every night. The one thing he couldn't give her. He had a duty to fulfill. Touching and tasting this woman was not part of it, much as he wished otherwise. Mired in guilt, he broke all contact, tearing himself away from her and jumping off the bed. He stood, staring down at her, fighting for control. And losing. Her taste was still in his mouth.

Her cheeks were flushed like the barest rose. Moonlight caught the moisture on her lips, making them glisten, beckoning him to sample them once more. Getting near her again was pure folly, he thought with self-disgust. Yet every instinct he possessed screamed that she was his. That she belonged to him and was his sole reason for living. Her conquest—no, her *surrender*—would be his greatest victory.

But even as he entertained the wild thoughts, he denied them.

Javar had fallen to a woman. Many years ago, his former tutor had taken a female dragon as his bride. She had softened Javar, made him lax in his duties. He became less cautious with the mist, no longer so quick to kill. That laxness had most likely earned him death. Or worse. Even now Javar might be imprisoned somewhere, being tortured for his knowledge and authority over the mist.

Darius could not allow the same for himself. Softening would mean the destruction of Atlantis.

Irritation raged through him—for what he couldn't have, for what he shouldn't want. How could the merest touch of Grace's lips and body reduce him to a fire-lizard focused solely on sensation? And how did just being with her let him glimpse everything missing from his life? Warmth. Love. An escape from the darkness.

Allowing himself to know the sweet joy of being in her arms, in her body, could destroy everything he'd striven so adamantly to build. She was life and light, and he was death and shadows. Joining their bodies would be more folly than simply allowing her to live with knowledge of the mist.

"We must stop," he said, the words ripped from him. He summoned all of his strength, all of his resolve.

"No. No stopping." She sat up slowly, a frown marring her features. Her eyes were still heavy-lidded from sleep, still relaxed from the peace spell, and she blinked. "I want you to make love to me. I *need* you to make love to me. I'm close. So close to climax."

"Cover yourself," he said, the words even harsher than before. If she didn't, he might beg her to strip completely.

The front of her shirt gaped open, revealing those perfect curves. When she didn't rush to obey, he leaned down and gripped her shirt, careful not to brush her skin. He was pushed past his endurance already, and one more touch… Whether his will was weakened because of his distance with Atlantis or because of Grace herself, he didn't know. Sweat ran down his brow as he tied the ripped hem together, partially covering her breasts, yet leaving a tempting amount of cleavage.

"What are you doing?" she asked, staring down at his hands, seeing the same image he saw. His darkness against her paleness. His strength against her femininity.

He pulled away, not responding.

Grace blinked. Shook her head. Heady passion still held her in its wondrous fog. She ached. God, she ached. At first she'd told herself Darius was nothing more than another figment of her imagination, but she'd known the truth. She knew it now. He was real, and he was here.

He promised he'd come after her and he had.

A shiver raked her spine. How she'd ever convinced herself those few hours with him in Atlantis had been nothing more than her water-deprived imagination, she didn't know. And it didn't matter now. It didn't matter why he'd come. All that mattered was that he *was* here and he wanted her, too.

Grace's gaze traveled the length of Darius's body. He wore the same black leather pants as before. Instead of being shirtless, however, he wore a black T-shirt that showcased every muscle, every ridge of sinew.

As she watched him, the peaceful lassitude woven so delightfully into her blood began to fade. The corners of her lips turned down as a lone beam of moonlight struck Darius's face, making the golden-brown of his eyes gleam. She paused. Golden? Before, in Atlantis, his eyes had been blue. Ice-blue and as cold as the color implied. Now they were a warm, golden-brown and hinted at untold pleasure, but also an inner pain so staggering she was amazed he hadn't buckled under the burden of it.

His features tightened, and his eyes lightened. Lightened until that cold, crystalline gaze was back in place. How odd, she thought, shaking her head.

"There is much we need to discuss, Grace," he said. The rough edge of his voice sliced through her musings. "When you finish covering yourself, we will begin."

Here she was, offering herself to him despite everything, yet he didn't want any part of her. The rejection hurt deeply.

She must have hesitated too long, because he added, "Do it. Now." His jaw clenched.

Unease dripped past every other emotion working through her, withering her relaxation a bit more. This was the man who had threatened to hurt her. This was the man who had chased her and locked her away. This was not the man who'd held her tenderly, who'd kissed her so passionately.

"Darius?" she said with a wisp of uncertainty.

"Use the sheet," he said.

"Darius," she repeated, ignoring his dictate.

He flicked his gaze to the ceiling, as if praying for divine intervention. "Yes, Grace?"

"What's going on?" It was a silly question, yet she could think of nothing else to say.

"I told you I would come for you, and so I have."

She swallowed. "Why?"

Before she had time to blink, he unsheathed a small blade from the waist of his pants and held the razor-sharp tip at her neck. The contact was light, not enough to draw blood, but enough to sting all the same. She gasped and whimpered, the sounds blending and echoing off the walls.

Darius arched a brow. "We are going to have a chat, you and I."

"You didn't travel all this way to talk," she said. And he hadn't traveled here to make love to her, either. What exactly did he want from her?

"For now conversation is all I require of you." His blade stayed suspended in the air for another fraction of a second before he slid it back into its sheath. "Do not forget how dangerous I am."

Yes, he was dangerous. And if now was for conversation, what was later for?

Fighting a cold sweat and a timorous shake, Grace scrambled up. Her sheet and comforter whisked to the floor in a tangle at her feet. Darius remained in place, as if he feared nothing she could do. Determined, she reached into the backpack on her nightstand, knocking down the empty wineglass in her haste.

She withdrew her Mace and without any hesitation, sprayed him in the eyes. While his roar reverberated in her ears, she bolted out the bedroom door.

CHAPTER ELEVEN

EVERYTHING HAPPENED within seconds.

One moment she was racing through her living room, the next Darius tackled her from behind. He slammed into her, propelling her facedown. They landed on top of her couch, and the impact squeezed every molecule of oxygen from her lungs. As she struggled to breathe, he flipped her over and locked her wrists above her head. Still a favorite position of his, obviously. She didn't have time to panic.

"My soul belongs to you, and yours belongs to me," he chanted, his voice strange, hypnotic. His gaze clashed with hers, ice-blue calculation with turquoise uncertainty. The rims of his eyes were red and swollen, but as she watched, all hint of the toxic spray vanished.

"What are you doing?" she gasped, growing increasingly light-headed.

"Bound we shall be," he continued, "from this moon to another, then set free."

Her blood whirled inside her veins as a strange, dark and oddly compelling essence invaded her. Dark, so dark. Scattered thoughts flashed through her, motionless images in black-and-white—images of a child's terror, hurt, and search for a love never found. Images of desolation and an ultimate withdrawal from emotion.

The child was Darius.

She was poised on the periphery of a vision, gazing down at a bloody massacre. Men, women and children were lying motionless in pools of their own blood. The boy—Darius—knelt over one of the children. A little girl. Long black hair formed an inky river around her face and shoulders, blending with the blood dripping from her neck. She wore a sapphire-colored dress that was bunched around her waist. Her eyes were closed, but there was a promise of beauty in every line of her softly rounded features.

Gently Darius fitted the hem of the dress around her ankles, covering her exposed flesh. He remained kneeling and gazed up to the crystal dome. He slammed a fist into the dirt and howled, the sound more animal than human, more tortured than any child should ever have to endure.

Grace wanted to sob. She found herself reaching out, hoping to wrap the boy in her arms. But even as she moved, she was whisked back to reality. Darius still hovered above her.

"What did you do to me?" she cried.

He didn't answer right away. His eyes were closed, as if he were lost in a vision of his own. When he finally opened his eyelids, he said, "I have bound us together." He looked smug. "For one day, you must remain in my presence. There will be no more escaping."

"That isn't possible."

"Isn't it? Can you not speak my language? Did I not travel here—Gracie Lacie?" he added softly.

She gasped. "How do you know that name?"

"Your father called you that."

"Yes, but how do you know?"

"I saw inside your mind," he said simply. He pushed to his feet, and she scooted backward to the edge of the couch. "Go to your room and dress," he said. "Wear something that covers you from neck to toe. We have much to discuss and not a lot of time."

"I'm not moving."

His gaze slitted. "Then I will change you myself."

With that threat ringing in her ears, Grace jumped up and scurried around him. When she reached her bedroom, she quickly shut and locked the door, then raced to the nearest window. She unlatched the fastener, raised the glass and attempted to throw one leg over.

An invisible wall stopped any movement outside.

Nearly screeching with frustration, she kicked and pounded at the wall but couldn't break past it. Finally, panting, she gave up. How dare Darius do this! she seethed. What had he said? A binding spell. How dare he cast a binding spell, locking her within his grasp.

A hard knock sounded at her door. "You have five minutes to dress, and then I am coming in."

He'd do it, too, she thought. Even if he had to kick in the door. Even if he had to take the apartment building apart brick by brick. With a humorless chuckle, she leaned against the ledge and rested her head on the wooden frame.

How had such a lost little boy grown into such an uncompromising man?

She didn't want to believe those flashes of his life were real, but he'd known her father's nickname for her. And she hadn't shared that information with anyone. Darius's childhood, those things she'd seen, had happened. She didn't like knowing he'd once had a family. She didn't like knowing about the pain he had endured at their deaths. Knowing made her long to comfort him, to protect him. To stay with him.

"I don't want to change while you're inside my house," she called. "I don't trust you."

"That matters not. You will do as I have commanded."

Or he'd do it for her, she mentally finished. Grace dragged her feet to her dresser and tore off her ripped tank. She quickly jerked on her largest, plainest turtleneck sweater and a pair of plain gray sweatpants. He didn't want to see her skin, and she didn't want to show it to him. Glowering, she donned socks and tennis shoes—better to kick him with.

When she was completely dressed, she paused. *What do I do now?* She would go out there, Grace decided, and she would be civilized. She would answer his questions honestly. Afterward, he would leave her, just as he'd found her. The boy he'd been would allow nothing less. She hoped. He'd certainly had the opportunity to hurt her: while she slept, while they kissed. A shiver of remembrance trickled through her, and she scowled. How could she *still* desire him?

Gathering her scattered wits, she unlocked the door and pulled it open. Darius towered a few feet away, his shoulder propped on the opposite wall. His expression was as cold and merciless as ever; his eyes could have been chipped from an Alaskan glacier.

"Much better," he said, eyeing her clothing.

"Let's go into the living room," she said. She didn't want a bed anywhere near them. Without waiting for his reply, she swept around him. She settled on the recliner—so he couldn't sit next to her—and said the first thing that popped into her mind. "Are you going to eat me?"

"What?" he half growled, half gasped. He settled onto the couch, as far away from her as possible.

Was he just as leery of her as she was of him? The thought shouldn't have bothered her, but it did. She had done nothing, by word or deed, to earn his dislike.

"Your friends," she said. "They're cannibals and wanted to eat me." She shuddered at the memory.

His lips curled in what could either have been amusement or fury. "They will never do so. That I can promise you." He schooled his features until they were as blank as a brand-new chalkboard. "Where is the medallion, Grace?"

Uh-oh. Confession time. "I, uh, lost it."

"What?" he roared, jolting to his feet.

"I lost it?" she offered more as a question than a statement.

He sank back into his seat and rubbed a hand down his face. "Explain."

"While I was inside the mist the second time, it ripped from my neck." She shrugged. "I tried to get it back, but failed."

His gaze pierced her with its intensity. "If you are saying this in an attempt to keep the medallion for yourself, I will—"

"Search my home if you want," she interjected defensively.

He massaged his temple with two fingers and continued to stare over at her. Then he nodded as though he'd just come to a monumental decision. "We are going to take a small trip, Grace."

"I don't think so."

"We're going to the cave. We will not stay long."

Heat drained from her face and hands, leaving her cold and pale. Did he hope to send her back into Atlantis? To lock her up? To either kill/torture/molest her—okay, the last one appealed to her in a way it shouldn't have—in his own surroundings?

"Do not think to protest," he said, as if reading her thoughts. "I must go, therefore you must go. We are bound together."

"Atlantis is—"

"Not where I'm taking you. I wish only to visit the cave."

She relaxed, soothed by the ring of truth in his tone. Another trip to Brazil might actually be beneficial, she realized, remembering the postcard Alex had sent her. She could take his picture with her, something she hadn't had last time, and walk through town, asking people if they had seen him. Because maybe, just maybe, whatever lead he'd found, whatever he'd done in Florida had directed him back to Brazil. God knows that's where the portal resided and that portal was what Alex was looking for.

"If I go with you," she said, purposely omitting her change of desires, "will you help me find my brother?"

"You do not know where he is?"

"No. And I've looked. His coworkers haven't seen him. He hasn't been home. He hasn't even called our mother, and he usually does. Someone sent me an e-mail supposedly from him, but I know it wasn't because I found a postcard Alex had written telling me he was in trouble. This entire situation is a mess! The only people who know I'm looking for him are his coworkers, but they're looking for him, too, so I don't know why they'd want to stop me. I just want my brother safe."

A flash of guilt stole through Darius's eyes. "I cannot stay here long, but you have my word of honor that while I am here, I will help you find him."

"Thank you," she told him softly. Why the guilt, though?

He stood and held out his hand, palm up.

"We're leaving *now?*"

"Now."

"But I need to call the airline. I need to—"

"You need only take my hand."

Blinking up at him in confusion, she swallowed, then forced herself to stand. "Give me just…" She rushed to her storage closet. "One…" She withdrew a photo album. "Second." She peeled Alex's picture from the slot, folded it and shoved it into her pocket. She raced back to Darius and, with a half smile, placed her hand in his. "I'm ready."

"Close your eyes." The deep baritone of his voice was hypnotic.

"Why?"

"Just do what I say."

"First tell me why."

He frowned. "What I'm about to do can be jolting."

"There. That wasn't so bad, was it?" She closed her eyelids, total darkness encompassing her. A full minute ticked by and nothing happened. What was going on? "Can I look now?"

"Not yet." His voice was strained, and his hand clenched around hers. "I do not have full use of my powers, so the trip is taking longer than usual."

Trip? And why didn't he have full use of his powers?

"You may look now," he said a moment later.

His dilemma forgotten, she fluttered open her eyelids and gasped. Bleak, rocky walls surrounded her. Water dripped in a constant procession, the sound ghostly. A thick, smoky mist billowed around them, cold and dreary, dusting everything it touched with chill. She was suddenly grateful for her sweatpants.

The only light came from Darius. Even through his shirt, his tattoos glowed bright enough to light a football stadium.

"How did you do that?" she asked, awed. "How did you bring us here so quickly, without walking a single step?"

"I am a child of the gods," he said, as if that explained everything. "Do not move from that spot."

Since that suited her desires perfectly, she nodded. She wasn't going near the mist.

His eyes scanning, searching, he stalked around the cavern, his muscles rippling beneath his clothes with every movement. She easily recalled how all that strength and sinew felt beneath her fingertips. Her mouth watered, and she shifted from one foot to the other. No matter what this man did, he oozed danger and excitement; it seeped from his every pore. He was far too menacing, far too unpredictable, and far too powerful. He'd promised to help her while he was with her, and she believed he would.

If anyone could find Alex, it was this man.

He tried to lift a large branch out of his way, but his hands ghosted through it. As she watched, her eyes widened. She turned toward the wall and ran her own hand over the jagged surface. Shockingly her fingers disappeared inside the rock. "We're ghosts," she croaked out, spinning to face Darius.

"Only while we are here," he assured her.

Knowing she was not a permanent phantom eased her worry, and she relaxed. She was used to new experiences. Most times she went out of her way to have them. But with Darius, things just sort of happened—weird things she could not possibly prepare for. He was excitement personified.

"Are you looking for the medallion?" she asked when he continued his search.

A long silence fell between them. Obviously he didn't want to answer.

"Well?" she persisted.

"I *must* find it."

What was it about that chain? Even she had fought to possess it, had felt its strange, unquestionable draw. "You want it, Alex wanted it and someone once tried to steal it from him. Other than unlocking your bedroom door, what makes that thing so valuable?"

"Dragon medallions are handcrafted by Hephaestus, the blacksmith of the gods, and each one holds a special power for its owner, like time travel or invisibility. What's more, it unlocks doors to *every* room in every dragon palace—as you saw for yourself," he added dryly.

"If I'd known it offered special powers, I might have held on to it more tightly," she said. Time travel. How cool was that? "My favorite novels are time travels, and I've always thought it would be cool to visit the Middle Ages."

"If you had known of the medallion's powers, you would *not* have lived long enough to travel through time."

Well, that certainly put things in perspective, didn't it? "I guess that means I shouldn't ask what yours can do."

"No, you should not. You and other surface dwellers should not even know the medallions exist."

She sighed. "Alex found an ancient text, the *Book of Ra-Dracus*. That's how he knew about them. That's how he knew about the portal into Atlantis."

Darius's chin whipped up and he faced her; his eyes narrowed. "I have never heard of this book. What else did it say?"

"He didn't mention much, but did say the book told of ways to defeat the creatures inside. Alex gave no mention of specifics, though. I'm sorry."

"I must see that book." *I must destroy it,* echoed unsaid.

"Shortly after he found it," she said, lifting her arms in a helpless gesture, "someone stole it from him."

Darius rubbed his neck as he knelt before a muddy mound. "Atlanteans are dangerous beings, stronger than your people and far more deadly. Why those on the surface continually try to invade our land is beyond me. Those who do always die. Every time."

"I didn't," she reminded him softly.

His head snapped in her direction for a second time. Silence. Then, "No," he finally said, "you didn't." He continued to stare at her, and she shifted uncomfortably. His attention wavered between her mouth and her curves. If his eyes became any more heated, her clothing would be incinerated, panties and all. "Where did your brother find the book?"

"Greece. The temple of Erinys," she said, snapping her fingers as the name popped into place.

"Erinys, the punisher of the unfaithful." His brow furrowed. "A minor goddess. I do not understand why she or her followers would possess such a book, a book that tells of ways to defeat us."

"Maybe she wanted to punish those in Atlantis," Grace offered.

His nostrils flared. "We are not, nor have we ever been, unfaithful to anyone."

O-kay. Sore topic. And one she wouldn't bring up again. "I'm sure you weren't, big guy," she said, hoping to placate him.

"We do not attempt to conquer the surface. We serve our gods faithfully. We do nothing to earn ourselves punishment."

"Well, now, that's not exactly true." Even though she'd just promised herself she wouldn't bring this up again, she found herself saying, "You obviously did *something.* Your entire city was cast into the sea."

"We existed. That is why we were hidden in the sea. The way I understand it is we were never meant to be created, yet Zeus cut off his father's—" he paused "—manhood, causing Cronus's blood to splatter upon the earth. He meant to create man, but we were the first to form. Though he was—is—our brother, Zeus feared what we could do, so he banished us from the land he viewed as his playground. We were not unfaithful."

"You were created by the blood of a god?" she asked, beyond curious about him.

"No," he answered. "My parents conceived me through the more traditional manner. My ancestors were the ones created by a god's blood." His lips pressed together firmly, stubbornly, and she knew he'd say no more on the subject.

His parents were dead, she remembered from her vision, and she ached for him. Ached because he'd been the one to find them. Ached because they'd been murdered in ways so cruel she cringed from the thoughts. She knew how devastating losing a loved one was. He'd lost everyone close to him in one fatal swoop.

"Your brother," Darius said, effectively changing the subject. "You said he's been missing for several weeks."

The mention of Alex served as a cold reminder of why she was here. "He hasn't been home, hasn't called, and that isn't like him."

"And there were men chasing him through the jungle, trying to obtain the medallion from him?"

"There could have been, yes. The theft attempt I mentioned was from before."

"Perhaps you should tell me everything that happened before and after you escaped me."

She told him what she knew, leaving out no detail.

"These men," he said, "the Argonauts who found you in the jungle. Would they harm your brother if they knew of the medallion?"

"I would hope not, but..."

Darius pursed his lips as he wondered just how many were involved in this tangled web of mystery—which was becoming more complicated every time Grace opened her mouth. "I wish to find and speak with them." He pushed to his feet. "The medallion is not here," he growled. "I have searched every inch of the cave."

"I didn't lie to you," she assured him. "I lost it in the mist."

He jerked a hand through his hair. Once again he was left unsure whether to believe Grace. Her motives seemed pure, the protection of her brother; yet her claim of losing the medallion seemed too convenient.

As he stood there, warring within himself, his heated tattoos illuminated a dark object, glinting in the corner of his eye. He'd seen the object during his search, but had ignored it. Now he bent down and studied it. Grace's weapon, he realized. The same sort of weapon the human guards carried at Javar's palace. He must have tossed it through the mist.

"Why did you carry this?" he asked her. His fingers drifted through the metal.

"The gun?" She closed the distance between them and knelt beside him. Her heady essence wrapped around him.

"A gun," he echoed. "Why did you carry this?" he asked again.

"To protect myself. I bought it from a peddler in Manaus."

"What does it do?" His voice was solemn, deep. "As I recall, you tried to wound me with it, but nothing happened."

"The cylinder wasn't loaded. If the cylinder *had* been loaded, bullets would have shot out when I pulled the trigger and slammed into you, causing injury. Maybe even death."

Intrigued, he eyed the gun with new expectations. A complicated piece of weaponry, to be sure. The coil, the thin shaft. "I would like to see this in action."

"I just bet you would," she muttered.

He flicked her a glance. "If I make it so that you can hold this weapon, will you show me how to work it?"

"I don't have any bullets," she said.

"Get some."

"Where? We're not exactly in the bustling heart of a city, with eager merchants hawking their wares."

"Later, then. When we return to your home. You can obtain these bullets and show me how this weapon works."

"All right," she said. Though Grace wasn't sure she wanted him to handle a loaded gun. Nor was she sure she wanted to take him to a gun range. "But how are we going to get it home? We can't even pick it up."

He turned back to the gun, letting his hands hover over the top, and closed his eyes. One minute melted into another. Lines of strain bracketed his mouth, and his bronze skin paled. Grace didn't utter a sound, didn't move. She didn't know what he was doing, but she was loath to interrupt.

Finally, he let out a breath and opened his eyes. He scooped his hand under the gun and lifted. Instead of sinking past an immaterial palm, the gun remained cradled.

"How did you do that?" Awe laced her voice. She took the weapon and tucked it in the drawstring waist of her sweats.

He ignored her question. "Come," he said, stalking to the entrance. "I wish to find these Argonauts."

"They have guns of their own," she warned him. "I saw them."

The dire warning didn't cause him a moment's concern, though his gaze gleamed with a tiny flicker of pleasure that she sought to offer it. "They will not even know we are here. We are like ghosts, remember?"

They were forced to crawl on their hands and knees until they reached the cave's entrance. Grace loved the way her knees glided through every rock and twig, but wondered why Darius didn't do his instant transfer thingy. They reached the end, and she eased to her feet. The heat and humidity of the Amazon threatened to roast her, and she was no longer so thankful for her sweats. Familiar scents drifted to her nostrils: dewy foliage, orchids, and recent rain.

"How does one protect oneself from a gun?" Darius asked, ushering her beyond a flourishing green bush.

"Kevlar vests. That's what the police use, anyway."

His expression turned pensive. "I would like some of these vests."

"Maybe we can order you some on the Internet. I'll do a search—"

Her body tingled in strange rippling waves, and she gasped. A piece of fruit had sailed through her and smashed into a tree. Laughter drifted to her ears, not human, but amused all the same. Two more missiles sailed through her as Darius whipped around. He launched himself at her, tossing her to the ground. His weight crushed her.

"How have you been spotted, woman?" he demanded.

"Those damn monkeys!" She glared up at him, blaming him for her trials, slowly becoming aware of the perfect fit of their bodies and the warm, seductive scent of him. "You said no one would know we were here."

"Monkeys are responsible?" His lips compressed, and if she weren't mistaken, amusement twinkled in his golden eyes. She paused. Golden again? The only time they'd been golden like this was right after he kissed her. What made them change? "Animals can see what the human eye cannot," he said.

"Are you laughing at me?"

"Perhaps."

"What I want to know is why he didn't throw anything at you."

"My guess is that he knew I would have him for my next meal if he did so."

She liked this side of Darius, playful and teasing. Grace smiled.

His gaze veered to her lips, and heat suddenly seared his eyes. All traces of merriment fled from his expression. Her own smile faded. Memories of the last time he'd lain on top of her licked through her mind. And just like that, she wanted him again.

The knowledge angered her. How could she desire this man?

She must have moved, must have arched her hips, because Darius hissed a torrent of air between his teeth. His muscles were tense, and he was leaning toward her. Closer, closer still.

In one swift motion, he jerked to his feet.

"Up," he commanded, his tone inexorable. "You're wasting time."

Wasting time? Wasting time! Her? Irritated, Grace stood and anchored her hands on her hips. "It's going to be nothing but good times with you. I can tell."

Darius led her around for the next hour. The heat obviously agreed with him. While he looked as refreshed and vibrant as if he'd just stepped from a yoga class, dirt glued itself to her clothes and body. Even her hair was weighted down and wilted. She was a ghost. Wasn't she supposed to stay clean and untouched by the elements?

"I hate this place," she muttered. Already she was tired and thirsty. And cranky. "I need a coconut smoothie."

The man responsible for her distress finally halted. "There are no Argonauts here."

No shit, Sherlock. Yes, definitely cranky. "I'm telling you, they *were* here."

"I believe you," he assured her, as if that had never been in question. "Their footprints are everywhere." He scanned the trees. "Do you know the names of the men who helped you?"

"Yes. Jason and Mitch. And Patrick," she added.

"I need their surnames, too."

"Sorry." She shook her head. "They didn't offer, and at the time I didn't care to ask."

Darius fought a wave of disappointment. He'd hoped to find the men, question them and finally gain at least some of the answers he sought. The sooner he finished this, the sooner he could reclaim Javar's palace—and the sooner his life returned to normal. No more chaos. No more unquenchable desires.

No more Grace.

His lips lifted in a scowl. She was quickly propelling him to the brink of madness. The way she moved, sultry, swaying. The way she spoke, challenging, lilting. The way she watched him with hunger in her eyes—hunger she couldn't quite hide.

She didn't want to want him, but want him she did. Very much.

And he wanted her right back—alarmingly so.

After he'd uttered the binding spell, he'd seen inside her mind and knew she ran from her own desires. Knew her brother, Alex, did the same. They'd watched their father slowly deteriorate, then quickly die. Grace had loved her father for the kind, gentle man he'd been, but watching him fade had been so painful she'd retreated to fantasy, imagining herself anywhere but home. Imagining herself in all kinds of exhilarating situations. A crime fighter of unequalled strength. A lady pirate who sailed the high seas. A siren who lured men to her bed and pleasured them into unconsciousness. The last intrigued him most.

She craved excitement and passion and all the things she'd created in her dreams, but so far life had offered her none of those things. Nothing managed to live up to her expectations. She'd known one disappointing adventure after another...until she stumbled through the mist. Then she'd finally found the exhilaration she had always craved.

How could he consider ending her life, when she was only just now beginning to experience her dreams? The question plagued him because he knew the answer; he simply could not accept it. Though he might want her to live, he would fulfill his oath.

Darius sighed. He was wasting time here, time that he didn't have to spare. His powers were already weakening. He wasn't sure how much longer he had before he weakened completely.

"Let us journey back to your home," he told Grace. He didn't wait for her response, he simply wrapped his fingers around her wrist.

"Wait. I want to head into town and ask around about Alex," she said. "That's why I brought his pic—" Before she could finish her sentence, he pictured her home and those very walls materialized around them.

CHAPTER TWELVE

THE NEW YORK MORNING announced its presence by shooting rays of sunlight through Grace's living room windows. Cars honked outside; the people above her stomped across their apartment, shaking her ceiling.

"You have got to stop popping me in and out of places. I'm this close—" she told Darius, pinching her thumb and finger together "—to having a heart attack. And besides that, I wasn't ready to leave," she snapped. "I wanted you to take me into town so I could show Alex's picture around and ask if anyone had seen him."

"I did not deem it necessary," he said, releasing her. His face was pale and those lines of tension were back.

He did not deem it necessary, she silently mimicked. What about what *she* deemed necessary? Scowling, she padded to the kitchen, placed her gun inside a drawer and poured herself a tall glass of ice water. She drained every drop. Only after she'd consumed three more glasses did she offer Darius a drink.

"Have you anything other than water? Something with flavor?"

"I could make lemonade." Not that he deserved it.

"That will suffice."

She withdrew several lemons from the refrigerator, beat them against the counter to release the most juice, then sliced a hole in the top of each. She squeezed the tangy liquid into a glass and added sugar substitute—she did *not* keep real sugar anywhere near her—and water. She slid the drink across the counter.

Having watched her mix the contents with a leery eye, he lifted the glass and sipped tentatively. She knew the exact moment the sweet-and-sour flavors blended into his taste buds, knew the exact moment he wanted to howl with pleasure. His strong fingers gripped the cup, curling around the glass with surprising gentleness; his eyelids grew heavy, causing his inky lashes to dip over the sensuous planes of his cheekbones.

As he swallowed, his throat moved. A wicked shiver dripped along her spine, and she had the sudden urge to lick him there. *I'm turned on by a man's trachea. How pathetic am I?*

"Surely that is ambrosia," he said. Thankfully his color had returned. He reluctantly set his empty glass on the countertop.

"I don't mind making more if you're—"

"I would like more," he rushed out.

If he reacted like this to lemonade, how would he

react to chocolate? Spontaneous orgasm? Maybe she had a Hershey bar hidden somewhere...

He consumed two more glasses of lemonade in quick succession. He requested a third, but she'd run out of lemons. His disappointment was palpable, but he shrugged it off.

Watching her with heated eyes, he licked the last drop from the cup rim. "You asked me earlier what power my medallion possessed. I will show you now," he said. "First I will need your brother's surname."

"Carlyle. Like mine."

He arched a brow. "Is that common here? To share names?"

"Yes. You didn't share the same name as your family members?"

"No. Why should we have? We are each individuals and our names are our own."

"How do you show your family relationship, then?"

"House affiliation. My family was House of Py." Darius removed his medallion, and as he held it in his open palm, it glowed a brighter, eerier red. "Show me Alex Carlyle," he said to the dragon heads.

Four beams of crimson sprayed from both sets of eyes. They formed a circle in the air, and the beams grew wider by the second. Grace watched with fascination as the air began to crystallize.

"What's happening?" she whispered.

Alex's image appeared in the center of the circle, and all questions were forgotten. Her jaw dropped open in shock. Dirt, sweat and bruises covered her brother from head to toe, and as she took in his appearance, her blood ran cold. He was pallid, his skin so pale she could see the faint tracings of his veins. He wore only a pair of ripped, stained jeans. His eyes were closed, and he huddled on a muddy floor. Tremors raked him. From cold? From fever? Or fear? The room was sparsely furnished with a small bed and a chipped wooden nightstand.

With one hand she covered her mouth and with the other she reached out, hoping to smooth his brow, hoping to reassure him that she was here. Just like in the cave, her fingers drifted through like a mirage. Feeling helpless, she dropped her hands to her sides. "Alex," she said shakily. "Where are you?"

"He cannot hear you," Darius said.

"Alex," she said again, determined to gain his attention in any way necessary. How long since he'd last eaten? What had put those bruises on his skin? What had made him so pale? She bit back a deep moan of distress.

"Do you recognize this place?" Darius asked.

"No." Lips trembling, gaze never straying, she shook her head. "Do you?"

"No," he sighed.

"It's a motel room, I think. Find him," she beseeched, watching in horror as her brother rolled to his side, revealing two bloody puncture wounds on his neck. Vampire? From Atlantis? Had he made it inside? "You said you would."

"I only wish it were that easy, Grace."

At last she switched her attention, flashing Darius an accusing glare. "You found me."

"We were connected through the spell of understanding. I simply followed my own magic. I have had no contact with your brother, nor does anything bind me to him."

Alex's image began to waver just as a woman approached him. She was the most beautiful woman Grace had ever seen. Where Alex was long and lean, the woman was small and delicate with flowing silvery-blond hair. Pixie features, porcelain skin. She crouched beside him and gently shook his shoulders.

"Who is that?" Grace demanded sharply.

Darius narrowed his focus. "That is Teira," he said, an undercurrent of incredulity in his tone. "Javar's wife."

"I don't care whose wife she is, as long as she leaves my brother alone. Is she cruel? Will she hurt him? What's she doing to him?"

Just as quickly as it appeared, the image faded completely.

"Bring them back," Grace commanded.

"The medallion shows me a vision for only a small period of time, and never the same person more than once."

No. *No!* She controlled the urge to stomp her foot, to whimper. To cry. "Take me to Alex."

"I wish that I could, but I do not know the surface."

"You said you found me because we're connected. I can give you one of Alex's belongings. Or a photograph of him." Nearing a point of desperation, she jerked out the photo of Alex from her pocket and wrapped Darius's fingers around the folded edges. "You can connect with this and find him."

"That is not how my powers work, Grace." There was no emotion to him now. He'd reverted to his indifferent, unperturbed self, the part of him she so longed to shatter. Blue eyes hard and cold, he set the photo aside.

A single tear slowly ran down her cheek. "You have to help me." Gripping the fabric of his shirt, she said, "He's sick. I don't know how long he's gone without food or water. I don't know what that woman planned to do to him."

"Teira will not hurt him. She is ever gentle and caring."

"He needs *me*."

"I have given you my word that I will help you find him while I am here. Do not doubt me."

"I don't doubt that you'll help me, Darius," she said brokenly. Hollowly. She stared up at him with watery eyes. "I just wonder if we'll get to him in time."

At that moment, Darius knew she meant Atlantis no harm. Knew she only wanted her brother safe and whole. Her emotions were too raw. Real. He hated himself for it because he could not let that change his purpose. He might loathe the man he'd become, the man he willingly was—a killer and a user—but that changed nothing.

When Grace learned that he was helping her only to destroy Alex, as well as Grace herself...

Tensing, he forced his mind on the matter at hand. Why was Teira with a human? Where were they being held? Their cell was a surface dwelling, yet Alex had been bitten by a vampire—a fact Darius wouldn't tell Grace.

The female dragon's presence added a new complication. Was she prisoner or captor? A loving woman who possessed a sweet nature and giving heart, she would not make a good captor. Yet Javar would never allow his wife to be taken. Unless he were dead.

That Darius once again found himself back to that line of thought unsettled him. He had, perhaps, another day here before he must return, yet he was no closer to answers than he had been when he first arrived. Instead the mystery had sprouted new, twisted limbs.

"The key is the medallion," he said. "I must figure out which human has the most to gain by possessing it."

"Not necessarily a human." With a shuddering sigh, Grace sank onto a stool. "Any of the creatures in Atlantis could use it to sneak inside your home and steal your valuables. For God's sake, you own jewels of every kind and size."

That's exactly what those humans had been doing inside Javar's palace, stealing, using the gods' tools to pry out the jewels. "Atlanteans must only ask and we share. There is no reason to steal."

"There is, too, a reason. Pure greediness. And I know for a fact that the emotion is inherent to all races, gods and humans alike. All of our myths and legends expound upon such things."

Now *he* sighed. "Humans are responsible *this time*." He thought back to the messenger's words and the gun the boy had drawn. "Humans are even now inside my friend's home, wielding guns and the gods only know what other weapons."

"Could the humans be working with this friend?"

"Never." He would not consider the possibility. "Javar loathes humans as I do. He would never aid one."

She averted her gaze from him, shielding her expression. Several seconds ticked until she said, "Do you loathe *all* humans?" A trace of hurt leaked into her voice.

"Not all," he admitted reluctantly. He liked one tiny female more than was wise. A female with silky red curls and softly rounded curves. With lush breasts and high-tipped nipples.

A female he craved in his bed more with every moment that passed.

"Well, then," she said, straightening her back, pretending she had not a care. "We'll concentrate on humans. I'm willing to bet the same humans who are inside that palace are the ones Alex wrote about. The ones who tried to steal his medallion. The ones who *did* steal his book."

"Wrote?" he lashed out, concentrating on that one word. He could not allow any written record of his home. He already had the *Book of Ra-Dracus* to contend with. "You said he *told* you."

"He did. In his journal. He kept a log of his search for the mist. Would you like to read it?"

"Where is it?" he asked sharply.

"I'll show you." She walked from the kitchen, and Darius followed close on her heels. She led him down a small, narrow hallway laden with the calming scent of chamomile. They entered her bedchamber and it took only one glance at the bed for his stomach to tighten. She stopped at the desk and held up a can for his view. "This looks like an ordinary hairspray can, right?"

"Of course," he said, though he had no idea what hairspray was.

"Well, it's not." With quick, precise motions, she untwisted the end and out popped a key. Her lush, pink lips lifted in a half smile, revealing the hint of straight white teeth.

His stomach didn't tighten this time, but reached up and devoured his throat.

How could one woman possess so much beauty?

With a graceful flick of her fingers, she hooked tendrils of hair behind her ears. She bent down and inserted the key underneath the desk. "My father was too sick to hold a job—that's why we moved from South Carolina to New York, so he could be close to Sloan-Kettering. Anyway, to pass the time and make money in the process, he carved and sold furniture. He built this for me a long time ago."

"I am sorry for your loss."

GENA SHOWALTER 203

"Thank you," she said softly. "My dad built one for Alex, too, though his secret compartments are different. I think. We used to get into each other's stuff, which made both of us furious. Alex would read my diary, and I would steal pictures of his friends. So my dad made us each a desk where we could successfully hide our treasures."

The melancholy in her voice remained long after her words faded away. Darius very nearly dropped to his knees and vowed never to hurt her or her brother if only she would smile again. He stayed the impulse, knowing such a promise was impossible to keep.

Inside the secret drawer lay a thin, plain book bound by black leather. As Grace traced her fingertips over the surface, she caught her bottom lip with her teeth, slowly releasing it. She handed the book to him, retaining contact until the last possible second.

He flipped through the pages, frowning at the unfamiliar script. While his spell of understanding gave him complete comprehension of Grace's spoken language, it did not provide him with an understanding of the written. He'd never been concerned with others' opinions of him, but he did not want Grace to perceive any weakness in him. He wanted her to see him as strong and capable, all that a woman could desire.

He handed the journal back to her, saying, "Read it to me. Please."

Thankfully she made no comment, merely

accepted the book and stood. "Let's get comfortable in the living room."

Once there, Grace situated herself on the scarlet couch, and he eased beside her. Perhaps he should have chosen another chair, but he craved physical contact with her and saw no reason to deny himself. Not while he hungered for her scent in his nostrils. Hungered for her touch. Even this, as little as it was.

His thigh brushed hers, and she sucked in a breath and tried to scoot away. Did she think to deny him this minor connection? After everything she'd already allowed? Only hours before, the woman had kissed him as if she couldn't live without the taste of him in her mouth. She had let him suck on her nipples, had let him bury two fingers deep inside of her.

He spread his knees, straightened the wide width of his shoulders, both actions consuming all of her space.

"Do you have to sit so close?" she asked on a ragged breath.

"Yes," was his only reply.

"Want to tell me why?"

"No."

"I don't like it," she insisted, scooting from him for the second time.

He moved closer. "Want to tell me why?" he parroted.

"No," she parroted right back, her expression stubborn.

"Then you may begin reading."

She examined her cuticles and yawned prettily. Only the needy gleam in her eyes gave her away.

"What are you doing?" he asked. "I do not have time to waste. Begin."

"I'm waiting."

He arched his brows. "For?"

"For you to move."

Scowling, Darius stayed where he was for a long while. This was a minor battle of wills, yet he did not want to lose. Did he have any other choice, though? Teeth grinding together, he inched slightly away from her. As he moved, the sweet scent of her lessened and the heat she emanated faded. He wanted to howl.

"That's better." She settled into the cushions and opened the book. Her fingers smoothed over the first page, and a look of sadness filled her expression. She began reading, despair reflected in her tone, as well.

He leaned his head back, locked his hands under his neck and closed his eyes. Her melodious voice floated over him, as gentle as a caress. There was something so peaceful about listening to her, as if her voice, despite its melancholy, was a reflection of joy, laughter and love. As if all three were his for the taking, if only he would reach out and grasp them. But he knew they would never be his. Warriors like him were destined to roam life alone. It was the only way to preserve his sanity.

A cold-blooded killer needed absolute withdrawal.

Much too quickly, Grace closed the journal with

a gentle flip of her wrist and glanced over at him. He worried two fingers over his jaw. "Tell me again where your brother stole the medallion."

"At a charity gala hosted by Argonauts."

Again Argonauts, Darius thought, his determination to speak with them increasing. Alex had stolen it, had almost had it stolen from him, and had been followed.

He frowned as a thought occurred to him. "If you knew someone wanted the necklace," he said to Grace, his voice growing harsher with each word, "why did you even go to Brazil?"

"Did you not hear the last passage? Alex found the hint of danger exciting. And so—" she jutted out her chin in defiance "—did I."

He was furious as he leaned toward her, putting them nose to nose. Their breath mingled, swirling together and becoming a single essence. Exactly what he wanted for their bodies. That quickly he lost his fury in a haze of lust. His dragon's blood roared to life, clamoring for her. Aching for her. Frenzied for her.

"That would-be thief could have found him, could even be the one holding him. Tell me, do you still crave excitement?" he asked softly, menacingly. "Do not think to deny it because I know you do," he added when she opened her mouth to protest. "I sense the need inside you. I sense it pulsing through your veins even now. Such a thing is dangerous for you, but..."

Her throat constricted, and she gulped.

Dismay whirled in the turquoise cauldron of her

eyes, but he also saw hunger, a tempest of desire. She would never be happy with an ordinary life. She needed adventure, needed her deepest fantasies realized, and though it was irrational, he wanted to be the one to give her those things.

His gaze swept to her lips. He found himself closing the rest of the distance, a heartbeat away from possessing her mouth with his own. She jack-knifed to her feet, turning her back toward him, granting him a tantalizing view of her cascading curls.

A lovely view to be sure, but not the one he craved.

"I'm sorry." Grace fingered her lips. Darius hadn't kissed her, had only come within a whisper of her, but still her lips throbbed for him. Of all the things he'd done to her, of all the things he'd made her feel, she feared this the most…this seemingly unquench-able desire she had for him. This need for him, and only him. This consuming ache for his touch that made her forget the only thing she should care about. Her brother.

But…

The more time she spent in Darius's presence, the more she saw past his cold, callous mask and into the heart of a vulnerable man. And that made her want him all the more. That *scared* her all the more. Such intense longing bordered on obsession. No man should have that much power over her. No man should be able to wrap sultry coils around her and consume her every thought.

Most women dreamt of having such a strong, sensual man at their fingertips. A week ago, she would have been in their ranks, thinking there was nothing more a woman could want than a man who looked at her with undeniable hunger, as if there were no other woman who could make him feel that way. Right now, Grace felt too exposed, too vulnerable.

"I'm not ready for this," she said. "Not ready for you. Last night, and even in Atlantis, everything seemed surreal. This…doesn't. This is real and in-your-face and can never be undone. I'm just not ready," she said again. "More than that, the timing is horrible. My first concern has to be my brother's welfare. Not my own…desires."

While she rattled off her list of reasons she shouldn't bed him, Darius's mind formed a list of all the reasons she should. And only one of them mattered. *She's mine,* he thought. His instincts had tried to warn him, had actually screamed it was so when he last kissed her. This undeniable tug had been between them since the beginning, and it wasn't going away. He admitted as much now. He wouldn't forget his oath, but he *would* have this woman. Where she was concerned, he could fight his needs no longer.

He would be doing himself a favor, he rationalized, if he took her and rid himself of this growing curiosity to know what being with her would be like.

He wanted to rise and reach out to clasp her by the

waist. He forced himself to remain in place, hands at his sides. He would take her, yes. But he would take her when it was *she* who was desperate for their loving. Not him. Beads of sweat popped onto his brow and dripped from his temples. He fisted his hands in the soft couch cushions.

Needing a distraction, Darius stood and liberated the journal from between her fingers. She gasped at the sudden loss and spun to glare at him. As she watched, he tossed the little book into a bowl and ignited a fire—with his mouth. He was surprised when the fire quickly dwindled to nothing, and he frowned. The fire should have lasted much longer. His powers must be weaker than he'd realized.

"Fire flew out of your mouth." Grace gaped. "Fire really and truly flew out of your mouth."

"Yes."

"But fire flew out of your mouth."

"I did tell you I was a dragon."

"I just didn't expect fire to fly out of your freaking mouth." Grace struggled to form a proper response. Darius really was a dragon. The concept was laughable—or should have been. All of it should have been laughable. Atlantis, misty portals, the gods. Yet she'd skipped right along, accepting every fantastical experience tossed her way.

But this… She expected her brain to shout *it's too much. I can't accept another implausible happening.* Surprisingly enough, her mind didn't shout. Her mind welcomed.

She toyed with the ends of her hair and expelled

a breath. When she was a little girl, her father had read her a book every night. His favorite had been the story of a long ago prince who rescued a princess from a fierce dragon. Grace had never liked that story. She'd always wanted the dragon to defeat the puny prince so the princess could sail through the clouds on his back. Now a real, live dragon sat in her living room.

"What else can you do?" she asked, her voice raspy.

He merely lifted a brow, a wouldn't-you-like-to-know glint in his eyes.

"Well?" she demanded.

"When you are prepared for the answer, perhaps I'll tell you. Until then..." He shrugged.

"Fine," she huffed. "If you won't tell me about your abilities, at least tell me why you destroyed my brother's journal. I wanted to give it back to him."

"There can be no record of Atlantis." As he spoke, the blue of his eyes swirled and churned with a life of its own, like the very mist he guarded. "I decided to either destroy the book or destroy you. Perhaps I made the wrong choice."

She preferred the other Darius, the honey-eyed Darius. The man who made her blood sing and her deepest fantasies cry for him. The man who twisted her into knots.

"You will obtain the vests now," he told her, crossing his arms over his chest.

Her nose crinkled. "What vests?"

"The ones you promised to buy for me in the cave. The ones that protect against guns."

That's right. She *had* promised him. With a sigh, Grace loped down the hall and into her room. After she booted up the computer—with Darius standing over her the entire time, his hands on either side of her armrests, his chest pressing into her back—she found a site that specialized in guns and other equipment.

"I like this thing," he said. "This computer."

With him so near, she had trouble concentrating. "The vests are two-hundred-and-fifty dollars each," she said, squirming in her seat. Maybe she should turn on the air conditioner. Her skin suddenly felt too tight for her body. "Do you still want to buy one?"

"One? No. I wish to purchase twenty. For now."

"Twenty! Where will you get the money? I doubt you brought any with you."

"I will allow you to pay for them."

Of course he would. "You want extra large, I take it?" Doing this was probably going to place her on the FBI's most-watched list. But Darius wanted the vests, and what Darius wanted, she would acquire for him. They were helping each other, after all.

She placed the order and had to use both of her credit cards. She also requested overnight shipping for double the mailing expense. "They'll arrive in the morning."

"I want to visit the Argonauts," Darius said. "Afterward, we will purchase bullets and you will show me how to use them."

Such a dictator, she thought, and wondered, foolishly, if he'd be that demanding in bed. She stole a glance at the hard angles of his profile. Oh, yes. He'd be demanding and the knowledge made her shiver. With a gulp, she flipped off her computer and swiveled in her chair, dislodging his hands. "Do you think they know more than they told me?"

"Perhaps. Perhaps not."

Which told her nothing. But she had her suspicions. They were not as innocent as they appeared. They couldn't be, and she hated herself for not realizing it sooner. Worry had clouded her mind, she supposed, but that didn't make it easier to take. "If we leave now, we can be there within the hour."

"Not quite yet." He leaned down, replacing his palms on the arms of her chair. Her knees bumped his thighs as his gaze traveled all over her. Burning her. Devouring her in a way that should have been illegal. He saw past her clothes, she suspected breathlessly, and saw the hard pebbles of her nipples. "First," he said, "you will bathe. Quickly," he added.

Blazing red heat stained her cheeks. "Are you saying I—" her mortification was so great she almost couldn't finish her sentence "—stink?"

"You have dirt smudges here." He ran his fingertip over the side of her mouth. "And here." That finger moved to her chin, and his nostrils flared. "While you are beautiful to me as you are, I thought you might wish to wash."

He thought she was beautiful? As she was? Grace nearly melted into her seat. Most men found her a little too plump, a little too red and freckly.

She struggled to form defenses against him, and

reminded herself that she wasn't ready to handle such a dangerous man. "I won't take long." Her legs trembling, she pushed up and raced to the bathroom. She slammed the door shut.

Just in case he entertained any notion of slipping inside, of stripping out of his clothes and getting into the tub with her, of letting the warm, wet water deluge their intertwined, naked bodies, she twisted the lock. She pressed her back against the cool wood, her breathing shallow.

Damn if she didn't pray Darius would burn the lock away.

CHAPTER THIRTEEN

ALEX CARLYLE was hot and cold at the same time.

A single guard shoved him inside his newest prison. A single fucking guard because he was too weak to be any real threat. The drugs his captors were pumping through his system were hell on his body. They kept him compliant, groggy and dependent. Kept him uninterested in escape.

Kept him stupid.

Or maybe his weakness stemmed from low blood supply. Vampires were allowed to suck from his neck anytime they wanted, as long as they didn't kill him. He almost wished they'd finish the job.

For months he'd done nothing but breathe and live Atlantis. He had finally acquired the proof he'd wanted of its existence, but he no longer gave a damn.

He shivered. The room was cold. So cold frost formed every time he breathed. Why, then, did his skin burn? He sank to the hard floor. Another tremor scratched down his spine like long, sharp fingernails.

A woman was shoved into the cell. The only exit slid shut behind her.

Alex closed his eyes, too tired to care. Within moments, small, delicate hands grasped his shoulders and gently shook him. His eyelids flickered open, and he found himself staring up into Teira's beautiful, ethereal face.

"You need me?" she said.

He'd lost his glasses, but he didn't need them to see that her pale brown eyes were alight with concern. She had the longest lashes he'd ever seen, as light as her waist-length hair. She claimed she was a prisoner, just like he was. The two of them had been "escorted" so many places he didn't know where he was anymore.

This newest cell was stripped bare, as if someone had recently scraped everything off the walls. "I'm fine," he lied. "Where are we this time?"

"My home."

Her home. He inwardly sighed. Somewhere in Atlantis, then. *If* she was telling the truth. He didn't know yet if he could believe a word out of the woman's gorgeous mouth.

He didn't know whom he could trust anymore.

Lately he'd been swindled and double-crossed by everyone he encountered. Every member of his team had betrayed him, willingly giving away his location and his purpose for a few hundred dollars. The guide he'd hired to see him safely through the Amazon had been a paid mercenary. Now he had to contend with Teira.

She was beautiful, exquisitely and guilelessly so, but beauty often hid a mountain of lies. And she was too concerned for him, too eager to learn about him. Perhaps she'd been sent to seduce the location of the medallion from him, he thought irritably. Why else lock her in a cell with him? He laughed humorlessly. Why else but to fuck the answer out of him.

Well, the joke was on her. Teira wasn't his type. He preferred women who wore too much makeup, and tight clothes over their even tighter, surgically enhanced bodies. He preferred women who screwed hard and left the same night without a qualm—if they didn't speak to him in the meantime, even better.

Women who looked like Teira terrified him. Instead of makeup and tight clothes, they wore an air of innocence, a marry-me-and-give-me-babies kind of wholesomeness that unnerved him.

He'd spent too many years caring for his sick father, too afraid to leave the house in case he was needed. He stayed as far away from wholesome women as he could. Just the thought of being permanently grounded made him nauseous. His captors should have locked him up with a slutty-looking brunette. *Then* he might have talked.

His jaw clenched. He never should have acquired that damn medallion.

What had Grace done with it? And why the hell had he sent it to her? He hadn't meant to involve her; he simply hadn't realized the extent of the danger until it was too late. He didn't know what he'd do if she were hurt. There were only three people he gave a shit about, and Grace was at the top of the list. His mom and Aunt Sophie claimed a close second and third.

Teira gave him another gentle shake. Her fingers were like ice, and he noticed her teeth were chattering.

"What do you want?" he barked.

She flinched but didn't back away. "You need me?" she asked again. Her soft voice floated over him, as lilting as a spring breeze. Her English wasn't very good, but she'd managed to learn the basics—and quite quickly, too. How convenient.

"I'm fine," he repeated.

"I help warm you."

"I don't need your goddamn help. Go to your side of the cell and leave me alone."

Her innocent features dimmed as she scooted away.

He fought a wave of disappointment. He would never tell her, would never admit it aloud, but he liked her nearness. Dirt might streak the smoothness of her skin, but she still smelled as exotic as a summer storm. The scent comforted him—but scared him, too. She was not his type, but he often found himself gazing at her, yearning to hold her, to touch her.

As if she sensed his inner longings, she moved back to him and smoothed her trembling fingertips over his forehead, down his nose and along his jaw, her touch light. "Why will you not let me help?" she asked.

He sighed, savoring her caress even while he knew he should make her stop. Cameras were probably hidden everywhere, and he didn't want anyone to think he'd finally caved where this woman was concerned.

"Do you have a syringe? Do you have whatever the hell they're giving me?"

"No."

"Then you can't help me."

She began tracing strange symbols over his cheek. An intense concentration settled over her features.

His tremors gradually slowed, and his coldness receded. His muscles relaxed.

"Feel better?" she asked, a trace of weakness to the words.

He managed to give her an indifferent frown and lift his shoulders in a shrug. What symbols had she drawn and what did they mean? And how in God's name had they helped him? He was too stubborn to ask.

"Why you not like me?" she whispered, biting her lower lip.

"I like you just fine." He wouldn't admit that he would have died without her. His captors, the same men who had chased him through the jungle, then plucked him from one location to the other, had been brutal. He'd been beaten, drugged and nearly drained, and shuddered with each memory. Always Teira was there, waiting for him, comforting him. Holding him with her quiet strength and dignity.

"Why do they have you locked in here?" he asked her, wishing immediately that he could snatch the words back. He didn't want to watch her features cloud with deceit as she spun a web of lies. He knew why she was here. Didn't he?

Softly, gently, she lay beside him and wrapped one arm around his waist. The woman craved bodily contact like no one else he'd ever met, as if she'd been denied it most of her life. And he'd be lying if he said her little body didn't feel good curled up next to him.

"They kill my man and all of his army. I try to... what is the word?" Her brow scrunched as she searched her mind.

He gazed deeply into her eyes. They were as devoid of duplicity as always. "Defeat them?"

"Yes," she said. "Defeat them. I try and defeat them."

Whether he believed her story or not, he didn't like the thought of her being tied to another man. And he liked even less that he cared. "I didn't know you were married."

She looked away from him, past him, over his shoulder. Sorrow and grief radiated from her, and when she next spoke, her pain was like a living thing. "The union end too quickly."

He found himself reaching out to her for the first time. He wrapped his fingers around her palm and gave a light squeeze. "Why did they kill him?"

"To control the mist he guarded and steal his wealth. Even here, in this cell, they removed the jewels from the walls. I miss him," she added softly.

To control the mist he guarded... Alex had known she was from Atlantis, though he had failed to realize she was the wife of a Guardian. Or rather, *former* wife. God, he felt stupid. Of course she would be kept alive. She would know things about the mist that no one else knew.

He studied Teira's face with fresh eyes, taking in the elegant slope of her nose and the perfect curve of her pale brows. "How long has your—" Alex couldn't bring himself to say *husband* "—has he been gone?"

"Weeks now. So many weeks." Reaching up, Teira traced the seam of his lips. "You help me escape?"

Escape. How wonderful the word sounded. How terrifying. He'd lost track of time and didn't even know how long he'd been imprisoned. A day? A year? At first, he'd tried numerous times to flee, but he'd always been unsuccessful.

He rolled onto his back, and the action made his bones ache. He groaned. Teira wasted no time tucking her head into the hollow of his neck and placing her leg over his.

"You are lonely like me," she said. "I know you are."

She fit perfectly against him. Too perfectly. As if she'd been made specifically to match his body curve for curve. And he *was* lonely. He stared up at the flat ceiling. What was he going to do with this woman? Was she a heartless bitch who only wanted the medallion and was willing to sell her body to get it? Or was she as innocent as she appeared?

"Tell me about you."

She'd made the same request a thousand times before. It wouldn't hurt to give her *some* information about himself, he decided. Nothing important, just a tidbit or two. He wouldn't mention Grace, of course. He didn't dare. His love for his sister could be used against him, and that he wouldn't allow.

"I'm twenty-nine years old," he told Teira. He placed his hands on her head and sifted his fingers through her hair. Not only did the strands look like pearly moonlight, they felt like it, too. "I've always had a passion for fast cars." And even faster women, but he didn't disclose that part. "I've never been married, and I don't have children. I live in an apartment on the Upper East Side of Manhattan."

"Man-hat-tan," she said, testing the word on her tongue. "Tell me more."

He didn't mention the crime or the pollution but gave her the details he knew she craved. "No matter what time of day or night, crowds of people wander the streets as far as the eye can see. Buildings stretch up to the sky. Shops and bakeries never close. It's a place where every desire can be indulged."

"My people rarely stray to the surface, but your Man-hat-tan sounds like a place we would enjoy."

"Tell me about your home."

Dreamy remembrance clouded her eyes, making the gold darken to chocolate. She snuggled deeper into his side. "We are inside a dragon palace, though you cannot tell by this cell. Outside, the sea flows all around. Flowers of every color bloom. There are many temples of worship," she said, slipping into her native tongue, "but most of us have forgotten them because we ourselves have been forgotten."

"I'm sorry." While he was coming to understand

some of her language, he wasn't close to fluent. "I only understood a little of what you said."

"I say I wish I could show you."

No, she'd said more than that, but he let it go. How wonderful it would be to trek through Atlantis. If he met the inhabitants, studied the homes, wandered the streets and inundated himself with the culture, he could write a book about his experiences. He could—Alex shuddered when he realized he was diving back into his old pattern of thought.

"I wish I had the power to help you understand my language," Teira said. "But my powers are not strong enough to cast such a spell." She paused, traced her fingertips over his jaw. "Who is Grace?"

Horrified, he leapt up and away from her as if she were the devil's handmaiden come to claim him. He swayed as a wave of dizziness hit him, wincing as a sharp pain lanced through his temples. He stumbled to the pitcher of water in the corner and sipped. When he felt more steadied, he glared over at Teira. "Where did you hear that name?"

She was trembling as she sat up and pulled her knees to her chest. "You said while you sleep."

"Don't ever say her name again. Not ever. Understand?"

"I am sorry. I never mean to upset you. I simply—"

The door opened.

Dirt flung in every direction as three men stalked inside. One carried a small table, one a chair and the third a platter of food. Soon a fourth man joined them, cradling a semiautomatic in his hands. He pointed the gun at Alex and grinned, daring him to move. Their arrival meant he'd have his drugs, so he was incapable of fear.

Teira's trembling increased. Every day these same men brought him food, a simple meal of bread, cheese and water. Every day they escorted Teira from the room, leaving him to eat alone. And every day she fought them, scratching and screaming. Alex had always assumed her resistance was an act, that they were taking her away to find out what she'd learned from him that day, but as he looked at her, really looked at her this time, he saw the signs of true terror. Her already pale skin became pallid, revealing the faint trace of veins beneath. Her eyes became impossibly round, and she pressed her lips together—to keep from whimpering?

The table was placed in front of Alex. Hands now free, the guard who'd been holding it strode to Teira and clasped her firmly by the forearm. She didn't protest as he wrenched her to her feet. She merely gazed over at Alex, silently pleading with him to help her.

"Time for you to be by yourself for a while, sweetheart," the man told her.

Whether she worked for or against these people, Alex realized her fear was real. "Leave her alone," he said. He latched on to her other arm, making her the rope in a vicious tug of war.

One of the guards scowled and stalked to him. Something was slammed into Alex's temple. His vision blurred. His knees buckled, and he went down. Hard. Teira cried out, tried to reach him, and Alex watched in growing horror as she was slapped across the face. Her head whipped to the side, and he caught the sight of blood on her lip.

Fury consumed him. Hot, blinding fury, giving him strength where he should have had none. With a roar, he sprang up and tackled Teira's tormentor. All three men flew at him, and he found himself subdued and pinned, helpless once again.

"Alex," Teira cried.

Get up, his mind screamed. *Help her.* As he pushed to his feet, someone grabbed his arm. He experienced a sharp sting as a needle was shoved into his vein. Familiar warmth invaded him, calming, relaxing. The ache in his bones faded. His dry mouth flooded with moisture. When he was released, he sank to the ground, the will to fight completely deserting him.

Teira was dragged away.

He closed his eyes and let his mind float away to nothingness. Footsteps echoed in his ears, tapering to quiet as the rest of the men vacated the room. A new set of footsteps suddenly sounded, these coming closer and closer to him.

"Enjoying the woman, are you?" a man asked, his voice familiar.

Alex fought past the fog webbing his brain and blinked up. Hazel eyes peered down at him, the same hazel eyes that belonged to his boss, Jason Graves. Jason wore an aura of self-importance that was almost palpable. He also wore a dragon medallion around his neck.

Alex's eyes narrowed. He'd never considered the man a friend, but he'd been a dependable employer for the four years he'd worked for him. Betrayal washed over Alex, bitter and biting, as he realized just what this meant.

He'd suspected this, but having actual evidence still managed to shock him. *I never should have stolen the medallion,* he thought again.

"I'm nothing if not hospitable," Jason said. His eyes gleamed bright with smug superiority.

Shards of his fury renewed, sparking past the complacency of the drugs. If only his body had the strength to act. "What are you doing to Teira?" He shuddered at the answer that leapt into his mind, certain now that she wasn't working with anyone, but was merely trying to survive. Just as he was.

"Nothing she doesn't enjoy, I assure you."

If he had a weapon, Alex would have committed murder just then. "Bring her back," he growled. "Now."

"First, you and I are going to have a tête-à-tête."

The extent of his helplessness shone as brightly as a neon sign. He closed his eyes. "What is it exactly that you want from me, Jason?"

"Call me Master," his boss said. "Everyone here does." He claimed the chair that had been set in front of the table and removed the lid from the platter of food.

The scent of spicy meat and fresh fruits wafted in the air, making Alex's mouth water. This wasn't the bread and cheese he'd expected. But then, the meal wasn't for him. How long since he'd last eaten anything that smelled so divine? he wondered. Then he laughed. What did he care? "How about I call you Bastard instead?" he said.

"Do it and I will have you strangled with your own intestines," Jason said easily, almost happily. "Afterward, I'll have the same done to Teira."

"Master it is, then." *Bastard.* Wincing, he pulled himself to a sitting position and crossed his arms over his chest.

Jason swirled his fork in what looked to be pasta and said, "You have been stubborn, Alex, holding out on us."

A prickle of unease worked through him, and he fought to remain expressionless. "What do you mean?"

"Your sister, Grace." Casually Jason bit into his food. He closed his eyes and chewed slowly, savoring the taste. "The picture you have of her on your desk is of a ten-year-old girl."

Alex's unease quickly mutated into terror, and the cold air seeped all the way into his marrow. "So what," he said, striving for nonchalance.

"A voluptuous, very mature Grace was found looking for you in the jungle. She's pretty, your sister." Jason licked creamy white sauce from the fork.

Alex tried to spring up, tried to wrap his hands around Jason's neck. His body refused to cooperate, however, and in midair, he simply collapsed back into a heap on the floor. "Where is she?" he panted. "Did you hurt her? Did you do anything to her?"

"Of course not." Jason's tone actually held an element of affront. "What kind of man do you think I am?"

"You really don't want me to answer that, do you?"
He scrubbed a hand down his face. "Where is she?"

"Don't worry. We let her fly back to New York.
She's safe—for the moment. We left her an e-mail
from you, saying you were okay, and for her sake, I
hope she's content with that."

His jaw clenched. "Leave her the hell alone."

"That depends on you, doesn't it?" Jason placed
his elbows on the table and leaned toward him.
"Where's my medallion, Alex?" he asked, his voice
growing harder, harsher.

"I told your men, I lost it. I don't know where it is."

"I think that's a lie," Jason said smoothly. He held
a pineapple slice between his fingers and sunk his
teeth into it, causing the juices to run down his chin.
He dabbed at the wetness with his napkin, mimick-
ing a proper Southern gentleman—the kind of man
he'd often teased Alex of being.

"What do you want it for, anyway? You already
have a new one."

"I want them all."

"Why? They aren't crafted from gold or silver.
They're crafted from metal filigree. They're a worthless decoration, nothing more."

They both knew he lied.

Jason shrugged. "They offer the wearer power
beyond comprehension, though we haven't yet
learned how to harness that power. In time," he said
with confidence. "In time. They also open every
door in this palace, offering a banquet of riches.
You could have been a part of this… I would have

asked for your help eventually, but you chose to work against me."

"You think you can just blithely steal from these people and walk away unscathed?" He snorted. "They are children of the gods. I, at least, meant only to study them."

"No, you meant to expose them. Did you think that would have done them any good? Did you think the entire world could resist coming here and stealing the overabundance of treasures?" Now Jason was the one to snort. "To answer your question, no, I didn't *think* I could blithely steal from them. I knew I could. Quite easily, too."

Alex shook his head at such blatant arrogance. "I suppose you're going to tell me just how you did it. We can have ourselves a Bad Guy Confession Time."

A hard glint entered Jason's eyes, but his need to brag far surpassed his anger. "Before entering the portal in Florida, I tossed in enough fentanyl gas to put a legion of men to sleep. Then I sent in my troops. Most were killed, but casualties of war are expected. The Guardian of the Mist might have been strong, but he couldn't survive multiple rounds of firepower and he quickly bled out."

"What about his men? The *Book of Ra-Dracus* speaks of each Guardian possessing an army of dragons inside his palace."

"Ah, the *Book of Ra-Dracus*." All arrogance, Jason lifted a jeweled goblet and sipped the contents. "Have I thanked you yet for the book's acquisition? It changed my life."

"You stole it from me," he accused, his eyes narrowed.

"Of course. Just like you stole from me. The irony is beautiful, isn't it?" Smiling smugly, Jason added, "You made the mistake of typing your notes into your computer. I keep tabs on all of my employees."

"You hack into their personal lives, you mean."

Jason shrugged. "When I realized exactly what you possessed, I knew I had to have it. So I paid someone to 'acquire' it for me."

"I stole the medallion from you, yes, but I always intended to give it back. I didn't think you even knew what it was."

"Oh, I knew." A soft rumble of laughter escaped. "I'm slowly emptying this palace of every jewel, every piece of gold, every fine fabric and selling them on the surface. How else do you think I afforded those new buildings? My designer clothes?" He paused, tilted his chin. "And I'll do the same to the other dragon palace. But we digress. How did we kill the dragon army? The same way we found them. *Ra-Dracus*. We learned they are weakened by cold and bullets. Quick. Simple."

"You're a monster," Alex whispered, horrified by what Jason had done—and all he would do.

"A monster? Hardly. Those that dwell in Atlantis are the monsters. In fact, let me tell you a little about Teira, the sweet Teira you so wish to protect. She's a dragon. A changeling." He studied Alex's waning color and nodded with satisfaction. "I see you know what I am talking about."

"I read *Ra-Dracus* in its entirety."

"Then you know what happens when you infuriate a dragon? It transforms into a beast. A killer."

"If Teira is a dragon, why hasn't she changed? Why hasn't she freed herself?" He paused. "Why hasn't she killed *you?*"

"She has seen what our guns did to her people, and she fears us. Fear will keep the fiercest of creatures submissive."

"Or maybe that's why you keep it so cold in here. To keep her weak because *you* are afraid of her."

Eyes narrowed, Jason said, "Dragons can go days, weeks without food. Then, suddenly, an intense craving comes over them. Do you know what they eat when this craving comes upon them, Alex?"

He swallowed. He didn't know, but he could guess.

"They eat whatever is in sight," Jason answered, leaning back in his chair. "And do you know what Teira will crave when the hunger hits her? You, Alex. You. She won't have to change to dragon form. She'll just start biting."

A wave of dizziness hit him as he shook his head in denial. "She wouldn't hurt me." He didn't know when he'd started to think of Teira as his ally. He didn't know when he'd lost his animosity toward her. He only knew that hers was the only kindness he'd known these last weeks.

"You sound so confident. So stupid." Jason laughed. "I know the nature of the beast, and I know beyond a doubt that when the time comes, she will feast on your body because you will be the only food in sight. She may not want to, she may hate herself for it, but she will do it."

"Why are you doing this? Why go to all this trouble? Kill me already and get it over with."

"Tell me where the medallion is, and I'll let you go. We'll forget this ever happened."

Liar, he almost shouted. Unless Jason meant to let him go with his head detached from his body.

Lethargy began to weave through the dizziness, and he closed his eyes. "I don't know where it is," he said. His voice sounded far away, lost.

"Need I remind you that I'm not above using your mother? Your aunt? Your sister? Patrick, one of the men who found Grace, would like nothing more than to spread her legs before he kills her."

Alex couldn't manage to open his lids; they were simply too heavy. He said weakly, "If anyone touches a single member of my family, I will—"

"You will what?" Jason said mockingly.

He didn't respond. There was no threat great enough...and there was nothing he could actually do. Not here, not now, and not while the drugs crawled through his system. Not while his body suffered from blood loss. Sleep, he just wanted to sleep.

"We've searched your home, Grace's home and even your mother's home. No one's been hurt yet. That can all change in an instant, Alex. I'm running out of patience." Jason pushed to his feet and walked around the table. He knelt in front of Alex. He gripped his hair and forced his head back, forced him to stare up into his eyes. "Do you understand?"

"Yes," he whispered hoarsely.

"You're pathetic."

His hair was released, but he didn't have the neck strength to keep his head from slamming into the ground. He rolled onto his side and knew nothing more.

How long passed before the sweet fragrance of seawater invaded his senses, he couldn't fathom a guess. But when he opened his eyes, Teira was curled beside him, sleeping peacefully. Instinctively he jerked away as Jason's words flitted through his mind. *She won't need to change into dragon form, she'll just start biting.*

Teira's pale lashes fluttered open, and the corners of her lips gifted him with a sleepy smile—a smile that did odd things to his stomach.

She studied his expression, and her smile slowly faded. "What wrong?"

As he studied her in return, he lost his trepidation. A bruise marred her cheek, barely visible under the dirt covering her. "Nothing's wrong," he said, his throat scratchy. Still a bit groggy, he reached out and gently caressed the discoloration.

"You look in pain," she said.

"How long did I sleep?" he asked.

She shrugged.

His fingers moved from her cheek and cupped her jaw. "What did they do to you?"

"They not hurt me," she assured him. "I think they fear I hurt them."

He chuckled, a low rumble that reverberated in his chest. She looked so delicate, it was hard to imagine her as a fearsome dragon.

"How you feel?" Concern glinted in her golden eyes. She placed her hand over his heartbeat.

"Better." Much better now that she was here. But the shakes would come again, he knew, and so would the need. "Teira." He sighed. "I'm sorry for how I've treated you." Born to a staunchly Southern father, he was ashamed of his behavior toward her. He might live in New York, but like every gentleman, he still opened car doors, still paid for meals and still called women when he said he would. Not that the ones he dated expected it. "I thought you worked for them, but that's no excuse."

Her gaze skittered shyly away from him. "I like being with you."

Her confession pleased him, warmed him as surely as a winter coat. She wasn't his type, but he was attracted to her all the same. A powerful attraction he couldn't hide anymore. Didn't *want* to hide anymore. "I like being with you, too," he admitted. He liked her more than he should.

Leaning up, hesitant, she placed a soft kiss on his lips. He knew she meant it as a chaste peck, a swift kiss of solace, but he pried her lips open with his own and swept his tongue deep. At first, she stiffened. But when she relaxed, she went wild in his arms. She came alive, plunging her tongue into his mouth, moaning her demands, fisting her hands in his hair and fueling his own response.

The air around them sizzled and that sizzle simmered in his blood. Her body pressed to his, her lithe curves a perfect fit. He'd gladly sprint to his death if only to die with her taste in his mouth. He reveled in her flavor, sweet and guileless, like the purest ocean, and unlike any female he'd ever tasted.

With a groan, he gripped her by the waist, clenching the fabric of her sheer gown in his hands. He settled her on top of him. He didn't care if cameras watched them. He didn't care that she was wrong for him. His need for her was too great. He deepened the kiss, exploring more of her mouth, running his tongue over her teeth. He allowed his fingers to trace a path down her spine, allowed them to cup her bottom and anchor her snugly against his growing erection.

She gasped his name, and the moment she did, she seemed to snap out of her haste. She tore her face from him. Their gazes locked, all hot and needy; their ragged exhalations blended. He fought the urge to tug her back down.

"Alex?" she said on a fragile catch of breath.

His hands shook as he smoothed pale strands of hair out of her face. "Yes, Teira." God, yes. His voice sounded slow and slurred, yet it had nothing to do with drugs and everything to do with the woman in his arms. His need for her surpassed any he'd ever known.

She caught her bottom lip between her teeth, and he watched as its plumpness tugged free. His shaft jerked in response. Then she leaned down, placing her lips next to his ear. "I can take us to freedom."

He paused, absorbing her words. "How?" he whispered fiercely, his arms tightening around her.

The corners of her lips turned up in a wry grin. "I stole a medallion."

Alex's smile matched hers. He laughed. They just might be able to escape. Which meant he could feed this woman real food—then spend the next few days with her in bed.

CHAPTER FOURTEEN

DARIUS GAZED at the sights around him.

Buildings towered as far as the eye could see, stretching toward the skyline—a skyline that was wide and open, cloudy, not filled with crystal and water. Colors, so many colors. They glowed from signs; they blurred together as masses of people strode past him. Even the sun shone brightly of yellow, orange and gold. What struck him most of all, however, was the multitude of scents that intermingled and cloyed the air.

The overload to his senses was strangely welcoming.

This place did not offer the lush, green foliage of his home, yet New York was beguiling and lovely in its own right. A place that called out to the beast within him—just as Grace did.

When this was over, he would— No, he could not think that way. He could not allow himself to envision Grace in his future. He must finish this.

Some of his men were surrounding Javar's palace, preventing the humans from spreading their violence further. Still…his fists clenched. The fact that they lived offended him.

And he did not like to be offended.

Beside him, Grace skirted around a table over-flowing with photos. "We'll be there soon," she said, glancing up at him. "Are you okay? You look pale."

She had changed into new clothing after her bath. *She* looked edible. Pale blue pants clung to her legs and a sea-green shirt molded itself to her breasts. She was like an ocean wave, utterly captivating, magical. He could have drowned in her and died happy. "Do not concern yourself with me."

"You could whisk us to Argonauts and save us the walk," she said. "I'm anxious to question them again."

Darius, too, was anxious to question them, but he couldn't whisk about in this city. To do so, he had to visualize his target. He knew nothing of this area, he thought, letting his gaze scan. A trickle of sweat dripped into his eyes, and he wiped it away.

The sun continued to beat down upon him, grow-ing hotter with every step he took. Usually his body embraced heat. Now he fought a deepening lassitude. He stumbled when his foot caught on a rock. One corner of his lips lifted in a scowl as he steadied himself. He despised frailty of any kind, especially his own.

"You're not okay," Grace said, her concern more concentrated. She clasped his arm and tried to pull him aside.

He shook off her hold and kept walking in the direc-tion she'd given him earlier. A woman's concern was not something he knew how to deal with. *This* woman's concern was something he *couldn't* deal with.

I'm going to bed and kill you before I leave, he almost shouted. *Don't waste what's left of your life caring for me.*

Scowl solidifying, he stepped out onto the street. He wanted his peaceful, emotionless existence back. No more of this I-want-her I-can't-hurt-her nonsense.

No more!

Pain suddenly flashed through his head. A pain more intense than anything he'd ever experienced. He doubled over with it, cursing the gods all the while.

"Darius!" Grace shouted, grabbing him by the arm and jerking him toward her. "Look out."

A honk sounded. A whiz. Cars swerved out of the way.

Fear halted Grace's heartbeat as a taxi nearly clipped Darius's side. The organ kicked back into gear only when she had ushered him to the safety of the sidewalk. Along the way, she accidentally bumped into a young woman headed in the opposite direction. "I'm sorry," she said, jumping out of the way to avoid the coffee spilling from the girl's cup.

"Watch where you're going," the girl fumed, never actually slowing.

"Darius, talk to me. Tell me what's wrong." Too afraid to release him, she clenched his hand and faced him. "We're not moving from this spot until you do."

"My time here is running out," he said.

She studied him. His sculpted features were taut, his lips tight, and the fine lines around his eyes strained. "You've said that before. What happens if you stay too long?"

He shrugged. One minute ticked into another, but he didn't move. Didn't speak. Didn't acknowledge her again in any other way. He simply watched as men, women and children continued to skip past them, some talking and laughing. Some arguing.

Maybe he thought she would use the knowledge against him. She didn't know, but was determined to help him. "Look at me, Darius. Please look at me."

His gaze descended gradually, falling from the building tops, to the neon signs, and finally to her. When their gazes connected, her jaw dropped slightly. As she looked at him, she saw many things. Heart wrenching things. She saw pain in his eyes, as well as traces of guilt and sadness. And, beneath it all, was the slightest glimmer of…hopelessness?

"When we returned from the cave," she said, "you were weak and pale, but after you drank the lemonade you felt better. If you'll wait here, I'll buy you something to eat."

The guilt in his eyes increased, and she wondered at its origin. But he nodded slowly, and her concern for him overrode everything else. "I will wait," he said.

She raced inside the bakery. Fresh ground coffee beans, with a hint of vanilla, and a mouthwatering array of muffins fragranced the air. She claimed a place in line. When her turn arrived, she ordered a bottled water and raisin granola bar for herself. For Darius, she ordered a sinfully rich chocolate éclair and espresso.

With sack and beverages in hand, she rejoined Darius. He hadn't moved from the spot where she'd left him, and he was still too pale.

"Here," she said, handing him the éclair and coffee. Her gaze lingered lovingly on the chocolate. How long since she'd had such a treat? Too long. She and Alex used to spend their allowance on box after box of éclairs. They'd eat as many as their stomachs could hold, and sometimes more.

She blinked away the memory, her determination to find him growing.

"Come on," she said to Darius. "We'll walk and eat at the same time."

As they trudged into motion, Darius sipped at his drink. Some of his color returned, and his steps became more fluid. Men gave them a wide berth, and women gave them, or rather *Darius,* a second—and sometimes third—glance. Grace knew those women were wondering if he looked this savage simply strolling down the street, how savage would he be making love? In his tight black shirt and tight black pants, the man reeked of sexual pleasure.

Darius pinched the éclair between his fingers, studying the sumptuous pastry from every angle. She watched him while she chewed her tasteless granola bar. "Just eat it," she said.

"It looks like creamy mud."

"If that's your attitude, you deserve to eat my granola." Mouth watering, she slapped the bar in his hand and confiscated the éclair.

"Give that back," he said.

"Over my dead body."

"I am hungry."

"Well, so am I."

She was just about to place the chocolate reverently on her tongue, was just about to let the Bavarian cream slide right into her mouth, when Darius ripped the dessert from her hands.

"That is mine," he said and handed her back her granola bar.

Ready to pounce on him, she growled low in her throat.

His lips twitched. "Why did you not buy yourself one of these if you want it so badly?"

"Because— Just because!" Grace chugged down her water, letting the coldness of the liquid bring her back to her senses. *I'm a rational being,* she reminded herself, *and I don't need the extra fat grams. Besides, what does one dessert matter in light of all that has happened lately?*

"Do all the women on the surface refuse to buy themselves the food they want to eat?" Darius asked.

She recapped the lid on the water bottle. "I'm not talking to you right now. You've tackled me to the ground, you bound me to your side, and...and you cast some sort of magic lust spell on me." Once she said the words, Grace blinked in astonishment. Of course! A magic lust spell explained her seemingly unquenchable desire for him, as well as the fact that she often found herself thinking of him when she should be thinking of ways to find her brother.

Slowly his lips inched into a true smile of amusement. The first he'd given her. There was a hint of possessiveness in that smile, too. His eyes darkened to gold. "You lust for me?"

"No, I do not," she ground out, her cheeks scalding hot. "I suspect you're capable of such a despicable deed, that's all."

His nostrils flared in a way that proclaimed he knew, *knew,* exactly how she felt about him—and knew the lust was entirely her own. "If we did not have so much to do this day, I would take you back to your home, sweet Grace, and explore this magic lust spell. Very, very thoroughly."

While she floundered for some type of rejoinder, he at last bit into his food. He stilled. Utterly and completely stilled. Chewed slowly. Closed his eyes. Opened his eyes, revealing a joy tantamount to orgasm. Chewed some more. Swallowed. "This is—this is—"

"I know," she grumbled. She finished off her granola. "It's not mud."

The taste was amazing, Darius thought, and helped restore more of his vigor. What had Grace called this culinary treasure? An ay-klare. The delectable morsel wasn't quite as flavorful as Grace herself, but close. Were he to slather her body with it and lick away every trace, he might find release before he actually entered her.

For so long he'd tasted nothing, and now he tasted everything. He knew Grace was responsible, that she was the catalyst. He just didn't know how. Or why. And he was no closer to the answer than he had been before. But he didn't care. He reveled in these new experiences. When she was dead—was gone, he corrected, not liking her name associated with death—he wondered if he would ever taste again. Or if he'd want to. Without Grace…

He took another bite of the ay-klare and noticed Grace eyeing his mouth with longing in her turquoise gaze. His stomach tightened. Did she crave *him?* Or the food he ate? Most likely the food, he mused, and he bit back a self-deprecating chuckle. She'd very nearly bitten off his hand when he'd snatched the dessert from her, reminding him of a female dragon who'd gone far too long without food.

He waved the remaining piece under her nose, and her eyelids became heavy and sultry. "Would you like to share this with me?" he asked.

She moaned as if he'd just offered to make her dreams come true. Dreams that were forbidden, coveted. Dreams she couldn't acknowledge but craved with every ounce of her being.

"No," she said, that single word sounding raw, like it had been ripped from her throat.

She obviously wished to partake, and quite desperately, so why did she think to deny herself? No matter, he thought in the next instant. Before she could pull away, he placed the food at her lips. "Open," he commanded.

Automatically she obeyed. Then she gasped. Bit. Savored. As she chewed, she made noises of pleasure. Breathy noises he'd only heard from women in his bed. His blood heated, rushing from his head and into his shaft. Gods, he wanted this woman. His responses to her were coming more quickly now. A bit more intently, too. Where she was concerned, he was all beast. Primitive and un-apologetically barbaric. One moment he wanted her slow and easy, tender. The next he wanted her rough, hard. Now.

He needed to sate himself on her. Soon.

Her fingers curled around his hand, holding the ay-klare in place. "Oh, my God," she said, eyes closed. "That is so good."

At the first touch of her fingers, white-hot heat speared him. He jerked away from her, then found himself reaching out again, reaching to take her by the base of her neck and yank her to him. Reaching out to kiss her, hard and deep and wet. He dropped his hands at his sides. Teeth grinding together, he in-creased his speed.

He had to remain focused where this woman was concerned. The time for making her desire him would come after he'd learned all that he could from her and the other humans. Damn this!

"Slow down," she huffed after a few minutes.

He tossed her a glance over his shoulder and noticed a dark smudge marring the edge of her lip. Before he could stop himself, he extended his arm and swiped the smudge away with his fingertip. He

kept the contact light, quick. If he lingered, if he pro-
longed the contact, he would strip her. Penetrate her.
He was near his breaking point already.

He turned his face from her so she wouldn't see
him lick the morsel he'd swiped from her off his
finger.

"Slow down," she said again. As she dictated directions, she had to pump her arms and jog to keep up
with him. "Will you slow down already? I've had
enough exercise these last few days to last me a
lifetime."

"You may rest when we have completed our
mission."

"I'm not one of your men. And just so you know,
the outcome of this is just as important to me as it is
to you—if not more so—but I'll be no good to
anyone if I collapse."

He slowed.

"Thank you," she said. "I didn't even move that
quickly when I thought I was being followed yesterday."

Darius ground to a halt, causing the couple behind
him to slam into his back. He remained in place,
absorbing the impact without moving an inch. With
muttered curses, the glaring pair scurried around
him.

"You were followed?" Darius demanded, glaring.
"By whom? Man or woman? Were you hurt?"

When Grace realized he was no longer beside her,
that she'd actually passed him, she had to stop and
backtrack, hopping over a piece of chewed gum,

then scurrying around a vender selling pirated DVDs until she reached his side. "I'm not sure," she said. "A man, I think, though I never saw him. And no, he didn't hurt me."

"Then he might be allowed to live another day."

Oh, my, Grace thought, breathless again for a reason that had nothing to do with exercise. Sunlight couched Darius's features, giving his cheekbones and nose a harsh sort of radiance. When he turned on the intensity like this, going all commando, her belly did strange things. Her *mind* did strange things. Like try to convince her to throw herself in his arms, sweep her tongue into his mouth, and rub herself against him, all over him, and forget about the rest of the world.

"I will hold sentry at your side," he said, his gaze already scanning the area, searching. "If this man comes near you today, I will eliminate him. Worry not."

She nodded, fighting an involuntary shiver. Despite everything, or maybe because of it, she knew Darius would keep her safe. As they jolted back into motion, he continually watched the world around him, taking in every detail and missing nothing. Like the guard he'd promised to be, he remained on alert.

If they were being followed, he would know—and she pitied whoever it was.

CHAPTER FIFTEEN

ONLY TWO MINUTES passed before Darius dragged her into a nearby souvenir shop, shoving people aside in his haste to enter.

"I'm so sorry, ma'am," Grace said. "You, too, sir." To Darius, she demanded quietly, "What are you doing?"

The fierce gleam in his ice-blue eyes made her swallow a lump of apprehension. "You were right," he said. "You were being followed." He glanced over his shoulder. "You still are."

"What!" she gasped, just as he pinned her against a rack of T-shirts. She'd felt no menacing presence today, felt no watchful eyes on her back.

"I would have noticed sooner," he said wryly, keeping his gaze trained on the store window, "but my mind was not where it should have been."

"What should we do? Who is it?"

"A human male. Short. He's wearing some type of coat, yet the day is warm."

Grace tried to peek over Darius's shoulder, but it proved too broad and too high. "Can he see us?"

"No, but he's waiting outside this shop."

"Let's go out the back. He'll never know, and we can—"

"No." Darius skimmed his hands inside his pockets, gave a flick of his wrists, and plucked out two daggers. The thickness of his hands and forearms kept the blades concealed from the public, but *she* knew they were there. He gripped each jeweled weapon tightly. "I wish to have a...conversation with the man."

Stunned, horrified, she only managed a choked gasp in response.

Good Lord. There might be a bloodbath this day.

"You can't kill anyone," she whispered fiercely. Her gaze darted around wildly. Tourists were staring at them like they were the morning's entertainment. "Please," she added more quietly, "put the knives away before someone notices them."

"The knives stay," he said, his voice cold, unfeeling.

"You don't understand. This—"

"No, Grace." He pinned her with a glare. "*You* don't understand. Purchase something from this store. Anything. Now."

Too nervous to care what she bought, Grace shakily lifted a plastic replica of the Empire State Building. After she paid for it, she gripped the bag and walked with Darius to the door. Her stomach had yet to settle.

"Good choice," he said, motioning to the small building. "Use the tip as a weapon if you must. Jab his eyes."

Jab his eyes? Grace gulped. *I should have bought a snow globe.* She didn't mind using Mace; that was a spray, for God's sake. But using a model of the Empire State Building, the centerpiece of Manhattan, to blind a human being…

I'm just a flight attendant on extended leave, she thought dazedly. *I do not jab people.*

Darius must have sensed her unease because he stopped just before they stepped outside. Facing her, he said, "I would leave you here if I could, but the binding spell does not permit it."

"Having a *conversation* with this person really isn't necessary." Even to her own ears, she sounded timid, and she winced. She just didn't want Darius injured or in trouble with the law. "I've seen enough movies and read enough books to know that sometimes the safest course of action is to retreat."

"And sometimes the safest course of action is the wrong one."

"When I asked you to help me find Alex, I never meant to place you in danger."

His features softened at her admission, but that flash of guilt was back. "This man might have information about your brother. He could be the one who tried to take the medallion, the one who locked him away. Do you really want to let him go?"

"No," she said quietly. Then more firmly, "No."

"I will be safe. And so will you."

"Let's use violence as a last resort, though. Okay?"

A long, protracted silence enveloped them. "As you

wish," he said reluctantly. "In return for that concession, I want you to stay behind me. And do not speak again until I give you permission. You will distract me otherwise."

Resisting the urge to link her fingers through his, she followed him into the sunlight. A warm breeze greeted them as they began stalking forward. At first she thought Darius meant to lead their tail to a private alley, but her warrior didn't even try to pretend ignorance. He approached the man clad in a brown trench coat who was standing in front of a store window pretending to look inside. At maternity dresses? Puh-lease.

Watching their reflections, the man realized Darius meant to grab him. He stiffened, gasped and jolted into motion, running from them as fast as his booted feet could carry him.

"Run, Grace," Darius called over his shoulder, as he, too, started running.

An invisible force wrenched her behind Darius, forcing her body into action. Her feet barely touched the ground as she flew, literally flew, after him. Damn this binding spell!

Darius followed the man through traffic lights and around cars, past people and over commerce tables. Irritated grunts and surprised screams echoed in her ears, blending with the sound of her own panting. Was that a police siren? Air burned her lungs. She clutched the plastic Empire State Building as they ran on and on.

If this kept up, she just might be a luscious size six by the end of the month.

When Darius finally came within arm's reach, he grabbed his target by the neck, quickly cutting off any screams of protest. Using only one hand, he lifted the man up and carried him into a nearby alley. There, he dropped him, watching the flailing man fall onto his butt and scramble to the wall. Darius crossed his arms over his chest, daring him to make a move.

Behind them, Grace huffed and puffed to a standstill, then hunched over, gasping for breath. If she survived the day, she was going to treat herself and Alex to a triple dip hot fudge sundae. Or perhaps a banana split. Or maybe fresh doughnuts dripping with chocolate glaze. Maybe all three. She straightened and saw several men huddled against the brownstone wall. Their clothes were threadbare, and their faces dirty and scared. Did they think they would have to face Darius next?

Forcing a smile, Grace handed one of the men her Empire State Building—she was *not* jabbing anyone today—and reached into her wallet. She withdrew several bills. At the sight of cash, the alley men lost all interest in Darius.

"For you," she said, paying them to go away and keep this "their little secret." *I'm aiding and abetting a criminal,* she thought, an unexpected wave of excitement crashing inside her.

Excitement? No, surely not. Skiing in Aspen hadn't excited her. Paragliding in Mexico hadn't excited her. Most likely what she felt so intently was fear. Any second she expected the police to show up and haul her and Darius away.

"I'll scream."

The threat came as the man pushed to his feet.

Both of Darius's brows winged up. A sheen of sweat glistened on his neck and face, but his expression did not portray a hint of weakness. "Are you a woman, then?" he said. "First you hide in the shadows, and when you are caught, you scream?"

"You lay a single hand on me, the cops will be all over you."

Darius grabbed him by the shoulders, angling his wrists in a crisscross and pressing his knives subtly into the man's carotid artery. Not enough to break the skin, but enough to sting.

That's when Grace received her first good look at the man. Shock held her frozen for a long while. "Patrick?" she said when she finally found her voice. This man worked with her brother; he'd even escorted her to the boat, and had engaged her in several conversations about her family afterward. "What's going on? Why were you following me?"

Silence.

"Answer her questions," Darius demanded. When Patrick still refused to speak, Darius increased the pressure of the blades, making small pricks and drawing blood.

"You won't kill me," he said smugly.

"You're right. I won't kill you. Not with blades, at least." Darius dropped his weapons and wrapped his hands around the man's neck. "You would die too quickly."

"I—I wasn't following her. I swear," Patrick sputtered, his face slowly fading from pink, to white, to blue. He kicked and clawed, losing his smugness with his need for air.

Eyes wide, she glanced from Darius to Patrick, from Patrick to Darius. Intimidation was a good tactic for getting what they wanted, but she knew Darius wasn't trying to intimidate. He really would kill Patrick without a single qualm.

"You are lying, and I do not like liars," Darius said, his voice so bored he could have been commenting on the mating habits of flies. But then his eyes slitted and his voice deepened, no longer dripping with boredom, but with rage. "I recognize you. You are the one who touched Grace while she was sleeping."

Patrick's eyes nearly bugged out of his head. "No, no," he gasped, struggling to loosen Darius's grip. "I didn't."

"I watched you do it," he said, his teeth bared.

Were those fangs? She shivered as she stared at the long, sharp incisors. Then their words sank into her brain. "He touched me?" she gasped, hands anchoring on her hips. To Patrick, she ground out, "Which part of me?"

"Your cheek," Darius told her. "But he wanted to do more. Would have, if his friend hadn't stopped him."

Her jaw gnashed in fury.

"You couldn't have watched me," Patrick said to Darius. "You weren't on the boat."

No, he hadn't been on the boat, but then, Darius hadn't needed to be. He'd used his medallion on her like he'd done to Alex, she realized, not liking that he'd seen her and she hadn't known.

Patrick made a gargled sound, and his battle for freedom intensified. His legs flailed, and his hands slashed.

"Were we in my home," Darius said, "I would have your hands removed for such an offense."

"I didn't hurt her," Patrick squeaked. "You know I didn't hurt her."

"Wrong again," Darius said. A flash of green scales pulsed over his skin. "You touched my woman. Mine. For that alone I want to kill you."

Grace's heart stopped. Literally stopped, suspended in her chest. Which should she react to first? The scales or the "she is my woman" statement? Neither, she decided. Only Alex mattered right now. Not her shock at the fact that there were actually dragon scales under Darius's skin, and certainly not her unwanted joy at his words.

Tamping down her emotions, she forced her attention to Patrick. His lips were moving, but no sound emerged. "I think he's trying to say something, Darius," she said.

Several seconds passed before Darius loosened his hold. "Have you something to say?"

"I—" Patrick sucked in a deep breath. "Just need—" deep breath "—a moment."

"You're supposed to be looking for my brother," Grace told him. "Why aren't you in Brazil?"

"Alex might already be dead. We found evidence to suggest it right after you left. I'm sorry."

Had Darius not shown Grace proof that Alex lived, she would have sunk to her knees and sobbed. Of all the things to say, of all the things to feign remorse about, that was the cruelest. She didn't ask what evidence; she didn't even ask why no one had given her such news before now. She didn't want to hear more upsetting lies.

Her eyes narrowed. "You may kill him, Darius."

Darius flicked her a startled glance, staring at her lips as if he couldn't quite believe what they'd proclaimed. He grinned slowly, then turned that grin to Patrick.

"What the woman wants," he said, "I give her."

Both of Patrick's palms pushed at Darius's chest, but the action had no effect. "I can't tell you anything. I'll lose everything, damn it. Everything!"

"So you would rather lose your life?"

Darius increased the pressure. Patrick gurgled, his mouth opening and closing as he tried to suck in air. Grace snapped out of her murderous inclinations. Thinking about a death and actually witnessing it were two totally different things.

Not knowing what else to do, she laid her hand on Darius's arm. "Perhaps I spoke too hastily," she said. "Let's give him one more chance."

Darius glanced at her hand, then brought his gaze to her face, never releasing Patrick. The blue in Darius's eyes had faded substantially, making them appear almost completely white.

"Let him go. Please." Her hand inched upward, and she stroked her fingers over his cheek. "For me."

She didn't know why she'd added those last words and didn't expect them to work. Yet color began to return to Darius's eyes, not ice-blue but gorgeous golden-brown. The color she was coming to love.

"Please," she said again.

He released Patrick in the next instant. The gasping man collapsed on the dirty concrete, wheezing as he tried to fill his lungs. Red handprints encircled his neck, changing to a blue-black as she watched. She and Darius waited side by side, silent, as Patrick breathed life back into his body.

"Why were you following Grace?" Darius demanded. "I will not give you another chance to answer, so consider your words carefully."

Patrick closed his eyes and leaned his shoulders into the wall. His fingers massaged at his throat. "The medallion," he said, his voice hoarse, broken. "I followed her for the medallion."

"Why?" Every muscle Darius possessed stiffened. "What did you hope to do with it?"

"My boss…he wants your jewels," Patrick choked out. "That's all."

Darius stiffened. "How do you know what I am?"

"You're like the others. The ones we…" His words trailed off. "I was only to keep track of Grace's whereabouts, to record where she went and who she talked to. I wasn't to harm her in any way. I swear."

"Give us a name," she said sharply, though she had already guessed the answer.

His shoulders slumped, and he laughed, a humorless, I-can't-believe-this-is-happening rasp. "I'll tell you, but you know what? You'd better be prepared to wade nose-deep in shit because that's what he's going to throw at you. He's the greediest son of a bitch I've ever met, and he'll do anything, *anything* to get what he wants."

"His name," she insisted.

"Jason Graves." He paused, adding gruffly, "Alex's boss. The owner of Argonauts."

A cold shiver of dread attacked Grace. Argonauts. Jason. Bits of information began to piece together in her mind. Trembling inside, Grace bent down until she and Patrick were eye-to-eye. She cupped his chin with shaky hands and forced him to face her, to stare her directly in the eyes. "Is Jason Graves holding Alex captive?"

Patrick nodded reluctantly.

"Where?" The word lashed from her. "Here in the States? Brazil?"

"Different places. Never the same place for long."

"Was he in Brazil while I was there? Is that why you guys were so eager to send me home?" Why hadn't they hurt her? Why hadn't they threatened Alex with her life? There had to be a reason.

"We didn't want you involved or stumbling on company business. You were to go home and sing our praises for doing all we could to find your brother. Other than that, I'm as clueless as you as to where he is," he added. "I'm told on a need to know basis, and I don't need to know that."

"How long has he been a prisoner?"

"A few weeks." Patrick wheezed, then coughed.

"You were supposed to find the e-mail we sent you and stop searching. Why the hell didn't you stop searching?"

His question was rhetorical, so she didn't bother with a response. The postcard she'd gotten from Alex had been sent a week ago. He must have escaped, sent it, then was recaptured. Her poor brother! "What does Jason plan to do with him? Kill him? Release him later?"

"Who knows?" he said, but the truth was there in his eyes. Alex would never be released. Not alive. "Last I heard, he was fine."

Shoving to her feet, Grace looked up at Darius. "We have to go to the police," she said. "We have to tell them what's going on."

"What are police?"

When she explained, he said sharply, "No." He shook his head, causing black locks of hair to brush his temples. "We will involve no one else."

"They'll help us. They'll—"

"They will only hinder our search. I would be unable to use my...special skills. I will find your brother on my own."

He was asking her to trust him absolutely, to place her brother's life in his hands. Could she? Dare she? Her gaze fell to the ground.

"What will you do with these police of yours?" Darius demanded. "Will you tell them the myth of Atlantis is true and your brother hoped to prove it? Will you tell them you have traveled there? Will you bring more of your people and heartache to my land?"

Her eyes closed for a brief moment. She mentally sighed. Did she dare trust him? she asked herself again. Yes. She dared. No man was more competent. And no other man possessed the magical gifts that Darius did. He could do things the law couldn't; he could take her places the law couldn't. "I trust you," she said. "I won't go to them."

He nodded as if her answer had meant little to him, but she saw the flood of relief in his eyes. He whipped his attention to Patrick, but said to Grace, "Step beyond the building. Don't ask why, don't hesitate, just do it, please."

Shaking, Grace did as he'd commanded. When she turned the corner, she heard a whoosh, a grunt, a thud. She gasped, but didn't look. Necessary, she told herself. Darius's actions were necessary.

Eyes glowing ice-blue, Darius joined her. He wavered suddenly, but righted himself. Grace gripped his arm to help steady him. His skin was pale again as he secured his weapons inside his pockets. He wound his arm around her waist and curled his fingers possessively on her rib cage.

"I kept my word to you," was his only explanation. "Let us pay this Jason Graves a visit."

CHAPTER SIXTEEN

ARGONAUTS WAS HOUSED in a towering building of glass and chrome, and as Grace rode the elevator up to the forty-third floor, she brooded, thinking the company should have been housed in a hut of shame and greed.

Did Jason Graves actually think he could lock her brother away and go unpunished? Her hands fisted at her sides. Underneath her anger, however, were tendrils of fear that refused to leave. She remembered how cold and sick Alex had looked.

"I'm scared, Darius," she whispered.

He remained curiously silent. Solemn, actually.

Grace turned toward him and blinked. Though some color had returned to his cheeks, the lines around his lips were taut, and there was a new hollowness to his cheeks. She didn't like to see this hard, strong, extraordinarily capable man weakened in any way. Not because it made him less able to help her, but because she cared about him. Darius. About all the things that made up who he was. Seeing him distressed was worse than experiencing it herself.

The realization rocked her because it meant…

Oh, God. She didn't just care about him. She loved him. Grace groaned, and Darius cast her a sharp glance. She offered him a forced half smile. Of all the silly things to do. To fall in love with this mighty warrior like a jumper from a plane. No parachute. No landing mat. Just…splat.

When she'd told Darius she wasn't ready for him, she'd meant it. He was too intense. Too stubborn. Too much everything. So how could this have happened?

Don't worry about that right now. Just feed him. Get his strength up. Her hands shook as she dug in her purse and pulled out a tin of mints. Keeping her focus away from his face—she did *not* want him to know what she was thinking—she reached down and grasped his hand. His palm was warm and dry, thick and rough.

He jerked away from her touch.

Before she had time to react, he was reaching out and stiffly relinking their fingers. "Don't do me any favors," she snapped and tried to tug her hand away. She'd just realized she loved him, and he didn't want her to touch him. "Just so you know, I didn't want to hold your hand. I wanted to give you a mint."

"Be still," he said, at last deigning to speak with her.

"Let go of—"

"Close your mouth, or I will close it for you. With my own."

Eyes narrowed, she lifted her free hand and stuffed several mints in his mouth, effectively shutting him up. Close her mouth, would he? His nose wrinkled as he chewed, but his grip on her hand strengthened.

Someone behind them chuckled, reminding her that two men carting briefcases and files were in the elevator, as well. She darted a gaze to them and gave each one a quick, forced smile.

Not about to heed Darius's warning, she whispered to him, "When we get there, let me do the talking. I don't want anyone to know that we know what's going on."

He frowned. "I will allow you to do the talking, since these are your people," he said loudly, uncaring about their audience. "If they do not answer to my satisfaction, however, I will be forced to act."

"You can't threaten everyone who refuses to answer your questions," she told him, still maintaining her sense of quiet. "Or you'll end up in jail—or a dungeon—or whatever you call it."

"Sometimes, sweet Grace, your innocence amuses me. As if *I* could be held in a prison." His frown deepened. "Will this contraption go no faster? We have wasted enough time already." With his free hand, he jabbed his finger into the wall of buttons.

The elevator stopped on the next floor. As well as the next...and the next.

"The stairs would have been faster," one of the businessmen muttered, his voice laced with irritation.

Grace flashed him another smile, this one apologetic.

The man glared at her, as if it were all her fault.

As if she could control a six foot five hulk of a warrior who— Oh, my God! Darius was displaying his fangs again, this time at the poor, innocent businessmen. When the elevator stopped yet again, the two scurried out with fearful gasps—but at least they were alive.

"Did you see that?" one of them said. "He had saber-teeth."

When the doors closed, leaving her and Darius alone, silence gripped them in a tight fist. Over and over the elevator halted. When someone tried to enter, Darius gave them the same scowl he'd given the businessmen and every one of them retreated and waved them on before the doors closed.

After the eighth jostling stop, Grace's stomach threatened to rebel, and she tugged Darius from the elevator and onto the floor. Twenty-nine, she realized with dread.

"Excuse me," she said to the first person she saw, an older woman who carried a tray of vanilla scented cappuccinos. "Where are the stairs?"

"Down the hall. Last door on your right."

"Thank you." Only when they were inside the empty stairwell did Grace speak again. "Perhaps now is a good time to tell me about your dragon peculiarities," she said, chewing her lip nervously. Her voice echoed from the drab walls. "I need to be prepared...just in case."

As they climbed, she retained a firm hold on his hand. He didn't ask her to release him, and she allowed herself to think it was because he needed the contact as much as she did, that they were connected in some intangible way and the physical contact strengthened that bond.

"Dragons can fly," he said on a sigh.

"With wings?"

"Is there any other way?"

"There's no reason to be snide. There's no bulge in the back of your shirt to indicate the presence of wings or any other type of…" She searched her mind for the right words, ending with, "Flying apparatus."

"They are hidden in long slits of skin. When the wings emerge, the skin is retracted. Perhaps I will show you. Later. When we are alone."

There was a promise of something in his voice, something hot and wild and erotically wicked, and she pictured him without his shirt, pictured her fingertips tracing down the muscles and ridges of his back. She shivered. His scent chose that moment to surround, envelop, and submerge her, awakening her to a deeper level of need.

She had to change the subject before she did something foolish, like ignore the outside world and her responsibilities and drag him home. "Are there humans in Atlantis?" she asked.

"Some. The gods used to punish humans by sending them to our land. Not long after their appearance, the vampires ate most of them."

"Gross." She spied a peek at him through the shield of her lashes, then quickly refocused on the stairs before she tripped. "Have you, well, have you ever dated a human woman before? Not that you're dating one now," she rushed on. "I just meant—" She compressed her lips together.

He jumped right to the heart of the matter. "By dated do you mean bedded?"

"If the question doesn't offend you, then yes."

"Are you sure you wish to hear the answer?"

Yes. No. She sighed. She *really* wanted to know. "Yes."

"There's only one human I would willingly bed, Grace, and I have plans to do so." One of his fingers heatedly caressed her palm.

Oh. Ribbons of pleasure wound around her, and her lips lifted in a soft smile she couldn't stop.

By the time they topped the forty-third floor, Grace's thigh muscles burned with fatigue. She'd always dreamt of being a perfect size six, but the torture required for such a task was getting to be too much. Exercise…how she was coming to loathe the word. It was a thing more foul than low-fat ranch dressing.

Darius held open the door, and she swept past him, finally releasing his hand. She stepped inside Argonauts, the carpet beneath her feet a plush burgundy wool. Her gaze scanned the offices. On the wall hung Picasso, Monet and Renoir. Guards manned several corners, and security cameras roamed in every direction. A small rocky waterfall filled the center of the waiting area, and an expensive, exotic perfume floated on the air, drifting like clouds over the sun on a perfect spring day. Both were peaceful, and both mocked her.

That bastard! There was no doubt in her mind how Jason Graves afforded these things. A surge of rage boiled deep inside her. When Alex had first begun working for Argonauts, he'd barely made enough money to pay the rent on a little efficiency in Brooklyn. The past few months he'd brought home substantially more and had moved to his decadent new apartment in the Upper East Side.

Argonauts, too, had moved from their small offices in Brooklyn to here.

Yesterday, or even an hour ago, she had thought this success was because of recent mythological discoveries. Now she knew the truth. Jason Graves afforded these luxuries through the rape of Atlantis.

She stalked to the reception desk. Three women manned phones and computers. The first, the one Grace approached, had short black hair and heavily but perfectly made up features. She wasn't pretty in the traditional sense, but attractive all the same. She frowned with impatience at Grace, then dropped her jaw in awe when she saw Darius. That damn sex appeal of his!

"One moment please," the woman said into her mouthpiece, speaking to a caller. To Darius, she said, "May I help you?" Her voice was cultured, ritzy.

Grace fisted her hands to keep from unleashing her claws.

"We will see Jason Graves now," he said.

So much for doing all the talking, she thought with a mental sigh.

"What's your name, sir?"

"Darius en Kragin."

The woman's fingers flew over her keyboard, her long, oval nails tapping away. Without glancing up, she asked, "Which company are you with?"

"I come on my own behalf."

She finished her typing, read over the computer screen, then leveled him with a stare. "Mr. Graves isn't in today. He's out on business."

Grace rubbed a hand down her face. She was tired of delays and was completely out of patience. "When do you expect him back?" she asked more sharply than she'd intended.

"End of the week. Possibly beginning of next. If you'll leave your name and number, I'll make sure he receives the information when he returns."

Unwilling to wait that long, Grace said, "What about his assistant? Is he in?"

"That would be Mitch Pierce," the woman said. She propped her elbows on the desk, linked her delicate, tapered fingers, and perched her chin in the cradle her hands provided. "And yes, he is."

Mitch...another Argonaut who had *helped* her in the jungle. She contained a scowl. "We'd like to see him. Today."

Arched brows and a superior smile met her words. "Do you have an appointment?"

Grace opened her mouth to say no, but stopped herself. Admitting she didn't have an appointment was the fastest way to get shown to the door. However, she'd be caught in a lie if she said yes. "I'm

Grace Carlyle and if he discovers you let me walk out of here, you'll be looking for a new job."

The receptionist ran her tongue over her teeth. "I'll see if he can fit you in."

One hand rapped at her computer while the other punched a series of numbers in the telephone pad. After requesting Mr. Pierce's schedule, she hung up and glanced at Grace. "He'll see you within the hour. You may wait through the double doors on your left."

"Thank you," Grace said. Trying unsuccessfully to suppress her triumph, she ushered Darius into the waiting room. They were alone in the room. A round, glass table occupied the center and was piled high with books and magazines; along the farthest wall sat a couch and several chairs. All elegant, and all expensive.

During their wait they endured several peek-in visits from security guards. She flipped through a few magazines. (According to the current *Cosmo* love quiz, she and Darius were *not* compatible.) In one of the magazines, there was a feature article about Jason Graves, his recent discoveries, and his recent accumulation of wealth. The article told how he had purchased an apartment building on the Upper East Side and allowed all of his employees to stay there—which was where Alex lived. That she'd known. Jason himself stayed in the penthouse. That she hadn't.

Darius spent the short time splayed out in his seat, his hands locked behind his neck. He kept his eyes closed. She suspected he was gathering his strength and mentally preparing himself for the coming confrontation, which had to be the reason he didn't barge through the offices, demanding to be seen *now*. Or maybe his spirit was ghosting through the building, watching, listening, ensuring their safety.

Finally a woman, slightly older and less hostile than the receptionist, entered and said, "Mr. Pierce will see you now. If you'll follow me…"

Grace jumped to her feet, Darius right beside her. They shared a glance before exiting. Side by side, they strode down a hall and around a corner. The woman stopped and swept her hand out in front of her. "Last door on the right," she said.

Gliding past her, Grace eyed every door she encountered. She didn't see Alex's name. Where was his office? "I'm so ready to nail the Argonauts to the wall," she muttered to Darius.

A genuine smile played at the corner of his lips. "I had not realized before what a bloodthirsty wench you are. Try to contain your bloodlust long enough that we might question this Mitch."

"Bloodlust?" she gasped, then realized he thought she literally meant to nail Mitch to the wall. "I meant—oh, never mind." Whether she meant it or not, the idea had merit. "I'll try to contain myself."

At the end of the hallway loomed a single door. The nameplate in the center announced Mitch's name in bold, black letters. "That's the one," Grace said, smoothing her shirt and jeans. She didn't know what she'd say or do when she saw him.

Darius didn't bother knocking. He simply shoved open the door and strolled inside.

She followed right on his heels. Mitch sat at a large mahogany desk. There was no clutter, no papers scattered around him. He was as average looking as Grace recalled, with broad shoulders and lean limbs, pleasantly attractive with slightly gray hair that gave him a distinguished air. Only one thing about his appearance captured her interest. Sweat beaded atop his brow.

He was nervous.

Very interesting. Her gaze cataloged the office, taking in the sea of wealth and indulgence. Art, vases, glass and wood figurines. Carpet so light her feet felt as if they were traipsing on clouds.

With a visibly forced air of nonchalance, Mitch folded his hands together—hands that were shaking slightly—and propped his elbows on the desk surface. There was something about his eyes, something she hadn't noticed before…they were beady and shallow. Greedy. He offered them a pleasant, if false, smile. "It's nice to see you again, Grace," he said. "You look well after your trials in the rain forest."

"Thank you." Bastard. She didn't offer him the same compliment.

"Please, have a seat." He coughed and flicked a nervous glance to Darius. "Did you really feel it was necessary to bring a bodyguard?"

"He's a friend," she said. "He's staying with me for a while."

"I see. Well, again, please have a seat."

Darius crossed his arms over his massive chest, stretching the material of his black shirt taut over his muscles, silently communicating his refusal. Only a fool would underestimate his capabilities.

Mitch used a plain white handkerchief to wipe at his brow. Obviously he was no fool.

Grace remained beside Darius. She only prayed his dragon fangs were retracted. Watching Mitch pee his pants was not how she wanted to begin this meeting. The only time she might, *might,* be glad to see those fangs was in bed. While he was naked. Looking down at her. Moving into her.

For God's sake, concentrate.

"Very well, then," Mitch said. "How may I help you?"

"Darius," she said, knowing the big guy intimidated him, "feel free to begin."

"Where is your leader, Jason Graves?" Darius demanded.

"Out of town. Still in Brazil, I'm afraid. I'm more than willing to help you with anything you might need." Mitch laughed nervously.

"I want to know why you had a man following Grace." He stressed the word *had,* making it clear Patrick would be following them no more.

With an audible gulp, Mitch leaned back in his seat. Too lost in his apprehension, he didn't try to deny it. "I suppose you cornered the man. May I ask what he told you?"

"He would tell us nothing," Darius lied. "Only that you had sent him."

Mitch's shoulders relaxed. "We *did* send someone to follow Grace, but we did that for her own protection. We feared something had happened to Alex, and we didn't want the same fate to befall Grace."

"You say 'feared,' as in past tense," Grace pointed out. "Do you now know that nothing *has* happened to him, then?"

"No, no. That's not what I meant." The smile he gave her was weak. "As I told you, we've still got men looking for him, both in Brazil and here. I came back because someone has to oversee the company. Don't you worry, though. We'll find him and bring him home safely."

"I'm sure you will." She gripped the edge of her jeans tightly and twisted, wishing it was Mitch's neck instead.

"Is that why you're here?" he asked. "To inquire about our progress with Alex? You should have called me. I could have saved you a trip."

"I'm here because I'd like to search his office, if I may."

"Oh, uh, I'm afraid that's impossible," he said, his smile slipping. "Only Argonauts' employees are allowed in the offices. Client confidentiality, and all that." He laughed shakily. "Are you looking for employment, Grace?"

Her brows raised. "Are you offering me a job, Mitch?"

He paused. "We're always in need of good employees."

Probably because you kill them all, she thought

snidely. She heard Darius suck in a breath and wondered belatedly if she'd actually said the words aloud.

"On your way out," Mitch added, his demeanor unchanging, which meant he hadn't heard her comment, "ask the receptionist for an application. If you're anything like Alex, you'll make a fine addition to our staff."

"I'll be sure to do that." Regarding him sharply, she tilted her chin to the side. "I'm curious. If you suspect something bad has happened to Alex, why haven't you called the police?"

"We don't want to involve the U.S. authorities until we have more concrete information."

Like a body? she mused. "What *have* you done to locate him?"

"Jason can give you more details about this when he returns. Perhaps you should contact the police on your own."

Her eyes widened as a thought occurred to her. Mitch wanted her to go to the authorities. Why? What possible good could that do him? Unless…could they be planning to make her look like a fool, an overly concerned sister? Or worse, guilty of a crime? Blame the sister. Of course. That would be the reason they'd let her leave Brazil, the reason they kept her alive and didn't wave her in front of Alex as an incentive to talk.

The realization rocked her. She owed Darius. Bigtime. He'd saved her from making a huge mistake, from playing right into Jason's hands.

"I haven't yet, no," she told Mitch. "Perhaps I will."

"That might be wise," he said, for the first time offering her a genuine smile. "There's only so much we can do." He paused for a breath. "Would either of you care for a drink?"

How casually he reverted to pleasantries. Suddenly Grace wanted to stomp her foot, to shriek and rail that she knew they had her brother hidden and locked away. She wanted to leap across the desk, magically will on a pair of brass knuckles, and smack Mitch right in his beady eyes. Too, she wanted to find the medallion and offer it on a silver platter. Just return my brother, she inwardly screamed.

It depressed her that she could do none of those things. If they suspected that she knew the truth, they might kill Alex. If she found and gave them the medallion, they might kill Alex. Destroy the evidence of their misdeeds, so to speak. Either way, he could die.

Never in her life had she felt more helpless.

"No drink," she said, surprised at her calm tone. "I do have some questions for you, though. When was the last time you heard from Alex?" If she kept him talking long enough, perhaps he'd slip and inadvertently disclose crucial information.

"I believe I've already answered this question. A few weeks ago," Mitch said. "He called to let us know he was entering the jungle."

"What is the name of the man your search team found? The one who had last seen Alex? He was gone when I woke up on the boat, so I didn't get a chance to talk to him." And now she knew why.

Mitch gulped. "I, uh, can't recall."

"You can't recall an employee's name?" She gave her jeans another hard twist. "Didn't Argonauts fund Alex's trip? Shouldn't you have records with the names of the men you hire?"

"We didn't fund the trip," he offered quickly. Too quickly. "Perhaps Jason can tell you the man's name when he returns."

"In the jungle, I wanted to stay and look for Alex, but was told he'd already bought a ticket home. Do you know which airline he used?"

He chuckled, the sound strained. "I'll be honest with you, Grace. I'm not sure where he is. I wish I could help you, but…" He shrugged. "He could be anywhere."

At least he didn't try to feed her the "he is dead" line. "So tell me, while you were in the jungle, did you happen to run into any…creatures? Hidden lands?"

"I—I—I don't know what you're talking about."

Liar! She wanted to scream. Grace glanced at Darius. His expression was blanketed, stoic, yet she had the distinct feeling he yearned to stalk across the room and beat Mitch into the carpet. Obviously Mitch received the same impression; he shifted uncomfortably in his chair.

With Mitch's complete attention centered on him, Darius strode casually about the office, lifting vases and figurines as if they were no more important than dust mites. His fingers pinched at them, dismissed them, then replaced them on their perches with complete disregard. Mitch tensed, gulped. However, not a single protest oozed from his mouth.

"I do not like you," Darius told him, weighing a jewel-studded goblet in his palms. He offered the words with a kind of still repose, a natural assurance only the most confident of people possessed. "You remind me of a bloodsucking vampire."

Mitch pulled at his plain blue tie. "There, uh, are no such thing as vampires."

"Nor dragons, I'm sure," Darius answered.

All color drained from the man's face, showcasing the thin hollows of his cheeks. His gaze widened, and he transferred his attention between Darius and the goblet. "That's right," he said brokenly, reaching out instinctively for the artifact.

Darius *tsked* under his tongue. He tossed the cup in the air, caught it, then tossed it again. When he caught it for a second time, he said casually, "Since you are an unbeliever, you'll never have to worry about being eaten alive by a dragon." He arched a brow. "Will you?"

On a strangled gasp, Mitch shoved to his feet, his chair rolling behind him as he anchored his palms on his desk surface. "Set that down before I call security. All I've done is try to help, and this is how you treat me. You may show yourselves out."

"I have seen these objects before," Darius remarked, staying right where he was and giving the goblet a few more tosses.

"In *Archeologist Digest,* I'm sure." Mitch cast a desperate, fleeting glance to Grace.

She struggled not to glare at him.

"Now, please," he added. "I have work to do, and I'm sure you don't want to take up any more of my time."

After replacing the goblet, Darius palmed a vase boasting a colorful array of dragons etched around the edges. "Where did you find this?"

A pause. A cough. "Madrid. I really need to get back to work."

"I would swear on my life it belonged to a friend of mine. Perhaps you have heard of him. His name is—or was—Javar ta 'Arda. He gifted his wife, Teira, with a vase identical to this one on the eve of their mating."

"Perhaps you should put that down." Mitch nervously licked his lips. "I meant it when I said I'd call security. I don't want to, but I will."

Darius returned the vase to its perch, letting it wobble ominously at the edge. "As I was saying a moment ago, I do not like you. But Grace has asked me to use violence as a last resort. Still," he added after a loaded pause, "I can say with certainty that you and I will have a reckoning."

With that, he strode from the office. *That's my man,* Grace thought proudly.

"Have a nice day, Mitch," she said, flicking him one last glance. His features were so pallid he resembled a ghost—or vampire. He was reaching out, racing around his desk in his haste to save the vase from annihilation.

As she chased after Darius, she heard the shatter of porcelain, the howl of a man. Both buoyed her spirits, and she bit back a smile.

LOST IN THE INTENSITY of his thunderous emotions, Darius stared straight ahead as he and Grace strode toward her home. "Do you think Alex is okay?" she asked, her voice so low he had to strain to hear.

"For now. He has something they want. Otherwise, they would have killed him long ago."

That kept her quiet for a long while. "Where do you think he's being kept?"

"Atlantis."

She paused midstep, before jumping back into stride. "But you checked. You said he wasn't there."

"He wasn't. Then. The vision of Alex confirmed that, for he *was* here on the surface. However, after meeting the cowardly Mitch I suspect he has already been moved."

"How do we find out where he's being kept in Atlantis? Interrogate Mitch? Break into Argonauts?"

"No," he answered. "We are more likely to find what we need in Jason Graves's place of residence." But more than that, breaking into Jason's home would supply him with a better understanding of the man he would soon fight.

Oh, yes. Fight Jason he would. His anticipation grew with every second that passed.

"You're right." Grace brightened and curled her lush, rosy mouth with anticipation. Her features were so lovely his chest hurt when he looked at her. "Since he's out of *town*," she sneered the word, "today is the perfect day to let ourselves into his apartment."

"We will go tonight, when the shadows can hide us."

"After that are you," she faltered, "are you going home?"

"I must obtain the vests first."

They neared Grace's door, and she withdrew a key. "I want to go with you when you return."

"No. Absolutely not."

Her eyes narrowed.

"Get inside. Now." He gave her a gentle shove past the entrance. "There is something I must do before I join you." A dark storm churned inside him. He needed some type of release, needed to plan his next move. But more than that, he needed some sort of distance from Grace and his growing feelings for her.

He did not give her time to ask him any more questions. He simply closed the door in her stunned, beautiful face. "I will be right here if you need me," he said through the wood.

Perhaps it was his imagination, or perhaps he was seeing more clearly than ever before, but in his mind's eye he watched her fingertips caress the slat of wood, watched her press her lips together, and her gaze sadden. She didn't know what was happening within him and that worried her. This was not the first time she'd worried for him, and each time it touched him deeply, softened him somehow.

He waited until he heard the lock click in place before he stepped away and began pacing back and forth through the hallway. He would have liked to explore this New York, but the binding spell prevented any great distance between him and Grace. Occasionally humans strode past him and gave him a curious stare, but no one stopped and questioned him.

I want to go with you, Grace had said.

He blanched at the thought of taking her back to his home, even as joy flooded him. How he would have loved to splay Grace upon his bed, her naked body open and eager for him. He craved the reality of that.

The thought of being without her left him cold.

And the acknowledgment of that coldness left him reeling.

Tomorrow he would have to leave. He had moments of utter strength, and moments of utter weakness. No matter what he learned or didn't learn, no matter what he acquired or didn't acquire, he would have to return home in the morning, or he didn't think he'd have the strength to transport himself to the mist. Yet he still had so much to do.

He still had to kill Grace.

Could he, though? Could he harm her?

Darius didn't have to think about it. No. He couldn't.

The answer sliced through him as sharply as a blade. He could not hurt sweet, innocent Grace in any way.

She captivated him on so many different levels.

He was coming to depend on her in a way he'd once considered impossible, craving the emotions she made him feel with the same ferocity he'd once hated them. Without her, he was not fully alive.

He'd watched her stand up to that man, Mitch, and he'd felt pride. She hadn't backed down. She'd questioned him without revealing her hurt, without crumbling under the need to administer justice. She was a woman of strength and honor, a woman of love and trust.

His woman.

Silently his boots pounded into the carpet. He drew in the rich scent of food that seemed to encompass this entire building, this city, and steered his mind on to his own home. Javar and all of the dragons of that unit were dead. Dark sorrow wove through his blood as he at last admitted the truth. He'd known it beyond a doubt the moment he spied the treasures of Javar's home displayed so mockingly inside Argonauts.

His friends were dead, he repeated in his mind. They'd died by guns, most likely. Guns...and vampires. Perhaps the *Book of Ra-Dracus* had even helped. No matter what had happened, no matter what had been done, he would have vengeance.

This was what came of allowing humans to know of Atlantis; *this* was what Javar warned him of.

While Javar had not been an easy man to know, he had been like a father to Darius. They had understood each other. When Teira entered Javar's life, the man had softened and the bond between tutor and student had deepened, even as it widened. What a senseless death. A needless death. He'd lost no one close to him since the murder of his family. And now trickles of pain, both past and present, rose within him like a tide of water, seeping insidiously past his defenses and eroding the very fabric of his detachment. A sharp ache stabbed him, and he gripped his chest.

Deny your tears and keep the hurt inside you, boy. Use it against those who mean us harm. Kill them with it.

Javar had said one variation after another of those words. He wouldn't want Darius to mourn him, but mourn him Darius did. He would not have survived those first years without Javar, without the purpose his tutor had given him.

He should have killed the human man, Mitch, Darius thought dispassionately. He should have killed both human men. Mitch and Patrick. They each had knowledge of the mist, had most likely entered and had played a part in Javar's death. Had he destroyed them, however, he felt certain Grace's brother would have been killed in retaliation. So he'd knocked Patrick out—punishment for what he'd wanted to do to Grace—and walked away from Mitch. What was wrong with him?

He knew the answer. Part of it anyway. He hadn't wanted Grace to view him as a killer. Protector, yes. Lover, most definitely. But ruthless slayer? No longer.

He could only guess at how she would react if she

fully beheld the beast inside him. Tremble with fear and disgust? Run from him as if he were a monster? He didn't want her scared of him; he wanted her pliant. Welcoming. He just wanted her, all of her. Now…and perhaps always.

He'd come so close to losing control with the one called Patrick, and it had required a conscious effort to calm himself. Coming face-to-face with the man who had run his fingertips over Grace's sleeping body had infuriated him. Only he was allowed to touch her. Only he, Darius, was allowed to gaze at her luscious curves and imagine her stripped and open, ready and eager.

She belonged to him.

He wished to give her the world, not take it from her. He wished to fill her days with excitement and her nights with passion. He wished to protect her, honor her and devote himself to her needs. He could not let her go, he realized now. Not ever. He needed her for *she* was his heart. His emotions had never been mild where she was concerned but as unstoppable as a turbulent storm.

I'll never be able to harm her. The admission solidified inside him. His deepest male instincts had known since the beginning. The woman was a part of him, the best part, and hurting her would destroy *him*.

There was a way to have it all, he decided. A way to keep her from harm, a way to keep her for himself and still honor his oath.

He had only to figure out what that was.

CHAPTER SEVENTEEN

WITH THE STOLEN MEDALLION in his pocket, Alex clasped Teira's hand in his, grateful for her warmth, her softness and her strength.

A tremor racked him. Not from the cold or blood loss, but from the forced drug-induced hunger. He craved, oh, how he craved more of that damning substance. His mouth was dry. His head pounded, creating a dull ache he knew would soon become a raging inferno of pain. He needed those damn drugs and was appalled that a part of him wanted to stay here and await another dose.

The other part of him, the saner part, flashed pictures of his sister and his mother through his mind. Next came an image of Teira being dragged away, being hurt in the worst possible ways. This picture lingered, fueling a spark of anger. And that anger overrode the hunger.

He was leaving this place tonight.

Saving Teira was necessary for his peace of mind. He owed her. They were in this together; they had only each other.

"Are you ready?" he asked. They'd waited for the

palace above to quiet, and now silence held them in its grip.

"Ready," she answered.

"I'll keep you safe," he promised her, praying he spoke true.

"And I will keep you safe," she replied, her tone more assured than his own.

How could he ever have doubted her? Alex wondered. He gave her hand a squeeze. "Let's do this."

Together they stepped toward the doors, and the thick ivory barriers slid open smoothly, as if they'd never offered any hindrance. *How simple,* he thought. *Carry a medallion and come and go as you please.* Drawing in a steadying breath, Alex hurried Teira from the cell. He kept his footsteps light, but all the while his heart thudded in his chest.

The deeper he roamed from the cell, the more frigid the air became, chapping his skin. Fog billowed about like a frenzied snowstorm, so thick he could only see what was directly in front of his face. Dry ice, he realized, recalling how Jason had bragged about sending bags of it through the portal. The shards crunched beneath his boots.

He was grateful for the fog. It embraced him in its chilly depths and kept him hidden from view. Using his free hand, he trailed his fingertips over the wall, letting the rough texture be his guide.

Beside him, Teira's body shuddered. He released her hand and wrapped his arm around her slim waist, pulling her into the warmth of his side, rubbing his hand over her ice-cold arm. Her delicate scent wafted to his nose, heating his blood. He wished he could see her face, wished he could see the glistening fog create a halo around her because he knew beyond a doubt that it would be the most erotic sight he'd ever seen.

"I'm here," he soothed.

"The cold...it makes me weak," she said, stumbling.

His own weakness had him stumbling, as well, but he used his weight to hold them both steady. "I'll get you warm," he said. As they trekked deeper through the palace, Alex expected alarms to erupt. He expected men with guns to surround them. Instead, silence.

The wall ended all too quickly, and he was left with only air and fog to guide him. Where did he go from here? The ghostly whiteness was too thick. Protective, yes, but also slowing.

A lone figure suddenly parted the fog and rounded a corner.

Unseen, Alex forced Teira quietly behind him, waiting until the man closed the distance. The hairs on the back of his neck prickled with tension as each new second passed. When the guard stepped close enough, Alex didn't allow himself to think. He simply slammed his fist into the man's exposed trachea, cutting off his air. Gurgling, he went down hard and fast. Alex didn't know if he'd killed him, and he didn't care.

Motions shaky, he removed the man's coat and fastened it around Teira's shoulders. The thick brown material swallowed her slight frame. He looked for a gun, but didn't see one. When he spotted a fallen fire extinguisher, he hefted it up and looped the straps around his shoulders. Not a great weapon, but it would have to do.

"Which way is the portal?" he whispered to Teira.

"You cannot use the portal here. I tried to escape before, when they took me from you. Too many guards. Too many weapons."

He uttered a frustrated sigh and pushed a hand through his hair. He hadn't come this far to be stopped now. "We'll have to take them by surprise." Though how the two of them were going to pull that off, he didn't know.

"There's another way," she said. "A second portal on other side of the island. Darius en Kragin is Guardian there and we will con-convince—is that right word?—him to allow you to pass. He will destroy these men."

A grin of relief lifted the corners of his lips. He placed his face so close to hers their noses touched, and he gazed into her golden eyes. "You lead the way, baby. I'll follow you anywhere."

She returned his grin, though an air of sadness clung to the edges of hers. "I do not want to lose you," she said. "I do not want you to go."

"Then come with me." When she opened her mouth to protest, he interjected, "Don't give me your answer now." He didn't want to lose her, either, he realized, and would actually fight to keep her with him. After clinging to his freedom all these many years, he was finally willing to surrender it in favor of permanency with a woman. *This* woman. "Just think about it, okay. Right now we need to get out of here."

He curled his fingers through hers again, and Teira weakly led him up a winding staircase. The room they entered next was even more frigid, but not as thickly fogged. Alex surveyed these new surroundings. There was no furniture, yet there was more wealth than he'd ever seen. Ebony at his feet, jewels at his side, and crystal above. He halted midstep and could only gape.

This is why Jason desires the mist. Hell, I want it, too.

A sense of greed momentarily choked his throat. There had to be a way to take some of this home. Conceal a few jewels under his shirt. Fill his pockets. He'd be able to keep his family in luxury for the rest of their lives.

The thought of his family drowned him in a desperate need to see them. Jason claimed they were unhurt, but Alex couldn't believe a single word out of that murderer's deceitful mouth.

No one would ever have to know what he'd done, and that was a heady thought indeed. He reached out and traced his fingers over the jeweled wall. As he did so, the exotic scent of jasmine wafted around him, loosening the tightness in his throat and reminding him that he already held a treasure. Teira. He glanced down at her, and she smiled slowly up at him—a smile of trust. His hand fell to his side.

Atlantis had to be kept secret. Men like Jason would continue to plunder, never ceasing their quest for riches, killing men, women and children in the process. *God, how stupid I've been, how caught up in my own need for glory.* He'd endangered his entire family for *this*. For prestige and money. His stomach churned with shame, making him all the more aware of his body's need for drugs.

"Come on," he said. "Let's get out of here."

"Yes."

They maneuvered around corners, stumbled through empty rooms, making Alex feel like he was navigating a maze. Most walls were bare, ripped of all jewels. Several guards were posted throughout, but they never detected Alex and Teira, hidden as they were by fog and shadows.

Two ten-foot panels of glistening dragon-inlaid ivory ended their winding search. The pair of doors opened, welcoming them into the night. Crashing waves created a calming lullaby, and warm air laden with the fragrance of salt and sea cascaded gently. Teira stopped, allowing the warmth to thaw and strengthen her. Color returned to her cheeks, and her back straightened.

She dropped her coat and spread her arms wide.

Alex drank in the mesmerizing beauty of both Teira and Atlantis. There was a dusky glow over the breath-takingly lush green foliage and stunning array of colorful blossoms. Blossoms Teira seemed to be a part of. How did a city under the sea have night and day? There was no sun, no moon. Crystal prisms stretched above to form a dome as far as the eye could see.

Vibrancy and vitality pulsed all around, strengthening him to his very core, making him forget his dry mouth, making him forget his bitter need.

"If we follow the forest path," Teira said, her voice stronger than it had been inside the palace, "we can reach Darius by morning."

"Then let's go."

One of the guards scattered along the bastion noticed them. "Down there," he shouted.

Someone else called, "Stop them!"

Pop. Whiz. Bullets flew, peppering the ground a few feet behind them. Alex increased his speed, sprinting for all he was worth, the fire extinguisher slamming into his back. Later, he would feel the bruises. For now, he felt only the blessed numbness of his adrenaline rush.

Still hand in hand with Teira, he forced her to keep pace beside him. He launched into the safety of the trees before finally slowing. Alex liked to think he was in top physical condition, or had been, thanks to his daily workouts. But right now his breathing was ragged, and his pulse leapt like it was connected to a live wire.

"You need rest," his companion panted. "We are safe here. We can stop—"

"No. No resting. Keep moving."

She claimed the lead, and he forced his suddenly heavy feet to step one in front of the other. Forced his mind on the task at hand and not the drugs he was leaving behind. For a moment, his vision blurred and he swayed. Teira glanced at him over her shoulder, her expression concerned.

"Keep moving," he said again.

When they swerved around a large elm, a giant of a man jumped from the shadows, followed quickly by another. Their features weren't visible in the growing darkness, but Alex felt the anger coiled so tightly in their bodies.

Teira screamed.

Acting instinctively, Alex sprayed the liquid nitrogen, spinning in a circle as he did so. A thick foam of white coated the men, and they growled indistinguishable curses as they wiped at their faces. He tossed the red canister to the ground and jerked Teira through the thick foliage. Then they ran. Ran around trees and bushes, flowers and stones. They waded through two crystalline rivers along the way, and through it all he heard the men racing in pursuit, their footsteps fast, determined.

"Which way?" he called.

"East," she said, panting a little. The white gown she wore swished and swirled around her ankles, and her moonbeam pale hair whipped behind her. "There is…a town…nearby. We can lose ourselves."

Alex veered east, pushing himself past his endurance. The longer he ran, the less he heard of his followers. Either he'd lost them or they'd given up. Or were somehow able to silently follow. He didn't relax his defenses. Only when Teira was safely en-

sconced inside his apartment would he rest—after he
made love to her. Several times.

After what seemed an eternity, they reached the
town. One moment they were surrounded by dense
forest, and the next by shimmering gold and silver
buildings. He slowed when he found himself on a
crowded stone road. Throngs of people strolled in
every direction. No, not people. Winged men, bull-
like animals and horned women. Interspersed
throughout were tall, lean humanoid creatures with
skin the color of new fallen snow. They glided rather
than walked.

Alex felt their dynamically surreal eyes boring
into him hungrily, as if they could already taste his
every drop of blood. Vampires. He shuddered. They
moved with fluid, catlike grace, mere slashes of
white skin and flowing, black clothing. The only
color they possessed was in their eyes, an inhuman
blue that hypnotized and promised every desire satisfied.

His shudders intensified, and he reached up and
massaged his neck, covering the marks of his last
encounter with a vampire. The *Book of Ra-Dracus*
told of their insatiable thirst for blood—more so than
earth legend proclaimed. He knew that firsthand.

"In here," Teira said. She ushered him inside the
nearest building. "We will hide here until we are
sure we are safe."

Loud music, more fluid than rock, less structured
than classical, boomed in every direction. Voices and
laughter blended with the music as people mingled

and danced. He and Teira swept through the crowd, trying to remain unnoticed. There, in the back, was an empty table, and they hurriedly claimed it.

He plopped into his seat. The adrenaline rush he'd experienced in the forest had helped mask his need for drugs, but now, as the surge receded, he became increasingly aware of his shaking hands and aching temples.

A woman approached them and clanked two glasses onto their table. Two small brown horns protruded from her forehead. She gave them a brittle smile and said something in the same language Teira sometimes used. He was beginning to catch on to its unusual inflections and pronunciations, so he didn't need an interpreter to know the waitress had said, "Drink up and leave, or tonight will be your last," before she flittered away, suddenly lost in the crowd.

"There are many vampires here," Teira said, gazing around. "More than usual."

A wisp of dark cloth. A shiver of electrifying power. Then someone was there, standing behind Teira, caressing her shoulder. The laughter and music slowly tapered to quiet, and the patrons stared over at them.

"You smell good, little dragon," a vampire male said, his voice hypnotic and dark. Seductive. "I wonder, though, how you will taste."

It took Alex a moment to translate. When he did, he saw red. He didn't care how much stronger the vampires were, he didn't care that he might be inciting a fight, he would not allow threats to Teira's life. "Back off," he said, glaring up at the blood-sucker. "Or it will be *your* blood that is spilled this night."

The vampire snickered.

"I taste like death," Teira finally responded. Her gaze flicked from Alex to the vampire nervously. "Now leave us. We wish only to rest. We will depart soon."

"No, you won't. Not until I've sampled both you *and* your human."

Another vampire joined them, his mouth a blood-red frown. "We are not to harm the human, Aarlock. You know that."

"I will not kill him. The dragon, however..."

Still another vampire approached, crowding their table further. "The human doesn't wear the mark. We can kill them both if we so desire."

All three bloodsuckers glanced at Alex's neck. The one called Aarlock smiled slowly. "No, he doesn't wear the mark of the other humans. He is fair game."

Alex could almost see the knife and fork clanging together in their minds, and he wondered what mark Jason and his minions wore to prevent vampire attacks. *I have to do something,* he thought, vaulting to his feet. Not knowing what more he could do, he drew back his fist. Before he had time to blink, the vampire caught his arm and held him in a bruising grip. Those eerie eyes turned to him, gazing deeply, probing.

A strange lethargy worked its way through him,

as if he'd been shot full of those delicious drugs. Suddenly he wanted only to feel this vampire's fangs sink into his neck, wanted only to give himself to this powerful man.

Dainty, gentle Teira, who loved tender contact, snarled a sound more animal than human, jolted up and bared amazingly sharp claws. She shoved the vampire backward, causing him to stumble as he released Alex.

"Do not touch him," she snarled. "He is mine."

The rest of the vampires gathered around them, some baring their fangs, others hissing. Alex shook himself out of his stupor just as Teira flashed her own set of fangs, hers longer than the vampires. Alex's eyes grew round. He'd known she was a dragon changeling, but he hadn't really expected her body to physically change.

"We must leave," Teira mouthed, once again speaking his language, never taking her attention from the creatures in front of her. "We will need a distraction."

Determination rushing through his veins, his palms sweating, he glanced around, searching for a spear, a torch, something. Anything. When that failed, he looked for a back door—not that they could have used it. The vampires had formed a circle around them, their bodies nearly transparent and vibrating with hungry energy.

His protective instincts sharpened. He'd have to use his own body to divert their attention. He'd never battled a vampire before—obviously—but he'd always welcomed new experiences. "I'll distract them." His muscles tightened, readied. "Run, baby, and don't look back."

She sucked in a breath. "No. No!"

"Do it!"

The front doors burst open, saving her from another reply.

Three of the largest men he'd ever seen tramped inside. An air of menace surrounded them, as dark as their clothing. Their faces were red, their eyes puffy from some sort of toxin. Alex concluded almost instantly that they were the giants from the forest.

The vampires uttered a collective hiss and inched away.

Teira peeked over his shoulder, and when she saw who had entered, she gasped. "Braun, Vorik, Coal!" Smiling with relief, she waved with one hand and laced the other on Alex's shoulder. "They will help us."

The three men flicked them a glance, gave a barely imperceptible nod, then spread out and assumed a menacing come-and-get-me-you-bloodsuckers stance.

Alex had yet to fight past his shock. "You know them?"

"They are Darius's men."

"Then why did you scream when they approached us in the forest?"

"I not realize who they were. Come. We go to them."

While he was grateful for the help, Alex was oddly disappointed. He'd wanted to be the one to save Teira. He'd wanted her praise to be all his own. How foolish, since he wouldn't have lived to hear such praise.

As Alex and Teira skidded toward the front door, the vampires and dragons divided the bar, each group taking one side, facing the other. The moment Alex came within striking distance of his rescuers, he was roughly shoved behind them. Teira was gently lifted out of the way.

"What were you doing in the forest, Teira?" one of the warriors asked. He never removed his piercing gaze from the enemy.

"Escaping," she answered.

A hard, dangerous glint consumed his golden eyes. "Escaping? You will tell me more of this later." He motioned toward Alex with his chin. "What of the human?"

Teira cast a glance at Alex. *What of the human?* The question had plagued her over the last weeks. If only he were like the others of his kind, she could have ignored him. If only she hadn't been so completely drawn to him... He was nearly as tall as a dragon warrior, with wide shoulders and a lean, strong body. Short, curly red hair framed a strong, square face. His lips were wide and soft, his jaw angular. But it was his eyes that truly captivated her. They were big and green and filled with so many dreams. Those dreams called to her in so many ways.

"He's my friend," she said to Vorik. "No harm is to befall him."

Having listened to the conversation, Braun whipped around, facing her, radiating fury. "What of Javar?"

She hated to give him the news, here and now, like this, but she would not lie or evade. "He is dead," she said sadly.

"Dead!" all three dragons exclaimed at once.

Remorse flitted over Braun's expression, but he quickly hardened the emotion into determination. "There were other humans at the palace. They carried strange objects that fired some type of disc."

"Those discs stayed inside the dragon bodies, keeping their flesh open and preventing them from healing."

"That alone would not—"

"That alone *would*. The palace has been made into an ice land. When our strength was drained, the humans attacked us with their weapons." She remembered how easily her people had been destroyed. One moment, healthy, happy and whole. The next, gone. Murdered.

Her hands clenched, making the sharpness of her claws bite into her flesh. She barely felt the sting. Why the humans kept her alive and imprisoned, she could only guess. A threat to Alex, perhaps? A bargaining tool? They had kept her weakened by the cold, had tried to keep her hungry, as well, but she'd stolen bits of food here and there. More than anything, however, the humans had kept her frightened. For herself, for Alex.

She would not rest until the intruders were destroyed.

She had loved her husband, had loved the time she spent with him, and even missed him, but he had never filled her with such great longing as Alex did, as if she couldn't breathe without him near. She sighed. What was she going to do with the handsome human? She wanted him to stay here, with her. Wanted him to hold her in his arms every night, and wake to his kisses every morning. If he wouldn't stay, she would lose him. She could not survive on the surface.

The sound of guttural curses sliced at her reverie.

"You are not welcome here, dragons," a vampire snarled.

"We came for the human and the woman," Vorik said calmly. He kept his hands over the hilts of his swords—swords that could pierce a vampire's chest, sending poison through the creature's body and striking a lethal blow. "We mean you no trouble."

"We claimed them first. They belong to us."

"Perhaps you'd like to fight us for them." Coal offered his opponents an anticipatory smile.

"That is an invitation we cannot refuse." The vampire offered his own anticipatory smile.

Dragons were stronger, but vampires were faster. Years ago, the two had warred and the dragons had emerged the victors. But both races had suffered horribly. If they fought now, Teira was not sure a single man would be left standing.

"Let them go," a vampire said to his brethren, surprising her. "These dragons will bow to us soon enough."

"We will never bow to you," Braun spat.

The words, "We shall see," were delivered with supreme confidence. "Yes, we shall see."

Vorik arched a brow. "We shall see *now*."

Without emitting a single sound, the dragons flew at the vampires, teeth bared and gleaming a hungry white, a vision of silent death as they transformed from man to beast. They dropped their swords, relying instead on their natural reflexes. Vampires moved quickly, gliding to the ceiling, then launching themselves at the dragons before gliding upward once again. It was a dangerous dance.

There were snarls and grunts of pain, the sound of ripping cloth. The flash of claws, and the scent of blood and sulfur.

"The stench of dragon can be smelled miles away," one of the vampires snarled, lashing out with his sharp nails as he slipped past.

"Since you can smell me, Aarlock, you might as well feel my flames." Vorik spat red-orange sparks out of his mouth, catching the vampire in the side.

A tormented scream erupted, blending with the sound of sizzling skin. Eyes glowing with hatred, the vampire retaliated, attacking straight on, fangs bared. Before Vorik had time to move, their bodies slammed together and Aarlock sank his teeth in Vorik's neck. Vorik gripped him by the neck, ripped him away, and tossed him to the ground.

"I see you still bite like a girl, Aarlock," he seethed.

"I see you still breathe like a hatchling."

They were on each other again.

"Hand me a dagger," Alex said to Teira over his shoulder. When the fight first began, he'd shoved her behind him. He didn't know if he'd be any help, but he couldn't let these dragon men fight alone. He had to do *something*.

She tried to maneuver around him for what seemed the hundredth time. The woman wanted to guard *him* instead of the other way around. "No," she said. "We must not interfere. We would only distract them."

Alex continued to search for a weapon, catching glimpses of the brawl at the corner of his gaze. Each of the species fought hard and cruel, biting and slashing. The dragons drew blood with teeth, claws and tails, while the vampires relied on speed, moving from one end of the bar to the other to slash and run. Their rusty-brown blood dripped onto the dragons, acting like acid.

In the end, speed and poison blood weren't enough.

The more fire the dragons produced, the stronger they became. Even Teira seemed to soak up the heat like a flower turning to the sun. All color had returned to her cheeks. Alex wiped at the sweat dripping from his face.

When the battle finally ended, burning embers and vampire ashes littered the ground. Braun, Vorik, and Coal were still standing. They were covered in blood and wounds, but by God, they were standing.

One of the dragons, Braun, pushed Alex outside. The others, Teira included, followed. She quickly made the introductions. Alex had never been more aware of his human frailty. The men he knew did not behave like these warriors, ready and eager for bloodshed.

"What do the humans at the palace want, Teira?" Vorik asked.

"The riches. They are taking them back to the surface."

"Damn this," Coal snarled. He threw a withering glance toward Alex.

Alex backed away, palms up. "I'm not with them. I'll help you in any way I can."

"He was a prisoner, like me." Teira met each man's stare. "Are there other warriors with you? Can we retake the palace tonight?"

Braun shook his head. "We cannot act until Darius returns. Our orders are to stay outside of the palace, detaining any who try to enter or leave."

Vorik frowned down at her. "The time for war will come, and then we will act. Until then, we do nothing." His gaze became piercing. "Understand?"

"When will Darius return?" she demanded. "I am eager for vengeance."

Ignoring her question, Coal exchanged a concerned glance with Braun. "As are we. As are we."

JASON GRAVES STUDIED the vampire stronghold with assessing eyes. While this fortress lacked the same magnitude of wealth as the dragon palace, it held enough to capture his attention. Silver walls. Gold inlaid floors. A violet ram's fleece rug.

Perhaps he needed to rethink his alliance with the vampires.

They had supplied the tools necessary to strip the dragon walls of their jewels, as well as the location of coins and other treasures. And in return, Jason was to slaughter the dragons. A good bargain, in his estimation. Or so he'd thought. He was beginning to suspect that the moment the dragons were exterminated, the vampires would feed off of him and his men, the alliance forgotten. He swallowed, allowing the idea of striking first to take root in his mind. That way, he would not only save his own life, but also gain vampire riches. He had heard they knew where to find the greatest treasure of all. The Jewel of Atlantis. A powerful stone, granting the owner unimaginable victories.

Right now, his unlikely allies knew that any human wearing a medallion was to be left alone. Jason had made it clear in the beginning that if one of his men were harmed, just one, he would join forces with the dragons instead.

That threat would no longer work when the dragons were gone.

"You have defeated Javar," Layel, the vampire king, said. He stroked deathly pale fingers over the seam of his red lips and leaned back in his throne. A throne comprised of bones. "It is time for you to defeat Darius, as well."

"We haven't emptied out the first palace yet," Jason hedged. He stood in the center of the room and shifted nervously. He hated coming here and never stayed longer than necessary. Knowing his men waited outside the throne room doors, weapons cocked and ready, did not soothe his unease. Layel could have his neck ripped open before he managed a single scream for help.

"No matter. I want them killed immediately." The king slammed a fist onto his armrest—a femur, Jason thought. "The dragons are cruel, evil murderers. They must die."

"And they will. We just need a little more time. I cannot divide my forces, and I will not leave the first palace until it is completely emptied."

Heavy silence encompassed them.

"You dare tell me no?" Layel said quietly.

"Not no, exactly. I'm merely asking you to have more patience."

Layel slowly ran his tongue over his razor-sharp teeth. "I knew you were greedy, human. I didn't know you were also stupid."

Jason scowled. "You are more than welcome to fight the dragons on your own." He didn't need the vampires anymore—he already possessed the tools. But they both knew Layel *still* needed him. Jason might be intimidated by this creature, but damn if he didn't enjoy what small power he held over him.

Intense fury blazed in Layel's eerie blue eyes. "How much longer?" he ground out.

"A week. Two at most."

"That is too long! The only reason you were able to defeat Javar was because you surprised him. Without that surprise, you will not defeat Darius." In a hiss of rage, Layel hurdled his jeweled goblet at Jason's head.

Jason ducked and the cup sailed past him. Barely.

"He is stronger than his tutor ever was," Layel said.

Jason glared up at him, a heated retort pressed at the gate of his lips. The doors burst open before a single word escaped.

One of his men ran inside. "Alex and the female escaped."

"What!" Jason shouted, spinning.

"Word arrived only seconds ago. They escaped through the forest."

"How?" Scowling, he strode toward his man and met him halfway.

"We aren't sure."

"Damn it! Search the forest. I want him found within the hour and brought back to me."

"Alive?"

"If possible. If not…"

The man hastened to do as he was bid.

Jason stood there, grinding his teeth. A part of him didn't care that Alex had escaped. The bastard would probably be found and killed by any number of vicious creatures. But the other part of Jason, the part that acknowledged wars could be lost by a simple mistake such as this, recognized the damage that could be done. Alex could stumble upon Darius, could warn him.

"Jason," Layel said.

The hairs prickled at the base of his neck, and

without looking, he knew the vampire king was directly behind him. Jason slowly turned, hoping his features remained emotionless. "Yes?"

"Fix this. Fail me and I'll add your bones to my throne."

CHAPTER EIGHTEEN

HOURS TICKED BY as Grace thinned the carpet in her tiny living room, pacing back and forth, from one wall to the other. The hallway had fallen silent half an hour ago. Every time she blinked, she pictured Darius sitting just beyond her front door, his eyes closed, expression pensive, his mind thinking of ways to leave her behind. She scowled. Darius might travel home in the morning, but not without her. Whether he approved or not, she was going.

Pushing out a breath, Grace rubbed her temples. Her shoulders slumped dispiritedly. *What am I going to do?* Beneath her frustration with Darius hovered a constant fear for Alex, and she knew that was the true catalyst to her riotous emotions. Helplessness ate her because she knew there was nothing she could do but wait and pray Darius was right. That Jason Graves would keep Alex alive because her brother had something he wanted.

The medallion.

She laughed humorlessly. It always came back to that. If she'd suspected the true value of that damn chain, she would have held on to it tighter. Where the hell was it?

She needed Darius. She needed him to reassure her. She needed him to wrap his arms around her and reaffirm wrongs would be righted and life would continue with promises of pleasure and happiness.

"Darius," she said in frustration. What was he doing?

The air in front of her thickened and blurred, sparkling with crystallized raindrops. A whisper of heat, a waft of masculine scent, then Darius materialized right before her eyes. His features were taut as his gaze darted left and right. "What is wrong?"

"I need you," she said. "I need you. That's all."

His visage relaxed, fraying his worry but leaving behind lines of tension.

Their gazes locked. She stood frozen, drinking him in. More than strained, he looked…changed. Different somehow. Sexier than ever before. Scorching. Needy. He sensed her growing desire, perhaps, because his nostrils flared and his eyes lit with fire.

Grace's heart flip-flopped in her chest. Darius didn't resemble the man who accosted her in the cave, a sword raised over his head, death in his gaze. Nor did he resemble the man who had nearly choked the life from Patrick. Right now he reminded her of the man who found delight in colors and chocolate, who had tenderly kissed her lips, savoring her every nuance. He had licked her palms and soothed her bruises.

Oh, God, how she wanted *this* man.

But guilt swam through her, locking her in place. How could she want him, *enjoy* him, when Alex was hurt?

"You cannot help your brother right now," Darius said, as if divining her thoughts. His gaze reached across the space between them, caressing her with quiet strength.

"I know," she said softly, yearning for him all the more. She tried to absorb his comfort from a distance, but that wasn't what she needed. Only full-body, skin to skin contact would work.

He stretched out his hand. "Then come here."

Without another word, Grace launched herself into Darius's arms. He caught her with a *humph* and banded his arms around her waist, anchoring his hands on her bottom and backing her into a wall. Instantly he smothered her mouth with a kiss. No, not a kiss. A devouring. He worshipped her taste, and she reveled in his, and as their tongues danced, she became a part of him. He became a part of her. She moaned, and her legs tightened around him.

He pulled away. "I will not stop this time," he said raggedly.

"Good, because I wasn't going to let you."

He trapped her earlobe between his teeth and gently tugged. The time had come; the wait was over.

One hand cupping his neck, the other kneading his back, she fit herself against his erection. The contact sizzled. A tremor moved through her, leaving a desperate arousal in its wake. He reclaimed her lips in total possession, branding her very soul.

She was his woman, and he was her man.

His tongue swept inside her mouth, and her desire raced toward the point of no return. No, that wasn't exactly true. She'd reached the point of no return the first moment she saw him.

She quivered with the force of her need, with the intensity of his heat, and the consuming ache to finally know him. All of him.

"Darius," she whispered.

"Grace," he whispered back.

This is where he belonged, Darius thought savagely, gazing down at Grace. Right here. With this woman. He'd never felt more alive than he did right now, in her arms. She showed him a world he'd never thought to see again, a world of colors and tastes… and emotion. True emotion. And he exalted in it. In *her*.

Slowly, seductively, her fingers crawled up his chest. She smiled a feminine smile. He nearly spilled his seed just then. The deepest, most primitive part of him had recognized her the moment she'd stepped through the mist. She was his mate.

His reason for being.

He would wed her, Darius decided in the next instant.

As he continued to watch her, Grace licked one of her fingers and drew a moist heart around his right nipple. Air hissed between his teeth.

By mating with him, Grace would become a citizen of Atlantis. His oath stipulated only that he kill surface dwellers who passed through the mist. If she were Atlantean…gods, yes. He would make her Atlantean.

The relief, the joy, resonated through him like a torrid rain.

He claimed her mouth with more ferocity, growling his need. She responded by weaving her hands in his hair and slanting her lips over his more fully. She rubbed herself against his erection, gasping, taking, giving. Their clothing only added to the friction. His fingers dug into the soft roundness of her buttocks, quickening her rhythm, and their kiss continued, hard and fast, then slow and tender.

"You are so beautiful," he said brokenly.

"No, I—"

"You are. I burn for you. I flame."

She melted against him. Into him. Her breasts meshed against his chest, her nipples pearled, waiting. Tasting them became as necessary as breathing. In all of his other couplings, Darius had rushed. He'd been savage, giving the woman pleasure, taking pleasure for himself, but offering nothing more. Never more. There would be no rushing now.

He wanted to savor and give.

"I will take care of you," he whispered. "Do you trust me?"

"So much, I ache."

With her legs still wrapped firmly around him, he sank to his knees and laid her tenderly on the carpet. He gently gripped her chin and forced her to meet his gaze. "This will not just be a coupling, sweet Grace. I am giving you me. All of me." He paused and studied her features. "Do you understand?"

Something he couldn't read leapt into her eyes. Uncertainty? Or excitement? She chewed on her bottom lip, then shook her head.

"I want to make you mine for now and always," he explained.

Her brow crinkled. "Do you mean...get married?"

"More than that. Life mates."

"There is a difference?"

"One that cannot be explained. One that must be shown."

"And you want to do this here?" Her eyes widened. "Now?"

He nodded.

Grace gulped. Surely he wasn't serious. He had to be teasing her. But the lines of his face stretched, determined, and an air of vulnerability clung to his shoulders. He refused to relinquish his hold on her gaze.

He meant every word.

And she didn't know how to react.

Grace en Kragin, her mind whispered.

Though she didn't understand what had brought him to this decision, the thought tempted her on every level, and a great need welled inside her. She'd already admitted that she loved him. Why deny her feelings in this? *I want to be his wife.* She did. Now and always, like he'd said.

How wonderful to be the one who snuggled in bed with him each night, the one he pulled tightly to his side, his breath on the back of her neck, his whispers of love in her ears. How wonderful to be the one who gave him children. Her mind easily supplied the image of a plump baby. Their baby. A boy as strong as Darius, or a girl as intense and focused.

"You saw the violence of my past," he said, mistaking her silence. "You know the things I've done and can guess the things I will do. I'm asking you to accept me regardless. If you can do this, I will give you my life, my riches and my vow to always protect you." The last words left his lips with all the desperation inside him. With all the longing. With all the need.

Her expression softened; her lashes dipped to half-mast. "I don't need your riches," she said. "Only you."

At her words, the possessiveness Darius had always felt for Grace raged to the surface. Raw, primal arousal burned inside him, hotter than ever before. Everything inside him cried for her. Not just part of her, but her entire essence.

He joined their hands, palm to palm.

Not pausing for a moment, lest she change her mind, he uttered, "To you I belong. My heart beats only for you." He held her gaze with the strength of his own. "No other will tempt me, from this day and beyond. To you I belong."

As he spoke, the places where his body touched hers warmed, became blistering, and a strange swirling unfurled in the pit of Grace's stomach, sweeping through her from head to toe.

"Say the words back to me," he intoned harshly.

Yes. *Yes.* "To you I belong. My heart beats only for you." As she spoke, he inched his lips closer to hers. "No other will tempt me, from this day and beyond. To you I belong."

The moment the last word left her mouth, he fit his lips directly over hers. She cried out, and he caught the sound. His eyes tightly closed as his entire body clenched and bowed.

A part of her soul ripped out of her body and into his. Instantly the void filled with his essence, sweeping through her like wildfire. The exchange was powerful, wholly erotic. Her stomach heated and tingled, and she lay there, panting. The fine hairs on her body clamored for him.

"What happened?" she asked between breaths.

"Our joining."

No more needed to be said because she understood. They were joined, not physically—not yet—but joined in a way that was even more tangible. Undeniable. She didn't understand the implications or mechanics of it. They were not two separate entities. They were one. She'd needed him before, but now she would die without him. She sensed it, knew it in the deepest part of her being.

"I am nothing without you," he said, echoing her thoughts. "Do you feel how much I hunger for you?"

She did. God, she did. His hunger mingled with her own, purring within her veins.

"You are more important to me than air," he said. "More important than water. You, Grace, are my only necessity."

"I love you," she said, at last giving him the words in her heart. As she spoke, the contentment that had always remained elusively out of reach was suddenly there and hers for the taking. So grasp it she did, holding Darius closer. He encompassed everything missing from her life: danger, excitement, passion.

Fire flashed in his eyes. Reaching back, he peeled his shirt over his head. "I'm going to give you everything you crave, sweet Grace." His lips lifted in a fleeting smile. "Everything."

Anticipation shivered through her. She threaded her palms up the strength of his chest, over his ribs and nipples, over his tattoos. He sucked in a breath. His tattoos were slightly faded, not as red and angry as before, but still there. Still sexy and warm. Her mouth watered for a taste of them, and she rolled him onto his back. Leaning down, she licked a path along the colorful dragon wings, savoring the salty taste. His muscles jumped at the first stroke of her tongue.

He slithered his hand between her legs and played; the fabric of her jeans created a dizzying friction. She moaned, arched her neck, and became lost in the breathtakingly sensual caress. Everything within her sprang to life, even places she hadn't known existed, starved for more of his attentions. She ached to be filled. By Darius. Only Darius.

He claimed he had done horrible things, but deep down she hungered for that fiercest part of him. For the wildness. The danger. She might have tried to deny it upon occasion, but she'd always known the truth. He was her every fantasy; his presence alone offered her more excitement than any challenge or adventure. When she was with him, she felt whole. She felt alive.

She felt vital.

"I want you naked." Darius didn't wait for her response, couldn't. Impatient for her as always, he did exactly what he'd done before. He gripped the neck of her shirt and ripped. Underneath he found lacy green fabric, her sexy belly ring and a light outline of a dragon tattoo.

He traced the edges with his fingertip. "Look," he told her.

Lost in sensation as she was, a moment passed before she obeyed. When she did, she gasped. "What the— I don't understand. I have a tattoo." Shock dripped from her tone, and her stunned gaze went from the tattoo, to him, to the tattoo. "I've never gotten a tattoo in my life."

"You bear my mark," he said, rolling them over once again and easing her down. "I am a part of you forever."

He tore the green material in half, just as he'd done to her shirt. Her breasts were lush and lovely, and the sight of them made him tremble. Tremble like a boy. He palmed one then the other, loving the way her eyes closed and her back arched, a silent entreaty for him to continue. He moved down her body and sucked a nipple into the hotness of his mouth. She gasped his name like a reverent prayer.

He sucked harder.

"Oh, God," she groaned.

Her knees clenched around his waist; her hands gripped his hair. He continued to knead one glorious breast, abrading the pearled nipple between his fingers while he laved and sucked the other. Like raspberries, they were, pink and rosy, sweet and delicate. One of his hands gravitated to her belly, fingering the delicate silver loop.

Losing control of his resolve to go slow, he teased himself between her legs. She moved wantonly against him, then with him. When she was gasping, begging, he jerked at her shoes, then her pants, tugging them down and kicking them from her ankles with his foot. The sight of her, lying under him in only a pair of lacy emerald panties, nearly made his heart stop. Such beauty. *His* beauty.

He drove his fingers past the delicate lace and found the silken heat of her. She was wet and hot. Ready. But he wanted her beyond ready. He wanted her desperate. Using the tip of one finger, he smoothed her moisture over her soft folds, gently grazing the center of her desire.

"Yes," she said, curving into his touch. "Yes. Touch me there."

"You need to be filled, Grace."

"Yes. Please."

He slowly sank one finger inside her, then another. "Are you ready for more?" A bead of sweat trickled down his temple. He bit her neck, making a small sting, then he licked it away as he thrust those fingers in a delicious rhythm.

She cried out and lifted her hips. His shaft strained for her, but he worked another finger inside her. How he loved the feel of her tightness. Her moist heat.

Soft, mewling sounds escaped her lips when he circled his thumb around her clitoris.

"I'm ready," she said. "I promise I'm ready."

With a growl, he latched on to her mouth and drank from her. He didn't deserve her, but the gods had given her to him and he was going to do everything within his power to make her happy. She would never regret giving herself to him.

"I want to kiss you here," he said, again circling his thumb around the very heart of her wetness.

Her eyes closed in surrender. As generous as she was, his Grace wasn't content to take pleasure only for herself; she insisted on returning it. "I…want to kiss…you here," she said, between panting breaths, slipping her own hand between them and cupping the long, thick length of him. "Who gets to go first?"

Those beads of sweat grew into a fine sheen over his entire body. She craved excitement, he thought, and so he would give it to her. "We will both go first."

Her tongue shot out and traced her own lips, taking in the residual taste of himself he'd left behind. "Really? How?"

In a total of two seconds, he removed his pants, then her panties, leaving them both completely naked. He gathered her into his arms and settled on his back, placing her on top. He'd never given a woman a chance to take him in her mouth. Picturing Grace's red curls spilled across his abdomen, over his thighs and cock, picturing her teeth grazing his length and her mouth sucking him deeply, nearly made him come.

"Straddle me," he said, surprised he still possessed a voice. His need pounded through his veins. "Do not face me. Face the other direction."

Her nipples pebbled further, and she gazed down at him with an expression of utter longing. Slowly she did as he instructed. Her back was long and slender and perfectly proportioned. He caressed a fingertip down each vertebra, and tiny bumps of pleasure appeared on her skin.

He clasped her hips, tugged, scooting her closer and closer to his waiting mouth.

"Now lean over," he instructed.

Languidly sensual, she moved her mouth toward his thick erection. Her warm breath fanned his heavy testicles as he lifted his head and licked into her slick heat.

At that first contact, Grace screamed her pleasure. Not an orgasm, but close. So close. Her hands clenched Darius's hips. He continued to lave her, and she inched the thick length of him into her mouth—and almost screamed again. The eroticism of having his shaft nestled in her mouth while Darius tasted her very essence proved earth-shattering.

"This is what I meant when I said I wanted to eat you," he rumbled, the vibrations resonating into her.

His words and actions combined, bringing her swiftly to a torturing climax. Her body jerked and quivered as a thousand lights sparked past her mind. Pleasure, so much pleasure. She tore her lips from him as his name ripped past her throat. "Darius, Darius, Darius." The heat of it branded.

When her climax faded, she should have been sated, completely fulfilled. But she wasn't. She wanted him buried deep inside her, so deep he'd leave his mark on her for days.

Desperate, Darius lifted her and spun her toward him. He tumbled her over and gazed down at her. "Now?" The word emerged hoarse and eager. Frantic. He needed to be inside her.

She spread her legs wide, fitting his hard length where it belonged, almost—but not quite—at the sweet edge of penetration. "I'll always be ready for you."

"You're my woman. Say it."

"I'm yours. Now. Always."

"And I am yours." He slanted his mouth over hers at the same moment he impaled her. He cried out at the joy of it, the heady bliss, his enjoyment so intense his wings burst unbidden from his back, stroking a heated draft over their bodies. Those majestic wings stayed suspended in the air for a breathless moment, two deceptively sheer extensions that at last lowered, surrounding him and Grace in an iridescent cocoon.

Shocked, he stared down at her. Her eyes were closed, and her lips pressed together. Instead of a pained cry, she murmured in surrender.

For Grace, the sharp pain of virginity left as suddenly as it appeared, leaving only the thickness of him. The hardness.

"You are…this is…I am your first lover," he said, when the realization struck him. "Only lover." A possessiveness more potent than orgasm shuddered through her.

"Don't stop," she said. "Mmm. You feel so good."

"Your only mate," he said with awe. He moved slowly at first, but that wasn't enough for her. She gripped his hips, raised her own and ground herself into him. He needed no more encouragement. He clasped her bottom and pumped into her, over and over, again and again.

He rode her hard, unable to slow. His kisses grew fervent, plunging in sync with his powerful thrusts. Exquisite tension held her in its grasp, held tighter, tighter, then suddenly exploded, gifting her with the most shattering gratification she'd ever experienced. She shuddered with it, gasped and screamed with it.

"By the gods, you are sweet," he said through clenched teeth. Anchoring her legs atop his shoulders and sending him deeper inside her, he quickened his strokes further and joined her, chanting her name.

Unexpectedly she climaxed again.

DARIUS CARRIED GRACE to bed and neither of them rose for several hours.

He wanted to spend the rest of his life right here in her arms, her plump backside nestled against him, but knew that wasn't meant to be.

Midnight had settled over the land.

Moonlight crept through the windows, its silvery fingers intertwining with darkness. The city pulsed with life, even at this later hour. Time to leave. Still...

He allowed himself a few more minutes of quiet luxury, of holding Grace in the protective shield of his embrace. Her intoxicating scent surrounded him, and her warmth seeped into his bones. Virgin. She had been virgin. This beautiful, sensuous creature had given him what she'd given no other man.

She was a treasure more rich and satisfying than any other. He would protect her with his life.

"Darius?" she sighed, snuggling closer.

"Hmm?"

"Are we married? I mean, we didn't sign anything or—"

"We are joined. Never think otherwise."

"I'm glad." She eased up on her elbow and offered him a satisfied smile.

"As am I," he said.

"What we did—I don't think there's even a word to describe the bliss."

He nipped the softness of her shoulder with his teeth. "I meant to go slowly, wife, meant to savor you."

Her eyelids fluttered down. "Say it again."

"I meant to go—"

"No. The part where you called me your wife."

His arms tightened around her. "We belong together, wife."

She rolled onto her side and faced him. "Just so you know, I happened to like it the way you gave it to me, *husband*."

His cock should not have stirred for hours—perhaps days—but as he looked at her and basked in her words, need unfurled through him. If they did not get up, he would take her again, and he knew he wouldn't have the strength to leave afterward.

"Get dressed," he said, patting her bottom. "Time for us to visit Jason Graves."

Grace lost her dazed expression. The sensual reprieve ended as real life intruded. She lumbered to her feet and stumbled to her bathroom. Wincing at the soreness of her body, she took a quick shower and slipped on a pair of black pants and a matching black, short-sleeved shirt.

When she glanced up, Darius stood in the bathroom doorway, watching her through intense, golden eyes. Golden eyes! Her pulse fluttered in time with a single thought: *he is my husband!* His pants hung low on his waist, giving him a sexy, rakish air. She found herself taking a step toward him, intent on slipping her fingers beneath the black material and—she stopped that line of thought before it was too late. Before she lost herself in him.

He didn't appear aroused in any way. He looked…pained, like that strange weakness afflicted him again. Proud as he was, he didn't say a word.

"Come with me," she said. She led him into the kitchen. There, she hurriedly fixed him a sandwich, and once he finished eating, he leaned back in his chair. He looked the same. Why hadn't that helped? She frowned and took his hand, meaning to gauge his temperature. But as she held his palm in hers, his color returned. It wasn't food that strengthened him, she realized, but her. Her touch.

"You have to tell me what's going on," she said, holding his gaze and retaining her grip on his hand. "What causes your illness?" When he remained silent, she persisted. "Tell me."

He sighed. "When the gods banished us to Atlantis, they bound us irrevocably to the land. Those that try to leave, die."

Her stomach twisted, and her body went cold. If staying here meant his death, she wanted him gone. "You have to go home. Now." She allowed all of her concern, all of her anguish at the thought of his demise, to seep into her voice.

"I will return in the morning as planned."

"I'll search Jason's home on my own, then fly to Brazil. I can be in Atlantis in two days."

"No. On both counts."

"But—"

"No, Grace."

She had to convince him to leave. But how? She released him and began clearing away the dishes, keeping her back to him. In seconds, he was directly behind her, holding her captive between his arms.

"You are upset," he said.

She paused, saying, "I'm scared for you. I'm scared for Alex. I want this to be over."

An undercurrent of menace suffused his voice when he said, "Soon. Very soon."

CHAPTER NINETEEN

BRIGHT NEON LIGHTS blazed from nearby buildings. Grace sucked in a deep breath as her gaze darted left and right. *I'm a criminal. I'm breaking and entering—or committing a B and E as the arresting officer would say.* She pursed her lips together and fought a shiver. She'd never admit this aloud, but hidden beneath her nervousness surged an intense adrenaline rush.

She and Darius stood outside Jason's swanky apartment building. A slight breeze drifted past, cooling her heated skin. She pressed her back to the brownstone, and cast another glance to her right. Unfortunately Darius couldn't magically teleport them inside. He had to visualize a room first, and he'd never been inside Jason's. She wondered, though, how he planned to get them in undetected.

"What if we set off the alarms?" she asked softly. Did the people strolling the streets suspect the truth? She was wearing all black, after all. Criminal colors.

"We will not," Darius answered confidently.

"Security guards observe screens of every corridor, maybe every room."

"That does not matter. I will cast a spell to guard

us before we set a single foot inside." He leveled her with an intense stare. "Are you ready?"

She gulped, nodded.

"Put your arms around my neck and hold tight."

After only a slight hesitation, Grace intertwined her shaky fingers around his neck, pressing her breasts into the hardness of his chest. Tingles raced through her nipples. "We could get into serious trouble for this," she said. "I don't know why I suggested it."

He grazed her lips with his own. "Because you love your brother."

Ripping fabric drifted to her ears a split second before Darius's shirt fell to the ground. His long, glorious wings unfurled. Her heartbeat galloped as her feet lost their solid anchor on the ground. *Whoosh. Whoosh.* A cool breeze stirred.

"What's happening?" she gasped, but she knew the answer. "Darius, this is—"

"Do not panic," he said, his grip on her tightening. "I have not forgotten how to fly. All you need do is hang on to me."

"I'm not panicked." She laughed. "I'm exhilarated. We're flying on the Darius Express." They moved quickly, smoothly, higher with every second that passed.

He uttered a chuckle of his own and shook his head. "I expected fear from you. Will you ever cease to amaze me, sweet Grace?"

"I hope not." She looked down, loving how the cars and people appeared like small specks, loving the giddiness of hovering in the air.

The moon loomed closer and larger, growing in intensity until she could only gape at its luminance. Darius chanted under his breath, and a strange vibration unfurled from him, a vibration that began as nothing more than a slight tremble, then grew into an intense shaking through the entire apartment building. No one below seemed to notice.

The shaking stopped.

"We are safe now," he said.

She didn't ask how exactly since they had reached Jason's upper balcony. As his wings glided them slowly forward, Darius set her firmly on the ground. The action drew a grunt from him, and she glanced up at his face. His cheekbones stretched taut and lacked any color. He kept his gaze from her as he drew in a shaky breath.

"You're weak again," she said, concerned. "Perhaps you should go home and—"

"I am fine." Irritation—with her or himself?—lashed from his tone.

She gulped, determined to get him out of here as quickly as possible. "Let's hurry, then."

White gauzy drapes billowed around the French double doors. Grace brushed them aside and tried the knob. Locked. "Do you know how to pick these?"

"No need." Darius ushered her aside, positioned himself in front of the doors and spewed rays of fire. The wood around the glass panels quickly charred. The tinkle of glass erupted as the panels fell and hit the ground.

"Thank you." Stepping over the jagged pieces,

Grace waved her hand in front of her nose to whisk away the smoke. Unabashedly she entered Jason Graves's home. "It's so dark," she whispered.

"Your eyes will adjust." He didn't use a breaking-and-entering voice. He used a why-are-you-whispering-you-silly-woman voice.

Even as he spoke, her vision opened and objects became clear. A chaise longue, a glass coffee table. "What about motion sensors and security cameras?" she asked. "Are we one hundred percent protected from those?"

"Yes. The spell disabled them."

Allowing herself to relax, she padded throughout the living room, tracing her fingertips over the paintings and jewels—yes, jewels—hanging on the walls. "So much wealth," she said. "And none of it belongs to him. It's like we've stepped through the mist and into Atlantis."

Darius remained at the threshold, his teeth bared in a red-hot snarl as he took in the stolen Atlantean artifacts.

"I know you're a child of the gods," she said, hoping to distract him from his fury, "but you're not technically a god. Where does your magic come from?"

"My father," he said, losing his infuriated edge. He entered, his steps clipped. "He practiced the ancient arts."

The image of his parents' lifeless bodies flashed in her mind again, exactly as she'd seen them in her vision when he'd cast his binding spell. She ached for the little boy he'd been, the child who'd found his family slain. She couldn't imagine the pain he must have suffered—and still suffered.

"I'm sorry for their deaths," she told him, letting her remorse and sorrow seep out with the words. "Your loss of family."

Darius stilled and glanced over at her. "How did you know they were…gone?"

"I saw them. In your mind. When you cast the binding spell."

His shoulders straightened, and surprise flashed through his eyes. "They were my life," he said.

"I know," she said softly, aching for him.

"Perhaps one day I will tell you of them." The offer emerged hesitant, but there all the same.

"I would love that."

He nodded, a little stiff. "Right now, we must search for any information this Jason has about Atlantis and your brother."

"I'll check the library for the *Book of Ra-Dracus.*" She looked around. "I'm willing to bet *he's* the one who stole it from my brother."

"I will search the rest of the home."

With a last, lingering glance, they branched off. The floors were polished mahogany panels, and the decor something out of a medieval home and garden magazine. Upstairs, Grace quickly found the study. Piles of books littered every corner, and some appeared old and well used. She flipped through each one, finding references to dragons and liquid nitrogen, magic spells and vampires, but none were the *Book of Ra-Dracus*. A large walnut desk consumed the center and a world globe made completely of…what was that? Some sort of jewel, perhaps? Purple, like an amethyst, but jagged like crystal. She studied it more closely. In the center, a waterfall churned around a single body of land. Around Atlantis. And a pulsing sapphire.

Though she wanted to study it more closely, she forced herself on the matter at hand. She moved toward the desk and shuffled through the papers on top. Finding nothing of importance, she withdrew a letter opener and, after struggling for several minutes, pried open the drawer locks. Inside the bottom drawer, she discovered photos that shocked and repelled her. She covered her mouth to muffle her horrified gasp. The graphic images depicted dragon and human warriors covered in a white foam, blood flowing from multiple bullet wounds. Some showed Alex and Teira. The two were lying in a jewel-encrusted cell, dirty but alive. Several held grotesque imprints of tall, pale creatures with eerie blue eyes feasting off the dragon bodies. The humans standing off to the side watched, their expressions a mix of fear, disgust, and titillation.

Why take photos of his crimes? As a memento? To prove the existence of Atlantis? Or did he hope to write a book, *How I Like to Kill?* She scowled.

She replayed the vision of her brother that Darius's medallion had supplied. This room wasn't the one Alex first occupied. This was a different room, one she knew resided in Atlantis. Those jeweled walls were very similar to what she'd seen inside Darius's home. When her husband returned to his home, she thought, more determined now than before, she was going with him.

Perhaps Darius sensed her growing disquiet, because the next thing she knew, he stood over her.

"What do you—" He paused, then very slowly, very precisely, reached over her shoulder and slipped the photos from her hands. She tried to pry them from him because she didn't want him to see the travesties done to his friends. He held tightly. "This is Javar and his men. And these are vampires."

Vampires. She shuddered. Having proof of their actual existence settled like lead in her stomach.

"I'm so sorry," she said, turning to face him. His eyes narrowed, but even from those tiny slits she could see their color glowed ice-blue. Fragments of grief radiated from him and into her.

"What else is in there?" He set the photos aside with one fluid motion, a deceptively calm motion.

Allowing him to change the subject, she said, "That's it. Did you find anything?"

"More artifacts from Atlantis." Radiating cold determination, he clasped her hand. "Jason Graves deserves so much more than death. He deserves to suffer."

Another shudder worked through her, because she knew he would do everything in his power to see that Jason got exactly what he deserved.

And she planned to help him.

GRACE WANTED TO BANG her head against the wall.

She and Darius arrived home several hours ago, yet he still remained rigid with tension. He refused to speak. She hated this, hated the remorse radiating from him.

He sat on the couch, his head back, his eyes closed. Not knowing what else to do, she quietly approached. "I want to show you something."

His eyelids reluctantly opened. When he offered no reply and made no move to rise, she added, "Pretty please with a cherry on top."

Not a single word left his lips, but he stood. Grace wrapped her fingers around his and ushered him into the bathroom. She didn't explain her actions; she simply removed his clothing, then her own. He was in need of loving—and she was going to give it to him. All the loving he could stand.

After turning the knobs and allowing the water to heat, she stepped inside the tub and tugged Darius in behind her. Still he remained silent. Hot water cascaded down their naked bodies, and as she stood in front of him, she lathered his chest with soap.

"I've got a joke for you," she said, mentally converting jokes she knew into dragon jokes.

He frowned—his first reaction. It didn't matter that he'd only given her a frown. She'd take anything she could get.

"What did the dragon say when he saw a knight in shining armor?"

His brow wrinkled, and he sighed.

"Oh, no, not another canned meal."

Slowly, so slowly, his lips inched up in a smile.

I did that, she thought with a surge of pride. *I made him smile.* She basked in the warmth of it and all the while his smile continued to grow. So sweet, so endearing, it lit his entire face. His eyes darkened, becoming that golden-brown she loved. He traced his fingertip over her cheekbone.

"Tell me another one," he said.

She nearly sank to her knees in relief at the sound of his rich, husky voice. Grinning happily, she slipped behind him and traced her soapy hands over his back. "It's long," she warned.

"Even better," he said, tugging her in front. He nibbled on her ear, dragging the sensitive lobe through his teeth.

"There was a dragon who had a long-standing obsession with a queen's breasts," she said, growing breathless. "The dragon knew the penalty to touch her would mean death, yet he revealed his secret desire to the king's chief doctor. This man promised he could arrange for the dragon to satisfy his desire, but it would cost him one thousand gold coins." She spread her soapy hands over his nipples, then down his arms. "Though he didn't have the money, the dragon readily agreed to the scheme."

"Grace," Darius moaned, his erection straining against her stomach.

She hid her smile, loving that she had this much power over such a strong man. That she, Grace Carlyle, made him ache with longing. "The next day the physician made a batch of itching powder and poured some into the queen's bra...uh, you might call it a brassiere...while she bathed. After she dressed, she began itching and itching and itching. The physician was summoned to the Royal Chambers, and he informed the king and queen that only a special saliva, if applied for several hours, would cure this type of itch. And only a dragon possessed this special saliva." Out of breath, she paused.

"Continue," Darius said. His arms wound around her so tightly she could barely breathe. His skin blazed hot against hers, hotter than even the steamy water.

"Are you sure?"

"Continue." Taut lines bracketed his mouth.

"Well, the king summoned the dragon. Meanwhile, the physician slipped him the antidote for the itching powder, which the dragon put into his mouth, and for the next few hours, the dragon worked passionately on the queen's breasts.

"Anyway," she said, reaching around him and lathering the muscled mounds of his butt, "the queen's itching was eventually relieved, and the dragon left satisfied and touted as a hero."

"This does not sound like a joke," Darius said.

"I'm getting to the punch line. Hang on. When the physician demanded his payment, the now satisfied dragon refused. He knew that the physician could never report what really happened to the king. So the next day, the physician slipped a massive dose of the same itching powder into the king's loincloth. And the king immediately summoned the dragon."

Darius threw back his head and barked with laughter. The sound boomed raw and new, and she fell deeper in love with him at that moment. She'd never heard anything so precious because she knew how rare such amusement was for him. She hoped he found such joy every day they spent together.

When his laughter subsided, a sensual light glowed in his eyes. His features were so relaxed, so open. "I'm intrigued by this breast feasting," he whispered, rubbing his nose against hers.

"I am, too," she admitted. "I have an itch."

"Allow me to help you." He pressed his lips to hers in a lazy, delicious kiss. His fiery flavor, his heat, his masculinity, still managed to enthrall her. Need and desperation wrapped around every inch of her body, and she threaded her wet hands around his neck.

His palms caressed a slippery path down her spine and stopped at the small indentation at the base. When those scorching fingers dipped lower, cupped and pulled her tightly against him, she sucked in an eager breath. She pressed her lower half into him, cradling his erection. Her nerve endings were alive with the memories of making love, and longed to repeat the experience.

"I'm going to have you again," he said.

"Yes, yes."

"Tell me you want me."

"I do. I want you."

"Tell me you need me."

"So much I'll die without you."

"Tell me you love me."

"I do. I love you."

She was living passion in his arms, Darius thought, and she was all his.

"Kiss me. And don't ever stop kissing me," she said.

He did more than kiss her. He gifted her with sweet nips and erotic licks, then proceeded to suck every drop of water from her body. He invaded her senses until all she could see, all she could feel, all she could taste was him. She shivered when the tip of his tongue swirled along the edge of her ear.

Suddenly he paused. A slow, suspended moment dragged by. "Help me forget the past," he whispered brokenly.

She nuzzled his neck and dipped her hand over his ridged abdomen. When she clasped his thick erection, he hissed in a breath. She didn't hold him long, just long enough to stroke him up and down. Then she released him, granting him one last fleeting, teasing caress before cupping the heavy sac of his testicles.

While her fingers gently tugged, she swirled her tongue around his nipples. They felt like little spikes in her mouth, and she lapped at the masculine taste of him mingled with the water.

"How am I doing so far?"

"I need more time to decide," he said roughly, raggedly. His fingers tangled in her hair, then massaged her neck…her breasts.

The sight of his strong, bronze hands on her soft,

white flesh proved the most erotic thing she'd ever seen. Once more she curled her fingers around his length. He was so hot and big, so hard. Up and down, she tormented him. She wanted so badly to fill his days with happiness, to help him "forget" his pain, as he'd said. No, not forget, but heal. She would do whatever was necessary to give him the peace he craved.

"What's your naughtiest fantasy?" she murmured against his collarbone. She bit down, not hard enough to break the skin, but hard enough to leave her mark. "Perhaps I can make it come true."

"You are my fantasy, Grace." His hands cupped her jaw, and he forced her to look up at him. "Only you."

If she hadn't already loved him, she would have fallen just then. "I have a fantasy," she whispered. She licked the seam of his lips. "Want to hear?"

He trailed his hands down her back, making her shiver, then cupped her bottom and jerked her into him for deeper contact. "Tell me."

"Well, I like to read books about big, strong warriors who love as fiercely as they fight, and I've always wanted one for my very own."

His lips twitched. "Now you have one."

"Oh, yes." The warm water made their skin slick and she rubbed against him, letting the peaks of her nipples abrade his chest, letting the plump head of his penis catch between her legs. "What I fantasize about is my big, strong warrior lifting me up, pressing my back into the shower tile and filling me."

He pressed her back against the cool tile and shoved inside her, deep and hard and scorching. Steam billowed around them, but it was the spicy scent of dragon and soap that filled her nostrils. He felt so good inside her, more exciting than climbing a mountain or bungee jumping from a bridge.

He pumped in and out of her, and she wound her arms around him. His strength beneath her palms filled her with heady power. He bit her neck, making her shiver. He spread her knees wider and pounded harder. She panted his name. Moaned his name. Gasped his name.

"Grace," he growled. "Mine."

And she was. Completely.

DARIUS HELD A SLEEPING Grace in the tight clasp of his arms.

She possessed inner strength, a giving heart and a deep capacity for love. Her smile gleamed brighter than the sun. Her laughter healed him. Actually *healed* him.

As he lay in the stillness of the night, with hazy moonlight enveloping him, he remained weak and sated from their loving. Long forgotten memories finally resurfaced, bits and pieces of his past, pieces he'd thought buried so deeply they'd remain lost forever. He didn't fight them, but closed his eyes, saw his mother laugh down at him, her smile as gentle and beautiful as the pristine waters that surrounded their city. Her golden eyes flashed merrily.

She had caught him with his father's sword,

brandishing the weapon through the air with a dramatic flourish, trying to mimic the warrior strength his father possessed.

"One day," she said in that sweet, lyrical voice of hers, "your strength will far surpass that of your father." She claimed the sword from him and leaned the gleaming silver against the nearest wall. "You will fight beside him and protect each other from harm."

That day never came.

He saw his father, strong and proud and loyal, striding up the cliff that led to their home. He'd just come from a battle with the Formorians, had washed away the blood on his skin, but his clothing still bore traces. When he spied him, his father smiled and opened his arms. Seven-year-old Darius ran to him and threw himself into the waiting embrace.

"I've been gone only three weeks, but look how you've grown," his father said, squeezing him tightly. "Gods, I missed you."

"I missed you, too." He fought back a tear.

His strong, warrior father wiped the moisture from his own eyes. "Come on, son. Let's go greet your mother and sisters."

Together, they walked side by side into the small house. His three sisters danced around a fire, laughing and chanting, their long dark hair bouncing about their shoulders. They each possessed identical features, plump cheeks and such innocence it hurt to gaze at them.

"Darius," they called when they saw him, running

to him first, though they'd seen him only a few hours ago. They shared a special bond with him that he could not explain. It had always been there, and would always remain.

He hugged them close, drawing in the sweetness of their scents. "Father has returned. Give him a proper greeting."

Their faces lit with their grins and they propelled themselves at the warrior.

"My precious hatchlings," he said, laughing through more tears.

Their mother heard their mingled joy and rushed inside the chamber. They spent the rest of the day together, not a single member of the family straying far.

How happy they'd been.

Here, in the present, a lone tear slid from the corner of Darius's eye. He did not wipe it away, but allowed it to trickle down his cheek and onto his ear.

As tuned to him as she was, Grace sensed his torment. She shifted to face him, her features alight with concern. "Darius?" she said softly. "It's okay. Whatever it is, it will be okay."

Another tear came, then another. He couldn't stop them, and wasn't sure he wanted to. "I miss them," he said brokenly. "They were my life."

She understood immediately. "Tell me about them. Tell me the good things."

"My sisters were like sunlight, starlight and moonlight." Their images filled his mind once again, and this time he nearly choked from pain. And yet…the pain was not the fearsome destroyer he had expected, but a reminder that he lived and loved. "Every night they created a small fire and would dance around the flames. They were so proud of their ability and were determined to one day create the biggest fire Atlantis had ever seen."

"They didn't fear being burned?"

"Dragons welcome and thrive in such heat. I wish you could have seen them. They were all that is good and right."

"What were their names?" she asked softly.

"Katha, Kandace and Kallia," he said. With an animalistic growl, he slammed his fist into the side of the mattress. "Why did they have to die? Travelers tortured and killed my sisters as if they were garbage."

Grace wrapped her arms around him and laid her head in the hollow of his neck. There was nothing she could say to ease his anguish, so she held him more tightly.

He rubbed at his stinging eyes. "They did not deserve such a death. They did not deserve what they suffered."

"I know, I know," she cooed.

He buried his face in the hollow of her neck and cried.

At last, Darius mourned.

CHAPTER TWENTY

GRACE RIFFLED THROUGH the box of Kevlar vests she'd picked up downstairs. Darius knelt on the other side and pinched one of the heavy black vests between his fingers. His lips curled with distaste.

She watched him. His eyes shone with vitality, alive with gold, glistening with contentment. They had been like that since last night and hadn't changed. Hadn't even flickered with blue. The fine lines around his eyes and mouth had relaxed, as well, and there was an ease about him that warmed her heart. Oh, he still possessed that dangerous aura. Danger would always be a part of him. But the coldness, the hopelessness, were both gone.

How she loved this man.

"Try one on," she said.

Frowning, he tugged the material over his shoulders. She leaned over and worked the Velcro for him. "It's too tight," he said.

"If a bullet smacks into you, you'll wish it was even tighter."

He snorted. "How can these do any good?"

"Maybe you'll understand better after I show you

how to use a gun." She raced to her kitchen and dug out the gun she'd stuffed into one of the drawers. She doubled-checked to make sure no bullets rested in the cylinder.

"This is a revolver," she explained when she stood behind Darius. Wrapping her arms around him, she placed the cold metal in his hands and curled his fingers in the correct places. "Hold it just like this."

His shaking fingers squeezed.

"Gently," she said, noticing how unsteady he suddenly seemed.

He tossed her a glance over his shoulder. "Who taught you these skills?"

"Alex. He said a woman should know how to protect herself." Fighting a wave of sadness, Grace steadied Darius's wrists by locking her palms underneath them. He might be more relaxed and at ease than ever before, but he battled that damn weakness and she didn't like it. The only time he seemed to recover his full strength was when he was sexually excited.

Grace wet her lips and purposefully meshed her breasts into the hard ridges of his back. "You want to keep your finger on the trigger and pick a target. Any target. Do you have one?"

"Oh, yes." His voice grew stronger and deeper. If she allowed her hands to slide inside his pants, she knew she would find him hard and thick.

"Good," she said. "Aim down the sight on the barrel."

Pause. Then, "What?"

She blew on his neck. "Aim down the sight on the barrel," she repeated.

Another pause. "How can I concentrate when your body is pressed to mine?"

In response, her fingers tickled up his arms. If sexual arousal kept him strong, she'd use everything in her power to arouse him. "Do you want to learn how to shoot or not?" she whispered huskily.

"I do," he ground out.

"Is your target in sight?"

He felt the heat of her, Darius thought, the sizzle of her, throughout his entire body. Yes, he had his target in sight. The couch. Exactly where he wanted her, naked and open.

He flicked a glance to the window. The sun arrived hours ago, vanquishing the binding spell. He should have left for his homeland. He possessed everything he needed from the surface. Atlantis called him, and it was long past time he destroyed her invaders.

But he wasn't ready to say goodbye to Grace.

He couldn't take her with him. She would be safest here, and her safety mattered more to him than anything else.

When this whole mess with the Argonauts ended, he would come back for her. He would whisk this woman, *his* woman, his *wife*—gods, he liked the sound of that—to Atlantis. They were going to stay in bed for days, weeks, perhaps months, and they were going to make love every way possible, then invent some new ways.

"Target in sight," he said.

"Squeeze the trigger," she said.

He easily recalled how she had squeezed him. How her inquisitive fingers had slipped beneath the hem of his shirt and skimmed the taut flesh of his lower abdomen. He ground his teeth together.

"Darius?"

"Hmm?" he bit out.

"Squeeze the trigger." She blew in his ear.

He squeezed. He heard a *click*.

"If the couch were human, and this a loaded gun, a bullet would have shot out and punctured skin, causing grave injury," Grace the temptress said. The woman who had sneaked past his defenses and infiltrated his senses. The woman who had captured his heart. "The lining inside these vests stops bullets and keeps them from entering bodies."

Darius spun, keeping her arms locked around him. The gun fell from his hands. He wrapped his fingers around her wrists and directed her aim lower.

"I have another target in mind," he said. And he kept his "target" busy for the next hour.

SATED AND REDRESSED, Grace tucked her gun in the waist of her jeans, filled her pockets with bullets and helped Darius gather the remaining vests. With that done, they squared off, facing each other. Neither moved.

"It's time to go," he finally said.

"I'm ready," she said with false confidence. She

raised her chin, not removing her gaze from him, but daring him to contradict her.

He regarded her silently for an inexorable moment, his expression blank. "You will remain here, Grace."

She bit back a scowl. She'd known he would do this, but knowing didn't stop the anger, the hurt. "Wrong," she said. "Alex is my brother, and I'll help find him."

"Your safety comes first."

"I'm safest with you." Her eyes narrowed, showing him the first sign of her increasing ire. "Besides, I'm your wife. Where you go, I go."

"I'll return for you and bring back your brother."

She gripped his shirt, tugging him close. "I can help you, and we both know it."

Pain flashed in his eyes, but was quickly overshadowed by determination. "This is the only way. I must lead my dragons into war, and I will not allow my woman near battlegrounds."

"What about the binding spell?" Ha! She watched him with almost smug expectation. "I can't leave your presence."

"The spell broke when the moon disappeared."

Her shoulders dropped. She racked her brain, searching for anything, anything at all, that might change his mind. When the answer arose, she smiled slowly. "Perhaps you're forgetting the Argonauts. That they had me followed."

Arching a brow, he crossed his arms over his chest. "What are you saying?"

"They could have me followed again. They

could try to hurt me this time, instead of simply watching me."

He stroked his jaw as he considered her words. "You are right," he admitted darkly.

She relaxed, thinking she finally convinced him of her point—until he next opened his mouth.

"I will simply lock you inside my palace."

Her earlier scowl broke free, and she poked him in the chest. "I like this macho thing you've got going on. I really do. But I won't stand for it."

Without a word he clasped her wrist with one hand and held the handle of the suitcase with the other. The air around them began to swirl. Bright-colored sparks flickered like dying lightbulbs, then quickly sped past them. The temperature never changed, the wind never kicked up, but suddenly the cave closed around her.

Grace didn't have time to catch her bearings. Never breaking his momentum, Darius pulled her inside the mist. The moment she realized exactly where she was, she threw herself in his arms.

"I've got you," he said.

His voice soothed her racing heartbeat. Only a minute or two passed before Darius unhooked her hands from his neck, gave her a quick kiss and ushered her into another cave.

Not even slightly dizzy, she cataloged her newest surroundings. A man—Brand, she recalled—stood off to the side. He held a sword above his head, and there was a deadly gleam in his eyes as he stared at her. Before she could utter a protest, Grace found herself shoved behind Darius.

"Brand," Darius barked.

At the sound of his voice, Brand's gaze finally flicked away from her. He glanced at Darius and relaxed. He even lowered his sword. "Why does the woman still live?" he demanded.

"Touch her and I will kill you."

"She is from the surface," he spat.

"She is my mate."

"She is—"

"My mate," he said firmly. "Therefore, she is one of us."

A childish part of Grace wanted to stick her tongue out at Brand. She hadn't forgotten that he'd once called her a whore.

Brand considered those words, and his fierce expression softened. He even grinned. "Tell me what you learned."

"Gather the others and meet me in the dining hall. I will tell you when I tell them."

Brand nodded, and with a final glance in her direction, he rushed off.

"I am glad to be home," Darius said. His strength had returned in its entirety the moment he'd stepped through the mist, and now he breathed deeply of its familiar essence. "I need you to demonstrate the gun and vests to my warriors."

She shook her head. "Not unless you're willing to compromise with me."

"I do not compromise." His tone was as stern as his expression. "Come."

She glared at him the entire way to the dining hall.

The dragon warriors were gathered around the table, standing with their arms locked behind their backs and their feet braced apart. When they spotted her, they each glanced to Brand who wore a smug, I-told-you-so frown. The youngest of the group offered her a smile, if you could call baring of teeth a smile. She waved nervously.

"Hi, again," she said.

Darius squeezed her hand. "Do not be scared," he told her, then glanced pointedly at each man present. "They will not muss a single hair on your head."

In the next instant, questions were hurled at Darius. "Why did you take a human for your mate? When? What happened while you were gone? What happened to Javar?"

"Give him a minute," Grace told them.

Darius smiled at her and tenderly kissed her lips.

Madox gasped. "Did you see that?"

"I did. I saw," Grayley said, awed.

"A human female has succeeded where we failed," Renard said. "She made Darius smile."

"I've made him laugh, too," she pronounced.

Darius rolled his eyes. "Show them what we have brought."

Despite his failure to compromise, she did as he asked. His safety, and that of his people, came before her sensibilities. "This is a Kevlar vest," she explained, demonstrating how to maneuver the Velcro fasteners.

"You must remain in human form to wear it," Darius said. "Your wings will be trapped by its wrappings. However, it will protect your chest against the enemies' weapons."

"I have a more important part I'd like to protect," Brittan said with a smile of his own.

A round of laughter followed.

"Now demonstrate the gun," Darius said.

Grace nodded and withdrew the gun from the waist of her pants. "This expels bullets, and those bullets cut through clothing and skin and bone, and sometimes lodge themselves inside the body. You can't see them, but they leave a hole and make the victim bleed. If you want to survive, you must dig them out."

Silence reigned as they considered her words and actions.

Each of the men wanted to view the gun. She once again double-checked to make sure she'd removed the bullets, then passed it around. "They come in many sizes, some much bigger than this, so be prepared."

After everyone viewed the weapon, Darius returned it to her. "Guns such as this were used to destroy Javar and his army."

Some warriors gasped. Some hissed. Some blinked in shock. "So they are dead?" Madox asked sharply.

Darius didn't flinch his gaze. "Yes. Both humans and vampires seized the palace."

Their fury became a palpable force, wrapping around each of them. "Why did you make us wait? Why did you not let us slaughter the vampires days ago," Tagart shouted.

"Had you approached them, you would be dead," he said flatly. "Vampires are already powerful, but aided as they are by the humans…"

Tagart had the grace to nod in acknowledgment.

"An entire dragon army wiped out," the tallest said, shaking his head. "It hardly seems possible."

"We will claim vengeance this day," Darius said. "We will reclaim Atlantis, our home. We go to war!"

Cheers of anticipation erupted.

"Gather what you need," Darius finished when the cheers died down. "We leave within the hour."

"Wait!" Grace called as the warriors shuffled out of the room. They paused and glanced back at her. "There's a man, a human with red hair. He's my brother. Keep him safe."

They looked to Darius. He nodded. "He is to be protected and brought to me."

The men filed out. All except Brand. He approached Darius's side. "The men need you to lead them. I will remain behind and guard the mist."

"Thank you," Darius said, and clapped him on the shoulder. "You are a true friend."

When they were alone, he turned to Grace. "Come," he said, an order he'd obviously become quite fond of.

She didn't protest as he led her to the entrance of his room. "Are you sure you don't want me to guard your back?" she said as he hustled her inside.

His golden eyes darkened. "I do not mind a woman going into battle. I mind *my* woman going into battle."

"Darius—"

"Grace." He closed the distance between them and meshed her lips with his. His tongue swept inside, conquering. She wound her arms around his neck, accepting him fully. Loving him completely. When he pulled away, they were both panting.

"Darius," she whispered again.

His heated gaze met hers. "I love you," he said.

Of all the times to give her those words!

"Tell me what I want to hear," he demanded.

"I love you, too," she sighed. "Here, take my gun."

He already had bullets.

He took it and gave her one final kiss. Without another word, he left her in his room. Alone. The doors slid firmly shut behind him, and Grace looked down at her hands. They were shaking, not from the lust that sluiced through her body; that was always there and would never go away. This time a gut-wrenching fear caused her tremors. Fear for Darius. For her brother.

She had thought about stealing a medallion, but had changed her mind at the last moment. Waiting here would be hard, but she would do it. For Darius. She would pray and she would plan, because one way or another vampires and Argonauts were going down. Hopefully, her men would not be harmed in the process. If they were…God help the citizens of Atlantis. Guns would be the least of their worries.

CHAPTER TWENTY-ONE

DARIUS STOOD in the forest, gazing down at the carnage before him. He'd flown here at lightning speed, only to learn the unit he'd sent to guard Javar's palace had been bested. They were covered in a white film and blood streamed from bullet wounds. Some were alive. Most were dead. His wings retracted and he dropped his vest. His hands curled into fists. Those humans *must* be stopped.

"Find the survivors," he called. Then he and the dragon warriors branched off, searching for the living.

He cursed under his breath as moans of pain filled his ears. How many more would die before this ended? Frowning, he strode over to Vorik, who lay prone and still. He knelt down.

Vorik's eyelids opened slowly and Darius pushed out a breath of relief that his man lived. He withdrew a sharp silver blade from his back scabbard and blew fire on the metal. When it cooled, he dug out the bullets just as Grace had shown him. Vorik grimaced and tried to pull away.

"Tell me of the attack," he said to distract him.

"Their weapons…" Vorik said, calming. "Strange."

Renard approached and crouched beside him just as Vorik fainted. "What happened to them?" He touched the white, dusty coating and jerked his hand away. "What is this cold substance that covers their bodies?"

Darius turned stark eyes in his friend's direction. "I do not know what it is. Don gloves if you must, but do as Grace advised and dig out the bullets."

The carnage reminded him of the day he'd found his family slaughtered, and as he worked, he had to bite back a groan. Had he not shared his pain with Grace, he might have collapsed from the weight of it now. With shaky hands he continued on to body after body. The dragon's recuperative blood helped them heal as soon as the small bullets were removed. If only Javar had known this, how many of his warriors could he have saved?

When he finished, Darius gazed down at his blood-soaked hands. He'd had blood on his hands before, and hadn't reacted. But this affected him. How much more blood would he wear before this day ended? He knew the answer: by the end of the day, blood would flow like a river. He only prayed the blood did not belong to his own forces, but his enemies.

He shoved to his feet, gripping the hilt of his blade. "We must reclaim what belongs to us," he shouted. "Who will fight with me?"

"I will." "Me," rang out. Every warrior standing wanted the chance to avenge the wrongs done.

"May the gods be with us," he said under his

breath. His wings sprang from his back. He swooped up his vest, gripping the black material and smearing it with blood. Using the strength in his legs, he pushed off the ground. The glide of his wings kept him in the air and moving higher, faster. His army followed behind him. He heard the rustle of their wings, felt the intensity of their determination.

Human guards roamed the top of Javar's palace. When they spotted Darius, they shouted, aimed and fired. In the air, he dodged the multiple rounds of bullets and spewed his own fire. His warriors did the same, burning the humans and their weapons. Then, one of his warriors grunted and was suddenly falling from the sky. He didn't see who it was, but continued breathing his fire.

A gong sounded, loud, high-pitched.

The humans atop the ledge didn't live long enough to hear it. Their scorched bodies withered into ash and floated on the breeze. Darius settled his feet on the jagged crystal. His wings retracted, and he quickly drew on his vest and fastened the straps. When his warriors were properly protected, as well, he met each of their stares one by one and waited for nods of readiness.

He withdrew a long, silver blade with one hand, the gun with the other, and approached the dome seam. Sensing his medallion, the two sides silently parted. He gazed down, but could not see anyone inside, surrounded as they were by a thick fog. He heard the shuffle of their panicked footsteps, however, and the murmur of their fear.

He would have preferred *flying* into the unknown, but the vest would not allow it.

He jumped.

His men quickly followed suit.

Down, down he fell. When his feet hit the ground, his entire body reverberated with the impact. He grunted and rolled.

Humans screamed and scrambled out of the way. Their shock delayed their reaction, and Darius used that to his advantage. He jolted to his feet, sword raised and struck his first victim. The human gurgled in pain, clutching his chest, then collapsed.

Behind him, his warriors fought valiantly. Breathing fire. Always breathing fire. He didn't pause, but advanced on his next target. A look of sheer terror contorted the young man's features when he realized Darius was coming for him. The man aimed a long black gun at Darius's chest and fired. One bullet after another slammed into Darius, causing only pinpricks of pain. He laughed. Eyes widening, the man dropped his gun and gripped a thick tube that rose from a red canister on his back. White foam sprayed out and over Darius's skin, so cold his blood hardened with ice crystals. His dark laughter increased.

A Guardian of the Mist welcomed cold. Was strengthened by it. He raised his own gun and fired, aiming for the head. The man's body spasmed, then sank lifeless at his feet.

The alarm grew louder, screeching in his ears and soon blending with the sound of gunshots. He winced at a sharp sting in his thigh, glanced down, and saw trickles of blood where a bullet had pierced. Never slowing, he rocked forward, using the momentum to slay an enemy with his blade.

Having destroyed every human within striking distance, he darted his gaze throughout the room, searching where to fight next. He watched through horror-filled eyes as Madox fell, his body covered in white foam, blood seeping from numerous wounds in his arms and legs. Darius emptied his gun of bullets, all of them slamming into a human many yards away.

He didn't know if his friend lived or died, and his stomach twisted. With a growl of pure rage, he raced forward and spewed a stream of fire, catching the last of the humans and igniting them like a bonfire. They did not dodge it fast enough. Their screams echoed from the walls, and the scent of burning flesh filled his nostrils. He tossed his gun to the ground.

The moans soon quieted and smoldering corpses littered the floor. With the battle over, he counted how many of his men still stood. Only three had fallen. He carried Madox outside and laid him on the ground. The others followed, some limping, some relatively unharmed. Renard rushed to his side and examined Madox, then helped remove the bullets.

"He'll live," Renard announced with relief.

Filled with his own relief, Darius gripped the dagger he held and sank the tip into one of the wounds on his leg. He grimaced. The bullets hurt more coming out than they had going in, but he welcomed the pain.

As he continued to work the knife in his other injuries, he realized he and his warriors reigned victorious. Yet…where was the sense of joy and accomplishment he should have had?

"What do we do next?" Renard asked, sitting down beside him.

"I do not know. Their leader, Jason, was not here," he fumed.

"How do you know?"

"The cowardly bastard is—" Darius did not finish his sentence. Something stirred in his soul, something dark, and he knew Grace was in danger. His blood curdled. He ripped off his medallion and held it in his hands. Because he couldn't call on Grace's image, he said, "Show me Jason Graves."

The twin eyes lit with glowing red beams. Jason's image formed in the middle. He was standing in front of Grace—who was chained to a wall. Vampires surrounded the two, eyeing Grace hungrily. She struggled against the chains. "What have you done with my brother?"

"I recaptured him and that dragon whore of his. And if you don't shut your mouth, I'll kill him while you watch," he said with an evil smile. "Mitch told me how protective Darius is of you. I wonder how much he's willing to give up for you."

"Leave him out of this," she spat, then pressed her lips together. Her face and clothes were dirty and her bottom lip was swollen. Darius's world darkened to one emotion: rage. It was a cold, calculated rage that wanted Jason's blood drenching his hands. They had sneaked into his home and taken her. They would pay.

He forced himself to study the rest of the vision, searching for clues as to where Grace was being held. When he saw Layel, king of vampires, he knew—and his fear for Grace grew in intensity.

The vision faded all too quickly.

He squeezed his fingers over the medallion. "Those who are well enough, come with me. We fly to meet the vampires. *Now.*"

Wings sprouted from his back, ripping away his vest. Every dragon still breathing unfurled his wings, as well. He experienced a moment of pride. These warriors were injured, but they remained faithfully by his side. They would fight—and die if they must.

THE VAMPIRE STRONGHOLD loomed on the horizon.

Black stone gave the large structure a haunted aura, casting shadows in every direction. Even the windows were blackened. No foliage grew here, for no living thing could thrive among the destruction and decay. Drained bodies hung from pikes, acting as a visual warning of the death that waited within, ready to strike.

Grace was inside.

Swallowing back his fear for her, Darius flew to the highest window and motioned for his warriors to do the same. The thin railing provided no ledge to stand upon, so he simply hovered there. A cold sweat covered his skin, and his teeth gnashed together. He was a man who liked to wait and study his enemy before attacking. But he couldn't—wouldn't—wait. Not this time. His warriors watched him, floating on silent wings. He couldn't see through the darkened glass, but could hear voices.

A woman's scream filled his ears. *Grace!*

He immediately gave the signal. Glass shattered as they propelled inside. Vampires hissed and humans aimed their guns. No longer protected by the vests, the dragons were vulnerable—and they knew it.

Darius pushed, shoved and sliced his way toward Grace. Careful not to burn her with his fire.

When she spied him, she struggled fruitlessly against her chains. "Darius," she called, her voice weak, hollow.

Jason Graves stood beside her, his expression one of shock and rage. Seeing Darius, the coward trained his gun on Grace's temple. Darius did not allow himself to look at his wife's face; he would have crumbled, and he had to stay strong. So it was then that he saw the blood oozing down her neck and onto her shirt.

"We both know I'm going to kill you this day," he told Jason, deceptively serene. "Your actions merely dictate whether you die quickly." His gaze narrowed. "Or whether I make you suffer endlessly."

Jason's hand shook as his gaze darted between Darius and the raging battle. Dragons breathed fire, scorching vampires and humans. Howls and shrieks blended together, creating a symphony of death. Sulfur coated the air.

"Kill me," Jason said, desperate, "and you'll never recover the *Book of Ra-Dracus*."

Intent only on saving Grace, Darius stalked toward him. "I care not for the book."

"One step closer, and I'll kill her. Do you hear me?" he screamed. "I'll kill her!"

Darius stilled completely. Yet…intense fury boiled in his blood, hotter and hotter until finally transforming him into his dragon self. He howled at the suddenness of the change, at the way his body elongated and sharpened. Scales armored his skin. His teeth lengthened and thinned, honed to razor-sharp points. His claws unsheathed. He felt the heat of the change and welcomed it.

Jason's eyes grew round, filling with undiluted terror. "Oh, my God," he gasped. He whipped his gun to Darius and squeezed the trigger.

Darius absorbed the impact of each bullet and launched himself at Jason. He twisted in the air, slashing the man's face with his tail. The bastard screamed, collapsed to the ground, blood seeping from the deep gashes, jewels tumbling from his pockets. Darius reached for him again, but gunfire came at him from a different direction. Another bullet pelted his arm, and he spun, spraying fire at this other enemy. Protecting Grace.

Having regained his breath, Jason scrambled up and stuffed the fallen jewels back into his pockets, the battle forgotten in his greed. Darius swung back to him just as Jason glanced up. Their gazes clashed for one startling second, terror against determination, before Darius bit his throat. Unsatisfied with that, Darius lashed him with his tail, clawed with his hands and slammed the man into the wall. A sickening crack followed as Jason's neck snapped, and he collapsed to the ground in a lifeless heap.

Jason's eyes stared transfixed upon a huge blue sapphire, and his fingers gave one last twitch, perhaps reaching for the sparkling diamond that rolled across the floor toward Grace's boot.

It happened too quickly and wasn't nearly enough. Not for the harm Jason had done. But Grace whimpered, and he suddenly didn't care. Vengeance didn't matter. Justice didn't matter. Only his wife mattered.

"Grace," Darius said, Jason already forgotten. His concern overshadowed all else as he rushed to her. His scales receded, revealing smooth skin. His fangs retracted. His wings curled into his back. When he reached his wife, he ripped her bonds from the wall, and she sank into his arms.

"Darius," she murmured. Her eyes were closed, her face pale.

He laid her gently on the floor and crouched beside her. As if sensing his vulnerable state, the vampire king swept before him, his eyes glowing that eerie blue. His sharp, white teeth were bared, ready to strike. The urge to leap up and attack was there, but Darius resisted. He wouldn't risk hurting Grace further.

Layel dove for him. Darius hunched over, protecting Grace with his body. He made no other move toward his opponent. The vampire's teeth sank into his shoulder, but as quickly as Layel attacked, he withdrew.

"Fight, you coward," Layel growled. "We end this here and now."

He glared up at him. "You cannot provoke me. The woman's life is more important, and I will not risk it. Not even to rid our world of your existence."

Blood dripped from Layel's mouth, slashes of red against his pale skin. He looked ready to pounce again, but instead offered, panting, "What are you willing to do for me to save your woman?"

"Call off your bloodsuckers, and I will not burn down your home."

"Burn my home and I will ensure your woman burns with it."

Grace uttered another whimper. Darius smoothed his hand over her brow, whispering soft words in her ear, though he never removed his gaze from Layel. "My warriors will disengage as soon as the woman is safe."

"I like having your warriors here. Easier to kill them." As he watched them, something indistinguishable came over Layel's expression. Something… almost human. He licked the blood from his mouth. "You love her?"

"Of course."

"I loved once," he said as if he couldn't hold back the words.

Darius studied the taut lines of Layel's features. "Then you understand."

The vampire king gave an almost imperceptible nod, then closed his eyes for a long moment, pensive. When he refocused, he said, "To save the woman, I will allow you and your men to leave my castle in peace. But there will not always be a woman to shield you and we will fight again, Darius. That I promise you."

"I welcome the day."

Layel unfurled his cape and turned, but he wasn't about to leave without offering one final blow. "I now possess many dragon medallions. Won't be long before your home is mine," he said, grinning over his shoulder.

Before Darius could reply, smoke erupted around him, and the vampire disappeared. Just like that, the rest of the vampires disappeared, as well, and the dragons were left in midbattle stances. Confused, they swung around, their expressions feral as they hunted for their opponents.

"Search the dungeons," Darius called. He continued to hold and rock and coo at Grace, willing his strength into her body.

Long moments later, Renard dragged a human man by the arm. Teira raced at his side, shouting that he was not to be hurt. Alex, Grace's brother, Darius realized. The human paled when he saw Grace.

"Grace," he shouted and fought to free himself. Renard held tight.

"These two were in the dungeon," Renard said. "This is the man your woman spoke of, is it not?"

"Release him."

The moment Alex gained his freedom, he sprinted to Grace. "What have you done to her," he snarled, trying to rip her from Darius's arms. "Let her go."

"If you do not remove your hand from my wife, I will remove it for you," he snapped. "The woman is my mate. *Mine*. That you are her brother is the only reason you will live. No one touches her but me."

Wisely Alex dropped his hands to his side. He lost his fury and desperation, both replaced by confusion. "Your mate?" He knelt beside them. "Is she…"

"She lives. She is merely weak from blood loss."

"She's pale."

"Give her time," Darius said, gazing down at this woman he loved and caressing a fingertip down her nose.

"I'm awake," she said quietly. "I'm sorry I let them get me. I tried to fight, but…"

Relief shuddered through him, and he couldn't hold back his next words. "I love you, Grace Carlyle."

"That's Grace en Kragin." Her eyelids fluttered open, and she smiled slowly. "And I love you, too."

Darius didn't know where Javar's medallion was, how many medallions Layel had or when the vampire would try and use them. Nor did he know where the *Book of Ra-Dracus* was, but he had Grace, and that's what mattered.

"I was so afraid…"

He cupped her cheeks in his hands. "Hush. All is well. Your brother is here."

To verify this, Alex leaned into her line of vision and grinned. "I'm here, sis. I'm here."

"Oh, thank God." With a grimace, she sat up and wrapped her arms around him, hugging, her grip fragile. "I missed you. God, I was so worried about you."

Darius allowed her a few minutes to reunite with her brother, then reclaimed her in the circle of his arms, exactly where she belonged.

She glanced up at him. "So what do we do from here?"

"I want you to live here with me. We can build a life together and raise our children."

Her eyes filled with tears. "Yes. *Yes.*"

Chuckling, he smoothed back her hair, then kissed her nose, her lips, her chin. "I think your brother will be staying, as well."

"Really?" Grace glanced at her brother curiously.

Alex wagged his brows and motioned to the beautiful blonde. "He means," her brother said, putting his arm around Teira, "that I've found love, too. Grace, I'd like to introduce my future wife, Teira."

She and Grace shared a secret smile, then Grace turned to Darius. "We can't leave my mom and aunt Sophie on the surface without us."

"I'm sure Layel has room for them."

"No!"

He smiled at her, a true, genuine smile. "I was teasing, Grace."

She stilled. Blinked. Darius? Teasing? How… shocking.

"You do find teasing acceptable, do you not, sweet Grace?"

"Of course. I just didn't expect it from you."

A tender light consumed his golden eyes. "You thought I lacked humor?"

"Well, yeah," she admitted. She drew in the masculinity of his scent, closed her eyes and savored. "But I love you anyway. You'll adore having my mom and aunt with us."

His lips twitched. "I'm not sure my men are prepared," he said with an undercurrent of humor. "But for you, anything."

"I love you," she said again. "Have I told you the one about the dragon who couldn't say no?"

* * * * *

You asked for Layel's story...
And now the wait is over.
In March 2009,
return to Atlantis in
Gena Showalter's
THE VAMPIRE'S BRIDE.

Turn the page for your sneak preview!

NIGHT HAD LONG since fallen.

The air was warm, fragrant and fraught with danger. The insects were eerily silent, not a chirp or whistle to be heard. Only the wind seemed impervious to the surrounding menace, swishing leaves and clicking branches together.

Delilah's every survival instinct remained on high alert. No telling where the other creatures were. She'd spied a few here and there as she'd gathered stones and sticks. And then they had disappeared, hiding amongst the shadows. She could have hunted them down, could have challenged them, but she hadn't.

The gods' warning refused to leave her mind. What if she killed one of her own team members? To begin at a disadvantage would be the epitome of foolish. She'd been foolish a little too often lately.

She and Nola had opted to sleep in the trees, making them harder to find, harder to reach. Right now she was stretched atop a thick branch, legs swinging over the side, handmade spear clutched tightly in her palms. Wooden daggers were strapped to her legs, waist and back.

Sharp bark dug into her ribs, helping keep her awake, alert. What were the other creatures doing just then?

What was *Layel* doing?

Layel…beautiful Layel. She'd only interacted with him twice, yet that had been enough to utterly, foolishly fascinate her. He was like no one she had ever encountered. Constantly she found herself wondering what his body looked like underneath his clothes, what his face would look like lost in passion, what he would feel like, pumping and sliding inside her.

He despises you. He is best forgotten.

Forget that his skin was pale and smooth as silk? Forget that his eyes were blue like sapphires and fringed by black lashes that were a striking contrast to his snow-white hair? Forget that he was tall with wide shoulders and radiated a dark sensuality women probably salivated over? Impossible.

What kind of females did he enjoy? What type of females had he allowed into his bed?

Sparks of something…dark flickered in her chest. Jealousy, perhaps. She wanted to deny the emotion, but couldn't. *Mine,* she thought. He might want nothing more to do with her, but no way in Hades would he be allowed to have another woman. Not while they inhabited this island.

What's come over you? Men were no longer something she prized. To her, they were something to destroy, a threat to her loved ones. Since her one and only mating had ended so disastrously, she had not thought to find herself possessive of a male. How many times had she watched her sisters fight over a particular slave? *He's mine,* they would shout. *It's my bed he will warm this night.* A clash of daggers always followed, as well as cut and bleeding warrioresses. How many times had she watched those "prized" men leave when the loving was over? Without a backward glance at the brokenhearted they were leaving behind.

Delilah had thought herself immune. Until now. She'd straddled the vampire's shoulders and he'd looked between her legs with undiluted heat. A shiver followed the thought, drowning her in another wave of that deep and inexorable desire. What would it be like to be bedded by Layel? Would he be gentle, taking her slowly? Or would his passion be as ferocious as his wild, blue eyes promised? Perhaps even a little wicked?

"You're aroused, Amazon. Why?"

Layel's whispered entreaty was so close, so husky, she wasn't sure if she'd imagined it. She stiffened, fingers tight on the spear, as she searched the darkness for him. Only treetops and night birds came into focus. Not even where thin slivers of golden moonlight seeped through the canopy of leaves overhead did she make out the form of a man. Slowly her muscles released their vise-hold on her bones.

Why am I aroused? Because of you, she wished she could tell this fantasy.

"Well?"

She gasped. Too real, too real, too real...

Before she had time to react, however, a hard

hand settled over her mouth while another shoved her to her back. A heavy, muscled weight slammed into her body. She lost her breath, barely managing to remain on the branch.

In seconds, Layel had her stretched out and her legs restrained. Her eyes widened as her spear was torn from her grip and thrown to the ground. A mocking *thump* echoed in her ears. She balled her hand and moved to strike him, but he released her mouth to catch the action. Next he caged her arms between their bodies.

"You will not hurt me," he said.

"I'll do anything I want."

"Try."

One word, but it was so smug she longed to slap and kiss him at the same time. She didn't panic. Yet. Nola was nearby. Probably sneaking up on Layel...now. But no. A moment ticked by, then another.

Nola never arrived.

Delilah's heart began to drum erratically in her chest. Her blood rushed through her veins with dizzying speed, and need quivered in her belly. Here was her fantasy, in the flesh. Hers for the taking.

You are an Amazon. Act like one. Forcing herself into action, she raised her head and sank her teeth into his neck until she tasted the metallic tang of blood. He hissed in her ear, the sound one of pleasure and pain. *You are biting him to escape, yes? So why are you writhing?*

Mmm, so good... Her tongue flicked against his racing pulse.

His hands now free, he fisted her hair and jerked her away. He was panting, anger and arousal bright in his eyes. "Think yourself a vampire, do you? Or are you half vampire? I know your kind consorts with all races and your father could belong to any of them."

She opened her mouth to respond but he shook his head, stopping her. "Scream and you'll regret it."

"As if I would scream," she muttered, offended that he thought so little of her abilities. *You did allow him to sneak up on you.*

Oh, shut up.

He blinked in surprise, as if he'd expected her to scream despite his threat.

Her irritation intensified, and she glared at him. "Did you hurt my sister?"

"She was gone when I reached you. I did not touch her."

"Then I will allow you to live. For now. But very soon I'm going to grow tired of letting you overpower me."

He snorted.

"Be thankful I haven't already killed you."

"Do not fool yourself, Amazon. You would be dead right now had I not stayed my hand."

There was fury in his voice and hate in his expression. Stayed his hand? So he *had* come here to kill her? Bastard! Except, despite everything he had said, despite the genuine loathing directed at her, his legs were between hers and she could feel the length of his shaft hardening, growing, filling.

Just like that, her blood sizzled another degree.

Blistered her veins. *I am callous, and I care for no one but my sisters.* If they were in Atlantis, she might agree to take him as her slave. If only for the month males were allowed inside the Amazon camp. But here on this island, with a dangerous competition in the works, they might very well be enemies.

"Afraid, Delilah?" he asked silkily.

Her name, spoken on those red lips…a hot ache bloomed between her legs, moisture pooling here.

"Of what?" The words emerged breathless, wine-rich.

"Dying. Pain."

"No," she answered honestly. Dying didn't scare her. Pain didn't scare her. But her reaction to this man petrified her. He made her feel vulnerable, as if she couldn't rely on herself. As if she needed him to survive. He'd already overtaken her thoughts.

"You should be very afraid," he said….

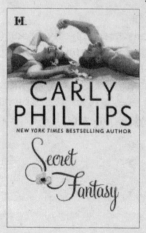

HQN™

We *are* romance™

New York Times bestselling author

SUSAN MALLERY

Sparks fly when Gracie's legendary youthful
bad-boy crush, Riley, returns home seeking
respectability. Gracie's determined to keep her
distance, but she's quickly discovering that first love
is sometimes better the second time around.

FALLING
for
GRACIE

Available January 2009 in bookstores everywhere!

www.HQNBooks.com

PHSM420

REQUEST YOUR
FREE BOOKS!

2 FREE NOVELS
FROM THE ROMANCE/SUSPENSE
COLLECTION PLUS 2 FREE GIFTS!

YES! Please send me 2 FREE novels from the Romance/Suspense Collection and my 2 FREE gifts (gifts are worth about $10). After receiving them, if I don't wish to receive any more books, I can return the shipping statement marked "cancel." If I don't cancel, I will receive 4 brand-new novels every month and be billed just $5.49 per book in the U.S. or $5.99 per book in Canada, plus 25¢ shipping and handling per book plus applicable taxes, if any*. That's a savings of at least 20% off the cover price! I understand that accepting the 2 free books and gifts places me under no obligation to buy anything. I can always return a shipment and cancel at any time. Even if I never buy another book from the Reader Service, the two free books and gifts are mine to keep forever.

185 MDN EF5Y 385 MDN EF6C

Name _____ (PLEASE PRINT) _____

Address _____ Apt. # _____

City _____ State/Prov. _____ Zip/Postal Code _____

Signature (if under 18, a parent or guardian must sign)

Mail to **The Reader Service**:
IN U.S.A.: P.O. Box 1867, Buffalo, NY 14240-1867
IN CANADA: P.O. Box 609, Fort Erie, Ontario L2A 5X3

Not valid to current subscribers to the Romance Collection,
the Suspense Collection or the Romance/Suspense Collection.

Want to try two free books from another line?
Call 1-800-873-8635 or visit www.morefreebooks.com.

* Terms and prices subject to change without notice. N.Y. residents add applicable sales tax. Canadian residents will be charged applicable provincial taxes and GST. Offer not valid in Quebec. This offer is limited to one order per household. All orders subject to approval. Credit or debit balances in a customer's account(s) may be offset by any other outstanding balance owed by or to the customer. Please allow 4 to 6 weeks for delivery. Offer available while quantities last.

Your Privacy: Harlequin is committed to protecting your privacy. Our Privacy Policy is available online at www.eHarlequin.com or upon request from the Reader Service. From time to time we make our lists of customers available to reputable third parties who may have a product or service of interest to you. If you would prefer we not share your name and address, please check here. ☐

BOB08R

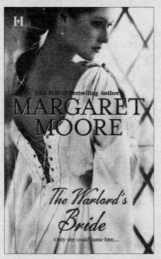

Gena Showalter